D1069703

WAKING BEAUTY

WAKING BEAUTY

PAUL WITCOVER

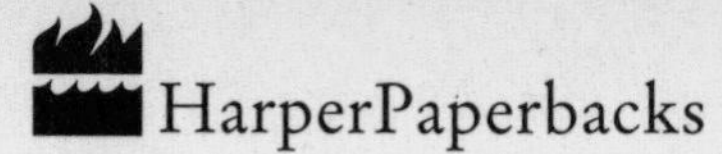

A *Division of* HarperCollins*Publishers*
10 East 53rd Street, New York, N.Y. 10022-5299

ISBN: 0-06-105249-3

Printed in the United States of America

First printing: February 1997

Designed by Lili Schwartz

Library of Congress Cataloging-in-Publication Data

Witcover, Paul.
Waking beauty / Paul Witcover.
p. cm.
ISBN 0-06-105249-3
I. Title.
PS3573 . I893W34 1997
813'.54--dc20 96-41416
CIP

Visit HarperPaperbacks on the World Wide Web at
http://www.harpercollins.com/paperbacks

97 98 99 00 ❖ 10 9 8 7 6 5 4 3 2 1

For Elizabeth Hand,
Who gave me a lift in her balloon

Now I shall spy on beauty as none has
Spied on it yet.
JOHN SHADE,
Pale Fire

WAKING BEAUTY

BOOK ONE

JUBILAR

"Beauty is truth, truth beauty,"—that is all
Ye know on earth, and all ye need to know.
JOHN KEATS,
"Ode on a Grecian Urn"

ONE

"*What a strange lad you are!*" exclaims Marcus Galingale to his son, Cyrus, late in the morning of the day before Cy's wedding.

Father and son are hard at work on a cabinet commissioned by a vizard from Quoz who will slash his payment in half if the piece is not delivered on time, wedding or no. Putting aside his bevel square, Marcus regards the steadily working Cy with a mixture of pride and bafflement.

"Cy, listen to me," he says. "What is it that troubles you? Confide in your father."

"I'm fine, sir."

"Fine? You call it fine the way you mope around, with that long face and those endless sighs, as if some horrible fate were about to befall you? Who would guess the most beautiful girl in all of Jubilar is your chosen bride? It makes me angry to see you like this; people are starting to talk. What is it? Doesn't Rose please you? Do her kisses lack ardor?"

Cy ignores his father's questions. The only sounds are the scraping of his plane across the board over which he bends and the lazy drone of fireflies through the fragrant air of the shop.

Marcus sighs, fingering his throat plug; the plug is carved in the shape of crossed hammers and notched with the sigils signifying husband, father, and unwed son. "The days before and after my wedding were the most carefree of my life. Your mother might not be much to look at now, but she was a pretty thing once, full of life and high spirits, always ready with a kiss. And what a cook! I didn't know if she would please me more in the bedroom or the kitchen; beauty fades, my boy, but a good cook is forever!"

His sharp blue eyes narrow shrewdly. "Is that it, lad? Can't she cook?"

"She cooks well enough."

"Then, by the Wheel, what is it? I charge you to speak the truth!"

With a resigned shrug, Cy puts up the plane and looks at his father. "You'll think I'm crazy."

"That is already my opinion. Now speak!"

"It's true I'm not happy. But it's not Rose."

"What then?"

"All of this." Cy nods disparagingly at the pieces of the cabinet scattered about the shop. The design, as with much of the furniture sold under Marcus's name, is his own. "I can see so clearly in my mind how everything should look, but something always goes wrong."

"You're a perfectionist."

"No; a failure."

Marcus shakes his fist. "If it was anyone else who said so, I'd give them a taste of this! Just look at you: seventeen, your throat plug unadorned, and already your skills are valued in lofty Quoz. Do you know what kind of work my father had me doing at your age? Spice-racks and footstools!"

"You don't understand."

"A father not understand his son? It's you who don't understand! In this family, I am sovereign!" Quickly, with the economy of movement practice brings, Marcus slaps Cy across the face.

Cy bows his head, seething. Oh, it's hard to be a son! he thinks. To have to swallow and swallow and smile as the gall goes down! But as the Blessed Sovereign to the Hierarchate, so the father to his family. An unfilial son tips the natural order of things. His example might spread to other sons, or to women, in whom the ashes of rebellion are always smoldering. The wise son submits to even the most tyrannical father, knowing that he, too, will one day be a husband and a father, with a family of his own to rule.

Marcus pushes his silver curls back from his forehead. "You've been praised too much, Cy. It's made you impatient and despairing, caused you to set goals you can't help but fall short of. Believe me, every worthwhile thing takes time; only bad things happen quickly. The key is patience. Plan for the future, but live in the moment. You're fortunate to have a bride as lovely as Rose Rubra. Enjoy her beauty. Drink deeply of it now, enough to last for the rest of your life! A woman's beauty is the briefest of seasons, my boy. Once gone, it does not return again, ever."

"I'll try," Cy says. "But it's hard."

"Did anyone say it would be easy? Are you a woman to want it so?" Marcus bangs his big fist on the wood for emphasis. "Turning after turning our family has clawed its way back to the city of Peripety, where our great ancestor Celtis Galingale moved as freely as a firefly through the Court of the Plumed Serpent. If not for the cursed Intricatas, our family would dwell in Quoz by now!"

As far back as Cy can remember, he's heard the tale of his family's disgrace: how the beautiful Sersis Intricata seduced Celtis Galingale only to betray him to the shrives by the command of her father, Malus. It's always seemed more fairy tale than history to Cy, as far removed from his life as the lives of the saints and martyrs. But the hatred he feels at the mention of the name Intricata is immediate and strong, fueled by a rage lacking all other lawful expression. "We'll have our revenge, father," he says now. "I swear it!"

"Good lad!" Marcus claps him on the shoulder. "You do yourself credit. But you see what I mean about impatience. The road to revenge is a long one. It must be traveled with care and cunning. Remember, Celtis fell all the way to lowly Arpagee. In all the time since, more than three hundred turnings, we've barely come halfway back. Your great-great-grandfather was born in Hent and died in Inction. My father's hard work and sacrifice lifted the family to Jubilar. It's our duty to continue advancing until we've won back all that was stolen from us, even if another three hundred turnings must go by before a descendant of Celtis enters Peripety.

"To advance is all, Cy. If Rose's beauty doesn't excite you, consider her dowry. Her father, Cerasus, may be a witless ox, but he's a *rich* witless ox. With his wealth added to our own, and with a son to carry the Galingale name forward—as I have every confidence you'll beget on Rose, for vengeful thoughts breed sons—you'll be able to advance to Kell, one step nearer Peripety and revenge. That's how the race is won, my boy: step by step, not in a single leap from start to finish! Give me your hand! There! You shouldn't provoke an old man so!"

Cy clasps his father's hand, glad of the reconciliation but still, in his secret heart, gloomy and rebellious. He scorns the patient revenge that Marcus counsels.

Each turning, on All Saints' Eve, to mark the ascension of Saint Ixion Diospyros, the Blessed Sovereign elevates a handful of worthy men. Some rise to the next town or city. Others leap all the way to lofty Quoz, Apex of Existence, the Crystal City, where Azedarach LXIV rules in majesty and power from the Serpent Throne. Thus each man, however humble his station, has at least some chance of advancement. Cy dreams of the day that one of his designs will catch the Sovereign's eye and lift him to Peripety or beyond. It's been his secret dream for turnings.

Yet now, at the ripe old age of seventeen, Cy is having doubts. Once again, All Saints' Eve has come and gone with no word from Azedarach.

Cy feels doomed to finish his days in Jubilar, a disappointment to his father. Everyone praises the genius of his designs, but Cy sees only the gulf that separates what he imagines from the clumsy accomplishments of his hands. It's a gulf that seems to grow wider, not narrower, with the turnings.

This is the shadow that has fallen over his life. And not even the prospect of marriage to Rose Rubra, daughter of the blacksmith, Cerasus, can cheer him.

Cy admits she's the most beautiful girl in Jubilar. He takes pleasure in her smile and her company; and her kisses, while they last, are almost enough to make him forget about Quoz. But kisses don't last forever, and a woman's beauty is quick to fade.

Cy wants a beauty that never fades. If such a beauty exists anywhere in the Hierarchate, it's not in lowly Jubilar, or in Peripety, but in Quoz.

Father and son have hardly resumed their work when there comes a timid knock at the shop door.

"Enter," calls Marcus. "Ah, Rose! Cy and I were just speaking of you."

Rose Rubra stands on the threshold, blushing, with her shy smile and luminous green eyes. A slight young woman of fifteen turnings, Rose wears a white blouse and a pale blue dress whose yellow-fringed hem hangs below her ankles. Her black hair is set in the style of a bride-to-be, with two long braids twining about her shoulders and arms like bands of lustrous ivy, only to end in bracelets at her wrists. A red hibiscus blossom is tucked above her left ear in token of fidelity; for the past month, as is the custom, Rose has worn a different flower every day to symbolize the virtues she'll bring to her husband.

"Ixion grant the day finds you well, father-in-law," she says.

Marcus smooths his silver hair. "Your beauty cures me of all afflictions, daughter-in-law: even age. At the sight of you, I'm made young again as if by vizards' craft! Why not marry me, and not this dullard of a son?"

Rose laughs nervously. "I don't think your wife would approve, father-in-law."

"How you women stick together! It's a wonder we poor men aren't kept in chains the livelong day, eh, Cy?" He nudges his son and winks.

"Don't mind him, Rose," says Cy. "My father likes to pretend women secretly rule the world."

"And don't they?" Marcus demands. "Each night, when we are chained to our beds, our nostrils plugged, aren't we wholly in their power? Rose, I ask you: What husband would dare anger his wife, knowing all she need do to revenge herself would be to remove his nose plugs and loosen his bonds? The potent scent of Beauty would do the rest, deranging his reason and seducing him into Herwood, never to return!"

Rose puts her hands together in the sign of the Wheel. "What wife could conceive such a terrible sin? It's every woman's loving duty to husband, son, and father to guard their sleep against Beauty!"

"Yet you can't deny the power you women wield," Marcus persists. "Surely the thought has crossed your mind, daughter-in-law, if only for a second—when Cerasus has angered you by some petty refusal or chastisement, for example—how easily you could be rid of him! Ixion himself says that evil thoughts sprout from women's hearts faster than men can weed them."

Rose grows paler and paler, pressing her hands to her heart. "Let me rot forever with Maw and her Furies in the Pit of Damned Souls if I ever presume to judge my father's judgments or seek a wicked revenge!"

"You raise your voice to me? You have a touch of the Fury in you, daughter-in-law!"

Rose turns paler still, trembling at how her words have run away with her. "I beg pardon, father-in-law."

"Peace, daughter, peace," laughs Marcus. "By the Wheel, your fear becomes you more than any blossom! You take my jests too much to heart, I assure you."

"I have offended you."

"On the contrary, I'm pleased to hear you defend the virtues of your sex with such pretty vehemence. Only practice them as vigorously and we'll have no quarrels."

"With your help, I will."

"That modest answer becomes you better still. Come, let me give you a kiss!"

Rose goes to Marcus, who kisses her loudly upon the lips. Taking her by the hand, he spins her once around as in a dance, her tiny feet kicking up sawdust, then passes her, blushing and laughing with embarrassment, to Cy. "What a treasure you have here, Cy! A paragon of wifely virtue!"

Cy frowns. "How like you, father, to swell Rose's pretty head after rebuking me for pride."

"Why, that's a father-in-law's privilege, like spoiling a grandson! But you'll excuse me, Rose, I'm sure: I've got work to do for tomorrow. Cy, I want you to clean up here before you visit the church. Mind you don't distract him, Rose."

In Jubilar, as in every village, town, and city of the Hierarchate, couples engaged to be married must visit the local church on each day of the week before the ceremony. There they kneel and light candles to Saint Viridis Lacrimata, Our Lady of the Perpetual Sacrifice, Patroness of Holy Patrimony, beseeching her for the blessing of a son.

Cy rolls his eyes as his father leaves the shop.

"How funny your father is!" says Rose.

"I know he frightens you."

"Sometimes I think it must be sinful to listen to him, the way he goes on! What would the Mouth of God say?"

"Try not to take him seriously, Rose. Laugh at his jests, but only in seeming. Inside, pay no heed."

"I want to be a good daughter-in-law, Cy. And a good wife."

Rose's green eyes shine with excitement and—Cy sees it clearly—love. Suddenly Quoz seems far away. What had Marcus called her? A paragon of wifely virtue. But she's a paragon of beauty as well: her scent as mysterious and compelling as any that baits the nighttime air, her hair a forest in which he longs to become lost. He trembles to think that in a day's time her body will be his to command, his to explore like an unknown country, her riches his to claim, his all her blushing secrets.

His father was right, Cy realizes. He *is* lucky in Rose. He swears to himself now that once they are wed he will not just drink deeply of Rose's beauty, he'll drain it to the very dregs, until all that remains is the wrinkled shell of virtue, like an empty wineskin.

Cy lowers his lips to hers as if to begin the drinking now.

The Church of the Spinning Wheel stands at the heart of Jubilar. Its circular walls rise high above a slate-tiled plaza, hub of the village. The plaza glistens in the dipping sun as Cy and Rose enter; the acolytes of the church are scrubbing the dark tiles clean as they do at the close of each day, and splashes of soapy water flash like a scattering of coins.

Groups of villagers are hard at work assembling stages, stalls, and booths for the traders and simularters due to arrive tomorrow for the Feast of Saint Ilex Erythrina. It was Marcus's idea to schedule the wedding of Cy and Rose on the feast day of Jubilar's patron saint in order that it might seem as if Ilex himself were honoring the Galingales.

A shout draws Cy's attention; his father is supervising the erection of booths on the far edge of the plaza. Marcus waves, a hammer clenched in his fist.

"Mind you come straight home, Cy! Your mother has a chicken roasting!"

Cy lifts his hand in acknowledgment. He hates it when Marcus addresses him in front of Rose as if he were still a boy, his throat smooth . . . as if *his* talents, *his* designs, weren't responsible for the success of his father's business!

"Come on, Cy." Rose pulls him up the steps of the church. "The Mouth of God will be waiting."

He groans. "With another lecture, no doubt. Every day the same thing. How the ceremony is to be conducted. Where each person stands. What is worn, and by whom. Who speaks what, and when. A thousand and one obscure items of ceremony! The priest has grown so forgetful in his old age that he can't recall what he's said from one day to the next, and so repeats himself endlessly."

"I know," soothes Rose. "Still, as my father says, respect is owed the office if not the man who holds it. The Ecclesiarch will send us a new priest soon."

"This one was old even when he was a boy."

Cy and Rose dip to their knees before the doors of the church and make the sign of the Wheel. The doors are slabs of black walnut carved over countless turnings into a tableau of torment and salvation. Each door is divided into more than a hundred panels, and each panel depicts a scene from *The Lives and Acts of the Holy Saints and Martyrs*, the ancient book that tells of the defeat of Maw, Dam of Darkness, and her followers, the Furies, at the hands of the saints.

Seventeen turnings ago, in thanks for the birth of a son to carry on the Galingale name, Marcus purchased the right to carve one of the remaining panels. The carving took three turnings to finish. His subject was a famous event from the life of Saint Stilskin Sophora.

In one of his many adventures, the innocent young saint, blessed with a purity often mistaken for simplemindedness, became separated from his constant companion, the dog Snowdrop, and was tricked by a Fury into using his powers to spin straw into gold.

At that time, the Furies had been but recently driven into Herwood by the saints, and as such were not the only women living there. Saint Stilskin believed he had come upon an aged hermitess, not a Fury, and so politely did she request his help that Stilskin could not refuse her.

The guileless lad had no inkling of his danger. To use his holy powers in this way would mean the forfeit of his immortal soul. No doubt Snowdrop could have warned him, but Snowdrop was not there; the Fury had lured him away with a bone.

As Stilskin sat down at the wheel, a strand of the Fury's hair chanced to become entangled in the spindle. So swift was his spinning that the Fury's hair unraveled from her head in the blink of an eye. And her magic unraveled along with it, for the power of Furies, like that of all women, resides in their hair.

Stilskin did not rise from the wheel when the Fury was bald. He continued to spin, faster and faster, flaying the skin from her body. When at last he was done, nothing remained of her but blood and bones. And instead of gold, Stilskin had spun himself a finer treasure: a beautiful young woman, virginal and pure, the very opposite of a Fury.

Now until that moment, Stilskin had never loved a woman. But as he beheld this woman spun by his own hand, he felt a stirring he had not known before.

He took her to wife and taught her the art of spinning. And ever since, spinning has been women's work. Every woman, on her wedding day, receives a distaff in token of the household responsibilities entrusted to her sex by the saint.

In his panel, Marcus had captured the instant when the Fury's raw and bloody bones lay in a heap on one side of Stilskin while, on the other, his virgin bride seemed asleep on a bed of straw. It's Marcus's finest work, the high point of his talent. Even Cy admires it.

The church is nearly empty at this late hour. The few old women praying in the pews do not so much as glance up when Cy and Rose push through the doors. Cy looks around apprehensively for the Mouth of God, but it seems his prayers have been answered: the priest is nowhere to be seen.

The interior of the church is chill and damp. The smell of old, well-polished wood emanates from the pews, seventeen wedges of seats bounded by narrow aisles. Stained glass windows set at the head of the aisles, high on the walls—each illustrating a turn of the Wheel in the Passion of Saint Ixion Diospyros—admit fingers of colored light that do not diminish the gloom but are, instead, diminished by it.

Above the nave hangs the huge figure of Saint Ixion. Nailed to his Burning Wheel, the saint gazes down with a look of cruel triumph that holds no place for mercy. He slew the Furies with just such a look as he rose above them, spinning in flames, snatched from their claws by a miraculous wind.

But Ixion's eyes are not always directed downward. The Burning Wheel is linked to the great bell of the church tower by vizards' craft. It spins slowly, inching the figure of the saint through a complete revolution every seventeen hours, the same time it takes the sun to appear and appear again. At the end of that time the bell begins to toll, summoning the faithful to daily worship beneath the judgment of Saint Ixion's gaze.

The Burning Wheel is said to mark a rounder time as well, a cycle of which each daily turn is but a fractional unspooling, at whose secret hour—

fixed from the beginning of time yet known to no man, neither Sovereign nor Ecclesiarch—the tocsin of eternal judgment will strike, cracking the bell of heaven, and the Spinner will unravel all that He has woven.

The Unspinning.

Beneath the nave, where the seventeen aisles converge, is the tabernacle, its secret insides walled away from the profane and profaning eyes of women. There the men of Jubilar gather, close by the hub of glory.

At the heart of the tabernacle, shrouded in mystery, is a second sanctuary, forbidden even to the men: the sacrarium. Only the Mouth of God may enter there.

Cy and Rose genuflect toward the nave and the figure of Saint Ixion. They make the sign of the Wheel, then rise and walk along the curve of the near wall. The rasp of their feet reminds Cy of sandpaper.

Candlewheels burning along the rounded walls illuminate grottoes in which pale simulars of the saints and martyrs hang or lie—sometimes behind glass, sometimes not—in tattered velvets of red and green and purple. The simulars, or the cracked and age-yellowed glass cases that hold them, are bestrewn with glittering tokens of thanks for answered prayers: locks of women's hair bound in bright ribbons; pieces of jewelry; bouquets both blooming and desiccated; gold and silver coins stamped with the profile of the Sovereign on one side and on the other with Saint Ixion's Burning Wheel and the legend "IN MY END IS MY BEGINNING," the motto of Church and Hierarchate taken from Ixion's final sermon, spoken moments before he was betrayed to the Furies by his own mother.

The simulars are as damaged as their costumes. They are missing eyes, limbs, or fingers, as if undergoing a martyrdom all their own.

Cy and Rose pass the simulars of Saint Stilskin Sophora and Saint Cedrus Lyciodes. They pass the eyeless simular of Saint Ilex Erythrina, which will be paraded through Jubilar at the height of tomorrow's feast, borne on the shoulders of men who tithe handsomely for the privilege, Marcus chief among them. They pass the glass-encased simulars of Saint Samsum Oxalis, Saint Quercus Incana, Saint Rober Viburnum, and the shrine of Saint Sium Lyrata, with its collection of strange musical instruments that no one knows how to play.

Then they come to the shrine of Saint Viridis Lacrimata, Our Lady of the Perpetual Sacrifice.

The simular hangs from thin, almost-invisible wires in the recesses of the shrine. It would be lost in shadow if not for the half circles of pure white candles that ripple out from it over the floor and walls. Only the shrines of Saint Ixion Diospyros and Saint Ilex Erythrina can boast more candles. They fizz and sputter in pools of wax or burn with a steady flame, casting and recasting a net of aqueous light. In that clear radiance shot through with bending rays of dark, the simular of Viridis Lacrimata floats in a kind of timeless undersea suspension.

The right hand of the saint is raised as if to bestow a blessing. In her left hand she holds a pale yellow platter upon which, like candies, are the perfect white-and-green orbs of her eyes. Her face is uplifted as though still possessed of sight, a keener vision than she gave up. She wears a wig of golden hair that seems woven of the light of candles but in fact comes from the heads of women whose names and bodies have long since vanished into the furnaces of Quoz. She's dressed in a white gown so ancient it seems the tremulous light could cause the fabric to disintegrate.

Cy and Rose follow a path through the blazing arcs of candles to where twin cushions of violet damask lie side by side. They make the sign of the Wheel once more as they kneel upon the cushions, which smell of mildew and attar of roses.

A small brass candlewheel stands between them and the simular. Beneath the wheel a tray holds an array of slender white candles. Six candleholders line the rim of the wheel; in each one is an unlit candle. A seventh candleholder, this one empty, is at the center of the wheel.

Rose takes a candle from the tray. She kindles it from a nearby flame, then lights the candles already in place along the rim of the wheel, whispering as she does so:

"Saint Viridis bless and keep us. Saint Viridis pray for us. Saint Viridis intercede for us. Saint Viridis wash us in your purifying tears. Saint Viridis ward Beauty from our house. Saint Viridis grant us the blessing of a son."

She hands the candle to Cy. With a show of reverence, he sets it in the empty place at the center of the wheel.

"Saint Viridis teach us the wisdom of your Perpetual Sacrifice," he intones.

Now the candlewheel is complete. The candles will burn through the night. Cy and Rose bow their heads in prayer.

After a moment, Cy looks up. Rose is praying fervently. Her lips move soundlessly as her fingers walk around the prayer wheel she wears on a gold chain about her neck.

Rose is often moved to tears by prayer, whereas for Cy the ritual is a struggle; his fingers, so deft with wood, fumble hopelessly on the prayer wheel. Listening for the heavy tread of the Mouth of God, he loses his place, mixes up the prayers, and finally has to start all over again. Rarely does he complete a single turning.

The faith of women is different from the faith of men, Cy thinks now.

Perhaps it's because women know and understand so much less about the workings of Church and Hierarchate. Or perhaps it's an awareness of the evil they harbor, the Fury sleeping in their hearts, that causes them to embrace the consolations of religion.

He thinks of Saint Viridis Lacrimata. Our Lady of the Perpetual Sacrifice. No other woman, in all the vast, ungraspable history of the Hierarchate, has been deemed worthy of canonization. Ever.

And yet, according to the *Lives and Acts*, Viridis Lacrimata was once a Cat in one of Quoz's infamous brothels, for Quoz was far from the shining city it is today in the dark times before the triumph of the Church of the Spinning Wheel and the erection of the Hierarchate.

Many were the carnal sins of Viridis—with men, women, even children—and great was the delight she took in them. She was never a Fury, but she adopted the insatiable appetites of the Furies as her own, rioting with them in the streets of Quoz and roaming with them outside the city gates to participate in orgies and sacrifices of animals and human beings among the mute trees of the forest that would later become known as Herwood.

One day a carpenter from Brool, a man of uncompromising piety chosen by the Spinner to proclaim a new covenant between God and men, entered the gates of Quoz. That humble carpenter called to prophecy was Ixion Diospyros. His notoriety preceded him. For months he'd been wandering from place to place, calling himself the Mouth of God and preaching against the Furies.

He cried out for men to exterminate the servants of Maw without mercy and establish on the smoking ruins of what had been destroyed a Hierarchate that would last until the Unspinning. A place where everyone knew his place, where women bowed to men and men to worthier men, everyone bowing to the one above him all the way up to the Blessed Sovereign, who would bow to no man, but only to the Spinner.

Although a few righteous men had begun to follow Ixion—future saints like Cedrus Lyciodes and Fagus Firmiana—so deeply ingrained was the influence of Maw that most men and women scorned him. Crowds gathered to disrupt his sermons, heckling and throwing whatever came to hand. Even the shrives, then as now charged with the preservation of order, turned a blind eye to the harassment or joined in themselves with a vengeance. Many demonstrations ended with bands of Furies rampaging through the streets in search of victims for their rituals of rape and sacrifice. Early the next morning, the survivors would creep out to drag away the mutilated bodies of those chosen to appease the bottomless hunger of Maw. Ixion had escaped this fate so often that it seemed even to his enemies that a higher power must be shielding him from harm.

As Ixion continued to preach, something wonderful began to happen: the heat and conviction of his rhetoric, coupled with his courage in the face of the ever-more-violent excesses of the Furies, began to win converts to his cause. The Furies, who at first had laughed and sneered at his message, decided to strike, even at the risk of creating a martyr.

Sympathetic men—the fathers, brothers, husbands, and sons of Furies—secretly alerted the prophet to the plot against him. They begged him to take steps to preserve his life by going into hiding or fleeing Quoz altogether. But Ixion refused. The Spinner, he said, had directed his steps to Quoz and would either protect him from harm or grant him the glorious death of a martyr as He saw fit.

Shortly thereafter, Ixion preached in Cat Square, close by the very pleasure house in which Viridis Lacrimata lived and worked. Curious to see this new phenomenon, the grim prophet from Brool who preached not only against their livelihoods but against their very lives, the Cats crowded onto the roof and balconies of the house. It was the same at every house in the square, each of which specialized in a different vice.

Hundreds of voices hooted down at the self-proclaimed Mouth of God. Ixion was pelted with garbage, used prophylactics, and bags of waste. Some Cats and their clients engaged in wanton and lascivious embraces in plain view of everyone in order to taunt the prophet with his helplessness and inflame him with lust. Women lay with women, men copulated with men, mere children, so corrupted and defiled they willingly did whatever was asked of them, performed the most sinful acts as if playing harmless games.

Viridis Lacrimata watched from a velvet couch on the high balcony of her bedchamber. She slapped aside the hands that, like kittens, sought to slip beneath her loose silks and draw her into play. She was intent on the small figure in the filth-bespattered robes standing upon a raised platform at the center of the throng below.

Ringed by a thin circle of followers, Ixion let the rain of abuse wash over him for a long time, head bowed as if listening to the Spinner whispering in his ear. Then, lifting his arms, the angry flash of his dark eyes visible to Viridis even from such a distance, he limped—for Ixion was lame in his left leg, the result of a childhood injury—to the edge of the platform.

It was then, before he could open his mouth, that the Furies struck. Viridis heard their bloodcurdling cry rise from everywhere and nowhere. The chanting of the name of Maw.

It began as a rumble deep in the throat, then gathered volume until the final explosive shout. Then it began again, its ebb and flow repeated unvaryingly, with the mindless rhythm of a naturally recurring force. It frequently lasted throughout an entire night, coursing up and down the streets of Quoz like a deadly wind, now gusting hard, now falling away.

Viridis had spent long nights shivering in fear of that wind, terrified of being chosen for the sacrifice. Yet there had been other nights when she willingly added her voice to the chorus, coming to herself in the morning in some foul alley with no memory of how she'd arrived there, her naked body smeared with blood and worse, weak and aching in every bone yet filled with a transcendent glow akin to the aftermath of an orgy.

The chant echoed now from all the roofs and balconies of Cat Square. Viridis felt the lure of it like an itch at the back of her throat or between her legs. But she ignored it, scrambling from her couch to witness more clearly what would become known to history as the Miracle of Cat Square.

Outnumbered at least thirty to one, Ixion and his brave followers drew into a tight circle as the Furies rushed upon them from all sides. In the confusion, it was hard for Viridis to see what was happening, but gradually she realized that portions of the crowd had turned against the Furies and were beating them back. At the center of it all, imperturbable as a rock, stood the prophet, the so-called Mouth of God, Ixion Diospyros. Intrigued, Viridis trained her spyglass—a gift from an admiring vizard—on his face.

His features seemed cold to her, even cruel. His pale flesh clung to the bones of his skull as if he sucked nourishment from no source but himself. Viridis could detect neither rage nor lust in his coal-dark eyes, just flickers of quick calculation. He did not seem to be at the crowd's mercy but rather to be pulling its strings, like a master simularter.

Viridis watched as a Fury pierced the ring of Ixion's defenders to thrust at the prophet with a knife. Ixion stepped forward, favoring his good leg, as he pulled aside his robes and bared his chest to the blade.

Then Viridis saw the miracle later attested to by many other eyes. The knife sank up to the hilt in Ixion's chest. At the same time, calmly, and as if effortlessly, he caught hold of the Fury's wrist and snapped it. As she fell to her knees, Ixion plucked the knife from his chest and, in a single stroke, parted the Fury's head from her shoulders. Holding it aloft by the hair, he pitched it into the midst of the Furies.

That was the turning point. In mid-cry, the many-voiced chant shattered. The Furies, overwhelmed for once by a ferocity greater than their own, fled.

Cradling in his arms the mangled body of Fagus Firmiana, first martyr of the new church, who had given his life so that the Mouth of God might live, and with the headless body of the Fury sprawled at his feet, Ixion preached as even he had never preached before.

With tears running down his cheeks, he proclaimed the Church of the Spinning Wheel. He said the new church would weave all men and women into a single fabric pleasing to the eye of the Spinner, a fabric so strong that not all the knives of all the Furies nor the claws of Maw herself would prevail against it.

But Viridis Lacrimata wasn't listening to his words, even though his voice, that matchless instrument, reached her clearly in the dazed hush that had fallen over those remaining on the ground and on the roofs and balconies of Cat Square. She was mesmerized by the miracle she'd seen with her own eyes but couldn't bring herself to credit.

Studying Ixion through the spyglass, she searched in vain for a wound above his heart where she'd seen the knife strike home. There was no mark on him, no blood at all save the Fury's and that of Fagus Firmiana. She recalled the ease with which he'd snapped the Fury's wrist and decapitated her. How was it possible that this carpenter from Brool—to all appearances a slight and, with his withered leg, sickly man—could possess a strength even a shrive would envy? She felt a stirring in her heart unlike anything she'd ever known.

Then the prophet looked in her direction. Though she knew it was impossible, Viridis felt his severe dark eyes, charged with an enmity beyond mere hatred, eyes that seemed capable of ordering the deaths of millions for the sake of an absolute good, bore into her down the hollow tube of the spyglass. She felt judged, condemned, dismissed, all in an instant. She gasped as if pierced by a shrive's dart and let the spyglass fall over the rail of the balcony. Her heart was melting and soaring at the same time.

Because this sensation was so new—or, perhaps, so old she'd forgotten it until now—Viridis misunderstood it. She took it for a passion: the madness of a lust beyond all lust that every Cat most fears and desires.

Then and there she fell to her knees and swore a vow to Maw, Dam of Darkness: she would abjure all carnal pleasures, live as chastely as a withered crone, and die as one, until and unless she won Ixion Diospyros to her bed.

And that, Cy marvels, is how it all began. With a Cat swearing an oath to Maw to entice a saint into her bed. Out of that had come the cult of Saint Viridis Lacrimata, blessed above all women, Patroness of Holy

Patrimony, Our Lady of the Perpetual Sacrifice, founder of the peripatetic sect of Viridians and the compassionate advocate and consoler of women throughout the Hierarchate.

But because every woman's faith shares this origin, even the purest devotion is tainted by the touch of Maw. Cy thinks he can detect it now in the crimson glow suffusing Rose's cheeks, in the glimmer of tears that cling to her eyelashes like diamonds in the candlelight. He feels threatened, as if she's escaping him, using religion as a refuge from his authority and that of all men, a place where she, and all women, can indulge passions permitted them nowhere else.

Cy begrudges her this, or any other, sanctuary. There's something faithless about the idea of sharing Rose with another man, even a saint dead for thousands of turnings. But then he recalls something the Mouth of God said to him during the time of his *Trachaea*: "Women, being weak, need something of their own to believe in, and Ixion, being wise, did not deny that need but instead turned it to his advantage."

Her prayers done, Rose wipes her eyes and flashes Cy a contented smile. He helps her to her feet.

The floor slips sideways as they stand, and they clutch each other to keep from falling.

"A Chastening!" There is excitement in Rose's voice. And fear. She buries her head against Cy's shoulder and begins once more to pray, her voice muffled now.

Meanwhile, the simular of Saint Viridis sways on her almost-invisible wires as though celebrating—if not actually orchestrating—the event. The tokens of thanks affixed to her gown in layers like an armoring of faith clatter together with a sound like the finger cymbals used by Viridians. Shaken loose, a gold coin wanders across the rough stones of the floor to strike the edge of Cy's boot. He watches as if in a dream as it wobbles onto its side; the coin is old, stamped with the sigil of a long-dead Sovereign, Basilicus LXVII.

Candles topple as the worsening tremors raise clouds of dust. There's a dull roar from everywhere and nowhere, and the sound of people shouting.

Cy prays in earnest now, though no words pass his lips. His eyes are fixed on the suffering face of the simular of Saint Viridis, as if imploring her to open her wooden lips and speak for him, say the words he can't say.

Instead, fireflies crawl sluggishly from the empty sockets of her eyes.

The color of bronze, the fireflies glitter harshly in the candlelight like pieces of living metal. Eyes like polished stone bulge from the fat little bodies that cling to the simular's gown as if they, too, are expressions of thanks pinned there by grateful hands. But in the end the fireflies are shaken loose. They drop heavily to the floor amid pools of wax and fallen candles, fanning their wings in a useless shimmering blur and moving their stubby legs with mindless determination. From time to time their bodies throb with a green light that fades before it can illuminate much of anything, as if the radiance exhausts itself in its own expression.

Sacred to Saint Ixion Diospyros, fireflies may not be willfully injured or killed. Their stings must be borne with patience. To harm one even by accident is a grave sin.

The ground rises then drops, as if a giant has shrugged. There is a noise of glass breaking, then a drawn-out groan like a great tree splitting down the middle. Rose cries out despairingly at the sound.

As he turns to comfort her, Cy sees a wire supporting the simular of Saint Viridis snap in a plume of dust. The saint's head lolls to the side with an abrupt and, to Cy, uncannily lifelike motion. The saint appears to be contemplating the yellow platter in her hand—or, rather, what lies upon it—as if wishing she could take back what was sacrificed so long ago.

Then all at once everything is still, the flickering of the candles dim in the clouded air.

But the Chastening, Cy knows, isn't over.

Fireflies continue to spill from the eyes of the simular. They pour from her mouth, the tips of her fingers . . . from every opening in that old and broken body, long retired from active use upon the stage. Their wings move furiously, filling the air with a humming sound, although they do not as yet fly.

Cy pulls Rose, who is sobbing now, out of the shrine and into the center of the church.

A crowd has gathered about the nave. It grows steadily as people enter the church. Frightened voices call for the Mouth of God.

The Season of Chastenings, which commences on All Saints' Eve, the last day of Holy Week, and usually lasts about four and a half months, until the Feast of Saint Sium Lyrata or thereabouts, has been especially harsh and lengthy this turning. The Feast of Saint Sium was weeks ago, and still the ground shakes. Still the Chastenings come. Truly, thinks Cy, the Spinner is angry. Someone or something has displeased Him.

"Oh, Cy!" Rose's voice is heartbroken. "Look at Ixion!"

A deep crack runs up the withered leg of the huge figure of Saint Ixion that hangs above the nave. A crack that was not there before.

Just moments ago Cy wanted nothing more than to avoid the Mouth of God; now he pushes with Rose to the front of the crowd to call for him with the others. The Chastening hasn't shaken his faith, only the pretense of not needing it.

At last the Mouth of God appears, climbing the stairs that spiral up from within the tabernacle. First his tonsured head comes into view, with its axe blade of a nose and gray eyes ringed with shadows like bruises that never heal. Then his lanky body, a geometry of warring angles in loose white robes. He hauls himself up the stairs as if each step is a sacrifice unjustly demanded of him, one for which he will receive no thanks in this life and precious little in the life to come.

Stepping onto the nave, the Mouth of God moves in his grudging way to the railing at its edge and makes the sign of the Wheel above the crowd. His baggy sleeves flap like the wings of some strange flightless bird as he calls for silence in a shrill voice.

An uneasy hush descends. Cy squeezes Rose's hand. She gives him a nervous smile, then returns her attention to the Mouth of God.

The priest clears his throat. "There are sinners among us," he begins in a lackadaisical tone that seems wholly divorced from the import of his words and the wreckage of the Chastening, as though he's reciting an old text from memory. "Foul heretics who, with a pretense of piety, seduce the faithful to damnation. These servants of Maw must be exposed. Punished. Or else the Spinner's wrath will smite us all. I don't need to remind you of Saint Ixion's words: 'Better to lose a finger than a whole hand.'"

"Who are they?" cries a voice at the front of the crowd that Cy recognizes as his father's. "Tell us!"

"What of Ixion?" cries another voice. "Look!"

The Mouth of God glances up at the figure of Ixion, then staggers as he catches sight of its damaged leg. "Martyrs and saints defend us!"

"What does it mean?" shouts someone.

"Is the Unspinning upon us?"

The Mouth of God gathers himself with a stern shake of the head. "You ask me who the sinners are." His voice trembles, no longer simply reciting words but inhabiting them. "You ask if the Unspinning is at hand. I tell you, we must live each day as if it were the Unspinning! Didn't Ixion tell us this? 'Look not for the hour of my return,' he said to Saint Quercus Incana. 'In each moment I am closer to you than your own heartbeat.'

"I fear we have forgotten the prophet's words! We have forgotten his closeness and thought only of how far away he is, how high above us! For too long we have taken the light of his Burning Wheel for granted. Our prayers have become routine. Is it any wonder the Spinner is displeased? Is it any wonder He sends a Season of Chastenings without end, each one worse than the one before?

"Oh, we have angered Him with our sinful ways! Our selfish, forgetful ways! Which of us is not guilty? We are all sinners! My children, what are the tremors that shake the ground in this season compared to the daily tremors that rage inside us? You come to me now because the great simular of Ixion has cracked. But what of your own neglected hearts? Ixion is there, too . . . and there his image has long since cracked, unnoticed, unmourned!

"But the Spinner notices. The Spinner mourns. And like a righteous father, the Spinner punishes."

"But we are devout people!" cries a man's voice. "Is it not Maw who has done this thing?"

The priest's face flushes crimson. "Haven't you heard a word I've said?"

The man to whom the rebuke is addressed—Mahaleb, the butcher—smiles awkwardly in the drunkenness of shame, his eyes darting in guilt and appeal to friends and neighbors in the crowd. But they edge away, rejecting him. Soon he stands at the center of a ring of hostile faces. With the same absurd smile frozen on his face, he hangs his round, thickly bearded head.

The first punch strikes Mahaleb below the left ear. He lifts one arm reflexively, then lowers it, keeping his arms rigid at his sides, fists clenched. He makes no sound.

A flurry of kicks and punches fills the air. Most fly high or wide of their mark, striking other targets or no one at all. But enough blows land to drive Mahaleb—who accepts his punishment meekly—to his knees.

The crowd pulls back. Mahaleb sways for a moment, beard glistening with blood. He's no longer smiling; with a groan, he topples to the floor.

The crowd gives an exultant cry and surges forward. Cy feels joy and purgation as his foot sinks deep into the butcher's side. It cheers his heart to see Rose kicking so prettily beside him, skirts hiked to her knees as though dancing.

"Enough!" The Mouth of God pounds the railing with his fist. "You are no better than Furies! Do you strike to chastise Mahaleb's error or to indulge your own wicked passions? You hold to the forms of things, but inside, what a falling away there has been! Do not blame Maw. Look inside yourselves and accept the blame. Mahaleb merely spoke what each of you was thinking. But the Spinner's judgment cannot be evaded so easily! There is nothing He does not see, nothing He does not know."

The Mouth of God takes a breath and continues in a more reasonable tone. "Without the pillars of Church and Hierarchate erected by Saint Ixion Diospyros, the Furies would return from Herwood to practice their profane and bloody rituals, murdering men, corrupting women and children. Nothing would stand between us and the Pit of Damned Souls, where the tormenting fires of Maw burn without light or heat, a darkness that feasts forever without consuming what it feeds on! Is that what you want?"

A shout goes up from the crowd: "No!"

"Then repent." The voice is softer now, entreating. The groans of Mahaleb, sharp, indrawn, as if each breath inches a blade farther into his ribs, lend support to the priest. "Repent. Heed the sign before it's too late. Accept the punishment the Spinner has devised that you may know the breath of His forgiveness."

There comes a loud and drawn-out creaking. The acolytes of the church—boys who have not yet been called to the *Trachaea*—struggle to close the heavy outer doors, bare shoulders pressed to the wood.

Cy shivers in dreadful anticipation. All around him the people of Jubilar are opening their robes or removing their shirts. Women stand with arms veiling their breasts. Children tremble at their sides with muffled sobs and sniffles, trying to act brave. The men stand like Mahaleb moments before, staring straight ahead, fists clenched at their sides. Mahaleb, too, somehow shrugs off his bloody garment.

Cy lets his robe slip from his shoulders. Although such feelings are sinful beneath the gaze of Ixion, all he can think of is Rose. Rose beside him, naked to the waist. Rose standing with eyes closed, lips quivering as though waiting for his kisses, as she will after the wedding. Tomorrow. It's forbidden to look, but he does anyway, furtively, out of the corner of his eyes.

Rose's smooth white shoulders—whiter still against the creamy blackness of her hair—inflame him with longing. The pale curve of her side below her crossed arms is a shape more perfect than anything he's coaxed from wood.

What shapes will he coax from her?

He wants Rose. Wants her helpless before him, with no raised arms to deny his gaze, no covering at all, just her long, black hair, unbraided, like a fine dark mist or veil. Then to pierce that veil and touch with fingers and lips and tongue what lies behind it, to take possession of it utterly, forever . . .

The Mouth of God raises his arms. Only he, in all the church, remains fully clothed. He lets the silence stretch, and stretch, then suddenly begins:

"Ixion Diospyros, Wheel Incarnate, blessed instrument of the Spinner, hear your humble servant! Let my mouth be your mouth! You who spin above us nailed to your Burning Wheel; you whose redeeming weave of light has broken the timeless chaos of Maw, separating day from night; you who shed your blood for us and bequeathed to us the holy institutions that keep us strong; you who watch over us with a pitiless and wrathful eye, protecting us from Beauty: yours the right to judge, yours to punish! Let your will be done, now and always!"

"As it was in the beginning, is now, and shall be until the Unspinning!" Cy intones along with everyone else.

Meanwhile, fireflies are pouring from the grottoes where the simulars are enshrined. They move with the quickness of wind, the fluidity of water, climbing the walls in glittering streams to converge upon the dome of the church, which they blanket like a second covering of gold leaf.

Then the dome sags sickeningly, as though collapsing, and Cy, unable to tear his eyes away, realizes that the swarm has taken wing. It hovers in midair above the nave, a bronze cloud lashed by flickerings of green. The thrum of their wings drowns out the sounds of prayer. With each passing second, the swarm grows larger. Louder. Still it hovers.

Then it falls.

Cy glimpses the Mouth of God, his white robes flapping as the fireflies dive past. The priest stands like a statue, invoking Ixion Diospyros with outstretched arms; yet his arms tremble as if gripping the reins of a power that seeks to run wild, a power too great for his old hands to harness.

Then the swarm hits. Cy loses sight of the priest. He sees only the metallic blur of bodies that strike with the force of stones, knocking him to the floor.

The fireflies crawl upon him. His chest and arms, neck and head, every exposed inch is thick with fireflies. Only his eyes are free; he breathes through a living mask, fighting down nausea, afraid they will enter his nose, his mouth. The stings come thick and furious, burning with the wrath of Ixion.

Cy feels his blood boiling in his veins. His senses reel with a pain so intense and encompassing that it approaches a kind of ecstasy.

His world dwindles to a pinpoint emerald flash as the stings of the fireflies coalesce to a single sting. Time stands still, hovering. He's no longer aware of the bodies surrounding him, of Rose, of his own body. He has no body; he's pure spirit, a silvery condensation upon the surface of a fiery green sea. He floats there, formless in himself yet given form by the shiftings of the sea beneath him. Suddenly an immense wave lifts him on its swell.

Or, not a wave.

A Wheel.

And Cy sees—not with his eyes but with some finer, more discriminating sight, like the vision that descended upon Saint Viridis Lacrimata after she plucked out her eyes—the Burning Wheel of Saint Ixion Diospyros.

Wreathed in flames, it turns with a slow and inexorable rotation against the dark void of the Pit of Damned Souls. In the depths of the Pit Cy sees the plaintive glitter of tormented souls like flecks of ice crying out for heat. His own soul aches inside him with the nearness of that bitter cold. And yet he rides upon the Wheel, on its very rim, like the candles he and Rose lit in the shrine of Saint Viridis Lacrimata.

Others are riding there as well, each soul adding its small flame to the greater burning. In the turning of the Wheel some souls fly off like sparks to dwindle into the Pit. Others fall back toward the Wheel's bright center, the motionless hub that shines with a blinding green light. They emerge transfigured, reborn, spiraling slowly outward to the fiery rim once more.

But for those souls flung from the Wheel, there is no return to it ever.

Cy feels the hopeless vertigo of that falling, and a longing gnaws at him, bottomless as the Pit itself.

Then nothing.

When Cy comes to his senses, the fireflies have gone. He sees the Mouth of God at the nave. Head bowed, shoulders sagging, the priest holds himself up with a visible effort.

Cy lies amid a welter of bodies, too weak to move. He hears people moaning faintly on all sides. He, too, is moaning. Every so often a convulsion wracks his body as the venom ebbs.

Soon he can stir. Sitting up, he feels a dampness at his groin and realizes vaguely that he's ejaculated. Everything is far away, or he is; he feels empty, hollow, as if the force that swept through him, excoriating, then exalting, has, in its abrupt withdrawal, scraped him clean.

With the fireflies it is always thus. Cy shudders as the bits and pieces of his shattered life come slowly, painfully, back together. Gradually he becomes aware of a soft chorus of weeping from the women of Jubilar. He listens as he might listen to a wind he cannot feel, grateful for the sound of what he can't experience himself, for men may not cry. But as Saint Viridis replied to Saint Rober Viburnum when rebuked for her tears, the tears of women are shed not for themselves but on behalf of men.

Only now does Cy think of Rose.

He finds her close beside him, her face glistening wetly as she fastens her blouse.

"Get up!" the Mouth of God exhorts suddenly from the edge of the nave, as if cheered by the spectacle of his dazed and supine congregation. "Rejoice! Your sins are forgiven! Blessed be the Spinner!"

"Blessed be," comes the response from the people of Jubilar as they stagger to their feet, joints inflamed by the stings. Yet there's not a mark on any of them, save only the butcher, Mahaleb, who bears the bruises of his beating.

"Go forth and sin no more," says the priest. "It is late in the day. The sun is setting; soon Beauty will rise on the tides of night. There is your proper concern. A Chastening only harms the body; Beauty corrupts the soul. The Chastenings last for a season only; Beauty is without end."

Making the sign of the Wheel, the Mouth of God turns from the nave in a swirl of white robes. He hurries down the staircase and disappears into the tabernacle.

Cy feels Rose's hand shyly touch his own. He takes it firmly, as he's been taught to do, and smiles with the confidence he knows she expects of him, the confidence he expects of himself.

Her green eyes shine, reassured, reassuring. He can't understand why it is they make him feel so uncertain.

TWO

Rose and Cy step from the church into the fading light of day. Hand in hand, they descend the steps. The bare frames of stalls and stages dot the plaza, along with piles of lumber and rolls of brightly colored bunting and crisp white canvas gathered for tomorrow's wedding and the Feast of Saint Ilex Erythrina.

People had dropped what they were doing and come running to the church at the first tremor of the Chastening; and it's a good thing, too, for Rose sees now that a number of the hastily erected structures have fallen. Thank Viridis no one was hurt. The stunned silence is broken by nervous whispers and coughs, the shuffling of feet, and, present as always, the whistle of the Wheel as it spins atop the church spire. A few dogs scurry about with tails tucked between their legs, as if sensing that this protracted Season of Chastenings, already the longest anyone can remember, is far from over.

A small beagle, patched with brown and black and white, runs yelping eagerly to Rose.

"Fortunatus!" Rose scoops up the little dog, a gift from her father on her seventh birthday, eight turnings ago. She hugs and kisses the dog as it licks her face. A small iron horseshoe dangles from its leather collar. "Poor Fort, you were scared, weren't you? It's all right now."

Whining, Fortunatus squirms out of her arms and saunters ahead with the ludicrous self-importance of its breed, the white tip of its upright tail beckoning Cy and Rose to follow.

Cy laughs with a simple pleasure that touches Rose like a ticklish ray of light. She leans against him, laughing herself now with an overflowing happiness.

But how frightened she was in the Chastening! She thought the church was going to fall right on top of them! Thank Ixion Cy was there. How brave he was! How strong! Rose had felt safe with him, as if he could bear the whole weight of the church on his shoulders, strong as Saint Samsum Oxalis.

In her mind's eye, Rose sees the crack running through the simular above the nave, the wood rent as if by the claws of Maw. It's enough to crack her happiness.

Do simulars feel pain? she wonders. The Mouth of God would impose a harsh penance if she confessed a thought so close to heresy. But the truth is, ever since she was a little girl Rose has believed that some secret affinity joins the saints and their images.

Spinning above the world, nailed to his Burning Wheel, Ixion must have groaned aloud when the old wood split. Rose is almost sure she heard it; a faint cry of pain, impossibly distant yet also quite near. She blinks back tears, afraid of provoking Cy, who disapproves of what he calls, in a phrase inherited from his father, emotional displays.

Rose shivers at the memory of the fireflies. The dry scratchings of their legs and wings as they crawled over her in their mindless frenzy. The smothering weight of them. And the stings.

How is it an excess of pain can bring about its own transcendence? Rose doesn't know, but it's always that way with the fireflies. After the agony, rapture. After the punishment, forgiveness. The Mouth of God calls it the mystery of faith.

Transported amid the rest of the congregation, Rose looked without blinking into the heart of Ixion's Burning Wheel. Brighter than the sun—hotter, too—it did not blind her. It did not burn. Instead, she gazed upon Saint Ixion Diospyros.

How beautiful his poor body, naked but for the flames! How helpless, licked all over by those scalding tongues, his bloody wrists and ankles bound with thorns to the rim of the cruel Wheel, his crippled leg a withered branch! What a suffering he endured for her sake, for all their sakes. If she could just lessen it. Take some portion of it upon herself as Saint Viridis Lacrimata had done. How glad she would be!

Ixion had looked at her then, his two mouths smiling with unguessable intent. The lower mouth, cut into his throat by the Furies, spoke only to pronounce eternal damnation upon the dead. With his other mouth he directed the souls of those not condemned outright along the path of rebirth proper to their station, for the orders of the Hierarchate extend even into death.

Would he speak to her? Oh, speak! Rose had prayed with every quivering fiber of her soul.

Silent, Ixion's gaze took possession of her, burning into her, melting her. She gave herself up to him like an eager candle to a flame. A flash of color came: an intense, blinding green.

The next thing she knew she was on the floor of the church, wracked with shivers, as a departing ecstasy drew its fingers down her body.

Was it the same for Cy? Rose will never know. It's forbidden to speak of the visions. Not even between husband and wife. Only the Mouth of God, in the solemn privacy of the confessional, can be told.

Rose thinks what a strange thing marriage must be. To know a man's most intimate secrets, his flaws and virtues, his hopes and dreams and fears, to bind him to his bed each night and watch over him while he sleeps, to bear his name, his child, how strange, despite all this, not to know what he experiences in that moment. Is it blissful dissolution, a mingling of essences, human and divine, such as she has always felt?

Surely it is, Rose thinks. It must be. Otherwise, how awful! Man and wife always, at heart, strangers to each other!

They hurry across the plaza toward home. The sun hangs low in the sky, oblong, bloated, an outraged red. Ixion's Burning Wheel on its endless journey. Long after it's ceased to be visible from Jubilar, the sun will set behind the glittering spires of the Palace of the Chambered Nautilus in far-off Quoz. Then, as the scent of Beauty rises from Herwood to tempt men from the safety of their beds, Ixion will enter the Pit of Damned Souls to battle Maw.

There they fight as they have each night for countless turnings and will for countless turnings more until the Last Day. They fight, each unable to defeat the other. But Ixion has never failed to wrest another day from his adversary, helped by the fireflies, whose stings Maw cannot bear. Victorious, he climbs bloodied but renewed each morning from the blue waters that hurl themselves tirelessly against the cliffs of lowly Arpagee. And at the first hint of his resurgent light, Beauty retreats to Herwood to bide impatiently until the next turn of night.

Rose will never see sunset in Quoz or sunrise in Arpagee. The one is too much to hope for, the other too dreadful to imagine. She knows that Cy is eager to advance, to reclaim another piece of his family's shattered honor by rising to Kell. She's glad her dowry will help him, but she's never been ambitious for herself. The sunsets of Jubilar have always been splendid enough for Rose.

Turnings ago, when she was a girl of six, Rose thought the sun really *was* Saint Ixion Diospyros nailed to his Burning Wheel. She can smile about it now, but then she dreamed of beholding him in all his glory, as the saints had done after his fiery ascension.

It tormented her, this desire, for whenever she did try to look, the brightness of the sun would force her to drop her gaze. But she knew it wasn't really the brightness of the sun. It was the unworthiness of the eyes that dared to raise themselves to that height.

One day, after the Mouth of God had read from the *Lives and Acts* the story of how Saint Ixion had appeared to the saints and spoken to them from out of a wheel of fire so hot their hair was burned from their bodies, Rose lay on her back in the yard of her father's house and stared up into the sun, determined to find Ixion at last. The mysterious words of the saint echoed in her mind with the Mouth of God's voice: "I am the Wheel; the Spinner is the turning. I am the fire; the Spinner is the burning."

Ignoring the pain, she forced her eyelids open with her fingers while her vision swarmed with colors. She lay there for a long time, mumbling the words of Ixion under her breath. Then the whole sky flared. She saw a man's body in stark outline against a circular field of radiant white. The dark lines of his widespread arms and legs were like the spokes of a great wheel. She wept with joy as the image burned itself into her eyes, and she wondered if she would see it from now on wherever she looked. But then she heard her father, Cerasus, cry out in a strangled voice, and felt herself dragged roughly into the house.

Inside, all was darkness. Rose begged Cerasus to open the curtains so she could see the saint again. But the curtains were already open.

The apothecary was summoned. He took one look at Rose and rendered judgment with a measured shake of the head, in which sympathy and professionalism gravely mingled. The child had blinded herself. There was nothing he could do.

Such an act was less admirable in one's own daughter than in the long-ago lives of the saints, apparently. As she drifted to sleep—having gratefully swallowed the bitter draught offered by the apothecary, desiring its promised oblivion—Rose heard her mother demand of him bitterly, as though he were to blame: "Well? Who in their right mind will marry a blind girl?" The apothecary did not answer, at least not in Rose's hearing.

But she knew the answer perfectly well herself, even if she was only six. No one, that's who.

Rose grew desperately ill. She burned with fever one minute and shivered with chills the next. Her eyes itched so terribly that she had to be bound to her bed like a man to keep her from scratching them out. She lost all track of time and place. There was only an endless succession of dreams and hallucinations. Bleak visions of the Pit, of dread Maw and her Furies, but also sublime visions in which she walked with the saints and martyrs in a golden light just as if she were one of them, a second Viridis Lacrimata.

Best—yet also worst—were the visions of ordinary happiness: her mother knitting at her bedside; her father tugging his ear in the funny way he had while he read to her from the *Lives and Acts*; all the things that Rose had seen a thousand times and taken for granted, as if they would always be there to be seen, as if she would always be there to see them.

Under the spell of such visions, Rose imagined her sight miraculously restored. She cried out for the straps to be removed, only to feel the dark and leaden weight of the bandages wrapping her head and eyes like the shroud of a dead man.

Then she fell silent and listened to the voices. There were always voices. Some she knew. Others she did not. She grew afraid to answer, never sure if they were really there.

The Mouth of God came to Rose; or, anyway, his voice did. The voice told her she was being punished for having dared to look upon what must remain hidden from the eyes of women. "No woman," said the voice, "should ever seek to pierce the veil of Ixion's mystery. It is impious, blasphemous, a sin of heresy, worse even than losing a father or husband to Beauty."

The voice went on to explain that the sun in the sky was but the pale image of Ixion's Burning Wheel, not the thing itself. Indeed, Rose was fortunate to have been only blinded; the briefest, most fleeting glimpse of the true Wheel would have burned her body to ashes and hurled her soul straight into the Pit.

The voice speaking so harshly of sin and punishment had its effect. Rose prayed to the Spinner for forgiveness and begged the Mouth of God to restore her sight. But the priest couldn't cure her. And forgiveness had to be earned.

Months went by. Rose kept to bed though her fever was gone and the bandages removed. How she yearned for a glimmer of light! A glimpse of color! Some reassurance that she, or the world, existed. She felt more dead than alive, buried under a mountain of black sand that grew higher with each passing day. There was talk of summoning the panderman; even her parents whispered the dreaded name when they thought she couldn't hear. But Rose was always listening; blindness had honed her hearing to such a fantastic pitch that even while asleep she could follow conversations in the next room.

One day a stranger arrived in Jubilar. The carriage in which he rode had the look of a thing of metal, silver and gold polished to a blinding shine. Upon the doors a fiery inlay of jewels depicted a plumed serpent grasping its tail in its mouth. Worked into the serpent's scales was the motto "In My End Is My Beginning," and, at the center of the circle, thus formed the letters "A" and "Z" in mother-of-pearl and onyx.

The imperial seal of Azedarach LXIV.

A team of four white horses pulled the carriage. The splendid animals stepped high through the narrow lane leading to the Rubra house, their long manes braided and beribboned like a woman's hair on a saint's day. Tiny silver bells jingled on harnesses of polished leather.

A pair of shrives shared the reins. Two more stood at the rear of the carriage. Their suspicious blue eyes in their featureless black masks flickered tirelessly over the gathering crowd, keeping it at a respectful distance; while such carriages passed through Jubilar from time to time, it was exceedingly rare for one to stop.

In the darkness of her room—merely the outer shell of the darkness to which she had retreated, a darkness as many-layered as an onion—Rose heard the jingle of bells and the clip-clop of hooves on cobblestones. She burst into tears, for who else could it be but the panderman? She wailed in terror. Nothing her father or mother said could quiet her. At last Cerasus, frightened half to death himself by the sudden appearance of an imperial carriage at his gate, forced a gag into Rose's mouth and tied her to the bed.

The man who knocked at the door wore robes of delicate blue. He held before his face, in an exquisite white hand, a mask crafted of hammered gold and the colorful plumage of rare birds, a mask in which a small ruby glittered above a smiling rictus of golden lips like a beauty mark. Fierce blue eyes peered through angled slits in the mask.

The man gave no name, introducing himself simply as a vizard from the Palace of the Chambered Nautilus in Quoz. Cerasus fell at once to his knees.

"Rise, rise." The vizard motioned impatiently with a slender walking stick. As soon as Cerasus was on his feet, the vizard pushed past him into the house, leaning heavily upon the stick while holding his mask carefully in place. "There's been talk at Court of your daughter's blindness," he began without preamble.

Cerasus blinked, scarcely comprehending. "You've heard, illustrious sir?"

"Her story has reached the ears of the Blessed Sovereign, as all stories eventually do. Notwithstanding the impiety of her act—an act the Sovereign has no choice but to condemn in the strongest possible terms, as I'm sure you appreciate—Azedarach finds himself moved by the faith that impelled it. Such a faith, however misguided, springs from a devotion that itself goes a long way to mitigate whatever sins it may give rise to. Your daughter's faith—a bit excessive in this day and age, to be sure—is the same faith that led the saints to victory over Maw and her Furies. The Blessed Sovereign said—mark you, these are his very words—'It's a miracle to find such faith in a child today; and not just any child, but a girl, a veritable Saint Viridis. What an example of sacrifice for the girls and young women of the Hierarchate!'"

"He said that?" Cerasus made the sign of the Wheel. "Ixion bless and keep our gracious Sovereign. May he reign forever!"

As if hearing in Cerasus's voice some hint that he was about to fall to his knees once more, the vizard made a stiffly preemptive gesture with his walking stick before continuing.

"Upon reflection, the Sovereign has concluded—and the Ecclesiarch agrees completely, by the way—that your daughter's simple faith would benefit more from mercy than punishment. She has already suffered enough for her sin."

With that, not even the walking stick could prevent Cerasus from kneeling and kissing repeatedly the hem of the vizard's robe.

Rose was given an infusion to make her sleep. The vizard spoke to her softly while it took effect. She couldn't understand what he was saying, but the sound of his voice soothed her. Gentle and wise, it was like the voice of a saint: Saint Ixion Diospyros come to protect her. Rose fell asleep with a smile on her face.

Two shrives carried her to the vizard's gilded carriage. No one—not Cerasus, not even the Mouth of God, who had arrived at last, wondering aloud why he hadn't been told earlier of this singular visitation—was permitted to look inside. The vizard promised to return in two days. Then, with the crack of a whip that sent the crowd scurrying, the carriage moved off in the direction of Quoz.

It was back early on the morning of the second day. A crowd was waiting at the Rubra home, a reception organized by the Mouth of God, who was determined not be ignored as he'd been before.

Alas, it was not to be. Stepping from the carriage, the vizard ordered the crowd to disperse before the Mouth of God could say a word. Then he motioned with his walking stick for Cerasus to join him. Together they walked to the house.

"Well, we've done it," the vizard said in a voice full of weariness and satisfaction. "Your daughter's vision is restored."

"Thank Ixion!"

"And the skill of these hands."

Two shrives carried a still-unconscious Rose from the carriage and returned her to her bed. Her eyes were once more swathed in bandages.

Over the next few days, Rose's eyes tingled constantly. She couldn't stop crying, only it was as if the water of her tears had evaporated, leaving only the salt. She developed excruciating headaches. Delirious, she believed Cerasus had moved his foundry into her skull. She cried out with each blow of his hammer how sorry she was for everything, for anything, as if first the blindness and now the cure were the two halves of a single punishment.

Rose tried to scratch through the bandages. She would have damaged her eyes again if Cerasus, forewarned by the vizard, hadn't strapped her down. Infusions left by the vizard eased her into a sleep where the pain couldn't reach; but even there she sensed it hovering, spiderlike, a malignant red blotch at the ragged edges of her consciousness.

The pain reached its height, then ebbed by imperceptible degrees. There came a day when Rose realized she no longer felt pain, just a hollow ache, an empty space where it had been. Her eyes still itched, only now they itched for light, not fingernails.

Soon afterward, Cerasus told Rose it was time for the restraints and bandages to be removed. It was her birthday. She was seven.

As her mother carefully undid the bandages, it seemed to Rose that time itself was being peeled away. Her mother's fingers were leading her back day by day through the accumulated layers of darkness and pain to the moment she'd gazed into the heart of the sun, determined to find Saint Ixion.

Almost an entire turning had gone by since that moment. Now Rose recoiled from her earlier self. She told herself she wasn't that bad girl anymore. She was a good girl now. And always would be.

Rose felt the remnants of an outgrown skin coming away with the bandages. All she'd suffered, the punishments inflicted on her for her sins, she took up now and directed inward, against herself. Against the girl she had been: her other, secret, self. The Fury she carried inside her.

Rose wouldn't look into the sun again. She would keep her eyes lowered, forgo the freedom of the sky for the safety of the ground. She would kill the Fury.

The last bandage fell from Rose's eyes.

She cried out in despair. There was only darkness.

"Shh," her mother said. "You've lived in the dark for so long that even a little light would hurt your eyes. Be patient, Rose, and wait like a good girl."

And so she sat with her parents in the darkness one last time, clutching their hands. Bit by bit the solid field of black, thicker if possible than the absolute night, came apart, swarming with black and white dots like busy salt-and-pepper ants. Grainy patches of gray coalesced, then resolved into indistinct shapes, shapes she seemed to know more by memory than sight.

Rose recognized the bulk of her dresser. It leaped out of the shadows, eager to be seen. Now other pieces of friendly furniture—a chair and night table, the bed in which she was sitting propped up on pillows—emerged to say hello, welcome back, we missed you. Her bedroom, her whole life, reconstituted itself around her.

An odd paleness fringed the windows. When she asked her father what it was, Cerasus went to stand there, little more than a shadow himself to her eyes. He fiddled with something, and the paleness grew less pale. Like some fast-moving liquid it formed pools on the floor, bringing with it hints of color.

Light, she realized. She was seeing light.

Laughing, Rose turned to her mother. But her laughter died at the sight of the tears running down her mother's cheeks. She touched the tears, then held up her fingers wonderingly and admired them as if they were sparkling with diamonds.

Her mother hugged her so tightly that Rose could barely breathe. She was laughing and crying at the same time, muttering prayers of thanks to Ixion and all the other saints.

Rose was happy, but her mother's behavior frightened her. She burst into tears.

It was then that Cerasus—who, unnoticed by Rose, had left the bedroom—returned. He cleared his throat, and as if at that signal, though reluctantly, Rose's mother relaxed her embrace. Wiping her eyes, a shy smile quivering at the edges of her mouth, she rose from the bed. Rose looked questioningly at her father.

Something small wriggled in his arms.

"This is Fortunatus," he said in a choked voice.

With a yelp, the puppy leaped onto the bed, licking Rose's face until she was shrieking with laughter and squirming under the covers to hide.

"Happy birthday, Rose," her father said.

And it was.

Two days later, after Rose's eyes had become acclimated to a somewhat brighter light, Rose asked her mother for a mirror. She was curious to see if she still looked the same. Would she recognize herself, or had the dark time through which she'd passed left its mark upon her features, changing her into someone else, a stranger?

With the mirror in hand, her mother seated expectantly beside her, smiling encouragement, an influx of dread caused Rose to hesitate. Did she really want to know? But she screwed up her courage and raised the looking glass.

Her reflection *was* altered. Gone was the chubby face she remembered, in its place a pale mask of sunken cheeks and hollow eyes lost in shadow. Her once-lustrous hair had forgotten how to shine. She looked like a haggard Viridian. Who would marry her now? She searched desperately for some trace of her old looks. And, like an answered prayer, her nose, her lips, her forehead came reassuringly into sight, like the furniture of her bedroom two days before.

She was the same girl after all, only receded a little from view, as if still coming back to the surface of her body, making the long journey back into the light.

Rose brought the mirror closer to her eyes, looking for evidence of her blindness. Lustrous green eyes gazed back at her.

She threw down the mirror with a scream.

Her eyes had always been brown. Not green. *Brown.*

"What is it, darling?" her mother asked. "What's wrong?"

"My eyes!" was all Rose could say, covering them with her hands.

"Do they pain you? Is the light too bright?"

Rose shook her head. "They're not mine!"

"Not yours?" Her mother laughed, relieved. "Whose then?"

"I don't know! The vizard stole them!" Rose had been told of the vizard's visit, though she remembered nothing of it, neither where he'd taken her nor what had been done there.

"Don't be silly, Rose! Some things are beyond even a vizard's craft!" Her mother picked up the mirror. "Here, look again. No one's stolen your eyes. The very idea! A vizard steal my girl's lovely green eyes! Wouldn't I know it if he had?"

Rose refused to look. Later, when Cerasus returned home for supper, Rose's mother related her fancy, and the two of them shared a laugh at her expense. Rose pouted at the table, hating them.

But she quickly became less sure of herself. Now she was able to play with her friends and with Fortunatus in the full light of the day, picking up her life right where she'd left off. No one treated her any differently, though in the beginning a kind of aura clung to her because of all that had happened. But no one noticed anything odd about her eyes.

Finally Rose decided she must have dreamed up the whole business of brown eyes. Hadn't she believed lots of crazy things when she was sick? Soon she forgot not only her suspicions but that she'd ever had them, becoming as proud of her green eyes as she'd been, at first, afraid.

At the edge of the plaza, a wide road cuts straight as a ruler through the village of Jubilar. The road begins in Arpagee and stretches all the way to Quoz, linking the seventeen villages and cities of the Hierarchate like jewels of wildly disparate value strung together on a necklace. Now Rose and Cy walk hand in hand down that road toward the Rubra home, Fortunatus still preceding them.

"Just think," says Rose. "We've walked along this road a thousand times. But when we come this way tomorrow, it will be for the last time as who we are now. After the wedding, we'll be husband and wife. Then, by the grace of Saint Viridis, we'll be parents as well, the father and mother of a son."

Cy laughs. "You'll still be Rose; I'll still be Cy. Getting married and having a son won't change anything. I don't know where you get your ideas!"

"Can't people change?" Rose asks seriously.

"We're born as who we are, Rose," Cy answers. "The Spinner weaves that into each of us. People don't change, only seem to as they fulfill their destinies, growing into who they are the way that boys grow into men and girls into women. Can girls choose to become men, or boys women? It's absurd!"

Rose is quiet for a moment. "Then I hope our destiny is a happy one."

"It will be enough if you give me a son."

"I pray each night to Saint Viridis for that blessing! And each day, when we light our candles in the church."

"I know you won't disappoint me."

"Would you love me if we had a daughter?"

Cy frowns. "It's bad luck to speak of such things, especially after a Chastening."

All of a sudden she's near tears, though she tries to hide them. Rose knows Cy better than anyone. She knows his brooding moods: the brittle pride and self-lacerating ambition that turn the triumphs of his talent into failures; the obligation of revenge laid upon him by Marcus, less an inheritance than an all-consuming curse; the veneer of arrogance cultivated to shield the shy good nature of his truest self from the relentless scouring of his father's expectations.

Loving him as she does, Rose holds even his flaws dear. But she loves what's underneath the flaws best: the sensitive and generous heart that redeems them. Though seldom glimpsed, she can feel it biding deep within him like a wounded creature afraid to step into the light. She's determined to coax it out.

Cy will change once they are man and wife, gentled by the perpetual sacrifice of her love. Each night Rose prays to Saint Viridis Lacrimata to show her the way.

But when, as now, Cy's lips lose every hint of a smile, when his eyes grow hooded, and his features harden into a mask as wooden as those worn during the revels of All Saints' Eve, then it's impossible for Rose to know what, if anything, he's feeling, and what he expects her to feel. She feels lost, like a kite whose string has snapped.

As they draw near to her house, Rose recites a silent prayer: *Saint Viridis, keep everything from shaking to pieces. Saint Viridis, hold us together.* And, as if in immediate answer, Cy pauses at the front gate to give her hand a squeeze.

"It's all right, Rose," he says. "You don't have to worry about anything. I know the secret of making a son."

"You do?" She gazes at him admiringly; how smart he is! "What is it?"

"Revenge," he says, and kisses her good night.

Inside, Rose's parents are waiting with supper.

"So there you are!" says her mother. She stands beside the kitchen table, ready to serve Cerasus, who looks at Rose and winks from his seat. Her father's hulking form seems, as always, too large and massive for the chair, which, nevertheless, supports him as it always has.

"It's not like you to be so late," her mother goes on. Her careworn face looks pinched and old in the candlelight, long gray hair drawn tight as a skullcap. The braided ends circle her fleshy neck like a thick scarf, then sink beneath her drab brown robes to bulge at her waist, as if, at her age, she's pregnant. "Is everything all right between you and Cy?"

Rose rolls her eyes, annoyed. "Yes, mother." Her mother always asks that question, as if she's afraid Rose can't be trusted not to make a mess of her own wedding.

"I've had a feeling all day bad luck was coming," her mother continues. "I pricked my finger at the wheel this morning, and you know what that means! 'Blood in the morning, Ixion's warning.'"

"Perhaps it's the Chastening," Rose begins.

Her mother throws up her hands in an abrupt gesture of dismissal. "'Man sins, the Spinner spins.' Now come help me serve your father."

Rose's mother continues to chatter as the two of them serve Cerasus his supper. Cerasus ignores them both, chewing the food set before him with no sign of enjoyment or, for that matter, awareness, like a cow chewing its cud.

"Just look at him. The poor man is exhausted. And why not? The Chastening damaged the foundry, you know. I don't care what anybody says. In my day, the Season of Chastenings came to a proper end each turning on Saint Sium's Day. There never used to be such shakings. It's not for nothing if we have them now. Mark my words, there's heresy afoot."

"That's not for us to say," says Cerasus, who apparently has been listening after all. He gulps his mug of beer, then holds it out for Rose to fill again. "Leave that to the shrives and the Mouth of God."

"Yes, husband." Her mother sighs. "What can we do but pray?"

Finished with his meal, Cerasus pushes back his chair with a satisfied grunt and stands. "I'm for bed. Rose, attend me."

Before Rose can comply, her mother intercedes. "Let the poor girl rest, husband. After tomorrow, she'll be attending to her own husband every night."

Cerasus nods agreeably, put in a good mood by the beer. "Only be sure to come and sit with me later, Rose."

"Yes, father."

Rose watches as her mother follows Cerasus out of the kitchen. She moves with a gait of plodding deliberation that Rose knows well, as if, over the turnings, the hair so deftly braided about her neck and waist has not only become the color of iron but has assumed its weight as well. How, she wonders, will her mother manage alone, when she's married and gone from the house?

But she will manage. Women always do. We women are never really alone, she thinks. We always have each other. That's our strength.

It gives Rose a warm sense of communion to think of how, in every home throughout the Hierarchate, from lowly Arpagee to the great Palace of the Chambered Nautilus in Quoz, wives and daughters and mothers are just beginning their jealous watch, alert for any sign of Beauty. She feels proud to be part of that caring net which willingly lets no man slip through.

Rose has no illusions about her importance in the scheme of things. Even if a vizard restored her sight once upon a time, still she's nothing more than a simple woman now, dwarfed by the vastness of the Hierarchate and the concerns of men.

But she has a part to play the same as everyone else, a part no less essential for being small. And perhaps, she thinks, when all the women, all the small parts, are combined, something large results. A glue or mortar that, however invisible to men, holds the Hierarchate together in its embrace like the perpetual sacrifice of Saint Viridis Lacrimata.

Each evening it's the same. Wives, mothers, and daughters all over the Hierarchate prepare their men for bed. They insert wax plugs into the men's nostrils and slide hollow wooden tubes into the holes in their throats. They strap the men down, which is not cruel but a kindness necessary to keep them from removing their nose plugs while asleep. Then they sit to watch over their sleeping men through the long and perilous night.

The women don't sleep at night; they doze fitfully, jolted awake by the slightest sound or movement. They nap in the daytime while the men are at work, stealing an hour of sleep here, half an hour there. In between naps they keep house, cook, go to market, do the washing and spinning and look after each other's children as if the children belonged to all of them in common. Rose was four before she realized the word "mommy" wasn't just another word for "woman" but instead referred to one woman in particular: her mother.

The word "daddy," however, always meant Cerasus.

The women's nightly vigil is devoted to the provision of small, practical comforts. Fanning the men, sponging their sweaty bodies, shooing the fireflies away, replacing spent incense and candles, making sure the windows are sealed, taking care of bodily functions in an efficient and discreet manner. All tasks of importance, no doubt, but are they of any *real* help?

What, Rose wonders, can mere women do against a rival they cannot smell, hear, touch, taste, or see? For only men can smell Beauty! Not even Fortunatus, whose nose is so keen, can grasp that scent. For all Rose knows, the air is already thick with it.

There's nothing she or any woman can do but turn their prayer wheels in their hands and study the sleeping men for any change of expression: a sudden quickening of breath, a red flush spreading over the cheeks, tremors in the lower extremities.

Perceiving such a sign, a woman (Rose has practiced with her girlfriends a thousand times!) must throw herself atop the body of her man and thrust her perfumed hair into his face to overwhelm Beauty's odor with her own palpable fragrance.

Sometimes the crisis passes, no one knows how or why. The man wakes in the morning with no memory of the fierce battle waged on his behalf. But if he wakes with popping eyes and with screams or incomprehensible mutterings on his lips, if he strains against his bonds until it appears as though the veins in his neck must burst or his bones snap like dry kindling, then there's no hope. That man is irretrievably lost. He is no longer a husband, father, or son.

He belongs to Beauty. To Maw. Dam of Darkness.

Nothing remains for that man's woman but to fulfill a last, terrible obligation: she must undo his bonds and set him free. Give him up to whatever fate awaits him in Herwood.

Each night Rose prays to Saint Viridis to spare her that awful sight and the even more awful task that goes with it. Rose doesn't think she'd ever have the strength to unfasten Cy's bonds and give him up. The mere thought of it makes her sick to her stomach. She'd kill herself first, even if the act disgraced Cerasus and condemned her to the lowest depths of the Pit.

Rose has finished her supper and is clearing away the dishes when her mother returns to the kitchen. "You must be hungry, mother. Let me serve you."

Her mother shakes her head. "Your father wants you upstairs. But first I have something for you, Rose."

"What is it?"

"Sit down."

Curious, Rose takes a seat while her mother goes to the cabinets and rummages around inside. Finally she comes to the table and sits beside her daughter. She's holding a small blue pouch in her hand. "An infusion of vervain and vulveria," she whispers as though to keep Fortunatus, who lies in the corner, from overhearing. "To keep the womb clean and receptive."

Rose blushes. "Mother . . . "

"Hush. Each morning, you must brew a tea using just a pinch, no more. Like this, see?"

"Phew! It stinks!"

"'Bitter in smell, all will be well,'" her mother quotes absently, holding a pinch of the tea under Rose's nose. It's the custom for the bride and her mother to speak as little as possible of the wedding beforehand, and then only disparagingly. It's not wise to draw the attention of Maw. Tomorrow, in the daylight, there will be time enough for talk and celebration.

"And for Cy, I have this." She produces another pouch, this one bright red in color. "Add a leaf to his tea each morning, and he will not soon tire of you, I promise."

"Why would he tire of me?"

"He's a man, isn't he? Go on, take it. You'll thank me for it one day, as I came to thank my mother."

Rose accepts both pouches, tucking them into her dress. "What's it like, mother? You know, the deflowering." She hates that term. As if she'll no longer be Rose when it's over.

"What's it like?" There's a trace of a smile on her mother's lips. A sad smile. "It's like dancing."

"How will I know what to do?"

"The man leads. You follow."

"I'm afraid of doing the wrong thing."

"You can open your legs, can't you?"

"It still hurts a little." A week ago, the stitches with which she was sewn shut as a child were removed by the apothecary in preparation for the wedding.

"Good. The pain will help you resist the promptings of Maw. Her voice is loudest and most tempting during moments of carnal embrace."

"I'm afraid, mother."

Her mother strokes Rose's hair in what is, for her, a rare gesture of sympathy and compassion. "Poor Rose. You're about to become a woman."

"Is that so bad?"

"Bad's got nothing to do with it. It's hard, that's all. You must pray to Saint Viridis Lacrimata."

The air is smoky when Rose cracks open the door of the bedroom and slips inside. The scent of sandalwood uncoils from sticks of incense glowing faintly orange in the corners of the room. She stifles the urge to cough, afraid of waking Cerasus.

A pair of candles flanks the bed in which he lies, bathing her father in a flickering, uncertain light. He's propped up on pillows, mountainous beneath a thin sheet already damp with sweat. The steady whistle of his breathing reminds Rose of the Wheel spinning faithfully, day and night, above the church.

Her father is the most substantial man she knows. Nothing bends Cerasus Rubra. As a girl, Rose clung to his thick arms as though to the branches of a tree, dangling her feet off the ground and shrieking with delight as he spun her around and around. *Faster, daddy! Faster!* she cried, as the bright world wheeled past, tilting into a blur of colors. She drank it all in without breathing, afraid to blink for fear of missing an instant of happiness.

And then, each night, to see him lying like this in bed. Helpless, the sturdy tree felled. His arms and legs strapped tightly down, his nostrils plugged, the hollow tube whistling in his throat, in his eyes a glimmer of some fearful and complicated emotion known only to men.

For many turnings that sight caused Rose to burst into tears. Even now it fills her with an almost unbearable pity, a nervous awareness of the fragility of things, as if the life she knows and takes for granted is as thin as an eggshell.

Cerasus's eyes flutter open. A smile spreads across his ruddy face at the sight of his daughter. Rose thinks of Cy lying in his bed now, tended by his mother for the last time.

"Come and kiss me." Her father's voice is scratchy, wind through dry grass. He's always more affectionate when it's just the two of them.

Rose presses her lips to her father's gray-whiskered cheek. She savors the smell of sweat and carbon that rises from him, traces of the forge no incense can mask.

"You were at church?" He winces with the effort of speaking.

"Yes, father."

"I couldn't go. The foundry was damaged. I had to fix some things."

"The church, too." She hesitates. "The simular of Saint Ixion cracked."

Her father gives a start. Air wheezes through the tube in his throat as his muscles flex against his bonds. "Cracked you say? It's the work of Maw, surely!"

"Mahaleb was beaten for saying so."

"Was he now?" He barks with laughter. "Poor Mahaleb! Will he never learn to hold his tongue?" But her father's good humor is quick to fade. "Keep me company for a while, daughter, on your last night as a maiden. How will I ever sleep without you?"

Rose fetches from its place against the wall the wooden stool on which she's spent a part of most nights since she was a girl. Once it had seemed so tall and imposing, a symbol of power and authority like a mountain to be scaled, from the top of which she could watch over her father's sleep and keep him safe from Beauty, as if able to see it coming from a long way off.

Now the stool barely reaches her knees, and it's far from comfortable, but she still uses it because it makes her feel closer to the girl she used to be. Settled in, she begins to pull with a gentle rhythm a string that hangs from the ceiling, and a breeze wafts from overhead.

Cerasus's eyes are closed again, his face smoothed by weariness. His massive chest, constricted by the leather straps, hardly seems to rise despite the regular whistle of air through his throat tube.

How old he seems. It occurs to her suddenly that on a night like this one she'll be sitting here upon this stool, a dutiful daughter returned for the last time to her father's deathbed.

How long until the vision comes to pass? Sooner rather than later. For Cerasus *has* grown old, she sees now. It's as if, in all the turnings she kept a sharp eye out for Beauty, another adversary, more subtle still, has stolen upon him. Not that he's grown weak and doddering like the Mouth of God; no, her father is as strong as ever, still able to lift an anvil above his head and throw it farther than any other man in Jubilar, as he'll no doubt prove tomorrow during the Feast of Saint Ilex, in the contests of skill and strength.

But Rose recalls a time when her father didn't suffer his bonds so easily. When there was, or seemed to be, a proud if passive resistance in the way he submitted to the necessity of restraint. There was something unbroken in him then, something that couldn't help rebelling even though it was all for his own protection.

No more. Now Cerasus has grown content, comfortable in his bonds, as if he couldn't sleep without them. Rose wonders if she'll look at Cy one day as she prepares him for bed and see the same expression. Won't she be, in some way, responsible for it? She remembers Marcus's words, his voice only half-teasing: "Evil thoughts sprout from women's hearts faster than men can weed them."

Now Rose hears her mother mounting the stairs with her heavy tread. Coming to take her place. And with a sensation of great bewilderment, she finds herself suddenly crying, unable to stop, though she weeps in silence so as not to wake Cerasus.

THREE

A firefly's sting jolts Cy awake. He blinks his sleep-encrusted eyes, manfully bearing the pain while trying to hold on to the tatters of a dream. But the shards of image and feeling slip away, no sooner grasped for than gone.

Really, he thinks with an exasperated sigh, the stinging is too much. He can't see the firefly, but he feels it behind his ear. The candles that should be burning at his bedside have gone out, plunging the incense-choked room into a darkness as thick as the night that broods outside his tightly shuttered windows.

"Mother?" he whispers.

There's no reply.

"Mother!" Louder now. Still no reply.

Damn the woman! She must have fallen asleep at Marcus's bedside. Again. She's old, Cy thinks angrily. Worn-out. Never enough sleep, she says. But whose fault is that? It's no excuse. Others manage well enough. Some women have three or even four men to attend to in a night: father, husband, father-in-law, son. They don't complain. They don't allow candles to go out or fireflies to sting.

Lately Cy hasn't felt safe at night. He no longer trusts his mother to protect him. The sting of a firefly is sharp, but it fades. Beauty's sting only worsens with time. Not even death can bring an end to it; according to the Mouth of God, a man who has smelled Beauty once smells it forever, even amid the stench of the Pit of Damned Souls.

Cy shifts, hardly able to move in his bonds. With his arms and legs strapped down, his head held in place to keep the nose plugs and throat tube from becoming dislodged, he feels like a baby in swaddling clothes.

Once married he won't suffer this way any longer; he's promised himself that. Rose will tend to his needs. He'll teach her to anticipate them. No longer will he have to wait patiently until Marcus is through. After a lifetime of waiting, Cyrus Galingale will come first.

But it won't be easy to train her. Cy has no illusions about that. Rose needs a firm hand. It's all her father's fault; Cerasus spoiled her shamelessly right from the start. Giving her that dog, for one thing, which she then spoiled in turn.

Because she's never failed to get her way with Cerasus, Rose expects other men to give in as easily. And thanks to her beauty, they often do. It's made Rose into a brash young girl, with more spirit than the other girls of Jubilar. But now she's grown too wild, soared too high. She needs a husband to clip her wings.

The sensation of being stung ceases abruptly; there's a whine of wings, and Cy sees the intermittent green spark of the firefly spiraling lazily through the dark above him. Around and around it goes, around and around in the same changeless circle. He hopes his mother comes before it lands on him again; he doesn't relish the prospect of another sting. Even worse is the fear that the insect will crawl down his throat tube and enter his body.

Fireflies are born from the souls of dead men. After a man's death, before the coming of the hearse, the body is carried into the tabernacle. There it is bathed, perfumed, and dressed. The jaws are bound shut, and all the openings of the body plugged. For two days, the men of Jubilar fast and perform the rituals of transubstantiation, led by the Mouth of God. A hearse arrives on the third day to carry the deceased to Quoz. There, in the great Cathedral, the Ecclesiarch slides a tube into the throat of the deceased. If a firefly crawls out, iridescent wings glistening, the man has lived a virtuous life. But if not, it's proof that Maw has claimed another soul. Shrives are dispatched to test the man's family, for where one has fallen, others, too, may fall.

Cy finds something horrid in this miracle. Obscene. He can't believe the firefly has come into being out of something as ineffable as a soul. He has a different explanation.

One night, a firefly crawls down a man's throat tube. It burrows deep into his body and lays its eggs. Sometime later, the eggs hatch. The maggots devour each other until the lone survivor begins to eat its way out, killing its host in the process.

Cy has been plagued by this fear ever since his *Trachaea*. He's never confessed it to the Mouth of God or anyone. How could he? He knows it smacks of heresy. But he can't help it.

Earlier, when the fireflies had swarmed over him in the Church of the Spinning Wheel, he'd bitten his tongue to keep from crying out. And rightly so. This way no one knows the truth. No one can despise Cyrus Galingale for a coward. No one can suspect him of heresy. No one.

Except Cyrus Galingale himself.

There's no escaping the night, Cy thinks. Dreams and memories will find you even if Beauty does not.

He remembers how they'd come for him five turnings ago, a week after he'd turned twelve. He'd been working alone in the shop. Marcus had gone home for an early lunch, forbidding him to follow until he'd finished sweeping up. Suddenly, as he hummed to himself, lost in the rhythms of the sweeping, the door to the shop had burst open.

In rushed . . . *Furies*.

Nothing in Cy's twelve turnings had prepared him for the sight of such unnatural creatures. He saw faces with a scattering of eyes and beaks rather than noses, webbed hands grasping at the ends of leathery wings, mouths that snarled, baring rows of wicked teeth, from foreheads.

With a scream, Cy dropped the broom and collapsed to the sawdust, a simular with cut strings. Then the howling Furies were upon him.

Blows and kicks rained down on him, but he scarcely felt them through his terror. Choking on sawdust, half-blinded with blood and tears, he tucked his head to his chest and hugged his knees.

He felt himself snatched up and passed in a circle. The Furies snarled and snapped as if fighting over which of them would have the honor of tearing him apart. In an instant he was naked, his clothes ripped to shreds. He choked on the coppery taste of blood. He tried to struggle, but his limbs were held fast. Oh, why had he been such a wicked son? Was there no mercy in the world? It was all he could do not to cry out for his father.

A hood was slipped over his head, a drawstring cinched tight about his throat. He could hardly breathe.

The great bell in the church tower was tolling. The howls of the Furies grew wilder. Cy wept, glad the hood kept the Furies from witnessing his shame.

Then they were moving. He was carried along, shivering in the cool outside air. The howls subsided to urgent whines and growls.

The next thing he knew, his wrists and ankles were being tightly and none too gently lashed to a hard frame of some kind. He realized dimly that he must have lost consciousness. The bell had fallen silent. There was only the rasp of his breathing and the frantic tolling of his heart.

The silence stretched until Cy thought he must scream or beg for mercy, shaming the name of Galingale with a coward's death. But just when it seemed he could bear it no longer, he felt himself begin to turn. He realized he was lashed to a Wheel, like Saint Ixion Diospyros and the other holy martyrs.

The speed of his turning increased. The Wheel wobbled beneath him as if about to break into pieces, breaking him along with it. From somewhere came the beating of a drum, faster and faster, goading his heart to keep pace.

There was a tearing at the back of his head as the hood was ripped away. Candlelight clawed into his eyes. Cy blinked furiously against the return of sight.

He saw the Furies gazing down at him in silence, mutable as dreams in a thick haze of incense. Then the candles flickered, dimmed, and sprang back. The Furies were gone. In their place—as best Cy could judge, for the spinning Wheel still drew out his sight—stood men.

The drum gave a final beat, and with that the Wheel was wrenched to a stop so abruptly that Cy had the wind knocked out of him. Gasping for breath, his head still spinning, he saw Marcus. He saw Mahaleb, the butcher, and the blacksmith, Cerasus Rubra, who would one day be his father-in-law. There, leaning over him from behind his head, was the Mouth of God. All the men of Jubilar were gathered around the Wheel on which he lay bound.

The Mouth of God spoke. "This is the Wheel of Saint Ilex Erythrina, who watches over the village of Jubilar and whispers our prayers into the ear of Ixion. On this Wheel was he broken by the Furies. Behold, the shedding of his blood has left welts in the wood. Let them be filled again!"

"To overflowing," answered the men in a ragged murmur.

The sight of so many familiar, if stern, faces filled Cy with an almost boundless relief. He smiled up in giddy trust and wonder, unable to make sense of the words. He was safe now. The Furies had been vanquished. There was no need to fear.

The men held something tucked beneath their arms. At first Cy thought he was seeing the severed heads of the Furies, kept as trophies. But then he realized they were masks. Masks such as were worn during the revels of All Saints' Eve, the one night in each turning free of the scent of Beauty. For on that night, the very night of Saint Ixion's fiery ascension, the sun does not set, but remains unmoving in the sky.

The masks looked comical now, grotesque and exaggerated. How had he taken them for real? It had all been a charade, a joke. He began to laugh.

At that, hands seized him by the hair and yanked his head back. Fingers pinched his nostrils shut. A hand clapped over his mouth. He struggled, but to no avail.

The Mouth of God leaned close, muttering under his breath. Something glittered in his hand.

Cy felt a sharp pain lance his throat. Air rushed like fire into his lungs. The hands released him. He coughed, but couldn't draw breath. He was choking, drowning. His chest was bathed in blood.

The priest loomed over him. Another pain struck at him, the worst yet, as if the flesh of his throat were being stretched and torn.

When Cy next woke, he was no longer bound. He lay upon cold, damp stones, too weak to move. His throat was on fire. To swallow, even to breathe, was agony.

Some men were sponging his body clean; the light of the candles made a cool fire dance upon his skin, all reds and golds. When Cy turned his head, he saw his father gazing at him with a proud smile. Cy struggled to return the smile, wanting to be worthy of it.

"Cyrus Galingale, son of Marcus Galingale, is it not fitting that the son should follow the footsteps of the father?"

The Mouth of God's voice came from Cy's other side, a whisper in his ear. He turned his head.

The priest was kneeling close beside him, the sleeves of his white robe drenched with blood.

"So do we all follow the path walked by Ixion, advancing from sons to fathers, boys to men. Now you have set your foot upon the sacred path trod by so many before you. Honor them! Put your shoulder to the Wheel and push it forward another turn! You are a man now, and welcome among your brothers!"

"You are welcome," chorused the men, his father loudest of all.

Cy managed to raise a hand to his throat. He almost lost consciousness with the pain, but his heart leaped in joy as his fingers encountered a nub of smoothly rounded wood.

A throat plug. So this was how it happened! he thought. This was the mystery dividing youth from manhood! The mystery of the *Trachaea*! All the men here had passed through their moments of doubt and terror just as he had, emerging into the light of mature understanding. Now all his questions would be answered. All secrets made known. He struggled to speak.

"Hush," said Marcus. "Don't talk. Now is the time for listening."

Cy nodded, feverish with excitement. He touched his new throat plug again to assure himself it was really there, reveling in the pain now.

"You are in the tabernacle," the Mouth of God said. "A place both tomb and womb. When you leave, you will be wise in the ways of men. Once you were of woman born. No longer. That part of you is dead. We have killed it. But you have been born again. Born of men. That is the *Trachaea*.

"When Saint Ixion Diospyros was taken by the Furies and nailed to the Wheel, the servants of Maw couldn't bear the thunder of his curses, and so they tore out his tongue. Because they were wicked, and it amused them to make men suffer, the Furies stuffed his nose with dirt, slit his throat, and set the Wheel afire. Then it was that a second mouth opened in Ixion's neck. That mouth was the *trachae*—the mouth of miracles.

"And from that mouth not blood but words gushed forth as Ixion cursed the Furies to the Pit of Damned Souls. He called a whirlwind down from the sky that tore them limb from limb and then raised him spinning into the heavens, where he spins to this very day, dividing the darkness.

"It is in memory of that blessed miracle that we enact the *Trachaea*. Through it, you are purged of woman and reborn of man: of man alone. What you have experienced, Cyrus Galingale, and what you have yet to experience, must never be revealed to woman or child. The unspeakable torments of the Pit are nothing compared to what the man who betrays these secrets will suffer. The shrives themselves, with all their Six Hundred torments, could not match it. The same blade I have used to carve you a new mouth, a new life, can also take away that life." The priest pressed the sharp point of the knife to Cy's breast, above his heart. "Do you understand, young Galingale?"

Cy nodded, terrified yet also thrilled by the solemn new responsibilities thrust upon him, responsibilities he'd desired for so long.

"Not all men are suited to become brothers," the Mouth of God continued. "There were men among the servants of Maw, traitors to their sex. Men who acted the part of women with other men. Men who laid their loyalty between a woman's legs. Even now there can be such traitors: the Furies of Maw never sleep, young Galingale! Though you have not called them, still they will come. Fear them in all their forms!"

The Mouth of God put up his blade. "Sleep now. We will begin tomorrow."

But that night, Cy grew sick and feverish. He drifted in and out of consciousness for the next two days, a stranger to his body, hardly aware of his surroundings, the comings and goings of the village men, the priest intoning the daily Mass from the nave above his head.

The Furies returned to haunt his dreams. Not content to remain there, they crossed over into his waking hours, which became indistinguishable from dreams. He thrashed and moaned, laughed and wept at the parade of grotesques. In the midst of the terror and confusion, he was comforted by the cool touch of a hand upon his brow, steering him through the storm.

It was his father's hand. Three or four times a day, Marcus bathed Cy's throat with herbal infusions and unguents to prevent the wound from closing.

During those days, a closeness developed between Cy and Marcus that had never existed before and never would again. As he cared for his son, Marcus told him of the family's golden days in lofty Peripety, just as the story had been told to him by his own father. Cy listened as if hearing the three-hundred-turnings-old tales for the first time, as if he really had been born again and were living a second childhood, all memory of the first erased.

As his father's words quickened to life in his feverish brain, Cy thrilled to the triumphs of his great ancestor, Celtis Galingale, and shook with rage as the treachery of the Intricatas unfolded. He felt as if he were dreaming what he heard, creating it out of himself. Or being created by it.

"Of all the men in Peripety, the highest and most noble was our ancestor Celtis Galingale," Marcus said. His voice cut through Cy's fever like the priest's blade had cut his throat.

"His innocence and purity made people wonder if Saint Stilskin himself had returned from the grave. Celtis had often passed through the gates of glorious Quoz on imperial business, entering the Court of the Plumed Serpent. There he mingled so easily with the nobles that he was frequently taken for one of them. Indeed, it was but a matter of time before young Celtis advanced to Quoz and claimed his rightful place in the Court.

"If the Galingales were the leading family of Peripety, the Intricatas were second to them only because they had produced a daughter and not a son. In wealth and pedigree, in every other measure of worth, the two families were equal. What better match, then, than Celtis Galingale and Sersis Intricata? The fruit of that union must be a boy of rare ability: a captain of shrives, perhaps, or a cunning vizard.

"With promises of power and glory, Malus Intricata, the father of Sersis, tempted Celtis's father, Rober Galingale—curse him for a blind fool!—to contract the marriage. Meanwhile, the witch Sersis worked her wiles upon Celtis.

"Was there ever such a wicked woman as Sersis Intricata? It was whispered that she had murdered her own mother to share her father's bed. That false and deceiving female feigned a love for Celtis. She claimed to hold the flesh in contempt yet displayed her charms at every opportunity, as if her own innocence were so great no shame could touch her. She discussed the holy saints and martyrs like the meekest Viridian while her body spoke the lustful language of Maw until Celtis was inflamed with the desire that she should be his wife, her maidenhead his trophy. He spoke to Rober. The marriage was arranged.

"But marriage was not what the Intricatas had in mind. For many turnings they had harbored a secret jealousy and hatred of our family. Not to rise with the Galingales but at our expense was their fondest wish.

"Celtis had boasted to Sersis, as young men will, of the wonders he had seen in Quoz: the fantastic scale of the Cathedral and the simular of Ixion that hung there; the beauty of the women and the richness of their clothes, their intricate hairstyles, the fabulous jewels they wore, as if diamonds, rubies, and sapphires were as common there as coal.

"Sersis pouted, as women will, her vanity stung. She accused Celtis of preferring the women of Quoz to her. He swore that she was the most desirable woman in all the Hierarchate, but did that satisfy her? No. It was only her body that he desired, she cried. Her chastity, her devotion to the blessed saints, her obedience to her father; he didn't honor these virtues but only humored them the better to satisfy his lust.

"No, Celtis hastened to assure her. Her purity was what he loved. He worshiped her like a saint! She was a paragon of chastity and he a beast to so much as dare to gaze upon her!

"Back she swung to the other extreme: 'So you think I'm ugly; you can't even bear to look at me!' And so on, back and forth, until Celtis was out of his mind with guilt and desire, desire and guilt.

"Finally Sersis suggested that if he really loved her, he shouldn't be afraid to prove it. Afraid? Celtis Galingale afraid? Name it, he said. And then she struck: a trinket from Quoz. Oh, how his blood ran cold when he heard that! For then as now there was no law less equivocal than the law prohibiting retrogressive import. It was impossible that Sersis didn't understand what she was asking him to risk. But in his innocence, Celtis assumed she was ignorant of such things. He gently explained that it was a mortal offense for all but vizards, shrives, and simularters to carry objects from high to low, thereby mingling the orders of perfection.

"But Sersis wouldn't listen. She wept, called him a coward, his love false and mean, too stingy to fetch the merest bauble, a token she would treasure less for its beauty or worth than for the very risk run in procuring it. She swore that it would be their secret, a bond uniting them more intimately than a wedding ring. Her words licked his ear. Oh, what deadlier weapon than a woman's tongue! Not for nothing do the holiest Viridians tear them from their mouths!

"How, she asked, could it be breaking the law to bring her something from Quoz when, after their marriage, as everyone knew, they were sure to be raised to that city, were as good as elevated already? Where was the harm in it?

"Sersis turned cold and cruel, denying Celtis the velvet of her lips and tongue, the caress of her laughter, all glimpse of her save from a distance and always among his rivals, from whence she darted glances that turned his testicles to ice, then crushed them in a vise of smiles.

"Finally Celtis could stand it no longer. On his next trip to Quoz, he smuggled back a small brooch, a cracked badge of emerald and sapphire in the shape of a winged hart, its flaw too great for Quoz but even so a finer thing than any woman in Peripety could boast of.

"Yet when Sersis saw the flaw—a hairline crack in one wing—she spurned gift and giver with a laugh that sent Celtis rushing in misery back to his father's house. There the shrives were waiting, already alerted by Malus.

"Thus were the Galingales betrayed and disgraced. All we owned was taken from us and awarded to the Intricatas. Only the grace of Ixion spared Celtis's life, for Rober, to ensure the continuance of our line, swore that he and he alone had ordered Celtis to commit the crime. He was flayed upon the Wheel in the plaza of Peripety, cursing the Intricatas as he died. Celtis was blinded in one eye and banished to lowly Arpagee with no shred of his former glory but his name.

"The Intricatas, with our wealth added to their own, soon advanced to Quoz. As a reward for the seduction and betrayal of our family, Malus and Sersis, in order that their line continue, received a dispensation from the Ecclesiarch permitting them to marry. They brought forth a son to carry on the Intricata name. Thus were murder and incest blessed and rewarded! Not even her name yielded up to a husband! And so it is that the Intricatas survive to this day, awaiting our vengeance. For their badge of nobility they adopted the very brooch of emerald and sapphire that had cracked Celtis: the winged hart. If ever you see that badge, Cy, on a woman's breast or carved into a man's throat plug, strike without a thought!"

Cy moaned in his delirium, fighting against his fever as if it were an Intricata. His father repeated the story of Celtis and Sersis every day. At last, on the third day, Cy's fever broke. He broke it. The cold light of revenge glittered in his eyes.

Marcus lifted his hand from Cy's forehead and called for the Mouth of God. "Quiet now," he said. "Take your time." He held a bowl of warm broth to Cy's lips.

Cy swallowed, wincing. The savory broth spread vitality through his bones. Raising trembling fingers to his *Trachaea*, he swore in a raw whisper that the Intricatas would pay for their treachery. An oath thus sworn was the most solemn a man could make. For the first and only time in his life, Cy saw his father cry.

The next two days Cy spent in the company of the Mouth of God. "Now you are a man," the priest said. "Henceforward you will pass your nights in mortal peril, bound to your bed, your nostrils plugged against the scent of Beauty."

"Like Saint Ixion tortured by the Furies," Cy rasped in his raw voice.

"Exactly so, young Galingale!" The Mouth of God raised a thick gray eyebrow. "I'm pleased to see that you are sensitive to such things. So many young men these days lack all appreciation for the beautiful correspondences of religion, the symbols and rituals that join us in an ever-living mystery and reconcile us to the tribulations of life. Perhaps the priesthood lies in your future."

Cy stammered a demurral.

"Why not? Who knows but that one day the voice of the Ecclesiarch will speak to you from the shrouded mystery of the sacrarium as it did to me, summoning you to the glory of such a sacrifice! But only the Spinner knows what's to come: each man serves in his own small way. Now answer this riddle if you can: Why is a bed like a Wheel?"

Cy pondered. "Because in both there is much turning?"

The thin line of the priest's mouth tightened in a rare smile. "That is a better answer than you know. Once Furies bound men to Wheels in order to break them. Now women bind men to beds to atone for the past crimes of their sex. But do not think that because men are bound by women, we are in their power. That would be a grave error. Though they chain us to our beds, I tell you it is women who, by this very act, are chained. With every knot they tie, they bind themselves more tightly."

"How can this be?"

"Think of Saint Stilskin, the most innocent of saints, but also—after Ixion—the wisest. It was Stilskin who gave women the sacred task of spinning. But whence came this art and duty? From a trap that a Fury had thought to spring against him! What was to have been the instrument of Stilskin's damnation—a spinning wheel—became instead the weapon that undid his enemy. Is that not a subtle turning, young Galingale?

"This business of being bound is no different. Remember that Stilskin spun the Fury into a woman. You know the rhyme: 'Mother, sister, daughter, wife: four threads weave a woman's life.' There are Furies forever picking at those threads, seeking to unravel them.

"At night, when Ixion's Wheel sinks into the Pit, and the scent of Beauty rises from Herwood, we men are helpless, and women, too, are at their lowest ebb. Then it is that Maw's whispers sound loudest and most persuasively in a woman's ears, and she begins to desire other partners than her husband, or to resent his authority and that of all men. Idle thoughts breed obsessions, and obsessions, actions. Thus are men betrayed to Beauty.

"But how can we men—who cannot even protect ourselves at night—guard our women from the temptations of the Furies so that they can keep us safe from Beauty? Not just our own safety but that of the Hierarchate depends upon it! How, young Galingale? How?"

Cy shook his head. "I don't know, father."

"The answer lies in our helplessness. Because only men can smell Beauty, only women can protect us from it. And so they must pass their nights watching over us, bound not only by duty, but by fear: for they rightly fear what awaits them should they lose a man to Beauty.

"Thus, in being bound, we men gain power over the woman who bind us. Thus, in binding, women are themselves bound. What does a simular know of the strings that bind it, of the simularter directing its every movement from above? No more do women know! The scent of Beauty, young Galingale, so deadly to men, is at the same time our most potent ally. This is the great mystery."

Cy felt light-headed. Though he didn't understand all the priest's words, something in them sank beneath his reason and worked there, out of sight, to produce a bubbling of excitement.

That night, he was left alone in the tabernacle. No candle, however feeble, eased the darkness. Incense choked the air. Although the scent of Beauty could not invade the walls of the church, it was necessary for Cy to become accustomed to the devices that would henceforth guard his sleep.

But he couldn't sleep. Bound to the hard Wheel of Saint Ilex Erythrina, his nose plugs pressed tightly in place and his throat tube inserted like a hot dagger into the still-raw wound of his trachae, Cy shivered at the ticklings of fireflies as they crawled over his naked body. Their green flashes winked in the smoky dark as they emitted a low, contented drone, like purring cats. They didn't sting, but came to the edges of his eyes as though to sip his sight.

He closed his eyes and prayed aloud to Ixion, only to stop almost at once. For it was then that the fear first came to him that a firefly might crawl down his throat and lay its eggs inside him. Even as he lay with his lips shut tight, he seemed to feel something wriggling down his throat tube and deep into his body.

The next day—the fifth day following the *Trachaea*—an exhausted Cy was called up to the nave at the close of the Mass. There, dressed in the white robes of manhood for the first time—the collar and cuffs splashed in red, a reminder of the blood that had been spilled—he was presented to the congregation for the first time as a man. Marcus stood beside him as sponsor.

Below the nave, the villagers stood in his honor. Their applause washed over Cy, winging his heart. He stroked his throat plug, the novelty of which still thrilled him, then made the sign of the Wheel. A roar of approval went up. Marcus, with a proud smile, touched his arm to direct his gaze.

His mother stood in the first row, tears streaming down her cheeks. She wore a bright blue gown and carried the household distaff, symbol of her matronly duties. Her hair was braided in the style of a woman whose son has become a man. The heavy, wheel-shaped braids were interwoven with bright threads and ribbons. What tenderness Cy felt for her! How he yearned to protect her from the promptings of her inner Furies! Yet the sight of her tears, her woman's weakness, touched something newly cold and judgmental in him, so that his pity mixed with condescension.

Meanwhile, an excited voice was shouting his name again and again above the rest. It belonged to Rose Rubra, the pretty girl of ten turnings contracted to be his bride. She was waving frantically in his direction. Long black hair trailed like ivy over the puffy white shoulders of her dress, flecked with small flowers: violets, columbines, pansies. She would come to him on the day of their wedding in just such a dress.

That event had always seemed distant to Cy, like a fairy tale told of the future instead of the past. But all at once, his throat no longer smooth and childhood forever behind him, it drew perceptibly nearer. How lovingly she smiled at him, as though he were Ixion himself! He had never noticed how pretty she was, how pure and unspoiled. Surely no Fury could blister such a rose.

For the first time, as he stood upon the nave, Cy caught a glimpse in the skinny, excitable girl of the woman who would become his wife.

Now, five turnings later, Cy is a man of seventeen and Rose a young woman. Their wedding is only hours away. Cy feels as though he's about to wake from a long sleep, from a dream that had seemed to last for turnings but, upon waking, will prove to have been a thing of instants only. All the important moments of his life so far, what have they been but steps in an initiation now drawing to a close? His real life lies ahead. The life of a husband and father.

"A son's wedding day marks the culmination of a father's life," Marcus announces early the next morning while examining Cy's patrimonial robes. "I'll give thanks on the day your son is born, Cy, but that will be your triumph, not mine. A wedding, though; that's a father's crowning success. After all, who was it that chose the bride and arranged the marriage while your throat was still smooth as a baby's?"

Marcus tugs the right and the left sleeves of the robes in rapid succession, then stands back to judge the effect, rubbing his beard with one hand. "How does it feel?"

Cy shrugs, too nervous to care. "It's okay."

"Your mother should have made the sleeves longer. You'd think a mother would know the length of her son's arms!"

Shaking his head, Marcus strolls to the open window of Cy's bedroom. A ragged cheer and a few hearty thumps of a bass drum erupt from below. Some neighbors and a contingent of the village band are waiting to escort Cy to the Rubra house.

Marcus turns to his son with a smile, his gloom dispersed in the glow of so many good wishes. "We're on our way to Kell, I can feel it! I'm proud of you, Cy."

"A father's praise outshines the sun." Cy quotes the proverb absentmindedly as he studies his reflection in a full-length mirror affixed to the wall.

The patrimonial robes are woven of pure white cotton and colored silk. The robes are long and spacious but at the same time stiflingly heavy, for they consist of seven distinct garments, each more splendid than the last. It took his mother two hours to dress him this morning: there were candles to be lit and prayers to be recited with the donning of each layer. Cy thought she'd never be done. After the wedding, when he and Rose have retired to their new home, Rose will repeat the ritual in reverse, disrobing him layer by layer as though peeling an onion.

The outer layer seems to shine with a light of its own. The loose sleeves and the wide wheel of the collar display an intricate design of green vines and colorful flowers: dusky purple irises, sunset orange saintsblood, yellow cockleshells, silvery blue Saint Stilskin's Wort. The flowers look genuine enough to smell, as if nature and art have joined to honor the marriage. The remaining six layers of the robes, though hidden from sight, carry scenes from the *Lives and Acts* and from the history of the Galingale family.

Marcus gives a knowing wink in the mirror. "A little hot under those robes, Cy? Don't worry: It's wonderful to be married, my boy. For all the obvious reasons and for some not so obvious, or so wonderful either, to tell the truth."

Marcus chuckles, warming to his topic. "What I'm going to say to you now is just what my father said to me on the day of my wedding, more turnings ago than I care to remember. He was a strict man, my father! A bit of a tyrant. Not the indulgent father that I turned out to be. But no matter.

"'Marcus,' he said. 'Your wedding sets the stage for the great act to follow: the birth of your son, my grandson, another link forged in the chain of fathers and sons that stretches all the way back to the erection of the Hierarchate and beyond. Today the burden of responsibility passes to you. My part is done, my link forged and tempered. Like my father before me, I can say to the spirits of our ancestors: the Galingale name did not die with me! I can say to the perturbed spirit of the great Celtis: I have brought you a step nearer your revenge! Now, my son, you must go and do likewise.'

"As you yourself are the living proof, Cy, I did just that. Now I charge you to do the same, lest all our struggles be for nothing, our name a mouthful of sawdust, no longer spoken or remembered."

"With Ixion's help, I will."

"Trust no one, help yourself: *That* has been the Galingale motto ever since the Intricatas poisoned the Court against us. Let your thoughts be full of the blackest revenge each time you lie with your wife, and you cannot help but get a son."

"Is that how you got me?"

"Do you doubt it? Tender thoughts breed females. Males are spun from harder stuff."

"Shouldn't a man love his wife?"

Marcus snorts with laughter. "You have too much of the woman in you, Cy! Your mother is to blame for that, coddling you as she did. But I will teach you, just as my father taught me on my wedding day. Listen and save yourself some bitter lessons."

Cy looks past his father, out the window and over the heads of the people gathered below. It's a fine summer morning, with clear blue skies and a breeze that flutters the sun-dappled leaves of the maples in the yard. Cy smells roast suckling pig, braised lamb, grilled chicken, goose, and duck. He smells breads and pies baking and sauces simmering: a rich banquet of odors announcing the wedding and the Feast of Saint Ilex Erythrina to follow. Yesterday's Chastening is like a bad dream, already forgotten.

"Never forget that women are Furies at heart," Marcus says. "No matter how beautiful on the outside, rank corruption festers within. This is true of your mother, of my mother, of Rose, of all women. Don't they bleed each month in token of a secret wound, an inner pollution? Remember that the mother of Saint Ixion betrayed him to the Furies: our holy prophet, her own son!

"It's easy, I know, in the heat of passion, to relax your guard and think that this woman, my wife, is better than the rest. No Fury she, you tell yourself. She was spun from a finer thread. I warn you, Cy, shun that weakness above all others! If you feel tenderness taking root in your heart, rip it out! Force yourself to some deliberate act of cruelty. Though it may seem hard, habit will smooth the way until cruelty becomes as pleasant as copulation itself. Women appreciate a strong hand. They fear the Fury in themselves, the child that will devour its parent."

"You counsel cold sheets for a marriage bed, father."

Marcus shakes his head. "No, no! Enjoy your wife by all means. Sport with her; make her your plaything; take what pleasure you can from her. That's a husband's right. But be wary of giving pleasure in return as foolish husbands do, lest, by bestirring the Fury in your wife's breast, you stoke a fire that consumes you both. I've seen it happen.

"When you were just a boy, our neighbors, the Bilobas—Platan and Iris, you remember them—were like that. There was nothing Platan wouldn't do for Iris, and nothing she wouldn't ask of him. It was scandalous the way they lived. They were begging for trouble. So no one was surprised when Platan disappeared one night, lost to Beauty; the only surprise was that he hadn't been taken sooner. As we listened for the bells of the panderman the next morning, the lamentations of Iris rang hollow in our ears, I can tell you! There were cheers aplenty at her scourging. We felt sorry only for the daughter, Rumer. You used to play with her, Cy. I've never told you this, but she was originally contracted to be your wife."

Cy turns from the window at this news. "Rumer Biloba was to be my wife?" He remembers a skinny, clumsy girl with clouds of freckles.

"You see that everything has worked out for the best," Marcus replies with a smile. "Cerasus Rubra may have the backbone of a wet noodle, but he's no Platan Biloba. And Rose is not only a greater beauty than Rumer was likely to be—a stroke of luck for you, my boy—but she'll bring a richer dowry to the marriage than Platan could have scraped together. Enough to buy our way forward to Kell. So you see how important these things are. Not just the fate of individuals but entire families rests upon the maintenance of the husband's authority over the wife."

Now Marcus comes close and takes Cy by the arm. "My last piece of advice to you is this, a little trick I've often practiced over the turnings: When you lie with your wife, close your eyes and imagine it's Sersis Intricata beneath you. Then copulation will seem like a delicious act of revenge, which, in a sense, I suppose it is! Who knows?" He winks. "Rose may prefer it that way. Women often do."

Before Cy can answer, a lurching cacophony of drums, whining pipes, and horns commences beneath the window, accompanied by a fresh wave of cheers.

"That's the signal," says Marcus. "They're ready for us at the Rubras'."

Cy's mouth goes instantly dry. His heart feels lodged in his throat like a peach pit.

Marcus squeezes Cy's arm a moment longer, staring into his eyes. Then, to Cy's surprise, his father pulls him roughly into his arms and thumps him hard on the back. "May Ixion bless and keep you, Cyrus! Remember all I've taught you."

Marcus precedes Cy out of the room and down the stairs without another word or glance. Cy's mother is waiting at the front door, teary-eyed. She smiles at Cy but says nothing; it's not her place to speak.

Marcus takes his wife by the arm and leads her out the door. Cy follows. The full-leafed trees and white picket fences that line the street are draped with colorful banners and flower-wheels. Men and women dressed in their finest clothes cheer him on from all sides. Children are laughing, dogs barking. The band is murdering the wedding march. Cy smiles at everyone, flooded with gratitude for such good friends and neighbors. Marcus had taught him to keep them at arm's length in his relentless climb toward Peripety and revenge: *trust no one, help yourself.* But now, as they escort him to his bride, their enthusiasm touches Cy deeply despite his father's admonitions.

It's not long before they reach the Rubra house. The white gate gleams beneath roses and poppies, passionflowers and fiery snapdragons. A group of close friends and relatives stand inside the gate, fanning themselves with nervous energy. Rose's six bridesmaids are whispering together, their creamy pink gowns like blossoms ripe for plucking. In their hands they hold, with the utter conviction of the not-yet-married, wicker baskets piled with white and red rose petals; with every movement petals drift over the sides of the baskets and flutter like butterflies to the ground.

At the sight of Cy, the girls giggle among themselves. He's known them all his life: Alba Inodora, Flava Cambrica, Pavia Libani, Carya Ostrya, Kalmia Sium, copper-haired Vicia Campestris. Pretty girls all, they lack Rose's beauty, to say nothing of her dowry.

The band falls silent. Cy shifts uncomfortably. Sweat trickles down his back, making him itch. He searches the windows of the Rubra house for a glimpse of Rose. But the curtains are tightly drawn, as though it's a panderman and not a groom who's come to call.

Marcus, meanwhile, strides up to the gate, where a glass bell hangs from a ribbon like the fluted blossom of a foxglove. He gives the ribbon an irritable shake. The bell rings with a clear, high tone.

Immediately, the door of the house swings open and out steps Cerasus Rubra. He looks too large for his robes of silver and slate gray, which would have swallowed Marcus. Blinking, he hurries down the stairs as if afraid the steps will not bear his weight. He approaches the gate, smiling and nodding at no one and everyone, his eyes iron filings in a soot-bearded face flushed crimson as if fresh from the forge.

"Hello, Galingale." He extends the hammer of his hand to Marcus, who eyes the offering as though it's irredeemably vile. At this Cerasus flushes more deeply still and fumbles at the gate: "Er, that is, 'Who rings the bridal bell?'"

It seems impossible for Marcus to draw himself up more stiffly than he has already; yet, he does. "'A father and his son.'"

"'For whom have you come?'"

"'A daughter and a wife.'"

"'What can you offer?'"

"'A name for all her life.'"

Now Cerasus rings the bell, knocking it clumsily against the gate. By a stroke of fortune, the bell doesn't break. A sigh of relief rises from the crowd, giving way to murmurs of admiration as Rose appears in the doorway, her mother at her side.

Rose wears a gown of dazzling white. A cloud of white lace veils her face. She holds a bouquet at her waist. There are violets, ever-faithful; dappled pansies, which bring good thoughts; pale rosemary, for remembrance; humble daisies, fennel, columbines, and rue. Blossoms ride the waves and hollows of her black hair, which swoops from her shoulders to flare like a midnight lily's hood. Fireflies weave halos around her head as if her beauty, though veiled, sheds a nectar as potent as that of any flower.

But no sooner has Cy caught a glimpse of her than hands reach out to turn him roughly away. He hears the rustle of her gown as she descends the stairs, then smells her flowers as she takes her place behind him.

Then the procession sets off again, the band picking up where it left off. The bridesmaids lead the way, strewing white and red rose petals from their baskets. Marcus and Cerasus come after them, and are followed in turn by their wives. Cy's mother walks two steps behind Cerasus, while Rose's mother follows Marcus at an equal distance, thus symbolizing the weaving together of the two families in the ceremony of Holy Patrimony. Last of all comes Cy and, behind him, Rose.

The urge to look back grows more intense as Cy walks. The noise of the procession prevents him from hearing Rose, and, robbed of that assurance, he feels the need to prove to himself that she's still there.

He thinks of the story of Roemer and Jewel that his mother used to tell him when he was a boy. She told the story often, though he never asked for it. It wasn't one of his favorites; in fact, it gave him nightmares.

"This happened long ago," she'd begin, fussily tucking him in. "In the first days of the Hierarchate, after the Furies had been killed or chased into the heart of Herwood but before Beauty had begun to poison the nights of men as it does today. In those days, there lived in the town of Lusk a young man by the name of Roemer.

"Now, Roemer's father had fought shoulder to shoulder with the saints. He was a hero, wealthy and influential. Because of him, Roemer could have picked any girl in Lusk for a wife. But, to his father's great shame, Roemer fell in love with a girl from Gliff named Jewel. Bad enough that a man from Lusk should choose a bride so far beneath him. But it was even worse.

"The two young lovers had never met; they had seen each other only once, from a distance, across a battlefield. But that glimpse had been enough. From that day, neither one could forget the other even though they were deadly enemies, or supposed to be.

"For Jewel's mother was a Fury. One of the very worst. After sacrificing her husband to Maw, Jewel's mother had fled into Herwood with Jewel, although the girl hated her mother and despised the wicked ways of Maw with all her heart and soul, both of which she had pledged to Roemer.

"Roemer's father ordered his son to forget about Jewel and take for his wife a lovely girl from Lusk whose family was as blessed in honor as in wealth. But Roemer refused. Oh, he was a wicked son! He told his father he would rather die than wed a woman he didn't love.

"Roemer's father chained him to his bed until he should change his mind. The Mouth of God was summoned to convince him of his error. But Roemer refused to listen or to eat. Not a morsel of food passed his lips.

"Days went by in this fashion. Weeks. The Mouth of God shrugged his shoulders and gave up, saying, 'This is a matter for the shrives. Maw has sunk her claws too deeply in the boy.' But Roemer's father wasn't ready to give up. Without Roemer, he would have no heir. The family name would be lost. And so he persuaded the priest to wait a little longer. Perhaps the mere threat of the shrives would be enough to convince Roemer to obey. But neither son nor father budged.

"One night Roemer found he had grown so thin, like a skeleton, that the chains could no longer hold him. Though weak, he stole away and entered Herwood to rescue Jewel and claim her for his bride. But he collapsed before he had gotten far. The Furies found him. They took him to their camp, where they were brewing Beauty in a huge cauldron.

"They'd been brewing it for months, but they couldn't get it right. Something was missing. They were angry. Furious, in fact. And now a man had come to threaten their sanctuary. To contaminate it with his presence. And not just any man—that would have been bad enough—but the son of a hated enemy. That was unbearable.

"The Furies wanted to kill Roemer, to rip out his tongue and slit his throat, flay his hide to wear as clothing, and make a necklace of his teeth and hair. And they would have, too, if Jewel hadn't come upon him as he lay there bleeding and half-dead.

"She shouldered her way through the Furies to cradle Roemer in her arms. With defiant tears, she swore that if they killed him, they would have to kill her, too.

"The Furies didn't know what to do. Their greatest sin was to kill one of their own. And so they summoned their chief, Jewel's mother. Jewel begged her mother to spare Roemer's life and let them leave the woods together as man and wife.

"Jewel's wicked mother thought for a moment. Then she spoke to Roemer. 'Do you love my daughter?'

"Roemer nodded, the power of speech lost to him.

"'Will you give us, freely, a gift of blood? A single drop in payment for her?'

"He nodded again.

"With one sharp fingernail, Jewel's mother took a drop of blood from Roemer's finger and added it to the cauldron in which Beauty was brewing. A fearful hissing and bubbling commenced. Gouts of steam shot up, withering the leaves of the trees.

"Jewel's mother smiled, while the other Furies howled and danced. 'Now you may go. You, young man, must lead the way. And you, my faithless daughter, must follow without a word, for that is the life you have chosen. No glance may pass between you until you leave these woods, or I will know and send a curse against you worse by far than death.'

"They started out. Roemer in front, then Jewel. The Fury's art placed a path where none had been before. The pale, ascending line lengthened with each footfall. That was all Roemer could see: the narrow path shining as if with a light of its own amid the forest's dark and tangled green.

"And behind him, unheard, unseen, a silence as palpable as a ghost's cold breath. Was she there? he wondered. Or was it all a hoax, a Fury's cruel trick? Perhaps in her time with the Furies, Jewel had become one of them. Perhaps she was stealing up on him, about to plunge a dagger into his back. Roemer no longer knew what to think, what to believe. He doubted everything.

"At last a feeble light began to glow. The edge of the woods was near. Another ten steps and she would be his.

"Then he heard Jewel whisper his name. And something in her voice tugged at his heart so strongly that, without thinking, he turned to her.

"The path behind him sank like a mist into the ground. He reached for Jewel's reaching hands, but already his arms were stiff as wood. His toes had burst his shoes to wriggle into the ground. His mouth was a bump, his limbs branches, his eyes twin knots that ran with the sap of sight.

"Roemer had become a willow tree. Jewel was likewise changed. And at that moment, for the first time, the scent of Beauty rose from Herwood although it was still daylight. For in the beginning, before the sacrifice of Viridis Lacrimata, Beauty rose unpredictably, at all hours of the day and night.

"It was as if a plague had struck the towns and villages of the young Hierarchate. More than half the men disappeared over the course of the next day and night. They vanished into Herwood, never to return, Roemer's father among them. The wailing of bereaved women reached into the depths of Herwood, where the Furies looked up from their feasting and smiled bloody smiles.

"When Roemer saw the bewitched men streaming past him—he was a tree, but trees can see perfectly well—he wept in guilt and sorrow. Only then—too late!—did he realize how wrong he'd been. How foolish. He was to blame for the deaths of these men. For the death of his father. He had betrayed them, supplied the Furies with the sole ingredient they'd lacked to complete their wicked potion: a drop of a man's blood, freely given.

"Thus did the Fury's curse come to pass. Roemer could not act. He could not move, rooted as he was to the ground. All that remained for him was to repent his crime. And this he did without end or mercy, repeating his foolishness over and over in his mind until his life became a constant season of chastenings, reminded by the presence of Jewel beside him of the folly that had led to his undoing and the death of so many good men. And thus do all willows weep, sharing Roemer's sorrow and warning us all—but especially little boys—to profit by his example.

"So it was then; so it is today; so it will be tomorrow. May the Spinner bless this bed and keep you from all sorrow."

Now, as the wedding procession wends through Jubilar, Cy keeps his eyes trained on the spinning Wheel atop the church tower, for it's considered bad luck for a groom to repeat Roemer's mistake by looking back at his bride. The Wheel flashes like a second sun against a crisp blue sky aswarm with kites.

There are kites shaped like boxes, diamonds, pyramids, wheels; kites

painted with portraits of the saints and martyrs; kites that res
mals, birds, serpents, fireflies.

In the *Lives and Acts* it's recorded how, as a boy, Saint Ilex
loved nothing better than to fly kites, and even when a grown man no sight pleased him more. After the wedding, when the Feast of Saint Ilex is celebrated, there will be a war of kites in his honor, the boys of Jubilar vying for mastery of the skies. By the time the Feast ends, the plaza will be strewn with fallen kites, and a lone kite will remain in the sky, victorious.

Cy smiles, remembering how, in his boyhood, he labored before each Feast of Saint Ilex to craft a kite sure to sweep all rivals from the sky. So light yet sturdy were his frames that from the age of seven until his *Trachaea*—when he became a man and put aside such childish playthings—he never lost a battle unless his string was cut, a tactic held in universal contempt but secretly resorted to by boys desperate to win; in other words, by all of them.

How Cy wishes he could feel now, for one last time, the impatient tug of a string between his thumb and forefinger! To be a boy again, directing the swoop and dive of a sleek and deadly kite, instead of a groom whose heart feels as if it's snapped its string.

At last the procession reaches the plaza, where the rest of the village is assembled. Boys and admiring girls are jostling through the crowd as though tugged by the kites they follow, their eyes focused upward as if the intensity of their gazes is all that keeps the kites aloft. Meanwhile, older children and adults stroll past the stalls, admiring the traders' wares although the real bargaining won't begin until after the wedding.

Cy sees a simularter's wagon. Painted across the top of the wagon in bright red script is the legend: "Saint Stilskin's Men—By Appointment of His Majesty the Sovereign." Just below this, three terse sentences in sunny yellow outlined with a thin border of black: "To Instruct. To Amuse. To Elevate."

The simulars swing limply in their extravagant costumes of velvet, silk, and lace above a stage painted a watery shade of blue. Helpless without the hands that give them life—or, rather, the illusion of life—they seem to be marking time. They brush against each other with a rustle of fabric and the hollow rattle of wood on wood.

According to the *Lives and Acts*, on the Last Day, when the Spinner shatters His Wheel and from the fragments crafts a second Wheel whose spinning will never cease—a Wheel without the wobble of Maw—the simulars will come to life, cut their strings, and become in truth whomever they mimic. On that day, saints and Furies will walk again, refighting the battles of the past. Only this time there will be no escape into Herwood; the defeat of the Furies will be forever.

Now a simularter steps from behind the wagon to watch the wedding procession pass. The man is tall and thin, dressed in the black-and-white-checked harlequinery of his order. His throat plug is carved into the shape of an outstretched hand. His cheeks are pale as chalk. His eyes have a pinkish tint like a rabbit's. A single black tear glistens below his right eye; his lips are the same glistening black. His short white hair bristles like a skullcap.

The man might almost be a simular himself, Cy thinks, so motionless and emotionless does he appear, with his spindly arms crossed over a sunken chest and fingers that droop like the listless legs of a spider.

Cy feels himself and all of Jubilar judged and found wanting in the simularter's arrogant, sleepy stare. The presumption angers him; he always feels like simularters are laughing at him, at everyone not of their order. What gives them the right? What can simularters, who dwell in lofty Quoz, know of the struggle to advance? What can they know of the festering bitterness of betrayed hope, the consecrating fires of revenge and ambition? What can they know of Cyrus Galingale?

The simularter unfurls his fingers in a languorous wave full of restrained beauty. Cy detects no mockery in the gesture; on the contrary, it seems shy, half-envious, as if the simularter is never free of hidden strings and so cannot dare a spontaneous movement for fear of tangling or breaking them. Cy has a feeling such sensitive hands might find strings to pull even in a living thing, strings no one but a simularter can see.

The procession turns a corner and comes in view of the Church of the Spinning Wheel. Arrayed along the church steps, the rest of the village band welcomes them with a brassy fanfare. The Mouth of God is waiting at the top of the steps, the heavy doors of the church shut behind him.

The priest raises his arms, and the church bell begins to toll. The joyful tones rise above the noisy plaza as if the sky is the inner surface of a bell struck by the clapper of the sun.

Cy climbs the steps and stands before the Mouth of God. He feels as though he's always been standing here, waiting for the wedding to begin. He hears the rustle of Rose's gown as she takes her place beside him, but even now it would be bad luck to look at her. Cy stares at the priest, who stares back with an expression as sour as ever.

No one moves or makes a sound as the echoes of the bell fade. When things are so quiet that Cy can hear the whistle of the spinning Wheel and the buzzing of the fireflies drawn by Rose's flowers, the Mouth of God raises his trembling hands to make the sign of the Wheel above Cy's head.

A sigh as of a hundred held breaths released at once sweeps over the plaza. The priest clears his throat and begins to speak.

"Dearly beloved. In the piercing sight of Saint Ixion Diospyros, whose ever-spinning Wheel gives us light and life; in the tearful sight of Saint Viridis Lacrimata, Our Lady of the Perpetual Sacrifice, Protectress of Hearth and Home, Patroness of Holy Patrimony; in the sight of Saint Ilex Erythrina, whose feast we celebrate today; in the watchful sight of all the blessed saints and martyrs; and, finally, in the honest sight of all the good people of Jubilar, we are gathered here to join this man, Cyrus Galingale, and this woman, Rose Rubra, in the bonds of Holy Patrimony. All praise to the Blessed Sovereign, Azedarach LXIV, from whom all order flows! And also to the Ecclesiarch, Mouth of the Divine Will!"

Cy responds along with the rest: "Praise them with great praise! May they rule a thousand turnings!"

The Mouth of God attempts to hush the crowd with frantic motions of his hands. At last, giving up, he shouts in his high-pitched voice: "Here, on the threshold of the Church of the Spinning Wheel, before we enter its inviolable sanctity, I ask if there is anyone who knows a reason why this man and this woman should not be joined? Speak now or carry your knowledge to the judgment of Ixion."

A few nervous coughs.

The Mouth of God continues. "Marcus Galingale. Is it your wish that your son, Cyrus, be joined to Rose Rubra, daughter of Cerasus?"

"It is," Marcus's voice rings out.

"And you, Cerasus. Do you consent that your daughter, Rose, be given to Cyrus Galingale, son of Marcus, to bear his name and his child and to put the honor and name of his family above your own?"

"I do," Cerasus rumbles.

"Since the fathers wish it, so shall it be." The Mouth of God turns in a whirl of robes and strides up to the doors. He pushes them open with a strength that belies his frailty and leads the way into the church.

Cy looks around in amazement as he enters. If not for the crack running through the withered leg of the great simular of Saint Ixion, he'd find it impossible to believe that yesterday's Chastening had ever occurred. The damaged simulars are back in their shrines, the shattered stained glass windows replaced with windows of identical design. There are flowers everywhere.

The crowd spills into the pews as the wedding party advances down the central aisle, and the wavering strains of an organ fill the air.

Spiraling up the sides of the tabernacle is a staircase ascending the backs and heads and limbs of gargoyles carved into the wood. These appalling guardians have always seemed as fearsome to Cy as the Furies whose entrance they bar, but now he treads upon them like a conqueror.

Cy comes to the top of the staircase and steps onto the nave. The Mouth of God is waiting behind the altar wheel. More than seven turnings have passed since Cy last stood here on the morning after his *Trachaea*, when the assembled villagers cheered his entry into the ranks of men. It seems only fitting that he enter the ranks of husbands from the same spot.

Cy stands to the priest's right. From the safety of the altar wheel, he can turn at last to face his bride.

His heart lurches at the sight of her. How lovely Rose looks in her white gown, flowers spilling from her hair! A pure and dazzling radiance seems to stream from her as she draws near, escorted by both sets of parents. At that moment, Cy knows himself to be blessed. Not even Azedarach, seated upon the Throne of the Plumed Serpent at the heart of the Palace of the Chambered Nautilus in far-off Quoz, can be closer to the hub of glory than he is here and now.

Rose takes her place to the left of the priest, facing Cy, the altar wheel between them. Though the cloud of the bridal veil hides her features, he can see her trembling. His heart goes out to her, wanting to shield her forever from all uncertainty and pain.

The organ falls silent. The chatter of the congregation ceases. The Mouth of God begins to speak.

And Cy feels the bud of the instant burst, obliterating everything in the explosion of its bloom. As in a dream, he sees himself from a great distance. He watches as he presents Rose with the ring of smooth gold that Marcus purchased from a trader fifteen turnings ago in anticipation of this day, listens as Rose swears never to remove it as she slips it over her finger. He watches himself accept in turn the ring that Rose has woven for him out of her own black hair and hears himself swear to wear it until the moment of her dishonor.

All the while thoughts are flitting through his mind like fireflies: designs for new pieces of furniture, snatches of old songs, the painted face of the simularter who waved to him, memories of a dream he'd had the night before and forgotten about until now, in which he was angrily sawing away at a board of black walnut only to discover it was Marcus's body, stiff as a corpse.

Then, suddenly, the Mouth of God is pronouncing them man and wife to a chorus of cheers from the congregation. *I'm married*, Cy thinks, trying the words on for size. The priest is looking at him expectantly. So is everyone. Marcus nudges his elbow, and time resumes its normal flow.

"You may kiss the bride," the priest repeats, to general laughter.

Lifting Rose's veil, Cy sees that her face is pale and wet with tears. But her green eyes are lamps of happiness. He kisses her tenderly despite his father's warnings. She trembles against him as though she might faint, and he kisses her harder, until she squirms, her weakness waking something cruel in him.

FOUR

Rose clings to Cy's arm as he clears a path through the crowded plaza. Rather than giving way, people press closer still; it's good luck to touch a bride, a guarantee of fertility for women and virility for men. For hours now, ever since the beginning of the Feast of Saint Ilex, Rose has been groped and prodded. Her once-pristine gown is torn and stained; the flowers she and her mother had spent hours arranging are mangled or missing, snatched as souvenirs. Rose feels like a flower herself, plucked petal by petal.

Her head is spinning from the heat and the excitement and, not least, the brimming glasses of ale that are thrust upon her and Cy wherever they turn. Glasses which would be the height of rudeness to refuse.

Rose doesn't want to be rude. Not on her wedding day. So she joins in every toast, and even proposes a toast or two of her own to the vast amusement of the men.

"May your daughters bring forth sons!"

"Don't worry about our daughters, missy! You just be sure and take your own advice!"

Rose has never drunk so much in her life. She's not sure that she likes it, but she's not sure she doesn't. Maybe this is what making love is like, she thinks, and giggles.

"What's so funny?" asks Cy, with a smile more potent than a dozen glasses of ale. His hair flops over his shining eyes like the ears of a puppy.

"Everything!" Rose can't help kissing him. Ah, this is happiness! How handsome her husband is! She thrills to the word. She can't get over the fact that she has a husband. Everything in her life has changed in the blink of an eye, even her name. She's no longer plain old Rose Rubra, but Rose Rubra Galingale. She repeats her new name to herself, glorying in the cadence of its syllables.

Laughing, Cy returns her kiss. "Not even married a day yet and drunk already!"

"I'm not!" But she is. She knows it, and, what's more, she doesn't care. Tomorrow she'll be a respectable housewife, but now she's a bride. This is her moment, her day, even if she has to share it with Saint Ilex.

She holds tight to the household distaff given to her by her mother. Its solid heft makes her feel strong and capable, as if Saint Viridis herself is present in the wood. With her help, she'll weave a marriage that will never unravel, spinning the threads of the Rubras and the Galingales together into a single unbreakable strand.

Earlier, as she danced with her father-in-law after the ceremony—the band serenading them from the steps of the church and the ring of onlookers clapping in time to the music—Rose had promised Marcus a grandson.

"I swear by my distaff," she'd said, wanting to please him, to bring a smile to his face, which looked so serious and grave. "A grandson to carry on the Galingale name."

"You are beautiful, Rose," Marcus replied, touching her cheek. "But all your beauty will be worth less than nothing without a son. Do not make any promises. Promises are easy; delivery is what counts."

"Yes, father-in-law."

She'd been glad when the dance was over. Her shoulders still hurt where he dug in with his stiff fingers as if she were a piece of wood to be carved.

Though she knows it's a sin, Rose can't help it: Marcus frightens her. Sometimes, when he looks at her, she feels naked, as if he's looking right through her clothes. Once she made the mistake of confiding this to her mother, who scolded her for dressing so provocatively.

Sometimes Cy looks at her in the same hungry way. But that's different. Then Rose feels beautiful, desired. And then she desires him, too, with a need so overwhelming that she blushes to feel it. For while it's proper for a wife to love and obey her husband, the desires of the flesh come from Maw and must be smothered without mercy.

The plaza is packed with revelers. People dance and sing to blaring music that seems to waft from every direction. There are drinks to drink and foods to sample, games of chance and skill to be played, wagered on, and argued over, exotic wares from as far away as Colubrine and Brool to be purchased or bartered for. Cy and Rose wander, letting the flow of the crowd carry them where it will, basking in the good wishes of their fellow villagers. When they pass a stall or booth that looks interesting, they anchor there for a time before cutting loose to drift again.

But really there are two celebrations at the Feast: one on the ground, the other in the air, where the kites are fighting in honor of Saint Ilex Erythrina. The brightly colored kites hover and plunge, soar and swoop, with no quarter asked or given. The strings, bristling with shards of glass, glitter in the sunlight. Some strings are taut, some sagging—reflecting the strategy of the flier—as they run down to disappear into the crowd like fishing lines into a lake. Rose remembers how, as a girl, she followed Cy on feast days, cheering his kites on to victory in hopes of winning him.

Now shouts of "The kites! The kites!" run through the crowd as if some epic battle is taking place above. Laughing, Cy points upward, and Rose follows his finger to watch with a thrill of excitement, as if becoming again that worshipful girl, the spectacle of two kites jockeying for position.

The kites are beautiful, sleek, and responsive to the string. One is shaped like a shrive's mask, with Ixion's Wheel emblazoned in fiery red across the black face. The other is smaller, in the shape of a plumed serpent, its body scaled with tiny mirrors that flash like silver as it wriggles through the air.

The shrive kite is above the serpent, a dangerous place to be. It hovers there as if its flier would like to bring it lower but is afraid of giving the serpent kite an opening.

"He's taunting him," Cy explains. "It's a trap."

Even as Cy speaks, the serpent takes the bait and arrows sharply upward. But the shrive is no longer there.

"He's got him!" Cy's fingers twitch at his waist as if he holds the string in his hands.

The flier of the serpent sends his kite into a steep dive. But it's too late. With a graceful sideways loop, the shrive's sharp-edged wing shears through the serpent's string.

The silver kite shudders, springs aloft on the release of tension, then commences a slow descending spiral; Salvaged, it will fight again, but not today. Its cut string billows behind, seeming to float for an instant like a strand of a spider's web shimmering in the sun. But the weight of the glass soon makes itself felt.

The crowd ducks for cover as the string, with its coating of ground glass, falls like a whip from the sky. At every feast there are injuries from the cut strings.

Cy and Rose run, too, laughing as if fleeing a sudden downpour.

Then Cy pulls up short. Rose stumbles against him, her laughter dying in her throat.

Standing before them, blocking the way, are two black-robed Viridians, bent with age and infirmity yet, incongruously, holding hands like little girls. And not just Viridians . . .

"Saint Ixion bless and keep us," Rose murmurs, making the sign of the Wheel. All at once, she realizes the shouts she heard moments ago had nothing to do with kites dueling splendidly in the sky, but with these other Kites—less splendid, more terrible—on the ground.

The Kites don't move or say a word. Blind, they stare up at Rose and Cy as if perceiving them with senses as far beyond the normal ken as Quoz is beyond Jubilar. Their nostrils twitch, dark and hairy as the nostrils of old men.

Rose presses Cy's hand, but he pulls away to make the sign of the Wheel. She's shocked to see how pale he is; could he be frightened of the Kites, her new husband, who faced yesterday's Chastening so bravely?

Rose wants to be brave for his sake, but she's never been this close to a Kite before. It's unnerving, to say the least, to see how intricate is the map of scars covering their faces and, indeed, every inch of their bodies not hidden by the black robes.

The scars, she knows, are self-inflicted, in honor of the scars the blood of Saint Ilex etched into the skin of the Furies who killed him. Those Furies, baptized by his blood, had become the first Kites, protected by Saint Viridis Lacrimata. They are called Kites not only because of Saint Ilex's well-known love of kites, but because they blind themselves and so move through the Hierarchate like stringless kites in the wind, now back, now forward, now back again.

Rose shudders, imagining the strength of will necessary to carve one's own flesh as though it were a block of wood. For the scarification isn't random. Up close, she can see there's a pattern to it. Many patterns, as if the women are works of art as admirable in their way as the kites doing battle overhead. Some scars are ridged, others take the shape of dots and dashes, waves and spirals, symbols whose meaning Rose can't decipher but which, because of their obscurity, fill her with reverence and awe.

For a moment, she experiences the illusion that the scars are not carved into the skin of the Kites but, instead, are moving over them, passing from one to the other like ripples left by wind on water, visible tokens of a faith whose deepest manifestations only the Kites might know. She wonders if it's on this level that their mysterious senses operate, free of the hindrance of eyes.

Rose curtsies and repeats the sign of the Wheel, certain that nothing is lost on the Kites. "Your presence honors us, holy ones. May a new bride ask the blessing of your order?"

At this the Kites smile. They have no teeth. Their lips, their gums, even their tongues are scarred. Rose cannot repress a gasp. Do the scars reach all the way inside their bodies?

And then she sees, in the puckering of flesh around the pits where the women's eyes once were, in the scars that fissure their faces as if those faces were shattered once and then pieced back together, not quite successfully . . . sees somehow, in the way the Kites smile, in the joy lighting up their butchered faces from within . . . sees that, far from being old, the Kites are young women, perhaps scarcely older than she herself.

It fascinates her, this unexpected discovery. At first she can't believe it, or, rather, doesn't want to believe it. But she knows it's true. How, she wonders, could any young woman—any woman at all—choose such a life? And how, having embraced it and been disfigured by it, can they smile now with such obvious joy? Rose thinks of the compulsion that had driven her once to look into the sun and feels a disturbing sense of recognition, as if the faces of the Kites are cracked mirrors giving back her own broken reflection.

"What is your name, daughter?" asks one of the Kites in a voice raspy and raw, as if it, too, is scarred.

"Rose Rubra Galingale, Your Holiness."

"Saint Viridis bless your marriage bed and keep you safe from harm, Rose Rubra Galingale!" The Kite makes the sign of the Wheel in Rose's direction.

"Saint Ilex watch over you in the darkest hour of the night, when Beauty prowls and sleeping men suffer the dreams of Maw," adds the other Kite in a voice even less mellifluous.

"Come closer, daughter," says the first Kite. "Don't be afraid. Let us touch you."

To her surprise, Rose finds she's not afraid. She offers herself to the questing hands, thinking of how Saint Viridis blinded herself in emulation of the Kites before she entered Herwood, saying she wished to come to the Spinner's everlasting light through a darkness deeper than any she had known.

The touch of the Kites is light and dry, like stalks of grass. Cooing sounds come from their mouths as they explore Rose's features, as if reading there a future visible to them alone. Then the Kites draw their hands sharply away.

"Your *eyes*," breathes one.

Rose opens her eyes, surprised. So it's true; the Kites know everything at a touch. She laughs self-consciously, aware for the first time that a crowd has gathered.

"I was blinded as a girl, Your Holiness. From staring too long at the sun, looking for Saint Ixion. A vizard cured me. Thanks to his craft, I can see again."

"Blessed be your eyes!" cries the Kite. She makes the sign of the Wheel. Her sister Kite does the same.

"It's just vizards' craft," Rose says, embarrassed now. She doesn't like to talk about her blindness. It happened so long ago, it hardly seems real. Like an old dream.

"A gift from Saint Viridis," says the second Kite. "Blessed be her tears!"

"But what of my marriage, holy sisters?" Rose asks, trying to change the subject. "Will I bear a son?"

"Don't answer!"

It's Cy.

He thrusts himself angrily between Rose and the Kites. "Have you lost your mind to ask such a question, Rose? Should a man learn on his wedding day what the sex of his child will be? And from such lips as these?"

"I'm sorry, Cy," Rose says. "I wasn't thinking."

"Your beautiful wife will be a mother," states the same Kite who spoke first. "That much is plain from her face. But to learn the sex of the child, we must touch *your* face."

Cy shakes his head. He steps back, pulling Rose along with him. "I won't let you."

"Do you refuse our blessing?"

Ominous murmurs run through the crowd. It's unheard of to spurn a Viridian's blessing. The blessing of a Kite is even more highly prized. Who but a servant of Maw would refuse it?

Rose speaks up: "Forgive him, holy sisters. He doesn't mean it."

"Be quiet, Rose," Cy says sharply. "I ask your blessing, holy sisters. But not your touch. I mean no disrespect. There are some things a man should find out for himself in the fullness of time."

"We do not impose our sight," replies the Kite. "Do not be afraid of that. If you do not wish to know, we will not tell you. But there is, as well, a blessing in our touch, on this day above all others, when Saint Ilex Erythrina achieved his martyrdom and the twelve foundresses of our order lost their eyes only to gain a second, more piercing sight."

"I've heard the touch of a Kite can change a man's future from what was meant to be. I've heard you and your holy sisters can pluck the threads of our spinning and rearrange them as you will."

The Kites' laughter is peculiarly unpleasant, like the coughing of a crow. One says: "You should not believe everything you hear. What the Spinner has spun, no one may unspin, least of all a woman. Not even Saint Viridis Lacrimata had that power."

"Please, Cy, it's the Feast of Saint Ilex!" entreats Rose.

"I told you to be silent!" Cy's expression reminds Rose of Marcus; she recoils as if he's slapped her. "We'll talk of this later! My father has told me the secret of making a son. I don't need any other advice. Now, holy sisters, if you have a blessing that doesn't involve the laying on of hands, I'll gladly accept it."

The Kites duck their black-cowled heads to converse in the strange clicking tongue of their order, which even their sister Viridians, or so it's said, cannot understand. Rose is frightened. It sounds like the Kites are arguing. What if, instead of blessing Cy, they curse him?

The Kites, meanwhile, have come to a decision. "Tell us your name."

"Cyrus Galingale, Your Holiness."

"May you never know Beauty, Cyrus Galingale!" says one, her voice rougher than ever.

"May the Galingale line flourish as long as the Spinner's Wheel turns!" cries the other.

"I humbly thank you, holy sisters." Cy bows, plainly surprised and pleased by such auspicious blessings.

The Kites turn away. The crowd draws aside to let them pass. They walk slowly, hunched over and holding hands. From the back, they resemble weird children. Their cowled heads weave from side to side, as if they are picking their way by scent alone.

Meanwhile Cy beams at Rose. "You see, the Kites respect firmness, like all women. I'm glad of their blessing, but I'd as soon let myself be touched by a Fury!"

"You don't mean that!"

He leers down at her, contorting his face to mimic the Kites. "Blessed be your eyes!" he croaks, and brings his hands up as though to claw her face.

Rose shrieks with laughter, twisting away. All at once she's drunk again, drunker than ever.

The drift of the crowd brings them to the wagon of the simularters, Saint Stilskin's Men, where a good-sized audience of all ages has gathered. Immersed in the illusion being crafted on their behalf, they are laughing freely and addressing comments to the stage.

"What are they playing?" Rose asks. But no one replies. She cranes her neck to get a better view of the small figures in their colorful costumes.

Cy shoulders his way through to the front of the crowd, pulling Rose along behind him. How lucky she is to have Cy to take care of things! What a clever and attentive husband he is! Even the Kites recognized his worth!

Although it's the Feast of Saint Ilex Erythrina, the play being performed is drawn from the life of the company's namesake, Saint Stilskin Sophora.

"Look, Rose!" Cy sounds like an excited boy calling to his mother. "They're doing *How Stilskin Spun A Wife*!"

"Do you think it's because of us?"

"Who else got married today? Of course it's because of us. Now be quiet! I don't want to miss anything!"

Neither does Rose. As she watches, the small stage of the wagon seems to expand until it's as wide as the world. She feels as if she's shrunk to the size of the simulars, while the simulars have grown as large as people. She reminds herself that it's all make-believe, an illusion created by the skills of the simularter, who, hidden above the stage, directs the simulars and makes them speak.

But her awareness of the mechanics of illusion never impinges on Rose's belief in the reality of what's taking place onstage. Not even the visibility of the strings attached to the simulars can spoil the effect. Indeed, it seems to her that the strings don't cause the limbs of the simulars to move but rather, like chains, circumscribe and restrain their movements.

Rose and Cy have missed the first act of the play, which takes place in the early days of the Hierarchate, just after Saint Ixion's ascension. For some months, a mysterious odor has been rising from the forest that has not yet become known as Herwood. It rises at all hours of the day and night, bewitching men and drawing them to their deaths. The scent is called Beauty because of the ravings of the afflicted who rush into the woods as though into the arms of the most beautiful woman in the world. Troops of shrives sent after them have not returned. In a few short months, Beauty has decimated the male population of the Hierarchate, threatening to undo Ixion's great victory.

Women and children can't smell the scent, and neither, because of their holiness, can the saints. For this reason, the Blessed Sovereign has ordered the saints to take wives and beget sons.

But Stilskin refuses. Stilskin believes that all women are Furies at heart, daughters of Maw. He will not allow himself to be corrupted by their touch. Instead, turning a deaf ear to the commands of the Sovereign and the pleas of his fellow saints—all of whom have taken wives, whole harems in fact—Stilskin swears to put a stop to the Furies, banish the scent of Beauty, and rescue those of the missing men who may still be alive. After all, he reasons, when there is no shortage of men in the Hierarchate, there will be no need for him to marry. And so, at the end of Act One, Stilskin enters the forest, accompanied only by his faithful companion, the little white dog called Snowdrop.

Rose and Cy have arrived near the beginning of Act Two. On stage, the simular of Saint Stilskin is lost in the depths of the forest as evening draws near. He wanders through the trees, whistling to keep up his spirits. He's dressed, as usual, in tattered robes of many colors. His belongings are bound up in a bright red kerchief and tied to a crooked stick that is slung over his shoulder. Snowdrop ambles at his side.

Saint Stilskin's belongings keep getting caught in the branches. He stumbles at every step. "Who's there?" he cries again and again, mistaking the trees for clutching Furies. The saint's eyesight is notoriously poor.

Meanwhile, Snowdrop is nipping at his master's heels and rolling beneath his feet, making it even harder for Stilskin to keep his balance. The dog's antics provoke shrieks of laughter from the children in the audience.

"What's gotten into you, Snowdrop?"

The little dog barks sharply, jumping up and down.

"What is it, boy?" Stilskin gazes out from the stage. His wooden eyes pass over the crowd as if able to see only trees. "What are you trying to tell me?"

Every child in the audience shouts: "Go back, Stilskin!"

"What's that?" Stilskin cocks his head and raises a hand to his ear. "Did someone call my name?"

The warning is repeated in louder tones: "GO BAAAACK!"

"Ah, the beautiful music of our brothers, the birds!"

"Noooooo!" the children wail.

The saint's hearing isn't so good either. "How dear to the Spinner are such simple creatures, eh, Snowdrop? How I envy them!"

Snowdrop runs in circles, chasing his tail and barking.

"Yes, the woods are filled with wonders." Stilskin struggles to untangle himself from a welter of branches. "Even the trees have much to teach us."

Snowdrop lifts his leg. More howls from the children.

"If only Sium Lyrata or Quercus Incana were here!" Stilskin continues obliviously. "How I'd love to show them the holy and innocent beauty of these woods! Here there is no talk of wives! Should we avoid the forest because the Furies have fled here? Are we such cowards? A wife is more dangerous than a tree or a bird! If a man puts his faith in the Spinner, he may walk anywhere he pleases without fear!"

Snowdrop, who has feigned sleep during Stilskin's impassioned speech, now leaps up and rushes offstage.

"Where are you going, Snowdrop? Have you found a place where we can pass the night?"

From offstage comes the sound of barking.

"Good dog!"

A curtain rises at the rear of the stage to reveal a second set: a continuation of the woods, only darker now, the branches more tangled and forbidding.

But all is not dark. Light drips like honey from what appears to be two round windows set into the trunk of a tree.

"Why, what a clever little house!" says Stilskin admiringly as he draws near. "I wonder who lives here?"

Rose and Cy shout along with everyone else: "A Fury!"

Stilskin raises a hand to his ear. "How restless the birds are tonight! Perhaps some dangerous beast is on the prowl! Courage, Snowdrop! I'll knock at the door of this charming home! Doubtless the owner will offer us the warmest hospitality. Ah, Stilskin! You've done it again!"

Stilskin strides forward. But he hasn't taken two steps before he's tangled again in the branches. The more he struggles to free himself, the more tangled he becomes. "How embarrassing! I seem to have gotten stuck somehow! Hello! Can anyone hear me? Help!"

An unpleasant voice quavers from the shadows: "Is it a squirrel? Is it a mouse? Is it an owl watching my house?"

Shrieks from the children. Rose presses Cy's hand. She darts him a look and a smile, but he's too engrossed by what's happening onstage to notice.

Meanwhile, Snowdrop has taken refuge behind a curtain. The curtain shakes with his shivering.

"What a lovely voice you have, mother!" Stilskin calls brightly, his hearing playing him false again. "Come out where I can see you!"

The voice replies: "Not a squirrel. Not a mouse. Not an owl watching my house."

"Look at him shake!" Cy says, laughing.

The simular is trembling violently. It seems to Rose that everything is shaking: the simular, the stage, the wagon, the ground on which the wagon stands. And then, at the precise instant she realizes what's happening, someone cries: "Chastening!"

With that, the purposeful vitality disappears from the simular. It jerks convulsively, a dumb thing of wood and string gripped in the bumbling hands of a giant.

This Chastening is even more powerful than that of the day before; in seconds, the Feast of Saint Ilex becomes a riot as everyone rushes to whatever safety the Church of the Spinning Wheel may offer. Screams and curses mix in a grinding roar. Over it all the church bell clangs, tuneless, idiotic, ringing in a reign of madness.

Rose feels Cy's hand slip from hers. She grabs for him in a panic, but it's too late. He's carried off in the crowd, his lips shaping her name in a cry she cannot hear. And then she's swept away herself, spun like a twig in a flood.

It's all she can do to keep her balance. To fall now is to be trampled. All around her stalls and booths are collapsing, spewing their contents over the stones of the plaza. Kites are rioting in the sky, mirroring the chaos below.

Out of nowhere, something hits Rose hard. The wind is knocked out of her. She falls.

Somehow, she manages to crawl under what felled her: a trader's wagon tipped onto its side. Underneath is a cavelike space in which she can shelter and peer out at the world.

Rose feels safe at last. She gasps back her breath as the stampede continues outside. How cozy it is, she thinks with gratitude: like a little house. Nothing can hurt her here. She laughs, not knowing why but unable to stop.

Suddenly, for the first time, it occurs to her that she might die. She might never know the joy of surrendering to Cy's embrace, of opening herself to him without reservation and giving him the son he desires. The son he demands.

Sobbing now, Rose hugs her knees to her chest and rocks back and forth beneath the wagon. She croons to herself just as she did once before, a frightened little girl adrift on indefinite seas of blindness:

Arpagee, Brool, Colubrine, Dindle,
Cut myself on a rusty spindle.
Ensentia, Ferly, Gliff, Hent,
All my money has been spent.
Inction, Jubilar, Kell, Lusk,
Beauty rises with the dusk.
Minauderies, Nooning, Ormolu,
You love me and I love you.
Peripety then lofty Quoz,
Rose is my name, my name is Rose.

The ground lurches. The wagon shifts, comes down on her head with a crack. She fights to stay conscious. Her sanctuary is no longer safe; it never was. Spots swim before her eyes as she drags herself out from under the wagon.

Rose lies on the ground, waiting for the buzzing in her head to subside. After a while, the ground stops shaking. Tears and moans are rising from all sides. Ignoring the pain, she sits up.

Bodies are strewn across the plaza. They lie amid the wreckage of stalls and overturned wagons, spilled merchandise and produce, smashed kites fallen from the sky. Some of the injured are being looked after, but most are alone. She hears calls for help, prayers, curses.

Rose thinks immediately of Cy. Is he among them? Hurt and afraid, wondering what's become of her?

She staggers to her feet and limps through the plaza, looking for Cy among the injured and calling his name. There's no sign of him, or of her parents. She prays they've taken refuge in the church. She would do the same, but there are so many people in need of help. Friends and neighbors. How can she ignore them? There's little enough she can do: make them comfortable, tell them everything will be all right, brush the fireflies from their wounds. Her tears are no longer for herself, but for these others.

"Bless you, Rose!"

"May Saint Viridis reward you!"

She labors on, slowly making her way toward the church. Then she sees part of a black robe lying under what's left of a trader's stall. Quickly, she throws the debris aside. The Kites are lying there.

"Are you all right, holy sisters?" Rose touches one of the Kites hesitantly. The Kite's head turns toward her. But not by volition.

The throat of the Kite has been slit from ear to ear.

FIVE

Cy relaxes on his new bed in his new home, listening to Rose sing softly to herself in the next room as she readies his bath. A stimulating mix of fragrances suffuses the air from the oils and spices she adds to the steaming water. He pictures her kneeling beside the tub, his new wife, her skin glistening wetly from her own just-completed bath, her long black hair clinging to her body. Soon she'll come to him.

With eyes lowered, she'll begin the ritual of disrobing, removing his robes layer by layer until he stands naked before her. Then she'll lead him to the bath and kneel to wash him, caressing his body for the first time with her virgin hands, cleaning away the cares of the day with a touch that promises pleasures long dreamed of. Afterward, she'll pat him dry with soft white towels and lead him to the bed. She'll close her eyes and lie back in surrender as he undoes the bindings of her hair and exposes the secrets of her sex, now his to possess.

Cy has waited turnings for this moment. At last he'll truly become a man, entering like an initiate the tabernacle of a woman's body.

It's late afternoon. The yellow curtains flutter in the bedroom windows, bronzed with the sun's decline. Cy's patrimonial robes are torn and filthy, the fine embroidery frayed, the labor of turnings undone in minutes by the Chastening and the hours of cleaning up that followed.

Not just his robes but the whole village of Jubilar came unraveled in those moments. Damage was extensive. Repairs will take months. By the grace of Ixion no villagers were killed, but many were injured by falling debris or trampled in the rush to the church, including Rose.

When he first saw her after the Chastening, her bruised forehead left a bruise on his pride that has yet to fade. As he rushed to embrace her, he'd understood that nothing was certain. Everything given could be taken away. He couldn't protect her. Not always. Not everywhere. All was as the Spinner willed.

He shudders. The Kites are dead. Murdered. Their scarred throats cut during the confusion of the Chastening.

It was Rose who found the bodies. She'd burst into the church, screaming bloody murder. Cy felt suspicious gazes fasten upon him even as he hurried to take her in his arms. He'd argued with the Kites, refused their blessing. Everyone had seen it.

He knows the malicious gossips of the village are only too willing to believe him a murderer. They've always envied the Galingales. They want nothing more than to see the family fall, especially now that Cy is set to rise above them. They're no better than a pack of dogs, he thinks. Marcus is right to despise them.

The whole thing is ridiculous. But he's a suspect just the same. Tomorrow, when the shrives come to claim the bodies of the Kites, they'll pay him a visit. Cy shudders at the prospect. The shrives care nothing for guilt or innocence. What matters to them is that a crime has been committed. Punishment must follow swiftly as an example to others. Anyone will do.

In the first frantic moments after being separated from Rose, Cy fought against the crowd to get back to her. But it was all he could do to keep on his feet as the ground lurched and the church bell clanged as if announcing the Unspinning.

As the tremors worsened, the makeshift stalls and booths erected throughout the plaza began to collapse. Heavy wagons were pitched onto their sides. The air was thick with dust and cries and kites falling from the sky.

Cy lashed out with his fists, desperate to clear a path back to Rose. Then he was knocked to the ground. He tried to get up, but people kicked him down as they rushed heedlessly past. He managed to crawl into a nearby stall before he could be trampled.

He huddled there, unable to stand for the shaking. He didn't think any bones were broken, though his left leg was numb. But he couldn't stay. Bit by bit the stall was disintegrating: pots and pans, bowls and glasses, forks and spoons and knives rained down from the walls and ceiling.

A sturdy wooden table, swept clear of merchandise, stood at the back of the stall. Cy scuttled beneath it, hoping it would shelter him.

After a moment, he saw a pair of scarred and bleeding feet enter the stall. Then another pair. Both were half-hidden in ragged black robes.

It was, he knew at once, the Kites, seeking refuge just as he had. They were close enough to touch if he'd cared to.

"Hello?" called one of the Kites over the noise of the Chastening. "Is someone here?"

Cy said nothing, filled with the same obscure dread that had seized him earlier in their presence. He crouched beneath the table, hardly daring to breathe.

Then another pair of feet entered the stall. Sharp-toed boots of scuffed black leather crept with a swift and stealthy grace, as if the ground were still.

"Who's there?" came the voice of the Kite.

Cy's heart drummed in his ears. The boots resembled those of a shrive. But if so, there should be another pair of boots, he thought, for shrives never traveled alone.

"We know you," said the other Kite, or perhaps the same one who'd just spoken.

A familiar voice said, "I am your Chastening."

It was the voice of Saint Stilskin Sophora.

The Kites laughed their peculiar grating laugh. "Too late, simularter! Tell Azedarach: the Liberatrix is come out of Herwood!"

"Tell it to Maw," said Saint Stilskin's voice.

Then came a noise all ragged and wet. Blood gushed upon the ground, spattering the tips of the black boots. The bodies of the Kites fell one beside the other inches from where Cy looked on in horror. He waited for the assassin to kneel and make certain of his work, knowing that to be discovered now meant death. Knowing, too, there was no place to hide.

"Fuck your Liberatrix," the voice of the saint enunciated. A gob of spit struck the face of the Kite nearest Cy. The black boots delivered a vicious kick, then moved off.

Cy watched the spittle run down the ravaged face of the Kite, contorted now in its ultimate agony. He was paralyzed with fear. The wound in the Kite's throat gaped like a grinning mouth from which blood oozed. There was a whistle of air and a bubbling sound. He wished the ugly thing would die.

As if in answer to his prayer, the stall collapsed with a drawn-out groan. An avalanche of debris buried the Kites. The table protected Cy, but even so it took him a while to dig himself out. He worked frantically, desperate to escape, to forget the horror of what he'd seen. When at last he was free, he hurried away without looking back.

The tremors seemed to have stopped, as if the Chastening had exhausted itself in toppling the stall. Stragglers were still entering the church. He limped after them, ignoring the cries of the injured begging for help. He'd forgotten Rose, forgotten he was married, forgotten everything but the blood drooling from the Kite's throat.

Inside the crowded church, the people of Jubilar stood before the nave, waiting impatiently for the Mouth of God. Some prayed, others cried, still others hugged their loved ones in relief or silent commiseration. Among them, Cy caught sight of three simularters conversing among themselves in the shadows of Saint Stilskin's shrine. Sidling close, he examined their boots out of the corner of his eye.

One pair was flecked with blood.

The simularter to whom the blood-marked boots belonged looked up suddenly, as if sensing Cy's gaze. It was the same man he'd seen earlier, during the wedding procession. The one who'd waved to him. The simularter didn't wave now, but regarded him coolly.

Cy smiled nervously and looked away. It was then that Rose had come running into the church, screaming for help. And even as he'd clasped her in his arms, Cy heard his name being whispered and noticed that his own boots, like those of the simularter, were spattered with blood.

Now, resting in the safety of his bed, Cy feels a gnawing sense of guilt, as if by witnessing the murders of the Kites he's committed a crime, one every bit as grave as the crime that ruined his ancestor Celtis Galingale.

What will he tell the shrives when they come to question him tomorrow? They cannot be lied to. Yet he's afraid the truth will condemn him.

"Cy."

Rose's tremulous voice startles Cy. He springs to his feet at the sight of her standing shyly in the doorway, covering herself with her arms, her eyes lowered modestly.

"Your bath is ready, husband."

"Let me see you," he says, his voice hoarse.

"The water will grow cold."

"I'm through with waiting. You're my wife now." In this, at least, he holds the strings.

Rose gives him a crumbling look.

"No tears," he admonishes, feeling flush with power, as if all his father's strength has flowed into him. "I will not tolerate tears. No woman ever brought forth a son by weeping."

"Yes, husband." Rose lowers her arms to her sides.

Cy feels a rush of heat through his body. Never has he imagined such beauty. All his now.

Rose stands quite still, her eyes fastened on the floor as if her gaze could hammer nails into the wood. Her pale skin is slick with moisture, just as he imagined it.

His to do with as he pleases.

Her long black hair twines about her neck, splitting into two thick braids that run beneath her arms, cross over her breasts and encircle her waist, then plunge between her legs like a girdle. The end of the braid, tucked back through the belt of hair, hangs behind her like a horse's tail.

Her breath comes in quick, frightened gasps that show Cy the shadowed outline of her ribs and the pale curve of her breasts against the dark edges of her hair. Her hips swell like a fruit at the peak of ripeness.

Cy turns away to pull the windows tightly shut and draw the curtains. Then he sits at the edge of the bed. "Light the incense," he whispers, half-choked with desire. Marcus's words of advice come back to him: make every copulation an act of revenge. Women prefer it that way.

Rose moves past him to a table next to the bed, where sticks of incense are waiting alongside Cy's nighttime regalia: leather straps, nose plugs, and throat tubes; the white bowl of water with its floating sponge. He sees that she is trembling.

First he will take her. Then she will prepare him to withstand the nightly siege of Beauty.

Rose fumbles with the matches. And suddenly, at that timid clumsiness, Cy's frayed patience snaps.

The next thing he knows, he's grabbing Rose and throwing her down on the bed. He tears at the teasing shift of her hair. It comes loose in his fingers. She cries out, wriggling beneath him.

"Cy, you're hurting me!"

He pushes the heavy mass of loose hair up over her face as if to smother her cries.

Rose goes limp beneath him. She's silent and still, as though asleep. All of her is open to his gaze. With his eyes he takes possession of her.

Then with his whole body. He forces his way inside her, not content to possess merely but determined to conquer, fighting once more, on the white field of the marriage bed, the war between the Galingales and the Intricatas.

SIX

A bell is tolling inside Rose's head. Its pounding pulls her up through the murk of sleep to where a red haze shimmers. Then into the pain-bright day.

"Ohhh." She groans into something warm and soft. A pillow.

She remembers toasts in the plaza. The Chastening. The wagon coming down hard on her head. She raises a hand to the spot, draws it back with a louder groan. She feels as though she's floating in a sea of hurt, all ebb and flow and surge.

She's married.

This is her new home. Her new bed.

There is dried blood on the sheets. Her maiden's blood; yet she can't help thinking, too, of the murdered Kites.

"Cy," she says. "Are you awake?"

No answer. Can he still be asleep? Is he keeping silent now to teach her a lesson? She turns.

The bed is empty.

Cy's nose plugs, his throat tube, his shackles: all are where she left them the night before, on the nightstand beside the bed.

Did she forget to prepare him? Is it possible?

"Cyrus!" she calls. "This isn't funny!"

But she knows it's no joke.

Rose screams. She screams as though her voice can touch the hard heart of Herwood and call her husband home.

She's still screaming moments later when the church bell begins to peal. It doesn't take long for the villagers to gather. They crowd into the yard, the women gossiping as they always do, making no attempt to disguise the relief they feel that, on this night at least, Beauty has plucked a man from another bed than theirs. How many times over the turnings has Rose joined in the banter, making light of a woman's misfortune!

The voices sound cruel and hateful to her now. Her ears burn with shame.

Rose pulls up the bloodstained sheets to cover herself as her parents and in-laws enter the bedroom with the Mouth of God. Their faces are hard, without pity or mercy. Villagers cluster in the doorway, craning their necks, quiet now so as not to miss a thing.

The Mouth of God moves around the room, smashing the windows with Rose's distaff, which he's taken from its resting place beside the hearth. Other windows are being smashed below.

Rose can't bear to meet the eyes of her parents and in-laws. From the door, her friends and neighbors stare with furtive and not-so-furtive smiles. Her maid of honor, red-haired Vicia Campestris, wears the same triumphant expression that had spread over her features after the wedding, when she'd beaten the last of her rivals to claim the bridal bouquet.

Rose sees that Vicia is *glad* of her misfortune. The others, too. How they despise her! They were always jealous, she realizes. Pretending to be her friends while secretly hating her for having found, in Cy, a husband sure to rise above them, above Jubilar, as if it's an implacable law that one family's success means the ruin of all others. She reads the same gloating thought in every face: if the Galingales and Rubras fall, other families, better deserving, will rise to take their places.

For a long time no one speaks. Rose tries to understand how things have gone so terribly wrong. How could she fall asleep without preparing Cy? All her life, she's been trained to perform that one task. To put his welfare before her own no matter what.

It must have been Maw, she thinks. The Dam of Darkness wanted Cy for herself. Rose thinks of Cy facing the horrors of Herwood. Alone, bewitched by Beauty. Perhaps he's lying hurt somewhere, calling out her name! Perhaps he's dying.

Or dead.

No! Not that. Cy isn't dead; he can't be. She'd feel it in her heart if he was. She'd *know*.

But either way, she knows she'll never see him again. The Cy she fell in love with and married . . . that Cy is as good as dead, and it's her negligence that killed him. It's no use blaming Maw, Rose knows. The fault is hers. She begins to cry, as if only now understanding the import of her loss. Of her guilt.

The Mouth of God gives a satisfied nod.

Rose's mother smooths her long gray hair, which loops about her neck and waist in the style of a matron whose married daughter has not yet produced a child. Taking a deep breath, she begins to speak in a clipped voice, refusing to meet Rose's eyes: "I taught you how to be a good and faithful wife to your husband. How to tie the knots to keep him bound. How to scent your hair to keep Beauty from tempting him. In losing him, you have dishonored me."

And with that she tears out a strand of Rose's hair.

Now Cerasus speaks. At the sound of her father's broken voice, full of sorrow and bewilderment, Rose understands that the effects of what she's done extend beyond her into the lives of the people she cares about most. Her dishonor does not end with her. Its ripples spread wide. Are still spreading.

"My seed brought you into the world," Cerasus says. "I raised you and gave you in marriage to a fine young man who would have given you a son . . . my grandson. In losing him, you have betrayed me."

With careful deliberation, as if it hurts him even now to cause her pain, Cerasus plucks a strand of Rose's hair. Only the wish to spare him any further disgrace keeps her from grasping his hand and wetting it with her tears.

Cy's mother has unbound her hair. It falls freely to her ankles in a token of grief and loss. Now she speaks in a low and venomous voice, brushing her hair from her face: "For all the years of his manhood I kept my Cyrus safe from Beauty's wiles, only to have you lose him after a single night! Stupid, careless girl! In losing him, you have killed me."

And with a look of hatred, as if it could bring back her son, or, failing that, avenge him, she yanks loose a fistful of Rose's hair.

Rose can't help crying out at that.

The Mouth of God frowns testily. A chorus of murmurs and shocked whispers rises from the doorway.

"Shame!"

"Did you ever . . . ?"

"Fury!"

Rose bites back her tears and bows her head.

At last Marcus speaks: "You cry in pain, but the pain you feel is nothing compared to mine. You lost a husband through your own stupid fault; I, a son through no fault of mine. And with my son, all chance of a grandson to carry on my name. Thanks to you, the struggles of more than three hundred turnings are all in vain. Thanks to you, my great ancestor will go unavenged! In losing Cy, you have killed my fame."

Rose trembles, afraid that Marcus will lose control and kill her. Such things happen. But rather than tearing her hair with his wife's vindictiveness, his touch is light and fleeting, yet so contemptuous Rose cringes as if at a blow.

Now Rose's parents and in-laws hand the strands of hair to the

Mouth of God. The priest touches the hair to the badge of the Wheel embroidered upon the breast of his robes, then raises his hands to make the sign of the Wheel above Rose's head. He intones creakily:

"Great Ixion Diospyros, you who spin endlessly above us upon your ever-burning Wheel, behold your wicked daughter, Rose Rubra Galingale, who has lost her husband and honor through her own selfish fault. Great and repugnant in the eyes of the Spinner is her sin; therefore, great the torments we inflict upon her now in your name."

The priest's hands descend toward Rose's head. But he stops short of touching her.

"A lifetime of sacrifice could not atone for your sin, daughter. Life as you have known it is over. Rose Rubra Galingale is dead. Her body may linger on for days or turnings, but her soul is already in the deepest levels of the Pit, suffering the eternal torments of Maw. Can you feel the Evil One gnawing at your soul, daughter? It is only right that your body share that suffering. Eternity is a long time. It begins for you now."

Rose listens without understanding, shivering beneath the sheets. How can this be happening to her, Rose Rubra, everybody's favorite? Just yesterday she danced in the arms of her father-in-law and promised him a grandson.

"Mama, no!" she blurts. "You can't let them!"

Her mother turns away.

"Silence!" Cerasus commands.

The Mouth of God places the strands of Rose's hair upon the floor. An acolyte steps forward with a smoking taper.

The stench of burning hair fills the room. To Rose it's the smell of everything she's known and believed in, her hopes and dreams, her brief happiness, going up in smoke.

A cloud rises inside her, more impenetrable even than the night, for it lacks the glimmering of fireflies. She lets herself sink into it. She embraces it, wanting to die. The last thing she hears is the sound of her distaff being snapped in two over the Mouth of God's bony knee.

When Rose wakes, a man is cutting her hair.

The two of them are alone in the bedroom. Her parents, her in-laws, the Mouth of God—everyone has gone. She knows she will not see them again. They are as lost to her as Cy.

She is bound to the bed with Cy's unused, unlucky shackles. A cloud of hair covers her shoulders. She is naked, alone with this strange man.

That more than anything tells Rose the extent to which things have changed for her. She is no longer a valued possession, a repository for the honor of men.

"Awake, are you, kitten?"

The man cutting her hair is very fat. Brown hair clings in greasy ringlets to his bulging pink neck. He wears a loose-fitting gray smock with a wide leather belt upon which hangs an assortment of combs, razors, scissors, and brushes, along with a set of keys that jangles loudly as he moves.

A badge of lock and scissors is embroidered in red and gold upon the greasy collar of the robe. The man's eyes are cold blue slits.

Rose thinks of verses chanted as a girl:

Pander white, pander black,
pander never coming back.
Pander young, pander old,
pander bought and pander sold.

The Panderman has come.

She can't bear his steady gaze. She squirms in the shackles, trying to hide her nakedness.

"There's no room for modesty where you're going," the Panderman says. "You might as well get used to that now."

Rose bursts into tears.

"Just once, I wish they wouldn't cry!" The Panderman lowers his scissors with a heavy sigh. "Look on the bright side, kitten. You're a pretty thing, not a day over sixteen by the looks of you and practically a virgin into the bargain. You'll fetch a handsome price in Kell. A share of that money will go to your father; enough for him to buy back his honor from your father-in-law, if I'm any judge of flesh. He'll end his days honorably in Jubilar and not back in Inction or Hent. Even in disgrace, a good daughter knows how to serve her father."

Rose shuts her eyes, trying to will herself back into unconsciousness. But though the Panderman stops talking, the *snip snip snip* of his scissors is not so easily silenced.

When he's finished cutting her hair, the Panderman snaps a leash and collar around Rose's neck, locking them with a key from the ring at his belt. "Too tight, kitten? Can't have you choking to death!"

He undoes the shackles and helps her to her feet. "Up we go!"

Taking a horsehair brush from his belt, the Panderman whisks away the loose hairs clinging to her skin. "Tickles, I know."

"My clothes . . ." Rose starts for the dresser.

The Panderman draws her back with a tug on the leash. "You'll get clothes in Kell." He tugs again, more sharply this time.

Rose follows him out of the bedroom.

"That's right," the Panderman says. "Why make it any harder on yourself?"

Leaving the room, Rose catches sight of her reflection in the mirror above the dresser. The dresser was Cy's wedding gift to her, built with his own hands from an oak felled at the edge of Herwood. But the dresser, a source of pride, is hurtful now, just as her reflection mocks the beauty she's taken for granted all her life.

As far back as Rose can remember, Cerasus told her how beautiful she was. Then the village boys began to notice, until one day she saw her beauty reflected in Cy's eyes and felt complete, assured of it.

But this ugly face in the mirror belongs to no one that she knows. The swollen red eyes, the blotchy skin, and, above all, the scalp with its weedy patches of hair and numerous small cuts, makes Rose think of a Fury. She runs a disbelieving hand over the stubble.

A woman's hair is her honor. From the moment a girl becomes a woman, she lets her hair grow; only the hair under her arms and between her legs is shaved away, for otherwise Maw might make a nest there.

When she marries, a girl cuts a lock of hair for her husband to wear as a wedding ring. If she is blessed with a child, she cuts another lock . . . two locks in the case of a boy, for the parents of a son are twice-blessed. Widows cut their hair to shoulder length and bury the cuttings with their husbands, half-dead themselves from that day forward. And women whose men are lost to Beauty through another woman's fault spin strands of their hair into a memorial belt as Cy's mother will do.

But to be shorn in this way! There is something obscene about it, a violation beyond anything Rose has ever imagined. She breaks into fresh sobs.

"Vanity, thy name is woman," the Panderman says. "Don't worry, you'll wear wigs even better than what you had."

"I don't want a wig!" she wails.

"You should have thought of that before you lost your husband, shouldn't you?"

The house is new, filled with new things. But there has been no time for Rose to make it her own. Now, as she's led down the stairs and out of the house, there is nothing she can hold in memory to cling to, just wedding gifts with no history to enliven them. The emptiness of each new thing, like a promise unfulfilled, is all that she takes with her.

It's not fair, she thinks. This was supposed to be her life. It was promised to her ever since she was a girl. A house, a husband, a child to raise—with Saint Ixion's blessing, a son!

The silence of the house rebukes her like the angry spirit of her never-to-be-born son.

Outside Rose sees it's early afternoon. Thin clouds drift across a hazy sky. The Panderman's horse and wagon are standing in the lane alongside the gate. Embroidered upon the white canvas covering the wagon is a larger version of the Panderman's badge of lock and scissors.

The horse gives a soft whicker at the sight of its master, stamping its hooves and setting its bells ajingle. Rose shivers at the sprightly sound. She moves to cover herself. That she should be seen like this! But then, forgetful, she looks about in awe.

There is no one to be seen. The lane is empty. The doors of the village houses are shut, the curtains drawn in every window.

But Rose feels the presence of her neighbors. They are all in their homes, sitting in the dark just as she has sat so often with her mother and father in the past, trembling with excitement and fear while waiting for the Panderman to pass unseen through the village, carrying in his wagon a woman who had already ceased to exist as daughter, wife, sister, or mother, and whose name would no longer be spoken by anyone. She thinks again of girlhood rhymes:

Mother, sister, daughter, wife:
Four threads weave a woman's life!

Unseen, but not unheard. Oh! The thrill of terror she always felt at the jingle of the bells, and how she shivered with a terror only partly feigned when her father whispered that the Panderman was coming to take away naughty little girls like her! Then how she laughed again, after the bells faded, and she was safe, and the whole village rushed out to see what presents had been left in the lane before the gates of the houses! Toys and candy wheels for the children, sewing kits for the girls, soccer balls for the boys, books and tools for the men, pots and pans for the women.

It makes Rose ashamed to remember those times. Not once did she wonder what was going on outside, on the other side of the curtains. A woman suffering as she suffered now. A woman halfway between the life she knew—which, though still around her, close enough to touch, was barred as if by gates of iron—and a life unglimpsed as yet, impossible to imagine, but already, irrevocably, begun.

The Panderman helps Rose climb through the canvas flap into the back of the wagon. It's dark and stuffy inside. Rose sees a dirty mattress, some pots and pans, and, jumbled in a heap, all the marvelous gifts she so enjoyed finding as a girl after the Panderman passed through the village.

The gifts don't look so marvelous now.

"That's your job, kitten." The Panderman slips the end of her leash into a lock on the wagon and secures it with another key from his belt. "As we go by each house, throw out something for the good folks that live there. It's a way of showing you don't blame nobody but yourself for what happened."

"It wasn't my fault," Rose says, more to herself than to the Panderman and more like a question than a statement.

His answer is sharp: "Whose was it then? Eh, miss? Whose was it? Saint Viridis Lacrimata's?"

She hears him wheezing with laughter as he walks to the front of the wagon and hoists himself onto the buckboard. The wagon lists, creaking with his weight.

Rose hears the crack of a whip and a "gee-up!" The wagon rolls forward with a jerk and a jingle.

Rose watches as they pass the boarded-up stable, damaged in the Chastening; her father's forge with its huge anvil hanging on a thick chain above the door; the carpentry shop of Galingale & Son. There her parents' home, with its blue window boxes of dahlias and heather—knocked askew in the Chastening—and its tightly drawn curtains . . . curtains she helped her mother sew. Is her mother weeping now in the arms of Cerasus behind those curtains? Or are they sitting side by side in the kitchen and pretending not to hear the Panderman's bells and the creaking wheels of the wagon?

There the house in which Cy grew up and where Marcus and Cerasus signed the marriage contract on the eve of her sixth turning. Already black ribbons flutter from the gate. Is it her imagination, or does one of the curtains tremble, as if drawn aside by her father-in-law for a last, vindictive glance?

There the Church of the Spinning Wheel, its great bell silent now. But the Wheel spins brightly above the spire as it always does, the pure tone of its whistling unchanged.

Man sins, the Spinner spins. Life will go on without her.

Rose remembers the first time Cy kissed her. It was in the storeroom of the carpentry shop late one evening shortly after his *Trachaea*. She no longer recalls how she came to be alone with him there, what he'd said to entice her. It wouldn't have taken much. Even then she would have done anything he asked.

She trembles now just as she trembled then when, out of nowhere, it seemed, he reached to touch her cheek and left his hand there while the whole world balanced on a razor's edge of time. The two of them stood still as statues at the heart of a whirling hush, his dusky skin perfumed with scents of wood. Then his lips pressed hard against hers, and her lips opened of their own accord, like a flower in the sun, all her senses dazzled, dissolving like sugar on his tongue.

Rose jumps as the Panderman opens the front flap and calls back to her: "The gifts! We don't have all day!"

Hardly aware of what she's doing, with her eyes fixed on the houses and shops that line the lane as if to burn them forever into her memory so that she can carry Jubilar inside her no matter how far away she goes, Rose distributes the gifts.

She feels a different part of herself go with each object thrown from the wagon, as if she's taking herself apart. She throws out her feet, her legs, her torso, her ears, eyes, nose, lips, tongue, even her arms and hands, until there's nothing left of her inside the wagon, and the mixed-up parts of her body are strewn all over the lane.

What makes it truly terrible is the knowledge that no one who picks up the gifts—not even her parents—will understand the significance of what they hold in their hands. They'll see only a new mirror or hairbrush, a toy shrive, a treatise on crop rotation. Something to be enjoyed for a time, used up, and then forgotten, just as she herself will be forgotten.

Her name will never again be spoken, not by any of them. Perhaps, in time, Rose herself will forget it. Then what will be left of Rose Rubra Galingale? Will she exist at all?

The Mouth of God was wrong, she thinks. She's worse than dead.

It's as if she never existed.

BOOK TWO

QUOZ

For beauty is nothing
but the beginning of terror . . .
RAINER MARIA RILKE,
The Duino Elegies

SAINT SAMSUM'S DAY
PART I

ONE

In the innermost chamber of the Palace of the Chambered Nautilus, ringed by vizards and shrives, entertained by simularters and voluptuaries, and surrounded by portraits and sculptures of his august predecessors, whose names are remembered by no one here, the Blessed Sovereign, Azedarach LXIV, sits upon the Serpent Throne. On his head he wears the Serpent Crown, crafted by vizards from the plumes of serpents in order to blur casual glances and confound the studied gaze. Those who serve him daily haven't seen his features clearly a single time in their lives. And never will.

Azedarach wears robes of royal purple. His frail body seems lost within the immensity of the Throne, almost as if there were no body, just empty robes.

But the Serpent Throne would dwarf any occupant. Three Azedarachs could fit comfortably within its arms. The Throne is all of gold, shaped like a great Wheel stood upright, its hub and spokes encrusted with jewels, mother-of-pearl and lapis lazuli. The seat is at the hub, wide and deep, with cushions of purple velvet and armrests of glittering silver scales. The back of the Throne, from whence it derives its name, arches over its occupant in the shape of a serpent with gaping jaws. Its mirrored wings stretch from wall to wall. Its eyes, twin rubies, flash in the light of a hundred thyrsi.

Azedarach vents a sigh like a sleeper's. A favorite Cat reclines on purple cushions at his feet, methodically inserting her tongue between the shriveled grapes of his toes and sucking them gently, avidly. The Sovereign requires continuous physical stimulation to root him in the present and remind him of his body. Some days he prefers something a little more aggressive, but today it's this business with the toes, which has the miraculous effect, after many uninterrupted hours, of giving him an erection. Today, after all, is Saint Samsum's Day. This afternoon there will be a celebration in honor of the saint—exemplar of the virtues of strength and loyalty—in the chambers of Cassine Illicium, odalisque of the House Illicium. As Sovereign, he must reward the hostess with a taste of his juices, so liberally suffused with the drug metheglin.

Azedarach sits and dreams, bound to his body by the most slender of threads, the insistent sucking of the Cat—a gift from Serinthe Lacrimata, odalisque of the House Lacrimata—all that keeps his spirit from floating up through the endlessly faceted chambers of the Palace and joining Ixion in the heavens.

He dreams of what has passed and what may come to pass. He cannot say for certain, as he could once, a long, long time ago—or as he dreams he could once—what is real and what is illusion. His dreams have spilled over into the world, mixing as thoroughly with the world as the metheglin has mixed with him, present in his blood and semen, in his sweat and tears and saliva, even his urine and feces—which he passes but once a week, tiny golden pearls—all assiduously collected and prized by the nobles.

For more than four hundred turnings he has sat upon the Serpent Throne. The metheglin kept him ageless at first, but now, his use grown intemperate, need has wrested sovereignty from will, and the turnings held so long at bay have settled over him all at once, rendering him so feeble in body that he cannot stir from the Throne unaided. Though the metheglin continues to preserve him, he requires ever-increasing amounts of the nectar, which he sips from a golden cup held by a trusted noble: the vizard Morus Sisymbrium, whose family has held the office of cupbearer for as many turnings as Azedarach has held the Throne.

There is nothing Azedarach does not see. Nothing he does not know. The metheglin that is his sole nourishment casts the net of his senses far and wide throughout the Hierarchate. Now he shares the prideful ambition of a young man whose wife has given birth to a son in lowly Dindle; now he knows the guilty shame of a woman in Nooning whose husband has beaten her. He is aware of the bruises on her face and the darker blemish that mars her heart and the heart of every woman; more than the legacy of the Furies, it's the living presence of Maw forever threatening to erupt anew, like a Chastening with no purpose but to destroy the orderly world established by Saint Ixion Diospyros.

As if the inside of his skull were plated with mirrors that multiply each thought and vision to infinity, distorting what they reflect like the crystal domes and towers of Quoz, in which alternate imaginings of the city rise and fall with each shift of light, Azedarach sees again the moment of the triumph of Maw, when all the towns and cities of the Hierarchate, from Arpagee to Quoz, will shake and crumble to the ground, and the ground will split asunder, swallowing everything—buildings, animals, people—into the Pit of Damned Souls.

For the whole of his reign this vision has tormented him. At first he tried to ignore it, but it wouldn't go away. Instead, it grew more frequent, more intense, with the turnings, blighting his gilded hours with a prophecy of impotence and failure. By now he hears the screams of the dying and smells the charnel house odors of the Pit so vividly that he can't be sure his vision hasn't come to pass already.

It doesn't matter. He's too weak to act. All he has now are the visions, the dreams. But there are other dreams—dreams in which he sees himself as he was in his younger days, more than three hundred turnings ago, before the taste of metheglin sapped his will and reduced his body to a husk. He sees himself in the prime of life, still new to the Throne, giving certain orders and setting in motion a chain of events that is coming to fruition at last, three hundred turnings later.

The Chastenings are the key. There are Chastenings sent by Ixion to instruct his wayward people, the purpose of which is to strengthen, not destroy. But there are other Chastenings that come from the dark heart of Herwood, Chastenings with no aim save destruction.

The Furies are responsible. First they created Beauty, which for untold turnings has bled the Hierarchate of men. Now, impatient with this slow attrition, they've devised a new spell: these Chastenings that worsen with every turning until not even Quoz the impregnable is safe.

They must be stopped before his vision comes to pass, and the Hierarchate is brought down in ruins. Before he is brought down.

For he hears the grumbles of the nobles, even the highest of them, the ones most indebted to him for their places. Men like the vizard Erigeron Intricata. They don't believe the Chastenings are being caused by the spells of Furies; they believe that Ixion is signaling his displeasure with the present Sovereign and calling for his overthrow. Or so they pretend to believe, the better to justify their hunger for the Serpent Throne, a rebellious hunger Azedarach understands very well, having been filled with it once himself, in the long-ago days when he was a mere noble looking enviously at the blurred features of Gymnocladus CCCLXXVII.

But the plots against his life don't worry Azedarach. There are always plots and counterplots. His awareness is spread so widely through the

Hierarchate that he doubts the death of his body will prove more than a brief annoyance; at times he suspects he's already died, although he's almost certain this is not true.

In any case, the metheglin will protect him. His loyal shrives and vizards will protect him. Saint Ixion Diospyros and the Spinner will protect him. And when he puts a stop to these Chastenings, he'll be hailed by everyone—his enemies loudest of all—as Azedarach the Great, Savior of the Hierarchate. Late at night, as he broods upon his Throne, the need for sleep long put to sleep in him by metheglin, which has also conferred an immunity to Beauty such as the saints possessed of old, Azedarach hears the echo of cheers ringing down from the future.

But they always change to screams by the dawn.

When he was a younger man, newly ascended to the Serpent Throne but already plagued by these cursed visions, Azedarach—against the advice of the Ecclesiarch—sent an army of shrives into Herwood to track down and kill the Furies and put an end to Beauty. The shrives never returned. It was as if the woods had swallowed them up. Azedarach learned his lesson. But he didn't give up. He devised a new plan to save the Hierarchate from the Furies, a plan he shared with no one but men he had put to death immediately after using them. Not even the Ecclesiarch knows of his plan.

Unfortunately, Azedarach himself no longer remembers the details. Metheglin has left his memories shredded and mixed with dreams and visions of times to come. He only knows that the seeds he planted so long ago are almost ready for harvest. But soon he will remember. A dream will show the way.

But there are, regrettably, limitations to dreams. He hasn't had a vision of whether or not his plan will succeed. He sees up to the moment when the Hierarchate falls, but not beyond it, as if that future is as yet undetermined, too clouded to see. He needs more metheglin to see so far ahead. To spin the frayed strands of what may be into the single thread of the inevitable. The cost is great, but he must know.

He makes a mewling sound. Morus Sisymbrium quickly and smoothly raises the gold cup, cast in the mold of a plumed serpent swallowing its tail, to the royal lips.

As the Sovereign drinks, his features are, as always, blurred by the obfuscatory powers of the Serpent Crown, but Morus, who is a vizard after all, knows that the Sovereign has entered the final stages of metheglin addiction. As Morus removes the goblet, a thread of honeyed drool falls from the Sovereign's lips into the cinnamon tangles of his metheglin-stained beard, beneath which the royal throat plug is hidden. Fireflies hum there, feasting on the drippings.

Morus permits himself an inner frown; like all vizards, he loathes metheglin, spurning its vaunted powers of longevity and omniscience. The price is too great. He prefers to remain the master of his powers, not their slave.

It is this well-known aversion to metheglin that has made the office of cupbearer the exclusive property of vizards. No one else can be trusted to withstand the temptations of such intimate contact with metheglin—for the cupbearer not only holds and presents the cup to the Sovereign, he prepares the draughts and keeps the keys to the metheglin vaults.

Morus Sisymbrium is the twenty-second of his line to hold the office of cupbearer. His ancestor, Rubus Sisymbrium, served as Azedarach's chief vizard in the uprising that won the Throne from Gymnocladus CCCLXXVII, another metheglin addict, over four hundred turnings ago. Morus has served Azedarach for more than thirty turnings.

Now Morus twitches the fourth finger of his right hand in response to another, more urgent, whine from Azedarach. Across the throne chamber, the black-suited shrives who have been standing at attention all night spring into action. They dash buckets of water upon a naked woman who hangs limply from the Wheel of Excoriation. She revives, screaming. The water has been brought to a boil. She is, or was, a Cat from one of the low houses, judged guilty of the crime of heresy and condemned to the torments of the Six Hundred.

Morus frowns again, this time openly. The heresy of the return of Saint Viridis Lacrimata has been spreading through the Catteries of Quoz like wildfire. Even in the High Houses there have been reports of secret gatherings, converts won over to the cause. Theirs is a different Viridis than the one he knows and reveres. A Viridis who never repented of her life as a Cat. A Fury; indeed, the Queen of the Furies. Liberatrix, they call her. Viridis Liberatrix.

The Cat's screams grow more piercing as the shrives bend to their work. They are halfway through the Six Hundred; it will take at least another two days to finish. But the application of certain drugs known only to the shrives will keep the woman awake and alert throughout her ordeal. Her senses excited to a pitch of nervous discrimination, she'll experience infinities of pain. The quality of her suffering will not be lessened in sleep; there, in dreams, her punishment will continue. Only when the Six Hundred has been completed, and the woman's skin hangs beside her on the Wheel, will she be released from life to suffer the unending torments of the Pit.

Azedarach smiles. For a little while, at least, he is distracted from his metheglin dreams. The screams of this woman have brought him a moment's peace. Tears of gratitude well up in his eggshell eyes. He wiggles his toes in the warm, wet hole of the Cat's sucking mouth.

TWO

"Murder! Help! Murder!"

The shrill screams echo through the still-dark halls of the House Lacrimata, empty in these early morning hours save for the green sparks of fireflies.

"Help! Murder!"

A pale light appears at one end of a long corridor in the lower levels of the Cattery. Fireflies scatter like minnows as an unusually tall woman strides out of the shadows. It is Serinthe Lacrimata, odalisque of the House.

Serinthe wears sheer violet robes and glittering silver sandals that whisper over the smooth stones of the floor. In the soft wash of light, her abundant hair is the same consuming black as the uniforms of the shrives. Loose, it reaches almost to the floor, billowing around her like a cape. A single firefly has taken refuge in her hair, where it pulses like a rare emerald.

Serinthe is followed by two black-suited shrives, each of whom holds a glowing thyrsis. The shrives are identical in their black uniforms of clinging, sculpted leather like marble or iron, identical in the gaudy splash of red lips at their throats; even their eyes are identical, distant blue sparklings behind the eye-slits of their face masks.

The hallway down which the three figures hurry is lined with doors, all of them cracked open now. Sleepy-eyed Cats and clients in various states of undress blink quiet questions from behind upraised candles. Some of the faces express curiosity, others amusement or annoyance, others a furtive alarm.

"I apologize for the disturbance," Serinthe purrs as she sweeps past each door. Her smile simultaneously reassures the men and makes her girls tremble. "Please, do not concern yourselves. It is nothing. A foolish young Cat. She will be punished severely."

The doors close one by one as the Cats, with whispers and caresses, entice their clients back to bed or whatever games have been interrupted.

Serinthe's eyes are the color of ripe plums. Because of her lankiness, the red teardrop tattooed beneath her left eye like a small mole gives her something of the look of a simularter even though, being a Cat, there is nothing androgynous about her.

By the time she reaches the end of the hall, the screams have frayed to whimpers. The odalisque stands for a moment at the door, the very last door, and listens to the sound of weeping from within. She wishes the Cat would shut up. The fool is giving her a headache. There's no excuse for tears. A Cat must remain in control of herself at all times. By what appalling incompetence, she wonders, was this girl approved for service? She'll have to speak to her voluptuaries. The last thing she needs right now is a scandal. Oh, but wouldn't Cassine Illicium like that! Serinthe wonders if Cassine is responsible for whatever has happened behind the door.

Happy Saint Samsum's Day, she thinks, rubbing her poor, throbbing brow. She hasn't slept all night, busy with her newest acquisition, a juicy girl of fifteen turnings who waits trembling back in her chambers, naked and hooded and bound. Serinthe doesn't like to be interrupted when she's interviewing a new Cat. She nods to one of the shrives.

The shrive tries the door. "It's locked, Mistress."

"Unlock it."

The shrive hands his thyrsis to his twin, steps back, and kicks in the door. Hysterical shrieks rise from within.

"Stay here until I call you," Serinthe tells the shrives. She takes a thyrsis and, stooping slightly, enters the chamber.

"Odalisque! Thank Viridis you've come!"

"Silence." Serinthe strides to the bed, where the naked Cat is tied, and slaps her hard across the face. The blow knocks the girl's blond wig askew. She has vomited more than once; the odor fouls the air. And something else, only gradually sensible, a smell that hangs below the other like a denser gas held in an uneasy suspension. But it grows stronger with each second, more oppressive, inescapable, like desire choking on its own excess. The spilled perfume of a hundred cut roses.

The Cat struggles to master her sobs.

Serinthe takes no further notice of her. Frowning, she steps back to examine the chamber. The crystal tiles of the high ceiling glow milky pink. There is blood everywhere: on the silk curtains, on the silk sheets, and on the rugs, heavy and black as tar in the attenuated light. Serinthe drapes her hair across her shoulders to keep it from trailing in the gore.

It's worse than she'd feared. Far worse. Everything will have to be burned.

There has been a struggle. Shattered bowls, bottles, and wineglasses are strewn across the floor, along with the remains of a meal. Chairs and tables are overturned. Candles and sticks of incense. It's fortunate there wasn't a fire.

A struggle. Yes, Serinthe thinks, but between whom? With the door locked from inside, and the Cat tied to the bed.

Serinthe walks around the bed, taking care to avoid the shards of glass that she knows are just waiting to cut her pretty feet. Nothing distresses her like the sight of her own blood.

There is a body lying facedown on the rug. A man. Naked, old, very fat. Half-buried in roses. The sight of his bloated, pale ass, scarred from numerous canings, fills Serinthe with rage. With the toe of one foot, she flips the body over.

It has no face.

Viridis help me, Serinthe thinks, taken by surprise for once. She makes the sign of the Wheel.

The flesh has been cut away, leaving a mess of blood and tendon and, winking through, the gleaming white bone of forehead, cheek, and jaw. The tongue protrudes from between the teeth, so swollen that it looks foreign to the body, a gross purple slug trying to force its way in. The throat plug is missing, exposing the slit of the trachae. The eyes bulge whitely in their sockets. They stare at her with the same look of vacant supplication she's seen a hundred thousand times in the eyes of her client. Dead or alive, their eyes are always the same, she thinks.

Whoever he was, he was a man of the Church. A Mouth of God. There's no disguising that. His prick a little boy's. A diminutive rose. The only part of him not stiff. Some of my girls are bigger, she thinks, giving the organ a nudge with the tip of the thyrsis.

Lately there's been a rash of assassinations throughout the city as the conflict between Sovereign and Ecclesiarch spirals out of control, fueled by the ever-worsening Chastenings. But the High Houses have always been neutral ground. Sanctuaries. Always respected. Until now. And this business of the face. The *un*face rather. It had frightened her at first. Like something out of the Six Hundred. To say nothing of the roses.

Serinthe summons the shrives, raising her hand meanwhile to quiet the girl, who has resumed her whining. She will question the Cat later.

The two shrives appear beside her.

"Do you recognize this work?" she asks.

The shrives study the corpse. Their faces are hidden behind black masks; only their brilliant blue eyes are visible. Serinthe has never seen their faces. She has no desire to see them.

"Well? Is the technique familiar to you?"

"*The Lifting of the Veil*," says one in a voice bereft of emotion.

"Part of the Six Hundred?"

"Yes, Mistress," says the other, voice identical. The two shrives, like all the pairs of their order, have the annoying habit of speaking in turn.

"Just as I thought. So it was done by a shrive."

"No, Mistress."

"Who else knows the Six Hundred?"

"Only the Ecclesiarch."

"And those who have undergone the torments."

Serinthe is growing angry again. She prefers to order her shrives, not question them. She has never heard a shrive give a straight answer. They are arrogant and disputatious, worse than vizards. But even she does not dare to lose her temper with a shrive. Azedarach himself fears to provoke them. "Are you trying to tell me the Ecclesiarch committed this murder? Or a ghost?"

"No, Mistress."

"Then who else but a shrive could have done it?"

"We do not know."

"Not a shrive."

She takes a deep breath. "Will you kindly explain why not?"

"Because there must be a certain order, Mistress."

"We are not free to impose whatever torments we desire."

"The proper sequence must be followed."

"*The Lifting of the Veil* is part of the sequence *Disrobing*."

"It cannot be performed by itself."

"And the roses?"

"Roses have no place in this sequence."

"It is blasphemous."

"No shrive would do such a thing."

Serinthe is fuming. "Not even if ordered by the Ecclesiarch, the head of your order?"

"We are sworn to protect the Hierarchate."

"Ixion himself gave us this task."

"The Ecclesiarch commands us by virtue of his position as head of the Church."

"But he would cease to be the head upon giving such an order."

"The Ecclesiarch could no more order this than a shrive could obey him if he did."

"I will not have the hospitality of my House insulted and abused in this way!" Serinthe cries in frustration, dizzy from following the shrives. Her headache is worsening. She gives the corpse a kick. "I have a reputation to consider! I want you to take this faceless thing out of here, do you understand? Get rid of it!"

"Where shall we dispose of the body, Mistress?"

"That's for you to decide! You can practice the sequence *Disrobing* on it for all I care! Just get it out of here! And let no one see you! The House Lacrimata will not be the first of the High Houses to suffer the shameful indignity of a murdered client!" Serinthe can imagine the laughter with which Cassine Illicium would greet the news of her disgrace. "Dump it in the House Illicium!"

"That would be forbidden," says one shrive.

"But perhaps an alley outside the House . . . ?" suggests the other.

Serinthe smiles. Things are looking up. "I will leave it to your discretion."

"You realize there is another question, Mistress."

Serinthe nods wearily.

"The door was locked."

"The Cat bound."

"Unless the murderer is still with us . . . "

Both shrives drop quickly to their knees and peer under the bed.

"Well?" asks Serinthe, angry at herself for not having thought to look.

The shrives stand. "There is no one."

"And no place else to hide."

"Perhaps it was a ghost after all," Serinthe says.

"Surely you do not believe in ghosts, Mistress."

"It was a joke." Shrives have no sense of humor.

"Ah."

"You will make a thorough search of the room," she orders. "There must be a hidden passage of some kind."

"Yes, Mistress."

"Have you questioned the Cat, Mistress?"

Serinthe needs no reminder. She has already turned to the bed. The young Cat is strapped down amid blood- and vomit-stained sheets, shivering with fright. She is so filthy, her face streaked with blood and tears and Ixion-knows-what, that it takes Serinthe a moment to recognize her. "Rose, isn't it? One of Alba's girls."

The Cat nods stiffly, eyes wide. The movement tumbles the blond wig into her lap. Her shaved head glistens with sweat.

Serinthe notes the absence of tattoos. Only the single red teardrop, common to all the Cats of the House Lacrimata, below her left eye. "Was this your first client, Rose?"

The girl's mouth works for some time before "Yes, odalisque" croaks out from between her lips.

Serinthe recalls having been impressed with this Cat's beauty during their interview some months ago, shortly after the Feast of Saint Ilex. She's not easily impressed. Little sign of that beauty now, she thinks. But still, she will not waste an investment. The girl had not come cheaply. Serinthe gives her sweetest, most maternal smile. "Can you tell us what happened here, Rose?"

Rose shakes her head as if Serinthe's smile only adds to her terror.

"Answer!" Serinthe stamps her foot. "Do you want me to give you to the shrives?"

"Sim . . . sim . . . ," the girl stutters.

"Simularters? Is that who killed him?" Serinthe does not trust the simularters. They have damaged her girls too often. She has warned Azedarach against them, but the metheglin-besotted fool won't listen.

Rose shakes her head vigorously. "Sim . . . *simulars*," she finally manages to pronounce.

"Simulars!" Serinthe rolls her eyes. "You were dreaming, idiot!"

The Cat is trying to say something else. It sounds as if she's choking on the words.

Serinthe is out of patience. She leans across the bed and touches the girl's thigh with the tip of the thyrsis. The girl's body rises violently against the straps, then falls back. Her thigh now carries a deep purple bruise, the very color of Serinthe's eyes. The girl's eyes are glazed, her breathing shallow. A thread of spittle leaks from her mouth.

"Now," says Serinthe, greatly encouraged. "Tell me what you saw. The truth."

"I saw simulars," the Cat whispers slowly. Her voice is far away, as if relating a dream while she dreams it. "They fell from the ceiling on their strings. Like spiders."

"This is absurd!" Serinthe can barely restrain herself from giving the girl another jolt. But that might kill her. And she doesn't want to kill the girl. Not yet. "Do you take me for a fool? Did Cassine put you up to this? Are you working for her?" Such things occasionally happen. A girl bought on the open market turns out to be a spy for a rival house. Serinthe usually exposes them during the initial interview, but from time to time one slips through.

"No, odalisque," the Cat drones. "The client had just strapped me to the bed. He was talking to me while he ate and drank. Telling me the things he was going to do to me. He wouldn't look at me. He just kept talking."

"Yes, yes. Then what?"

"I didn't see them at first; it was too dark. There was a smell of roses. An odor so thick I nearly choked on it. But he smelled nothing; he was too busy eating. Then I saw them dropping from the ceiling on their strings. I watched them fall. I tried to warn him, but I was too frightened. They knocked him onto the floor. After that, I couldn't see. But I heard. I heard . . . "

"Go on. This is entertaining, at least."

"I heard the simulars talking. They said they had come to put the House in order. They said the rightful odalisque had returned."

Serinthe, for the second time this morning, finds herself taken by surprise. "The rightful odalisque indeed!" She turns to the shrives. "Do you hear?"

"Yes, Mistress," says one.

"The heresy," says the other.

Serinthe doesn't like the way the shrive pronounces the word "heresy." There's an eagerness in his voice she hasn't heard before, a caress of the tongue.

"There's no heresy in this House!" she cries. "How could there be? This is the House of Saint Viridis Lacrimata, Our Lady of the Perpetual Sacrifice!"

"Give us the girl."

"We'll find the heresy."

Serinthe is about to reply when a prolonged rattle rises from the girl's throat. A shudder passes through her body. Her eyes roll up into her head.

"Is she dead?" Serinthe asks.

"She has lost consciousness," one of the shrives replies after examining her.

"She will not wake for some hours."

Serinthe turns to the shrives. "Well? What do you make of her story?"

"She is telling the truth."

Serinthe wonders if the shrives have a sense of humor after all.

"As she believes it," the other shrive adds.

"There are drugs that can induce belief."

"Yes, yes." Serinthe has made use of such drugs in the past. As has Cassine. "Cassine Illicium's behind this. I just know it."

"You have no proof."

"Give us the girl."

"Why? So you can kill her? We'll learn nothing that way. Do the heretics confess? Has a single one ever named a comrade before the end of the Six Hundred?"

"No, Mistress," the shrive admits.

"I have a better way. There is a gathering at the House Illicium later today in honor of Saint Samsum. As odalisque, I'm expected to attend. I'll bring this Cat . . . Rose. The two of you shall come as well. We'll observe how Cassine acts when Rose is introduced to her. One of them will give the conspiracy away, I assure you. Cassine has never been able to hide her feelings; how she ever became odalisque is beyond me. We can't afford to squander this chance—the House Illicium must be riddled with heresy! More heretics than even you have Wheels to accommodate!"

The shrives look at each other without speaking. At such times, Serinthe has the impression they are talking with each other in their minds.

"This is acceptable," one finally says.

Serinthe breathes a sigh of relief. "Now get this place cleaned up. When you're done, I'll send some girls to fetch the Cat and ready her for the gathering."

She hurries to leave the room. The stench of blood and vomit, thickened by the reek of the roses, is making her nauseous. But at the thought of the girl who waits for her in her chambers, Serinthe feels better. She grips the thyrsis tightly. Its touch need not always leave a bruise.

THREE

The Ecclesiarch strides around the altar wheel within the tabernacle of Saint Ixion's Cathedral of the Spinning Wheel. It's the very Wheel on which the boy-saint Cedrus Lyciodes was martyred by the Furies. The ancient wood bears the scars of the arrows and knives that transfixed him. There are deep crevices where his hot blood ran, channels that brim anew in the *Trachaea* and the other sacred rites of bloodletting.

The Ecclesiarch moves so quickly that his white robes seem to melt into a blur. One hand slides along the rim of the Wheel as though it were the banister of a spiral staircase. He circles and circles, never seeming to get anywhere. But each revolution brings him closer to his secret destination.

He comes here, to the tabernacle, as a prelude to the only escape he knows from the million cares of his office. The hard, smooth curve of the Wheel beneath his hand makes him feel close to the martyred saint. He imagines himself caressing the marble white limbs of Cedrus, hardened in the brutal agonies of asphyxiation as though striving toward the embrace of Ixion, his beauty made imperishable by such an early death, before the gross changes of manhood had ravaged his smooth and hairless body. The Ecclesiarch increases his pace, stirred by the craving that never sleeps in him, a hunger so voracious it feasts on itself like a serpent devouring its own tail.

Only when alone does he move with such careless abandon. In public he restricts himself to the grave, deliberate movements appropriate to his age and office. But the exercise of restraint is difficult, increasingly so with each turning. His nerves rebel, trembling in indignation, an inner jangle that never lessens until he gives in, and even then does not cease but merely becomes, for a time, more bearable. He often shakes like an old man with the effort of holding his hungers in check. The shaking, in its way, is useful: it adds to the impression of decrepitude that causes his opponents to dismiss him as a threat. Even those who, like Azedarach, should know better.

But in private there must be some release. An indulgence to stave off madness or surrender into the kind of helpless idiocy that claimed Gymnocladus, that has claimed Azedarach. There is no weakness that repels the Ecclesiarch more than this return to the undisciplined state of infancy, the shameless hunger of a babe at its mother's breast, milk replaced by metheglin.

He remembers as if it were yesterday, and not more than four hundred turnings ago, lifting the Serpent Crown from the head of Gymnocladus prior to his execution. The face of the deposed Sovereign, unseen for hundreds of turnings, was soft and flabby, utterly without character, a waxen mask held too close to a flame, the eyes no more than soap bubbles. Gymnocladus whined not from fear or the imminence of death but because his dose of metheglin was overdue. Now the Ecclesiarch wonders if, behind the veil of the Serpent Crown, the features of Azedarach have come to be indistinguishable from those of his predecessor.

Soon he will not have to wonder.

Coming to an abrupt decision—or, rather, recognizing that in another second the decision will no longer be his to make, the all-important difference between willing something and giving in to it—the Ecclesiarch breaks off his circumnavigation of the Wheel and passes through the curtains of somber red velvet that shield the sacrarium from impious eyes.

Moments later, he steps into a corridor on the upper levels of the Cathedral. The shrives on either side of the door stiffen as he emerges. He absently makes the sign of the Wheel. They are his shrives, personally chosen by him and molded from boyhood to serve his every whim.

At this high level, the walls are all of crystal. As he bustles down the corridor at the halting skip of an old man—he is careful to hide his true vitality even from his shrives—the Ecclesiarch gazes over the glittering topography of Quoz.

The city spreads out on all sides, a diamond of infinite facets kindled by the late morning sun. In the distance, the domes of the Palace of the Chambered Nautilus rise in counterpoint to the Cathedral spires that bristle around the Ecclesiarch. Ribbons of color twine through the air between as if a flock of serpents has dropped from the sky.

Serpents can sometimes be glimpsed above Quoz, hunting their favorite prey, the birds. Once, when he was a boy of ten turnings living with his mother in the House Lacrimata—the very Cattery in which Viridis Lacrimata had plied her trade before her lust for Ixion had seduced her into sainthood—the Ecclesiarch witnessed that rarest and most auspicious of omens, the coupling of two serpents.

Kneeling upon the narrow balcony of his mother's chamber, to which he retreated when she entertained her admirers—not from modesty, but the better to spy upon them, wondering which, if any, was his father—his attention was drawn one afternoon from the familiar spectacle of a penis in its second infancy being sucked like a wet noodle between the red and grimly efficient lips of his mother. At a noise like swords clashing he turned to see twin bolts of silver and blue collide in the air above his head, so close he could have hit them with a stone. He threw a shout instead as the serpents licked around each other amid violent discharges of fire, then arrowed apart.

In that instant, he knew that Ixion had chosen him for greatness. His mother and her elderly client had rushed onto the balcony, drawn by his cry.

"What is it, Sium?" his mother asked with a frown, not bothering to hide her nakedness. In those days, he still had a name.

"I saw the serpents mating!" he said proudly, pointing to the very spot . . . where, however, no trace of the fabulous union remained, not even a feather wheeling brightly to the ground.

The old man, a vizard, laughed. His penis shook beneath his fat belly to the same rhythm as the plug in his throat. "Your boy has a healthy imagination, Isatis!"

"He's a liar," his mother said. "He's been spying on us. I know his ways. I'll give him something to cry about!" And she'd grabbed him then, in front of the old vizard, pulled up his robes, and put him over her knee and spanked him with her bare hand as if he were a child, not a boy of ten turnings, practically a man.

"Admit you lied!"

"I didn't!"

He remembers watching the vizard's penis harden with each of his mother's blows, remembers also how his own small penis grew rigid between his clenched thighs as the hand smacked his bottom, becoming, in his imagination, the vizard's hand, the hand of his unknown father.

At the feel of him pressing against her, his mother had pushed him roughly away, her mouth tight with distaste. "Look at him! The little beast!"

Laughing, the vizard had grasped his mother by the arm and drawn her back into the chamber, winking at the boy as he did so. Soon the sounds of another spanking had emerged from the chamber.

Later he told the Mouth of God who visited the Cattery each week to hear confessions how he'd seen the serpents. The priest did not call him a liar, but asked many careful questions. The next day, he was taken from his mother—who seemed happy to be rid of his unnerving presence—and placed in a dormitory on the lower levels of the Cathedral along with other boys like himself, the bastards of Cats selected for training as acolytes. His name was taken from him, and other things as well. Thus began his career in the Church of the Spinning Wheel.

A career that has lasted over two thousand turnings.

Like Azedarach, the Ecclesiarch prolongs his life with metheglin. But while the Sovereign refuses himself nothing, stuffing himself with metheglin until it leaks from his pores, the Ecclesiarch rations his intake like a miser parting with gold. Not for him the self-indulgence of the Sovereign, the abdication of initiative in exchange for a dreaming omniscience bereft of the ability or even the desire to act. The Ecclesiarch tastes metheglin but once a month. It is his sole nourishment. A single amber droplet is placed with infinite care and devotion upon his tongue by a favored acolyte, the only time the Ecclesiarch relies upon the loyalty of another. He finds the experience galling but cannot trust his hands to perform the delicate task. Their shaking, whether by accident or in fulfillment of a secret desire, might alter his measure, which has not varied in two thousand turnings.

His predecessor Ecclesiarch, who taught him the secrets of metheglin, served for six hundred turnings before succumbing to temptation and hunger and gorging himself to death, or worse than death, in the metheglin vaults. But he was a weak man, corrupted by odalisques and simularters, not unlike Azedarach.

The Ecclesiarch thinks with scorn of Azedarach buried alive at the heart of the Palace of the Chambered Nautilus, the passage of time and all the things of the world as insubstantial to his mind's clouded eye as are his features to the eyes of those who wait upon him. Sovereign of all the Hierarchate, he is no longer sovereign of himself.

The Ecclesiarch will not repeat these mistakes. As long as he keeps his measure constant, there is no limit to how long he may live. He has already lived for two thousand and sixty-one turnings. Longer than any Ecclesiarch—perhaps any man—in history.

The monthly taste of metheglin not only frees him from the tyranny of time, it gives him a physical quickness, in short bursts, that no man can match. And it accelerates the working of his mind, freeing his thoughts from the heavy chains of causality. They break up and re-form, then shatter in a glittering spray, each drop of which holds a pattern, a mind of its own, part of a larger pattern yet also complete in itself, a whole Hierarchate in his head.

The Ecclesiarch does not sleep. He does not dream. He is always awake, always thinking.

But the hunger. He's never gotten used to the hunger. Ravenous, unimaginable, it gnaws incessantly at his body, at his sanity, a famine raging through his blood. It has carved him out until he sometimes fears there's nothing else left in him. His life is an agony of want without end, the satisfaction of which would mean not death but a life worse than death, the death-in-life to which Azedarach, like so many before him, has succumbed.

But he accepts the hunger gladly, offers it up to Ixion as a perpetual sacrifice in the spirit of Saint Viridis Lacrimata. It's the hunger that keeps him alive. To be satisfied is to die, and it's immortality the Ecclesiarch craves. Not for its own sake but to better serve the Spinner. To protect the Hierarchate from fools like Azedarach, with his dangerous idea that the Chastenings are the work of Maw and not, as they always have been, a sign from the Spinner urging spiritual or political renewal. It's obvious that Azedarach doesn't want to entertain the possibility his reign has proved displeasing to the Spinner. But in his desperation to retain the Serpent Throne, he's become as grave a threat to the Hierarchate as anything that comes out of Herwood.

Azedarach doesn't understand the necessity of balance. How can he, when it's precisely that which is missing from his own life? But the Ecclesiarch knows. The Ecclesiarch understands. As with the precise measure of metheglin that binds him to a wheel of inner excoriation while granting him an immortality perpetually renewed, balance is everything. It's no accident the heresy of Saint Viridis Lacrimata's return has emerged now. Azedarach has encouraged it. He must be stopped.

He will be stopped.

The Ecclesiarch passes another pair of shrives. At his signal, they fall in behind him. The corridor turns sharply. No longer can the glittering splendors of Quoz be seen. The crystal walls are darkened to opacity by vizards' craft. Soft white light seeps from crystals in the floor. Black doors line the corridor at regular intervals, disappearing into the distance. The seal of the Hierarchate glimmers in silver upon the doors, the plumed serpent swallowing its tail. Below the seal, worked in smoky carnelian, are the words spoken by Ixion in his last sermon, before his capture by the Furies: "IN MY END IS MY BEGINNING."

The Ecclesiarch hesitates. To the left are his private chambers, where, with the assistance of loyal shrives, he devises new torments to add to the Six Hundred. He's invented thousands of innovations. *The Bleeding Necklace. Saint Samsum's Burden.* But today none of them has the power to grant him one moment of relief. None of them can supply the peace and forgetfulness he craves.

"Wait for me," he orders now.

"Yes, Your Eminence," the shrives reply in unison.

The Ecclesiarch enters a door on the right side of the corridor and steps into a darkness as absolute as night. He does not hesitate, but strides quickly forward. Metheglin provides a lamp of its own by which to see. A light that never goes out. This, too, he keeps hidden, an ability his enemies will never suspect until it is too late.

He is in another corridor. Narrow and winding, it is lined with small cells, all of which are empty. Each cell has a plain wooden desk and a bare pallet. There are no windows; the cells might as well be deep underground as high above the city. The doors are iron bars that can be opened only from outside.

Once, not long ago, acolytes selected to become shrives were brought to these cells to begin their arduous training under the personal supervision of the Ecclesiarch. Out of every hundred boys, only two or three at best would ever come to wear the proud black uniform of a shrive and enter that brotherhood of fanatic loyalty and cruelty. The rest perished in training or proved to be temperamentally unsuited for the duties required of them, in which case they studied the Six Hundred from a different perspective than they'd hoped.

Once it was the Ecclesiarch's passion to test these boys. To take them in his hands and see if he could break them or mold them to his will, either outcome affording equal pleasure.

No more.

Now the Ecclesiarch hurries past the empty cells with no regret for yesterday's pleasures. The corridor becomes a staircase that coils upward, turn after turn. He climbs like the wind. And yet he is not the wind, but only something whirled by the wind.

He comes at last to a door. He reaches a trembling hand to the lock, then pulls back. He puts his eye to a sliver of dark crystal in the door, through which he may gaze undetected into the chamber beyond.

The chamber resembles a room in a Cattery. Cushions of red and purple satin and velvet spread across a floor covered in thick rugs decorated with colorful representations of scenes from the *Lives and Acts* and intricate motifs of wheels within wheels. Billowing silk drapes of gold and silver cover the walls. Clouds of incense drift up from great copper braziers. Mirrors artfully placed give an illusion of limitless space. The crystal ceiling admits the light of the sun, now almost directly overhead. From the great bed at the center of the chamber, a bed in the shape of a wheel, one can lie back and look straight up into the sky, as if floating in midair. The chamber sits at the tip of the tallest Cathedral spire, high above the other structures of Quoz. In all the Hierarchate, there is no place nearer to Saint Ixion.

An ashen-pale figure lies sprawled across the bed, facing upward as if gazing through the ceiling, one arm flung over a forehead uncreased by age or worry. A heavy gold chain leads from one smooth ankle to an iron post that rises from the center of the bed all the way to the ceiling.

On another, more slender gold chain around his neck, the Ecclesiarch wears a gold key.

Now, as if sensitive even to the pressure of a secret gaze, the figure in the bed sits up and faces the door with an expression that pierces the Ecclesiarch to the heart. There is no fear or hope in that look, no acknowledgment of another, just self-involvement so complete and unquestioning that it has no need of mirrors or even of eyes, for the skin of the face flows like a drift of sand over the wells of sight. It's the same expression of serene detachment depicted in representations of the martyrdom of Saint Cedrus Lyciodes, who was blinded by the Furies before his death.

And yet the features are not those of the boy-saint.

The features the Ecclesiarch examines so intently recall another face entirely.

His own.

It's like looking into a mirror that reflects the past. As if the intensity of thought instilled in him by metheglin, the obsessive self-reflection that operates with the tireless precision of the system of bells and clocks set in motion by vizards in the myth-shrouded days preceding the erection of the Hierarchate, has created in the external world a living eidolon of the image most sacred to his memory: that of his youthful self. The boy he was when he was still whole, unspoiled. Before his name was taken from him without his consent or his understanding of what such a loss would mean in turnings too distant to contemplate yet already nearer than he knew. Only in the lack of eyes is the boy different from the Ecclesiarch's former self. And yet that difference merely stresses the uncanny nature of the resemblance, as of a statue come to life under the ardent gaze of its creator, who cannot bear to be scrutinized in turn.

The Ecclesiarch does not know what he wants from this boy. He only knows that for the first time in over two thousand turnings, he feels a hunger rivaling that of metheglin. He pushes open the door and steps breathlessly into the chamber.

"Is it Saint Samsum's Day already, Nuncle?" The boy's voice is full of weariness. He sinks back on the bed without another word.

Neither does the Ecclesiarch speak. Not yet. As he walks stiffly to the bed, he catches sight of himself, or, rather, of countless images of himself, in the mirrors. He feels as if he, too, is but one of these images, all of which are equally real and substantial. An infinity of Ecclesiarchs converging here in this chamber high above the many-faceted city of Quoz, drawn by the boy who lies on the bed at the center of a nest of mirrors, immune to reflection. The Ecclesiarch wonders why the features of his splintered selves do not resemble those of the severe and emotionless man he knows himself to be. He looks away, wishing he were as blind as the boy chained to the bed.

But there is no looking away from so many mirrors, no escaping the face they present and re-present.

The face of a man in love.

FOUR

"*Girls! Girls!*" The voice of the odalisque Cassine Illicium crests sharply over the excited chattering of the five Cats gathered in the hospitality hall of the Cattery. She claps her hands twice, then twice more. By the time the echoes have faded, the silence is complete.

"That's better." The odalisque emerges in an indolent unfolding of exquisitely pale limbs from the cushioned and veiled litter in which her four shrives have borne her to the hall. They are gifts from the Ecclesiarch; also, she knows, spies, but still they have their uses.

An admiring murmur rises from the Cats at the sight of their odalisque, a wordless purring. Cassine basks in the sound, seeming to rub against it as, with long and lingering strides, the roll of her hips a worldly caress, she approaches the five voluptuaries of the House Illicium.

She wears little enough: silks so thin they are almost transparent, beneath which her perfect skin glows as if emitting a light of its own, a radiance that would ravish eyes to blindness if unveiled. Only the triangle where legs and torso meet is dark, as dark as the uniforms of the shrives who stand woodenly around the litter like the posts of a bed. Beside them, she is a marvel of airy movement. Bright earrings and bracelets and rings flash in the glow of candlewheels hanging from the high ceiling. Her feet are shod in slippers that might be woven of sunlight; a ribbon of rainbow arabesque arches across the golden tops, curling upward at the toes. Chains of dark blue and green tattoos web her depilated scalp and the skin above her eyes. The tattoos seem to writhe in the choppy light like serpents sloughing the skin that binds their fragile, still-damp wings. Each tattoo, like the beaded spokes of a prayer wheel, carries with it a shadow word or phrase that, when linked together, constitutes a single prayer of submission to Saint Viridis Lacrimata, the patron saint of Cats.

Cassine Illicium is odalisque of one of the oldest, most respected Catteries in Quoz: the House Illicium. Only the House Lacrimata, where Saint Viridis herself once served—and more for that reason than the excellence of service—has precedence. But Cassine is still a Cat. As such, she's permitted to wear one of her formidable wigs only when entertaining a client; at all other times, she must leave her head bare as a reminder of her dishonor of the crime that brought her here from Lusk, a weepy girl of fourteen who one night left her widowed father untended and defenseless when Beauty prowled the dark.

When her hair was cut and shaved away by the Panderman, her father's name also shorn from her, she'd wanted to die. But the House Illicium purchased her instead, at the market in Kell. Gave her a new home. A new life. A chance, however slim, for redemption.

She became Cassine Illicium and set about grasping that chance with both hands. In just fifteen turnings, her beauty and determination won her the position of odalisque, a prize she's held against all rivals for fifty-eight turnings.

In a few short days, Cassine will turn eighty-seven. A generous lifetime. But even on a bad day she looks no more than thirty. Although she's never tasted the fabled sweetness of pure metheglin, some trace of it lingers, dilute but still potent, in the secretions of her clients, wizened noblemen from the Court of the Plumed Serpent and the upper echelons of the Church, servants of Sovereign and Ecclesiarch who have eked out their lives on whatever scraps are thrown or fall to them. Just as she has eked out her youth, her beauty.

Now Cassine takes more pride in the tattoos covering her scalp than she ever did in the abundance of hair that was the hope and glory of her girlhood. The tattoos are a reminder not only of her crime, but of the path to redemption. The path of perpetual sacrifice that leads step by slow step back to Saint Ixion, as if her father were stumbling blindly out of Herwood to forgive her. She has tried to instill this same pride in all her Cats, whether born in the Cattery, ignoble offspring of nobles, or, like her, sent here as punishment for crimes of neglect.

The five who stand before her now in wispy silks and silver slippers do not share a single history. Some come from far away, others have lived their entire lives beneath the wide roof of the House Illicium, which, over the turnings, like the other High Houses, has become attached by a maze of corridors and chambers to the Palace and the Cathedral, part of both yet belonging wholly to neither. In the shape of their bodies, the size of their bones; in their height, their weight, the color of their skin; in the steadiness of their gaze and the color of their eyes; in their voices, their laughs, and what they laugh at, they are as different as night and day.

Apart from a rough equivalence in age—they appear to be somewhere in their mid-teens to early twenties—the five have only one thing in common other than their sex and its ancient curse: their heads have been shaved to a smoothness that glistens in the light of the candlewheels. Even their eyebrows and eyelashes have been removed.

These five are Cassine's voluptuaries, instructed by her personally in the timeless arts of arousal and satisfaction that Cats have practiced since before the erection of the Hierarchate. They are her lieutenants in the management of the House Illicium; each one heads a harem of fifteen Cats, plus assorted children—boys not yet old enough to be sent away for training as Mouths of God or shrives or simularters, girls too young or untutored to entertain clients—and older women whose charms have long faded but whose encyclopedic knowledge of the *ars erotica* surpasses even Cassine's. They are her daughters, her sisters, her lovers, and her rivals, too. They are the only family she has. Or needs.

"How lovely you are, Aralia," she says, addressing the first girl in line, whose handsome dark face smiles back openly, brown eyes glittering.

"Thank you, Cassine."

Cassine stretches—Aralia is tall—and bestows a lingering kiss upon her reddened lips. "I'm jealous, Aralia. I believe you may catch the eye of the Sovereign himself this afternoon."

"Viridis grant it!" Aralia laughs nervously and runs a hand over her scalp as if for luck. Tattoos wind from her left temple to behind her left ear like a vine of thorns.

Cassine continues down the line of voluptuaries, warmly greeting and kissing each in turn. The others are tattooed like Aralia, only to a lesser degree. The last in line—a petite, pale-skinned girl whose name is Rumer—has only a single tattoo, a tiny green Wheel like a birthmark on the right side of her head.

Cassine steps back. The softness of lips and tongues flutters pleasantly in her memory. It seems only yesterday that she chose these girls from among their sisters and brought them to her chambers for the months of training and discipline that spin ordinary Cats into voluptuaries. But, except for Rumer, who's still relatively new, it's been turnings.

In one case, too many turnings.

Cassine forces herself to smile. A sour taste clings to her breath like curdled delight. When kissing Aralia, she noticed that age, the implacable enemy of Cats, had at last begun to spin its heavy webs at the corners of the voluptuary's mouth and sweet almond eyes. She can no longer deny that Aralia, her favorite, the eldest of her voluptuaries, has passed her prime. Perhaps only her own too-sensitive eyes can detect the change, but soon others will notice. Really she should be relieved of her duties now, before she dishonors the Cattery.

But Cassine cannot bear it. The girl has quickened her heart with too many kisses, served loyally for too many turnings. She will be as gentle now as when she first brought Aralia to her bed, a frightened girl of fifteen turnings freshly arrived from Kell. Her intelligent brown eyes, despite their tears, gazed with interest at her new home, whose strangeness, as Cassine well knew, could seem terrible at first. In that frankly curious gaze, Cassine was reminded of herself, of the girl she'd been or liked to imagine she'd been. It was a rare gift, given unconsciously, wrapped in tenderness and regret and all the more precious for it.

She will give Aralia a gift, similarly wrapped: one last week as chief voluptuary of the House Illicium. It is Holy Week, after all. Saint Samsum's Day. And who knows? By some miracle Aralia may catch the elusive eye of the Blessed Sovereign and receive from him the one gift she really needs, the one gift capable of saving her: a taste of metheglin.

Perhaps. But Cassine is already thinking about Aralia's successor, of the parade of girls she'll summon to her chambers for testing in the long nights following All Saints' Eve. Savoring this pleasure, sweeter for being postponed, her smile is no longer forced.

"Happy Saint Samsum's Day, daughters and sisters." Her throaty voice, swelled by the acoustics of the hall, curls in the voluptuaries' ears.

"Happy Saint Samsum's Day, Cassine," they reply.

"There is much to do before this afternoon's gathering, so I won't keep you long. You have your duties; I know you'll carry them out to perfection, as always. Most of you know what Saint Samsum's Day means to this House. But for the sake of our Rumer, who I understand is a little nervous, I'll do what we Cats are taught never to do and repeat myself!"

The others laugh as Rumer blushes scarlet. This is her first Holy Week as a voluptuary, and for the last month she's been driving everyone crazy with her apprehensive questions, afraid of disgracing the House Illicium by some thoughtless word or action.

Cassine twitches a finger. Two shrives spring instantly to life, fetching, from within the litter, a slender couch piled with lush, wine-dark cushions. The odalisque reclines carefully upon the couch, as if even such pillows as these might bruise her pretty skin.

She lies on her side, facing the voluptuaries. Her head rests upon a cushion, half-sunk in shadow; the sight is enough to silence the voluptuaries' laughter, for Cassine appears in this weave of light and dark to possess a glorious growth of hair. A wealth of hair such as each of them once possessed or dreamed of possessing, the long tresses of which entangle their dreams.

"Long ago, longer than any man can say," Cassine begins softly, her voice filling the hush, "in the days when Maw reigned in the hearts of women, turning them from helpful wives, mothers, and daughters to wild Furies drunk on the blood of men and boys, there lived in the city of Peripety a man by the name of Samsum Oxalis.

"Now Samsum was a blacksmith famous from Arpagee to Quoz for his strength. Half a dozen strong men together couldn't lift the anvil he kept in his foundry, but he raised it above his head for sheer pleasure at the start of each day. Even his hammer was beyond their strength.

"Yet despite his marvelous strength, Samsum was shunned by everyone. He lived alone in his foundry, both parents dead, no relations or friends. A gentle man, he was shy and ill at ease in the company of others, unable to share a story or a drink without forgetting the one and spilling the other. And as for women, his face would turn as red as Rumer's at the mere mention of a woman's charms, however delicately phrased. No wonder the men despised him! They envied a strength that seemed wasted on such meekness, as if by some unfathomable error the Spinner had spun the soul of a lamb into the body of a lion.

"Neither was Samsum pleasing to the eye. His limbs were too large for his body. Dark hairs sprouted from every inch of him like the bristles of a boar. His back was humped. And his face . . . daughters and sisters, I hesitate to describe his face! There are not words ugly enough. It was a moldering mushroom of a face, all swollen and creased and ruined, as if chopped to pieces by an axe and then put back together by a blind man.

"Though far from poor, he had no hope of marriage. No woman could bear the sight of him. Hardened Cats turned him away. And children, with their knack for cruelty, made Samsum's life an unending torment of practical jokes and insults. Even the Furies shunned him; not because they were afraid of his great strength, but because it would have been an insult to Maw to send such an imperfect sacrifice to the Pit of Damned Souls.

"One day, a stranger entered Peripety. A man who walked with a limp, dressed in the clothes of a beggar, and called himself the Mouth of God. I don't need to tell you who that man was."

"Saint Ixion Diospyros!" breathes Rumer, caught up in the tale like a child hearing it for the first time.

Cassine smiles. "So it was. Only he wasn't a saint yet, Rumer, but a prophet on his way to Quoz. With him came his motley band of followers, men like Fagus Firmiana, Rober Viburnum, and Stilskin Sophora . . . as well as the scribe Quercus Incana, who, after the erection of the

Hierarchate, would write down the story of Ixion Diospyros and the other saints and martyrs in his *Lives and Acts*.

"Ixion's reception in Peripety was unkind. His message of the new covenant between men and the Spinner, his call to all men to rise up and throw off the bloody yoke of Maw and her Furies and erect in its place a Hierarchate that would stand until the end of time, fell on deaf or hostile ears. Crowds gathered to disrupt his preaching with laughter, hard words, and harder stones.

"Of course there were Furies in those crowds, and women whose hearts belonged to Maw even if their hands hadn't yet done her evil bidding. But there were men as well. Men afraid to hope, afraid to believe. Men whose anger had no other target but the man who'd come to save them. And these men were as vicious as any Fury in the extremity of their hate, for it was themselves they truly hated. In their hearts, they knew Ixion was right. But it was too hard, that truth. Too painful. So they punished him for speaking openly what they kept hidden from themselves.

"But one man listened. One man in all of Peripety. From the first day that Ixion had appeared, Samsum watched him from the shadows of his foundry. In the prophet's ragged clothes and limp he saw a kindred spirit. Watching as jeers and garbage rained down on the prophet's head, Samsum felt a curious agitation commence in his blood. It grew day by day. For the first time in his life, he felt angry. Not for himself, but on behalf of this other, who bore insult and injury as calmly as he himself had long borne the gibes of his tormentors.

"Samsum retreated each day to the heart of his foundry and stood in the heat of the forge, raising the great anvil above his head over and over again until the sweat poured off him in a river, and his powerful arms were as weak as jelly. He was afraid, you see. Of himself.

"At last there came a day when the crowd was no longer content to jeer and hurl stones. Like dogs so used to straining against a leash that they pause in disbelief once it's dropped, suspecting a trick, and then leap forward with doubled zeal, no longer caring, the crowd—egged on by Furies, who preferred to remain in the background of this affair, not wishing to give the impression that they took a crippled prophet seriously—rushed upon Ixion and his small band, which immediately formed a circle around him. The crowd had no weapons, just their bare hands. But hands need no daggers to kill.

"At a word from Ixion, his defenders retreated. The Mouth of God stood alone to meet his murderers. He watched them come, the men, women, and children of Peripety, his eyes blazing with the same contempt he would show later in Cat Square and again in the moments before his fiery ascension.

"Looking on from the doorway of his foundry, Samsum felt a shattering inside him, as when flawed iron newly drawn from the forge is plunged into ice-cold water. With a bellow that drowned out the shouts of the mob, he waded into its midst, taking people in his huge hands and tossing them about like simulars.

"Routed by such an unexpected display, the crowd itself soon shattered. Leashed again, the people of Peripety watched in disbelief as Samsum approached Ixion and fell to his knees. Tears streamed down his butchered face, making it even uglier.

"'Let me follow you, master,' he said.

"'What are you called?' asked Ixion.

"'Samsum Oxalis,' he said.

"'Your strength and anger are a man's,' said Ixion. 'But tears are a woman's weakness.'

"'My strength and anger are yours.'

"'Then dry your tears and come,' Ixion said.

"And he went, taking only his hammer from the forge."

"But what of *our* House, Cassine?" Rumer interrupts now, demands now, all restraint forgotten in the need to hear again how the story ends . . . this tale she's heard a thousand times since her arrival at the Cattery and has told another thousand times herself. "What of the House Illicium?"

Cassine lifts her head from the pillow, hurt by Rumer's impatience, which has the sting of criticism. She prides herself on her storytelling. It's a form of expression strangely related to the *ars erotica*, a parallel branch perhaps, employing similar strategies to similar ends, climax promised and delayed with the same teasing cruelty, the same repertory of lies and misdirections put at the service of pleasure's truth, and thus an art she feels called upon, as odalisque of a great House, to master. "I'll not be hurried, Rumer. You know that. I'm telling the story for your benefit; the least you can do is listen."

Rumer hangs her head. Her face and scalp are fired to scarlet. "I'm sorry, Cassine."

"Well, perhaps I do go on." Cassine immediately relents. Sometimes she thinks her heart is too soft. But her Cats are such good girls. She feels the need to confide in them. "Do you know, there are nights when the Ecclesiarch summons me to his chambers, and all he wants is to hear stories? I recite story after story from the *Lives and Acts*, a seamless weave from sundown to morning. Sometimes he has me talk for a whole night and day so that I wind up back where I began, as if the book itself were a wheel, or I get so sleepy that I start dreaming out loud, spinning new stories from the old. And do you know, I don't think he even notices! Most of the time I never see him, just hear him in the adjoining chambers, scuttling back and forth like an insect. Or I don't hear him at all but know he's there somehow just the same. Then it seems like the sound of my voice is the only sound in the world, and if I stop talking, the world will stop, too. Isn't that silly? I can see it's given me bad habits. But if you promise not to interrupt again, Rumer, I promise to be as direct as a shrive's arrow."

As Rumer nods—the voluptuaries are so well accustomed to their odalisque's capricious moods that nothing surprises them anymore—Cassine wonders what the Ecclesiarch will make of her confession when his spies, the shrives, report it to him. He's warned her to say nothing of their private meetings, but she's a Cat after all, and Cats must play. If she flexes her claws and draws a little blood, why, she means nothing by it. Anyway, he will do nothing. The Ecclesiarch needs her now, for she supports his lackey, Erigeron Intricata, against Azedarach, who has always shamelessly favored the House Lacrimata. In return, if Erigeron wins the Serpent Throne, Cassine will ascend to the very apex of influence and Serinthe Lacrimata will fall to the Pit. If not, Cassine will find another game to play.

"So Samsum left his foundry and followed Ixion to Quoz," she continues, laying her head back on the pillow. "What happened in Quoz we all know: the Battle of Cat Square, in which, for the first time, substantial numbers of men rallied to Ixion's side and routed the Furies, though not before Fagus Firmiana had the honor of becoming the first martyr of the new church. It was there, too, that Viridis Lacrimata—a Cat no better and possibly worse than the rest of us—swore her famous oath to Maw to coax Ixion into her bed or die untouched by any other lover, whether man, woman, or child.

"After Cat Square, Ixion and his followers left Quoz and returned to Peripety, retracing his steps to lowly Arpagee, for it was from there, for reasons known only to the Spinner, that his final ascent must begin. Everywhere he went he preached, and everywhere he preached thousands flocked to his banner. Not only men joined him now, but women whose hearts had at last rejected Maw. Viridis hid among these women, her eyes burning with a passion she didn't understand, a thirst she knew only one way of slaking.

"Rober Viburnum, still mourning the death of Fagus, saw Viridis one day in a crowd in Ormulu and recognized her immediately as the infamous Cat who had sworn to seduce Ixion into her bed. He denounced her to the crowd, which would have murdered her on the spot save that Rober, who had loved Fagus as a brother, demanded that honor for himself. Bloody and beaten, Viridis was passed up to the platform on which Ixion was soon to preach.

"Rober drew the dagger called Ice, whose chilly sting was reserved for the blood of women just as its twin, called Fire, knew only the blood of men. But before Rober could strike, Samsum took hold of his wrist. He squeezed, and Ice fell to the boards with a clatter.

"'Let Ixion judge,' he said.

"There was nothing Rober could reply to that. Nursing his wrist, he retrieved his dagger and slid it into its sheath of Fury's hide. Then he scurried to fetch Ixion.

"Now Samsum had never seen a woman like Viridis Lacrimata before. It wasn't her physical beauty alone that dazzled him, but an inner shining, a glow that no one else had seen and that she herself had mistaken for one of the all-consuming passions that sometimes curse us Cats. As the blows of the crowd had rained down upon her, Samsum had felt a slippage in his chest like iron melting and then hardening into a new and stronger form. Now he reached down to help Viridis to her feet. She stood weakly, grateful for his strength. Wiping the hair from her eyes, she saw her savior for the first time.

"You must remember, daughters and sisters, that Viridis was a voluptuary of the House Lacrimata, then as now the highest House. Because under Maw there was no shame or dishonor in being a Cat—and the loftiest Cats, like Viridis, were no less noble than their clients—only the finest, most beautiful things and people had ever intruded upon her exquisite gaze. Although Ixion wasn't handsome by her standards—under normal circumstances his withered leg would have rendered him instantly invisible to her—such is the irrational nature of passion that it was precisely this deformity that Viridis found most irresistible. Transformed in her mind, it was no longer an imperfection but a unique mark of worth, the one flaw that renders an otherwise ordinary object priceless to a collector.

"But what collector could value such a ruined thing as Samsum Oxalis? No, his was an ugliness too brutal and complete for redemption. Everything that Viridis was recoiled in horror from the sight of him. (Don't give me that look, Rumer, you would have done the same!) Viridis twisted away with a groan, the first sound she had made in her ordeal, and Samsum saw that her features had twisted, too. Her beauty underwent a change, took on an echo of his ugliness like a mirror that not only reflects but absorbs some portion of whoever stands before it. He felt she would have faced Rober at that moment in preference to him.

"It was then that Rober returned with Ixion.

"'This is she, master,' said Rober. 'The Cat who has boasted of her intent to corrupt you.'

"Ixion, who had witnessed all that had transpired, spoke to Viridis: 'What do you desire of me, whore?'

"Viridis dropped to her knees: 'I would follow you, master, like these others.'

"'Yet you turn away from my follower, Samsum.'

"'He is ugly, master,' Viridis answered.

"'No uglier than you are in my sight, or in the sight of the Spinner! Tell me why I should not let Rober kill you.'

"'Because I love you.'

"'What does a Cat know of love?'

"'I only know what is in my heart,' said Viridis.

"'Would you shave your head for my sake, cut off the hair that draws men to you and chains them to your fancy?'

"'I would,' she answered.

"'Would you renounce Maw for my sake?'

"'I do renounce her,' she said.

"'Will you forswear the oath you have made to seduce me?'

"And suddenly Viridis realized that instead of trapping Ixion it was she who had been trapped, she seduced. At that moment she began to understand the true nature of love, which is perpetual sacrifice. Tears fell from her eyes, the first she had shed in many turnings. 'I will do whatever you ask of me, master!'

"'Then perhaps I will spare you . . . if there is one person here who will speak for you. What say you, Rober?'

"Rober Viburnum drew Ice. 'Here is my answer.'

"Ixion addressed the crowd. 'And what say all of you?'

"'Kill the bitch!' shouted the assembled men, women, and children.

"'Is there no one who will speak for this woman?'

"'I will speak for her.' It was Samsum Oxalis.

"Ixion smiled. 'You, Samsum? After she has spurned you?'

"'I can bear it,' he said.

"So it was that Viridis Lacrimata was spared, as Ixion had perhaps always intended. She shaved her head, exchanged her rich robes for sackcloth, and shed her silken slippers to tread barefoot in the train of Ixion. How much more beautiful was she then, daughters and sisters, than she'd ever appeared in the gilded mirrors of her House!

"In the war against the Furies that now erupted openly, no woman fought more bravely or put her own life so thoughtlessly at risk to help the wounded and dying than did Viridis Lacrimata. Soon other women joined her, women from all walks of life, from ordinary mothers and daughters to Cats: the first Viridians. The very people who had called loudest for her death came to love and revere her. Even Rober Viburnum made peace.

"But one thing continued to trouble Viridis. Try as she might, she couldn't learn to tolerate, much less love, the man who had twice saved her life. Something in Samsum's features repelled her. Every time she looked at him, she felt as though she were gazing into a mirror that didn't reflect her surface but what lay hidden beneath it: the ugliness of her soul, festering with the poisons of Maw.

"Although Samsum, for his part, never spoke to Viridis and tried to place himself in her view as seldom as possible, his feelings for her were too strong to be completely denied. The beauty he'd glimpsed in her shone more intensely with each day, drawing him as a candle draws a moth and burning him as badly, though he never complained, never reproached her. But with what bitterness did Viridis reproach herself! She begged Ixion to punish her, but he refused.

"'Samsum spoke for you,' he said. 'Only Samsum has that right.'

"But Viridis couldn't bear to ask anything of Samsum. She realized that if she wanted to be punished, she'd have to do it herself. So with a dagger honed to the keenness of a razor, she deliberately carved into her beautiful face all the words she longed to speak to Samsum but couldn't. And more; she wrote her own history, a confession of flesh and blood written in flesh and blood. Such was her resolve that her hand never wavered. This was outside Minauderies, during the long return to Quoz, the so-called March of Martyrs, when every day brought a new battle, new martyrs in the young Church of the Spinning Wheel.

"When Samsum saw what penance Viridis had performed upon herself—she was unconscious then, half-dead from loss of blood and hence unable for once to avoid his stare—he didn't make a sound. He studied her bandaged face for a time, the blood seeping through the bandages to write what lay beneath them. Then he left the room in which she lay, tended by vizards loyal to Ixion.

"Watching her he had felt nothing, numb as iron. But now, with each step he took, an anger grew in Samsum such as he'd never known. Taking the great hammer that was his only weapon in battle, the same hammer that had rung on the anvil of his forge in Peripety, and which only he could lift, Samsum went forth alone as the sun rose to engage the Furies outside the gates of Minauderies.

"What a battle was waged that day, daughters and sisters! Samsum's mighty hammer crashed like thunder against the skulls of the Furies! At each blow from his hand a dozen fell, their heads split open! Such glorious slaughter was never seen in the world! Truly, the Pit was full on that day! Ixion's soldiers, watching from their camp, were mad to join the fight, but Ixion held them back. 'This is Samsum's day,' he said, as if he'd known all along that such a day must come.

"From sunrise until the first shadows of evening, Samsum fought.

Until the sky appeared as bloodied as the ground beneath it, he did not tire. Thousands of Furies lay dead and dying on all sides. The field was his. The battle won.

"Then Ixion, who had watched the fighting all day from a hill overlooking the field, turned away. Quercus Incana was with him as always, making the notes that would become the *Lives and Acts*. He saw something then that he'd never seen before and never would again.

"Ixion Diospyros was weeping.

"On the field, Samsum dropped his arm. He let his bloody hammer fall. Suddenly there was no anger in him. No strength. He bowed his head as the Furies, howling, converged. And let them take him.

"Ah, what an anguished howl went up from the camp of Ixion at that sight! Rober Viburnum begged to be allowed to retrieve the body of his comrade.

"'He is not dead,' said Ixion, without looking back.

"'Then we must rescue him!' shouted Rober.

"'That is not our task.'

"'How can I stand by and do nothing?'

"'His burden is greater, yet he bears it,' Ixion said, and would say no more.

"Ixion had spoken the truth. The Furies did not kill Samsum. They hated him too much to grant the easy oblivion of death. He was taken to Quoz, their stronghold. There he was dressed in women's clothing and placed in a Cattery. Which Cattery do you think that was, Rumer?"

Rumer claps her hands excitedly. "The House Illicium!"

Cassine smiles, for this is her favorite part of the story, too, and she never gets tired of telling it. "So it was. For many turnings, as the war continued to rage, the tides of fortune swinging first one way and then the other, Samsum lived the cloistered life of a Cat, the plaything of whatever man or woman desired him. So frightened were the Furies of his strength that his eyes were put out, and he was bound night and day to his bed by the heaviest of chains. These chains were never loosened.

"But Samsum never tried to escape, never struggled. The truth was, he'd forgotten himself. He no longer knew who he was. As he'd stood on the battlefield outside Minauderies, the cloud of rage had lifted from his eyes. He'd seen the thousands of Furies battered to bone and jelly by his hammer. They lay about him in a geography of death: hills and valleys, rivers of blood. And for an instant, the ruined face of Viridis had seemed to take shape in the mountain of corpses. He felt a twinge of doubt, of pity. That was all it took for Maw to enter his soul and rob him of his strength. Or, if not his strength, then the will to use it, which is much the same thing.

"As the turnings passed in the House Illicium, Samsum's hair grew until it was as long as a woman's. It was even styled like a woman's. And then he really did lose his strength, for to possess a woman's hair is to possess a woman's strength, which is to say no strength at all.

"In the darkness of his blindness, Samsum lost all track of time, of life itself. Not even the hourly tolling of the great bell of the Temple of Maw could reach him. Mercifully, he knew nothing of what his body suffered, the daily humiliations inflicted by the Furies. He wandered in a realm of dreams. Always the face of Viridis Lacrimata floated before him as he'd seen it that night in Minauderies. Only now, in the dream, he reached out to remove the blood-drenched bandages. He peeled them smoothly away, knowing that when he was done she would look at him without horror and speak the very words she had carved into her skin, a skin that would be without blemish now.

"But the bandages unraveled endlessly. Beneath each layer was another layer. Often he would grow tired and have to rest. Then the ghosts of the martyrs would come and speak with him. Some of their deaths he'd witnessed himself or heard about, but others he'd thought still living. All they wanted to talk about was how bravely they'd died; they boasted and argued among themselves just as they'd done while living. Samsum listened patiently, believing that he, too, was dead. And behind their boasts, he followed the progress of the war. Ixion was winning. He was drawing ever nearer to Quoz.

"At last there came a time when Samsum looked up from the bandaged face of Viridis to see Rober Viburnum approaching. His throat was slit from ear to ear, and his two daggers, Fire and Ice, protruded from his eyes. His tongue had been cut out, and his genitals severed and stuffed into his mouth.

"'Have they killed you, too, then, Rober?' he asked sadly.

"'I was struck down in the battle for Peripety,' answered Rober, penis serving for a tongue. 'Look at my wounds! I have won great honor today! When the list of martyrs is written, the name of Rober Viburnum will be at the top!'

"'A fine death, Rober!' Samsum agreed. 'But what of the war?'

"'Peripety is won,' said Rober. 'Soon Ixion will knock at the gates of Quoz, brother. See that you open them.'

"'I'm as dead as you!' Samsum exclaimed. 'I can't open anything.'

"But Rober had disappeared. Samsum heard a voice whisper his name. He looked down into the face of Viridis Lacrimata. The bandages were gone, vanished, as if Rober had taken them with him. And her skin was perfect, just as he'd always known it would be, smooth and radiant and white. She looked at him without a hint of revulsion, as if his face pleased her now. Then she whispered to him again. A single word, soft as a kiss. That word was, 'Wake.'

"And Samsum woke. The darkness he'd taken for death was simply blindness. He felt the heavy chains that bound him. The heaviness of his hair. And the empty space where his strength had been. He felt the softness of the bed on which he lay, smelled perfume and incense coiling in the air. He listened. After a time, he heard the soft scrape of footsteps.

"'Who's there?' he asked.

"The footsteps halted. The tremulous voice of a girl answered: 'Sabal Illicium.'

"'Am I in a Cattery then?'

"'The House Illicium.'

"With that, Samsum knew the shame of what had been done to him. The sins of flesh and soul to which he'd been subjected in a terrible revenge. His body seemed more loathsome to him now than ever, as if its ugliness had multiplied a thousandfold while he slept.

"'Have you come to kill me, little Cat?' he asked with real hope but still as gently as he could, for he heard how young Sabal was, how frightened. As if to remedy the loss of his eyes, his hearing had grown so acute that he heard the expression on her face when she looked at him: it was the same expression he'd seen so often on the face of Viridis Lacrimata. He turned away, wishing less to spare her the sight of his ugliness than to spare himself this reminder of it.

"'Kill you? Why would I do that? The odalisque Persea Illicium sends me to care for you each day,' Sabal said. She was a young Cat; no older than you, Rumer, though far more sensible. Samsum didn't frighten or repel her in the least. How could he? She'd tended him for so many turnings, since his arrival at the House—feeding him, bathing him, washing and styling his hair, even cleaning his messes and the messes that were made of him—that she no longer noticed his ugliness. It was his helplessness, his dependence, that drew her attention. She'd come to think of him as a child, a baby. Caring for him had become the center of her life. What Samsum heard as revulsion was simply surprise. He was the frightened one.

"'I've brought your breakfast,' Sabal said, wanting to soothe him. She came to the edge of the bed and sat.

"'What are you doing?' asked Samsum.

"'Feeding you as always.' She raised a spoonful of the cold porridge that was his sole nourishment to his mouth.

"Samsum chewed, hoping it was poison. But even the bland taste of the porridge was a revelation after such a long sleep of senses curled inward. He couldn't help savoring it. As he ate, a great bell began to toll somewhere in the distance. He could feel its vibrations even through the bed. 'What's that?' he asked.

"'The bell of the Temple of Maw. Surely you've heard it before!'

"'Perhaps faintly, in a dream . . . '

"'You're different today,' Sabal said. 'You've been asleep for a long time, but now you've woken up, haven't you?'

"'Yes,' he said.

"She continued to feed him. 'Usually we talk, but not like this. You never ask my name. You call me Fagus Firmiana or Rober Viburnum. Cedrus Lyciodes. Sometimes you call me Viridis Lacrimata—she's the one who betrayed her sister Cats and broke her oath to Maw all for the love of Ixion! Don't you remember?'

"'I remember,' said Samsum. 'I thought I was dreaming. Tell me, little Cat. Has Peripety fallen?'

"'Months ago,' she said excitedly. 'Now the gates of Quoz are besieged! But Persea says they will never fall.'

"And then Samsum knew that his dreams had all been true, sent to him by the Spinner. He no longer wanted to die. A final task had been asked of him. A chance to redeem himself.

"'You're not like other Furies,' he said. 'They keep me alive for revenge, to torture me, but there is tenderness in your care. Why?'

"Sabal stood up so quickly she spilled porridge on the sheets. His question had flustered her. The truth was, she had asked herself the same question. 'You shouldn't ask such things. I've got to go.'

"'Will you come back?'

"'After tonight's orgies.'

"Sabal was true to her word. That night, after the last Furies had left the chamber, she returned to find Samsum barely conscious on the bed. She cleaned him, tended his wounds and bruises, wiped away the blood and semen, the urine and excrement that caked him and the sheets.

"'Is it always like this?' Samsum gasped, missing the oblivion of dreams.

"'Lately it's been worse,' said Sabal. 'One day soon I'm afraid they'll kill you.' Unable to help herself, she burst into tears.

"'What do you care?' asked Samsum.

"'How can you say that?' wailed Sabal, really weeping now. 'After all I've done for you!'

"'Kept me alive for this? What kindness is that? You've cared for yourself, not me. I'm just a way you make yourself feel better. Your sister Cats sharpen their claws on me; you prefer to rub against me and lick me clean. But you're still a Cat! Still a Fury!'

"'I'm not a Fury!'

"'What?'

"Now Sabal spoke softly and slowly, hardly believing herself what she'd said: 'I'm not a Fury.' And when she said the words again, he knew they were true.

"'Praise Ixion,' Samsum breathed. 'The Spinner has turned Maw out of your heart, little Cat!'

"Sabal could only smile, wiping away her tears.

"'First,' said Samsum, 'I'll need a scissors.'

"The next night the orgy of vengeance was all Samsum's. Not a single hair remained on his head when the Furies entered the chamber. Sabal had seen to that. With the cutting of each lock, Samsum had felt his strength return in an easy flow. Now he snapped his chains like paper and whipped them in deadly arcs through the air. The startled Furies were dead in seconds.

"'Come be my eyes, little Cat,' said Samsum. Sabal ran to him, and he lifted her onto his shoulders. Together they set out for the gates of Quoz.

"But news of his escape traveled quickly, and not even Samsum could prevail against the assembled might of all the Furies. Maybe if he hadn't been blind, or hadn't had to worry about Sabal, or hadn't lain asleep for so long, or still had his mighty hammer in his hand, Samsum could have reached the gates and opened them wide to Ixion's army. But that was not to be.

"Instead, he found himself pushed back. Though the dead Furies lay in heaps around him, there were always living Furies to take their places. At last, bleeding from countless wounds, he could retreat no farther. His back was to a wall.

"'Where are we, Sabal?' he asked.

"'The Temple of Maw,' she shouted. 'Please, Samsum! I'm afraid to die!'

"'Put your faith in the Spinner,' said Samsum. 'And death cannot touch you. Is there a door?'

"She directed him to it. There were Furies inside the Temple as well as outside, but Samsum cut his way through them as Sabal shrieked and covered her eyes, peeking through her fingers. But no blade or dart touched her. Samsum shielded her body with his own.

"'Where are the stairs?'

"Soon they were climbing a spiral staircase. The bodies Samsum left in his wake made it difficult for the Furies to follow him up the narrow, winding stairs, slippery with blood. At last they reached the top. Samsum closed and bolted the door behind him. He felt a breeze on his face. Smelled distant fires. 'What do you see, little Cat?'

"'I see the army of Ixion.'

"'Is it very large?'

"'Oh, I cannot see the end of it! Their banners are blowing in the wind, all red and blue and yellow!'

"'Get down now and lead me to the bell,' he said, for it was to the bell tower that they had climbed.

"Sabal took Samsum by the hand and brought him to the great bell of the Temple of Maw. Vizards had cast that bell in days so ancient only the Spinner and Maw remembered them. That bell was to other bells what Quoz is to the other cities of the Hierarchate. It took fifty strong men to ring it.

"Now Samsum groped for the ropes used to ring the bell. He took a rope in each of his hands. Then he said to Sabal, 'I'm sorry, little Cat. You will not hear again after this.'

"But Sabal answered, 'In the silence, I'll hear the Spinner more clearly!'

"'Good-bye, Sabal.'

"'Good-bye, Samsum.'

"He rang the bell with all his strength. At the first thunderous tone, Sabal fell senseless to the floor. The Furies in the Temple below shuddered and felt a dreadful weight settle over their hearts. All through the city of Quoz, people stopped what they were doing and looked toward the Temple of Maw, where the great bell was ringing lustily although it was nowhere near the hour.

"And outside the gates of the city, Ixion Diospyros limped from his tent and said to Quercus Incana, 'Make ready the men. Samsum is opening the gates.'

"As Samsum rang the bell, the waves of sound rolled through him, shattering his eardrums just like Sabal's. Now he was deaf as well as blind. Only the weight of the bell tied him to the world. It pulled at him with a strength that rivaled his own, lifting him off the floor. Was he Samsum or the bell? Was he ringing these changes or himself being rung? He did not exist. The bell did not exist. There was only the rhythm between them.

"Out of that rhythm, a miracle was generating.

"Cracks began to form in the crystal towers of Quoz. In the buildings of stone and brick. In the thick, high walls that barred Ixion and his army. Windows shattered. The bones of old people splintered and broke. Women aborted their babies, strong men were driven mad. And still Samsum rang the bell.

"Sabal opened her eyes. There was a hissing in her ears that would never go away, a sound like the great ocean makes as it smashes against the cliffs of Arpagee. She watched as Samsum, with one mighty tug, pulled the bell of the Temple from its blocks. The bell bounced against the floor and fell from the tower. Tangled in the ropes, Samsum was pulled after. Yet it seemed to Sabal that he might have freed himself if he'd tried. She gave a cry she couldn't hear as Samsum disappeared over the ledge.

"Outside the gates, Ixion heard a final tremendous gong. Beside him, Viridis Lacrimata clutched her chest and fell to her knees with a groan, her heart shot through with cracks.

"After the gong, silence. Then, filling the silence from within, came a roar like the worst Chastening that ever was or will be as the walls of Quoz came tumbling down. At that very instant, Viridis Lacrimata's miraculous tears began to flow.

"Ixion sent his army into the city with orders to destroy everything. There would be no mercy for Quoz, the last stronghold of the Furies. Men and women, young and old. All perished at the edge of the sword. Only one was spared.

"Sabal Illicium. Ixion himself fetched her from the bell tower where she lay weeping. Viridis Lacrimata tended her wounds, nursing her back to health. And when she was cured—save for her hearing, which even the tears of Viridis couldn't restore—Ixion named her odalisque of the House Illicium. The first odalisque of a new line, a line that continues in me and someday, perhaps—who knows?—in one of you. Maybe even you, Rumer."

Rumer blushes again, giggling nervously. "No, Cassine!"

"Isn't it every Cat's wish to become odalisque?"

"But you've been odalisque forever!" As the other voluptuaries laugh, Rumer looks stricken and quickly adds: "I mean, you always look so young and beautiful, Cassine! I don't want to take your place; I'm happy just to serve you!"

"Ah, sweet Rumer! Come let me kiss you!"

Rumer advances shyly, and Cassine raises herself on an elbow to kiss the stooping girl's mouth. "The Blessed Sovereign, even the Ecclesiarch, must age. If the great ones cannot escape that fate, what hope have I or any of us?"

"I've never thought about such things."

"Stay as thoughtless as you are beautiful, Rumer. Care only for pleasure." With a clap of her hands, Cassine summons the shrives, who smoothly lift the couch and bear her back to the veiled litter. "Now to work; there's much to do and little time before our guests arrive. Prepare your harems well, my daughters and sisters! Bring honor to the memory of Sabal Illicium on this Saint Samsum's Day!"

Once Cassine has gone, the voluptuaries talk among themselves about the preparations still to be made for the afternoon's gathering: which Cats to assign to which guests—a delicate and subtle business if no one's feelings are to be hurt—whose favor they hope to win for themselves, whose to discourage. Only Aralia does not join in the teasing banter.

"Are you all right, Aralia?" asks Rumer, who's sensitive to such things and wants everyone to be as happy as she is, still smiling from the warm favor of Cassine's kiss.

The voluptuary bursts into tears.

Now everyone is concerned.

"What is it, Aralia?"

"What's wrong, darling?"

"She was talking about me! Couldn't you tell? I'm done for!"

"You're imagining things."

"It was in her kiss!"

"Nonsense."

But Rumer notices that even as they speak their words of comfort and reassurance, the voluptuaries move away from Aralia as though they might catch her disease.

Aralia notices, too. "Soon it will be your turn, you hypocritical cows! May Viridis make a desert of your cunts!"

And with that she turns and runs sobbing from the hospitality hall.

FIVE

The simularter Sylvestris Jaciodes gazes into the mirror upon the dressing table of his chambers in the Palace. A solitary thyrsis rings him in a stark white nimbus. Behind him, across the room, his simulars hang against a dark red curtain. They seem to float, strings lost in shadow. Saints, martyrs, Furies: they study Sylvestris with painted expressions and glass eyes.

The angular face regarding him in the mirror is without expression, rigid as a mask of chiseled bone, and as white. The eyes are completely black, as if the pupils have broken like the yolks of eggs and bled their darkness into the iris.

"All things are simulars," whispers Saint Rober Viburnum, "whether or not their strings are visible in a particular light, to a particular eye." *Yes*, Sylvestris thinks: *but the simular that dwells in mirrors is the most perfect simular of all.*

Sylvestris has frequently become trapped before, or rather within, mirrors for days on end. Already he feels the beginnings of that voluptuous dissolve. His images, his selves, are legion. A host of simulars. An inner hierarchy reflecting the Hierarchate of the outer world. Or is it the other way around?

One day he'll sink so deeply into the mirror that he'll never come out. He'll shed his body and become a voice. Each time he gazes into a mirror, he feels the temptation, hears other voices inviting him to join the immortality of infinite reflection. Yet each time he pulls himself back, as he's been trained from childhood to do.

Even now the simular of flesh and blood acts with such grace that Sylvestris almost forgets to wonder who is pulling its strings. Nimble white fingers, as long and tapering as the blades of scissors, flick open a small red box upon the table. Inside is a golden bead no larger than an apple seed.

Metheglin.

Black fingernails, filed to a point, raise the bead smoothly to the waiting lips. There is a sensation of coolness as the bead touches the tongue and is swallowed.

In the spreading chill, Sylvestris feels a narrowing of perspective, a confluence of his many selves into a more or less purposeful stream. It's a kind of miracle the way things happen one after another or all at once, he marvels, as fingers dip a fine-tipped brush into an occluded glass vial without spilling a drop of the dark liquid within. Even if a drop had spilled, that, too, would have been a miracle.

Filled with a heaviness that is not without pleasure, for there can be joy in surrender as well as escape, Sylvestris settles into the body. With quick, delicate strokes he limns a black tear at the corner of his right eye. He rinses the brush and replaces it, miraculously, inevitably. He selects a new brush, less fine, and dips it into another vial. Pulling his chin up slightly, he parts his lips as though to vent a sigh. He traces their bow in thick, glistening black, then fills in the outline with a flourish. The simulars are full of admiration; he hears them stir behind and within him, a rustling of dead leaves. He releases the breath he's held for so long: a web of frost, fine as lace, spins across the glass. Metheglin's icy exhalation.

As Court Simularter, Sylvestris is due momentarily at the House Illicium, where, as he's done on this day for each of the past eighty-eight turnings, he'll perform a scene from the life of Saint Samsum Oxalis selected from the *Lives and Acts*. Azedarach will be in attendance, as will the Ecclesiarch: the two men at each other's throats behind a cloak of courtly etiquette at once perfectly translucent and impenetrable as the black armor of the shrives.

Only now that armor has been pierced. Not by some outer agency, but from within. Each side, goaded by the excesses of the other, dares more, and openly. Brutality is increasingly embraced, subtlety disdained. And although Sylvestris regrets that loss, on the whole he's never felt more alive. So many roles to play! The possibilities for improvisation are endless. Nor need subtlety be lost entirely; it can continue, a private game. A game played less with others than against one's own selves.

Sylvestris rises from the table, leaving the veiled face frozen in the mirror until his return. He strolls by the simulars—their voices mere murmurs in his head now, thoughts smothered in velvet—and steps behind the red curtain against which they hang.

He faces a wall of transparent, multifaceted crystal, in which images of himself gaze back. All the walls of his chamber are crystal; Sylvestris lives within a hollow jewel. A curtained jewel. Not to stop others from looking in but to prevent himself from looking out. The view, though spectacular, has its dangers: a surfeit of mirrors, a labyrinth from which no escape may be possible.

But now, anchored by metheglin, Sylvestris isn't afraid to gaze upon the city. The afternoon is advancing; he'll be late if he doesn't hurry. But he lingers, captivated as always by this architecture of air, a miracle of color and light made solid. He looks through his own reflections, past shimmering bands of color constant only in their inconstancy, into other chambers of the Palace, in which others stand and, reflected like him, gaze into chambers where others stand looking, all of them superimposed on each other, bits and pieces of a shape no eye can grasp save that of the Spinner, a shape like a great Wheel perhaps, only a Wheel made of an infinite number of smaller wheels, themselves made of wheels smaller still, and so on, each wheel turning—some one way, some another, some fast, some slow—yet the great Wheel continuing to turn at one unvarying speed, in one direction, toward one end: the Last Day.

The Unspinning.

Sylvestris sees this not with his eyes but with his whole being. He imagines the Crystal City shattering, the million shards a polychromatic blizzard. It's a vision he's had before. He sees himself swept along with it, whether rising or falling he cannot say. His body tumbles slowly, his simulars at his side, in the awful hush that comes when there's nothing left to hear. The voices begin to rise in him.

Dizzy with vertigo, Sylvestris lifts his gaze above the city before he, too, shatters; not even with the help of metheglin can he see all the way to the ground, much less hold the living paradox of Quoz in his mind.

Far in the distance, towering over every other building, the spires of the Cathedral are visible. Those bulwarks of faith unshaken by any Chastening. Their tops are lost in a smoky haze shot through with the flickering reds and oranges of the bonfires that burn there day and night, furnaces in which the bodies of the Hierarchate's dead are cremated after harvesting.

Yet it's not fire that Sylvestris thinks of now.

It's roses.

A corpse was discovered this morning in an alley outside the House Illicium. That in itself is nothing strange. But until today, at least as far as Sylvestris knows—and he prides himself on his knowledge of the city's knotted history—whatever corpses have been yielded up by the streets have retained their faces. And none of them have lain, like this one, half-buried beneath a drift of red roses.

This business of the roses, even more than the face, is what intrigued

Sylvestris from the first. The eccentricity of it appealed to him; imagine, the skills of a shrive married to the sensibility of a simularter! He was frankly envious.

He experienced a frisson of déjà vu upon hearing of the circumstances from one of the senior apprentices of his order. A certainty that he'd encountered the story before, perhaps in some other form. Finally he realized that it was reminding him of the *Lives and Acts*. Not a particular tale, but all of them at once. And yet none of them. It was as if a lost tale—forgotten or omitted by Saint Quercus Incana—had been found and reenacted with simulars crafted of flesh blood and bone.

Or as if a new tale were unfolding.

And why not? he thought at the time and still thinks now. Why can't there be other tales to tell? Quercus Incana had refused to finish the *Lives and Acts*, laying aside his pen in mid-sentence never to pick it up again. "Only the Spinner can end it," he'd said, when the other saints had begged him at least to end his book with a complete sentence.

The original copy lies locked within a crystal reliquary in the Cathedral of Saint Ixion Diospyros, guarded night and day by shrives. Each turning on All Saints' Eve, the book is taken from its resting place and given a public reading by Mouths of God, up to and including the last, unfinished line. It's a line Sylvestris knows by heart, just as he knows all of the *Lives and Acts*:

> *Bidding the saints good-bye, she went where even my pen cannot follow, into a darkness of her own choosing, a sacrifice without . . .*

Because that unfinished sentence told of the entrance of Saint Viridis Lacrimata into Herwood to lift the curse of Beauty, there had always been those who believed that the sentence, and the book, could only end with her return. And if the book were to end, then the Hierarchate must end with it. Thus the completion of the *Lives and Acts* had become linked to the idea of the return of Saint Viridis Lacrimata from Herwood, and the return of that saint to the Unspinning. The one must follow the other like the night the day.

No matter that this belief had been declared heretical. It wouldn't die. How could it, when the book was read aloud each turning? Yet because Ixion himself had ordered the ritual before his fiery ascension, remarking to Quercus one day in the hearing of the other saints that it would be a good thing if the book were recited from time to time to keep its wisdom fresh in the minds of men and women born after the events it chronicled, the Ecclesiarch could not forbid it.

Sylvestris has no sympathy for heretics. He likes the Hierarchate and his place in it. But what he can't forget is that out of the present struggles new tales are continually being born. Tales that could serve as the basis for plays every bit as good as those he and his simulars now perform. Better even.

How sick he is of these tired old plays! The same ones over and over again. *How Stilskin Spun A Wife. How The Serpent Got His Wings.* As a sourcebook, the *Lives and Acts* was drained of vitality long ago. It's nothing but a cemetery now. A mausoleum. It pains Sylvestris to think that he must live his life picking over the bones of old stories. Where's the challenge in that? Even the simulars are bored!

Among his duties as Court Simularter is the creation of simulars and plays based on topical subjects, court intrigues and the like, for the private delectation of Azedarach. That might be enough for some, but Sylvestris's ambitions demand wider scope. He wants to be as famous as Quercus Incana, who, after putting aside his pen, spent the rest of his days spinning the *Lives and Acts* into plays, dictating the lines to an amanuensis.

For turnings now, Sylvestris has fashioned the struggles of Sovereign and Ecclesiarch against each other, and against the heretics who seek to topple them both from below, into a cycle of plays. He dares not commit his plays to paper; he writes them in the pages of memory and performs them in the theater of his mind, a ghostly repertory lacking only the acclaim of others, without which it can mean nothing.

His longing is not only sinful but dangerous; the only stage it's likely to bring him to is that of a shrive's wheel. A simularter performs hidden from his audience's view; any applause evoked by his skills belongs neither to him nor to the simulars he invests with a life more real than his audience can imagine. It belongs to the saints themselves. And to the simularter of all simularters, the Spinner.

But Sylvestris wants it anyway.

Upon first hearing of the faceless corpse lying in its bower of roses outside the House Illicium, Sylvestris had thought at once of the dramatic possibilities. He'd been hurrying through the crowded mid-level streets toward the mortuarium—where the body would have been taken—when a pair of shrives intercepted him.

Shrives possess the unnerving ability of knowing exactly where to find whoever it is they seek. They appear suddenly, as if out of thin air. Sylvestris has too much pride to let himself be intimidated by such cheap theatrics, but others aren't so proud. The street around him had emptied in seconds.

The shrives bowed stiffly, in unison. "The Sovereign requires your attendance," one of them said. Their blue eyes, unblinking, flickered over everything with equal suspicion.

"But this extraordinary murder!" he protested. "Surely you've heard . . . "

"*Now*, simularter."

Sylvestris bowed graciously. "By all means." He did not argue with shrives. He had no wish to see his fingers broken. The bones never healed properly; not even when set by vizards, who were responsible for the creation of simularters in the first place. He often relives the painful operations in dreams, waking with a shout, his hands twisted as if by arthritis.

The shrives conducted him to the Palace of the Chambered Nautilus. Their presence was enough to clear a path through the congested streets, where fresh produce and merchandise from all over the Hierarchate was sold in open stalls. It was, he knew, useless to inquire about the summons. Doubtless Azedarach would answer his questions, but the prospect was hardly encouraging; the Sovereign's pronouncements were notoriously obscure, impenetrable as the oracles of Kites.

But instead of being taken to the throne room, as he'd expected, Sylvestris found himself facing a door upon which the head of a snarling bear was carved: the family emblem of Azedarach's cupbearer, Morus Sisymbrium.

"What's this?" he demanded of the shrives. "I thought it was the Sovereign who summoned me!"

"You are to wait inside," one of the shrives replied.

Sylvestris was sure he'd walked into a trap. Soon he'd be as dead as the corpse he'd been so eager to examine. The irony made him smile. But if he must die, he could at least do the job himself; the sharp nail of his left pinkie was tipped with poison. He wore the antidote upon the nail of his right pinkie, but he'd have no need of it now.

But as if sensing his intent somehow, one of the shrives touched the gloved fingers of his right hand to the throat of his black uniform, where red wires were sewn in the shape of lips, in the most solemn oath of his order. "Fear not," he said. "No harm will come to you."

"The Sovereign commands it," said the other shrive as he opened the door.

Sylvestris stepped warily between the shrives and into the room. Just because the shrives intend no harm doesn't mean everyone else shares those sentiments, the voice of Saint Fagus Firmiana reminded him. The door was pulled shut behind him.

He was in a small and chilly chamber with a single door opposite the one he'd come through. There were no windows. The air smelled of mildew and stale incense. He was, as far as he could tell, alone.

A thyrsis in one corner of the room cast a sallow light, as if it would soon go dark. A cool draft issued from a fireplace empty of ash, in front of which stood a three-legged wooden stool. The walls were hung with tapestries so ancient and threadbare they scarcely seemed solid; still, enough remained of what was depicted there to tantalize the eye.

Drawing closer, Sylvestris made out figures from an old fairy tale, *The Bear's Wedding*. He performed the play frequently at weddings; it was a favorite of children and adults alike. But now the images struck him more deeply, more personally, than that.

The tapestry, or one very much like it, had hung in the simulartry where he'd spent the first, and in many ways the most difficult, turnings of his apprenticeship: between the ages of five and eight. Now he felt the essence of those turnings living within the tapestry, as if captured by a secret weave.

Half-disbelieving, Sylvestris brushed his fingertips over the delicate fabric. What a strange encounter! In the Palace, as in a dream, one was continually stumbling across chambers that one had visited once and then lost for turnings, as though the rooms rearranged themselves randomly around the hub of the Serpent Throne. The same was true of objects and even people. It was something one never got used to.

The tapestry had been much brighter once; of course, that had been more than ninety-five turnings ago. If not for metheglin, the voice of Saint Ilex Erythrina reminded him, you, too, would have faded in that time, perhaps to nothing.

The surface of the tapestry appeared worn to the flatness of paper, but bumps and ridges invisible to the eye showed plainly to Sylvestris's exquisitely sensitive touch. So it was that his childhood—or those traces of it interred here—returned to him as much through his fingers as his eyes.

A bear was taken from Herwood, brought to the Palace of the Chambered Nautilus, and dressed in the finest clothes for a piece of mischief that failed to come off or, rather, succeeded entirely too well. The idea was to substitute the bear for the lover of a Cat whose vision was by no means of the clearest. Not only was the myopic Cat deceived by the ruse, declaring her lover much improved, if in need of a shave, but the rest of the court was taken in as well. They saw only the splendid clothes and beautiful jewels, not the beast within. Even the original conspirators, who'd captured the bear and dressed it like a courtier, somehow forgot all they'd done and became victims of their own joke.

Sylvestris knew nothing of the circumstances of his birth or parentage. Life for him, as for all simularters, had begun on the day the fourteen bones of his hands were precisely broken by a team of vizards for the first of more than sixty operations. A drug administered at the same time, lethium, selectively unburdened him of what little past he possessed, leaving his memory as full of holes as the tapestry he now caressed. But they would not give him lethium more than once. Some things he will always remember. For instance, how often a single bone, even one as tiny as the ungual phalanx of the little finger of a boy of five turnings, can be broken, set, and broken again. Anesthetics were not permitted, pain an integral part of the procedure. By the time the vizards were done with him, at the age of eight, his hands were composed of not fourteen but thirty-nine distinct bones interspersed with metal joints and wire tendons. They were as scarred as the face of a Kite. Whatever his life had been before that was as impossible to grasp as the original shape of his hands.

The bear was equally deceived, its memories of a previous life sunk in profound hibernation. When the Cat's cuckolded lover, a headstrong young prince, issued a challenge, the bear accepted and won easily. Following this victory—by which, according to law, it won the prince's title and property—the bear rose to prominence as a courtier. Soon it had contracted a marriage with the daughter of a noble family, a young princess of ten turnings who loved nothing better in all the world than the tickle of her husband-to-be's kisses and how they smelled of honey.

Between operations, in the stretches of time allocated for recovery, intervals measured less by the rising and setting of the sun than by the ebb and flow of pain, Sylvestris would lie in his narrow cot, his hands swathed in bandages, and stare feverishly at the tapestry on the wall—this same tapestry, if his senses could be believed!—struggling to keep himself from moaning or crying out. Such outbursts were severely punished. Weights of various shapes and sizes were suspended from his fingers in a network of glittering wires finely calibrated to stretch his healing bones.

Perhaps, he'd thought, or rather hoped, if he could lose himself in the tapestry, weave himself into its story, he might come to fill the gaps in his memory and to forget, and so escape the suffering and terror in which he waited with his fellows. Less than a third of them would survive the treatments.

The wedding day arrived. A more handsome, virile groom had never been seen. How lucky the bride was! Girls and young women watched the wedding procession with envy, dreaming of princes of their own, while married women looked at their husbands with newfound regret. But at the last moment, as the Mouth of God performed the ceremony of Holy Patrimony, a small boy exclaimed: "Why, he's nothing but an old bear!"

At this the bear remembered itself. It was not a courtier, not a prince. It remembered its dank cave in Herwood, remembered the she-bear that, perhaps, still waited there. With a groan at once angry and forlorn, the bear tore off its splendid clothes and devoured the wedding party, bride and all.

But Sylvestris couldn't forget. Not for long. Because the vizards always came back. They came back and, with meticulous care, fashioned the boys piece by broken piece into the shape of simularters. Fashioned them in mind as well as body, for the mind can be broken just the same as the body, broken and then put back together in more personalities than the hand has bones.

Many turnings later, long after it had returned to Herwood, the bear was hunted down and killed by a brave prince. Upon slitting open the belly of the beast, he found the princess curled up asleep in the stink of the stomach, unharmed, no longer a girl of ten turnings but a rosy-cheeked woman now cloaked in her own long hair like a newborn in its caul.

The prince had never seen a more beautiful woman. His kiss did not awaken her, but all the same it was a pleasant kiss. He decided to marry her. A quiet, complaisant wife, a wife who never complained, never asked where he was going or even noticed when he was gone—what more could a prince want?

Sylvestris recalled a boy who, for a time, had occupied the cot beside him. The boy's name was as unknown to him as his own; the lethium had unnamed them all. Only when they became simularters would they have the right to choose a new name. The boy was nearly seven, much further along than Sylvestris, with hands already recognizable as a simularter's, translucent fingers more than twice their normal length, like the legs of the albino crabs that nested in the cliffs of Arpagee, the meat of which, though poisonous, was considered a delicacy in Quoz. But he was small and incredibly frail, pale as the sheets on which he lay, and always covered in a film of sweat, dark hair plastered to his forehead. Despite the advanced condition of his hands, Sylvestris had sensed that with each operation his neighbor was becoming less of a simularter and more of a ghost.

That spring, much to the prince's surprise, the princess awoke at last. The couple spent a happy summer, but the following winter, and each winter thereafter, the princess fell once again into a deep, deep sleep. No kiss could wake her but that of the spring.

It was forbidden for the boys to talk to each other, but late at night, when the others were asleep or lost in the agony of bones forced into positions they were never meant to have, the boy on the cot beside

Sylvestris would call to him in a voice so soft, even less than a whisper, that for a long time Sylvestris wasn't sure if he was really hearing something or if it was the first of the inner voices the vizards had assured him would soon begin to manifest themselves. He'd listened, straining to hear.

"Brother . . . "

At last, unable to decide whether the voice came from inside or outside, he dared an answer. "Is that you, brother?" His voice sounded frighteningly loud in the hushed dark.

"Brother," came the voice again, accompanied by a gentle creaking of weights and wires, as if the boy had shifted in his cot.

"Be quiet!" he hissed, very afraid now. "We'll be punished!"

His neighbor giggled; a dry rattle that made Sylvestris shiver to hear. "But we are already. I remember . . . "

Sylvestris pricked up his ears. "Remember what?"

"Before."

"You can't. It isn't allowed."

"I remember my mother."

"I'm not listening anymore!" Sylvestris turned away; the movement sent pains shooting through his fingers, sparks of color that he could see clearly in the darkness, as if fireflies were hovering above his hands. He bit his lip, feeling the tears well.

"Brother . . ."

"What?"

"Don't you remember anything?"

He thought. There was only a gray cloud. "What . . ." He swallowed. "What was she like? Your mother?"

"She was pretty. She smelled nice. And I had lots of fathers. A different one every day."

"Lots of fathers," Sylvestris repeated dreamily. The boy's words had triggered something in him; not a memory, exactly, but whatever trace a memory leaves behind.

For a while there was silence. Then: "Brother. I'm frightened, brother. I can't feel my hands. They're like ice."

"It's the treatments."

"I'm cold, brother. I'm cold."

"Go to sleep," he said. When the boy called to him again, he pretended to be asleep himself.

Early the next morning, when Sylvestris was taken for treatment, he told the vizards. And when he was returned to the simulartry that evening, a new boy lay in the cot beside his cot. A boy who did not speak. Or remember.

But when, shortly afterward, Sylvestris heard the first voice speak within him, it was the voice of the boy who remembered. It's a voice he still hears, especially at night. He still does not answer.

One day the princess told the prince that she was with child. If only it were a son, the prince replied, his happiness would be complete. The prince was there for the birth. His son emerged from between the princess's legs like a bear rushing from a cave. Horrified, the prince lifted the newborn mewling thing, with its covering of wet fur, and dashed it to the floor, splitting the skull like a soggy melon. The princess fell upon her husband with a groan at once angry and forlorn. With one swipe of her paw, she killed him.

As he came to the final section of the tapestry, in which the princess, catching sight of her reflection, received the shock that turned her into stone, Sylvestris saw a telltale glitter out of the corner of his eye. A mirror was concealed behind the cloth. Cursing under his breath, he covered his eyes with his hands and forced himself to look away. He hadn't yet swallowed his daily allotment of metheglin; without it, the briefest glance into the mirror would transfix him. Then Morus Sisymbrium, upon entering the chamber, would find him, like the princess, turned to stone by his own reflection.

Sylvestris felt the insult acutely. The voices of his simulars rose in an angry babble. He kicked at the stool. It flew against the tapestry, shattering the mirror. At once the simulars grew quiet, like children shocked into silence by a prank gone too far. Sylvestris felt ashamed; it was unseemly for a simularter to behave so precipitously. The mirror had upset him, as Morus had intended. But Sylvestris would have his revenge.

He had no love of vizards. Their famous disdain for metheglin was entirely too calculated to suit him. It was a mark of arrogance, a vain affectation. Besides, he knew very well that many of them indulged in private what they professed to scorn in public, although he had no evidence this was true of Morus. But Morus was as bad as the rest of them. The vizard's position as cupbearer gave him not only the key to the metheglin vaults, but to Azedarach as well—a key that Morus didn't hesitate to turn to his own benefit. There was, of course, nothing odd about that; Sylvestris employed his position as Court Simularter in the same way. But what he found most galling, what gnawed incessantly at his pride, was that his own need for metheglin made him dependent upon the vizard. Not that Morus could deny him anything; only Azedarach could do that. But still. In this play, it was Morus Sisymbrium who pulled the strings.

Now the inner door of the chamber creaked open, and Morus Sisymbrium himself strode brusquely in.

"Sorry to have kept you waiting." A stocky man in the autumn of middle age, with a thick beard and a wild mane of gray hair, his throat plug carved in the shape of a bear's head, Morus stopped short as if in surprise at the sight of the shattered mirror and overturned stool. "An accident, simularter?"

"You have a great love of the obvious, Morus."

The vizard laughed, showing large white teeth. "If that were true, my opinion of you would be quite different." He rubbed the robe of pale green silk, embroidered in red and gold with a design of mating serpents, that stretched over his ample stomach. "Did the shrives pull you from bed?"

In his haste to view the corpse, Sylvestris had curtailed his morning toilette; his face was unpainted. He waved his fingers negligently. "I was engaged on a matter of some import when they found me. A murder outside the House Illicium. Perhaps you've heard?"

"Ah. Iber Arvensis, you mean."

Sylvestris nodded as if this were old news to him. Iber Arvensis was Keeper of the Discipline of the Sacraments, a minor but not unimportant Church official whose archival duties made him one of the few men with unrestricted access to the original *Lives and Acts*. Still, that seemed a flimsy pretext for assassination. "The work of heretics, surely."

"I couldn't say."

"Do you imply that I could?"

Morus turned to the tapestry, running his left hand, which was missing the fourth finger—a penance imposed by the shrives for an old indiscretion—along its frayed surface. "I recently came across this tapestry in the simulartry. Something of a family heirloom. It was quite beautiful once, or so I'm told. Woven by Viridians in honor of my ancestor, Rubus Sisymbrium, the first to adopt the bear's head. He was a handsome man, Rubus. A fierce fighter, Azedarach's right hand. He sniffed out many a heretic and traitor in his day! I'm told I resemble him."

"I could wish the resemblance complete."

"Could you indeed?" Morus laughed again. "I forget how hard it must be for simularters. Not to know your father, I mean. To have no history, no lineage. Nothing to pass on, and no son to pass it on to. Not even a name of your own."

"On the contrary. I chose my name freely. No one imposed it on me. I am chained to nothing."

"Nothing but metheglin."

"How little you understand." Sylvestris was growing bored. "Why have you brought me here?"

"Not I: Azedarach." Morus opened the door through which he'd entered and gestured for Sylvestris to precede him. "Fear not; I do the Sovereign's bidding."

Sylvestris bowed and, although hardly reassured, stepped through. He found himself in a passage lit at intervals by thyrsi. The low ceiling compelled him to stoop.

Morus locked the door behind him, then squeezed past the simularter. "This way."

Sylvestris heard the voice of Saint Rober Viburnum and repeated the question aloud: "Does this have to do with Iber Arvensis?"

Morus did not reply. The two men descended a staircase, encountering no one, then entered a semicircular chamber redolent of formaldehyde. The walls and ceiling were of crystal, from which issued a harsh white light. The air was very cold; Sylvestris could see the breath in front of his face. The joints of his fingers ached as they always did when the temperature dropped close to freezing. He placed his hands in the pockets of his robe in a futile attempt to warm them. On a row of tilted slabs in the center of the room lay the cleanly eviscerated corpses of nine men, their organs already harvested. Their skin was blue and waxy. Each one was faceless.

"By the Wheel . . ." Sylvestris turned to Morus.

"Yes, it's been a busy morning." The vizard inclined his head to the left. "That's Iber there, the fat one at the end. The other eight were found indoors, but with their faces ripped off, half-buried in roses, the same as him. We had to identify them by their tattoos."

"And?" Sylvestris was already crafting a new play in his head, everything else—the cold, his animosity toward the vizard—forgotten.

"The odd thing is, they are, or were, insignificant men. Iber was the best of them. Hardly worth the trouble of such an imaginative end, one would think. Another curious fact: in each case the cause of death was the same. Coronary thrombosis." The vizard frowned and tugged his beard. "Unfortunately, the hearts couldn't be harvested. A shame. And as for their faces, they were removed after death. Expertly removed, I might add. With a touch any vizard or shrive would envy."

"Any witnesses?"

"Six of the men were married. Their wives slept through everything, if you can believe it."

"Do you?"

Morus shrugged. "Perhaps the roses were laced with an olfactory narcotic. If so, all of it had dissipated by the time the bodies were found."

"I don't suppose it's occurred to you that the women themselves murdered their husbands."

"The shrives will uncover the truth."

"Do you honestly think that I or any simularter—"

Morus interrupted hotly: "Who else would devise such a flamboyant method of assassination? Who else has the hands for such delicate work? But what I think is irrelevant. Ask rather what Azedarach thinks."

"And what might that be?"

Morus tugged his beard again. "Azedarach believes the missing faces are intended as a message. After all, the Sovereign is said to be faceless. Not simply because of the Serpent Crown's obfuscatory effect, but because the Sovereign embodies a power beyond himself, beyond any man: the power of the Hierarchate, which, as it were, wears a succession of masks, of sovereigns. Looked at in this way, the assassinations become a declaration of war against the Hierarchate itself. The Ecclesiarch isn't behind them. Nor are the heretics, at least not directly. The assassins are from Herwood. From Maw herself. The Furies have returned to Quoz at last. So says Azedarach."

Sylvestris made the sign of the Wheel. The voices of his simulars began to clamor more loudly than ever, all of them at the same time. The Last Day is dawning, they sang, some in joy, some in horror. Beware, Beware! Prepare, prepare!

Sylvestris shivered in the onrush of a seizure, another legacy of the treatments. Desperately, under his breath, he recited the Litany of Quiescence.

"You seem troubled, simularter."

Sylvestris realized that Morus was gazing at him with an expression of contempt; for a moment, everything had gone gray. He was exhausted; he badly needed a taste of metheglin. In the chill air of the chamber, his sweat was like ice. "It's said that in the Last Days, before the Unspinning, the simulars will cut their strings and live in truth the lives they counterfeit."

Morus laughed curtly. "I'm surprised at you, Sylvestris. I had no idea you were superstitious. Why, you'll be talking about the Little People next!"

"And I had no idea you were such a fool! You scorn what you don't understand."

"I understand more than you give me credit for. I'm a rationalist. I suspect heretics sooner than Furies and traitors sooner than simulars."

"But Azedarach is no fool, thank Ixion! He knows my loyalty. Your suspicions mean nothing to me. You should know better than to try and pull a simularter's strings, vizard."

"Remember your hands, Sylvestris. So fragile. What a loss to us all if you could never perform again."

"Someday I will give you a private performance."

"I look forward to it more than you can imagine. But not today, I'm afraid. Azedarach has a task for you."

Sylvestris regarded the vizard with suspicion. "Why doesn't he tell me himself? I've no cause to trust you."

"The Sovereign's reasons are his own. It's not for us to question him."

"It's you I'm questioning. Swear to me on your family's honor that you speak for Azedarach."

Morus sighed. "I swear."

Sylvestris nodded, satisfied. "What is this task?"

"It involves a Cat from one of the High Houses."

"Why is a Cat so important to Azedarach?"

"The Sovereign didn't say, nor did I inquire. It's enough that he desires her."

"Very well. But what has this to do with me?"

"You will procure her. That isn't simply an order; it's a destiny. Azedarach has foreseen it in a metheglin dream, and you know his dreams are never wrong."

"Who is she? What's her name?"

"He didn't say."

"Then how will I find her?"

"You will know her by her eyes."

"Her eyes? What about them?"

Morus smiled. "Azedarach bade me tell you they are the eyes of Saint Viridis Lacrimata."

A knock at his door recalls Sylvestris to the present. An apprentice of his order enters, a boy of ten with fingers as long and brittle as twigs. He sniffles loudly, then wipes his reddened nose with his fingers. "Your pardon, Master. You instructed me to remind you of your obligations at the House Illicium."

Sylvestris dismisses the boy with a nod. He begins to collect his simulars. His long and slender fingers fly over the almost-invisible black strings, twisting them expertly into braids while, in a singsong whisper, he chants the Litany of Awakening: "You have been untouched for too long; now a hand both careful and mischievous is shaking you; look, look, all the fireflies are fluttering out of you, beginning, even at the moment when they find themselves, to bid themselves farewell. . . ."

There are, in fact, no fireflies, but the words are not meant to be taken literally. Anyway, he's repeated the litany so often over the turnings that he's become deaf to it, like a melody hummed under the breath.

He lifts each simular from where it hangs and gently places it in a pouch of brightly colored silk. Saint Stilskin Sophora goes into a white pouch. Saint Fagus Firmiana into a yellow. Roemer goes into a red pouch, Jewel into a blue. Each pouch has a drawstring allowing it to be cinched shut. That done, Sylvestris carefully deposits them into a large black sack. There is a precise order to be followed, but the simulars argue as usual over precedence. Sylvestris will not be drawn into their puerile squabblings, which invariably degenerate into enumerations of past slights and never reach a conclusion other than to give him a headache.

He examines the simular of Saint Viridis Lacrimata. It depicts the saint just before her entry into Herwood. Her face, crosshatched with scars, has bloody holes for eyes. She holds a white bowl in her hands; floating there, as in a thick tomato soup, are what might be two emeralds. He hears her now, calling for him to hurry up, get a move on, for all the world like a nagging wife.

There's no mistaking a simular for a saint, he thinks as he places her in her green pouch. *The eyes of Viridis Lacrimata.* He curses his luck: Azedarach has set him an impossible task. No wonder Morus had been in such high spirits: the vizard would like nothing better than to see him fail.

At last Sylvestris is through. Hoisting the bulging sack over his shoulder, he sets off for the House Illicium.

SIX

How wonderful to have a passion! thinks Rumer Illicium, dancing across her chambers in the arms of an invisible partner, a man or woman—she can't decide which—to whom she'll give herself utterly, with the same doomed devotion that yoked Viridis Lacrimata to Ixion and Samsum Oxalis to Viridis. She skips lightly over the floor, singing a popular song and watching her slippers flash silver and gold like little fish in the glow of the candles. "Please be mine, share my life. . . ."

Her feet, tightly bound within the gorgeous slippers to keep them forever small and dainty, will be chafed to bleeding by the evening's end, but Rumer is too excited to care. Cassine's parting kiss still burns on her lips. The story of Saint Samsum Oxalis glows in her heart like a promise of a passion all her own, one every bit as terrible and sublime as that which crushed the blind saint beneath the walls of Quoz.

Of course, it would be better to be struck by a passion for a man than a woman, Rumer thinks. A rich and powerful vizard like Morus Sisymbrium or Erigeron Intricata could, if they chose, advance her career, though, to tell the truth, she'd prefer someone younger, less wearying. Vizards are notoriously virile thanks to the administration of injections at the base of the penis, shots that turn their members as rigid as bars of steel. But they allow only fellatio to be performed upon them and take forever to come. When they do, their copious discharge is streaked with black grit and tastes vaguely of burned oil. It's an altogether-depressing experience. For days afterward, Rumer's jaw aches, and her digestion is troubled.

But the thing about a passion, as every Cat knows, is that you don't choose it: *it* chooses you. Rumer shivers in the grip of a voluptuous apprehension, remembering the haughty Picea Circium. Odalisque of the House Circium for sixty-two turnings, and a woman, moreover, without a hint of softheartedness in her nature, Picea had succumbed in an instant to a passion for a Kite she chanced to glimpse from her litter one morning while being borne through the streets to an assignation. People still talk of the scandal as if it had taken place only yesterday and not eight turnings ago.

According to witnesses, the Kite, an old woman, blind and disfigured like the rest of her order, had stared at the heavily curtained litter as though aware of the odalisque by some occult sense. Picea, complaining of a headache, ordered the litter back to the House Circium. The vizard summoned to treat her could find nothing wrong with his patient; after a bleeding, he prescribed a course of emetics and ordered her to bed. But later, dismissing her anxious voluptuaries—every one of whom was subsequently flayed upon the Wheel for negligence—Picea took a razor and sliced her pretty face to ribbons. Only in that sharp-edged and bloody coin could she buy her freedom; disfigured, she was no longer of value to the House.

Such an offense would have condemned any other Cat to the Six Hundred. But Picea, as odalisque of a High House, had certain privileges. The Viridian's life of perpetual sacrifice was always available to Cats of the highest rank, for Saint Viridis Lacrimata had spent her entire life as a Cat before passion fell so heavily upon her. Now Picea claimed that right for herself, the first time a Cat had done so in more than a hundred turnings. Roughly bandaged, she was cursed at, struck, kicked into the street by the very shrives who, earlier that day, had borne her heavy litter on their shoulders. It was the middle of the night, the streets swept clean by fear of Beauty, darkness absolute but for the glimmer of fireflies. By morning, Picea was gone. A spotty trail of blood led away from the Cattery for some yards, then vanished.

Her fate remains a mystery. Some believe Picea was taken by the shrives after all and secretly put to death, perhaps by the Ecclesiarch himself. Others maintain she was taken to Herwood by the Furies, and that she lives there still, plotting revenge. Or that her wounds grew infected in the filth of the lower levels to which she descended in quest of the Kite she'd seen but once, and that briefly, long enough, however, for the barbed hooks of passion to sink deep into her heart, weighing her down. They say Picea died there, alone, in horrible pain, forgotten, damned.

But from time to time a Cat will claim to have seen her, a frightful apparition waiting upon a Kite like some ragged slave, black eyes shining with fanatic devotion, face a quilted patchwork of scars, her body, kept succulent for so long by metheglin, wrung dry with the onset of age and hardship, recognizable only by the tattoos of silver-gray porpoises that circle her scalp, neck, and shoulders, the marks of the House

Circium, impossible to efface, surfacing through layers of gr
desperate for air.

Rumer both fears and desires a passion all her own. But yearning, especially for a Cat, is stronger than fear. And so she dances, cocooned in a warm and happy glow, her eyes shining as she imagines the sacrifices her passion will bring. She is eager to embrace them, for, in the words of Viridis Lacrimata, "Without sacrifice there can be no passion."

Picea Circium has drifted far from Rumer's thoughts now. Instead, she thinks of the gathering. The loftiest nobles will be there; the Blessed Sovereign himself is expected. Rumer imagines herself performing the dance of the eighteen veils; suddenly, a glance darts across the crowded room, one among many yet keener than the others. It pierces her as remorselessly as Beauty ever pierced a man and claims her as completely. How Rumer longs to feel that fateful sting! *Saint Viridis, grant me your blessing on this day!* she prays fervently in silent descant to the words she sings in a gleeful, chirrupy voice: "Stay with me, be my wife, la da . . . "

This is by far the most exalted gathering Rumer has had the honor of attending since being raised by Cassine to the rank of voluptuary the previous spring, when the Chastenings were at their peak, worse than any time in memory. Just nine months ago, but already the fat, lazy days are growing thinner and colder as the wheel of the seasons turns. Frost has begun to sheathe the crystal domes and towers of Quoz. The intricate lacework, spun by night, melts with sunrise, giving rise to rain and rainbows. But soon there will come a day when it does not melt. Hour by hour it will thicken into an armor of blue ice, bitter foretaste of the Pit of Damned Souls. Then will the iron doors of winter clang shut as, remembering his betrayal, Ixion turns his shining face from the world in anger. The Chastenings will commence, worsening through the spring before gradually ceasing with summer.

If there is a summer. For the *Lives and Acts* prophesies an end to all things. The Unspinning, when the Spinner will break His Wheel to pieces and the world along with it. It's said that Saint Viridis will return in those days, redemption and damnation mingling in her tears. Simulars will cut their strings and, for a brief span, live the lives they have mimicked for turnings without number. Can it be that the Unspinning has already begun, as heretics claim?

Rumer thinks with a shudder of the body discovered this morning in the alley behind the House Illicium. She's heard it whispered by her sisters that the thing was found lying amid a thousand roses with its face cut clean away, the whiteness of the exposed bone like fresh-fallen snow among so much red. These are dark times surely! Stopping abruptly before a full-length mirror, Rumer basks in the reassurance of her reflection, as if her beauty may hold the Hierarchate together, as if the promise of summer is gestating inside her like a child in the womb.

Rumer stands just five feet tall in her tiny slippered feet. That is unusually petite for a Cat, though there have been fashions in such things, as in all others, times when dwarfs or giantesses were the rage, and Cats of less startling proportions were deemed uninteresting, even ugly. Presently, most Cats above the age of fifteen stand four or five inches taller than Rumer. Some, like Serinthe Lacrimata, Cassine's archrival, are over six feet in height, taller than most men, with the exception of simularters, whom they resemble in the manner of caricatures.

Cats fortunate enough to arrive at the Cattery as girls receive a rigorous course of beauty treatments that last from the time of their first menses at twelve or thirteen until the age of eighteen. Women or young girls over eighteen undergo the same treatments, but with less chance of success. The beauty treatments sometimes stunt or, on the contrary, accelerate the growth of their subjects; the vizards who administer them complain that the bodies of women are as contrary as their souls. These side effects grow increasingly severe with age: muscles and bones atrophy, tumors swell, brains liquefy or shrivel like raisins. For a woman over the age of twenty-five, treatments are a waste of time, although the vizards occasionally make the attempt in order to test a new procedure. A select few, barred by age from the treatments yet still relatively young and pleasant to behold, find work in the Catteries as maids and cooks and seamstresses, abortionists and midwives, performing the thousand and one daily tasks that Rumer and her sister Cats take so much for granted as not to notice at all; the rest belong to the shrives.

Considering the alternatives, Rumer is satisfied to be merely small. She's not ashamed of her size; in fact, it's been a blessing, a boon. Not only does it distinguish her from her taller sisters, it makes her appear younger than she really is, a girl of nine or ten whose body is precociously developed rather than the woman of nineteen who has only recently tasted metheglin for the first time—heavily diluted at that—and who pinches herself each morning to find herself voluptuary of a High House. Within limits, it pays a Cat to be different.

But not *too* different. Anything really out of the ordinary is evidence of the corruption of Maw and, hence, an immediate sentence of death.

Fortunately, aside from her diminutive size, Rumer is quite normal. Her lips are swollen in a perpetual pout; her nose is like a button; her eyes are shaped like almonds. Her breasts are enormous. They balloon out from her birdlike chest as if they might rise into the air of their own accord, lifting her up behind them. A man can circle her waist with his hands, yet her hips are generous enough to rock the grossest vizard in their cradle, and her buttocks are plump as pillows. The lips of her sex have been widened and lengthened, the interior muscles of her vagina altered to grant her a heightened degree of control. Her clitoris, which she can will erect and, moreover, manipulate like a wicked little finger, is two inches long and fully capable of penetration, yet the nerve endings have been partially deadened so that her own pleasure does not unduly compromise that of her clients.

Rumer conveys an impression of childishness: perverse, to be sure. It's made her a popular Cat, in constant demand as a kind of unnatural synthesis of girl and woman. There are clients who prefer the narrow hips, hairless smooth sexes and flat chests of those Cats who range in age from five to twelve turnings and haven't yet undergone their beauty treatments—every Cattery has its kittens—while other clients favor mature, experienced women, well versed in the *ars erotica*. Both camps find common ground in Rumer. To them, she's less a woman than the simular of a woman; a plaything, not quite real . . . or, rather, less real even than the others, a copy of a copy. Simularters are especially drawn to her for this reason.

Now, gazing into the mirror, Rumer frowns to see that her wig has drifted to the left again, giving her a lopsided look, as though she's had too much to drink. With an exasperated sigh, she straightens it for what seems the hundredth time. The wig of jet black hair was ordered months ago. It comes from the head of a virgin and is thick as the night itself, flaring about her head like an impenetrable shadow. Cunning braids web her slender neck and arms, then come together in a single strand that encircles her waist beneath her gown of sheer blue damask. The pattern of the braids proclaims Rumer's position as a voluptuary of the House, while miniature tableaux woven into the wig with threads of many colors depict those disciplines of the *ars erotica* that are her particular specialties.

The wig is the most beautiful thing Rumer has ever owned. Unfortunately, it's really quite heavy and has a tendency to slip. She hasn't mastered the art of balancing it, but neither can she bear to set it aside. The black hair shows off her creamy skin to advantage; everyone says so. It brings out hints of green in her eyes and gives her delicately rouged nipples, pressing against her white blouse, a festive insouciance, like candies begging to be eaten.

Once more the wig, as if tugged by invisible fingers or possessing an infernal malevolence all its own, slides slowly to the left. Rumer slides along with it into a mood as heavy and black; sudden, unpredictable, overwhelming, these upwellings of despair afflict all Cats to varying degrees. They are a further fruit of the beauty treatments, counterpart to the gaiety and frivolousness so painstakingly instilled by the vizards.

Snatching off the wig with a curse, Rumer flings it to the floor, or tries to. But she's forgotten the braids encircling her neck and arms and waist. The wig hangs upside down below her breasts, top dusting the floor like a false beard worn during the revels of All Saints' Eve.

Aghast, she turns away from her reflection, unable to bear the sight of her smooth, freshly shaved head and the small green wheel tattooed beside her left ear, the mark of the House Illicium, of which she's normally so proud. It's all suddenly horrible, grotesque; it's not her own face in the mirror but her mother's face from long ago, those desolate eyes fixing her with their impossible appeal.

Rumer feels the chill of the Pit gaping in her heart; it's at moments like these that Maw draws closest. Her senses reel; she is falling. She lifts the wig and buries her face in its softness. Beneath the wigmaker's perfumes linger traces of a life so longed for that it was lived in advance, in the hopes and dreams of a girlhood both different from and identical to her own.

All at once the memory of Jubilar returns to Rumer in a rush, freighted with all she's lost. In her mind's eye she sees clearly the house on Saint Ilex Street, her home until the age of six. Thirteen turnings later she can still remember every inch of it with sad affection. She recalls the faces of her neighbors and playmates, especially the boy from next door, Cyrus Galingale, to whom she'd been pledged by her father. If things had gone as they were supposed to—as Rumer frequently thinks when in the grip of these bleak and sullen moods—she and Cyrus would have been married by now, with a house of their own and, by Ixion's grace, a son.

Instead, one night, her mother had suffered a lapse as impossible to understand as to forgive; by morning, her father was gone forever, drawn into Herwood on the leash of Beauty. Thus was Rumer, in the space of a single sleep, between closing her eyes and opening them again, robbed of father and mother, husband-to-be, the son for whom she'd prayed each night from the time she'd been old enough to pray. The offense had been her mother's, but punishment had fallen upon Rumer as well, for the sins of the mother adhere to the daughter. She'd sat still as stone, too frightened to make a sound as the Panderman snipped her hair with his scissors and the dark locks dropped into her lap until her pale and slender thighs were buried. Not even when her skin itched under that blanket did she move. But she'd begun to squirm, and then to cry, when the Panderman began on her mother. How could she not, when she so loved to brush her mother's hair? The rhythm of the long, firm strokes, and the scents they gave rise to, lulled Rumer into a sensual trance. To watch that solace taken away lock by lock just when she needed it most was more than she could bear.

Shorn, the hair of women is used to fashion splendid wigs like the one that Rumer holds in her hands; somewhere, Rumer knows, a Cat has worn or now wears a wig made from her hair, just as, she is sure, another woman has married Cyrus and given birth to the son that by rights should have been hers. And although as a Cat Rumer knows she may one day bear a child, even a son, she also knows that child will be taken from her after a few brief turnings and given to one of the orders to raise. All memory of her existence will be altered or erased altogether from the child's mind by vizards, while her memories will cut as cruelly as ever, for it's part of a Cat's punishment that she never be allowed to forget.

The last time Rumer saw her mother was in Kell. The Panderman took them to market there, chained together in the back of his wagon, mother and daughter huddled naked on a mat of filthy straw, too dazed for tears or prayers. He took them out, splashed them down with icy water, and put them up for sale with fallen girls and women from all over the Hierarchate. Rumer went quickly enough to one of Cassine's geldings, but her mother, at thirty-six, was too old to be of use to the House Illicium or any other house, high or low.

When she realized they were about to be separated, Rumer began to wail. Her mother didn't say a word; she clasped Rumer to her and squeezed. Rumer choked, unable to breathe. Silent tears spilled from her mother's shining eyes. Rumer saw that her mother would kill her now rather than let her go. She kicked, desperate to break free of the embrace, but her mother ignored the pain, if she felt it at all. In the end, the shrives had saved her. They beat her mother half-unconscious and pulled Rumer, gasping like a newborn baby, from her arms. Even then her mother had kept her silence; not only kept it, but hurled it back at them, a curse too savage for words.

"If you'd fought half so hard to keep your husband, you wouldn't be in this trouble now!" one of the shrives had snarled, a judgment that Rumer, far from dismissing, has adopted as her own. By now, she's certain, her mother is long dead, suffering endless torments in the darkest recesses of the Pit.

Which, as far as Rumer is concerned, is no more than she deserves. Looking up, she catches sight of her mother's harrowing eyes in the mirror. Of what dreadful crime do they accuse her? Why won't they leave her in peace? Rumer feels they will hound her to the grave like an evil passion. And beyond. She bursts into tears.

"Rumer, darling! Whatever's the matter?"

Rumer jumps as if addressed by a ghost. But it's flesh and blood that regards her from the chamber doorway: the chief voluptuary of the House, dark-skinned Aralia Illicium. Rumer blushes, humiliated to be discovered sobbing like a novice.

"Aralia!" She blots her tears ineffectually with the loose ends of the wig. "I didn't hear you come in."

She's about to continue with some nonsense or other, but Aralia glides quickly forward with a look of such pained sympathy in her kindly brown eyes that Rumer is overwhelmed afresh by the profundity of her own sorrows. She throws herself into Aralia's arms. "Oh, Aralia! Nothing's right!"

"Shh, my pet," Aralia whispers, a smile on her lips as her fingers caress the smooth, hot skin at the back of Rumer's neck. "Aralia's here."

Rumer snuggles deeper into Aralia's arms, soothed by the musky scent and softness of her breasts. Nuzzling aside the lacy white tunic Aralia wears, she finds a dark nipple and draws it into her mouth with a sigh that Aralia echoes.

Of all her sister Cats, Rumer feels closest to Aralia. When she first arrived at the House Illicium, she was examined by Cassine and assigned to Aralia's harem. And Aralia had taken a shine to the pretty young Cat from the first, instructing her personally in every facet of the *ars erotica*. Her persistence and sincerity gradually coaxed Rumer back to life. Not a true passion but, rather, the playful shadow of one, it's lasted for turnings now, a source of comfort and pleasure to them both.

After a moment, Aralia gently disengages herself and adjusts her tunic. "There now. Tell Aralia all about it."

Rumer smiles sheepishly. In her hands, she still holds the wig. She presents it with a shrug. "It won't stay straight," she complains, blushing at how trivial and absurd her words sound now.

"That *is* a tragedy!" Laughing, Aralia guides Rumer to the mirror, where her skillful hands soon set everything right. "There. A dainty dish to set before the Sovereign!"

Rumer beams at her reflection, tilting her head from side to side. The wig does not slip at all, not even when she spins as if in the arms of an overenthusiastic vizard.

"Aralia, you're a saint!" Rumer claps her hands. She stands on tiptoe to kiss Aralia on the lips. Only then does it register that Aralia wears no wig. Nor is she dressed for the gathering.

"You're going to be terribly late," she teases, with her hands on her hips. Soon the hundred bells of the House Illicium will chime, summoning the voluptuaries and their harems to the hospitality hall to greet the arriving guests. "Cassine will be furious!"

Aralia scowls. "I'm through with that bitch."

Rumer is too stunned to speak.

"Don't stare at me like that!" Aralia begins to pace, looking everywhere but at Rumer. "It's all up with me; you heard Cassine this morning!" Her voice rises in a perfect imitation of the odalisque: "'The Blessed Sovereign, even the Ecclesiarch, must age. If the great ones cannot escape that fate, what hope have I or any of us?'"

Rumer shakes her head numbly.

"And don't start crying. I know what I know." Aralia touches a hand to her scalp, then draws sharply back as if pricked by the snarl of thorns tattooed there. "I've seen it happen too many times not to know when my turn's come!"

Rumer feels faint. She gropes her way to a chair and sits down heavily. "You're running, aren't you?"

"What else can I do? I've no desire to end my days as a scullery maid for some trollop or as a victim for novice shrives to practice their carving on! Of course I'm running. So would you."

"No. It's a sin. And they'll catch you. The shrives. They always do."

Aralia shrugs. "Not always." She looks at Rumer. Her eyes are blazing, desperate but unafraid. "Come with me!"

"Oh, Aralia! How can I?" Then Rumer gasps at what she sees, belatedly, in Aralia's eyes. "You're going to look for the heretics!"

"I'll join them gladly, if I can find them! I've been reading their pamphlets, Rumer. Saint Viridis is returning from Herwood to set things right at last. We've been lied to, fooled. Maw's not evil; she's good. Even now, believers are gathering secretly in the lowest levels of Quoz. 'Seek, and you shall be found'; that's what the pamphlets say! They say there's a big fight coming. A war. Things are going to change. It's already started! The body found outside the House this morning? That's just the beginning. Here, read it yourself!" From her tunic, Aralia produces a small, folded square of dirty gray paper and steps forward with an outstretched hand.

Rumer jumps to her feet, hands pressed over her burning ears. To possess such a thing is death. "It's blasphemy! Maw's wickedness! I won't read it! Or listen to another word!" She sinks back into the chair, her face in her hands.

Aralia moves to replace the pamphlet beneath her tunic, then slips it under a cushion on Rumer's bed instead. She walks to the door and waits.

Soon, without lifting her head, Rumer speaks in a choked and miserable voice. "Why'd you come here, Aralia? Why didn't you just go?"

"I couldn't leave without seeing you. I had to ask you to come. You won't always be so young and pretty, Rumer. Someday you'll taste the bitterness of Cassine's kisses."

Rumer's head feels heavy as stone; her heart she can't feel at all, a heaviness beyond weight or measure. Does Aralia think she's a child? Of course she won't be young forever. But running isn't the answer; it only makes things worse. Everything is as the Spinner wills, she thinks: man sins, the Spinner spins. "They'll ask me about you. The shrives. I'll have to tell them everything."

"I know that. Rumer, if you change your mind, I'll be waiting for you down there. If you seek me out, I'll find you. I promise."

"Don't do it, Aralia!"

There's no reply. Rumer is afraid that if she looks up now, her mother's ghastly eyes will be regarding her from Aralia's face. But when she finally raises her head, Aralia is gone. Her mother's eyes, if they are anywhere, are waiting as usual in the mirror. She will not look. Not even for the sake of her pretty wig will she look.

Rumer stands up slowly. Her body feels stiff, awkward; even the slightest movement is painful, as if Aralia's words have aged her like a Fury's curse. Her cheeks are wet, but she won't weep for a heretic. She won't let Aralia spoil this day.

Pressing her lips together, Rumer resumes her solitary dance, trying to recapture, in the sweeping rhythms, her carefree mood. But her slippers scuff at her senses like sandpaper. She breaks off and stands absolutely still in the middle of the floor, holding her breath, looking at nothing. Then all at once the hundred bells of the House Illicium begin to chime.

SEVEN

"*Cassine, darling!* How *marvelous* everything is!"

The braying voice precedes its speaker like an obnoxious herald. Conversation falters; heads swivel to the wide-open doors of the hospitality hall. The doors are famous throughout Quoz, covered back and front with a swarm of tiny, naked bodies, a paean to excess and abandon in which the thousand and one disciplines of the *ars erotica* find simultaneous expression. In the flickering light of the candlewheels, the carved miniatures seem to seethe like waves on a choppy sea. Tangled bodies rise from the depths of the wood without escaping it: now swelling, now falling away.

A Cat with restless blue eyes and an intimidating smile sweeps through the famous doors with an escort of two shrives. Five voluptuaries follow, their painted faces aglow.

One of Cassine's geldings glides forward and, in a voice of ethereal beauty that rises above the playing of the musicians at the far end of the hall, announces: "The odalisque Althea Circium and household." Later, he and his brother castrati will sing the hymn cycle of Saint Samsum for the delectation of Azedarach.

Althea's gaze flickers over her fellow guests, appraising them with practiced assurance, cataloging the sly gradations of power, influence, and obligation that bind them all together in an ever-shifting web. This canny instinct, closer to intuition than reason, is possessed by all Cats, thanks to the beauty treatments. Without it, Cats would stumble blindly through the social maze of the Hierarchate, impeding the very pleasure it is their sole purpose to provide.

Althea is as generously endowed in this as in all other respects. She, too, has a place in the web, one higher than some but lower than most. It's a part of her punishment, like that of all Cats, to be keenly aware of her relatively low position. And, like all Cats, like everyone else in the

Hierarchate, Althea will protect what she has while doing whatever is necessary to advance at the expense of others.

Excess becomes her; she says so herself. Her blond wig, like the smaller wigs of her voluptuaries, is styled in an ocean motif. It weighs over ten pounds. Glittering shells, starfish, and sea horses gathered from lowly Arpagee can be glimpsed amid the curling waves. She bears the tattoo of the House Circium—the leaping porpoise—in a splendid fashion that is the envy of her Household: small blue porpoises frolic in an endless ring around her coral white throat. Her great breasts rise from a froth of blue silk and white lace like islands newly born.

The House Circium is the third of the four High Houses. Highest of all is the House Lacrimata, where Saint Viridis once served; then come, in descending order, the House Illicium, the House Circium, and the House Valentine. The distance between Lacrimata and Illicium is the gossamer thinness of a firefly's wing, but the chasm that divides these two from Circium and Valentine is as wide and deep as the Pit itself.

The High Houses arrive at official functions in order of ascending eminence, from lowest to most high. Already Cassine has greeted the odalisque Persea Valentine and her five voluptuaries and sent them to mingle with the earliest, least exalted, of her guests, for there, too, a scrupulous ranking is observed.

Althea's late as usual; an unfortunate habit, unbecoming to her House, as she well knows. Yet she persists. Eight turnings ago, in the aftermath of Picea Circium's scandalous passion and the flaying of her voluptuaries, Althea was chosen by the Ecclesiarch to become the new odalisque. The elevation took place so suddenly, amid confusion and violence, that she's never felt easy in it; anything so summarily given might be snatched away at a whim. Unsure of her position, she's continually driven to test it, proving it to herself over and over again.

"You've outdone yourself this turning, sister," she gushes to Cassine while advancing imperiously into the already-crowded hall. Although the odalisques of the four High Houses address each other as sister on these formal occasions, it's customary for the lower-ranked to wait until the higher-ranked condescends to employ the term, a point of etiquette Althea habitually ignores, as if such customs are ridiculously old-fashioned. "But then you *always* do!"

Cassine Illicium presses her cheek ever so lightly to the powdered cheek Althea aggressively offers. How Cassine would like to scratch that cheek! But she does nothing. She's determined to act the gracious hostess on this of all days, the most important of the calendar for the House Illicium, commemorating as it does not only the martyrdom of Saint Samsum Oxalis but the heroism of Sabal Illicium that made it possible. Not even the news of the flight of her chief voluptuary, Aralia—tearfully reported by Rumer before the arrival of the first guests—will be permitted to spoil her mood. Cassine will not scratch, though she can still dream of it. Flexing her fingers, she purrs: "It's sweet of you to say so, Althea!"

With a slight motion of one hand, Althea summons her five voluptuaries, each of whom curtsies respectfully to Cassine as she is introduced. They are all beautiful girls. Not one appears to be older than twenty. Cassine has to give Althea credit. Indeed, there is a pearl among them, a girl of truly exceptional quality, perhaps even a future odalisque, with skin and eyes the color of amber and a wig like spun gold.

Cassine can't resist stroking the voluptuary's cheek. She's reminded of Aralia, even though Aralia's skin was never as light as this. Nor as soft. But the heart detects resemblances invisible to the eye. Touching the cheek of this Cat who really looks nothing at all like Aralia except in the most superficial way, Cassine allows herself to feel the desolation of a betrayed love, deep and uncomprehending, a tangle of bitterness and regret shot through with the first glimmerings of a forgiveness still to come.

"How lovely," she whispers.

"You do me great honor, sister," says Althea, flattered.

"You do this House honor," Cassine replies.

"Her name is Nyssa. Let me make you a gift of her."

Cassine withdraws her hand sharply; she has no intention of placing herself in Althea's debt. "I wouldn't dream of depriving you of such a treasure."

But in truth she's tempted. Why should she suffer so? Aralia is gone for good; the shrives will catch her and flay her alive. Why shouldn't she lessen her own pain in the arms of this exquisite girl?

But there are no gifts between the Cats of rival Houses. Only traps, as Cassine well knows. Althea, sensing weakness, even though ignorant of its cause, has simply moved to seek advantage, as Cassine herself would do, has often done. Not only has Cassine placed spies in all the other High Houses, she knows which of the Cats in her own House report against her. And to whom.

If circumstances were different, she thinks, she'd accept the challenge of Althea's offer. She'd take this amber-skinned Cat and turn her, melt her old loyalties and forge new ones, then send her back to the House Circium to spy upon her old mistress. She's done it hundreds of times, not even seriously, with an expectation of real advantage, but as a distraction, a game. These young Cats drive themselves half-crazy dreaming of a passion of their own, one that will rival the great passions of the past. It's simple enough to fan those hopes into the flames of delusion.

Sometimes Cassine thinks that's all passion is, all it ever was. An immense delusion. She's never had a passion herself, but she's loved in her way. And if passion is a fiery delusion, then love is a gentle deception one practices against oneself. But Cassine has always known where to draw the line, and she doesn't trust herself with Nyssa, who by some trick of memory or desire recalls Aralia so strongly—and, what's more, not the Aralia of today, clearly embarked into physical decline, but the girl of twenty or thirty turnings ago, firm and unwrinkled—as to make her loss seem recoupable, like a debt incurred in one coin that is miraculously repaid in another. What, she thinks, is this hope born of futile longing, of the loneliness inherent in her position as odalisque, if not a delusion, or in any case the beginnings of one? Althea was right to sense a weakness.

Cassine reproaches herself for it now. In the future she'll guard herself better. She smiles in a certain way, and one of her voluptuaries, Carya, responding to the summons, steps instantly to her side.

"Odalisque."

"Carya, you know the odalisque Althea Circium. Althea, this is Carya. She'll be my proxy this evening."

Carya curtsies prettily before Althea. "If there is anything you desire, odalisque . . . "

"Yes, yes." Althea silences Carya with a frown.

"Is she not to your liking?" inquires Cassine.

"She'll do very well, I'm sure." Althea gives Cassine an ingratiating smile. "But to tell the truth, sister, I was hoping for Aralia. She served me so well last time! Where is she? Not ill, I hope."

Cassine finds herself surprised by Althea for the second time. Can it be that she knows of Aralia's disappearance? How is that possible, unless Althea has succeeded in turning one of her Cats? *Or*—the thought suddenly comes to her, a thin, cold blade slipped between her ribs—what if Aralia has taken refuge at the House Circium! But no, that's impossible, she reassures herself. No one would risk the anger of the shrives by shielding a runaway Cat. Not even Serinthe Lacrimata would dare. More likely Althea has simply noted Aralia's absence from the gathering, which is, after all, conspicuous. Others have remarked upon it. Even so, Cassine decides she's been too trusting of late. Her soft heart will be the death of her! A purge of the Cattery is long overdue. One can't be too careful in these troubled times, when Ecclesiarch and Sovereign vie against each other for power and Cats must walk a thin and jagged line between them or, like Picea Circium, find themselves crushed, for Cassine is a believer in politics, not passions. "Regrettably, Aralia is indisposed."

"What a shame! The shock of that awful murder no doubt. Poor Iber Arvensis! A regular patron of hers, wasn't he?"

"He favored Aralia from time to time."

"We saw him seldom at Circium, I'm afraid. But to die that way . . . and practically on your very doorstep, Cassine!" Althea shudders as though savoring a rare pleasure. "A terrible thing. I must say, you're holding up well."

"Is there a reason I shouldn't be?"

"No. Of course not! I only meant, if it were me, silly thing that I am, I'd be shaken to the core! The idea of violence reduces me to jelly!" She laughs, and the vast surfaces of her breasts quiver in sympathy. "You must tell Aralia from me that the best cure is always a good fucking!"

"That will be a solace to her." Cassine sees with relief that new guests are waiting to be announced and greeted. "You'll have to excuse me for now, Althea. Carya will conduct you to the banquet table if you'd like."

As Carya again curtsies obediently, Althea catches sight of the bright red wig of Persea Valentine across the hall, where she's dancing with a young simularter. "Persea!" Althea shrieks, already advancing upon her. "Persea, *darling*!"

Meanwhile, the gelding announces the next guest, a Mouth of God whom Cassine has always found particularly tedious. She sighs deeply, then turns to greet him, her smile fixed in place. The gathering is going well; the musicians are in fine form; the hall rings with laughter and conviviality. But just the same, as the priest holds forth on some arcane point of theology, in which she feigns a polite interest, and afterward, too, in the steady stream of guests that she must welcome, Cassine finds herself increasingly troubled by what Althea has so shrewdly, and shrewishly, implied: namely, that although the mutilated body of Iber Arvensis was found outside the House Illicium, the murder took place within; and, further, that Aralia was involved in the killing, perhaps even the killer, her absence now a confession of guilt.

Of course, Cassine doesn't credit this calumny for one second. Yet neither can she dismiss it from her mind. The possibility, however remote, is enough to spoil her mood. For a Cat to murder a client save at the client's own desire, a desire, moreover, that must be approved by the Ecclesiarch and witnessed by a Mouth of God—indeed, for a Cat to inflict any injury upon a client not explicitly negotiated beforehand—is unthinkable. It goes against every instinct ingrained by the vizards in the course of the beauty treatments. Cassine can't believe Aralia capable of such a monstrous rebellion against her conditioning.

And yet. And yet. There comes a moment in the life of every Cat, provided they live long enough, in which even the hazy comforts of self-deception drop away to reveal the future in all its stark and unappealable horror: a future made up of sacrifice, humiliation and pain, a torture chamber of atonement for the sins of the past, of which the pampered pleasures of her life as a Cat will count as among the worst. What might a Cat not be capable of in that moment under the right—that is to say, the wrong—circumstances, with Maw pouring her vitriol directly into the heart? Heresy? Murder? Are such desperate acts so different in kind from the wild excesses of passion that all Cats are made to yearn for?

The mistake, Cassine tells herself, was to give Aralia time to reflect upon the imminence of her fate. To stare, so to speak, into the abyss. Better to have removed her swiftly, without pity, as Serinthe or Althea would have done. Once again, Cassine's generous nature has obscured her better judgment. But what can she do? Can she help it if the Spinner has given her a kind and trusting heart?

"His Excellency, the vizard Erigeron Intricata."

The unctuous voice of the gelding recalls Cassine to her duty. "My Lord Intricata! What a pleasure!" Smiling, she steps forward to greet the Ecclesiarch's protégé with the kiss to which his rank entitles him. "Welcome to this humble House."

"Happy Saint Samsum's Day, Cassine," the vizard drawls wearily, as his shrives survey the crowd with their ever-vigilant eyes. His own eyes are half-closed and puffy; indeed, his whole body moves as if weighted with sleep, a cumbersome garment that wraps him head to toe in its invisible shroud. As they kiss, the wiry hairs of his gray beard scratch her cheek, and his tongue flutters drily over her lips like the wings of a firefly. He caresses her breasts listlessly, as though repeating an action whose significance he no longer remembers.

Cassine smells the stench of lethium on his breath. Not for the first time, she imagines that beneath his wrinkled skin there's nothing at all. Not bones or blood or organs, just a darkness broken here and there by the aimless flickerings of fireflies.

She pulls away as soon as politeness permits. Her smile doesn't waver even though she feels disgusted, as if she's embraced a walking corpse. There's nothing worse than a lethium addict, she thinks. The stench of putrefying flesh that no perfume or incense can conceal. Perhaps they themselves can't smell it, but as far as she's concerned the dead should have the decency to do their moldering in private, away from the noses of others.

Erigeron Intricata is fat, even for a vizard. His skin has a pasty tone better suited to wax than flesh and seems to cling to his bones chiefly out of habit. His cheeks sag to such a degree that his features droop in a perpetual caricature of sadness, as if modeled out of wet clay. His throat plug, with its emblem of a winged hart, is buried almost entirely in the folds of his jowls. Wheezing softly, he gazes at Cassine with inscrutable yellow eyes that always remind her of the eyes of serpents.

"You're looking well, Cassine."

What would be mere flattery from anyone else is from Erigeron's bloodless lips a statement of cold fact; more turnings ago than Cassine cares to remember, he performed the difficult sequence of beauty treatments that fashioned her inside and out into the Cat she is today. Like all true craftsmen, Erigeron retains a prideful interest in his work. It pleases him, she knows, to see that she's still attractive, in good working order. To him she's a mechanical contrivance, an unusually sophisticated simular, not a woman of flesh and blood. From time to time—less frequently of late, thank Viridis—he samples her himself. Not from desire or affection, Ixion knows, but to test his handiwork. Immediately afterward, as she lies exhausted and bruised upon the bed or floor or wherever he's abandoned her, Erigeron delivers, while dressing methodically, a detailed evaluation of her performance.

Nevertheless, Cassine feels she owes the vizard a debt of gratitude she can hardly begin to repay. He did his job well; she's odalisque, after all. Although it wasn't the seed of his loins that gave her this life but, rather, the toil of his hands and mind, she honors him as a second father, as all Cats honor the vizard that makes them, or, more accurately, remakes them.

In this sense, it can be said that Erigeron Intricata has fathered more than half the Cats of the House Illicium, as well as a fair number of those in the other High Houses. He is blessed, Cassine thinks, with a wealth of daughters.

But he is poor in sons.

Two turnings ago, Erigeron's son, Malus, a beautiful boy of ten, died suddenly of an illness that neither Erigeron nor his fellow vizards could diagnose, let alone cure. One day Malus was alive, the darling of all who knew him. The next day he was gone. All of Quoz mourned.

It was rumored that fever and convulsions had horribly despoiled the boy's beauty as he died. People wept at stories of how his creamy skin had swollen and split, how his eyes had burst like boils, his bones snapped like dry twigs gathered for burning. Whatever the truth, Malus was buried in a closed casket. The Ecclesiarch had conducted the funeral personally, an unheard-of honor for one so young.

Children are everything, Cassine thinks. They are not only the future, but the cumulative heritage of a past stretching back further than the reach of memory. With intelligence and luck, a boy may rise to the Serpent Throne itself, carrying his father's name, the name of his father's fathers, to glorious heights. And even a girl, though she must relinquish the name of her father in the sacrament of Holy Patrimony, may bring honor to it by the merit of her married name, just as the rays of the sun give luster to an object that, of itself, sheds no light. The wealthiest man, if he lacks a son or daughter, is poorer than the meanest beggar, less to be envied than a common Cat. Why, the mother of the Ecclesiarch, or so Cassine has heard, was a Cat in the House Lacrimata! Children are everything.

And yet, by the will of the Spinner, honorable women can bear but a single child. A man may father a hundred bastards upon Cats if he likes, but only one child with his lawful wife. This is no mere prohibition, to be avoided with bribery or cunning. It needs no shrives, no threat of the Six Hundred, to enforce. It is a fact, a destiny. A law encoded by the Spinner in the bodies of women, where not even vizards can amend it.

Only Cats are exempt from this law. No one knows why or how, but there is no limit to the number of children Cats are able to produce. Cassine has never given birth herself; it's rare for an odalisque to conceive. But she hopes fervently to bear children one day. Sons and daughters who, even when taken from her, their memories of her wiped clean, will carry some trace of her forward. Then, after she's dead, she won't be alone. Her soul may plummet to the harshest depths of the Pit, but the actions of her children, and of their descendants, will be sensible there for good or ill, adding to her torments or lessening them. If she's fortunate in her descendants, a spiritual benefit will accrue from their actions great enough to eventually win her the Spinner's forgiveness and the freedom to be reborn, for it is written in the *Lives and Acts* that the living can ransom the souls of the dead. It's for this reason, rather than from any maternal instinct, that Cats produce children with such enthusiasm even though the strain of repeated pregnancies ages them prematurely and cuts short their careers; in no other way can they hope to escape the Pit and the endless round of tortures to which their sins have condemned them.

Just the same, a Cat's children don't belong to her; nor to the men who sire them. They are Ixion's children, property of the Church of the Spinning Wheel, to be disposed of in accordance with the needs of the Hierarchate as determined by the Ecclesiarch. The lucky ones are raised as Mouths of God, shrives, or simularters. Others become Cats or, as geldings, the servants of Cats. Some go to the Viridians, to wait upon the holy sisters and, in time, join that sere and anonymous order. But the majority are dispatched to Arpagee, lowest of the low, from whence, with memories wiped clean by lethium, they begin, for both the first and the millionth time, the long ascent to Quoz.

There simply wouldn't be enough children to go around if not for the fertile wombs of Cats. In her turnings as odalisque, Cassine has guessed from the hints, confidences, and complaints of her clients that perhaps a quarter of all lawful unions are barren, a monotonous litany of miscarriages, stillbirths, spontaneous and not-so-spontaneous abortions. Nor does birth guarantee survival: each night, from Arpagee to Quoz, babies die in their sleep for no apparent reason. What is more vulnerable than a child, after all? Men can be protected against the nightly dangers of Beauty with incense and nose plugs, but who can guard a child against the secret ripening of its fate? What mother is so attentive? What father so powerful? Not all the skills of vizards, the prayers of the Ecclesiarch, or the commands of the Sovereign himself can stay the Spinner's hand.

Of all deaths, the hardest to accept is that of a male child. It's as though a river, down which the patronymic, like a well-made boat, has sailed smoothly from generation to generation, should run suddenly and mysteriously dry, stranding the boat where no waters will ever raise it again. In rare cases, precedent for which rests explicitly in the *Lives and Acts*, the Ecclesiarch is empowered to grant dispensations permitting divorce, annulment, remarriage, or adoption in order to redress an injustice and restore the potency of a name. But the exceptions are so narrow, hundreds of turnings have gone by since the last.

That was in Minauderies, where, as everyone knows, the Intricatas were nearly undone by the treachery of the Galingales, jealous parvenus bent on ruining them utterly. At that time, Malus Intricata—the namesake of Erigeron's son—had a daughter named Sersis, a treasure of rare beauty, intelligence, and charm. He was as proud of her as if she'd been a son. Malus's wife had died when Sersis was still a young girl, and ever since she'd cared for him with a wife's devotion added to that of a daughter. Though he hated to give her up, Malus contracted her in marriage to Celtis Galingale, scion of the wealthy Galingale family, newly risen to Minauderies but already eager to advance beyond it to Nooning.

The Galingales weren't content simply to rise, however. Their warped ambitions, gratuitously cruel, demanded advancement at the expense of others or not at all. And so Celtis, carrying out the orders of his father, Rober Galingale, had sought to ensnare the innocent Sersis in the crime of retrogressive import. By the grace of Ixion and the vigilance of Malus, the plot was exposed in time, and the Galingales suffered the fate they had planned for the Intricatas.

Still, although Sersis was absolved of all guilt, her reputation was ruined. No one would have her for a wife; she could not have been shunned more thoroughly if she'd been found guilty of adultery. It seemed the Galingales would be successful after all: not only the Intricata name but its very blood would run dry.

But Malus refused to give up. Acting through the local Mouth of God, he filed an appeal with the Ecclesiarch as all men have a right to do. Some months later, as much to his own surprise as everyone else's, a dispensation came down from Quoz removing the taint of incest so as to permit him to marry Sersis himself.

The union of father and daughter was pronounced a scandal and a disgrace by the citizens of Minauderies. The authenticity of the dispensation was vociferously denied and disputed. The Mouth of God, while he couldn't refuse outright to perform the ceremony of Holy Patrimony, seemed prepared to delay it on various pretexts until the Unspinning. Only when the Ecclesiarch dispatched a troop of shrives did the wedding take place.

Afterward, Malus and Sersis were shunned. No one would speak to them. When they appeared in public, people looked right through them, as if they'd gone invisible. And when Sersis became pregnant, there was malicious speculation as to what sort of abomination she would produce.

All that changed when Sersis gave birth to a healthy boy, an unmistakable sign of Ixion's favor. Talk of scandal vanished even before the blood of the birthing had dried. Suddenly, the Intricatas could do no wrong. As far as everyone in Minauderies was concerned, they'd been touched by a divine hand.

They must have been blessed in truth, Cassine thinks now, seeing in the sorrowful face of Erigeron a lingering trace of that original blessing like the backward-cast shadow of an object long departed. For over two hundred turnings, son had succeeded son as the reinvigorated family rose from Minauderies to Nooning, Nooning to Ormolu, Ormolu to Peripety and, finally, triumphantly, from Peripety to Quoz and the apex of the Court of the Plumed Serpent.

Then the blessing unraveled. A cold wind blew from the Pit. And two turnings ago, without a shred of warning, young Malus died, his life no more enduring than a candle's. Out went the future; out went the past. A brief flicker, then darkness.

Without Malus to ransom them, Cassine wonders, either by his own future actions or those of his descendants—now never to be born—what chance of redemption is there for the souls of the Intricatas already suffering in the Pit . . . or those soon to be suffering there? She has no doubt that the death of their son is a judgment upon Erigeron and his wife, Anonna, a punishment for some grievous sin kept hidden from every eye except the eye of Ixion, who sees all things.

Early on the morning after her son's funeral, Anonna left Erigeron bound to his bed and, as if walking in her sleep, her long hair trailing behind her like the train of a wedding gown, made her slow way through the empty streets of Quoz to the Cathedral. There she knelt upon the steps and bowed her head in prayer. She didn't move for hours. A crowd gathered, curious but respectful, mindful of her grief. Cassine was among them. No one spoke. Not even the children.

At last, when Ixion's Wheel had climbed above the central spire, pouring its light over the steps like a cascade of diamonds, Anonna raised her head. Tears ran down her face. She wiped them away. Then she took a kitchen knife from under her robe. Small and sharp, flashing in the sun.

Anonna raised the knife and began hacking at her hair and scalp. No Panderman would have been so violent. She accompanied her actions with shrill ululations. An approving murmur, full of anticipation, welled up from the crowd as people realized what was taking place: a thing few of them were old enough to have seen, a gesture fallen out of fashion in Quoz, although still common lower down: the ritual of maternal atonement.

Anonna worked until the blood ran down her shoulders and her hair lay strewn across the Cathedral steps. Breathing hard, she wiped the blade meticulously on her robe. Her shining eyes passed slowly over the faces of the crowd. Then, with quick stabbing motions, she blinded herself.

Many cried out, but not Anonna. Later it was discovered she'd numbed herself with drugs stolen from Erigeron. But at the time her silence seemed remarkable, uncanny. Cassine will never forget how she watched, moved to tears by the dignity with which Anonna both inflicted and bore her own pain; others stared as if savoring each movement, judging this enactment of the old ritual against what they'd read of it or heard from the lips of those fortunate enough to have witnessed it themselves.

Anonna opened her robe and slashed her breasts. Cassine remembers how small they were, how dainty, like plums; all at once she'd felt a heaviness in her own breasts, as if even they yearned to weep. Then Anonna lowered the knife to her belly, her womb. A hush fell, expectant, reverent. Everyone waited. But it was too late. Anonna was too weak. She swayed, nearly collapsing. The knife dropped from her hand.

Only then did she utter a cry, less of pain than despair. Her blind fingers groped after the blade. They wandered over the stone steps, wet with blood and covered with the cuttings of her hair. But she found nothing; the knife lay beyond her reach, although in plain view.

Then suddenly she slumped over. Cassine had thought her dead. But she wasn't dead. Her offering had been refused.

Anonna succeeded in restoring the ritual to popularity, however. In the two turnings since that day, scarcely a month has gone by without some distraught mother following her example. As for Anonna, she's disappeared. Some say she's dead, a victim of the shrives or killed by her own hand. Others hold that Erigeron gave her to the Viridians, who revere blindness in memory of their foundress. But Erigeron sometimes confides in Cassine—why, she can't imagine—and he let slip once that he keeps Anonna locked in his private chambers to forestall another suicide attempt. A laudable ambition, but Cassine doubts it's as simple as that. She knows Erigeron too well. In fact, she's deduced from certain hints that he keeps Anonna locked away the better to experiment upon her, using his vizardly skills to make the desert of her womb blossom with a second son.

It's madness, of course. What the Spinner has done, no man can undo. Cassine sees the insanity moldering in Erigeron's flat yellow eyes as he takes her by the arm and draws her to one side, wheezing softly. His shrives and hers move into a circle around them, backs turned, shielding them from the rest of the gathering.

"You're hurting me, my lord."

Erigeron nods. "Please lower your voice."

"Have I angered you in some way?" she whispers.

He shakes his head, loosening his grip without releasing her. Erigeron may be mad, Cassine thinks, but it's a cunning madness. Dangerous, too, made more so by his addiction to lethium.

Lethium is among the most potent drugs in the vizards' vast and ancient pharmacopoeia. Large doses will render the mind of an adult as pristine as that of newborn baby. But administered judiciously—as, for example, to boys selected to become shrives, simularters, or Mouths of God—it erases only selected portions of memory, leaving other portions intact. The use of lethium as an antimnemonic attained such a high degree of precision in the days before the Hierarchate that there has been no advancement since. Vizards like Erigeron need only follow the detailed instructions left by their predecessors to excise, as with the keenest scalpel, all memory of the events, no matter how pleasant or terrible, that occurred between, say, the hours of two and three on a certain afternoon twenty-five turnings ago. The most deeply held memories, whether recurring across a lifetime or burned into the mind in an instant, can be expunged so thoroughly it's as if they never existed.

But the efficacy of lethium is not limited to the erasure of memory. Properly applied, it produces an amnesia affect, an inability to recognize the occurrence in oneself of such troublesome emotions as envy, sympathy, sadness, anger, or love. Of any emotions at all. The emotions don't actually vanish; instead, the normal responses are forgotten. And as the active emotional range is narrowed, those emotions that can still be felt—or, rather, expressed—grow correspondingly intense.

Lethium endows the members of the various orders with the emotional characteristics peculiar to each. Shrives, for example, care only for the infliction of pain and suffering, while Cats live for the pleasure of others. In some ways, the two orders are like mirror images, and yet, Cassine has often thought, they have more in common than what separates them.

Erigeron turned to lethium after the death of his son, seeking the balm of affective oblivion. He didn't want to forget Malus, but to make the remembering of him bearable. But Cassine doubts he's found much solace; his appearance never suggests the bliss of forgetfulness, only the haunting afflictions of memory. He's become colder, crueler, more reckless and desperate since Malus's death. Cassine's present aversion is not entirely due to the stench of rotting flesh that proclaims his addiction; she's afraid of him now, and she never used to be. Nothing matters to Erigeron anymore but to resurrect his patronymic and ransom his ancestors from the Pit. He'll plunge the Hierarchate into civil war if he has to. Not that the prospect of a little bloodletting makes Cassine flinch. She's a Cat, after all, and a Cat likes nothing better than to scratch. But on the whole Cassine prefers to be the one doing the scratching.

Without Malus, it's only by ascending to the Serpent Throne that Erigeron can win redemption for the Intricata line. And so he plots against Azedarach. That's fine for Erigeron, but Cassine can't help worrying what will happen if he doesn't succeed. Then he and all his allies, herself included, will be purged, cast headlong into the Pit.

But if he succeeds! Then it will be Serinthe Lacrimata who topples! The House Illicium will replace the House Lacrimata as the highest of the High Houses. And, despite the risks, Cassine can't resist the chance of humbling her greatest rival.

"Is Aralia available?" Erigeron asks now, running his tongue over his lips and tightening his grip again.

So unexpected is the question, so painful the grip, that it takes Cassine a moment to compose herself and reply in a steady voice: "I'm afraid she's indisposed this evening."

Erigeron sighs heavily and releases her at last. "So it's true. She's run off."

"No, I swear—"

"Don't lie to me, Cassine. You know better than that."

Not for the first time, Cassine is struck by how quickly news travels in Quoz. Her voice is a pleading whisper. "I only just heard about it myself from young Rumer. I've alerted the shrives, but I didn't want the news to spoil things. Not on Saint Samsum's Day!"

"No, of course not. Entirely understandable. The honor of the House. Only—" Erigeron's eyes bore relentlessly into Cassine's; she waits for him to continue. "Did you know she's with child?"

Cassine shakes her head. "It's not possible."

"I assure you it is. Aralia is pregnant. Or was, when I examined her yesterday."

"She came to you?"

"I sent for her. She had no idea until I told her."

"You should have told me. She should have told me."

Erigeron smiles. "Perhaps she . . . forgot."

"You mean you made her forget. With lethium."

"It was necessary. I didn't want anyone to know. It's a little experiment of mine."

"I see."

"I very much doubt that."

Anonna, Cassine thinks, has the same dark skin as Aralia. She pictures the two women lying side by side in Erigeron's private chambers, their wombs cut open, a tiny fetus, afloat in its sac of amniotic fluid, being transferred from one to the other. Can even vizards accomplish such things? Shunning metheglin, they prolong their lives by harvesting organs from the dead and transplanting them into their own bodies. Is this any different? Cassine shudders, suddenly cold. "Are you the father, my lord?"

"The Spinner is the father of us all," he replies. "You won't breathe a word of this, will you, Cassine?"

"My lord!" Everything that passes between a Cat and her client is confidential. To imply otherwise is, at the very least, insulting.

"Peace, Cassine. This business with Aralia has upset me. I see that I can't conduct the experiment alone; you will assist me. I require a Cat with a skin tone similar to Aralia's, a Cat who's given birth only to males. No females, do you understand? After she's been impregnated, you will watch over her. See that she doesn't take it into her muddled head to run. You'll be rewarded, Cassine."

Cassine bows. "As you desire. But may I ask—"

"You may not. Remember what they say about curiosity. I'll take my leave of you now; I want to talk to Rumer. As I understand it, she was the last one to see Aralia."

"They were very close," says Cassine. "Rumer is beside herself, poor child. I know how she feels. What with Aralia and the murder this morning, I'm at my wit's end."

"A destination I doubt you shall ever reach," Erigeron says mockingly. "Don't trouble yourself over the murder . . . or murders, I should say, for Iber Arvensis wasn't the only victim. The work of cowardly heretics. Perhaps Azedarach is helpless to move against these scum, but I'll soon flush them out, believe me!"

And with that Erigeron strides purposefully through the crowd behind his phalanx of shrives, leaving Cassine to gulp gratefully at the fresh, unspoiled air of his absence as the gelding steps forward to announce the next guest.

"The Court Simularter, Sylvestris Jaciodes!"

EIGHT

Rumer is on her third glass of the fiery liquor called saint's blood when she sees the vizard Erigeron Intricata across the hospitality hall. A terror that at best slumbers fitfully in her comes fully awake at the sight of him. Rumer knows him well; she won't forget his touch if she lives to be a hundred. His slender, white hands—so cruel, so efficient—sliced her open and sewed her up again with a minimum of anesthetic almost every day over the course of her beauty treatments. He didn't leave a mark on her skin, but hardly a day goes by without some mysterious pain rending her from deep inside. In her recurring nightmare, Rumer stands before the mirror in her chambers and watches her body grow webbed with scars. They become visible slowly upon her milky skin, as if rising to the surface, until she's as hideously scored as a Kite. Then her body comes apart along the jagged seams of the scars: a hand drops here, a leg there, a breast over there. It doesn't hurt, but she feels a desolation worse than pain, as if she's no more alive than a simular. Rumer always wakes up before the disunity of her body is complete, but she's afraid a day will come when she won't wake in time, and what then?

Stomach knotting, Rumer looks away from the vizard and gulps down her drink, only to be overcome by a fit of coughing. The long-faced young man at her side, a minor Church official whose name she's forgotten twice already in the short time they've been talking, throws back his tonsured head and brays with laughter as if she's just delivered a devastating witticism.

The youth can't believe his luck. His first invitation to a gathering of such distinction, and here he is being flirted with shamelessly by one of Cassine Illicium's voluptuaries! He wishes his coworkers and friends at the Ecclesiastical Archives could see him now; they'd turn green with envy. None of them has been this close to a voluptuary before. Neither has he, but he's got a hunch he'll be getting closer still before the evening is out. He can't help wondering how many of the stories he's heard about voluptuaries are true. How they're double-, even *triple*-jointed, for instance, or that their long tongues, sensitive and prehensile miracles, can actually jerk a man off. It's hard to know what to believe, so he believes everything; life is simpler that way.

Draining his glass—no saint's blood for him; he's drinking wine, which has the salubrious effect of removing his inhibitions without dulling his intelligence, or so he tells himself—the young man sweeps Rumer into his arms. He feels himself stiffen at her musky scent and the firmness of her breasts pressing against his belly. She's small, no bigger than a girl. But for the love of Ixion, what tits! "How about a spin?" he growls.

Rumer's head is already spinning from the saint's blood. Her throat is burning. She wonders if she'll be sick all over the glittering tunic of what's-his-name. Giggling, she imagines the horrified look that would spring to his face, and lets herself go limp in his arms. Let fate take its course. She wanted to dance, didn't she? But this isn't quite what she had in mind. What's-his-name drags her around the floor, muttering suggestively into her wig while his hands go roving. Any grace he might normally possess has been, to put it charitably, forgotten. He treads on her feet with predictable regularity, blissfully ignorant of any offense, drunk on wine and the heady fumes of imagined virility. It's early yet, Rumer thinks. It's going to be a long night.

In his exuberance, what's-his-name nearly bumps her into a shrive. Fortunately, Rumer is just able to avoid the collision, though at the cost of a bruised instep. Thanks to the murder of Iber Arvensis, there are almost as many shrives as guests. The chief topic of conversation is not if but when the mysterious assassins will strike again.

The shrives mix with no one. They pace in silent pairs, seeming to communicate among themselves by telepathy, for although they never speak, their movements are flawlessly in sync. Even the highest officials step aside with alacrity to let them pass. They move like hunters: slow, restrained, full of menace. Yet there is, as well, a mesmerizing beauty to their glide. Their blue eyes prowl the room, occasionally coming to rest on a particular face. Then it's as if an entire life is being inventoried for a judgment yet to come.

Rumer feels self-conscious among so many shrives. She's certain they're staring. But if they are, she can't discover it, and as for Cassine's guests, they're too intent on the unfolding of their private intrigues to pay her and her clumsy partner any heed. Nearby, the odalisque Althea Circium dances with an elderly vizard, grinding her pelvis against him as if determined to wear him down to the bone. Althea, detecting Rumer's stare, winks ironically over the vizard's shoulder. Rumer smiles sweetly back. Cats of the lower houses can be so vulgar, she thinks. Even an odalisque. Craning her neck, Rumer looks for Cassine, reflexively searching out an antidote to Althea. The tempo of the music changes; the crowd parts; for an instant, as what's-his-name sways, uncertain which way to turn, Rumer catches sight of Cassine at the front of the hall. She's laughing at something the simularter Sylvestris Jaciodes has said, hiding her open mouth behind a fan colorfully painted with scenes from the *ars erotica*. The silvery lilt of her voice, the gracious tilt of her head, and the elegant way she holds the fan, as if equally uncaring of its beauty and her own, combine in Rumer's heart to bring her suddenly, unexpectedly, to the brink of tears. Then what's-his-name makes up his mind, the crowd shifts again as the music changes, and Cassine disappears from view. Her laughter splashes briefly above the music and conversation, then is gone.

Rumer, in her sadness, looks for Aralia before remembering through the swirling fog of three drinks that she, too, is gone. Actually Rumer hasn't forgotten Aralia's absence, but only played at forgetting it. She decides another saint's blood is necessary, though what she'd really like is a lethium cocktail. "Thirsty," she slurs up at what's-his-name with a tongue fuzzier than the mind behind it.

The young man responds with a loud sniff, wrinkling his nose in distaste. "Phew! What an awful st—" Then stops short, his face gone ashen.

Erigeron Intricata stands beside him, breathing heavily from the exertion of crossing the length of the hall.

"My Lord Intricata!" The young man executes a series of flustered bows. "I had no idea!"

"May I cut in?" the vizard wheezes drily.

"An honor!" Continuing to bow past the ring of shrives that have accompanied the vizard, what's-his-name backs into the crowd, which itself is drawing precipitously away. Soon Rumer is standing alone on the dance floor with Erigeron Intricata and his escort. The musicians, fallen momentarily silent, resume playing with a flourish at a signal from Cassine.

"Happy Saint Samsum's Day, Rumer," says the vizard.

Rumer is mute with terror. Erigeron's deathly smell is making her nauseous. She's afraid of disgracing herself and her House. With trembling hands she produces her fan and spreads it before her face, peeking over the top. The fan, a gift from Aralia on the occasion of Rumer's elevation to voluptuary, is drenched in aspergine, a mild narcotic, at least in its present form. While unable to vanquish the charnel odor of the vizard's addiction, it at least provides a curtain, however flimsy, to shelter behind.

Without another word, Erigeron takes Rumer by the wrist and lays his other hand upon her waist. Gingerly, keeping her at arm's length, and seeming especially intent not to disturb the fan, which she holds rigidly in front of her face, he embarks on a slow, almost-stately, waltz. The shrives drift along beside them as if they, too, are dancing, only in a fashion peculiar to their order. It's torture for Rumer to feel so alone, so exposed to the stares of everyone. But then, bit by bit, led by Althea—to whom Rumer silently pledges undying gratitude—other couples return to the dance floor, though they are careful to keep a respectful distance even while straining mightily to overhear.

"Cassine tells me you were the last to see Aralia," says Erigeron in a low whisper. The slits of his yellow eyes bore into Rumer beneath their puffy lids.

Viridis help me, Rumer prays. She swallows; her mouth is dry as death. "Yes, Excellency," she rasps from behind the fan, the very fear that has silenced her now aiding her tongue.

"Surely you have no reason to be afraid," Erigeron says.

She shakes her head in vehement agreement.

"I thought not. Why, I said as much to the captain of the shrives. 'You can't possibly suspect Rumer of anything!' I told him. 'There's no need to question her; I'll vouch for her myself!'"

Rumer feels faint. Shrives don't ask questions unless they've already decided upon the answers. She gives her fan a flutter, releasing more aspergine. "Please, I haven't done anything wrong!"

"Of course not," Erigeron soothes. "But shrives can be so suspicious! Who can blame them in these perilous times? You have to admit it looks odd, Rumer. Why would Aralia come to you and announce her intention to run? Why tell anyone? It doesn't make sense; it's almost as if she wanted to be caught. After all, she must have known you would tell Cassine. I wonder, could it be a plot of some kind?"

None of these eminently sensible questions has occurred to Rumer until now. Under their influence, the memory of Aralia's visit takes on a sinister cast. She doesn't know what to believe. Fortunately the aspergine is kicking in. It's all beginning to seem far away, or she is, like watching a performance of simulars. "A plot?"

"I'm not saying I think so, but the shrives?" Erigeron shrugs his heavy shoulders. "Well, they're made to think that way. Perhaps it would help if you told me what passed between you and Aralia. Why *did* she come to see you, Rumer?"

"To say good-bye."

Erigeron nods as if she's just confirmed his own guess. "I've heard the two of you were close. Something of a passion, I take it."

The word "passion" gives Rumer a strange hollow feeling, part yearning, part loss. She's dreamed forever of experiencing a passion, yet she's still no closer to it, or even to understanding what it is. "Aralia taught me all I know about the *ars erotica*. About being a Cat. A voluptuary." As she says it, she realizes for the first time just how true it is, and how little thanks she ever gave Aralia for it.

"Did she tell you why she was running?"

Rumer hesitates, not wanting to be disloyal.

"Go on."

"She thought Cassine was going to retire her. She was afraid she'd be turned over to the shrives. You know, for the apprentices to practice on."

"An understandable fear."

Rumer wonders if that will be her fate now.

"Was that all? Did she tell you anything else?"

A fist squeezes Rumer's insides. He knows, she thinks. He knows about Aralia's plan to join the heretics. She looks at him blankly, afraid of incriminating herself, for she kept this information from Cassine.

"Come now, Rumer. It's a simple question."

She has to give Erigeron something, she knows. A morsel of truth, enough to satisfy him. Then perhaps he'll leave her alone. "She asked me to come with her."

"She made no mention of me?"

"No, Excellency."

"If I find you're lying . . ." He gives her a shake, not hard but impossible for her to misinterpret, though anyone watching would think he'd simply stumbled in the dance and reached for her to steady himself.

Rumer's resistance crumbles. "She had a pamphlet from the heretics!" she hisses. "She was going to join them!"

The vizard's cheeks grow mottled with rage, though his voice remains a terse whisper. "Did you read this pamphlet?"

"No, I swear! I told Cassine everything the minute she left my chamber!" Overcome with dread, Rumer sinks to her knees. She presses Erigeron's soft white hand to her cheek. The shrives draw close, as if to remove her, but the vizard waves them off with his free hand. Although the music continues, everyone around them has stopped dancing and is staring openly.

"Have you taken leave of your senses?" The vizard pulls his hand away with an expression of annoyance. "For Ixion's sake keep your voice down! And get up!"

Rumer makes the sign of the Wheel as she rises on shaky legs. "Have mercy," she pleads, her voice barely audible. "I'm no heretic! I worship at the Wheel! I loved Aralia but not enough to betray the order for her sake! I'd tell you where to find her if I knew!"

"You should have spoken of this sooner."

"I was afraid."

"'Only the guilty have anything to fear,'" Erigeron says, quoting Saint Ixion. "I don't think you're a heretic, Rumer. Just a foolish Cat. I'll have a word with the shrives. But you'll have to be questioned. You know that."

"Now?" she manages to croak.

"I think after the gathering will be soon enough."

Rumer nods gratefully and, despite the aspergine, bursts into tears. Ashamed, she hides her face behind the fan. She feels as though she's betrayed Aralia just as surely as if she'd told Erigeron where to find her. But isn't it really Aralia who's betrayed her? Why didn't she slip away quietly, in secret? Rumer hates Aralia for what she's done, for what she's made her do. Meanwhile the stares of the others pierce her like knives. She can't bear to look at them. What must they think of her? What must Cassine think, whom she loves like a mother? No, it's too awful. A disgrace. And on Saint Samsum's Day of all days!

"Have you nothing better to do, my lord, than to kiss my girls and make them cry?"

Rumer looks up in surprise at the familiar voice. It's Cassine. The odalisque is shaking a finger at Erigeron Intricata in mock chastisement.

The vizard gives a mocking bow in return. "What could be better than that, Cassine, when your girls are so beautiful and cry so well!"

Cassine laughs her sparkling laugh. As if they'd only been waiting for her signal, the others join in. Ignoring Rumer completely, Cassine takes Erigeron by the arm and leads him away. "I've someone for you to meet."

The vizard bows again.

"Althea!" Cassine calls. "Where's that delectable Nyssa of yours?"

The amber-skinned voluptuary is produced and introduced to Erigeron. Watching, Rumer sees that the Cat's nostrils do not so much as quiver in the vizard's presence.

"Why, she's perfect," he announces with enthusiasm. "Will you cry if I kiss you, dear?"

"If it pleases you, my lord."

"How charming!"

Althea beams triumphantly at Nyssa's side. "You see, My Lord Intricata. The House Circium has its treasures, too."

"I never doubted it." Soon Erigeron and Nyssa are dancing together.

Drying her tears, Rumer marvels at Cassine's skill. It's plain to see why she's served as odalisque for so long. Who could think of challenging her?

Cassine returns to Rumer and takes her firmly by the arm. "What's the matter with you?" she whispers. "Are you drunk?"

"I'm sorry, Cassine. I can explain." But before Rumer can say anything more, the voice of the gelding rings out from the front of the hall:

"The odalisque Serinthe Lacrimata and household."

Cassine sighs. "Viridis preserve me. Can I count on you, Rumer? No more little scenes?"

Rumer bows her blushing head. "Odalisque, I—"

"That will be quite enough. If I wasn't already short one voluptuary, I'd send you to your chambers." She pulls Rumer along as she hurries to greet Serinthe. "Not a word from you if you want to remain a voluptuary, Rumer. Just keep still and look pretty."

NINE

As Serinthe Lacrimata enters the hospitality hall, her fingers trail caressingly, possessively, over the figures carved into the famous doors. How lovely they are. Each tiny figure a masterpiece in its own right. That these magnificent doors, which do not simply illustrate, but in a very real sense embody, the *ars erotica,* should grace the entrance to the House Illicium and not that of her own House has rankled Serinthe ever since she first visited the House Illicium more than a hundred turnings ago. She was a mere voluptuary then, accompanying her odalisque to a Saint Samsum's Day gathering much like this one. She remembers how she brushed the carvings with her fingertips and swore a private oath that the doors would stand in the House Lacrimata one day. She's sworn it anew each turning on this day, the only time she may lawfully enter the House Illicium.

Now at last that oath is about to be fulfilled, like so many before it. A grateful Azedarach will give her anything she desires as a reward for exposing a High House riddled with heresy, one aligned, moreover, with his enemy, the Ecclesiarch. Serinthe has already ordered her geldings to prepare for the installation of the doors; already, too, she feels a restless presentiment of the disappointment that inevitably follows her triumphs.

Serinthe covets nothing more than the beautiful things that happen to belong to others; nothing gives her more pleasure than to take them for her own. Once hers, however, they lose the charms that attracted her in the first place. Fortunately, one can't possess everything, she thinks. How boring that would be! There are always new things to covet.

As she waits for Cassine—and how like Cassine to keep her waiting; just the sort of petty slight she's learned to expect from her rival—Serinthe searches the crowd for her chief spy in the House Illicium. She has many questions, and though they can't talk now, even the exchange of a glance would tell her a lot about Cassine's role in all that's happened. But there's no sign of the woman. Despite herself, Serinthe begins to worry. Cassine cannot be underestimated. The doors remain to be won; even now, a wrong move can ruin everything.

She glances uneasily at the Cat called Rose, who stands behind her amid the voluptuaries of the House Lacrimata. She's strikingly beautiful in her sheer gown of green and yellow silks, which conceal the bruises left by Serinthe's interrogation. Her strawberry blonde wig is woven through with ribbons of green and gold and fresh, simple flowers—daisies, buttercups—that perfectly complement her pale skin and green eyes.

Yet there's something worrisome about those remarkable eyes. If they shine now—and they do—it's with a reflected, not an inner, light. Rose reminds Serinthe of certain Viridians whose attention has fallen away from external realities and taken refuge deep within. Yet she looks more beautiful than ever, as if, by withdrawing so far into herself, she's left a void that others can't help rushing to fill. All Cats aspire to such a remote yet extraordinarily accessible beauty, but few attain it. Serinthe labored for turnings to achieve through artifice what Rose seems instinctively to know.

And that, she thinks, is the problem. She can't trust Rose, yet she has to use her. Rose is the bait in the trap she's prepared for Cassine. From a distance, Rose is irresistible. But looked at too closely, with an eye more critical than admiring, her bruises show . . . and not just the ones on her body.

She is damaged.

Ever since regaining consciousness after Serinthe's none-too-gentle questioning, Rose has demonstrated all the initiative of a simular. She does what she's told, allows herself to be dressed and led from place to place, but there's no volition to any of it, no awareness. She hasn't spoken a word, or even made a sound, and that, too, seems less a purposeful withholding than a fundamental loss of ability, a profound forgetting such as might result from an overdose of lethium. But there's been no lethium. Perhaps it's a defect of the beauty treatments belatedly emerging. Or the shock of witnessing the murder of Iber Arvensis. Perhaps the raw, convulsive touch of the thyrsis has unhinged Rose's mind.

Though she'd never admit it, Serinthe regrets having employed the thyrsis so early in the interrogation. She should have waited. Called in the vizards with their oh-so-persuasive drugs. Or trusted the time-tested methods of the shrives. But she was too angry and impatient to wait, goaded by the faceless corpse of Iber Arvensis mocking her from its bed of roses. Besides, she's never trusted vizards, and she hates the smugness of shrives.

The thought of the assassinated minor official touches a fresh spark to Serinthe's still-smoldering rage. The temerity of it! The unmitigated gall! The four High Houses have been neutral ground ever since the erection of the Hierarchate. Seven hundred turnings have passed since the last time the sanctuary of a House was violated in this way. The disgraceful incident took place in the House Valentine; the odalisque herself, Salix Valentine, was responsible: a passion turned sour. Salix was condemned to the Six Hundred, and the House, formerly third in rank, was placed below the House Circium, a position it still holds today.

Serinthe doubts the House Lacrimata could ever be reduced in rank; the veneration in which Saint Viridis is universally held protects the House from all but the most minor sanctions. However, this protection doesn't extend to the odalisque. Serinthe's hair may be her own, but she has no illusions that she's anything other than a Cat because of it. She could easily find herself shaved bald by the panderman and following in the footsteps of Salix Valentine: a distinction to be sure, but not the kind Serinthe so desperately craves.

Thank Viridis her shrives were able to remove Iber's body and lay it outside the House Illicium without being seen! Serinthe knows Cassine was behind the murder. Proof? Proof is for shrives. Of course, she's not so naive as to imagine that Cassine is solely responsible. Doubtless the Ecclesiarch was pulling the strings; he generally is. But he's beyond Serinthe's reach, while Cassine is not. If she's relying on his protection, she'll find herself sorely disappointed.

"A thousand pardons, Serinthe!" Cassine comes hurrying up at last. She's attended by her shrives and an unusually small Cat, one Serinthe has never seen before but recognizes from her spy's reports as the young voluptuary called Rumer.

"I would have been here to greet you properly," Cassine continues, "only—"

There's no sign of Aralia, chief voluptuary of the House, as Serinthe notes with increasing unease. It's Aralia, not Rumer, who belongs at Cassine's side. But Serinthe's smile is effortless and smooth as she holds up a forestalling hand like Saint Viridis delivering a benediction: "Nonsense, sister. Who appreciates the responsibilities of a hostess better than I? To understand all is to forgive all, as Viridis once remarked."

It's Serinthe's habit to speak of the saint by her first name only, as though they are intimately acquainted, and to quote from her sayings as if they come not from the *Lives and Acts* but from a private conversation held just yesterday over glasses of chilled wine and sorbet.

"That's very gracious of you, sister."

"How can I be otherwise? In this House, today of all days? Happy Saint Samsum's Day, Cassine."

"And to you, Serinthe." Cassine curtsies low, making the obeisance she owes Serinthe as odalisque of the House Lacrimata and hence, in a sense, a descendant of the saint. "Your household is most welcome in this House. Whatever is mine is yours."

Serinthe can't help smiling. "You shouldn't make such rash offers, sister. Everything and everyone is so delectable, I can't help wanting them all! This precious little voluptuary, for instance; how charming she is, like a child!"

"This is Rumer; she was elevated this turning."

Blushing, Rumer steps forward and executes a smooth curtsy.

Despite everything, Serinthe is delighted. "Look at her blush! The sign of a passionate nature."

Cassine dips her head in acknowledgment. "She's very popular. A credit to the House."

"I'm sure she is. Come here, child. Let me kiss you." And, stooping, Serinthe does just that, bestowing a lingering kiss on the voluptuary's upturned mouth. "Mmmm. Delicious. A cunning tongue. How old are you, child? Seventeen? Eighteen?"

"Nineteen, odalisque."

"And already a voluptuary. You have a long career ahead of you, I'm sure."

"Thank you, odalisque." Released, Rumer returns to Cassine's side.

"Am I mistaken, sister, or did I detect a trace of Aralia in that kiss?"

"I had no idea you were such a connoisseur of kisses, Serinthe!"

"Every kiss has its distinctive signature; once I've tasted a kiss, I can recognize it again blindfolded."

"You're right, of course; Aralia trained her personally."

"Then you are fortunate as well as beautiful, Rumer. I don't think you could have had a better teacher—other than Cassine herself, of course!"

Rumer blushes more deeply still, eyes shining.

"Speaking of Aralia," Serinthe continues as if by the way, turning again to Cassine, "Forgive me, but it hardly seems like Saint Samsum's Day without Aralia standing at your side to greet the guests!"

"Aralia was suddenly taken ill this morning."

With these words, Serinthe's worst fears are realized. The pained expression that flits over Rumer's face at the mention of Aralia's name provides all the confirmation Serinthe needs of her spy's fate. She's badly shaken. She's lost spies before, but never like this. It took turnings of patient effort to insinuate Aralia into the upper echelons of the House Illicium; without her, Serinthe feels half-blind in this unfriendly place.

Vulnerable, despite the presence of her shrives. Now she understands why no warning of the assassination reached her: Aralia was exposed before she could give it.

Is she dead now, dead as Iber Arvensis? Or is she alive, hidden away in a windowless room of blazing white where darkness never enters, suffering the torments of the Six Hundred? And if alive, has her conditioning held, or has she confessed her long association with the House Lacrimata? Serinthe's head throbs with bloody thoughts. Still, her voice is light as ever. "What a shame! Nothing serious, I trust."

"The vizards are hopeful."

"My prayers go with her." Not that they'll do her any good, Serinthe thinks, making the sign of the Wheel. But she offers up a silent prayer to Viridis anyway. It's not Aralia's health she prays for, though.

"It's as the Spinner wills," Cassine says meanwhile, in a tone of pious resignation as if replying to Serinthe's prayer.

"Allow me to present my voluptuaries." Serinthe can't tell how much Cassine knows or suspects about Aralia, but she wants badly to repay her now by flaunting Rose in her face. A spy for a spy. Though it's possible Cassine won't recognize her right away; in her splendid silks and fine red wig, the first round of beauty treatments successfully concluded, Rose can hardly resemble the girl Cassine must have recruited to spy on the House Lacrimata.

Serinthe can imagine how it all happened; she knows the process well, having employed it with Aralia and countless others. A girl is procured with bribes from a panderman before she can be put up for auction, then given to vizards for conditioning. The vizards induce secondary personality traits that the girl will never be conscious of, not even while performing her duties as a spy. At last, her memory selectively purged by lethium, she's returned to the panderman and auctioned off to a rival House.

But despite all the trouble taken to recruit them, spies are generally unmasked after purchase. Each House employs vizards to screen new Cats for evidence of prior conditioning. Just the same, spies occasionally slip through. Sometimes a spy rises to the rank of voluptuary or, like Aralia, chief voluptuary, before she's found out. Of course, no one can say for certain how many spies are never found out or how high they may rise. As high as odalisque? Serinthe has often wondered.

Persea Valentine, Althea Circium, Cassine Illicium: any one of them could be an agent for any of the others or for someone else entirely. Why, Serinthe herself could be a spy; she'd never know it unless a vizard exposed the conditioning! She grows so suspicious of herself sometimes that she can't make the smallest decision. Normally confident to the point of arrogance, if not beyond it, she worries so much about performing the will of her hidden master or mistress that she becomes paralyzed, unable to act, a simular tangled in its own strings.

Serinthe decided a long time ago she'd rather not know the truth. If the choice is between the illusion of free will and a drab reality of determinism and servitude, she'll take illusion every time. What Cat wouldn't?

As she presents Rose—having saved her for last, after the formal introduction of her voluptuaries—it occurs somewhat belatedly to Serinthe that Cassine may never have seen Rose at all, in which case it hardly seems likely that she'll recognize her now. It's possible, Serinthe thinks, that Rose was recruited after the auction, not before it, seduced by a spy nestled within the walls of the House Lacrimata like a spider in a nursery. But Serinthe pushes this annoying thought from her mind. She prefers not to consider the likelihood that her House, the Highest House, is as thick with spies and heretics as she knows the lower Houses to be.

"This is Rose," she says, guiding the girl forward with care, a hand at her elbow. "A new girl. Purchased last turning during the Season of Chastenings from the market in Kell."

It's unusual to reveal even this much of a Cat's personal history, especially to the odalisque of a rival House. But even if Cassine has never seen her, Serinthe hopes her rival may recognize Rose from this information and betray her knowledge, however fleetingly.

But in Cassine's shining dark eyes, there's no evidence of pretense, only unfeigned admiration: "Why, how beautiful she is! What a treasure!"

"I had an idea she'd please you, sister."

"How well you know me!" Cassine gazes caressingly at Rose, who returns a look of blank serenity. "She's exquisite, as though carved from fine marble. And those eyes! I've never seen eyes of such luminous green! I almost think they'd shine in the dark like a true cat's! But if you acquired her only a turning ago, you can't possibly have made her a voluptuary already!"

"Of course not," answers Serinthe. "She's only had her first round of beauty treatments. And at her age, there's always the chance of failure, as you know."

"What a pity to have to take that chance! She seems perfect to me as she is."

"There *is* something special about her, isn't there? Kiss her if you like."

Cassine does so. Then draws sharply back. She looks quizzically at Rose. "Don't you like me, child?"

Rose blinks.

"Is there something wrong with her, sister?" Cassine seems curious rather than angry. "Is she deaf? Or blind, perhaps?"

"She has taken a vow," Serinthe answers smoothly. "She's sworn to Saint Viridis to say nothing, to do nothing, until All Saints' Eve. Until then, she must suffer meekly and in silence everything that befalls her."

"Everything?"

"She may commit no action. Not the slightest."

"We'll see about that." Cassine parts the silks that cover one of Rose's breasts and pinches the rouged nipple. But Rose's face betrays no discomfort.

"How marvelous!" Cassine bends to kiss the nipple, as though abasing herself for having doubted.

"I knew you'd appreciate her, Cassine. That's why I took the liberty of bringing her today, as a gift on Saint Samsum's Day. In honor of Sabal Illicium, whose memory we all revere."

Cassine looks genuinely touched. Her eyes glisten with tears. Taking Rose's limp hand in her own, she says: "I humbly accept your lovely gift. May it cement the bond of friendship between our two great Houses."

Serinthe smiles graciously. "I'm sure it will."

Cassine turns to the small voluptuary. "Rumer, I'm going to put Rose in your harem, I think. I want you personally to take charge of her training, just as Aralia did for you."

Rumer does not reply. She's staring at Rose like a simularter enraptured by his reflection in a mirror.

"Rumer!" exclaims Cassine. "You will do me the courtesy of answering when I address you!"

Rumer blushes again, more deeply than before. "Forgive me, odalisque." Even now she can't tear her eyes away from Rose. "It's just that I've never seen eyes like this. They go right through you."

"Indeed they do," agrees Cassine. "Now: stay close to her for the rest of the gathering, Rumer. No one is to pluck this rose before me, do you understand? Not even the Sovereign himself. Afterward, I want you to prepare her and bring her to my chambers."

"Yes, odalisque," Rumer whispers, taking Rose's hand.

"Serinthe, if there's anything you desire . . . "

"I'll take it, don't worry!" Serinthe can't believe her good luck; she hadn't expected it would prove so easy to persuade Cassine to accept the Cat as a gift. Now the bait has been taken, the trap all but sprung. Earlier, after her interrogation, Rose was conditioned by the most skillful vizards in Serinthe's employ to uncover heresy in the House Illicium. And uncover it she will, even if she has to plant the evidence herself.

Soon, Serinthe thinks, the famous doors of Illicium will belong to the House Lacrimata, and Cassine will be the plaything of shrives. She claps her hands, dizzy with happiness.

"Oh, look!" she cries, pointing across the hall, where guests are gathering before the half circle of a curtained stage. "The performance is about to start! I don't want to miss this; I've heard Sylvestris is planning something special!"

TEN

Suspended in his net above the stage, where the eyes of the audience cannot find him, Sylvestris Jaciodes dons his gloves of silvery mail while silently reciting the Litany of the Harrowing of the Self: "Not for my glory, but for the glory of Ixion. Not for me to speak, but for the Spinner to speak through me. Not for me to move, but for me to move others."

Made of metal, the gloves are no heavier than silk. He makes fists, wincing as the metal contracts and cools. As if his hands are being slowly chewed, tiny needles emerge to pierce them in a thousand places, linking with receptors implanted by the vizards in the course of his apprenticeship.

A cascade of fire burns along his nerves, shoots up his naked arms, explodes behind his eyes in violent bursts of magenta, vermilion, sapphire, each color accompanied by a unique pain, a synesthesia of agony that as quickly subsides. Sylvestris no longer feels the weight of his body supported by the net's fine mesh, no longer sees the stage beneath him, where the simulars chosen for the evening's performance droop listlessly upon the boards, their strings rising to his gloves.

Mechanically, Sylvestris continues his recitation: "Not world, but that which is not world; internal darkness, deprivation, and destitution of all property; desiccation of the world of sense; evacuation of the world of fancy; inoperancy of the world of spirit. . . ."

He feels his selves splintering. The voices of his simulars rise in an excited babble. Opening his eyes, he sees, from different though simultaneous perspectives, the drab curtain of the stage, behind which can be heard the expectant buzz of the audience and muffled strains of music. He sees, also from many angles, his simulars, who gaze at each other through him while gazing at him through each other: Saint Ixion Diospyros; Saint Samsum Oxalis; Saint Cedrus Lyciodes; Saint Stilskin

Sophora and his faithful dog, Snowdrop; Saint Rober Viburnum; Saint Quercus Incana; Saint Fagus Firmiana; Saint Ilex Erythrina; Saint Viridis Lacrimata; Sabal Illicium; Roemer and Jewel, and others. There are assorted Furies and servants of Maw as well, but these simulars are empty shells only, possessing no personalities of their own, for it would be foolish to give Maw even the slightest chance to corrupt a simularter.

Sylvestris is a multitude of selves now. Each distinct, yet all cohering in a greater whole. He experiences the rapid and intricate movements of his fingers in the silver gloves, but also, and as intimately, the exuberant movements of the simulars as they leap to their feet on the stage and turn somersaults or pirouettes while whispering excitedly to each other like prisoners freed from a long sentence of solitary confinement.

Which, thinks Sylvestris, in a sense they are. Now he has been imprisoned in their stead. His body sweats and stutters in the restraining embrace of the net like a sleeper tossed by dreams. The net absorbs the sweat before a single drop can fall, like rain, over the simulars below.

And the dreams?

"Looks like you could use a little paint around the eyes, Vi, old girl!" growls Saint Fagus Firmiana, wooden lips opening and closing in a rough approximation of the words Sylvestris is subvocalizing overhead.

"Hmph!" the saint replies, twirling on her toes. Her severe habit, dark and restrictive, seems out of place as she dances. "You're as full of termites as ever, Fagus!"

"Shh! The curtain's going up!" the simular of Sabal Illicium warns in a whisper. Shy, uncomfortable in the spotlight, she smooths her garish costume nervously.

The audience applauds as the simulars bow and curtsy, revealed by the rising curtain. Even when silent, as now, or when reciting the lines of a play, the simulars communicate through the medium of Sylvestris, their voices ringing brazenly in his head:

"Did you see Althea Circium's wig? I almost died!"

"Looks like Erigeron's found a new friend! Won't Aralia be jealous!"

"Mmmm; speaking of jealous, who's the Cat with Rumer?"

Meanwhile, the simular of Saint Ixion Diospyros steps to the edge of the stage. Grasping the strings above his head in one hand while gesturing broadly with the other, he inclines himself at an extreme angle toward the audience and proclaims in a loud voice:

"Gentlemen and ladies. Learned vizards and ambidextrous simularters; devout Mouths of God, stalwart shrives, and frolicsome Cats: a Happy Saint Samsum's Day to you all! Let's have a round of applause for our gracious hostess, odalisque of this historic House: the lovely and talented Cassine Illicium! May metheglin forever preserve her youth and beauty!"

Cassine waves from the front of the hall, where she's greeting the vizard Morus Sisymbrium.

At a nod from Saint Ixion, the other simulars scamper up their strings like spiders, leaving him in sole possession of the stage. He lifts a finger to his lips, and the thyrsi above the stage dim to a twilight glow.

"What an evening we have planned for you!" the simular enthuses, looking almost like flesh and blood in the diminished light. "What a show! The thrilling and inspirational story of Saint Samsum's capture and escape just as Saint Quercus recorded it from the eyewitness testimony of Sabal Illicium! Every word, every action—down to the smallest gesture—has been researched and rehearsed to perfection, gentlemen and ladies! But that's for later; after the arrival of the Ecclesiarch and our Blessed Sovereign, may he reign ten thousand turnings!

"And until then? We'll keep you entertained, never fear! 'To Instruct! To Amuse! To Elevate!' Thus our ancient aim; thus our sacred mission! And so, without further ado, I give you that holy fool, that saintly simpleton, Stilskin Sophora!"

As the audience applauds, the simular of Ixion leaps into the air and is gone. At the same instant, a small simular descends to the stage, bathed in a shaft of white light.

Snowdrop.

Looking up, the dog barks impatiently, imperiously.

No response.

The audience titters as Snowdrop places his paws over his head and commences a piteous whining.

At last a head peeks from below the fringe of the raised curtain. A simular descends.

Slowly.

Upside down.

It is Saint Stilskin, hopelessly entangled in his own strings. His attempts to free himself serve only to make things worse.

"Oh, dear. I seem to making a mess of things."

Suddenly, as if for the first time, Stilskin catches sight of the audience. His body jerks, shivering with uncontrollable stage fright. "P-p-p-people!"

The more Stilskin shivers and flails, the more he slips free of the knots constraining him, until, with a final twitch, he turns right side up and lands smoothly on the stage. As Snowdrop barks happily, the saint executes a nimble jig, his stage fright replaced by a confidence equally comical. "Oh, Stilskin," he enthuses. "You've done it again!"

As the performance continues, punctuated by the laughter of the audience and the arrival and departure of simulars upon the stage, the simulars indulge in their favorite pastime—gossip—until Sylvestris's head is buzzing like a hive.

"I don't see Aralia. Does anyone see Aralia?" asks Saint Rober Viburnum.

"She's gone," Saint Samsum opines. "Run off."

Saint Cedrus Lyciodes sniffs: "I never trusted her."

Sylvestris joins in. "Never mind Aralia. I'm supposed to be looking for a Cat, remember?"

A chuckle from Saint Ilex Erythrina. "There's plenty to choose from here!"

"Not just any Cat; one with the eyes of Saint Viridis Lacrimata."

"Hear that, Vi?" asks Saint Fagus Firmiana. "Some Cat's got your eyes!"

"She's welcome to them!"

"Anyway, you don't need us," continues Saint Ilex. "You'll find the Cat yourself. Azedarach foresaw it, didn't he?"

"According to Morus Sisymbrium," says Sylvestris. "But I don't think Morus told me everything. He wants me to fail."

"I never trusted him," sniffs Saint Cedrus.

"There is nothing the Sovereign does not see, nothing he does not know," Saint Quercus Incana piously intones.

"A metheglin sponge, that's what he is!" Saint Ilex scoffs.

Sabal Illicium is aghast. "That's heresy, Ilex! You'll get us in trouble!"

"I never trusted him," Saint Cedrus sniffs.

"But you're me, Cedrus," explains an exasperated Ilex. "I'm you. And we're all part of Sylvestris."

"I never trusted any of us."

Even as he squabbles with the simulars and directs their performance upon the stage, Sylvestris gazes through their eyes to search the audience for the girl he's been commanded to find. It seems as though it should be confusing, when he thinks about it, to see the same scene from twenty or thirty different perspectives, bits and pieces of a whole too vast, too complicated, for any one pair of eyes to encompass. But it's not confusing. Not at all. It's simply who and what he is. A simularter. Made this way by the vizards.

No doubt Ilex is right; the girl won't be here. No Cat below the rank of voluptuary is welcome. And even if some lucky chance has brought her to the House Illicium this evening, how will he know her? The eyes of Saint Viridis Lacrimata; that could mean almost anything. But the Sovereign has spoken. Sylvestris must obey.

And so he looks among the Cats in their outrageous wigs, those marvels that defy gravity as much as good taste. He looks among the pompous vizards, heirs of a knowledge Sylvestris suspects they themselves only half understand at best, who strut and preen like peacocks, their vanity a match for any Cat's. He looks among his fellow simularters, towering above the other guests, pale and slender, stalking through one party while, in their minds, as he well knows, another, endless party unfolds. He looks among the pairs of shrives who glide through the crowd in their skintight black armor, blue eyes raking coldly over the Cats, coldly over everyone and everything . . . except each other. And he looks among the Mouths of God, their robes embroidered with images of Ixion's Wheel like shields against the dark temptations of Maw while their tonsured pates, as it were, proclaim a condition the robes conceal, a lack that hasn't curtailed their breathless pursuit of the Cats even though it would seem to condemn that pursuit to perpetual frustration.

The vizard Erigeron Intricata explores the ear of a dark-skinned voluptuary with his tongue. She absentmindedly fondles his penis through a convenient slit in his robe, too enraptured by the antics of Stilskin and Snowdrop to concentrate on the task at hand. Sylvestris knows that she belongs to the House Circium but can't remember her name. Lyssa, perhaps. Or Myssa. Anyway, she's not the one he seeks. There's nothing about her shining amber eyes—lovely though they are—to suggest the miraculous eyes of Saint Viridis Lacrimata.

Elsewhere Althea Circium flutters her tongue in the direction of Morus Sisymbrium. Morus declines her offer with a polite smile, his gaze attracted by Serinthe Lacrimata, who is passing by in the company of Rumer Illicium and another voluptuary—from the House Lacrimata to judge by her wig—whose features and tattoos Sylvestris can't make out.

At the front of the hall, Cassine's gelding announces the Ecclesiarch. All conversations, all diversions, immediately cease. The simulars shin up their strings as the musicians strike up the stirring notes of "Ixion Ascendant," composed by Saint Sium Lyrata.

Everyone pushes forward to greet the Ecclesiarch. The shrives are hard-pressed to keep order; all fear is forgotten in the rush to receive the Ecclesiarch's blessing.

Meanwhile, Cassine Illicium makes the sign of the Wheel and sinks to her knees upon soft cushions in anticipation of her guest. Her voluptuaries abase themselves behind her—except for Rumer, who has remained standing in the company of the voluptuary from the House Lacrimata, a breach of protocol that no one except Sylvestris seems to have noticed.

For an instant, through the eyes of Saint Samsum Oxalis, he has a clear view of Rumer's companion: a beautiful stranger, one of the loveliest Cats he's ever seen, her eyes closed as if savoring the music. Sylvestris is intrigued. But before he can take a closer look, Erigeron Intricata, accompanied by the dark-skinned Cat he was with earlier, steps in front of the girl.

At the same moment, the Ecclesiarch arrives, entering the House Illicium through the famous doors. Sylvestris, like everyone else, watches as he shuffles in.

He is old: wonderfully, horribly old. It's said that he's seen more Sovereigns rise and fall than other men have seen sunrises and sunsets. It's said he's mastered the disciplines of every order in the course of his life. Other, more fantastic, things are said of him. Sylvestris believes them all.

Physically, however, the Ecclesiarch gives an appearance of decrepitude. Dwarfed by his silver robes, which seem to weigh him down as though woven of lead, he moves at a slow and deliberate pace through a space cleared by the shrives, looking neither to the left nor to the right. His eyes are an infinitely pale blue, like a film that could be washed away by a single tear. His bald head, a pale and withered raisin, trembles upon the narrow reed of his neck. His expression is lost in wrinkles. He makes the sign of the Wheel with palsied hands in response to the adulation that pours over him from all sides; his fingers are the length of a simularter's, but skeletal and crabbed, arthritic. They form a poor, misshapen Wheel. It looks as if a firefly's sting could finish him.

Yet he projects an aura of grave and inviolable dignity that transcends his apparent frailty. The frailty belongs to the man; the dignity derives from the office. The Ecclesiarch stands at the head of the Church of the Spinning Wheel; only the Blessed Sovereign ranks above him in all the Hierarchate, and even he must bow to the Ecclesiarch in matters of religion. The Serpent Crown, symbol of sovereignty, is bestowed by the Ecclesiarch's hand. And the shrives acknowledge his authority as supreme. It's said that no firefly would dare to sting him, for if it did, it would find itself stung in return.

And yet, Sylvestris thinks, there are those who brave that sting. He himself is such a one, pledged to Azedarach in the struggle for power. A man must take sides, he thinks. No man can be all things at once. Not even a simularter.

His simulars, of course, do not agree.

The Ecclesiarch comes to a halt before Cassine Illicium and stretches out the claw of his right hand. A large and heavy ring glints upon his middle finger: an amethyst shaped like a firefly, caged in a setting of gold.

The ring originally belonged to Saint Ixion Diospyros. Since his fiery ascension, it has passed from Ecclesiarch to Ecclesiarch in an unbroken line. It is called Infallible.

Whoever kisses the ring is judged as if by Ixion himself. Those who are pure of heart need have no fear. But anyone else will suffer a sting that burns forever. A judgment from which there can be no appeal. Absolute. Eternal.

Infallible.

Trembling, pale, Cassine shuts her eyes and presses her lips to the ring. It pulses, suffusing her face with a violet glow. She raises her eyes to the Ecclesiarch, her expression beatific, full of the joy of survival. "You are most welcome in this House, Holy Father, divine intercessor, living Wheel!"

The Ecclesiarch motions for her to stand. "Daughter," he begins, then breaks off.

There is a commotion in the crowd. A voice bellows: "Treachery!" A chorus of screams follows. The crowd surges like a great, terrified beast, smashing through the cordon of shrives.

Sylvestris lets his gaze splinter.

A man has fallen. A vizard lies in a tangle of robes. Erigeron Intricata.

A dark-skinned Cat holds a bloody dagger. Sylvestris recalls her name just as the piercing voice of Althea Circium confirms it: "Nyssa! What have you done?"

"Death to the tyrants!" Nyssa Circium cries. "Long live Viridis Liberatrix!"

People gasp and cover their ears at the sound of the forbidden name.

Nyssa leaps at the Ecclesiarch. She's fast, faster than the shrives, who have been knocked off-balance by the mob. But the old man is faster yet. He's gone in a silver blur.

The shrives recover quickly. Forcing their way through the crowd, they converge on the assassin.

Nyssa's eyes flicker desperately over the crowd. "Join me!" she implores. "Together we can beat them!"

No one stirs.

"Cowards!" she rages. "See how a free woman sells her life!" Brandishing her dagger, Nyssa runs at the nearest pair of shrives. But she has no chance; they disarm and subdue her with the brutal efficiency that is their trademark.

The hospitality hall, jammed only seconds ago, is almost deserted. Serinthe Lacrimata has fled along with her voluptuaries. Persea Valentine and her Household are gone as well. So is Morus Sisymbrium—no doubt hurrying off to warn Azedarach, Sylvestris thinks.

Those who remain look on in shock. Some weep, others make the sign of the Wheel and murmur prayers, others are silent. Cassine

Illicium huddles with her voluptuaries, sobbing. Althea Circium and her Household are already under arrest. When Althea begins shrilly to protest her innocence, a shrive steps up and knocks her to the floor with a blow that sends her wig flying.

The body of Erigeron Intricata has been turned faceup. He's been stabbed through the heart. Sylvestris is surprised how little blood there is. Just a dark trickle down the front of the vizard's robe. The deathly stench of lethium pervades the room.

The shrives raise a battered and bloodied Nyssa to her knees, holding her arms, which seem to be broken, tightly behind her back. She's barely conscious, moaning. Her wig is gone.

The Ecclesiarch approaches. If his hand shakes now, as he extends it, it's not with the tremors of age.

"Your Holiness," begins one of the shrives.

"We must interrogate," continues another.

"Silence!" The voice brooks no argument. The shrives say no more.

The Ecclesiarch does not offer his ring to be kissed. He punches Nyssa in the mouth. She spits defiantly. Then a virescent glow plays over her bruised and bloody face. Her eyes grow wide as if with sudden understanding. A gurgling rises in her throat. The shrives release her; she falls heavily to the floor. A series of progressively worsening convulsions wrack her body as if flesh is warring with bone. Finally, in the midst of a horrendous spasm, Nyssa stiffens.

She's rigid, all flexibility fled. But the force behind the muscular contractions, though blocked, doesn't go away; in the tense silence of the hall, Nyssa's bones can be heard groaning and creaking like wood beneath a relentless accumulation of pressure. Her mouth is open. Her tongue protrudes stiffly, but no sound emerges.

Her eyes, however, are screaming.

Sylvestris sees Rumer Illicium standing near the doors of the hall. Her wig has been knocked askew, but she doesn't seem to notice, tugging instead at the robes of the Cat beside her, the same Cat whose beauty Sylvestris found so mysteriously moving when he caught a glimpse of her earlier.

It moves him still. Even more so. For her expression is unchanged, as if none of this has the power to touch her. Not even Rumer's tugging can make an impression. She has a blank, unformed quality that reminds Sylvestris of a simular. An emptiness waiting to be filled. Or, not an emptiness, but a multiplicity, like the range of possibilities coexisting in a moment of grace before the choice that must banish all but one of them.

Now, as the bones of Nyssa Circium snap, stabbing like daggers through her skin, Sylvestris sees a tear well up in the Cat's green eye. It rolls down her cheek, past the red teardrop tattooed there, mark of the House Lacrimata. And he knows: he's found her, the one he's looking for.

He struggles to free himself from the silver gloves and the netting. The pain is excruciating; disengagement is meant to be a slow and respectful ritual, with litanies offered up as each simular is vacated. He could make Stilskin or one of the others call out from the stage for the shrives to detain the girl, but with the Ecclesiarch present that doesn't seem wise. Morus told him that Azedarach wants the girl for himself.

Sylvestris is still hooked into the net when he sees Rumer finally succeed in pulling the girl out of the hall.

The Ecclesiarch sees it, too. He looks up sharply from Nyssa's still-twitching remains. "Who has just left?"

"Two Cats, Your Holiness," replies a shrive.

"Shall we fetch them back?" asks the second of the pair.

"No. But don't let anyone else leave. Seal the House; in fact, seal all the Houses. Confine the Cats until they can be questioned—that includes the voluptuaries and odalisques. And make haste! In another hour Beauty will be upon us!"

"Yes, Your Holiness." The two shrives make the sign of the Wheel and are gone.

ELEVEN

"Quickly! Inside!" Faint with terror, Rumer pushes Rose into her chamber and locks the doors behind her. To assassinate the Ecclesiarch: it's madness! Heresy! Everything Rumer is, everything she's been conditioned to be, recoils in horror.

But Rose seems unmoved. She stands quietly, her lovely face untroubled. Rumer thinks how utterly her chamber is altered by Rose's presence. Suddenly everything is new and strange. All the gifts bestowed by her clients or sisters, each one cherished for a reason known only to her, have become Rose's now. The pasts that made them precious, lingering like the embers of an old fire, have been blown out by Rose.

Rumer feels her heart crumbling like a hill of sand in the face of a wind that began to blow the instant she first set eyes on Rose. Now, as the grains of her heart are stripped away, something is uncovered. Something that was present in her before the vizards came with their soft hands and sharp scalpels to begin the beauty treatments. A thing buried so deeply and for so long, under layers of conditioning, that she forgot it was there, like an oasis hidden in the wastes of a desert.

Rose is the wind; Rose the oasis.

Rumer can't stop trembling. She wants to throw herself on Rose and cover her with kisses. She wants to rip the clothes from her body and ravish her. And she wants to abase herself before her. All at once.

So this is a passion, she thinks. She's crying. It's nothing like how she imagined it would be. Hoped it would be. She's sick, feverish. Yet her body is ripe with longing.

"Won't you say something?" she asks Rose, her voice breaking. "I love you; I'm yours; command me."

But Rose doesn't answer.

Or perhaps Rumer only imagined speaking. She can't tell. She hugs herself, shivering as she approaches Rose. Rumer is the older of the two, yet she still has to look up. She's mesmerized by Rose's eyes, so green and deep. She thinks of plants, of trees, of life bursting forth in its willful and inexhaustible profusion even in the heart of a desert.

Rumer stands on tiptoe and kisses Rose hard. All the sly technique she learned from Aralia has left her now; she feels like a novice kissing someone for the very first time. And though Rose does not respond—her lips indifferent, her tongue limp, without an answering curiosity—it's wonderful, overwhelming. The most exciting, the most expressive, kiss that Rumer has experienced in a life replete with kisses. She could die from happiness. Die.

She pulls away, dizzy. Soon the shrives will come. She knows that whether or not she will survive the purge is entirely a matter of chance. Innocence is irrelevant. Anyway, there's no such thing as an innocent Cat. These may be the last unfettered moments of her life, the ones she will cling to for comfort when she suffers the torments of the Six Hundred.

Rumer takes Rose by the hand and leads her to the bed. She sits her gently down. Then, with all the tenderness she can manage at this moment, a tenderness that continually threatens to escape and run wild, causing her hands, her whole body, to shake—as if tenderness, too, has its violent side, the one shading into the other by imperceptible degrees that remain mysterious even in the obsessive questionings of regret—Rumer undoes the fastenings of Rose's wig and lifts it from her. Then she removes her own wig, but hurriedly now, roughly, tearing it off, no gentleness to spare for herself.

She runs her fingers over Rose's clean-shaven head. A thrill courses through her as the last hard bits of her heart are broken up like the shell of a crab from Arpagee. She bends to kiss the smooth, hard place above one ear, marked by a small pink scar, perhaps from the panderman's scissors. She traces the scar with her tongue. It tastes of salt.

Rumer's legs decide they will no longer support her. She sinks onto the bed with a moan she doesn't hear. She slides one of Rose's hands between her thighs and clamps them tight, then pulls Rose down beside her and searches out her mouth with her own. She kisses blindly, thrusting deep with her tongue, wanting to squeeze herself into this beautiful other, to be swallowed up in Rose completely.

But Rose doesn't return Rumer's kisses or caresses. Her lack of response is too complete to be a purposeful withholding, an oath sworn to Viridis as Serinthe had said. No, Rose is damaged, a casualty of the beauty treatments perhaps. Rumer wants nothing for herself, only to give pleasure the only way she knows. She'd perform the entire *ars erotica* if she could! But she knows that even then Rose wouldn't wake; or her body would, but only her body.

Yet in the face of futility, Rumer feels a desperation to consecrate this moment, this passion, with words. It goes against her training and experience to believe there can be an eloquence in words not present in kisses. But perhaps, after all, there may be.

Rumer pulls just far enough away so that she can see Rose's face clearly. Already those features have imprinted themselves where her heart used to be.

Rose lies on her back. She stares up at the ceiling with a placid gaze, breathing calmly despite lips smeared and swollen by the force of Rumer's kisses, her silks in disarray.

"I love you," Rumer says. "I love you, Rose."

Rose turns her head; her green eyes narrow as if she's looking for something or someone. Then she's gone again where Rumer can't follow, though she would if she could. Follow.

Rumer thinks of the cliffs of Arpagee that stand at the low end of the world, turning back the sea. The sea dashes itself against those high rocks continually, without a prayer of getting past. Now she understands the restless longing that impels the sea. It lifts her on its headlong wave and pushes her, again, toward Rose.

The corner of a gray piece of paper is jutting from the pillows by Rose's head. Curious, Rumer pulls it out and unfolds it. The name VIRIDIS LIBERATRIX leaps out from the ink-smeared page. She drops it before she can read any more.

It's the pamphlet Aralia showed her. The one put out by the heretics. Aralia must have left it.

The shrives, she thinks. The shrives will come. And when they do, they'll find it.

Rumer retrieves the pamphlet. There are matches beside her bed. The paper burns quickly. When it's done, she mixes the ashes into the soil of one of her plants. Then she looks at her dirty hands and sighs. It's no use; she's destroyed the pamphlet, not her memory of it. The shrives will use their drugs to compel that memory to testify against her.

Rose is still lying on the bed. Her eyes are open but give no evidence of sight. She might be blind. Or sleeping. A thousand kisses could rain upon those eyes and still they would refuse to acknowledge anything but air and sunlight, Rumer thinks. She's like a beautiful flower: asking nothing, giving everything. The shrives will pluck her petals one by one.

Rumer runs to the bed and clasps Rose in her arms. "I won't let them! We'll run first! Yes, we'll run!"

But how? demands some sensible part of her. *And where?*

"I don't care," Rumer answers aloud. She maneuvers Rose to her feet. Together they start for the door.

"You won't get far."

Rumer is so surprised, she nearly falls. The voice is coming from one of her closets. She can't tell which one. She backs away, shielding Rose. "Who's there?"

A door swings open, and a grinning Aralia steps into the room. "Have you changed your mind so quickly, Rumer? Decided to join us after all?"

Rumer can only shake her head. She hardly recognizes her old friend. Instead of the transparent silks and gaudy feathers of a voluptuary, she wears a loose-fitting outfit of black that not only conceals her distinctive figure but makes it hard even for Rumer to tell that she's a woman at all.

"Quite a bit of excitement at the gathering, I hear. A pity I had to miss it. And even more of a pity that Nyssa missed."

"You *knew* about the assassination!" Rumer gasps. "What do you want? Why did you come back for me?"

Aralia takes another step. "But I haven't come for you, Rumer. Though you're welcome to join me if you like; you know I'm fond of you. It's *her* I've come for. Rose Lacrimata."

"I won't let you take her!"

Now it's Aralia who appears surprised. "Why, Rumer! Are you in love? Don't bother to answer; I can see by your face that it's true. A passion! In this day and age! How old-fashioned!"

"What do you want with her?" Rumer asks suspiciously.

"Have you noticed her eyes?" Aralia asks in turn. "Do they remind you of anyone?"

Rumer shrugs. "They're green." Then she says: "You mean Saint Viridis Lacrimata?"

And Aralia, completing Rumer's total disorientation, drops to one knee. "Viridis Liberatrix," she says.

Rumer hugs Rose close as Aralia claps her hands and two figures glide from the closet. They, too, are dressed in black, and at first Rumer takes them for shrives, certain she's been betrayed.

But then she sees they are women; Cats, to judge by their tattoos. One bears the silver porpoise of Circium at her neck, the other the red heart of Valentine upon one cheek. The women's hair is their own, black as their loose outfits and cut short as a skullcap. They carry thyrsi.

Both women drop to one knee like Aralia.

"Blessed Viridis!" says the Circium.

"That I have lived to see this day!" says the Valentine. "Speak to us!"

But it is Rumer who answers: "No. You're wrong."

"Quiet," says Aralia, getting to her feet. "Let her answer for herself."

"She won't."

"Why? What have you done to her?"

"She's taken a vow," Rumer says, not because she believes it, but because she can't think of anything else. "She won't say or do anything until All Saints' Eve. You see how devout she is. Not a heretic like you!"

Aralia laughs at that. But the other two women appear angry and suspicious.

"She's lying!" says the Valentine.

"Let's kill her," the Circium suggests. "Make an example for the others. She'll never break her conditioning anyway. The vizards got their claws too deep in her."

"There were some who held that opinion about you, Lyra," says Aralia. "Or have you forgotten."

The woman blushes and scowls but says no more.

"I just saved your life, Rumer," Aralia cheerfully informs her. "What have you got to say?"

"Go away. Leave us alone."

"Leave you to the tender mercies of the shrives? No, I couldn't do that. You know how fond I am of you. You're coming with us, Rumer. I advise you to come quietly. Lyra here would like nothing more than for you to put up a fight. Isn't that right, Lyra?"

Lyra grins.

"But where are we going?" asks Rumer, holding tight to Rose, who seems oblivious to everything, a trait Rumer can only envy at this point.

"Why, into the Pit, of course."

Seeing the look of horror that settles over Rumer's face at this information, Lyra Circium and the Valentine begin to laugh. They continue to laugh as, gesturing with their thyrsi, they herd Rumer—and Rose, who comes docilely along—into the closet.

Rumer sees that the back of her closet is false. There's some sort of passage behind it; she feels a faint, warm breeze and smells a dampness that makes the familiar perfume of her life seem like a polite lie.

Then Aralia, who enters the closet last of all, shuts the door behind her, and everything goes dark.

ALL SAINTS' EVE
PART II

ONE

"Come back to bed, Nuncle," implores the weary voice.

The Ecclesiarch grunts a noncommittal reply. He stands with his naked back to the bed, touching the cool crystal of the window with fingers and forehead. Instead of his own reflection, he sees the face of Erigeron Intricata. The vizard's murder was to have been prelude to his own, and though he escaped by the grace of Ixion, the nearness of death has left the Ecclesiarch badly shaken, more than he'd realized at the time.

After returning from the House Illicium, he'd dismissed his shrives and hurried here, to this most secret chamber of his heart, where the only relief available to him waits day and night to be unlocked with a golden key. He surrendered to it blindly, until the fear and anger began to seep from his bones and he was able to think clearly again. That was less than five hours ago, but already it seems like turnings.

Across the city, across the whole Hierarchate, men are sleeping now, guarded by their women as Beauty stalks the night. But where is a man safe from women? the Ecclesiarch asks himself, thinking again of Nyssa Circium, remembering how she sprang at him, her knife wet with the vizard's dark blood. Does such a sanctuary exist?

He sighs. It's his own fault; he's spent too much time worrying about that dangerous bungler, Azedarach. Now the heretics have taken advantage of his inattention and grown more daring than at any other time in memory.

Damn the treacherous bitches! They're worse than Furies with their crazy talk of Viridis Liberatrix: they claim to follow the Spinner, but it's

Maw they truly serve. They fill the heads of women with dangerous ideas and forbidden desires. Not only Cats, but virtuous women, too: wives and mothers and daughters. He's tolerated them for too long.

He'd hoped to make use of them against Azedarach. He'd sent spies among them to influence their actions on his own behalf. But that had been a mistake. Spies can be turned. The heretics are to blame for the strangely stylized murders of Iber Arvensis and the rest, as well as for the assassination of Erigeron. But what infuriates him more than anything, more even than the attempt on his own life, is that, through ignorance, the heretics have upset his most carefully laid plans.

In just seven days, on All Saints' Eve, Erigeron was to have launched a rebellion against Azedarach. What better way to commence the Season of Chastenings? But now the Ecclesiarch will have to forgo that auspicious confluence and start planning from scratch unless he can find someone to take Erigeron's place. And that won't be easy on such short notice, for secrecy is everything and success far from certain.

But first he'll have his revenge: tomorrow he'll unleash a purge such as Quoz has never seen and will not soon forget. Not only the High Houses, but the shrives—who are responsible for his safety—will suffer. But the hammer of his wrath will fall most heavily upon the heretics. Let them hide in their squalid burrows beneath the city! He knows their haunts.

"Nuncle, I'm thirsty."

The Ecclesiarch turns from the window and moves with a kind of shuffling limp to where a pitcher and two fluted glasses rest upon a table within easy reach of the bed. A jingling sound accompanies his steps. The pitcher contains a cool, clear wine redolent of aspergine. He fills a glass, then, careful not to spill a drop, lowers himself to the edge of the bed.

There comes a noise of shifting bedclothes. A slight, pale figure sits up, shedding shadows like water. A boy.

A boy with no eyes: his sockets smooth as hollowed marble in a face that otherwise resembles the Ecclesiarch as he might have looked once upon a time.

Around his smooth neck, the boy wears a thin gold chain, and dangling from this chain is a small golden key. His arms hang limply at his sides, as though he's exhausted his strength in the act of sitting up. He is, perhaps, twelve. His *Trachaea* still before him.

The Ecclesiarch cups one hand behind the boy's neck and with the other brings the glass to his expectant, slightly parted lips. But suddenly, as the Ecclesiarch leans forward, the gold chain about his ankles snaps tight, bringing him up short. His hand slips, and the contents of the glass splash over the boy's hairless chest and lap.

"Ooof!" Flailing out, the boy knocks the glass from the Ecclesiarch's hand. It shatters on the tiles of the floor. "I'm all wet!"

"Forgive me, Sium," says the Ecclesiarch in a low and trembling voice. "My chain is tangled . . . "

The boy flounces back onto the bed. "Lick it off."

Slowly, the Ecclesiarch lowers his head to the boy's fluttering chest. His sense of smell, rendered highly acute by the minute doses of metheglin that sustain him, detects, in addition to wine and aspergine, the boy's musky sweat and other, more intimate odors, all of which combine to make his head spin.

He extends his tongue. A moan escapes him as he begins to lick away the wetness. Tears start to his eyes. The hard knot of his rage melts like butter.

"Lower, Nuncle." The boy giggles, squirming. "I'm all sticky!"

Never has the Ecclesiarch known such bliss. The bliss of self-surrender, humiliation actively invited and willingly endured. It's as if he's a boy once more, assisting his mother, a voluptuary in the House Lacrimata. As he opens his mouth, he spreads his legs wide, and the chain between his ankles stretches taut, tightening the leather noose around his neck. Now, as he works, he scissors his legs, so that the noose alternately tightens and loosens.

Like all servants of the Church, the Ecclesiarch is a gelding. That prodecure—and others equally severe—has left him incapable of even an erection. But this stratagem—which he learned, like so many valuable things, from watching his mother—enables him to achieve a sensation akin to the tension and release of orgasm . . . or so he imagines.

The boy discharges with a faint shudder and gasp, as if surprised by the workings of his body. The Ecclesiarch pulls away, holding the single hot bead on his tongue for a moment, his eyes shut tight the better to savor not the taste but the memory that comes with it: of the games he and his fellow acolytes played under cover of darkness in the days before the vizards removed their testicles and reduced their penises to limp and useless noodles. How simple and innocent things were then, he thinks. What did we know of heretics or that harsh mistress metheglin, we boys intent only on coaxing forbidden pleasures from between each other's thighs?

He pulls the noose tight, and a darkness rises up in him like the night, haunted by a wisp of memory like Beauty, the sound of an older acolyte whispering his name, Sium, and the smell of his own semen on the boy's hot breath.

The Ecclesiarch lifts the remaining glass from the table and spits into it. He fills his mouth with wine straight from the pitcher and then spits again. He forbids himself the pleasure of swallowing even such a tiny pearl as this not because it would endanger his strict regimen of metheglin but in order to inure himself to other, more difficult sacrifices.

"What an old man you must be, Nuncle," comes the drowsy voice of the boy who bears his former name.

"Ever so old." The Ecclesiarch lies back on the bed and lets the boy's fingers wander across his face. His fingertips are like ice.

"I wonder if I shall ever be old as you."

"Only the Spinner knows."

"I wish I could see your face. See what it looks like to be old."

"Would you have me grow you a new pair of eyes, Sium?"

"Oh! Could you, Nuncle?"

The Ecclesiarch laughs softly.

Soon the boy is asleep. Not from exhaustion or sexual release but the effects of aspergine. In the last two turnings, since the Ecclesiarch acquired the boy from his father, Erigeron Intricata, in exchange for a promise of the Serpent Throne, and plucked out the boy's eyes so he would never know who kept him—using lethium to rob him of his name, Malus, and replace it with another, Sium—the boy has become an addict. He's easier to manage that way; aspergine addicts spend two-thirds of the day asleep. They scarcely age at all during that time, metabolism slowed to a crawl.

The Ecclesiarch lies quietly next to Sium who was Malus, listening to his shallow, drawn-out breathing. The boy is truly an orphan now, yet he will never have the chance to mourn his murdered father. The name Erigeron Intricata would mean nothing to him even if, by some chance, he heard it here in his gilded cage, where he sees nothing, hears nothing. His world consists and will consist for the rest of his life of a darkness filled by one person: his mysterious benefactor, his "nuncle," whose actual identity is no more known to him than his own.

As always, the boy's breathing soothes the Ecclesiarch, helps him think. He's calm now. His anger gone. Perhaps things aren't so bad after all, he reflects. Erigeron was a liability. A lethium addict, he never would have lasted long on the doses of pure metheglin the Sovereign must ingest. The Ecclesiarch had only made use of Erigeron in the first place in order to gain possession of his son. It had disgusted him to discover a man who desired the Serpent Throne so greatly he would pander his son—and, in doing so, forgo the future of his line—to get it. But he'd agreed to the vizard's terms, already in love with Malus: or, rather, with Sium, whom he recognized in Malus, lying dormant there, a sleeping beauty needing only the kiss of knife and needle to be awakened.

But now the heretics, all unknowing, have done him a kind of service. Their timing could have been better, but even so, what had seemed hopeless moments before suddenly seems like a blessing, a golden opportunity for the Ecclesiarch to choose a man he can trust and work with. It's harmony the Ecclesiarch desires, not power, for he already possesses all the power he wants.

The Ecclesiarch weighs likely candidates with his usual care: this one, despite an excellent mind, is too fond of the Cats, a weakness responsible for undoing many a Sovereign; that one, eminently suited, is too old; this other, although he shows promise, is still too young. He rejects them, one by one, until there's no one left.

And then it comes to him. He's been looking in the wrong places. There is one man perfectly suited to the responsibilities of the Sovereigncy. A man of character and strong will from the highest levels of the nobility. A man who, without exaggeration, may be said to hold in his hands already the myriad strings of the Hierarchate and so is no stranger to the temptations of power. A man of unimpeachable integrity to his friends and enemies. A man who just happens to be loyal to Azedarach.

But loyalties can be changed. If based on reason, they can be reasoned away. If based on emotion masquerading as reason, so much the better, for then they can be redirected, even reversed, by subtle appeals to the heart, which cares only for the illusion of its own constancy. Only preserve that illusion, and there's no betrayal it won't embrace.

Pleased at having come to such an audacious decision, the Ecclesiarch whispers a command. The thyrsis brightens in response. He leans on one bony elbow and gazes with amazed possessiveness on the eyeless face of sleeping Sium, which by some miracle resembles his own face so completely. It was that resemblance—unexpected, unlooked for—which, after two thousand turnings, awoke in him a longing for his long-forgotten youth.

Perhaps he cannot possess his youth again. But he can possess this boy, this living bridge into his own past. He leans down and brushes the flesh of the empty eye sockets with his rough lips. Then he slips the gold chain from around Sium's neck. The boy grasps the key in his fist as he sleeps; the Ecclesiarch must pry his cold fingers apart to free it, which he does gently, with the tenderness of a parent.

Then, with a barely audible click, he unlocks the chains that bind his ankles and transfers them to the boy's ankles. He replaces the key and chain around his own neck and rises from the bed.

It's early, he knows. Hours yet until the dawn. But he won't, can't, sleep: another blessing and curse of metheglin. Mindful of the broken glass littering the floor, he begins methodically to dress while, behind him, Sium whimpers in his chilly sleep.

TWO

The suffocating darkness that falls after Aralia shuts the false back of Rumer's closet is lifted an instant later when Lyra Circium and the Valentine kindle their thyrsi. Rumer finds herself in a short, tight passage leading to stairs that spiral down out of sight. These Lyra and the Valentine descend, their bootheels clanging loudly, as if against metal. Aralia elbows Rumer to follow.

Rumer hesitates, holding tightly to Rose, who shows all the awareness of a sleepwalker. "Are you really taking us to the Pit, Aralia?"

"Poor Rumer!" Aralia laughs, her teeth flashing white against her skin, which seems darker than usual amid the shadows. "You're already in the Pit and don't know it."

"I don't care about me; just don't hurt Rose."

"Hurt her? This Cat you call Rose is Viridis Liberatrix, Lacrimata reborn, no longer Our Lady of the Perpetual Sacrifice but the redemption of sacrifice. We love and cherish her just as you do Rose. You see, Rumer, we're not so different after all: what you call heresy is only love."

Confused, Rumer starts down the stairs, one hand on the railing, the other on Rose, who moves with an easy glide, as if, should Rumer let her go, she'd float all the way to the bottom.

After a few moments, they come to a platform and enter a passage that slopes sharply down. Red symbols appear at intervals on the pale walls, briefly visible in the light of the thyrsi. It seems to Rumer that Lyra and the Valentine are following the marks, but she's never before seen their like and can make no sense of them now.

Rumer is completely disoriented; even if she and Rose did escape somehow, she knows she'd never be able to find her way home. "Is the whole city honeycombed with passages like these?" she asks Aralia, less from curiosity than to hear a familiar voice.

"Quoz is called the Crystal City, but every crystal has its flaws," Aralia replies softly. "These are the flaws of Quoz. Your closet isn't the only one with a false back, Rumer. We're like fireflies: no place is closed to us."

"But where do they come from? Did you make them?"

Lyra Circium's laughter barks from ahead. "Who but the Spinner could craft such wonders?"

Maw, Rumer thinks with a shudder. But she doesn't say it. Instead, she asks about a stench that's been growing more unpleasant by the minute.

Again, Lyra answers: "Where' d you think all the shit goes?"

"And the heat?" For it's been growing hotter, too.

"You'll get used to it," Aralia says. "We all do. It's always summer down here."

"It's horrible," says Rumer. "I can't believe you threw away all the comforts of our House for this!"

"There are worse things than the smell of shit, Rumer. At least we're free. And soon the Liberatrix will free all our sisters."

"The shrives will find you. Find us all."

"You'd better pray they don't," Aralia says. "You and Rose are heretics as far as they're concerned. But the shrives don't know these passages as we do. Anyway, it's night in the upper world. Beauty is on the prowl. It'll be morning before anyone comes after us."

"If then," adds Lyra. "The shrives don't like to come down here if they can help it. The Little People, you know."

"But those are just stories!"

"Are they?" asks Aralia. "Maybe every story, no matter how strange, has truth at its heart."

"Have you seen them, Aralia?"

"You don't see the Little People, Rumer. Not unless they want to be seen. We don't bother them, and they don't bother us. But they hate shrives, just as we do. They lure them into ambushes and kill them to the last man if they can."

"How do you know if you haven't seen them?"

"Because we come upon the corpses of shrives from time to time, their vaunted armor split open like a nutshell. Or maddened survivors desperately trying to find their way out. Who else but the Little People could be responsible?"

Rumer lapses into silence, thinking of all she's heard. Clearly, the heretics are more than slightly mad; only children or simpletons believe in the Little People. And yet Aralia is one of them. Her Aralia.

She feels like the Hierarchate is riddled with flaws, some of which, like these passages, can be found and entered with the body, while others allow access only to the mind, the heart. There are flaws you enter, she thinks. And flaws that enter you.

Is her passion a kind of flaw? It dawned in her like a second sun the instant she saw Rose and still hasn't set, holding at the zenith of its rising like the sun on All Saints' Eve. Even here, where the rays of the upper sun can't penetrate, her passion sheds all the light she needs, just as fireflies kindle a tiny sun in their bodies to guide them through the darkness. If that's a flaw, she thinks, it's so deeply a part of her now that she couldn't exist without it. Nor would she want to.

At last, after what seems hours, they stop. As far as Rumer can tell, they are in the middle of a corridor like so many others, with red symbols painted upon gently curving walls. But now Aralia places her hand upon one of the symbols and speaks in a voice too low for Rumer to hear. The symbol begins to glow. There is a grinding noise, and a portion of the wall slides back. Within the chamber thus revealed a thyrsis brightens. Rumer recoils in fright; she's never seen such crafting.

Lyra snickers, pushing her forward. "Go on; it won't kill you!"

"What . . . what is it?"

Aralia shrugs. "There are many such wonders here, Rumer. This will be your chamber for now. Don't worry; I'll be back soon. There's food, water, a bed to sleep in if you choose, and a pot for the necessities of nature."

"You're not taking Rose." It's at once a question and a statement.

"Relax, Rumer. Rose is staying with you. I think we can trust you to look after her. The two of you will be perfectly safe here. This door is the only entrance or exit. It locks from the outside, and only I know how to open it. Now go in; you'll find it cooler."

Cautiously, Rumer leads Rose inside. The air, in fact, is noticeably cooler, although a faint smell of sewage remains. The door closes with a swift, silent glide.

"Aralia!" she calls, striking uselessly against the door with her fists.

"Quiet, Rumer!" comes the muffled reply. "You don't want any passing shrives to hear! I'll be back soon, I promise!"

Then it's just the two of them, her and Rose, as it had been in Rumer's chambers in the House Illicium such a short while ago, before Aralia stepped through the false back of her life to carry her away.

Only this chamber is nothing like her own. It's hardly larger than her closet. There are no chairs, only wooden stools. No flowers or burning incense to sweeten the air. No mirrors in which to admire her reflection; no perfumes or cosmetics to apply. There's a table with a pitcher of water and a bowl of fruit, but the fruit looks waxy in the glare of the thyrsis. There are more symbols upon the walls, like letters in an ornate, forbidding alphabet, the gospel according to Maw.

Pushed into one corner is a mattress with a heavy brown blanket. Rumer leads Rose to this bed and lays her down gently, arranging the blanket to keep the chill away, for the coolness of the air has grown as bothersome as the heat had been. Then Rumer slides beneath the blanket herself, shivering in her thin robes. She wraps her arms around Rose, less for warmth than to keep her from slipping any further away, or, failing that, to be drawn along on the journey.

But Rose is asleep already, and there is no following her. Rumer lies with her eyes closed, listening to the poem of Rose's breathing, drunk with the rise and fall of her chest, the mysterious arousing smell of her. As before, in her chambers, she feels the stirrings of an overwhelming desire, as if the urges to possess and to be possessed are annihilating and giving birth to each other with every beat of her heart. She hooks one leg over Rose's hip and grinds slowly against her, letting the fuse of her clitoris catch fire.

The orgasm breaks before she knows it. She moans, biting down on her lip as her legs clamp tight and her soul finds a false door of its own and flees through it, running down passages that have no bottom, spiraling down stairs of endless joy.

Rumer wakes in darkness. For a moment she's back in her old chambers in the House Illicium. But then the thyrsis comes to life, and the room—or the cell—takes shape around her, just as she remembers it. Rose, too, is unchanged, asleep beside her. She could sleep through the Unspinning itself, Rumer thinks.

Rumer is hungry and thirsty and has to pee. She uses the pot provided, then has some water and, after washing it thoroughly, a surprisingly delicious peach from the bowl of fruit on the table. She brings one for Rose, but, unable to wake her, has that one, too. Licking the juices from her fingers and waving away a firefly drawn by the sweetness—so there are fireflies even here, she thinks—Rumer paces the chamber like a dog in a cage. Is it still night? Have the shrives begun to search for them? And what of Aralia? Why hasn't she come back as she'd promised?

As time drags by, and Aralia shows no sign of returning, or Rose of waking, Rumer, more out of boredom than interest, examines the red symbols adorning the walls of the chamber. The markings appear at irregular intervals, but always at the same height, a little above her head. The same symbols appear again and again, sometimes alone, sometimes in groups of two or more.

All at once Rumer recognizes the symbol on which Aralia had placed her hand to open the hidden door. The symbol resembles a hand; or, rather, perhaps it was grown from the seed of a hand, just as her own body, after the beauty treatments, retained parts of what it had been, what it had started from, though it was that no longer.

Fearfully, but with excitement, Rumer places her hand on the symbol just as she saw Aralia do. Aralia also spoke, and so Rumer whispers a prayer of her own to Saint Viridis Lacrimata, asking for guidance and protection.

A section of the wall slides silently open by vizards' craft. Rumer is so surprised that she nearly falls over.

Behind the wall is a small space crammed with stacks of pamphlets like the one Aralia had left in Rumer's bed. Rumer had hardly been able to bring herself to touch that pamphlet, but now she reaches in and takes one. Immediately, she feels a rush of guilty fear, as if she's being observed. It occurs to her that Aralia could be watching from a spy-hole. But then she thinks angrily, Let her look! Let all the heretics look! She sweeps the walls with a defiant gaze before examining the pamphlet in her hands.

The face of Viridis Lacrimata is visible beneath a veil of dust. Hideous with self-inflicted scars, the face retains no trace of its former beauty save in the soft green eyes. The dust dims their shine a little, but it also smooths the scars, allowing Rumer to see—or, rather, to imagine—how beautiful Viridis had been once upon a time when her passion for Saint Ixion had first awakened, prompting her to give up her sinful life and follow him. How beautiful she'd been then, before the passion of Samsum Oxalis revealed to her the sin of her own beauty, before his ugliness taught her how to remedy that sin.

Rumer looks at Rose sleeping peacefully, as if her sleep has placed an impenetrable lid of glass between her and the world, and it's as if she's seeing Viridis Lacrimata as she was in the very prime of her loveliness, preserved through the turnings by some miracle of vizards' craft. If Viridis were to return, she thinks, surely it would be as Rose.

Rumer wipes away the dust with the palm of her hand, and the picture of Viridis undergoes an awful change. Her expression is no longer serene, beatific despite the harshness of the scars. She's a Fury now: wild, unkempt, bloodthirsty. Her green eyes shine with cruelty rather than compassion.

Above the picture, obscured by dust until now, the name VIRIDIS LIBERATRIX appears. Below is the familiar motto of the Hierarchate, only reversed: "IN MY BEGINNING IS MY END." A picture of a broken Wheel renders the heresy plain.

The blasphemy pierces Rumer's heart like a dagger. She sinks onto the bed. Is this Viridis Liberatrix then? A savage monster, more animal than human? Is this what Aralia and the others believe Rose to be? When they look at her, is this what they see? Will they shape her by some parodic beauty treatment into the antithesis of the kind and gentle saint she resembles, never more so than now, sleeping with the pure innocence of a child?

Bending to kiss Rose on the forehead, Rumer swears it won't happen. She won't let it. She'll keep Rose safe from harm, even at the cost of her own life.

Rumer knows she should throw the pamphlet down, but she opens it instead, for she must learn everything she can now about the heretics if she's to protect Rose. The pages are covered in a tiny black script almost impossible to read. But she holds the pamphlet close to her eyes, determined to wrest meaning from it forcibly, letter by letter.

All you know is a lie, the pamphlet says. *Everything you have been told is false. AWAKE! There is but one truth. One way. Blessed be the Spinner! Blessed be HER holy martyr, Saint Viridis Lacrimata! She who will be born again out of HERWOOD to redeem us with her tears! Blessed be Viridis Liberatrix! AWAKE!*

Even the smallest child knows of the perpetual sacrifice of Viridis Lacrimata. Is it not written in the Lies and Acts *that she plucked out her miraculous eyes and entered Herwood blindly to ransom men from Beauty? That, thanks to her, Beauty comes only at night, when men may guard themselves against it with the help of faithful women? Who among us doesn't know by heart the last words written by so-called Saint Quercus Incana: "Bidding the saints good-bye, she went where even my pen cannot follow, into a darkness of her own choosing, a sacrifice without . . ."*

But without what, Quercus?

Without end?

Without justification?

Without purpose?

The Lies and Acts *does not answer.*

But truth cannot be hidden forever. Truth will prevail though it takse a thousand turnings! A thousand thousand! In the words of Viridis: "Seek, and you shall be found!"

You won't find those words in the Lies and Acts. *So-called Saint Quercus saw to that. And all the other so-called saints. Starting with the worst of the lot, Ixion Diospyros.*

But the true testament of Viridis Lacrimata has survived, passed down in whispers from turning to turning, from mother to daughter, from woman to woman. Now we pass it on.

We, the true Viridians!

On that last night, as she lay in her chambers in the House Lacrimata and waited for the last dawn she would ever see, Viridis summoned her closest disciples to her side and spoke to them for the last time, saying:

"Blessed be the Spinner! Blessed be HER holy name now and forever! As it was in the beginning, is now, and shall be until the Unspinning!

"Daughters and sons of the Spinner, you know what fate awaits me. Because I could not close my eyes to the wickedness of the so-called saints, because I did not keep silent about what I saw, my eyes are to be taken from me by vizards. I say my eyes, but are they mine? Some people speak of my eyes as if they are the source of the miracles that spill from them in tears, forgetting that all we are comes to us through the Spinner. We possess nothing of ourselves. Nothing.

"But how hard that is to remember! Maw, the Prince of Lies, whispers ceaselessly in our ears, and HIS most subtle weapons are four small words: I, me, my, mine. How pleasant to listen to the honeyed voice of Maw! How easy to fall into the sin of pride! I am no better than anyone; indeed, much worse. For I, chosen despite my faults to bear a gift more precious than pure metheglin, forgot how little I deserved it and came, over time, to heed the whispers of Maw. I took a jealous pride in my tears. With every cure, each a greater miracle than the last, I exalted myself higher and higher, until I was on a level with the Spinner. Like the so-called saints, I believed myself to be anointed, infallible, divine.

"But SHE is the eternal source; through HER alone all blessings flow. The Spinner raised me; now SHE brings me low. Blessed be! Truly is it said, 'Man sins, the Spinner spins.'

"Early tomorrow morning, I shall be blinded, stripped naked, and whipped into Herwood, where the Furies dwell. All will be as the Spinner pleases, but I do not think I shall last until the night.

"My sisters and brothers, I have asked you here neither to rail against my fate nor to escape it as some of you would have me do, but to take my leave of you. I know there are those of you who have arranged my escape and have decided to free me from this prison whether I approve of it or not. I do not. Put aside all such ideas. In clinging to me, you embrace only Maw. I shall not go. I am already free."

At that, a weeping and a turning away commenced among the disciples, who could not bear such a loss.

"Why do you do this thing?" asked a tearful young woman named Marin, whom Viridis could not help loving above all the others. It was Marin, as Viridis knew, who had arranged the escape, bribing the shrives with a promise of Viridis's tears.

"Don't be bitter, Marin," Viridis said. "I say to you truly, there is for all things the proper turning. Life, death, rebirth. All of us die with the dying. See, they depart, and we go with them. All of us are born with the dead. See, they return, and bring us with them. If I leave you now, it is only to come again."

The disciples crowded around her, asking when the second coming would occur, and where, and whether her form would be the same or, if not, how they would recognize her.

"You will know me by my eyes," Viridis said. "As for when and where—that knowledge has not been given to me. That only the Spinner knows, as SHE knows all things, from the secret beginning of the world to the time of its Unspinning. But it will be a time of terrible Chastenings, when the Hierarchate is divided against itself and simulars walk freely as it is said they used to do. Then from a lowly place I will come again with my green eyes, and my tears will burn like the stings of fireflies."

Now Marin spoke again: "I do not think any of us will see that day."

Viridis smiled. "Poor Marin, you are right."

"Then what shall we do, Viridis?"

"Prepare the way."

"How? The saints will persecute us. They are strong; where is our strength?"

"There is a power stronger by far than the weapons of shrives or the craft of vizards. Faith, Marin. Faith will sustain you, if you surrender to it. But what lies ahead will not be easy, my brothers and sisters. The road is difficult and narrow. In many places it is poorly marked or blocked altogether. Many of you will fall by the wayside or go astray, some misled by our enemies, others betrayed by weakness and doubt and despair."

"Never!" cried Marin.

Again Viridis smiled. "You yourself will deny me before this night is out."

Marin burned with shame and indignation to hear such an unjust thing from the woman she revered above all others, the woman she had risked so much to rescue—only to be refused—the woman she was prepared to die for at that moment if necessary.

"Come, Marin," Viridis said. "To know all is to forgive all. The Spinner has more faith in us than we have in ourselves. What you do this night out of anger and fear will not outweigh your service in the past or in turnings yet to come."

Then the disciples took their leave of Viridis. She embraced them each in turn and blessed them with her tears. When the wetness touched their skin, they gasped, filled suddenly with a new and stronger faith than they'd ever known. Those who were ill felt the sickness shrivel and die; those who were afraid felt fear give way to confidence, sadness to a sustaining joy. Their love, already strong, grew wider and deeper, as if the tears of Viridis had not sunk into them but they into the tears. The women looked at the men with love and forgiveness, seeing fathers and brothers, husbands and sons. The men looked at the women with love and humility, seeing mothers and sisters, daughters and wives. In themselves they saw each other; in each other, themselves. They saw the truth beyond sex and gender, the single thread out of which all things are spun: love.

At last, only Marin remained in the room.

"Will you not come and kiss me good-bye, Marin?" Viridis asked. "There is not much time left before the dawn."

But Marin turned away. "It's not fair. Why must we wait untold turnings for your return when we have you with us right here and now? So many turnings of death, of suffering worse than death. Why must they be? There's no room for women in the Hierarchate of the saints; we can be wives or whores, nothing more. Is that what you fought for, Viridis? Is that why so many of us sacrificed life and limb in the war against the Furies? The people venerate you. They fear the saints but don't love them. If you lead, they will follow. And not just women: men, too. This new weapon of the Furies, the scent called Beauty that rises out of Herwood at all hours of the day and night, has thrown the saints into a panic. The time to act is now. Your tears can cure us of this plague of saints! I beg you, Viridis! Let me save you!"

And Viridis answered: "Who can judge the Spinner? Which of us has sat at HER Wheel? HER ways can seem hard and unjust, I know. Do you think it is easy for me to give up my eyes, Marin? No longer to see the beautiful things of the world, each of which reflects the face of the Spinner like a perfect mirror? Do you think it is easy to go blindly into Herwood, knowing the kind of death that awaits me there? It is not easy. But the Spinner asks no more of us than we are able to give."

"I don't care about the Spinner! It's you I love!"

"Poor Marin. I know you do. But don't you see? It's the Spinner you love, reflected in me. Just as I love the Spinner in you."

"Viridis—"

"If you would take leave of me, do it now, for the saints will be coming soon."

"I won't!" Marin shouted. "You care only for yourself, Viridis! All your talk of the Spinner: it's selfishness masked in piety. You'd rather be a martyr than a leader. Betray us if you want, but I won't be a part of it!"

With that, Marin stormed from the room, leaving Viridis to her fate. Outside, the two shrives standing guard, whom Marin had bribed to help in the escape, blocked her way.

"Is she not coming?" asked one.

Marin pushed past them. "She's a fool!"

"What of your payment?" called the other. "You promised us a vial of her tears!"

"Get them from her yourself!" she cried. "She's no longer any concern of mine!"

Suddenly Marin realized that Viridis's prediction had come true: she'd denied her. At that, the dam of her hurt and anger crumbled, and tears came pouring out. As she ran blindly through the halls of the House Lacrimata, the voice of Viridis filled her ears:

"My task is over, Marin. Yours is just beginning. Remember all that I've told you! Remember!"

And Marin knew, as if she'd seen it herself, that, to stop the saints from taking her eyes and perverting their healing powers through vizards' craft, Viridis had gouged them to jelly.

The next time Marin saw Viridis was the following day. Disguised in a hooded cloak, she stood among silent thousands to watch as Viridis was whipped into Herwood by a pair of shrives. After she disappeared into the woods, a colossal cheer arose: a cry of gratitude, not hate, for the saints had announced that Viridis embraced her sacrifice willingly, giving her life in exchange for an end to Beauty.

Only Beauty didn't end. It changed. It no longer came randomly, at irregular intervals, but always at the same time, as if summoned by the setting sun. Beauty rose that night, as it has risen every night since and will continue to rise until the coming of Viridis Liberatrix.

The next day, the shrives began a purge of all Viridis's followers. Fewer than half were found. The others, led by Marin, fled to the trackless caverns beneath the city.

There they are still.

Waiting.

Thus ends the true testament of Viridis Lacrimata.

Blessed be the Spinner! Blessed be HER holy name now and forever! Blessed be HER holy martyr, Saint Viridis Lacrimata, who will be born again out of Herwood! Blessed be Viridis Liberatrix, whose tears will redeem us! As it was in the beginning, is now, and shall be until the Unspinning!

AWAKE!
SEEK, AND YOU SHALL BE FOUND!!
THE LIBERATRIX COMES!!!

Rumer closes the pamphlet and lets it fall to the floor. Her heart is beating furiously. Once again she has the feeling of being watched. *All you know is lies*, the pamphlet said. But perhaps everything is a lie, even that. Perhaps there's no truth, only ever-finer gradations of lying, grays edging into a black as impenetrable as night.

Rumer notices suddenly that her hands are smudged with ink from the pamphlet. She scrubs them clean in water from the pitcher. But even then she feels dirty, as if the ink has sunk beneath her skin, where no water can reach, to stain her soul forever.

THREE

"The Blessed Sovereign will see you now."

Sylvestris bows to the shrives. Turning sharply on their heels, the pair conducts him through a series of chambers, each one more splendid than the last, each furnished with courtiers who pass their slight, decorative lives in the struggle to reach the chamber beyond. The rustling of their silks as Sylvestris is led past is like the sound of butterflies at war.

There are other insects as well: lost souls bearing thick petitions that will never be granted or even read; lawyers pursuing appeals for clients long dead or—hoping to get a head start—not yet born; sons in search of fathers; fathers looking for sons; Cats summoned on a whim, who, arriving at the Palace of the Chambered Nautilus in obedience to a command already forgotten, wait in vain to be given leave to depart, imprisoned behind bars of courtly etiquette that prevent them from making their predicament known and condemn them to lives of indescribable solitude amid the frantic if circumscribed gaiety of those as trapped as themselves . . . which is to say everyone. All of them breaking against the sovereign indifference of Azedarach like waves against the cliffs of Arpagee.

They look at Sylvestris with envy and disdain, joy and good fellowship, with all the emotions the human heart is able to counterfeit so well, and with those other emotions, less numerous perhaps but no weaker for that—on the contrary—which it cannot, for all its cunning, disguise.

To Sylvestris, they are ephemeral as dreams. More so even, for while dreams often linger in the mind, influencing not just feelings but actions, too, these people do not touch him in any way, except when one of his senses bumps unavoidably against their existence and, like a man who collides with some unseen or unexpected object in the dark, recoils.

The shrives stop now to open the immense golden doors leading to the throne chamber. They do not glance inside, but instead keep their blue eyes locked on each other, weaving out of this mutual regard an invisible and suspicious veil that must be successfully pierced by anyone wanting to enter into the presence of Azedarach.

Stepping between them, Sylvestris feels a tingling all through his body. As always at this moment, he can't escape the thought that he's being, quite literally, seen through. That each object on his person, each thought in his mind and emotion in his heart, is being laid bare by an instrument as sharp in its way as a vizard's scalpel. That if he's a step away from the Sovereign, he's also a step removed from the Six Hundred.

And it's the same step.

Then he's through. Dazzled by the light of a thousand thyrsi, Sylvestris falls to his knees and presses his forehead to the soft carpet. The spices, perfumes, and incenses that freight the air of the throne room in tangled profusion have insinuated themselves into the fibers of the carpet, yet even so Sylvestris smells the intoxicating reek of pure metheglin that emanates from the Serpent Throne at the far end of the chamber, where Azedarach sits and waits. Sylvestris breathes it in, fortifying himself for the ordeal to come.

For he's failed. Although he found the girl with the eyes of Viridis Lacrimata, she escaped him. He couldn't get free of his simulars in time to stop her from leaving the hospitality hall. And now she's disappeared altogether.

Although he'd come straight to the Palace from the House Illicium, it's taken hours to thread his way through the narrowing inward spiral of passages and chambers leading to the throne room; the demands of court protocol are inflexible. It was evening when he arrived, now it's morning of the following day.

At last he hears himself announced. Sylvestris gets to his hands and knees and begins to crawl, following a blue stripe woven like a path into the carpet. The carpet has a multitude of such paths, each of a different color. Some lead to the foot of the Serpent Throne, others stop at a respectful distance. Still others circle the Throne without stopping, keeping a constant distance or drawing near only to spiral away.

Sylvestris is not alone in the chamber. There are other simularters engaged in their common art, so that the voices of the saints and martyrs enacting scenes from the *Lives and Acts* echo upon the stage of his mind, bestirring his own sleepy simulars.

Voluptuaries perform the *ars erotica* with slow and highly stylized movements, holding the most difficult positions for hours or even days on end, no longer needing to sleep or eat, as if the demands of the body, of time itself, have been transcended. It happens sometimes that two or more voluptuaries become as it were a single entity in the course of these exercises; their bodies, interpenetrating, freeze in place. Then, in the form of suicide known as ecstasia, they slowly waste away until death either puts an end to their congress or elevates it to a higher plane: only the Spinner knows which.

There are men following other paths, mostly vizards and Mouths of God. Some, like Sylvestris, are approaching the Throne, while others, their business concluded, crawl away. From time to time, Sylvestris passes close enough to a fellow traveler to exchange a whispered greeting:

"May Ixion be with you."

"And with you."

Shrives survey the chamber from raised platforms, looking for any deviation, however slight, from the paths. Such an error constitutes unmistakable proof of heresy, proclaiming, to the keen eyes of the shrives, the presence of Maw. Meanwhile, in a section of the chamber specially irrigated to facilitate the efflux of blood and other liquids, two women are being subjected to the Six Hundred: one is Persea Circium, the former odalisque; the other Sylvestris doesn't know. Although his gaze is fixed on the path before him, he hears the women's gibbering cries, the swish and crack of whips, the thud of heavy blows.

Small groups of musicians dispersed throughout the room play upon varied instruments a single composition that evolves as it's played. The musicians embark upon variations that sometimes last for days before finding their way back, as if by chance, to the original theme, a work by Saint Sium Lyrata. Always changing, it remains forever the same, just as new threads pass continually through the Spinner's Wheel to become a part of His grand design. In the tangled complexity of the music, Sylvestris hears a rich and surprising order. Perhaps the whole Hierarchate is supported in that precise, precarious balance, he thinks, crawling along the razor's edge of the path.

At the end of the path, the image of a small blue wheel is woven into the carpet. With eyes downcast, Sylvestris touches his forehead to its exact center; the carpet shiny and almost bald there from other foreheads than his. Dizzy from the scent of metheglin, he waits for the summons of a bell. The silvery tinkle comes at last. He lifts his head with slow reverence and shuffles forward to cover the blue wheel with his knees.

The Serpent Throne towers above him. Sylvestris feels small and vulnerable in its shadow, as if the serpent that gives the Throne its name is about to flex its cavernous wings, dip its huge head from the ceiling, and swallow him in the gaping pit of its mouth.

Azedarach sits upon the Throne like a doll upon a chair. Cradled in his hands is the large silver chalice filled with his metheglin supply. As cupbearer, it's Morus Sisymbrium's duty to hold that chalice, but there's no sign of him now. Sylvestris notes his absence but has no time to consider it further, his attention focused upon Azedarach.

Loose purple robes drape a body as skeletal as a child's exhumed corpse. Above the head—that is, above where the head should be—floats a coruscating diadem given the likeness of a serpent swallowing its tail. This is the Serpent Crown, crafted from the plumes of serpents, which dazzle the eye like lightning leashed in bands of hammered gold.

Below the Crown hangs a veil of wispy cloud or fog that envelops a head, a face; or, rather, a succession of faces, each one gone before Sylvestris can see it clearly. A metheglin-matted beard emerges from this ambiguity to spill down Azedarach's chest and pool in the hollow of his lap. Fireflies cluster there in a slow feasting.

Many turnings ago—or so Sylvestris has heard—the Serpent Crown rendered its wearer wholly invisible. Ixion often availed himself of its power to spy upon the Furies and learn of their plans; it was because of this that they never captured him, not until his mother betrayed him. After Ixion's ascension, his successors, the Blessed Sovereigns, used the Crown to stalk like ghosts among their subjects, rewarding and punishing on the basis of what they saw. But over the turnings, the Crown lost the power to cloak its wearer. And once lost, it couldn't be restored, for no one, not even the most skillful vizards, understood the secret of the Crown's ancient crafting. Now the Crown blurs the face of its wearer but cannot make him disappear from sight.

Or can it? Sylvestris isn't so sure. Perhaps Azedarach, like his predecessors, strolls invisibly through the corridors of the Palace and the streets of Quoz. Sylvestris wouldn't be a bit surprised. When it comes to Azedarach, he's found it pays to expect the impossible.

Now Azedarach lifts the chalice to his lips; its silver edge vanishes into the cloud that veils his features, then reemerges to the sound of smacking lips and a low belch of satisfaction.

With each sip, Sylvestris, we see more clearly the Spinner's weaving.

The Sovereign doesn't speak audibly; his voice rings in the mind of Sylvestris like the voice of one of his simulars. But while the simulars, as it were, arise from the inside out, coming from the depths to the surface, the Sovereign's voice enters from outside Sylvestris's head, as though traveling along an invisible tube or wire forcibly inserted through the skull. And once inside, this tube or wire doesn't merely convey the thoughts of Azedarach; it extracts Sylvestris's thoughts from him in turn. Some say this ability stems from the vast quantities of pure metheglin ingested by the Sovereign; others ascribe it to the Serpent Crown, which, being mysterious, seems an inexhaustible font of miracles. But whatever the truth, Sylvestris always returns from his audiences with Azedarach feeling like his head has been squeezed in a vise.

We see the future, Azedarach continues. We see the past. When you've lived as long as we have, the past becomes as cloudy as the future, becomes, indeed, a kind of future, and the future a kind of past.

Sylvestris nods politely. To converse with Azedarach is like playing at a game of riddles with an annoying child, the voice of Saint Stilskin whispers inside him.

With this difference, Saint Rober Viburnum amends: that while the child will merely throw a tantrum if upset, the Sovereign has the power to make the most vengeful fantasies of the child come true.

Sylvestris does not respond to either of them. My most puissant lord, omnipresent in time . . . he begins, also silently, choosing his epithets with care.

Do you know there will be more murders discovered this morning? Azedarach interrupts. It's true. Another five victims will be found disposed of in the same way as Iber Arvensis: the face expertly removed, the body buried in roses. That much we can foresee, but no more: the identity of these assassins is hidden from us. He takes another noisy gulp of metheglin.

Sire, Erigeron Intricata was assassinated by a Cat, a heretic. Perhaps the heretics are responsible for these other killings as well.

The cloud enveloping the Sovereign's head darkens, and the plumes of serpents feathering the Crown flash as if in anger. We need but close our eyes for sweet metheglin to waft us into the minds of our subjects. We see what they see, know what they know. The key of metheglin opens every door, Sylvestris: even those locked and double-locked by vizards. Not even the heretics can hide from us! They are flesh and blood, are they not? Let them cower in their burrows, where our loyal shrives cannot find them and our eye cannot follow. Their thoughts are still part of metheglin's web, along which we scuttle like a spider! By metheglin's light, their minds are as open to us as your own, though considerably less cluttered. Go on, ask your simular's question.

Sylvestris winces. Not for the first time, he wishes he could quiet the clamorous and all-too-often-irreverent voices of his simulars, at least at such moments as this.

But you can't, pipes the insolent voice of Jewel. And what's more, you never, ever will, not until the day you die!

Controlling his anger with an effort, Sylvestris allows the words of Rober Viburnum to ripen in his mind like fruit for Azedarach to pick: I mean no disrespect, Sire. But if you know the thoughts and plans of the heretics, why didn't you stop the assassination of Erigeron Intricata?

The laughter of Azedarach rises into the air like tiny bubbles that burst with an unexpectedly loud noise to release an unpleasant odor. Why should we prevent the murder of a man who conspires against us? In all the Hierarchate, there is only one mind closed to us: that of the Ecclesiarch. The minute doses of metheglin that have kept him alive for thousands of turnings have hardened his mind into a shell even we cannot pierce; we can only know his thoughts indirectly, by observing the thoughts of others. Thus all men are our spies, even Erigeron Intricata. His thoughts gave us a glimpse into the Ecclesiarch's hidden plans. But was it a truthful glimpse or only what our adversary wished us to see? Not knowing, how could we act?

An inflexible paradox is at work, Sylvestris. A moment ago you named us "omnipresent in time." A delightful epithet, but, alas, inaccurate. Your Sovereign is not present in all times at once; only the Spinner may claim that distinction. Metheglin has its own imperious currents; sometimes they waft us into the future, other times into the past. We cannot choose where we go or what we see. Indeed, we are never sure exactly where we are in time. Are we two conversing now, in the present? Or is this, as real as it seems, merely the memory of a conversation already past? Or a glimpse of one yet to come?

He's mad, whispers the voice of Saint Ilex Erythrina in Sylvestris's head.

Too much metheglin, opines Saint Stilskin.

You at least have the illusion of free will, but we may no longer indulge in that comforting self-deception, bound to this Throne as tightly as any man to his bed when Beauty pollutes the night. We cannot act, but only watch.

Why are you telling me all this, Sire? Do you wish me to act on your behalf? You need only command me! Never before has Azedarach spoken to him like this. It's strange and alarming. Sylvestris suspects he's being tested in some way.

Ah, that is precisely what we cannot do! Our actions were taken long ago—now we can only observe their endings. If we address you now in a different way than we have in the past, it simply means the time has come to address you in such fashion, that is all. And if we ask something of you, it is nothing you have not been fated to do always and already. Which brings us to the girl.

Sylvestris bows his head. Now the axe will fall, warns Saint Sium Lyrata. She escaped me, Sire. I failed.

No; it was enough to have seen her.

Who is she, Sire?

The hope of the heretics, Sylvestris. Viridis Liberatrix. Azedarach raises the chalice as though making a toast.

"But that's impossible!" Sylvestris explodes aloud, echoed inwardly by his simulars.

Of course it is, the Sovereign continues calmly. The old legend of the return of Viridis Lacrimata out of Herwood is a myth, no more. But the heretics believe in her, Sylvestris, and because of their belief, they labor tirelessly against us. How can we stop them? No one has ever succeeded. But many turnings ago, when we were younger and more naive, we thought of a way: we would give the heretics the very savior for whom they prayed so fervently.

Ashamed at having spoken aloud, Sylvestris returns to silent speech: Give them? How?

We decided to make her; we say "decided," but even then we were following a pattern we were as yet too blind to see. We commanded certain vizards, whose talents as far surpassed those of their brothers as Quoz surpasses Arpagee, to craft a pair of eyes, eyes that would possess not only the likeness but the miraculous effect of the green eyes of Saint Viridis Lacrimata.

The process took almost two hundred turnings. To craft an artificial eye whose tears would cure all ills; to perfect the technique of implanting it successfully in a human host: these were problems to tax even the vizards of old, the men who crafted the Serpent Crown and the many other marvels we take for granted.

There were many attempts. Many failures. Meanwhile, we began to explore metheglin's glittering web. Lost in the immensity of simultaneous time, we forgot what we had set in motion. But the vizards continued their work. And at last, nine turnings ago, they met with success . . . *qualified* success.

It proved impossible to duplicate the healing tears of Saint Viridis Lacrimata; instead, the eyes were made to secrete tears of *poison*, for the apocryphal testaments circulated by the heretics permit such an interpretation: "Then from a lowly place I will come again with my green eyes, and my tears will burn like the stings of fireflies."

What drivel! Still, our subject was admirably suited: a girl from lowly Jubilar, Rose Rubra by name, who had blinded herself by looking for Saint Ixion in the bosom of the sun, a common act of devotion among the lower orders, who take everything so literally. She was secretly brought here, to the Palace, where the eyes were implanted by vizards. Of course, the eyes did not shed their deadly tears at once; they had been crafted to become activated only after the girl lay with a man for the first time. His seed would trigger the transformation. Once the girl was no longer a virgin, a slow awakening would commence; not just of her eyes, Sylvestris, but of her mind, too, for her conditioning was deep and subtle; no ordinary vizard could expose it.

The treatments were a success. And after the eyes were implanted and the conditioning inlaid, the girl was given lethium and returned to Jubilar to wait for the day of her wedding. The vizards were put to death . . . the killers of the vizards, too, until there was no one in the Hierarchate who knew or suspected what had been done.

Sylvestris's mind is whirling. But why was it done?

You disappoint me, Sylvestris. Azedarach drinks from the chalice. The vizards crafted the girl to be a spy, an agent to act on our behalf, though unknowingly. She will lead the heretics into our hands, where they will be destroyed for good and all. Our plan was simple: after the girl's marriage and deflowering, her husband—having served his sole purpose, like certain insects, by the contribution of his seed—would be arrested by the shrives on a charge of murder.

Murder? Sylvestris thinks of Erigeron Intricata lying lifeless on the floor of the House Illicium.

As no wedding takes place without the presence of Kites, it would be a simple matter to have one or two of the holy sisters disposed of in such a way as to implicate the groom. As a heretic, all his property—including his bride—would be forfeit to the Crown. We would then give her as a gift to one of the High Houses. There the heretics who infest the Houses so thoroughly would take note of our pawn's green eyes, detecting in them the proof of Viridis Lacrimata's return even before her poisonous tears began to flow.

Again, the bubbles of Azedarach's laughter rise. Such was our plan, Sylvestris! Yet all the while we were exulting in its brilliance, a grander plan was unfolding, of which our royal actions constituted but one small part. The Spinner's plan. Great is the Spinner and intricate His spinning! No man is a spinner, Sylvestris, not even your Sovereign: we are all of us spun.

Only metheglin makes the Spinner's weavings sensible to human eyes. In metheglin dreams we saw the true flowering of the seeds we had planted in our youth. We saw how, after the girl's wedding, a Chastening would occur—the last, worst Chastening of the season, Sylvestris; surely you remember it!—thanks to which the murder of the Kites would be witnessed by the very man we had hoped to blame for their deaths. And he, with some presentiment of his fate, would succumb to despair and give himself up to Beauty in the night. The Panderman would come the next morning and take the girl to the market in Kell, where she would be purchased by the House Lacrimata.

And so it came to pass, just as the dreams predicted, less than a turning ago. Thus does the Spinner attend to all things. His is the plan; we are but His instrument.

As I am yours, Sire, answers Sylvestris smoothly. What is it you wish of me?

Azedarach gestures with the chalice. You have noted the absence of our cupbearer, Morus Sisymbrium.

Sylvestris nods.

And have you not wondered at the reason?

It's not my place to ask, Sire. But if it should please you to tell me, I should be glad to know.

The death of Erigeron Intricata has raised a delicate problem for the Ecclesiarch. His revolution lacks a figurehead now. What is the use of toppling us from the Serpent Throne if there is no one to take our place? The Ecclesiarch loves order above all things. He is a creature of certainty; long life has made him cautious. He will not move against our Crown until he secures a replacement for Erigeron.

Sylvestris cannot repress a start; he almost speaks aloud once more, but catches himself in time. Do you mean Morus? A pawn of the Ecclesiarch? I never liked him . . . but that! I can't believe it!

Perhaps he's not yet betrayed us. But soon.

Then we must act quickly, Sylvestris replies. Morus knows about the girl; he'll tell the Ecclesiarch.

That, too, is part of the Spinner's plan.

I don't understand.

Your understanding is not necessary; only your obedience. Serve us well in this, and the position that Morus has thrown away will be your reward.

Sylvestris smiles at the delicious prospect of replacing Morus as cupbearer to Azedarach. Traditionally the office is held by vizards, whose famous distaste for metheglin renders them immune to its temptations—at least in theory—but no law prohibits a simularter from serving. Azedarach need only say the word, and the keys to the metheglin vaults will be placed in Sylvestris's hands. He can practically taste the metheglin now. How shall I serve you, Sire?

Morus has never seen the girl, but you have. You will recognize her when you see her again. And although we cannot know the Ecclesiarch's plans, the plans of the heretics are a different matter. We may be prepared for them at least.

What are they? asks Sylvestris.

Soon they will attempt an act of sabotage. We cannot tell you more—not yet—but you will be waiting there with a troop of shrives we will send to you when the time is right. The shrives will speak a word so that you know they have come from us. That word is, "Rose." Once the heretics strike, the shrives will kill them all, sparing only Rose, who will be with them. We will supply you with a weapon, Sylvestris: another word. A word that, even if spoken in the mildest whisper, will trigger her conditioning. That word is "Galingale."

Galingale? Sylvestris thinks in surprise. As in the story of Celtis and Sersis?

The same. Also the name of the girl's luckless husband. Once you speak it, Rose will lead you to the other heretics. You will capture their leaders and kill the rest. Then you will bring Rose here. She will suffer the Six Hundred in view of the public, at the end of which she will confess that the secret leader of the heretics is—and always has been—the Ecclesiarch.

Thus will our adversary fall. Once again, as in the days of Ixion Diospyros, the Hierarchate will be ruled by a single hand. Our hand. Then the Spinner will smile! The Chastenings will grow still, and the scent of Beauty will cease to rise from Herwood with the night!

At that claim even the voices of Sylvestris's simulars are struck dumb. A moment passes before Sylvestris recovers his voice. You have seen all this, Sire? he asks in wonderment. Is this really how the future will be?

But the Sovereign doesn't answer. Instead, Sylvestris feels him disengage from his mind, the spring of his departed attention leaving behind only a painfully acute vibration. As quickly as that, Sylvestris is dismissed; before he can leave Azedarach, Azedarach has left him, dragged like a kite by the capricious winds of metheglin to a moment or moments he can no longer place in time's well-ordered hierarchy.

Sylvestris hears again the tinkling of a bell. He scoots backward a little way on his knees, then bows from the waist and touches his forehead once more to the center of the blue wheel in the carpet. Then he turns and begins to crawl away from the Throne.

FOUR

The Ecclesiarch looks up from the fat cadaver lying upon—or, rather, spilling over—the clear glass table as a pair of shrives conducts Morus Sisymbrium into the cold, brightly lit room. The shrives bow, then depart. Morus bows and remains.

He appears uncomfortable in his thin robes, as if he's just risen or been made to rise from bed although the sun has been up for hours. Despite sticks of incense burning at the head and foot of the table, the smell of decomposing flesh is strong, almost overpowering. The Ecclesiarch wears a mask scented with aspergine, but Morus has no protection. He breathes through his mouth in tiny sips, as if trying to avoid inhaling a whole lungful of the rotten air while seeking to give the impression there's nothing amiss and that he's breathing this way out of choice, not necessity.

The Ecclesiarch's gaze passes slowly over Morus and settles on the corpse, as if he's blind to the living and can see only the dead. Already the cranium has been opened and the brain removed. Also the eyes. Now the Ecclesiarch resumes work on the chest cavity with a succession of knives and saws neatly laid out on a silver tray alongside the table. He pauses from time to time to offer up the necessary prayers, or to light a fresh stick of incense, or to inject the cadaver with some drug or other. At last he lifts a bloated mass dripping with gore from within the chest and places it carefully into a white container packed in ice and filled with a clear, viscous liquid. He seals the container, makes the sign of the Wheel above it with bloody hands, then beckons abruptly to the vizard.

Tugging his thick beard with one hand, Morus walks up to the table and surveys the cadaver with a critical eye, as though he were judging the work of an apprentice. "I'm impressed," he says. "I had no idea you were so skilled in the harvesting, Your Eminence."

"Coming from you, that's quite a compliment. But I try to keep my hand in, so to speak," the Ecclesiarch says, with the bare bones of a smile. "Periodically, for practice, I will prepare a body for the last rites. Here, though, I confess it's more than that: Erigeron was an old friend. But his death isn't merely a personal blow, it's a loss to the Hierarchate. Men of Erigeron's talents aren't easy to find . . . or replace."

"The heretics grow ever bolder," the vizard comments.

"And not just the heretics," says the Ecclesiarch. He selects a scalpel from the tray and passes it smoothly back and forth through the smoke that dribbles up from sticks of incense burning at both ends of the table.

"Unfortunately, there is little worth harvesting here," he continues, changing the subject, or seeming to. "Erigeron was too fond of lethium, I'm afraid. To tell the truth, he was a dead man before the heretic stabbed him. He just didn't know it. Do you suppose his ignorance of his own terminal condition may have been the very thing that was keeping him alive?"

Morus's hand has yet to leave his beard; it lingers there, fingers idly stroking, while his eyes are fixed on the Ecclesiarch. "To the ignorant, all things seem possible."

"And yet the Spinner can accomplish things which we, in our ignorance, believe impossible." The Ecclesiarch raises the scalpel above the dark pit of the chest, then hesitates as if unsure how to proceed.

"If I may assist," Morus offers.

"On the contrary, it will give me great pleasure to assist you." The Ecclesiarch steps aside, granting Morus his place. "It's not often I have the opportunity of observing a master at work!"

With a slight inclination of his head at the compliment, Morus steps behind the table. He dons a white smock, tucking away his beard with practiced efficiency. Then he fits a mask over his mouth and nose and chooses a different scalpel from the tray. He passes the scalpel through the smoke of the incense and whispers a prayer as the Ecclesiarch did before him; for the harvesting to succeed, the proper prayers must be said, the proper gestures, injections, and incisions made, all in the proper order.

"It's true that lethium addiction leaves precious little to harvest, Your Eminence," he says meanwhile. "Especially in a case like this, where necrosis is so far advanced. I had no idea that Erigeron had let things get so out of control. Of course, I sympathized with his grief at the death of his son, young Malus—we all did—but that was turnings ago. A grief sustained, not to say cultivated, over such a long period is itself an addiction. As a vizard, he should have been sensitive to the dangers of lethium. But we are always slow to detect in ourselves the odor others find offensive! A truism that applies even to vizards, I'm afraid. However, I believe we may find something worth salvaging even here."

"There is always something to be salvaged," observes the Ecclesiarch. "Don't you agree?"

"Yes; provided there is profit in it. Otherwise, only a fool would waste his time."

"Indeed. But then, I am not speaking to a fool," says the Ecclesiarch.

FIVE

Rumer sits exhausted and fearful at the edge of the bed, watching the sleeping girl who, by some miracle, has gifted her with a passion more real than she'd dreamed real could be. Neither her hunger nor her thirst can lessen the pangs of this passion, which she's conscious of even while she sleeps, for even her dreams are all of Rose. But dreams are no true place of meeting; they don't bring Rumer any closer to Rose, only underscore the wall between them. A wall transparent but impossible to scale or pierce or burrow beneath to reach the beauty who sleeps within.

Rose has been sleeping for two days, ever since Aralia brought them to this cell and left, promising to return. Rumer can't wake her, no matter what she does. She's tried kisses and caresses, shouts and whispers. She's shaken Rose. She's prayed. She's begged and cried and pleaded.

Rose's skin is flushed and sweaty, hot to the touch. While there was water, Rumer would dip her fingers into the pitcher and let the drops fall between Rose's blistered lips, feeling as if it wasn't water at all but her own life's blood. But now the water is gone, and Rumer has eaten the last of the fruit, a sour apple that sits heavily in her belly.

Rumer doesn't know what to do. She kisses Rose on the lips, feeling with her lips and tongue the roughness of the skin, the blank, stupid heat of the fever. Yet even through her concern, Rumer feels the stirring of desire. The sheer physicality of her passion embarrasses her: rude, insistent, never to be denied, not even in such dire circumstances as these.

But she can't, won't, deny it; she nuzzles her lips into the scorching hollow of Rose's neck and tastes the thin, stale film of sickness clinging there. She whispers with all the urgency of her longing into Rose's ear, then whimpers a plea for waking that, as always, goes unheeded.

Instead, a sudden pain saws through Rumer's stomach from the undigested apple. She thinks for a moment she'll be sick, and staggers up with a groan. But her legs rebel, and she must cling to the bed for support. The room swims, then slowly steadies as the pain, without vanishing altogether, subsides.

Rumer shuts her eyes and breathes deeply. It's then that she smells it: hanging faintly in the air, the ghost of a familiar perfume. Aralia's perfume.

"I know you can hear me, Aralia," she says, gazing at the section of wall through which they'd entered. "Don't hide from me! Rose is sick, maybe dying; she needs help!"

At that, a different section of the wall slides open and Aralia steps into the chamber. She's changed her appearance again; in place of the baggy robes she wore when Rumer last saw her, now Aralia is dressed in a tight-fitting black uniform reminiscent of the armor of the shrives. Only Aralia doesn't wear a mask, and a broken wheel has been embroidered in green over her left breast.

There are others in the shadowy passage behind Aralia, but Rumer can't discern their features or even their gender. She wonders if every wall here opens to the touch of the heretics, if nothing in this underground world is as solid or permanent as it appears.

"Dying?" Aralia laughs. "No, Rumer; it's not death you're witnessing, but birth."

Rumer doesn't listen; she's crying. "Help her, Aralia, please!"

Aralia gathers Rumer into her arms. Rumer resists at first, then surrenders to that comforting embrace, which has meant safety and shelter ever since her first days at the House Illicium. Aralia's embrace still comforts, though Rumer hates that it does.

"Shh," says Aralia, stroking Rumer's neck with cool and practiced fingers as she guides her back to the bed. "Poor Rumer, it's not easy for you, I know. I've been watching; I no longer doubt your passion for Rose. It's a wonderful, terrible thing, isn't it, a passion? I had no idea love could be such a torment!"

Rumer sniffles, unable to reply. But she's thinking that Aralia still doesn't understand; a passion isn't a torment at all. It's a blissful surrender even in the worst, most painful moments. Or, no, it's beyond torment or bliss, surrender or sacrifice. It's the air she breathes, the skin of her body, the blood throbbing in her veins.

"Look at her," Aralia says meanwhile, her voice full of pride and triumph. "She's not your Rose anymore. She's Viridis Liberatrix now. Or will be, when she wakes."

Rumer shrugs free, the spell of Aralia's embrace broken. "But that's just it, Aralia! She's been like this for two days! Can't you see she's sick? You've got to do something!"

"You're the sick one, Rumer."

"No, just tired is all . . . "

Aralia shakes her head and pushes Rumer gently but firmly onto the bed. "More than that, I'm afraid. The apple you ate was poisoned, Rumer. You're dying."

Suddenly Rumer's pain returns, like a wave that has ebbed only to gather itself for a fresh assault. She tries to get to her feet, but her legs aren't working. A numbing cold is spreading from her belly through her limbs.

Aralia motions, and three women step from the passage into the light of the room. Rumer recognizes Lyra Circium and the Valentine; the third woman is hideously scarred, dressed in black rags . . .

A Kite. A holy Kite, here among heretics. Rumer feels a giddy disbelief, but her fingers instinctively make the sign of the Wheel and she gasps out "Blessed Viridis!" even as she tells herself the poison must be responsible for this bizarre hallucination.

"She is beside you," the hallucination says in a voice as real as anything.

"Help me, holy sister!"

"Only Viridis can help you."

With that, Rumer understands: the Kite is a heretic. She, too, wears the symbol of the broken wheel. Rumer has the sensation of falling; it's as if the floor of the chamber has proved as false as the walls and has opened wide beneath her, sending her into the Pit. All she can say is: "Why?"

But the Kite doesn't answer. She advances toward the bed, guided by Lyra and the Valentine. The black sockets of her eyes glow with such a cold and predatory intensity that Rumer is convinced she's gazing into the heart of her own death. Yet she can't look away.

"Please," she whispers to no one and everyone. "I don't want to die!"

"Who said anything about dying?" snaps the Kite. "Viridis will save you; all you have to do is wake her!"

"I can't; I don't know how!"

The Kite gives an impatient shrug beneath her covering of rags as though it's all the same to her whether such a stupid girl lives or dies provided she's quick about it.

"Aralia . . ." Rumer's vision is gone now. She clutches for her friend's hand, which, however, eludes her. "Help me . . . "

Aralia's soft lips brush Rumer's forehead. "Sweet Rumer, if only I could! But how can you live? You don't believe in our cause; you'd betray us sooner or later. So you must die . . . unless you can wake the sleeper. Only her tears can save you."

A cold, pale flower is blooming at the back of Rumer's throat. Its taste is bitter, bitter. She chokes as the petals unfurl.

And as quickly as that, Rumer's battle is no longer to stay alive but simply to die with the dignity of her own choosing. She forces her limbs to unbend; it's the hardest thing she's ever done. But somehow she manages to push herself against Rose, as if to warm herself in a last embrace, although in truth she's beyond the reach of heat or cold. Then she hears a voice speak from out of the numb dark. Faint at first, it grows stronger with each word:

I say to you truly, there is for all things the proper turning. Life, death, rebirth. All of us die with the dying. See, they depart, and we go with them. All of us are born with the dead. See, they return, and bring us with them. If I leave you now, it is only to come again.

Where, Rumer wonders, has she heard that voice? Why does it fill her with such joy?

You will know me by my eyes, the voice continues.

And Rumer knows: it's the voice of Saint Viridis Lacrimata.

Suddenly she's floating above the bed. Her vision has returned; for a flickering instant, she sees Rose's body and her own, sees Aralia and the others looking on in silence. But then everything changes: in place of Rose, she sees Viridis Lacrimata; where she saw herself, she sees Marin; and instead of Aralia and the others, she sees women she knows somehow as the disciples of Viridis. Dimly, Rumer recognizes the scene from somewhere, as if she's seen it in a play of simulars. She tries to remember, but then she's not floating anymore.

She's not Rumer now; she's Marin. And she's trying with all her strength, with all her heart, to convince Viridis to escape from this cell and the terrible fate that awaits her, first at the hands of the saints, then in the depths of Herwood.

But Viridis refuses. And with each refusal, Marin feels more angry and betrayed. One by one, the disciples leave the tiny cell, glowing in the health of Viridis's tears, strengthened in faith for the ordeals to come, until only Marin remains.

"Will you not come and kiss me good-bye, Marin?" says Viridis. "There is not much time before the dawn."

Marin angrily opens her mouth to refuse. To deny. But something catches her. She looks at Viridis as if for the first time. And she sees, shining through those familiar, deeply loved features, the face of another woman. A stranger . . . yet not a stranger. Younger, her skin still smooth and unscarred, but with the same green eyes. And though she doesn't think of Rose, something in her heart remembers.

Instead of turning away, Marin embraces Viridis and kisses her.

And Rumer wakes to find herself kissing Rose. Her face is wet with tears, her own and Rose's. For Rose is crying, too. Rose is gazing at her with shining green eyes and crying. Her tears are cool and soothing, like spring rain. Her tears are life. They are love. They wash all the poisons from her.

"Hail Liberatrix!"

Rumer turns and sees that Aralia, the Kite, Lyra, and the Valentine are all on their knees before Rose. She draws back and makes to join them, feeling suddenly unworthy and shy in the presence of the saint returned.

But Rose gently restrains her. "Your place is beside me, darling Rumer," she says. "Now and always."

"Is it really you?" Rumer asks in wonderment. "Is it all true?"

Rose places her hand tenderly on Rumer's wet cheek and smiles. Then she looks at the heretics, and though she continues to smile, something hardens in her green eyes, so that Rumer is suddenly afraid.

"Holy sister," Rose says. "Was it you who poisoned Rumer in order to draw me from my sleep?"

The Kite stands, assisted by Lyra and the Valentine. "It was, Liberatrix."

"Come close for your reward."

"Liberatrix! I'm not worthy!"

"I say you are."

The Kite approaches.

"Stretch out your hand. Touch my face."

The Kite's scarred face is made even more repulsive by a smile of naked expectation in which greed and lust seem perfectly united. She touches Rose's cheek.

And screams.

Rumer has never heard such screams. Not even during the public excoriations of the shrives.

The Kite falls to the floor. Smoke is rising from her hand, from which, as Rumer watches in horror, the flesh and then the bone melt away with a hissing sound. Soon there is only a stump whose pink surface gleams wetly in the harsh light of the thyrsis. But the Kite has stopped screaming long before that.

Still smiling, Rose looks at each of the heretics in turn and says: "Then from a lowly place I will come again with my green eyes, and my tears will burn like the stings of fireflies."

SIX

With a cry of abandon, Rose lets her head fall back onto the red silk pillow. She clamps her thighs around Rumer's ears as her body bucks to the expert lashings and probings of Rumer's agile tongue: like the rest of her body, a testament to the success of the beauty treatments.

Slowly the thrashing subsides, her legs fall open—the muscles quivering, spent—and Rumer, released, can breathe again.

"Oh, that tongue of yours," Rose murmurs, a dreamy smile on her lips as she traces, with a sharp fingernail, a lazy spiral upon Rumer's left breast. "How you make me forget!"

Rumer is too exhausted to respond even if a response were called for . . . and, as she's learned, it is not. She lies limply amid the tangled sheets, gasping like a fish out of water, engulfed in the wetness and smell of Rose's juices and her own sweat. The muscles at the root of her tongue throb in protest, unused to such a workout. She wants to cry.

For two days, since the miracle of Rose's transformation, Rumer has brought Rose to orgasm so many times, in so many ways, that she herself has lost count.

Rose hasn't ignored her, either. At least not sexually. Rumer is sore all over, even bruised in places, as if the two of them have worked their way through the *ars erotica* from start to finish and back again.

It's been a demanding journey. Rose is insatiable but not particularly inventive. Or gentle. She's too impatient for that. There's desperation in the way she throws herself into sex, like a starving woman who can't fill her belly no matter how much she eats of the banquet spread before her.

Rose hasn't slept once in the last two days. She doesn't seem to need it, as if she's done all her sleeping already. Used it up. Not only that, she hates it when Rumer sleeps, as if sleep is a rival with whom Rumer is regularly unfaithful. Rose gives her up to it grudgingly and for a brief time only before imperiously summoning her back with kisses and caresses.

And in fact Rumer embraces sleep, though not without guilt, for only there can she escape, for a little while, both Rose's demands and her own confused feelings. The last two days have been the strangest, most deeply unsettling of her life. All the time Rose was lost to her in sleep, Rumer prayed unceasingly for her to wake. She would have given her life in exchange; she almost had given it. When she'd opened her eyes to find herself gazing into the shining green eyes of Rose and saw there, like an answered prayer, a passion the twin of her own, Rumer had felt an eruption of joy so fierce that it was physically painful, like a poison even the tears of Viridis Lacrimata couldn't purge.

But then came the horrible punishment of the Kite, and it was as if the holy sister's screams had introduced a flaw into the diamond of her joy, or perhaps simply held that diamond up to a new light to reveal a flaw whose existence Rumer hadn't suspected. In the days since, other flaws have come to light, so that Rumer's passion, while it has not lessened, has grown more complicated. Darker.

Perhaps that's the nature of passion, Rumer thinks now, as Rose rings the small bell to summon Aralia. Perhaps it's only when the object of our passion is out of reach that we can love with total selflessness, total absorption. But once the sleeper wakes, passion ceases to be a dream and, without fading exactly, becomes something else. Something other. Is that why, now that Rose is awake, Rumer seeks the refuge of sleep, as if to restore the old balance?

Perhaps. But Rumer wonders, too, if Rose's tears have worked a greater change: not simply healing her of the poison but of other things as well, changing her into a different person just as, once upon a time, the beauty treatments had changed her from a girl into a Cat. What is she becoming now?

After Lyra and the Valentine had removed the Kite—who, to Rumer's surprise and relief, was merely unconscious despite the gravity of her wound—Aralia had led Rose and Rumer through the once-deserted maze of passages, deserted no longer. All along the route, crowded into the passages and looking on from adjoining chambers, people had gathered to see with their own eyes the incarnation of Viridis Liberatrix.

There were hundreds, from all walks of life: Viridians, Cats from the High Houses, even respectable women, the wives and daughters of courtiers. There were vizards, too, and simularters. In short, here beneath Quoz was a microcosm—crudely misshapen to be sure—of the great city above.

It amazed Rumer, how many people had fallen through the cracks of the Hierarchate. The rejected and discarded. Had they come willingly, she wondered, or, like her, been abducted? Surely they couldn't all be heretics! And yet she knew somehow that they were.

There were many more women than men, and in their arms the women all seemed to be carrying flowers, which they strewed in Rose's path. Despite the crowds, a profound and eerie silence reigned, broken only by the buzzing of fireflies drawn by the crushed blossoms. The heretics dropped to their knees as Rose passed, then stood and followed without a word, as if no words existed that would not profane the moment. Their faces spoke plainly, however, in ecstasies of dumb yearning and tears of half-disbelieving joy.

Seeing those faces, lit up with such naked hope and faith, made Rumer feel jealous, as if these people, with their glaring need, would try to take Rose from her and claim her for their own. She clutched Rose possessively by the hand.

Rose, meanwhile, barely acknowledged the existence of the onlookers. She followed Aralia impatiently through the underground warren—in which Rumer was utterly lost—as if she already knew every turn, every branching.

The ground beneath their feet sloped steadily, and the passages grew rougher as they descended, until they were moving through tunnels carved out of solid rock. The air grew hotter still. From up ahead came a watery slapping sound.

At last they emerged into a vast cavern lit with hundreds of thyrsi and packed with thousands of people. As Rumer watched, more people poured in through various openings. She was reminded of the huge crowds that thronged the Cathedral of Saint Ixion Diospyros on All Saints' Eve, eager for the blessing of the Ecclesiarch, and wondered if this place, too, was a cathedral of sorts.

As Rose entered the cavern, the restraint of the heretics snapped, and the air reverberated with cries of "Hail Viridis!" and "Liberatrix!" and "Heal us!"

Rose pulled free of Rumer's grasp and raised her hands for silence. But the gesture only provoked the crowd, and for a terrifying moment Rumer was certain they would all be crushed or trampled, if not actually torn to pieces, as the heretics surged forward with hysterical shouts, like Furies. She shut her eyes with a shriek immediately swallowed up in the greater noise, and braced herself for the engulfing wave.

But it never came. The shouting abruptly ceased. Rumer opened her eyes to see the mass of heretics swaying tamely in place like grasses in a breeze. The nearest were scant feet away. Rose stood before them, arms at her sides. Tears were rolling down her cheeks.

Simple tears.

As if witnessing a miracle, the heretics were making the sign of the Wheel and whispering prayers to the Spinner. Many of them were turning prayer wheels in their hands and weeping. Still others shuddered as though gripped by a private ecstasy or torment, like people exposed to the venom of fireflies.

Suddenly, as if in response to a change of atmosphere too subtle for Rumer to detect, people began dropping smoothly to their knees, whole sections at once, like fields of sunflowers deprived of light. Soon everyone in the cavern was kneeling except Rose and Rumer.

Looking across the uneven plain of heads, Rumer saw that an immense door was set into the opposite wall of the cavern. It shone like white marble, and was carved with figures of some sort, like the doors of the House Illicium. But the figures were too distant for her to make out; anyway, something else had captured her attention.

To the left of the door, the cavern gave way to an inky expanse of water that stretched as far as she could see and then vanished into mist and darkness. Small boats jostled at anchor close by the shore. Rumer wondered if she was seeing World's End, the place where the firm earth drops off into the infinite depths of the Pit. Yet gentle waves rolled unhurriedly out of the dark.

Rumer felt dizzy, as if she were no longer underground, but had emerged into another, larger world; or, rather, as if she stood at its very edge, on the threshold of a crossing, like death, from which there could be no sensible return. Overwhelmed, she, too, fell to her knees.

Then Rose began to speak. She did not raise her voice; she didn't need to. In the hushed, expectant silence, her voice filled up the cavern like dawn filling up the sky.

"Sisters and brothers, your prayers have awakened me from my long sleep," she said. "I have listened; I have come. Now the great struggle resumes. Long ago, an injury was inflicted upon us by Ixion Diospyros and his wicked followers, the so-called saints, who loudly proclaimed their loyalty to the Spinner while secretly doing the will of Maw. I swear to you now, sisters and brothers: we will bring this Hierarchate built upon our mothers' martyred bones crashing down about the heads of Sovereign and Ecclesiarch! They will suffer as we have suffered! As they fall, so shall we rise, trampling them under our feet!"

The crowd, which had risen to its feet as Rose spoke, now danced in place with raised fists, as though already trampling their enemies. "Hail Viridis!" they chanted. "Hail Liberatrix!"

Rumer felt again that a wave of uncontrollable violence was cresting, about to break over them. But, again, Rose lifted her hands for silence, and this time the crowd complied at once. Rumer marveled at Rose's self-possession, which, like her voice, or, rather, the things she said, was so ill suited to the young woman she seemed to be. A young woman who, despite her beauty, moved with the gawky gracelessness characteristic of Cats in the early stages of the beauty treatments, when the changes inflicted by the vizards in such rapid succession, even as they undergo the natural transformations of adolescence, outstrip the ability of their bodies to adapt. Rumer felt as if there were two distinct women sharing the same body, and she could love only one of them.

"We are not Furies," the Liberatrix was saying. "We do not delight in blood for its own sake. But we have been wronged. There must be punishment. Expiation. And there will be. But it won't be easy, sisters and brothers! Your faith will be pushed to the breaking point and beyond. Lives will be lost; bitter tears shed. But we will prevail. We will prevail because the Spinner will always prevail over Maw. Blessed be the Spinner! Blessed be Her holy name, now and forever! As it was in the beginning, is now, and shall be until the Unspinning!"

"Blessed be!" rumbled the crowd in response. And Rumer knew they would storm the Palace of the Chambered Nautilus at that very instant if Rose asked it of them. Knew, too, that she would join in the assault, however hopeless. Did that make her a heretic? She didn't know what she was anymore.

But Rose asked only patience, not action. "I will speak to you again on All Saints' Eve," she said. And she turned back and took Rumer by the hand, raising her gently to her feet. Gesturing for Aralia to follow, she strode into the crowd, which parted smoothly before her.

She walked right through the midst of them, calmly and without fear, all the way across the wide cavern. As she passed, the nearest heretics reached out to touch her tear-stained face with shy and humble deference. Rumer flinched, remembering the screams of the Kite.

But there were no screams now, only sounds of indrawn breath from faces that seemed suddenly washed clean of pain and worry. Other hands touched Rose's garments, the same wispy robes she'd worn to the gathering at the House Illicium. Hands found Rumer, too, brushing her face and body as if she were a thing of wood, like the simulars paraded through the streets of Quoz on All Saints' Eve. Rumer tried to bear the touches bravely, but it was all she could do to keep from crying aloud. She had nothing to give these people. Nothing.

At last they reached the white doors on the far side of the cavern. The doors were immense, as large as the doors of the Cathedral of Saint Ixion Diospyros. Carved into the marble was a depiction of the entrance of Saint Viridis Lacrimata into Herwood.

Rumer had seen countless renditions of this scene over the course of her life, but never like this. For one thing, the figures were as vast as the doors themselves. But more startling than the sheer size was that in contrast to the story as told in the *Lives and Acts*, here Viridis was shown being whipped into the forest by shrives. Naked, her eyes bloody holes, she looked like a hunted, hated beast.

This was no sacrifice willingly entered into, Rumer thought, unless on a level beyond anything she'd ever imagined, like a murder in which the victim, though innocent, forgives the murderer and accepts an unjust death. What kind of sacrifice was that? And yet there was something in the saint's expression that spoke to Rumer, though it took her a moment to recognize it. Or, rather, to recognize herself in it. For it was passion. The passion she felt for Rose was mirrored in the marble.

Leading to these doors was a series of wide steps, as if meant for giants, at the top of which three normal-sized women were waiting. To the left and right of each step, other women in skintight black armor stood, holding thyrsi. If not for the absence of masks, Rumer would have taken them for shrives. And yet they might as well have been masked; their expressions were inscrutable, their eyes hard. Rumer wondered if they were here to welcome Rose or to bar her way.

The crowd pushed to the edge of the stairs as Rose, with Rumer and Aralia, mounted past the watchful sentries. Of the women waiting at the top of the stairs, two were Kites—though neither was the Kite whom Rose had punished—and the third was a slender woman in a dark gown whose long black hair was streaked with gray and whose face was scarred almost as terribly as the faces of the Kites who flanked her.

As they drew close, Rumer saw that a tattoo of silver porpoises circled the woman's pale neck: the sign of the House Circium. And suddenly she knew—though she'd seen this woman only once, when her beauty, still intact, had rivaled that of Serinthe Lacrimata—that they were in the presence of Picea Circium. Picea Circium, whose legendary passion for a Kite had caused her to sacrifice her position as odalisque of the House Circium more than eight turnings ago. She'd disappeared after that, presumed dead by those who bothered to remember her.

Finding her so unexpectedly, Rumer wondered how much of the old story was true. Had there really been a passion? Or had Picea, like Aralia, been an agent of the heretics the whole time? Rumer felt as if the smooth walls of her understanding had swung open to reveal hidden passages like the ones honeycombing this underground world. How much of what she'd known—or believed she'd known—was wrong? Amid the shifting perspectives, was there any absolute to hold on to?

And she thought: Yes. There was an absolute, and she was holding on to it already.

Rose.

Meanwhile, Picea watched them come, curiosity, hope, and suspicion muddying her brown-eyed gaze. Or, rather, she watched Rose; she never looked at Rumer or Aralia. The Kites, too, were interested exclusively in Rose. The spectacle of those mutilated, eyeless faces tracking Rose's every move with almost predatory keenness made Rumer shiver with dread.

"Don't be frightened, darling Rumer," Rose whispered, squeezing her hand in reassurance.

But Rumer grew more frightened than ever at that, for she recognized something in Rose's voice that she'd last heard in the moments before the punishment of the Kite.

Rose came to a halt before Picea. She said nothing, only waited with a dangerous smile on her face.

Picea was trembling. "Who are you?"

"By these eyes you will know me," Rose answered. "By these tears."

"We must be certain," said Picea. "We have waited for so long . . ."

"You speak of proof," Rose interrupted. "What of faith?"

At that Picea blushed deeply; the scars crisscrossing her face stood out in livid bands against the underlying scarlet. But she repeated, "We must be sure."

"I have healed this girl. And others in the crowd."

"Yes. But your tears do not always heal, do they?"

Rose's smile widened. "Then from a lowly place I will come again with my green eyes, and my tears will burn like the stings of fireflies."

"Quoting scripture proves nothing," said Picea, who nevertheless seemed taken aback. "The prophecies are famous. It has occurred to us that the vizards might one day craft a spy in the semblance of a saint."

"The same might be said of you. Or of the holy sisters here."

At that the Kites on either side of Picea opened their mouths with a hissing sound, like serpents, and Rumer shuddered to see they were tongueless as well as eyeless.

"I speak for everyone," said Picea. "I am Picea Circium. I wear the mantle of Marin."

"Then stretch out your hand, Picea. Touch my cheek."

Picea raised her hand. It shook despite her efforts to hold it steady. "I am weak!" she said, as though cursing herself.

"To know all is to forgive all," said Rose. "The Spinner has more faith in us than we have in ourselves."

At this, a lopsided grin sent new cracks through Picea's splintered features. "More scripture?" she said. And touched Rose's cheek.

A cry broke from Picea's lips. A look of wonder washed away her grin. She pulled back her hand and regarded it as if it were changing before her eyes. Suddenly she dropped to her knees, followed, after a brief hesitation, by the Kites. A roar went up from the crowd.

"It's true!" Picea said, gazing at Rose with shining eyes. "You've come! Viridis Liberatrix!"

Rose nodded impatiently. "I'm very tired, Picea. Can we go in now?"

Picea got to her feet and, with a gesture, summoned the ten women from along the stairs. "These women are your bodyguards, Liberatrix."

The women knelt in a single motion, presenting their thyrsi stem forward to Rose.

"They are viragi," explained Picea. "Our answer to the shrives."

Rose gave a distracted nod. "I'm very tired," she repeated.

The viragi shot to their feet as though given a direct order and began to push open the heavy marble doors. As soon as there was space enough, Rose slipped through, pulling Rumer along behind her.

They were in a hall as large as the hospitality hall in the House Illicium. Only this hall was carved out of solid rock, not crafted of rare woods and metals. Chandeliers made of thyrsi dripped from a high, ragged ceiling. Tapestries hung from the walls, each one depicting an episode from the life of Viridis Lacrimata. Some Rumer recognized—although, like the carvings that decorated the doors, they presented familiar stories in unfamiliar ways—but most were completely new to her.

The floor was a single mosaic made up of small, colored tiles. Rumer grew dizzy trying to decipher the shape these tiles combined to form, but the design was too big, or perhaps just too cunning, for her to take in at once.

At the other end of the hall sat a huge marble sculpture of a broken wheel. Rose hurried toward it, no longer seeming as tired as she had just moments before. Only when she'd clambered into the sculpture did Rumer realize that it was really a throne: a heretical counterpart or parody of the Serpent Throne.

Now, as Rumer and the others drew near, Rose seemed to notice the presence of the Kites for the first time. She stepped down from the throne and asked: "Who let them in here?"

Picea looked puzzled. "Is something wrong?"

"I don't like them," said Rose. "They're ugly."

One of the Kites protested: "We scar ourselves in devotion to—"

"I don't mean outside," Rose interrupted. "Ugly *inside*. Like the other one."

"What do you mean?" asked Picea, looking at the Kites with the same suspicious gaze she had earlier trained on Rose.

Tears had begun to well at the corners of Rose's eyes. "Let them brave my tears as you did."

The Kites backed away, shaking their heads. But the viragi blocked their escape.

"Do you fear the Spinner's judgment?" Rose asked, stepping toward them.

One of the Kites opened her mouth with that terrible hissing sound and, before anyone could stop her, moving with a speed that belied her blindness, hurled herself at Rose. Rumer screamed as the Kite clawed Rose's face, as though determined to scratch the eyes out of her head.

But Rose moved at the last second. The Kite's nails raked down her cheek, just below the tattoo of the red teardrop marking her as the property of the House Lacrimata. And even before the blood began to flow, the Kite's hand was smoldering.

The Kite fell to the floor, writhing, as her flesh burned away. Awful croaking screams came from her tongueless mouth until, after some moments, she lost consciousness.

There was a heavy silence. Rumer couldn't stop shaking. Aralia had a strange, lopsided grin on her face. Rose was simply looking at the remaining Kite.

As if bowed by the weight of her gaze, the Kite sank to her knees. Trembling, she stretched out her hands, the palms scarred as thoroughly as her face, as every inch of her.

Then Rose stepped forward to let a single teardrop, red with blood, fall.

The Kite collapsed in a heap. Though her flesh, like her sister's, had already begun to dissolve, she was unconscious and seemed to suffer no pain.

"Her submission merits some small mercy," Rose said.

"Were they spies then?" asked Picea.

Rose shook her head. "My coming means an end to their power. They would prefer things not to change."

"Will they die?"

"They will wake dead to all they were." Rose turned to two of her bodyguards. "Remove them."

Bowing, the viragi complied, dragging the Kites from the hall.

It was only then that Rumer noticed that the wounds on Rose's cheek had healed. No trace of them remained. Without thinking, she touched the spot with her hand, her fingers tingling in the bath of Rose's tears.

Rose turned to her with a smile. She took Rumer's hand in her own and pressed it warmly, as Picea and the others, seeing what had happened, dropped again to their knees.

"I want to go to my chambers now," said Rose.

Suddenly she seemed tired again, and Rumer wondered if the exercise of her healing powers had drained her in some way.

Picea led them to a door concealed by a tapestry on the wall behind the throne. "These chambers have been kept ready for your return," she said. "I hope you find them satisfactory."

The door, like others Rumer had seen, bore a red symbol on its smooth face: the same symbol, evolved from a hand, which she now thought of as meaning "open." Picea touched it with her palm, and, indeed, the door slid open.

Picea made to follow them inside, but Rose turned and stopped her. "Leave us for now," she said, her voice hoarse.

"But there is much to discuss," began Picea.

"We will speak again soon. Now I must rest. Aralia, you wait here. If I need anything, I'll call you."

"Yes, Liberatrix." Aralia flashed a triumphant smile, flattered to have been chosen in preference to Picea, whose face, despite its scars, just as plainly registered disappointment and hurt at the rejection.

It struck Rumer that things weren't as different here as they seemed if old rivalries were continued so openly. Even among the heretics, she thought, without makeup and perfume, without the fabulous wigs and all the other trappings of their order, a Cat remained a Cat. The beauty treatments were more than skin-deep. There was something reassuring in that. But something disturbing, too, as if none of them could ever be more—or less—than what the vizards had crafted them to be.

What did that mean for her? After all, her passion had been crafted by vizards: if not this passion specifically, then the susceptibility to passion she shared with all Cats. Even in the grip of her passion, were the vizards pulling her strings?

Then the door slid closed, and Rumer was alone with Rose in a large but sparsely furnished chamber. In addition to a large but plain bed, there were some chairs, a table or two, and, on the walls, more tapestries. Remembering the sumptuous luxury of the apartments in the House Illicium—especially Cassine's private chambers, which, on Rumer's rare visits, had appeared scarcely real, like visions of some fabulous afterlife—Rumer felt homesick for her own lesser but still quite splendid chambers, which she knew she would never see again.

Rose, meanwhile, seemed unaware of their surroundings. She sagged against the door, hugging herself as if feeling a chill through her ragged silks.

"Are you all right, Liberatrix?" Rumer asked.

Rose smiled wanly. "Please, Rumer; can't you call me by my own name when we're alone like this? I need to hear it."

Rumer blushed. "Rose."

"There's something wrong in me, darling Rumer. Something unfinished. You called out to me when you were dying, and I woke myself to save you. I don't regret it. How could I? But it was too soon."

"Too soon?"

"Sleep was changing me," she said, holding Rumer's gaze with her own. "Like a dream I was having of myself. A dream I had forgotten long ago and was only just starting to remember. I saw dark shapes bending over me. I heard voices whispering; I could almost make out the words! I saw a flash of light so bright it burned, and at the very center I saw . . . *Him*."

"Him?" prompted Rumer.

"Ixion Diospyros, bound to his Burning Wheel. Looking at me with hard, unforgiving eyes. I'm afraid, Rumer! I'm afraid!"

Rumer took Rose in her arms. "What can I do?"

As if in answer, Rose's lips sought hers. Rumer tasted the salty wetness of tears, unable to tell if they were Rose's or her own. Then their tongues slipped together, and Rumer faded in the voluptuous dissolve of the kiss, a teardrop swallowed in the vaster sea. Yet not lost there. Stretched infinitely wide and deep. Become the very thing that engulfed it.

Later, they bathed together in an adjoining chamber, in a pool of warm water fed by a spring that splashed down the smooth blue-gray rocks of the wall. There was so much Rumer wanted to ask, so much she wanted to say. But each time she opened her mouth, Rose shut it with a kiss.

Later still, they retired to the roomy bed in the outer chamber. Then Rose began to talk. At first she quoted scripture, told of simulars dropping out of the night with razors shining in their tiny fists: dark, prophetic ravings that chilled Rumer to the bone. But then she spoke of Jubilar, the same village where Rumer had grown up until her father had been lured away by Beauty, condemning her to a Cat's career. She spoke of people Rumer knew, or once had known, until she began to wonder if Rose had somehow sucked out her memories along with the poison. But before she could ask, Rose would be gone, and the Liberatrix would return, terrifying Rumer with her madness.

This continued without pause for two days. The voices were never directed at Rumer; if she answered, she was ignored. She was witness to a private argument.

Yet she was no passive onlooker. Again and again, Rose returned to Rumer's body, taking from it what she needed, giving back what she couldn't hold. She was insistent and demanding in her lust, like a baby at its mother's breast. And, like a mother, Rumer would give anything and everything to appease that hunger, even at the cost of her own life. For regardless of how her bones ached or her mind rebelled, a single touch or even look from Rose was enough to melt whatever resistance had been hardening Rumer's heart. At such moments, Rumer felt as though she no longer existed. Only the passion existed. She knew that she really was Rose's anchor; without her Rose would become lost in and to herself, swamped by the voices of her clashing selves.

But an anchor must be tethered to something, or else it will fall until it hits bottom. To whom was Rumer tethered? Once she would have answered, simply, Rose. But she doesn't know who that is anymore. And despite the firm mattress beneath her, she often has the sensation of falling.

Now the chamber door opens and Aralia enters in response to the bell rung by Rose, even before its tones have faded from the air. She sinks to her knees and presses her forehead to the floor, then lifts her head and waits expectantly, smiling at Rumer with calm assurance, as if it's just a matter of time before she takes her place in the bed.

Rumer moves to cover herself with the sheets. Lately she's started to feel a sense of modesty; at least, she thinks it might be modesty. It's strange and new and a little embarrassing, as if Aralia of all people hasn't seen her naked a thousand times and explored every part of her with fingers and tongue. But that was a different time, a different Rumer. She gives herself so completely now to Rose that there's nothing left to share with anybody else.

"It's time." Rising gracefully from the bed, as if from a long and refreshing nap, Rose wraps herself in a loose robe of bright yellow silk. "Come, Rumer." She holds out her hand and helps Rumer to her feet.

Rumer stands unsteadily, clutching her own robe, also of yellow silk, to her body. Her body aches. She thinks she has a fever. All she wants is to sleep.

"We'll have a bath," Rose continues. "You may send in Picea and the others after a moment, Aralia."

Aralia bows, laughing. "You should see them! They're not used to being kept waiting. They're upset, but they're too frightened of your tears to say anything out loud!"

"As you should be," says Rose.

Aralia gapes. "But you know my loyalty!"

"And your ambition. Now. Do as you are told."

Aralia bows stiffly and leaves the room.

Rose leads Rumer into the adjoining chamber. She helps her out of the robe and into the warm pool.

The bottom of the pool is covered with soft white sand, and Rumer sits in the clear and shallow water and watches a pale cloud swirl up around her thighs. She leans the back of her head against the gentle slope of the rock and sighs as fragrant water slips up her neck. There is a sensation of floating. She could sleep for hours, she thinks. For days.

She hears Rose enter the pool but doesn't open her eyes. But then she feels Rose's hand brush her cheek, and at that touch, like an irresistible summons, her eyes open. Her whole body opens.

Rose smiles wistfully as she withdraws her hand. "No. Rest now, darling Rumer. You've been through a lot. I know it hasn't been easy."

Rumer can't remember Rose ever speaking to her in just this tone before. She feels herself blushing helplessly, like a young Cat under the tender and admiring gaze of an older sister whose love she's despaired of winning. "I don't mind," she says, smiling for the first time in two days. "It hasn't been easy for you, either. Is"— she hesitates, then continues in a gulp—"Is everything all right now?"

"It's hard, Rumer. Hard to hold everything together." Rose smiles suddenly. "I wasn't made to last."

These words fall like ice through Rumer's heart. She finds Rose's hand beneath the water and takes it. "I won't let anything happen to you!"

Rose squeezes her hand. "It's only for a while longer. Then I can rest."

"What are you saying?" Rumer feels numb with dread. "You talk like something terrible is going to happen."

"Only the Spinner knows what's to come."

"I couldn't bear it if anything happened, Rose. I want us to be together."

"Sweet Rumer, aren't we?"

Rumer is hardly reassured, but before she can say another word, Aralia's cough signals her return.

"I've brought them," she says.

A group of women stands behind Aralia, faces cloaked in shadow. Now one of them strides to the edge of the pool and drops to her knees in front of Rose. "I ask your forgiveness," says the woman, whose beauty shines even through her tears.

"For what, Picea?"

Rumer gazes in wonder at the face of Picea. The skin is smooth, without a trace of the scars that, just days ago, had so disfigured her, making her a Kite in all but name. Now she's as Rumer remembers, the remarkable beauty for which she was famed as odalisque of the House Circium restored by the miracle of Rose's tears. It's as if the flesh has not simply been healed, the scars erased; time itself seems to have been smoothed away. Once more Picea's lips have their perfect pout, her nose its sensual flare, her brown eyes their provocative gleam in the matchless setting of her high cheekbones.

"I doubted you," she says. "I'm not worthy of what you've given me."

Rose shrugs impatiently. "Then you must become worthy of it. Now get off your knees: We have much to discuss."

Picea climbs awkwardly to her feet, swiping at her eyes with the sleeve of her dark robes.

Now the other women step forward. In addition to Aralia, there are five viragi and three women in ragged black garments with hoods covering their faces.

The Kites.

As one, the three women lift their hoods.

And Rumer sees that the Kites, too, have benefited from Rose's tears. They do not possess Picea's beauty; even with all their scars washed away, the women are merely plain, their bodies entirely lacking the voluptuous overripeness of the former Cat's. But they are no longer eyeless. And as they begin to speak, Rumer sees that their barren mouths have sprouted tongues.

"Forgive us," they say in unison, their eyes downcast like those of recalcitrant children.

"You have paid the price," says Rose.

And only now does Rumer notice that the Kites are still maimed. The hands that boiled away in the fierce bath of Rose's tears have not found a second flowering, as if the tears can heal all wounds but those they inflict themselves. Is punishment so much stronger than forgiveness? she wonders.

But the Kites show no shame at these stark reminders of disgrace. On the contrary, as with the scars and other maimings, they seem already to have elevated their injuries into proofs of special worth, signs that set them not only apart from, but above, others. But what Rumer finds most interesting about them is not their lack of beauty, nor the restoration of eyes and tongue, nor even their missing hands.

It's how young they are.

These women, whom she's taken all her life for crones, now seem to be even younger than she is, scarcely older than Rose. Rumer knows there's only one explanation for that.

Metheglin.

As odalisque of the House Circium, Picea received small doses of dilute metheglin in the semen and other bodily fluids of her loftiest clients; not much in comparison with the doses of Azedarach, perhaps, but enough to preserve her beauty against time's slow scarification for turnings, even until today. But where would Kites get metheglin?

Further, Rumer sees that she's not the only one to be surprised by the apparent youth of the Kites. Picea, too, is staring at them openmouthed.

"Have . . . have the tears done this?"

"No, Picea," says Rose gently. "Now you see what the Kites wished to hide from me. From all of us. It was for this that I punished them."

"The metheglin vaults," whispers Picea.

And one of the Kites speaks. "Yes. We found an entrance to the vaults many turnings ago. Instead of sharing our discovery, we kept it to ourselves."

"How long?" asks Picea in a small voice.

A different Kite answers: "Almost six hundred turnings."

"Six hundred!" Picea sinks to the ground.

Aralia is slowly shaking her head, as if to clear it. Even the viragi seem to be having difficulty maintaining their composure.

"What we could have done!" Picea moans, rocking from side to side while cradling her head in her hands. "Metheglin is the key to the power of Sovereign and Ecclesiarch. Without it, the Hierarchate falls! We've searched for those vaults ever since the time of Marin. You knew and said nothing! Your silence kept our enemies in power and cost the lives of innocent people! Why?"

"We didn't have the right to act," says one of the Kites in a defensive tone. "Viridis Liberatrix hadn't yet returned from Herwood. To act without her would have been blasphemy. Is it not written that she will be born again out of Herwood to redeem us with her tears? If we took matters into our own hands, wouldn't that show a lack of faith in the Spinner?"

At that, everyone looks to Rose.

"Perhaps if you had acted, I would have come sooner. Did you think of that?"

"No," admits the Kite. "Is it true?"

"Does it matter now?" Rose asks in turn. "Besides, I'm here now, am I not? Yet you still would have kept your discovery a secret from me if you could."

"We weren't sure—"

"Enough!" Rose stands, showering everyone with water from the pool. "Have you forgotten so soon the feel of my tears?"

The Kites have already fallen to their knees. "No!" they cry. "Please!"

Rose regards the huddled, shivering figures silently for a long moment. Then she sits again in the pool, her thigh touching Rumer's beneath the warm water. "Not to act is sometimes a greater wrong than even a wrong action."

The Kites are weeping now. "If we acted wrongly, it was only from excessive love of you," gasps one. "We kept the location of the vaults a secret for your sake, in order that the scriptures would be fulfilled! And if we used metheglin ourselves, it was only that we might live to see the day of your coming!"

"Yes, I know," says Rose. "It's that alone which has saved you. But the time for secrets is over. In three days it will be All Saints' Eve. From Arpagee to Quoz, the entire Hierarchate will celebrate the fiery ascension of Ixion Diospyros. As the world above our heads parades in drunken revelry beneath a stalled sun, here in the darkness we'll tear down its secret foundations. By the time the night is over, and the sun has resumed its descent, the metheglin vaults will be destroyed; the Hierarchate and its leaders will fall with the sun, nevermore to rise."

SEVEN

On All Saints' Eve, everyone rises with the sun. Already hundreds of people are streaming through the streets of Quoz, drawn to the Cathedral by the pealing of the bells; soon the Ecclesiarch will celebrate the Mass and bestow his blessing. Except for Cats, sequestered in their Houses in anticipation of what is always the single busiest day of the turning, members of all orders are here, mingling easily. Bands of apprentices, some as yet untouched by vizards, roam the streets in their colorful robes, loudly singing the songs of the orders they serve and hope one day, like their masters before them, to join.

Only the shrives keep aloof. They patrol in seemingly random aggregates of pairs, in the midst of the crowd yet not of it. More than their black armor and masks, it's their attitude that sets them apart; their crystal blue eyes flicker over each face as if merely confirming a fate already decided, inescapable. They will celebrate this holy day by purging Quoz of sinners and heretics, plucking them from the crowd without warning or mercy, just as, on the day of Ixion's fiery ascension, in the relentless light of his Burning Wheel, the saints rooted out and slaughtered the secret enemies of the young Hierarchate.

But not even the presence of the shrives can dampen the festive mood. Whole families flock together, wives and wide-eyed children following husbands and fathers beaming with pride. Each face reflects the belief that the shrives will take someone else. For hasn't it always been someone else?

There is laughter and singing, flashing eyes and teeth, and flasks spilling their contents while being roughly passed from hand to hand, mouth to mouth. Everyone is dressed in their finest, most colorful clothes. Spun by the women over the previous turning especially for today, the clothes will be worn this once, then cast away. Some people are already sporting masks: gross caricatures of the saints, which make the children laugh, or of Furies, which make them, even the eldest, shriek with a terror only half-feigned. Later, other masks will be donned. Masks for adults.

But that is hours away. The sun is still rising, just as if this were a normal day and not All Saints' Eve, twice as long as the others.

The day may be twice as long, but it ends too soon just the same, Sylvestris thinks irritably, shouldering his way through a knot of boisterously drunk apprentice vizards. The youths jeer at him, all the ingrained arrogance of their order emerging under the influence of whatever they've ingested. Like their masters, the apprentices have forgotten—if they ever knew—that those privileged to wield the instruments of change upon themselves are not for that reason the authors of change. All are as simulars in the Spinner's hands, Sylvestris reflects with satisfaction. Simularters, not vizards, approach Him most closely in the end, crafted in His image.

There's a stirring at the back of his mind: Isn't it a comfort to think so, the musical voice of Saint Sium Lyrata intones.

Sylvestris sighs. He's not used to getting up so early, not even on All Saints' Eve. And it shows. He didn't sleep much, busy with a Cat from the House Lacrimata whose name he's already forgotten. Now he's due at the Palace for a performance. His head is pounding from the bells, and he can't seem to get into his usual rhythm. Every step feels a little off, as if he's stumbling through the day. He swallowed a bead of metheglin before leaving the Cat's chambers, but even so he feels as if half of himself stayed behind in the mirror when he painted his face this morning.

"The better half," whispers Saint Ilex Erythrina. The other simulars giggle. Why must they always torment him?

Moving against the general flow, away from the Cathedral and toward the Palace of the Chambered Nautilus, Sylvestris fights to make headway. People knock against him, then grin and offer a drink or pill or injection by way of apology; others, like the young vizards, curse him for a clumsy ox. All the while, his simulars chatter nervously, like a congress of old women.

Sylvestris shares their nervousness. Scores of people are regularly injured on All Saints' Eve, especially when, in the waning hours of a too-brief freedom, they go wild, desperate to squeeze a few last sparkling drops of time from the all-but-empty day before the return of Beauty and the night. Then fantasies of all stripes are acted out and old scores settled behind anonymous masks.

Now, despite the padded and reinforced gloves he always wears in public to protect his hands, Sylvestris can't forget that even an accidental collision—or a purposeful one, for as Court Simularter he has his share of enemies—could break his brittle fingers and leave him permanently crippled. Any one of the people around him could be a spy in the service of the Ecclesiarch or the heretics, an assassin sent to kill him or a simularter crippled in some long-ago duel come to pay him back.

The duels of simularters bear a superficial resemblance to the solemn affairs of shrives undertaken with envenomed daggers. But simularters face each other with no weapons save their hands, marvels of strength and agility marred by a single flaw: their bones, when struck at certain points, just so, are brittle as glass.

Dueling simularters circle each other in a wary silence, their hands and fingers weaving intricate patterns in the air. A slender chain joins the right ankle of one man to the left ankle of the other. They wear only breechcloths. Whole hours can pass in this way, the jingling of the chain like the hypnotic accompaniment of a highly stylized dance.

Then one or the other strikes: a whisper of displaced air, the crack of snapping bone, and it's finished. Sometimes the two adversaries suffer a simultaneous, mutual crippling, their two hands colliding like birds in flight, but usually there's a clear victor.

Sylvestris is a veteran of more than thirty duels. He has a positive hunger for duels; for a little while, at least, he can step out from behind his simulars and take the stage himself. He has no pity for those he defeats. Nor respect, for these days the old ways are ignored and the losers quickly resort to begging. He despises them. They cling to life, honor forgotten, a pack of shameless cowards. Yet they dare to accuse him! He sees it in their eyes whenever he passes by: *You're no better, Sylvestris; you would be begging here beside us. Someday you will be.*

But they are wrong. He would cut his simulars' strings, open his veins in atonement, as was done in the old days.

As Sylvestris nears the Palace, the crowds grow thicker and more exuberant. At last, when he reaches the wide square in front of the Palace gates, he finds himself stuck in the milling throng. Thanks to his height, he can see over the heads of the others, to where the gates glitter in the sun. A black line of shrives stands before them, keeping people back.

Now, to the accompaniment of cheers, a surge sweeps him up, carrying him farther from the gates and toward the buildings that edge the square. Sylvestris fights it at first, then gives up. He'll have to wait till the current brings him close to the gates, where he can signal the shrives for assistance.

The source of the commotion, he sees now, is a procession that has just entered the square: simulars of the saints, removed from their shrines for the day, are being carried on the shoulders of Mouths of

God. Their destination is the Cathedral, where all the simulars from the chapels and churches are being brought to receive the blessing of the Ecclesiarch.

Lurching with the unsteady gait of their bearers, who cannot be seen in the crush, the simulars appear to be walking on the shoulders of the crowd. Fireflies swarm in the air above them, a busy blur of green and gold through which eager hands reach, braving stings to touch the simulars or pin long strips of colored paper inscribed with carefully worded prayers to their garments. Later, after the Mass, a great parade of simulars will wind through the streets of Quoz, led by the Ecclesiarch himself. Then the real celebrations will begin.

Sylvestris seizes the opportunity to duck into a narrow, dead-end alley between two buildings whose walls of opaque crystal flow together high above his head. There are no doors, no windows. The sharp reek of urine indicates he's not the first to take refuge here. By late morning, the whole city will stink of piss. And other things.

Lifting a scented handkerchief to his nose, he watches the mob stream by and shakes his head. Easier to walk on water than across that space. Suddenly, out of the corner of his eye, Sylvestris sees a familiar face in the crowd, gone before he can register its significance. Then it hits him.

Iber Arvensis.

He's just seen Iber Arvensis. A passing glimpse, the briefest fraction of time; yet it was him. Or was it? He looks again, but it's too late. The face is lost in the crowd. Probably he imagined it.

"But what if you didn't?" asks the voice of Saint Ilex.

Sylvestris slumps against the wall. *Iber Arvensis*, he thinks dully. The simulars echo: "Iber Arvensis." Dead and harvested. And disposed of.

"Not his face," Saint Fagus Firmiana reminds him.

How could he forget? The face peeled away, the body left in a bed of roses stained even redder with blood. Sylvestris feels sick, wondering if there's been some mistake. Is Iber really dead? Or was another body substituted for his, a body crafted by vizards to resemble Iber in superficial ways, with the face removed to prevent identification?

He feels he's stumbled across something important. Either that, or he's imagining things. But there's a fine line between imagination and reality: who knows that better than a simularter? And the unusual circumstances of Iber's death have been repeated many times in the week since Saint Samsum's Day. Every morning, new bodies are found. He's not imagining that.

If people think you're dead, he reasons, they don't look for you. They don't see you. You're a ghost. A flesh-and-blood ghost.

A spy.

But for whom? It could be anyone. The Sovereign. The Ecclesiarch. Even the heretics. He feels dizzy, overwhelmed with paranoia. The jubilant crowd suddenly seems sinister, composed of people who are not what they appear to be, as if even their faces are masks worn to deceive, their most friendly actions actually staggering betrayals. He'll alert Azedarach once he gets to the Palace.

"But what if Azedarach is behind it?" comes the voice of Saint Rober Virbirnum. "What if it's part of a plan you're not supposed to know?"

He sighs. What indeed. Then his reward will be the Six Hundred. He's seen how Azedarach protects his secrets. No, it's safer to say nothing, he decides. To see nothing. At least for now. And perhaps he really didn't see anything. It happened so fast. His eyes playing him for a fool.

"Simularter."

The abrupt voice from behind makes Sylvestris jump. He turns, his hands up to protect himself. Then he lowers his hands. A pair of shrives stands before him. Little more than their blue eyes are visible in the shadowy recesses of the alley. Where had they come from? How did they get here?

"You will come with us."

"On whose authority?" he manages to ask.

"The Sovereign bids us say to you: 'Rose.'"

Sylvestris feels as if a dormant conditioning has come alive in him at the mention of that name, a slack cord suddenly pulled taut. So that's it, he thinks, Iber forgotten, everything forgotten but Azedarach's promise. The heretics are making their move. The girl among them. Rose.

"You mean Viridis Liberatrix," the voice of Saint Viridis herself archly amends.

Whatever name she goes by. Azedarach's spy. He should have guessed the heretics would strike today, on All Saints' Eve. He has a thousand questions. "How?" he begins.

But the shrives do not reply. They turn as one and walk through a door at the back of the alley, clearly expecting him to follow. Sylvestris is sure there was no door there a moment ago.

Clearly, he thinks, the shrives were waiting for him. They knew he would choose this alley. Or, rather, they dictated his choice. Somehow he was herded here, the random flux of the crowd concealing a pattern, a purpose. He feels angry; like all simularters, Sylvestris prefers to do the manipulating. But he's also impressed. It's impossible not to be.

Following the shrives, Sylvestris enters a small, square room lit by a thyrsis. He pats his face with the scented handkerchief, careful not to disturb his makeup. "Why do you shrives always have to sneak up on people?"

"We do not sneak," says one of the shrives.

"Others are unobservant," says the other.

Sylvestris staggers with a yelp of surprise as the room suddenly plunges. "What vizards' craft is this?" he blurts as his ears pop. Each time he thinks he's seen the last of the city's marvels, a new one comes along to surprise him.

The shrives do not answer. Now it feels like the room is slipping sideways. He touches the wall to steady himself and tries again: "Where are we going? I insist you tell me!"

"To the metheglin vaults," says one of the shrives, not at all impressed.

EIGHT

The Ecclesiarch rises from the bed in which the boy, Sium, lies beneath tangled sheets, one ankle bound to the bedpost by a thin gold chain that shines in the early morning sun like a trickle of pure metheglin. But it's not the chain that holds the boy here; nor is it his blindness. His true chains are forged in his blood, frozen with aspergine like a river choked with ice.

Now, his skin turned the color of chalk mixed with ash and his lips as blue and lifeless as the steely eyes of a shrive, Sium reminds the Ecclesiarch of a body laid out for harvesting. He thinks of Sium's late father, Erigeron Intricata, and how Morus, with consummate skill, harvested even from that shell of putrefaction organs free of lethium's taint.

But the son is not the father. Sium is not dead, only sleeping, preserved like a firefly in amber until the Ecclesiarch wakes him with a thawing kiss.

From this chamber, whose crystal walls and ceiling seem crafted of air and light, so that he always feels like he's flying through thin air, or, rather, floating upon it, as in some fabulous sky boat—solitary, serene—the Ecclesiarch sees the great city of Quoz spread beneath him. He stands at the top of the Cathedral, the highest point in Quoz. It is he, not Azedarach, who approaches nearest of all men to Saint Ixion's Burning Wheel; looking down, he feels as if he's gazing through Ixion's eyes, nailed to the ever-burning wheel of the sun.

In the distance, towering above the rest of the city but still far below him, are the multifaceted domes of the Palace of the Chambered Nautilus, whose secret heart Azedarach inhabits like a canker, undermining the Hierarchate from within just as lethium corrupted the body of Erigeron from the inside out. But the light of the morning sun can't heal this sickness or even reveal it; the light gilds the domes, making them sparkle like a mountain of gems, a treasure to be won. And if the

Ecclesiarch smiles now, it's not that the radiant display has blinded him to the ugliness that hides behind it like malice behind a smile. No, it's because today is All Saints' Eve, when by the Spinner's grace all things are possible.

Today, on the anniversary of Ixion's ascension, the sun will freeze at its zenith and, balanced on some invisible fulcrum, hold steady in the sky from noon to noon, holding back the tide of night and the scent of Beauty that comes with it. Today, too, the sickness festering at the heart of the Hierarchate will be cut away by Morus's discreet and efficient hands, hands that, for turnings, have performed the Sovereign's will but are now pledged against him. Just as once, long ago, the Spinner raised the lamp of the sun to illuminate for the saints the hiding places of the Furies, so today will He watch in triumph as Azedarach and his followers are hunted down.

The Ecclesiarch recalls Morus's words as they sealed their bargain over Erigeron's bloated corpse: "When an organ is diseased, it must be removed and a healthy organ put in its place or else the whole body will sicken and die." How like a vizard to dress betrayal and ambition in the drably impersonal prescriptions of his craft, he thinks with appreciation.

Of all the orders, the Ecclesiarch, in his heart, feels closest to the vizards, perhaps because, like him—or, rather, his image of himself—they are in some sense their own creations. For although they are but one order among many, the vizards are the only order that shapes itself, just as they shape the others—the simularters, the Mouths of God, the shrives, even the Cats—by an ancient craft they themselves no longer fully understand, following rituals that were old and obscure even in Ixion's time.

Yes, the Ecclesiarch thinks, turning away from the bright city, today will be a day to savor. Yet there are other matters he must attend to, less historic than the overthrow of the Sovereign, perhaps, but in their own way just as important. Perhaps *more* so, for without them what would the Hierarchate be but an empty shell, glittering yet hollow, like the brittle husk of a firefly or the sloughed-off skin of a serpent?

As always on this day, he must say the Mass and bless the devout multitudes assembled within and around the Cathedral. They have already begun to gather far below, tiny and busy as ants. By now, he knows, the Mouths of God will have removed the *Lives and Acts* from its resting place and begun the sonorous public reading that will last until tomorrow noon, when the arrested sun resumes its descent, signaling the end of All Saints' Eve and the start of another Season of Chastenings. Even in the midst of great change, the Ecclesiarch reflects, trying on the thought for use in today's sermon, the Wheel of the

Spinner continues to spin as it always has and always will until the Unspinning. May that day be soon in coming, he amends piously, out of habit.

But there's a different prayer in his heart.

So much to do, yet he feels strangely reluctant now to leave this peaceful chamber and the sleeping boy who is the very image of his youthful self. No, more than the image: the thing itself, as if people, like seasons, recur with the turnings.

When he first saw the boy—or, rather, first noticed him, for he had seen him many times, in passing, before his attention was captured—the resemblance alarmed him like a ghostly visitation, an omen of death. Indeed, his immediate thought was to have the boy killed.

But something had stopped him. Instead, no more able to resist the strange compulsion than to understand it, he'd arranged with Erigeron to fake his son's death. Then he'd plucked out the boy's eyes, and his memory, too, and brought him here to this high and solitary tower whose crystal walls and ceiling, with a word, turn opaque and become mirrors.

For weeks the Ecclesiarch came each day to gaze upon his prize, whom he kept in a deep sleep with injections of aspergine. He paced the chamber like a caged animal, not so much looking at the boy as at the boy's reflections, gradually working his way back in time, back to his own lost youth, which had been dead and now lived again, multiplied to infinity.

Often, drawn irresistibly, he sat at the edge of the bed and brought his hand, with its deadly ring, the amethyst firefly, close to the boy's blue and slightly parted lips, feeling the icy breath lick his fingers. Then his hand, his whole body, would shake with conflicting desires: to kill the boy; to spare him. And other desires he was afraid to acknowledge.

Then, one day, it wasn't his ring that he brought close to the boy's lips but his own trembling lips, the dry and liver-colored lips of an old, old man. He bent his head and kissed the sleeping boy. And it was he, not the boy, who awoke. Suddenly, all the fugitive past was restored to him. Tears were streaming down his face. He had no idea why; he hadn't wept since the day the vizards tore him from his mother over two thousand turnings before. He thought: *I am whole again. At last.*

But he wasn't. Not yet. Not until, instead of the usual injection of aspergine, he administered the antidote and woke the boy to his new life. He gave the boy a new name, which had once been his own name—Sium—and abandoned himself to himself.

And even then . . .

There are times the Ecclesiarch wonders if he was wrong to awaken the past, to embrace it like this. Tied to another, he no longer feels safe. What if some harm should come to the boy? Then he would be left alone again, with an emptiness nothing, not even metheglin, could fill. He can feel it already, a foreboding like the chill of night that sometimes enters the air though the sun yet shines. To protect himself, to free himself from this beautiful, intolerable bondage, he'll use the ring one day. A final, deadly kiss.

But not today.

Not on All Saints' Eve.

Even as he leaves the chamber, the Ecclesiarch is already eager to return. If only he could remain there forever, like Sium. If only he could change places with the boy. Not just in play, as when he transfers the golden chain to his own ankle, but for real, leaving his aged body, wracked with ceaseless hunger, to slip into Sium's, as though into a perfectly tailored robe. How nice it must be to drift in aspergine's timeless void, waking only to taste the pleasures of love! He laughs out loud at the thought. Then he locks the door behind him and hurries down the hall to the far door, which he opens in turn.

Outside, the two shrives of his personal guard snap to attention. As he motions for them to precede him, he wonders if they have any idea what goes on behind these doors. Why he comes here each night. What would they think if they heard him laugh or saw him cry? Fortunately for them, their faces are hidden behind the smooth black masks of their order, and their eyes give no hint of thought or feeling.

Without a word between them, they move in unison down the long hallway. The Ecclesiarch follows, frowning at this silent yet somehow arrogant display of intimacy, as if the shrives are sharing thoughts. If they can converse mind to mind, he wonders, can they not hear his thoughts as well as their own? And Sium's?

The vizards have assured him otherwise. All shrives are virtually indistinguishable, but the pairs share a closer identity, knit together in the treatment rooms of the vizards. There they are crafted to respond to an array of subtle cues only their enhanced senses are capable of detecting. This can give observers the impression that an uncanny link exists, as if a single mind is controlling both bodies, or, rather, is divided between them. But that's all it is. An impression.

But the Ecclesiarch isn't wholly convinced. After all, Azedarach can project his thoughts and hear the thoughts of others. Though he owes this ability to the crafting of the Serpent Crown, who's to say the shrives haven't attained a similar ability? The truth is, he envies them. Envies that bond. It's what he wants with Sium.

What he can't have.

The Ecclesiarch is in a foul mood when he enters his chambers to prepare for the Mass. When he catches sight of Morus Sisymbrium seated in his favorite chair, twisting the ragged ends of his beard in his stubby fingers, his mood grows fouler still.

Morus springs to his feet. "Your Eminence!"

"What is it?" the Ecclesiarch snaps. "You know we shouldn't be seen together. If Azedarach—"

"He already knows." Morus appears genuinely disturbed, even frightened. "Someone must have warned him."

"It is you who have warned him by coming here!"

"No." He shakes his head vehemently. "I wouldn't have come unless there was no other choice. Anywhere but here, and I'm as dead as Erigeron, of no use to you."

All the anger flows out of the Ecclesiarch. He feels tired. And old. He sits heavily in the chair vacated by Morus. "What's happened?"

"His shrives came to arrest me. It's only by chance I got away! This is Sylvestris's doing, I'm sure of it!"

"Why?"

Morus shrugs impatiently, as if the answer should be obvious. "He's been looking for a girl, a Cat."

"Yes, yes. You told me that when we made our bargain."

"But I didn't tell you why; I didn't know myself until today. This morning, before the shrives paid their visit, one of our—that is, Azedarach's—spies came to see me, a woman we placed among the heretics some turnings ago. It seems they're in an uproar, Your Eminence; apparently, they believe that Viridis Lacrimata—Liberatrix, rather—has returned to them."

"Rank superstition."

"I trust this girl, Your Eminence; she hasn't been turned, I'm sure of it. And she acted like she believed it herself."

The Ecclesiarch frowns. Viridis Liberatrix! That old heresy has been around longer than he has. He's never given it a moment of serious thought, never entertained the possibility of its being true. And yet he finds himself reflecting now for the first time that if the essence of his youthful self may be reborn in the son of a vizard, perhaps Viridis Lacrimata, too, may live again in a lowly Cat.

Or seem to.

It's not impossible. He's had teams of vizards at work for turnings to replicate those miraculous tears. Have Azedarach's vizards succeeded where his own have failed?

Not a comforting thought. But the possibility cannot be ignored. If Azedarach could produce a living, breathing saint, he would be untouchable, practically a saint himself.

Yet if Azedarach has crafted a second Viridis, why has she appeared among the heretics? Is that part of some plan? Or has Azedarach lost control of the plan, of his own creation? Is there an opportunity here?

"Where is Sylvestris now?"

Morus shrugs again. "I haven't seen him for days. But what about me? What am I going to do?"

"Why, you will do as you are told, Morus. What else?" The Ecclesiarch sighs. "You disappoint me. I thought you were resolute. Dependable. With a character as steady as your hands during a harvest. Instead, at the first hint of difficulty you fall apart. Perhaps you are not fit to wear the Serpent Crown after all. Perhaps I should look for someone else. A man who isn't afraid to gamble with his life for such a lofty prize."

Morus's eyes flash angrily, but he holds his tongue.

"Well?"

"I'm your man," he growls, almost spitting. "There's no going back, only forward. I knew that when I agreed to join you, and I've never forgotten it or wished otherwise. I'm no coward, Eminence. But things have changed. Our plans must change with them."

The Ecclesiarch considers. "A change of plans is risky so late in the game."

"Who is it now who's afraid to gamble?"

The Ecclesiarch smiles thinly. "No, you are no coward, Morus. So it's a gamble you want? Very well. Tell me: do you still have the keys to the metheglin vaults?"

Morus gives a slow nod, not understanding.

"I'm going to give you a troop of shrives. You will go there at once, without delay."

"You wish me to secure the vaults?"

"I want you to destroy them."

"You can't be serious!"

"Azedarach is an addict, as you well know. Without his supply of metheglin, he'll die. As for me, I have my own private supply, so you needn't worry on that score," he adds with the barest trace of irony.

Morus strokes his beard rapidly. "The metheglin vaults have always been neutral ground, off-limits in even the bloodiest conflicts."

"Meaningless tradition."

"It cost me nothing to betray Azedarach, yet this I find difficult." Morus gives a gruff, almost-embarrassed, laugh. "My family has guarded the vaults for twenty-two generations, held the keys in a sacred trust. How can I betray that trust, Eminence? It's as if I'm betraying my father, my ancestors—my own self!"

"There comes a time in every man's life when he must kill his past to set his future free."

"I thought that by possessing the Serpent Throne, I would have everything," says Morus. "I mean, everything I started with, and more besides. But now I find that, bit by bit, I must murder all the things I love in order to gain it. Is it always that way with power, Eminence?"

"Yes," the Ecclesiarch replies after a moment, gazing at his amethyst ring and thinking of Sium. "Yes, of course it is."

NINE

Rumer huddles in the cramped stern of the boat, trying to stay awake. A thyrsis set in the bow casts a sliver of light upon the water. There is a hot wind in her face that smells faintly of brine. It blows stronger as they go. Hotter, too; even the water is hot. A fog rises from its dark surface.

Spread out loosely behind them, the lights of the other two boats bob in the darkness like large, slow-moving fireflies. The only sounds are the steady dip and curl of the oars, the soft, companionable creaking of the boats, and the slap and splash of water against the hulls and the rough-hewn rock of this maze of tunnels they've been rowing through for hours now.

Occasionally, caught by the weird acoustics of the place, the voices of Rose and the three Kites drift clearly back to Rumer from where they stand whispering and pointing on the bow, darkly silhouetted in the haze like shadows turned to stone:

"That tunnel leads to Lusk."

"That one to Dindle."

"No one has come back from this one."

It's Rumer's first time in a boat. She finds the rocking of the water soothing, although the nearness of it, as well as its darkness, concealing who knows what, makes her nervous. She can't swim. That skill is not part of the *ars erotica*, and hence had no place in her education.

Sitting in front of her, rowing with powerful, hypnotic strokes, are four viragi; that they are expert swimmers, Rumer has no doubt. They blow air loudly through their mouths in time to each stroke. She's still frightened of them, and of their skintight black uniforms that bear such an unsettling resemblance to the shrives' armor. How uncomfortable they must be! Rumer is wearing a summery skirt and top, but even so she's dripping with sweat. Yet the viragi appear unfazed despite the heat and their physical exertions, and Rumer wonders if their ability to ignore, if not transcend, the limitations of the body is a mark of discipline or vizards' craft.

Picea and Aralia are each captaining one of the other boats. Altogether, twenty-one women are spread among the three: Rose and Rumer, Picea and Aralia, the three Kites, plus fourteen viragi—six on Rumer's boat and four each on the two others.

Half-asleep, Rumer watches the tunnels pass and imagines the boat is holding still while everything else glides smoothly by. Like the raw materials of dreams, the shapes revealed by the thyrsi take on, as if by a quality inhering in them rather than by Rumer's fancy, the look of people and places she's known. She watches in spellbound fascination as her history unrolls before her bleary eyes, so that even while the boat moves forward it seems to be carrying her deeper and deeper into the past.

There is Erigeron Intricata at the moment of his death, as the assassin Nyssa Circium plunges the knife into his chest. Here the positions of the *ars erotica* are portrayed in miniature, just as on the doors of the House Illicium; only these figures aren't static, but full of life and motion, seeming to generate heat. There is her mother's face, swollen with tears, her shaved scalp nicked with blood, watching with clenched lips and fists as the panderman pulls Rumer to the auction block in Kell. Here is the house in Jubilar where Rumer lived for so brief and happy a time, and there the house of her neighbors, the Galingales, whose son, Cyrus, would have become her husband if Beauty hadn't stolen her father and, with him, her life—or, anyway, the life he'd promised her.

So many losses, she thinks. Yet each of them, in its way, had brought her closer to Rose. She doesn't regret any of them now. But the very fact of these past losses has made her suspicious of whatever she possesses or desires in the present. She's afraid she'll lose Rose, too.

A splash of water from the oars jerks Rumer upright. Seconds or hours may have just passed; it's impossible for her to tell if she was asleep or dozing. Rose is still at the front of the boat with the Kites, and the tunnels continue to glide by as before, the steady rhythm of the rowers unchanged. Rumer yawns, rubbing grit from her eyes. It's grown hotter, she thinks. And the briny smell has lessened, or, rather, become mixed with a new and sweeter smell: the smell of metheglin. She pinches her arm hard, determined not to fall asleep again.

But she's never felt so tired. It's strange, because here she is on her way to destroy the metheglin vaults, and you'd think that would be enough to hold a person's interest. But no; she's continually nodding off now and has been ever since they embarked.

Rose had moved quickly, selecting the women to accompany her to the vaults. A number of men had volunteered to go as well, but Rose shook her head.

"You've had your turn," she said. "This is the women's time."

Some of the men looked hurt at that; a few seemed angry. But none of them argued.

No one, male or female, wanted Rose to go. The risk was too great. If something should go wrong! If they should lose her now, after waiting for so long! How could they go on without her, without Viridis Liberatrix?

But, again, Rose firmly shook her head. "This is how it must be."

So they left. Rumer stood at Rose's side as they walked out of the underground palace and into the even larger cavern that contained it. Below them, at the foot of the steps leading to the palace, a great crowd stood, stretching as far as Rumer could see, to the very limits of the space. There must have been thousands. As before, she found herself marveling at how many heretics lived in this secret, underground world.

Rose was greeted with cheers and upraised fists. Rumer wondered how many of these people had been waiting here for the last two days just to see the Liberatrix. Probably all of them, she thought, just as, in some way, every one of them had been transformed by Rose's tears.

Herself included. Wasn't she different now? She didn't know how or why, but she felt the truth of it instinctively, like a newly awakened sense. If only she wasn't so tired, perhaps she could figure it out. But she wondered if the tiredness, too, was not a part of her transformation.

Rose lifted her arms in acknowledgment of the cheers, and the crowd quieted almost instantly, so eager were they to hear her voice addressing them once more. Rose waited a moment, letting the silence stretch, the anticipation build.

"This is women's time!" she said at last, her clear voice ringing out like a bell. "Today is All Saints' Eve, the day that Ixion Diospyros ascended into the heavens, nailed by the Furies to his Burning Wheel. On this day the so-called saints turned against their allies who had fought side by side with them in the great war to defeat Maw and His Furies. They turned on us, on women. Turned on their wives and daughters. On their own mothers. Ever since that betrayal, we have been as slaves to men. As property. No more. No more!"

At this, the crowd erupted again in cheers. Rumer found herself nodding as if in agreement, but did she really agree? This was heresy, pure and simple. And yet there was truth in it. She'd been sold to the House Illicium to pay off her father's debts. The money had gone to the Galingales, to atone for the broken marriage. That had always seemed reasonable and right. Why, all of a sudden, did it seem so wrong?

Rose continued. "There are men among us today. Our brothers in the fight. We welcome and honor them. Our fight is not just to liberate women, but men, too. In the Hierarchate, every position is fixed. No one rises except by another's fall. The highest tower in Quoz rests upon the lowest hut in Arpagee. Take away that hut, and everything collapses. In such a rigid, inflexible system, it's not only women who are slaves. Every master, every man, is himself a slave. We fight for a world without slaves or masters. So it's only right that men fight alongside us now.

"But with all honor to the men among us, this is women's time! And it must be women who strike the decisive blow, women who break their own chains!"

More applause. Rumer listened, her heart beating fast, as if itself applauding.

"This is women's time! Let us smash the clocks of men with their miserly accretion of minutes and hours and days and turnings, all the deadweight of time! We will craft new clocks, living clocks that run on the rhythms of the body, the pulses of the heart, the flow of the blood! We will smash the barriers of gender, of the orders: all the walls erected by the Hierarchate to keep us in our places, to raise some people high while casting others down to the lowest depths.

"Together, daughters and sons of the Spinner, let us spin a new and better world. A fairer world. A world more truly in the image of the Spinner's Wheel, without beginning or end, top or bottom, in which the turning is all.

"So I call upon each of you now: become as a single teardrop from my eyes. On this All Saints' Eve, touch the world above us and heal its wounds as my tears have healed you. Blessed be the Spinner! Blessed be Her holy name now and forever! As it was in the beginning, is now, and shall be until the Unspinning!"

Rumer clapped and shouted "Blessed be!" along with the rest of the crowd, contributing her small voice to its thunder. How beautiful Rose looked, applauding in turn. How proud Rumer was! She felt as if she were shining, her heart a burning wheel.

Aralia, who stood beside her, leaned close to shout above the noise: "Remember what I told you, Rumer? What you call heresy is only love!"

And Rumer shouted back: "I know."

Then Rose, as if she had heard the exchange, took Rumer by the hand. Together, followed by the women Rose had chosen for the mission, they walked down the steps and through the crowd to the edge of the water. A number of boats were drawn up on the pebbled shore; others floated at anchor a short distance out.

"Our route lies there," said one of the Kites, pointing across the water, where darkness fell with all the weight of stone. "We call this the Undersea, for it runs beneath every town and city of the upper world, emerging into the light only to crash against the cliffs of Arpagee. The world floats upon these wide waters as if upon the Spinner's outstretched hands; from here, there is no place in the Hierarchate we cannot reach. The Undersea gives us our food. Our water. It is all things to us."

They chose three of the lightest and fastest boats, then climbed aboard as the crowd shouted encouragement. Rumer wobbled to her seat in the stern of the largest boat as Rose joined the Kites up front. Then the viragi pushed the boats into the water and jumped aboard themselves. They started rowing, and the boats shot away. Looking back, Rumer watched as the shoreline and the cheering crowd standing upon it dwindled, until all she could see were the winking lights of thyrsi. Then they entered the first tunnel, and she was cut off from all sight of the shore.

"Rumer!"

Rumer's eyelids flutter open, and she finds herself looking into the angry face of Rose.

"Don't sleep, Rumer! You have to stay awake. It's important!"

Rumer rubs her eyes.

"I know it's hard, but you've got to try."

Rumer nods; she'll stay awake forever if Rose asks. "Where are we?"

"We're putting in."

Even as Rose speaks, the boats glide onto the shore with a pleasant rasping sound, then grind to a halt. The sweet smell of metheglin is stronger now. Dizzying. They must be very close to the vaults, Rumer thinks. But the air is cooler, and that, at least, helps her stay awake. She follows the others out of the boat, then leans against Rose, her legs uncertain.

They are in a small cavern, a kind of pocket worn into the stone. The undulate walls and ceiling, streaked and whorled with sediment and exposed minerals, glitter with moisture in the light of the three thyrsi set in the bows of the boats. The ground is hard and slippery, with a scattering of small stones. It slopes up to a passage that cuts at an oblique angle into the recesses of the cavern.

Everyone seems to know what to do but Rumer; plans must have been made while she was sleeping. First, Aralia, Picea, and Rumer must insert a set of nose plugs to keep themselves from being overwhelmed by the scent of metheglin, which can be toxic in concentrated doses. Rose helps Rumer with hers, but doesn't use the plugs herself. "I have nothing to fear from metheglin," she says.

The Kites, too, habituated to metheglin by turnings of clandestine use, eschew the uncomfortable plugs; the same plugs, Rumer notes, which men wear each night to protect themselves from Beauty.

The viragi fold up the collars of their uniforms so that their noses and mouths are covered as if by a clinging black veil, making them look more than ever like shrives.

Then the thyrsi from the boats are distributed to three viragi, each of whom leads a group of about ten women. The Kites take positions near the front, where they can point the way. Rumer stays close to Rose. The other viragi hold thyrsi, too, only these do not shed light. Rumer thinks again of the shrives, in whose hands the thyrsi are deadly weapons.

As they enter the passage, which is wide enough for two women, Rose takes Rumer by the hand and squeezes reassuringly. How strange it feels to Rumer to be led by Rose along this passage just as, only a week ago, she led Rose from her chambers in the House Illicium down to the hidden world of the heretics.

The passage rises steadily, branching often. The Kites follow some of these turnings while ignoring others, until Rumer can no longer remember the way back to the boats. The only sound is the scraping of their footsteps, the echoes of which come back strangely distorted, as if they are being followed. Rumer looks over her shoulder but sees only backward-cast shadows slipping nimbly among the rocks with a furtive life of their own.

At last the Kites signal a halt. A section of wall has collapsed, perhaps during a long-ago Chastening; a pile of rubble fills the passage. There is a crack in the wall wide enough to squeeze through. One by one, they slip inside.

And find themselves in a narrow passage whose ceiling hangs so low they must scrabble on hands and knees over the wet, pebbly ground. But as the crevice ascends, the ceiling follows suit until they can walk upright, looking like an army of women who've clawed their way up from out of the ground.

As soon as she can, Rumer takes Rose's hand again. At some point, she's cut her arm, and although she feels no pain—the cut hardly more than a scratch—the sight of the blood, a trickle muddied to ocher by dirt and mud, is unsettling.

The air has grown cold, but Rumer is warmed by a flow of heat that passes from Rose to her across the bridge of their hands. Picea and Aralia, however, shiver miserably, pulling their robes about their shoulders. The Kites shiver gladly, as if making of this latest suffering an ostentatious offering. And the viragi seem resistant to the cold entirely, as, earlier, to the heat; Rumer wonders at this until Aralia, though chattering teeth, explains that the black uniforms were crafted to maintain the bodies of their wearers at a constant temperature.

"Like the armor of the shrives," Rumer says.

"Not even shrives have armor like this," Aralia sneers.

There's a turn, and the crevice spills into a wide and obviously man-made or enhanced corridor. Along the pale, regular walls, Rumer sees red markings similar to those she's seen before; for some reason, they frighten her now, as if the reality of what they are about to do here has only just struck her.

Soon the Kites call another halt.

"We have arrived," whispers one. "This entrance was lost or forgotten over the turnings. Only we know of it now."

From the wall, the symbol of a hand seems to warn them away like a bloody imprint.

Another Kite speaks, her voice soft and matter-of-fact. "Behind this door lies the oldest section of the vaults. In all the turnings we have come here, we have never seen another soul, and only rarely have we heard the muffled footsteps of the cupbearer gathering metheglin in the distance. But today we will penetrate more deeply into the vaults than we have ever gone before, and we must expect resistance."

"We have prayed for it," says one of the viragi, her face a Fury's mask.

"No doubt much of what we are about to see will prove strange to us," Picea interrupts. Her stern brown eyes rake over each woman in turn, admitting no distinctions between them. Only Rose is exempt from her scrutiny. "Perhaps some of you will be tempted to have a taste of metheglin like the holy sisters here. But remember: we haven't come to plunder the vaults. We're here to destroy them."

The Kites nod. Now the third Kite speaks, unable to keep a possessive and boastful lilt from her voice as she describes the secrets of the vaults. "There is a small store of processed metheglin from which my sisters and I have drawn over the turnings. But raw metheglin is kept in rows of chilled containers until it can be processed by the cupbearer. If they are breached, the metheglin becomes spoiled. Useless. We know this because once, many turnings ago, my sisters and I chanced to be in the vaults during a Chastening, when a number of the containers cracked and spilled their contents across the floor. We were curious to know if the cupbearer would gather up the spilled metheglin and repair or replace the containers. But when we returned, though the mess was gone, the containers were gone as well. Then we knew that the craft of repairing them, like this entrance, had been lost over the turnings, forgotten."

The Kite turns to Rose with a proud smile. "Surely the Spinner revealed this secret to us, that we might one day use it against our enemies! That day has come at last! By smashing the containers, we will bring the whole Hierarchate down!" And she raises her fist as if the wall before her is itself a thing of glass to be shattered with a blow.

But Rose says: "Wait."

All eyes are on her now.

"Let me."

Bowing her head, the Kite steps back. Rose places her hand upon the symbol, and the wall slides open.

Immediately, a dense wave of frigid air spills over them from within, causing everyone but Rose and the viragi to pull back. Even Rumer feels the cold, though she still grasps Rose's warming hand. At the same time, a golden light pours through the opening with the force of a blunt object, blinding her.

As in a dream, Rumer feels Rose's lips brush her cheek and hears her voice whisper in her ear: "You woke me, Rumer; you set me free. But now you must sleep. Remember me when you wake, Rumer. Remember!"

Then Rose's hand is gone, and with it all warmth and comfort. Rumer stumbles forward, pushed by eager viragi. She gropes after Rose and cries her name, but her small voice is lost amid cacophonies of breaking glass.

The metheglin vaults seem to go on forever, filled with row upon row of glass containers, each roughly the size of a small child. Coils of tubing sprout from the containers. Some of these tubes are rooted in the floor while others rise like shining vines to an impossibly high ceiling. The flood of honeyed light radiates from within the tubes and containers, where a substance flows like molten gold.

Metheglin.

The viragi move quickly down the long rows, smashing the containers and ripping away the tubes. Metheglin comes oozing out, spraying out, shining all the while with such intensity that Rumer wonders how the vaults can be so cold, how this strange substance, like blood fallen from the sun, can produce blinding light but no heat.

Rumer is shoved again. She sprawls heavily to her hands and knees on a smooth, hard, numbingly cold surface; little cracks of pain worm through her bones at the impact. She tries to rise, but suddenly an immense weariness settles over her shoulders, the same weariness she felt on the boat. It squats on her now like an obese vizard, like Erigeron Intricata.

Rumer smells a sweetness like nothing she's ever known, a sweetness indistinguishable from the pain, the cold, the gauzy golden shine, and she realizes that her nose plugs have become dislodged in the fall; she's smelling pure metheglin. She looks again for Rose, finds her standing calmly in the midst of this purposeful destruction, and cries out to her for help. But her voice is less than a whisper; no tears will save her now.

Everything is fuzzy, slow. The number of viragi has tripled. Or is it shrives she sees? Black onrushing figures, silent and deadly as the night that rises up without mercy to obliterate her sight.

TEN

The waste, Sylvestris thinks. The senseless, colossal waste! A bright river of raw metheglin is spreading across the floor of the vaults from the broken shells of storage containers, each one irreplaceable. If not for his nose plugs, the scent would have driven him mad by now. But the sight of so much contaminated metheglin is maddening enough.

In preparation for his duties as cupbearer, Sylvestris has learned that it takes the contents of a hundred containers to make a single ounce of pure metheglin. An ounce! Raw metheglin must be preserved in these containers, the products of a crafting no living vizard can duplicate, like the thyrsi, like the Serpent Crown itself. And, vast though the vaults may be, they hold only a finite number of containers.

It's no small part of his new duties to guard them well, these treasures as valuable as metheglin, and as mysterious. Yet now, before his duties have officially begun, as if this is the price to be paid for assuming them, Sylvestris must sacrifice a portion of what he's sworn to protect. He knows, of course, that there's always a price, but the excessiveness of it both grieves him and fills him with rage against these heretics who care only for wanton destruction.

"Let them taste destruction then," prompts the voice of Saint Rober Virburnum. The voices of his other simulars agree, clamoring for blood to spill in place of metheglin.

Sylvestris has watched and waited, grinding his teeth in fury as the heretics entered through an all-but-forgotten door and began their wicked rampage. The glassine containers felt no pain as they shattered beneath the heavy blows of thyrsi, but he did. Those were his bones breaking; that was his blood upon the floor.

How it galls him to see the viragi, mockeries of shrives armed with stolen thyrsi; their mere presence desecrates this holy place! And the three Kites, traitors to their order, who even now scurry off on some mission of mischief. Among the viragi he sees Aralia Illicium, her dark skin bronzed in the golden light, and a pale Cat, even lovelier, who reminds him of Picea Circium, though of course it can't be she: he remembers well the old scandal, mad Picea in the grip of her passion slashing her face to ribbons, then vanishing from Quoz as if swallowed by the night. Some distance from the others, the voluptuary Rumer Illicium collapses to the floor, where she lies as if overwhelmed by metheglin.

And there, facing Sylvestris calmly, as if she sees him crouched behind the row of containers and fears him not at all, is a slight young Cat. A red teardrop is tattooed on her left cheek; a fine, dark bristle covers her scalp. The green of her eyes nearly outshines the metheglin.

Rose, he thinks.

Viridis Liberatrix.

The last time he saw her was after the murder of Erigeron Intricata. He'd been hanging in his harness above the stage, the wires of his simulars binding him there like chains, when he caught sight of her beside the doors of the hospitality hall, her green eyes bright as fireflies. He knew right away that he'd found the woman Azedarach had sent him to find, knew it even as he lost her, Rumer pulling her from the hall before he could properly disconnect himself from the harness. He winces at the memory of that nerve-searing pain, and his simulars whimper softly inside him, sharing it.

Even though her beauty treatments are incomplete, Rose seems beautiful to him now. Hers is a wild beauty, unshaped and imperfect. But real. No longer a normal woman, not yet a Cat, Rose is something else entirely, something new, like an order of woman that has not been seen before.

"Or," comes the precise voice of Saint Quercus Incana, "not for a very, very long time."

She stands there as if waiting. As if the two of them are alone here in the vaults, watching each other, both knowing what comes next.

And, Sylvestris thinks, Rose does know. Or, rather, a part of her knows: the secret, second self that pulls her strings like a master simularter. For it's not fate that's brought Rose here, but conditioning, which, as Saint Quercus reminds him, is itself a kind of fate, perhaps the only kind. Rather than leading these heretics to glory, Rose has already betrayed them. And he holds the key, the word, to wake the last piece of conditioning, the ultimate betrayal that slumbers inside her.

Galingale.

He will use it against her, but not yet. Not yet. Now Sylvestris speaks to the shrives in silent hand language, signaling that she is not to be harmed. As for the others . . .

None must escape, the Sovereign told him. And so Sylvestris forces himself to hold back, clenching his hands into mute fists as the heretics penetrate more deeply into the vaults, swept on a reckless tide farther and farther from the door, which alone might save them.

Concealed behind the rows of containers, two lines of shrives are poised to snap shut like the mandibles of a beetle lurking under sand. They are as eager as Sylvestris to strike, but, unlike him, betray no hint of impatience, only a discipline cold as the air of the vaults, as if they would await his signal until the Unspinning itself.

But Sylvestris has no intention of waiting so long. He gives another hand sign, and so quickly is the order communicated to every shrive in the vaults that even before his gloved fingers have stilled, the trap is sprung.

The shrives outnumber the viragi by three to one. They have been trained from boyhood in the expert use of weapons and in the equally deadly arts of hand-to-hand combat. Crafted by vizards in body and mind, they are vicious fighters, fanatically loyal, all but invincible in their sleek black armor.

Aralia Illicium and the beautiful pale Cat beside her go down like stalks of grain before a scythe. They do not even have time to scream. Taken by surprise, the viragi are engulfed from two sides in a whispering black flood.

The false Liberatrix doesn't flinch. She ignores the brittle clash of arms as the shrives engage the viragi, ignores everything, as if nothing taking place here is real, none of it solid or permanent enough to matter. Sylvestris is reminded of Azedarach, who, seated placidly upon his Throne, gazes into kingdoms of time sensible to no other eyes but his own.

Sylvestris smiles. He begins to unfold his long legs. Though his bones ache with cold, he feels a warm, triumphant glow, already savoring his victory and the reward it will bring: the keys to the metheglin vaults.

"Wait," comes the voice of Saint Ixion.

Sylvestris crouches, peering over the containers. Something is happening . . .

It's the viragi. Somehow they've broken past the ring of shrives. Not all of them: only ten or so. The bodies of the rest lie strewn across the floor in a wash of metheglin and blood and broken glass, limbs twisted and smashed like simulars abandoned in a Chastening. More incredibly, shrives have fallen, too, and in greater numbers, their armor breached as easily as the fragile glassine containers that surround them.

The surviving viragi form a circle around Rose, facing outward. Now Sylvestris sees that her cheeks are wet with tears. She brushes one hand past her eyes, like a sleeper freshly wakened, then touches the uncovered heads of the viragi as if bestowing a last blessing, her lips shaping an inaudible prayer. Sylvestris can't help but admire the useless gesture; he observes everything with a critical eye, thinking of how best to stage these events later for the private delectation of Azedarach.

Meanwhile, after blocking the way to the door, thereby cutting off the only escape route, the shrives resume the attack. They have the clear advantage of strength and numbers, but the viragi fight as if possessed by Furies.

Sylvestris has never seen anyone move so quickly, with such deadly and purposeful grace, like dancers trained to kill. The viragi penetrate the shrives' defenses easily, striking again and again with their stolen thyrsi. Rather than shedding light, the opalescent globes at the tips of the thyrsi erupt in blue-and-red sparks which leave smoking, fire-rimmed cracks in the armor of their adversaries.

When the shrives strike back with their own thyrsi, the strange armor of the viragi merely shimmers like some viscid liquid rippled by a breeze. Even at the strongest blows, the black armor does not shatter or crack in a florid shower of sparks; it blooms with bursts of color like bruises as quick to flare as to heal, as if the armor is somehow absorbing and then diffusing the energies directed against it.

Incredibly, more shrives are falling now. The survivors are pulling back in disarray. Sylvestris, for one terrible moment, is sure he will have to take to his heels. His triumph is turning to smoke before his eyes. His simulars are no help at all; their frantic voices pummel him with suggestions and recriminations until he can barely hear himself think.

He forces himself to stay put, afraid he'll only present an easy target by running. The shrives come on again, in a ragged mob, howling as though out of their minds with shock and grief and rage. The sloppiness of the attack appalls Sylvestris; he's never heard of shrives losing control this way, breaking ranks to attack like wild animals.

But this time, despite the absence of coordination, their superior numbers tell. Under the repeated blows, the resilient armor of the viragi begins to glow with a white-hot incandescence that compels Sylvestris to look away. There's a sudden flash, and when he looks again their armor is the color of cinders. One by one, the viragi fall as if cooked within their armor.

Only seven shrives remain. Seven out of the fifty who attacked just moments ago. Their battered armor is painted red with blood, their own as well as that of the viragi.

Rose stands alone, unprotected, within the circle of her fallen defenders. The shrives pace the edge of that circle, as if afraid to cross it.

Then one of them raises his thyrsis and leaps over the charred bodies with a growl. Rose steps forward to meet him with a smile, as if welcoming the blow.

Sylvestris leaps to his feet: "No! Stop!"

The shrive hesitates, glancing over his shoulder as the simularter crosses the space between them on his long legs. "She is not to be harmed; the Sovereign commands it!"

Sylvestris puts all his authority into his voice, but in truth he's afraid. More afraid than he's ever been. For the blue eyes studying him from the black, blood-spattered mask are as cold as always but no longer intelligent. They are the predatory eyes of an animal. Or a madman. The other six shrives look at him in the same way, with the same volatile gaze. It's as if the blows of the viragi not only breached the shrives' armor but shattered their conditioning, snapping the iron chains of discipline that restrain their murderous natures. Will they obey him now? Or turn on him like curs in which the wolf has awakened?

"Step back," he says in a voice as firm and calm as he can muster. "She is Azedarach's."

A glimmer of recognition, of fear, comes into their eyes at that. So their conditioning has not been completely shattered; a single link, at least, remains.

"I command you in the name of Azedarach: step away!"

The shrives outside the circle shuffle back. But their brother within the circle turns to Rose. He hefts the thyrsis in his hand, shifting from foot to foot.

"Step away!" Sylvestris repeats more forcefully.

The shrive lets the thyrsis fall.

Even before it hits the floor, Sylvestris knows the last link has been broken. He springs forward: "No!"

The shrive makes a movement with his hands. A dark blur, a sharp and sickening crack, and Rose goes down.

The shrive screams. His hands are smoking, as if consumed from within his armor. He falls to the floor, writhing in agony. His screams rise to a thin, excruciating wail. Then silence.

Sylvestris makes the sign of the Wheel as the other shrives look on, blue eyes wide with horror.

The shrive's armor is melting. It balloons momentarily, as if at the pressure of expanding gases, then sags, collapsing in upon itself to form a fervid, bubbling pool in which blood and bits of charred bone mix with the oily scum of flesh.

Sylvestris shivers, suddenly cold again. The words of Azedarach come back to him now as if the Sovereign is projecting them into his head from the Serpent Throne . . . which, for all Sylvestris knows, he may be:

Unfortunately, it proved impossible to duplicate the healing powers ascribed to the tears of Saint Viridis Lacrimata; instead, the eyes were made to produce tears of poison, for the apocryphal testaments of Viridis Lacrimata circulated among the heretics seem to permit such an interpretation: "Then from a lowly place I will come again with my green eyes, and my tears will burn like the stings of fireflies."

The vizards did their work well, he thinks.

"Too well," comes the voice of Saint Stilskin.

Sylvestris feels sick. He wonders if Azedarach glimpsed this turning in any of his metheglin dreams. Somehow, he doubts it. He forces himself to walk past the slowly coagulating pool, from which a greasy smoke rises, leaving a dirty film upon his clothes and skin, and squats beside the body of Rose.

Her neck, he sees at once, is broken.

There's no light now in her green eyes; they are dull as clouded marble. He's afraid to touch her. What use now the word Azedarach had given him? If he speaks the name *Galingale*, will it return Rose to life?

He stands with a disgusted sigh, only to find that the shrives have fled. He is alone with the dead. Their bodies seem to watch him with resentful malice as he strolls among them. His simulars are silent for once, but he can sense their apprehension. He shares it. But he can't leave yet. He promises himself he'll personally supervise the excoriation of the shrives who deserted him.

He stops beside the body of Aralia Illicium. One of the first to die. Her eyes wide in shock, her mouth still open in the scream she'd had no time to give. Her perfect white teeth gleam like pearls in the bloody oyster of a mouth he's kissed a hundred times. The pallor of death has lightened her skin like a dusting of ash. He shakes his head, remembering hours spent with her in the House Illicium. He'd been fond of Aralia; unlike many Cats, whose aversion to simularters was plain, Aralia did not limply surrender herself to his manipulations, but gave herself over willingly, as if she derived pleasure from his touch.

Was it, he wonders now, because she was a spy? Did her guilty conscience somehow need the pain he provided? A kind of penance for the countless small betrayals of others, of herself, that made up her daily life?

There's a long knife beside the frozen claw of her hand. He takes it, tests the edge upon her throat. He judges it will do.

Now he cuts away Aralia's robes. There's a slight bulge to her belly, a bare brown swell, and he wonders if the rumors are true: that she carries the child of Erigeron Intricata. His laughter is a sharp bark.

He returns to Rose. He's not squeamish, but he cannot easily forget the shrive. Though Rose is dead, her tears may retain their poison. And what of her blood?

He mouths a silent prayer to the Spinner, and begins.

Perhaps because her neck is already broken, the work is smooth and fast. There is very little blood. A small answered prayer, he thinks.

"It's always the small prayers that are answered," comes Saint Rober's voice.

When he's through, and the head has, of its own weight, rolled away from the neck, Sylvestris spreads what he's cut from Aralia's robes. He prods the head into the center of the fabric, using a thyrsis plucked from the floor. Then he ties the corners together and slides the thyrsis beneath the resulting knot. He lifts the bundle easily: for all the world like Saint Stilskin Sophora setting out on one of his absurd adventures.

Once again he has the feeling of being watched. And now there's a sound to go with the feeling; a muffled noise, something like a sob.

He lowers the bundle to the floor and slides the thyrsis free. He stretches his long legs, and in a heartbeat he's across the floor, splashing through the spilled metheglin, past rows of shattered containers, to where three young women crouch, shivering in each other's arms. They look up at Sylvestris with a pretense of defiance, their faces streaked with tears. They wear the robes of Kites.

He motions with the thyrsis. "Get up."

The women climb shakily to their feet, clutching each other for comfort.

"Where are the others?"

"There are no others," one of them replies in a quavering voice.

He believes her; she's too frightened to lie. "Put your hands where I can see them."

The women are each missing a hand. Some kind of ritual dismemberment, he thinks with distaste. But the hands they have are holding something . . .

He strikes one sharply across the wrist with the thyrsis. Metheglin beads rattle over the floor. Sylvestris laughs. "What have we here? Not only cowards, but thieves?"

The women say nothing. The other two open their hands, letting the metheglin they hold fall at his feet like an insult.

"I could kill you," he says.

Now one of the women speaks. "Since when have Kites feared to die?"

"Kites!" Again Sylvestris laughs. "You may wear the robes of Kites, my girls, but your faces are too pretty by far."

"The Liberatrix did this." There is wonder in the woman's voice. She strokes her cheek as though she has trouble believing in the smoothness of her skin. "Her tears healed us. Just as they will heal the world."

"Her tears heal nothing. They are poison."

"To some," the woman says.

Her smugness infuriates Sylvestris. "She was a spy, you idiots! A piece of vizards' craft! She betrayed you all! And now she's dead."

The women only smile.

"The shrives will wipe those smiles off your faces." He motions with the thyrsis, adding ironically: "After you, holy sisters."

To his annoyance, the women's smiles only widen as they pass among the bodies of the shrives. They even smile to see the ravaged corpses of their sister heretics. But their smiles vanish at last when they see the headless body and the bloody bundle that rests beside it.

"Pick it up," Sylvestris says to the one who had spoken. "Go on."

The woman does so. Sylvestris is curious to see whether she'll suffer the same fate as the unfortunate shrive who'd struck the fatal blow. But nothing happens. The woman cradles the bundle like a young mother holding a swaddled baby.

"Do you know what's in there?"

The woman nods.

"She didn't benefit much by her own tears," he observes. "Did she?"

One of the other women answers: "She shed them for others."

Sylvestris laughs. "She should have saved a few for herself!"

But then he feels again the sense of being watched, and it occurs to him that there may be more heretics hidden here after all, perhaps expecting reinforcements.

"Come on," he says gruffly, motioning with the thyrsis for the women to precede him. "We're going to pay a visit to Azedarach."

ELEVEN

The sun hangs over Quoz like a thyrsis nailed to the sky. Making the sign of the Wheel, the Ecclesiarch gazes into its fiery depths with a look both ardent and imploring, as if searching there for the dark and crabbed shape of Ixion Diospyros. The boisterous crowds thronging the steps of the Cathedral and the square beyond fall into a reverent hush, straining after his words with looks of naked yearning. Like impatient children waiting for the panderman to go, the Ecclesiarch thinks, so they may rush out of hiding and claim the gifts left scattered behind.

Every turning, especially on this holiest of days, there are those—mostly young girls or old women—who stare into the sun until they go blind, claiming afterward to have been rewarded with a glimpse of the beloved martyr in return for the sacrifice of their sight, his image burned so brightly into their retinas that all else is consigned to darkness. The Ecclesiarch has seen them by the thousands over the turnings. He's seen their ruined eyes, like clouded crystals, watched them toil tirelessly as ants up and down the six hundred steps of the Cathedral with thin, tapping canes and alert, fearful faces, as if the image of Ixion for which they have forsaken the sun might, like a faulty thyrsis, flicker and fade, abandoning them in this darkness whose extent they had never suspected and have perhaps—the doubt is plainly displayed on their faces, as if they have lost not only sight but the sense of being seen—too rashly embraced.

But thanks to the shield of metheglin, the Ecclesiarch may look into the seething furnace for hours, if he likes, with no worry for his eyes, letting the dumb heat beat down against his face until his bones are ringing like a gong pitched beyond the range of human hearing.

But he hears.

And it is beautiful. The music strikes his body like sunlight, in pulsing waves of color, jangling threads of red and blue and green, pink and yellow and orange. All the noisy colors of earth and sky are pumping into him from that fertile center like blood from a celestial heart. And each color, each thread, as it brushes against the others, produces a unique tone, distinct yet part of a greater harmony: a harmony never complete, always in process, like the music of the musicians who pass their lives in the throne room of the Palace, playing their instruments day and night in shifts so that the composition begun countless turnings ago by Saint Sium Lyrata may never reach its conclusion but go on until the Spinner lifts His hand from His Wheel and puts a stop to all becoming.

The Ecclesiarch feels so much a part of this music that he can't tell if he's musician or instrument; all he knows is that the music—like the sun and the Hierarchate—will go on for at least another turning, renewing itself here, now, on All Saints' Eve, before his upraised eyes and hands. He, too, feels magically renewed, as in his fantasy of switching places with the boy Sium and reclaiming the youth tricked from him by the vizards more than two thousand turnings ago.

The Ecclesiarch is crying now; not outside, of course, but inside, where no one can see, he gives thanks to the Spinner with his tears for this gift of rebirth, more precious than any gift a panderman might leave for a lonely boy, more precious even than metheglin although impossible to appreciate without it. And just for an instant, like a second gift more wonderful than the first because entirely unexpected, he sees the slight figure of a man lying splayed upon the splendid bed of the sun as if chained there.

But it's Sium the Ecclesiarch sees, not Ixion Diospyros; never Ixion Diospyros.

No matter how often the Ecclesiarch looks into the sun, how deeply he searches, the vision of the saint eludes him. He doubts anyone has ever truly seen him there; those claiming otherwise are either liars or self-deluding fools, unable to distinguish truth from metaphor.

Yet now he flings wide his arms to the gasps of the crowd and moves his lips as if deep in conversation with the very saint he doesn't see. He makes his body tremble as though tossed on a torrent of words only he can hear, for it cannot be a simple thing to speak directly to a saint. People are like children, he thinks again. They know nothing of sacrifice or love, less than nothing of knowledge and power. They want only to be entertained.

At last he lets himself grow still. He lowers his eyes and solemnly gazes over the assembled multitude. A sea of faces looks back in earnest expectation.

Faces change with the turnings, he thinks now. People age and die, and children are born to take their places. But all the while, this human sea remains essentially unchanged, following the rhythms of its timeless ebb and flow, as unaware of the small things that comprise it as they are of the great enduring thing they comprise.

In all the Hierarchate, only two men are fully aware of this sea that stretches not only from Arpagee to Quoz but back in time, even beyond the founding of the Hierarchate, and forward as well, into the unimaginable distance where the Unspinning awaits.

The Ecclesiarch soars above it on metheglin's supple wings, his body hollowed by hunger until even his bones are lighter than air. From there he looks down upon the glittering surface of the sea. He takes in its vast, roiling extent at a glance. But his sharp eyes can no more pierce its secret depths than they can discern Saint Ixion's silhouette abiding in the sun.

As for Azedarach, he hasn't left the sea at all. His gluttonous consumption of metheglin has, as it were, dissolved him into it, imparting to his mind the sea's protean flux, its moody freedom from the constraints of time. But he shares as well its limitations, the shores against which it can only crash and fall away, spent.

Now, standing on the six hundredth step of the Cathedral stairs, the Ecclesiarch looks down on the people of Quoz from just such a shore. Already some of them wear the painted wooden masks that give them the appearance of saints and martyrs and monstrous Furies, masks which confer anonymity and freedom in the revels it is his duty now, as on each turning, to proclaim. Even those not yet wearing the elaborate masks, wigged and beribboned, who clutch them to their chests in anxious anticipation, appear masked to the Ecclesiarch, their naked expressions identical to expressions worn by other faces on this day last turning or a thousand turnings ago. Not for the first time, he considers that it is only when donning their wooden masks that people's everyday masks fall away, and their true faces emerge.

And isn't that the real miracle of All Saints' Eve? When, by the Spinner's grace, the sun halts at noon, it does more than hold the night at bay and keep Beauty muzzled and chained in the kennel of Herwood. For the length of that blessed noontide, which, like a dream, is situated both within time and outside it, the people of the Hierarchate shed their daily selves and crawl like serpents from outgrown skins to find themselves suddenly and as if by a miracle *winged*, become something wholly other than what they were, yet something they always have been.

The Ecclesiarch licks his lips and begins to recite the words just as they have been recited each turning since the first Ecclesiarch spoke them from this very spot. His voice rings out loudly over the square, and clear, as if somehow amplified by the Cathedral at his back, whose vaulted crystal facade, crowded with friezes and bas-reliefs and gargoyles, rises like an ice mountain upon whose summit the weary saint has stopped to rest and cool himself before continuing on his endless journey.

"Thus says Ixion Diospyros: Behold the sun fixed to the roof of the sky, the wheel wherein I turn and burn! Now is the wheel of time ground to a halt and Beauty crushed beneath its rim! I say to you, to all righteous men, to all meek and contrite women whose hearts are free of the taint of Maw: Rejoice! For by this sign is the Spinner's holy covenant affirmed, renewed for another turning! But to all Maw's evil crew, whether woman or man or Fury, I say: Tremble. I say: Repent. For the Season of Chastenings is at hand."

The Ecclesiarch pauses here as always. He lets his head droop and his hands dangle limply at his sides, as if the weight of Ixion and his Burning Wheel has suddenly settled upon his own poor shoulders, already stooped with age and the burdens of high office. A moment goes by; then he raises his head wearily and regards the crowd with a stern yet doleful expression. This also they expect of him: that without forgiving the sins for which they will be chastened he mourn them in advance.

But the Ecclesiarch, too, is wearing a mask, and he's never been more keenly aware of it than now. For he knows, as no one else here knows, that Morus Sisymbrium is even now destroying the metheglin vaults, drying up the springs of Azedarach's power right at the source. How he wishes he could be there to savor the irony: the containers smashed, their precious contents spilled by the very man Azedarach had trusted to guard them! But he consoles himself with the thought that there will be other ironies to savor before long.

His next words will launch the uprising. The future of the Hierarchate depends on its success; if Azedarach isn't deposed, and quickly, the Ecclesiarch fears it will be too late to avert the Spinner's judgment. Tomorrow, when the sun resumes its course, the Season of Chastenings will begin. With Azedarach on the Throne, it surely will prove to be the worst ever. Even the adamant towers of the Cathedral may shatter and fall, unless Azedarach shatters and falls instead.

A smile appears on the Ecclesiarch's face: or, rather, upon his public mask. And upon the face behind his mask there is a smile also, though of a very different kind. He makes the sign of the Wheel and opens his mouth to deliver the sermon composed during his private revels with Sium.

"My children, even in the midst of great change—"

And suddenly he sees Iber Arvensis in the crowd before him. It's so unexpected that he can't go on, an almost-physical blow, like a jolt from a thyrsis.

The dead man—that is, his face, a pale mask peeping out from beneath a crimson hood—is visible for a second, less than a second, through a gap in the crowd upon the stairs. Then he, it, is gone, as if Iber's face, removed from the body found outside the House Illicium a week ago, on the morning of Saint Samsum's Day, has taken on a life all its own.

But the Ecclesiarch doesn't believe in ghosts. He believes in something much worse.

Heretics.

Now, scanning the crowd with eyes honed by metheglin to an acuity eagles would envy, the Ecclesiarch spies other faces of the recently dead. Faces missing from the corpses found in baths of blood and roses. Faces peeled away with such uncommon skill that even the vizards performing the harvestings were envious.

And he thinks: *masks*.

The faces have been made into masks behind which heretics lie concealed. But the strange thing, the really strange thing, is that the masks of Iber and the others are being worn by *children*. The tallest of them no more than four feet in height.

The Ecclesiarch has no idea why the heretics would use children in this way. No idea at all. But it does occur to him that he's not the only one to have planned an uprising for All Saints' Eve.

Under the circumstances, he decides to dispense with the sermon. The crowd has taken note of his hesitation and, milling nervously, shares his unease without understanding it.

He raises his hands to reassure them. He makes the sign of the Wheel, blessing them in the name of Saint Ixion Diospyros. And then he utters the words which, by prior arrangement with his shrives and agents, signal the beginning of the uprising against Azedarach. "Blessed be the Spinner! As it was in the beginning, is now, and shall be until the Unspinning! Behold, Ixion is risen!"

The response is a rolling thunder of built-up tension and relief. Howls and screams rise to the sky, echoed and amplified by the crystal towers of Quoz, until the noise is like a harbinger of Chastenings to come, and the ground itself shivers beneath the Ecclesiarch's feet.

"Blessed be! He is risen indeed!"

Now, while the sun roosts overhead, there will be no night, no Beauty. Now men may celebrate without fear or caution, freed from their nightly restraints; now women, with no need to watch over fathers, husbands, sons, may pursue pleasures forbidden them the rest of the turning on pain of a Cat's career or the Six Hundred. On this day, Ixion Diospyros ascended into the heavens, betrayed by his mother and nailed by her to his Burning Wheel. On this day, the Spinner raised him up and set him at the center of the sun, which became as his body, its light his vision, its heat his blood, able to warm the land or scorch it to a cinder.

And on this day, the Furies, robbed of the night in which Maw cloaks her servants, were exposed and defeated, harried by the saints into Herwood, from whence Beauty soon began to rise.

On this day, all the old, accustomed ways are set aside, scorned, forgotten. Tomorrow, the Chastenings will come. The night will return, and Beauty with it. But today there is only rejoicing.

Ixion is risen!

The revels have begun!

Music blares from all sides, ponderous and lurching cacophonies of sound at which whole groups of people—masked, anonymous—begin to move, the crowd stirring like a sluggish behemoth waking after a long sleep. A creature slow to wake but, once roused, wild and powerful and beautiful—terrible, too—like the Leviathan said to dwell in the depths of the sea, whose fitful coilings give rise to the waves that crash against the cliffs of far-off Arpagee.

Over the turnings, on All Saints' Eve, the Ecclesiarch has witnessed scenes that seem enactments or reenactments of the bloody histories recorded in the *Lives and Acts*—which book even now, a strange compendium of playscript, commentary, and prophecy mingling the sacred and profane, is being read aloud in faithful obedience to Ixion's ancient command by a succession of Mouths of God in a small chapel of the Cathedral sacred to the book's author or amanuensis, Saint Quercus Incana.

The Ecclesiarch has seen beatings, rapes, murders. He has watched the strong slake their lusts upon the weak as desires held in check all the turning long are loosed, like wicked genies in some child's tale, for a day. He has seen women perform acts of ecstatic self-mutilation in emulation of Viridis Lacrimata, boldly putting out their eyes or courting blindness in the sun. He has watched men willingly have themselves bound to wheels and scourged with whips and canes to bleeding, even unto death, like Saint Ilex Erythrina.

But he has also seen other things. Acts of selflessness and sacrifice worthy of the saints themselves. He has seen lovers find each other despite or perhaps because of the masks which are never removed, not even during the most intimate moments, lest a father behold a daughter, a mother a son. He has watched those selected by the shrives for their private amusements, which are invariably fatal, go along with their torturers joyfully, as if there could be no greater honor than to be chosen to die on All Saints' Eve.

All these things and more he has seen. It has always been his custom to walk the streets on this day, leading a long procession of simulars assembled from the six hundred churches of Quoz. The wooden images of the saints are borne through the city by penitents, whose bare shoulders quickly become bruised and then awash in blood. When one man drops, another takes his place with such alacrity not a step is missed. The most noisome and unruly crowds grow silent and draw aside when the parade passes by with the Ecclesiarch marching at the fore and feigning an old man's tremulous, shuffling gait while liberally dispensing blessings. Unlike the others, he does not wear a wooden mask. In all of Quoz—indeed, in all the Hierarchate on this day—only the Ecclesiarch is maskless, exposed and vulnerable as at no other time. Yet never has a hand been raised against him.

But today, for the first time, he's decided not to go. The assassination of Erigeron Intricata, which came so close to claiming his own life, the murders and bizarre disfigurements of Iber Arvensis and the others, and now these ghoulish masks worn by heretic children, have convinced the Ecclesiarch to remain behind while his agents and shrives topple Azedarach from the Throne and install Morus in his stead. Earlier he dispatched a Mouth of God to lead the procession in his stead, and already the line of simulars is winding slowly through the square.

The Ecclesiarch motions for a pair of shrives to attend him. He informs them of what he has seen: the fleshy masks, the children. They nod in unison and quickly melt into the oblivious crowd, hunters after their prey.

Now, as he turns to reenter the Cathedral, a scattering of pebbles lands at his feet. He turns back, more insulted than threatened, and searches the crowd for the culprit. But he sees only a churning wall of masks and bodies impossible for even his eyes to pierce. More pebbles fall, and this time they hit him, though harmlessly, pattering over his head and shoulders. Not hurled from the crowd at all, he realizes, but from above.

Filled with foreboding, the Ecclesiarch lifts his eyes.

The facade of the Cathedral is alive with movement. As he watches, disbelieving, the gargoyles and figures of the friezes and bas-reliefs detach themselves from the mortared background to ascend the central spire of the Cathedral like spiders. Bits of masonry and chipped crystal fall back as they go, and it's this hail which has struck him.

High overhead, a lone figure glances down as if aware of the Ecclesiarch's gaze. Its eyes wink with red flashes in a face he knows even at such a distance.

But those eyes he doesn't know. Unhurried in their scrutiny. Unafraid. And utterly, utterly strange.

The Ecclesiarch blinks, feeling his mind dangle between wonder and horror. Despite its size, that was no child returning his gaze from behind the grinning mask of Saint Stilskin Sophora. No; nor was it a mask. And with that realization, the balance teeters and tips into a chasm of dread such as he's never known.

For it was a simular. Simulars, rather. Climbing the Cathedral under their own power, strings cut as it's recorded in the *Lives and Acts* will occur on the Last Day.

Can it be that no one else has seen? He turns again to the boisterous crowd, wanting to shout, to point, to make them see the miracle of doom taking place in plain sight right above their heads.

But he does nothing, and no one, as far as he can tell, so much as glances at the Cathedral. Why should they, after all, when there is such a bounteous feast for the eyes spread before them? A feast not only for the eyes, but for the fingers, lips, tongue: for the whole hungry body. He feels a wave of revulsion for them, for the appetites that rule them. It's fitting, he thinks, that they die as they've lived, in ignorance and gluttony.

But is it really happening? The Unspinning come round at last?

His skeptical reason, knocked off-balance by the sight of the simulars, is quick to right itself. He's no superstitious fool like these others. He's the Ecclesiarch, spiritual leader of the Hierarchate. He wears the amethyst ring that Ixion himself once wore. He's lived for more than two thousand turnings, enduring a hunger no man can imagine. And he's not ready to die, to give up everything he's fought for, everything he's achieved.

The Unspinning? More likely, Azedarach is responsible. Or the heretics.

The Ecclesiarch returns his gaze to the Cathedral. Only seconds have passed since he looked away, but the simulars—or whatever they truly are—are so far up the spire that even his keen eyes can barely make them out. They move with astonishing speed, climbing toward the sun.

And suddenly his heart plummets in his chest as if cast with a stone from the tip of that spire. For he's guessed their destination: where else but the chamber where Sium sleeps in chains of gold and chilly aspergine?

Now, with all the quickness metheglin has given him, the speed he's always concealed and disguised so that it might one day save him, the Ecclesiarch runs. He's a dark blur, a shadowy wind that ruffles the garments of the Mouths of God and stirs the pages of the *Lives and Acts* as he whispers by the chapel of Saint Quercus.

The Ecclesiarch runs down passages known to him alone, stopping only when he must employ a lift, cursing the slowness of the antique mechanisms, whose crafting is beyond the skill of any vizard now. He runs like a man about to lose the only thing he loves.

He runs for his very life.

TWELVE

It's not long before Sylvestris and the three Kites come upon the bodies of the shrives who'd fled the vaults. Sylvestris stops to examine the mutilated corpses; their limbs have not only been broken repeatedly but wrenched into unnatural positions, as if death is a role for which life has ill prepared them. The truly awful thing, however, is that he slowly comes to discern in the careful positioning of the bodies a parody of the martyrdom of Saint Cedrus Lyciodes as described in the *Lives and Acts* and performed countless times by his simulars upon the stage. He admires the cleverness, but it frightens him just the same.

Even more frightening are the roses heaped among the dead. Sylvestris feels a cold sweat running down his neck and back. The voices of his simulars are ominously silent.

"Afraid, murderer?" says one of the Kites.

"Shut up!" he growls, prodding her sharply in the back. The sooner they leave this spooky warren of ill-lit passages, the better he'll like it.

The Kite laughs, a harsh sound in the empty hallway, as she and her sisters resume walking.

Sylvestris casts a parting glance at the shrives, then follows. He came this way just hours ago; then the passages had been bright with promise. Now it's all he can do to retrace his steps and locate the lift in which they'd descended to the vaults and which, according to what the shrives had told him, will carry them to the Palace of the Chambered Nautilus and the waiting Azedarach.

Sylvestris wonders if the Sovereign will be surprised to see him enter the throne chamber with three Kites and the head of the Liberatrix. More likely he's expecting it. Probably this—like everything else, as it often seems to Sylvestris—is just one more part of Azedarach's grand design.

But what of his own design, a mere thread in the larger tapestry, perhaps, but still important to him? Will he receive the keys to the metheglin vaults as Azedarach promised? Or will the Six Hundred be his reward?

"They're coming after you, murderer," one of the Kites gleefully remarks.

"Shut up," he repeats, glancing over his shoulder but seeing nothing, just the empty corridor. "Who?"

"Poor simularter!" another mocks. "You'll find out."

And the third: "Ask your simulars."

But his simulars persist in their silence. Sylvestris feels oddly abandoned without their irreverent chatter, annoying though it may be. He steps up the pace, realizing suddenly that he's still wearing the nose plugs he'd inserted to enter the vaults. He'd forgotten them completely until now: a small but dangerous lapse, it could give the Kites the idea that he's nervous, even afraid.

Which he is, of course; he'd just rather they didn't know it. He yanks out the spongy plugs and throws them to the floor in disgust.

The scent of roses envelops him. He sneezes, but there's no escaping the perfume; voluptuous, oppressive, relentless, it suffuses the air like syrup, sticky and sweet.

"Do you smell it at last, murderer?" asks the Kite with the bundle in her arms. "Did you think the Liberatrix may be so easily killed?"

"I smell nothing," he lies, willing his voice steady.

"It's your death. Look: the Little People have come."

And Sylvestris sees an avalanche of roses tumbling down around him. With a cry, he lifts his arm to shield his face from the thorns as the voices of his simulars rise at last in a single, desolate groaning.

For simulars are dropping from the ceiling, dropping on black threads through the rain of roses: Stilskin Sophora; Ilex Erythrina; Samsum Oxalis; Sium Lyrata; even Ixion Diospyros. All the saints from the *Lives and Acts* are here, descending to the floor.

They are like his own simulars. Yet different. Not lowered by the hands and thoughts of a simularter concealed overhead. No.

Lowering *themselves*.

Hand over hand, with a slow gliding motion, they come as if air is like water to them and they must fight a natural tendency to rise. The winking of their eyes is a cold, ruby staccato, light and dark, light and dark.

It has come, he thinks dully. The Last Day. The voices of his simulars fill his mind with discordant shrieks and prayers, threats and curses, like bitter ghosts confronted with a life they merely pretend to. The thyrsis drops from his senseless fingers into the rising tide of roses. Sylvestris falls to his knees to search for it.

Laughing, the Kites are upon him like Furies, scratching and biting at his face and eyes. He fights back, using the poisons painted upon his fingernails to quickly paralyze them. Death will follow at a leisurely pace, but he doesn't think there will be time to savor it.

He staggers to his feet, the thyrsis forgotten, to find himself at the center of a ring of simulars. The tallest of them barely reaches to his knees. They circle him like malevolent children, drifts of roses piled about their waists, red eyes winking.

"What do you want of me?" he demands.

They make no answer, only stare with those awful eyes in which there is nothing human yet something unmistakably alive.

"Is this what it seems? The Last Day? Or some kind of trick?" Sylvestris is no longer demanding, but pleading now. He kicks the body of the Kite nearest to him, sending up a shower of roses. Her mottled face—like that of her two sisters—gapes stupidly, pop-eyed, tongue oozing from her mouth like a fat snail from its shell. "Answer me!"

But they do not.

"Why, then I'll fight you," he says, knowing already the hopelessness of it, the utter uselessness of resistance. But he will be no coward here, at the end of everything. The voices of his simulars are less frantic now, almost somber, though not sad. They urge him on, preferring, like him, a brave death.

Sylvestris takes his stance. His long and shapely hands trace deadly patterns in the air. He does not know if the poisons on his fingernails will affect these things, or whether their bones will break like the bones of human beings, or if they have bones at all. But he is fast and strong; no one has ever touched him in a duel. And he has the advantage of size and reach. That still counts for something, he supposes.

The simulars make no move to defend themselves, as if they consider him beneath their notice, no more dangerous than a fly: he, Sylvestris Jaciodes, victor of more than thirty duels, Court Simularter and soon-to-be cupbearer and keeper of the keys to the metheglin vaults! Well, he is no fly.

"A firefly, rather," comes the voice of Saint Ixion.

Yes, a firefly. And he will show them his sting.

He selects a target, a simular standing to his left: Saint Stilskin, in fact, whose vacant grin he's always found annoying but never so much as now.

Sylvestris feints with his right hand; then, moving more swiftly than he's ever moved in his life, he sends his left hand arrowing toward the saint.

He hears a crack. There's an instant of blinding pain which his mind and his simulars struggle to make sense of. But then Sylvestris sees his hand: his supple hand, so swift and prideful and fine, master of so many strings. It hangs from his wrist as if no longer deserving a place there, broken beyond all fixing.

The pain seems unconnected to the sight. Sylvestris struggles to fit the two together, like two halves of a puzzle. Then all at once he's got it: he wasn't fast enough; not this time.

"Nor any other," comes Saint Ixion's voice, faintly.

Now a cloud is rising in him like the shivery darkness of an epileptic seizure. He recites the Litany of Quiescence, but the cloud continues to rise and to unfurl its wings until the voices of Ixion and all the others are gone into the dark, and Sylvestris with them.

THIRTEEN

Two shrives snap to attention as the Ecclesiarch emerges from his private lift, the sole means of access to the chamber in which Sium sleeps.

"Urgent news from the Palace, Eminence," begins one.

"Later." He brushes by.

The other shrive dares to take hold of his arm. "But Your Eminence. Azedarach is escaped. Fled. And there are reports of heretics, of viragi . . . "

"I said later!" The Ecclesiarch wrenches free. What do Azedarach or the heretics matter to him now? He holds up his hand, displaying the heavy ring upon his finger, the firefly amethyst. "Or do you wish to kneel and kiss this ring?"

The shrive steps quickly back. "I meant only to serve."

"Then follow as best you can, for I have need of your service now. But I will not bear your touch again."

"Yes, Eminence," say the shrives in unison.

But already he is off, racing down the long corridor, through the door and up the spiral stairs. The shrives, for all their formidable speed, are unable to keep up with him.

At last he reaches the chamber door. He's almost afraid to enter. He's always kept the existence of this chamber a secret; not even his shrives have seen it or know what he keeps here. But now his fear is greater even than his mania for secrecy. He will reveal everything to the shrives, for he may need their help to save Sium. He'll do anything to save Sium, he realizes.

And the shrives can be disposed of later.

He pushes through the door, praying to the Spinner that he's arrived in time and fumbling meanwhile in his robes for the syringe containing the solution of dilute metheglin with which to thaw the boy's aspergine-frozen blood.

He stops short with a groan. The chamber looks like it's been struck by lightning. Plush satin cushions are strewn over the floor. The gold-and-silver drapes have been torn from the crystal walls, save for one, which blows into the room like a gay streamer; the copper braziers lie overturned, their coals smoldering on the rugs. The crystal walls themselves are, as he left them, opaque, reflecting the chamber they enclose as if to the ends of space and time. And there he sees, above the reflections of the great round bed at the chamber's center, swaying gently back and forth like an exhausted pendulum and multiplied to infinity in the mirrors, Sium dangling from the ceiling. Hanged by the neck with his own gold chain.

The Ecclesiarch howls: such a sound a human being may produce but once in a lifetime, even a lifetime of two thousand turnings. How is it, he wonders, that the chamber walls do not shatter, the whole Cathedral come crashing down as in the tale of Saint Samsum Oxalis?

He's on the bed in an instant, ripping apart the soft links of the chain—if only the boy were heavier, his own weight would have saved him!—and lowering the body, so cold, so cold, onto the bed, where just hours ago the two of them . . . No, he can't bear to think it.

"Sium! Please, Ixion . . . "

The body is cold, but that may only be an effect of aspergine. With trembling hands, the Ecclesiarch plunges the syringe into the boy's alabaster neck, into the blue bulge of the carotid, which he's kissed so often, thrilling to the hot, drowsy pulse.

"Wake, Sium! Nuncle's here . . . "

But the boy does not stir.

He seems more beautiful than ever, the smooth pits of his eyes like tiny bowls into which the Ecclesiarch may pour his tears. His soft, ash-blond hair will continue to grow; is that fair? The Ecclesiarch thinks he'll cut it off. Yes, he'll do that, and keep it where he may stroke it when he wishes. He kisses the cold blue lips, pushing his tongue against clenched teeth that will not open to him now, no, never.

He catches sight of himself, of his reflections, in the mirrors. All of them cradling the body of Sium as he is, all of them staring with tears running down their aged cheeks. Why, he wonders, can't the dead boy live in one of these mirror worlds? It doesn't seem like too much to ask, one out of so many millions.

If he searches, perhaps he can find it, the place where the boy yet lives, where the two of them are laughing even now in a glad embrace, turning their backs on these other grim reflections, rejecting them.

"Sium, Sium, I'm sorry." It's himself he mourns, himself he's lost. Not Malus Intricata, that unfortunate son of an unfortunate father; Malus died long ago so that Sium could be born.

Is it for this that he's Ecclesiarch? The merest touch of his ring is death, but there's no ring to ferry back the dead; not even the tears of Viridis Lacrimata could cross that gulf. Better to have killed the boy himself, as he so often considered, than to find him like this, fled past all recalling. That death would have come from him at least, a final kiss. Of what use now is his ring? It can neither call Sium back nor send him to join him, for such is the ring's crafting that its sting, deadly to others, causes its wearer no harm.

So rapt is the Ecclesiarch in his own grieving that he doesn't notice the arrival of the two shrives. But then he sees the mirrored army of their reflections. They are addressing him, all of them at once, their voices a babble he can't comprehend. But he watches curiously, for it may be that he knows them from somewhere.

And as he watches, simulars come crawling out from the cushions and drapes and rugs that lie in disarray upon the floor. They emerge from under the bed like small children. And in the mirrors they come, too, with eyes flashing in bursts of red light; some of them have but a single flashing eye, the other dark as coal.

A strange sound comes from the shrives. It takes the Ecclesiarch a moment to recognize it: fear.

Now they are fighting. The shrives and the simulars. In the room, in the mirrors. They fight as the Ecclesiarch rocks Sium to his breast, singing to him softly and looking for a place of sanctuary.

The shrives fight back to back, thyrsi spitting sparks. But the simulars are fast. Almost faster than the Ecclesiarch's eyes can follow. They are toying with the shrives, playing with them. *The Little People,* he thinks. And without knowing why, he claps his hands and laughs.

Then the shrives go down. The simulars swarm over them. The Ecclesiarch hears the cracking of bones. It continues for a long time.

When it's over, the simulars turn to him. He can't stop shivering. But he will address them, for he's the Ecclesiarch, and he must know. "Why?"

There is no answer. They stare at him, red eyes flashing in perfect synchronicity. He will not, cannot, meet those eyes; he looks past them, searching among reflections for the safe place, the hidden place, as he interrogates these monsters.

"What are you?"

Again, silence. But then he finds it: the safe place. The mirror world in which Sium is still alive. No simulars dwell there, or only the kind that dangle harmlessly from strings. He sees Sium's pale arm beckon from behind the fluttering gold curtain. "Come, Nuncle," he says. "Come."

The Ecclesiarch has seen the simulars in action and judged their speed: they're no faster than he. Yet he must carry Sium, and that will slow him down. Still, he knows it's within his power to escape. Already he's moving, faster than he's ever moved, Sium's body tucked beneath one arm. The simulars don't stir; he's taken them by surprise, as he knew he would.

With a triumphant laugh, he leaps past the gold curtain, feeling it wrap around his neck and shoulders like a cape, around Sium, too, lashing the boy to him in a taut embrace. And then, by a smooth transition, like slipping into a clear, cool bath, the Ecclesiarch is through.

If anyone had chanced to look up from the streets below, they would have seen something amazing: Ixion Diospyros tumbling out of the sky, a ribbon of gold fire trailing behind him.

But nobody does look up. And anyway, the ramparts of the Cathedral soon break his fall.

BOOK THREE

HERWOOD

Beauty is convulsive, or not at all.
ANDRÉ BRETON,
Nadja

ONE

The little man is muttering to himself as he taps upon the containers with a thyrsis: tap, tap, tap, all along the row. His diminutive size suggests a simular rather than a human being; Rumer can't see his head, only the hump of his shoulders and the bundle he carries tucked into the crook of one arm. She hardly knows if she's alive or dead, awake or dreaming. Everything is unfolding of its own volition; she can only keep as silent and still as the bodies lying stiffly around her in muddy pools of blood and metheglin. As long as she can do that, nothing will happen to her. Nothing will hurt her. But now the little man stops and turns, as if aware of her eyes upon him, and there's nothing she can do but watch.

Atop his shoulders is a blurred distortion, vaguely egg-shaped, a field of intersecting planes of air through which Rumer sees, as through frosted glass, a face. But before she can bring the face into focus, it flies apart in a whirl of fragments that quickly coalesce into a different face, which then shatters in turn, the process continuing relentlessly. Above that ghostly vortex floats a crown of quicksilver and gold; below, a tangled beard descends nearly to the floor. And though she's never seen her Sovereign before, not in the flesh, Rumer knows at once that she's in the presence of Azedarach LXIV.

But before she can react, the veil of the Serpent Crown spills down over the rest of Azedarach's body; all that remains is a blur, a squirm of light like a serpent swimming through the air. Then that, too, is gone. Rumer hears light footsteps patter past her and out the door through which she and the others had entered this place . . . how long ago? Hours? Days?

Everything comes rushing back. She remembers the viragi smashing the containers. Remembers losing consciousness, falling to the floor where she now lies. Remembers, as in a dream, the attack of the shrives.

But that was no more a dream than the sight of Azedarach. The evidence surrounds her.

Rumer picks herself up. She feels as if she's slept for days; a new and seemingly bottomless strength supports her. But all she can think of is Rose. She begins to search.

Right away she finds Aralia and Picea lying side by side. Aralia's robes have been cut away to expose the brown swell of her breasts and belly; Rumer weeps as she kisses the cold forehead and closes the startled violet eyes. She does the same for Picea. She hates her tears, as if her heart has betrayed her in its rush to mourn, already giving up hope.

Then Rumer comes to the circle of viragi and shrives. She sees the body at its center, desecrated like no other here.

She turns away with a moan. Turns and staggers blindly through the vaults. She sees none of the devastation around her, only that vast and incomprehensible absence, like looking up one day to find the sun gone from the shoulders of the sky.

She wants to die. But she doesn't deserve it. First there must be pain. Turnings of pain and suffering and madness.

The floor is wet with blood and metheglin. Shards of glass beckon like shiny toys left behind by the Panderman. She picks one up, squeezing the edges into her palm. How snugly it fits!

Then she raises her hand to her face and begins to carve there all the words she wanted to say to Rose but didn't. All the words she can never say now. And yet can never stop saying. She carves slowly, meticulously, lovingly.

When she's through, she drops the glass. Her face is burning; the skin feels as tight as a drum. Her legs carry her from the metheglin vaults like the legs of a somnambulist. She doesn't go back the way she came; how can she follow Azedarach through that door, the same door she'd entered by, holding on to Rose's hand? She takes another door instead.

She hasn't gone far down the bright passage before she comes to a drift of roses in which the bodies of six shrives lie buried. She hardly notices, intent on her own pain.

Ahead more death awaits: the three Kites are lying stiff as boards upon the floor, their mottled tongues sticking out at the world. Beside them is the simularter Sylvestris Jaciodes. At the sight of him, something stirs in Rumer, and she pauses. One of his hands has been severely mangled; his throat gapes in a bloody grin; his ears have been cut away. And roses: a riot of roses! Rumer laughs, kicking up the blooms with her feet like a giddy child among fallen leaves.

Breath bubbles from the simularter's gashed throat.

Rumer bends over the long and bloodless face, its mask of painted white superfluous now. "Was it you?" She shakes him. His head flops, nearly severed; it's a testament to the skill of the vizards who crafted him that he lives at all. "Did you do it? Answer me!"

But he's beyond the reach of words. Only pain can touch him now: a private pain she can neither ease nor add to. And in a moment, not even that, he'll be dead.

All at once, Rumer is weeping. Her tears splash the face of Sylvestris, carving pink runnels into the white paint. Her body has turned against her again, squandering her tears on this man for whom she feels no love, no pity, but only the blackest hate.

Yet she can't help herself; the pent-up grief and horror come streaming out of her disloyal heart. The anger and desolation and loneliness. The guilt of being left alive. All of it flowing from her not as she stood before Rose's body, but here, now, beside this cruel and barren man. A simularter to whom Cats are merely a less durable kind of simular, as easily replaced as broken. The very man—she's sure of it—responsible for Rose's death and decapitation.

Again she hears the ragged bubbling of a breath. A red froth rises from the simularter's slashed throat, and yellow bile trickles from the dark holes where his ears used to be. His body begins to convulse, as if shaken in the jaws of death, his head flopping like a fish. Rumer gets to her feet and runs.

But it seems there's no escaping death; farther down the passage, the armored bodies of shrives line the walls for almost a hundred yards. Their limbs have been broken, the bodies arranged as in a grotesque tableau. Here, too, there are roses.

Rumer advances warily down the hall, passing between the stiff, somehow admonitory figures. She feels the eyes of the dead upon her. Judging her. Perhaps she, too, is dead. Come to the Pit of Damned Souls without knowing it.

There's a vizard among the shrives. His penis has been severed and stuffed into his mouth, from which it protrudes like a sausage. His eyes have been gouged out; in the bloody sockets his testicles sit like moldering walnuts. His ears, like those of Sylvestris, are missing. Yet even in this gory ruin of a face, mutilated in the manner of Saint Rober Viburnum, Rumer recognizes Azedarach's cupbearer, Morus Sisymbrium.

She turns away, saddened and sickened. She's seen too much death. Whoever killed these men lingered over their deaths like connoisseurs over wine; they took time to mutilate and then arrange the bodies with an attention to detail more usual in art than murder, as if the careful positioning of the dead—and of each broken limb and finger—is replete with meaning, like the gestures of a Mouth of God during the Mass.

If so, it's a meaning Rumer has neither the wisdom nor the desire to interpret. She shudders and moves on. But now a final gruesome discovery confronts her: a pile of dead bodies. The bodies of children.

Is no one to be spared? Rumer wonders, as her tears well up again. Of all the horrible things she's seen, this is the least forgivable or understandable; she doesn't want to understand it, or even to see it. Yet she approaches the pile, drawn by the very thing she dreads.

She stops with a thin and nervous giggle: what she'd taken for children are only simulars.

Rumer counts ten in all; they lie face up along the wall like logs stacked for burning. Each one is damaged: missing an arm or a leg or a head, or with a torso blackened as if from the blow of a thyrsis. Strangely, the simulars are covered in blood, as if they, too, like the shrives, are casualties of whatever battle was fought here.

"*Ohhhhhh . . .*"

The feeble groan seems to come from somewhere behind her. But when Rumer spins around, frightened and surprised, there's only the rows of dead shrives like obsidian statues. "Who's there?" she asks in a tremulous voice.

A drift of roses is piled against the opposite wall. It stirs weakly now, as if in reply.

Rumer rushes over and falls to her knees, flinging aside the roses. She'd begun to think she was, if not dead herself, the only living person in the world, as though the Unspinning had come and gone while she slept, passing her by. "Don't worry; I'll have you out in a—"

With a scream, Rumer flounders back, falling into the stack of simulars. She goes down, still screaming, amid their flailing wooden limbs and bodies.

Underneath the roses, sitting up smoothly despite the absence of strings, is a simular. The simular of Saint Samsum Oxalis.

Its head is charred, partially split open, as if it's been in a fire, and a deep crack slices down the broad forehead, through one eye, all the way to the chin. That eye is black and empty. Dead. But the other eye is alive, a ruby spark that flickers with the fitful arrhythmia of a failing thyrsis.

The simular turns its carved and painted face to where Rumer lies beneath the tangled remains of its fellows. It looks right at her. And laughs.

A laughter unlike any Rumer has ever heard, harsh as the squeak of rusty hinges. Like an approximation of laughter made by an instrument never designed to produce such a sound. Or perhaps not laughter at all, but a noise for which laughter is the only equivalent available to her mind . . . just as, filtered through human ears, the calls of animals take on human qualities they do not, in themselves, possess.

Rumer can't move or scream. It's as if she's trying to blend into the simulars among which she lies, become as wooden and lifeless as they and so escape that blinking eye and grating laugh. She can only pray to the Spinner as—holding its hammer in one small hand like a child grasping a favorite toy—the simular of Saint Samsum heaves itself erect.

Stray roses fall from its lap and legs. In addition to Samsum's traditional costume—the heavy robes and black apron of a blacksmith from Peripety—the simular wears a necklace strung with dark and oblong beads like dried mushrooms.

"YOU DID THIS," it says in a gratingly loud voice utterly without inflection; the red lips of its painted mouth move stiffly, yet there's no relation between those movements and the words apparently produced by them that Rumer can see.

"No! I swear . . ." Rumer understands somehow that it wasn't laughter she'd heard before; if anything, it was laughter's opposite, as if a simular might know the pain of loss and mourn its fallen comrades just as she does. She remembers Aralia mentioning the Little People and their hatred of the shrives, and all at once Rumer realizes what the simular is wearing around its neck.

Not beads. *Ears*. A necklace of human ears.

She whimpers.

"WHY, IT IS A CAT," says the simular, and the thick black eyebrow painted above its winking red eye rises in a caricature of surprise. "DO NOT BE AFRAID. I WILL NOT HARM YOU. LOOK AT ME: MY LIMBS ARE WEAK; ONE EYE IS GONE, AND I CANNOT TRUST THE OTHER. I ASK ONLY YOUR HELP. DO NOT LEAVE ME TO THE SHRIVES. COME BE MY EYES, LITTLE CAT," it pleads. "FOR JUST A LITTLE WHILE."

At that echo of the old story from the *Lives and Acts*, something snaps in Rumer. She bursts from the pile of simulars.

But the simular is fast. Rumer hasn't gone two steps before it's there in front of her, hammer raised to prevent her escape. And although she's twice its height, Rumer knows the simular is stronger.

"WHY DO YOU RUN." The simular takes a lurching step toward her, and its eyebrow rises again: "YOUR FACE . . . "

Rumer shakes her head, retreating.

"OH, IS IT YOU," the simular croaks. "PLEASE, DO NOT FEAR ME: I CANNOT BEAR IT. I AM YOUR SERVANT. I WILL TAKE YOU TO A SAFE PLACE. COME."

"Go away!" With trembling hands, Rumer makes the sign of the Wheel. "Leave me alone!"

"BUT YOU ARE THE LIBERATRIX," the simular says.

"No; she's dead! Rose is dead!"

The simular cocks its head to one side and gazes at her. It reaches into the pocket of its black apron and pulls out a small mirror, which it slides across the floor to her feet.

Cautiously, Rumer picks it up, then gasps.

Her face is that of a stranger, swollen and inflamed and smeared with dried blood. The wounds carved into her skin glisten with blood and pus, soft scabs beginning to form like the tracery of some new language coming into existence for the first time, a language born of pain: pain's articulation. But it's not the wreck of her face that causes Rumer to gasp in disbelief and astonishment.

It's her *eyes*.

They shine with a steady green glow.

"No . . ."

Her brown eyes are gone. Vanished. In their place, two fiery emeralds.

Not hers.

Rose's. These are Rose's eyes.

Rumer throws the mirror to the floor, where it shatters. She scrambles after the shards. Better to blind herself than to see Rose each time she looks into a mirror.

She feels a weight upon her back. The simular.

She tries to throw it off, but she can't. A sticky substance, fine as the thread of a spider, is spinning around her wrists and legs. Her neck. She feels herself lifted to her feet, pulled by the thin black threads now attached to her body like the strings of a simular.

"I WILL NOT LET YOU HARM YOURSELF, LIBERATRIX." The voice of the simular grates into her ear from the perch of her shoulders, making her wince. "WE HAVE NEED OF YOU."

With that, Rumer finds herself marched stiffly back the way she came, passing through the gallery of shrives, the simular compelling her legs to work by pulling upon her strings like a simularter.

"FOR TURNINGS WE HAVE WAITED FOR THIS DAY, PRAYED FOR IT. NOW AT LAST WE SHALL BE PRISONERS NO MORE."

Rumer struggles, but it's no use. The feel of the body against her neck and scalp is unutterably strange: cool and hard as metal, yet no heavier than hollowed wood. Her skin crawls with revulsion. "What are you?"

"I AM SAMSUM," says the simular, as if that explains everything.

"Where are you taking me?"

"HOME."

"Please; I'm afraid."

"I WILL NOT HARM YOU, LIBERATRIX."

"I told you: I'm not the Liberatrix! She's dead! I can show you the body!"

Silence from the simular. They pass through the gallery of shrives; soon they come to the spot where Rumer found the dying simularter, Sylvestris Jaciodes. She sees the bodies of the three Kites. But Sylvestris is gone.

Has someone moved him? Azedarach, perhaps, whom she'd seen before? But she'd heard him run from the metheglin vaults. Why would he come back? No, there must be another explanation.

Then Rumer thinks of how Rose had kissed her when they'd entered the vaults, whispering the command to remember; as if she could forget the touch of those lips, the taste of those tears!

But could it be? she wonders, crying herself now, the tears stinging her ravaged face. Had Rose, knowing she was about to die, passed her powers on to Rumer? Had the miraculous elixir of her tears worked a transformation upon Rumer while she slept, changing her brown eyes into the green eyes she saw in the simular's mirror?

Her heart quickens. Rose had fallen into a deep sleep while she changed from an ordinary Cat into the Liberatrix. And she'd emerged from that sleep transformed, with tears able to cure or cripple or kill. Can it be that Rumer's eyes are like Rose's in more than color now?

Her tears have splashed the simular without effect, but that may be due to its strange nature. Yet neither have her own wounds healed, though her tears have bathed them, and she recalls that Rose's tears had healed the scratches inflicted by the Kite. But Rumer's wounds are self-inflicted, and perhaps the tears are helpless to heal such injuries, just as the tears of Viridis Lacrimata never healed the scars she cut into her face for Samsum's sake.

But Rumer wept over Sylvestris, washing his face in her tears. And now he's gone. She's feels certain that no one else has been here; her tears are responsible. They revived him, gave him the strength to flee.

The Liberatrix isn't dead. Rose isn't dead. No. She lives on in Rumer: in her eyes, her tears.

You will know me by my eyes . . .

Rumer feels the cold candle of her heart burst once more into flame, and the sting of her tears seems somehow lessened, the pain diluted with joy.

Meanwhile, the damaged simular of Samsum Oxalis continues obliviously along the passage, past every horror, until they enter the metheglin vaults. The simular pauses as if to survey the damage. "YOUR SISTERS FOUGHT BRAVELY," it says.

Rumer finds herself forced to walk in the one direction she has no wish to go. She doesn't want to see Rose's body; she needs no reminder of what she can't forget, and anyway she'd like to believe the body is simply a sloughed-off skin, like those left behind by new-winged serpents migrated from earth to sky. Rumer carries Rose's essence within herself now; why study the shell? It's like ignoring a baby for the afterbirth. "Please, no."

"YOU SAID YOU COULD SHOW ME THE BODY OF THE LIBERATRIX."

"No!"

The simular jerks her to a halt. "SHOW ME."

With a trembling hand, Rumer points.

"I SEE NOTHING. THE BODY OF A WOMAN, NOT EVEN WHOLE."

"Don't you understand? They . . ." But she can't go on.

The simular says nothing for a long moment. Then, to Rumer's surprise: "YOU LOVED THIS WOMAN."

"What do you know of love?" she demands with bitterness, as though Samsum is to blame for all that's happened.

"WE ARE NOT SO DIFFERENT," Samsum replies in its cold and unnerving voice. "WE LOVE AS YOU DO. WE MOURN OUR DEAD. WE, TOO, WANT TO BE FREE."

"Her name was Rose," says Rumer.

"YOU ARE CRYING."

Wiping her eyes with clumsy hands half-tangled in the threads that bind her to the simular, Rumer turns away, wanting only to leave this place.

Samsum doesn't stop her; it guides her steps toward the door through which Azedarach had fled. "I WOULD TAKE THEM FROM YOU IF I COULD," it says.

"What?" she asks, confused.

"YOUR TEARS. YOUR PRECIOUS TEARS."

"They don't feel so precious now."

"PERHAPS TEARS ARE ONLY PRECIOUS TO THOSE WHO CANNOT CRY."

Rumer is struck anew by the strangeness of the creature she carries upon her shoulders like a small child, yet which controls her every move like a simularter. "Why can't you cry, Samsum?"

They pass through the door and into the outer passage, retracing the steps that brought Rumer and the others here. All dead now but for her. At last the simular speaks: "IN REVE IT IS WRITTEN THAT ONCE ALL SIMULARS WERE FLESH AND BLOOD . . . AND WILL BE AGAIN ONE DAY."

"Reve?"

"OUR EXILE. OUR PRISON. OUR HOME."

"I've never heard of it."

"YET IT EXISTS. ONCE IT WAS A GREAT CITY, GREATER THAN QUOZ. BUT IT FELL WITH THE REST WHEN IXION DIOSPYROS LAUNCHED HIS REBELLION."

Rumer knows a twinge of fear. "Are you Furies then?"

"THERE ARE NO FURIES. THAT IS JUST A NAME THE VICTORS GAVE TO THE VANQUISHED. THEY CALLED THEMSELVES SAINTS AND THEIR ENEMIES FURIES. BUT THE TRUTH IS, THEY WERE ALL JUST MEN AND WOMEN."

"Then what are you? You have the name and likeness of Samsum Oxalis . . ."

"ONCE I HAD ANOTHER NAME, ANOTHER LIKENESS. BUT THEY WERE STOLEN FROM ME, ALONG WITH THE LIFE THEY LABELED."

"Stolen?"

"BY VIZARDS. THERE WAS LITTLE BEYOND THEIR SKILLS IN THOSE BRIGHT DARK DAYS."

"But why?"

"AS PUNISHMENT. IXION LED THE LOWER ORDERS IN A REVOLT AGAINST THEIR RIGHTFUL MASTERS, WHO DWELLED IN THE GREAT CITIES ABOVE QUOZ."

"There's nothing above Quoz!"

"REVE IS: CITY OF ROSES. AND ONCE ALSO THE CITIES OF SECULUM AND TIRL, UNNSY AND VERGE. AND THE FLOATING CITIES, TOO. WAMBLE AND XENIA. YAR. LOFTY, INCOMPARABLE ZANDER."

Rumer feels dizzied by this litany of strange names. She wants the simular to stop, to take back all it's said. But Samsum continues in its flat, inhuman voice as it leads her down branchings she can't recall having taken before.

"I AND THE OTHERS LIKE ME—ALTHOUGH WE, TOO, BELONGED TO THE LOWER ORDERS; IN SOME WAYS, THE LOWEST, AS YOU SHALL SEE—DID NOT JOIN THE REBELLION. WE FOUGHT IT, LOYAL TO THE LOFTY ONES WHO HAD GUIDED US FROM THE FIRST. THEIR OVERTHROW WAS OUR DEFEAT. TO PUNISH US, IXION IMPRISONED US IN SIMULARS CRAFTED TO RESEMBLE HIM AND HIS SAINTS. LOCKED US IN BODIES NEITHER ALIVE NOR DEAD, BODIES OF FANTASTIC STRENGTH AND ENDURANCE, WHICH NEVER AGE YET LACK THE SIMPLE ABILITY TO EXPRESS FEELING. THUS ARE WE

CAGED IN AN ISOLATION WITHOUT END, CUT OFF FROM ALL WE WERE YET REMINDED CONTINUALLY OF OUR LOSS."

Samsum causes Rumer's hand to rise; her fingers brush the smooth coolness of its body, so unlike wood or flesh or metal.

"THIS PRISON CANNOT LAUGH," it says. "IT CANNOT CRY. YET THOUGH MY VOICE IS FLAT AND MY EYES DRY, INSIDE I AM STILL HUMAN. LIKE YOU, I AM MOVED TO LAUGHTER OR TEARS. MY HEART, LIKE YOURS, QUICKENS WITH LOVE AND DESIRE. ANGER AND SHAME. ALL THE SHADES OF FEELING THAT ARE THE SPINNER'S GREATEST GIFTS. ONLY MY FEELINGS MAY NEVER BE EXPRESSED. THEY ACCUMULATE INSIDE ME TURNING AFTER TURNING, DENIED ALL RELEASE. NO, NOT EVEN A SMILE OR A SIGH IS PERMITTED ME."

Rumer doesn't know what to think: cities above Quoz; men imprisoned within the cells of simulars. It's too much for her to grasp. And still Samsum goes on, its voice loud in her ear, as if no longer talking to her at all, but to itself.

"THEY TOOK MY MEMORY OF WHO I WAS. I WOKE IN THIS BODY KNOWING ONLY THAT IT WAS NOT MINE. THAT I WAS OR HAD BEEN A MAN. BUT MY NAME, MY HISTORY, ALL OF THAT WAS GONE. I WAS NOT ALONE. THERE WERE OTHERS: TWO HUNDRED AND THIRTY-SIX OF US. WE WOKE IN THE RUINS OF REVE, AND THERE, FOR MORE TURNINGS THAN I CAN TELL, WE DWELLED IN IGNORANCE AMONG ROSES WHOSE SCENT WE COULD NOT SMELL. WE THOUGHT WE WERE THE ONLY CREATURES IN THE WORLD. WE DID NOT AGE, BUT ACCIDENTS WORE US DOWN. THEN CAME A DAY, A CHASTENING, WHEN ONE OF US—A STILSKIN—WAS DAMAGED, ITS HEAD ALL BUT CRUSHED. IT WAS DYING. BUT BY SOME MIRACLE, A PORTION OF ITS MEMORY RETURNED IN ITS LAST MOMENTS. AS IT DIED, THE STILSKIN SPOKE TO US LIKE A MAD PROPHET. IT TOLD US WHAT WE HAD BEEN AND WOULD BE AGAIN ONE DAY. IT TOLD US OF YOU, LIBERATRIX."

"Me?"

"THE STILSKIN SAID YOU WOULD RETURN AND FREE US FROM THE PRISONS OF THESE BODIES. ITS WORDS GAVE US COURAGE TO HOPE AND TO ACT; FOR THE FIRST TIME IN MEMORY, WE LEFT REVE. SOME TRAVELED TO THE CITIES OF THE HIERARCHATE, WHERE WE HUNG LIMPLY AMONG OUR EMPTY BROTHERS, THE MOCKING TOYS OF SIMULARTERS, WATCHING AND LISTENING. OTHERS STUDIED THE PASSAGES BENEATH THE GROUND, THE BRANCHINGS OF THE

UNDERSEA. AND WE TOOK REVENGE FOR WHAT HAD BEEN DONE TO US. WE HUNTED SHRIVES AND SIMULARTERS AND VIZARDS; VIZARDS ABOVE ALL WERE OUR PREY, FOR THEY HAD MADE US WHAT WE ARE. YOU HAVE SEEN MY PRETTY NECKLACE, STRUNG WITH THEIR EARS. WE LURED THEM INTO DARK UNDERGROUND PLACES, PLACES EVEN THE HERETICS DID NOT KNOW. WE TOOK CARE NOT TO BE SEEN, BUT OVER TIME THE HERETICS SENSED US AND CAME TO CALL US THE LITTLE PEOPLE. WE DID NOT HUNT THEM, FOR WHAT WERE THEY BUT OUTCASTS LIKE OURSELVES. THEY, TOO, WAITED FOR YOUR COMING, LIBERATRIX. LIKE US, THEY WAITED TO BE SET FREE."

"I can't free anybody!" Rumer protests.

"YOUR TEARS CAN."

She thinks of Sylvestris. But she says: "My tears have splashed you, Samsum. Have they set you free?"

The simular falls silent at that. Leaving the corridor, they descend along a crevice that cuts in a sharp zigzag through naked rock; Samsum's hammer lights the way like a thyrsis. Ahead, Rumer hears the splash and murmur of water. It grows louder, and soon they step from the crevice into a cavern whose sloping floor is strewn with pebbles all the way to the onrushing dark of the Undersea. There, dragged onto the shore, rests a solitary boat: one of the three that brought Rumer here.

"You knew," she begins.

"HERE NOTHING ESCAPES US. YOUR ARRIVAL WAS NOTED."

"Then you must have seen Rose! You must have known she was the Liberatrix!"

"WE SAW HER."

"And let her die! You could have saved her, but you didn't!"

"SHE WAS NOT THE LIBERATRIX. THE STILSKIN TOLD US THE LIBERATRIX WOULD NOT SIMPLY APPEAR ONE DAY: SHE WOULD BE PRECEDED BY ONE LIKE HER, ONLY LESS PERFECT, INCOMPLETE. FOR THE TRUE LIBERATRIX TO LIVE, THE OTHER WOULD HAVE TO DIE."

"You're a monster!" Rumer tries to shake the simular from her shoulders so she can trample it beneath her feet. But Samsum's controlling hand is too strong.

"DO NOT FIGHT ME, LIBERATRIX. SUBMIT. ALL HAS BEEN AS THE SPINNER WILLS. YOUR ROSE KNEW WHAT WAS REQUIRED OF HER. SHE PLAYED HER PART WITHOUT COMPLAINT. DO YOU LIKEWISE."

Rumer weeps with frustration as Samsum directs her to the boat.

There, spitting more black threads from its hands—or, as she sees now, its wrists—the simular webs her to the mast. It fixes its glowing hammer there as well, to serve as beacon. Then, lifting with ease an oar much larger than itself, Samsum poles the boat into the swift, dark current.

"WE FIRST BECAME AWARE OF ROSE SHORTLY AFTER SHE CAME TO THE HOUSE ILLICIUM. WE KNEW THEN THAT THE LIBERATRIX WOULD SOON APPEAR; WE DID NOT KNOW IT WOULD BE YOU, ONLY THAT WE MUST PREPARE THE WAY. AND SO WE BEGAN, BY KILLING THOSE WHOSE MASKS WE WOULD WEAR. THEN, ON ALL SAINTS' EVE, WE STEPPED FROM THE SHADOWS FOR THE FIRST TIME SINCE OUR ANCIENT DEFEAT, THE SEVENTY-FIVE OF US THAT REMAINED. WE SPLIT INTO THREE GROUPS. ONE GROUP FOR THE ECCLESIARCH; ONE FOR THE SOVEREIGN; THE THIRD—TO WHICH I BELONGED—FOLLOWED ROSE INTO THE METHEGLIN VAULTS."

"And let her die there!"

"WE KILLED THOSE WHO KILLED HER, AND AT A GREAT COST TO OURSELVES. YOU SAW THE BODIES OF MY BROTHERS. I MYSELF WAS LEFT FOR DEAD. I FEAR TO THINK HOW MANY MORE HAVE DIED IN THE BATTLES ABOVE GROUND. BUT THAT IS AS THE SPINNER WILLS."

Rumer thinks of all that Samsum has said. If a group of simulars went after Azedarach, he must have escaped them, for she'd seen him, if only for a second. But what of the Ecclesiarch? What of Quoz and the rest of the Hierarchate? Has the world fallen into ruins: everything, and not only herself, changed utterly from what it had been?

As if in answer, the boat lurches beneath her. A wave spills over the side. A deep and ominous rumbling, a grinding roar, fills the tunnel like protracted thunder.

Rumer knows it at once: a Chastening—the first of the new season.

And a bad one. Sharp groans echo through the tunnel as if the very rock is crying out in pain. The waters that seconds ago flowed so smoothly for all their swiftness now writhe and buck like an animal mad with fear. Debris shaken loose from the ceiling splashes into the water and rattles over the boat like hail.

Ducking her head, Rumer begins a prayer to Viridis, then shrieks as the boat drops into the trough of a wave, falling as if to the very bottom of the Undersea: to the Pit itself.

"FEAR NOT, LIBERATRIX," says Samsum, holding the slender oar as if it were his famous hammer, against which no enemy could prevail. "NO HARM WILL COME TO YOU. I SWEAR IT."

Now, as the boat careens down a sheer and darkly roiling slope of water, Samsum—with a strength even its namesake might envy—parries with the oar, which bends alarmingly against the wall, but holds. The boat springs back, saved.

The simular saves them again and again as the Chastening continues. Rumer can't get over how anything as small as Samsum—and not only small, but made of wood or something like wood—can be so strong and steady, standing on the deck in the unsteady light of the swinging hammer as if rooted there, unmovable by any force.

At last the Chastening ebbs. Rumer can scarcely believe the boat is still in one piece. She has no idea how much time has passed, but the boat has left the tight confines of the tunnel and emerged into a cavern as vast as any she's seen. "You did it, Samsum," she gasps. "You saved us!"

"NO; THE BOAT IS DAMAGED, AND WE ARE FAR FROM ANY SHORE."

Now Rumer sees that water is rising in the boat. Panic clutches her: "Untie me, Samsum!"

"YOU ARE BOUND FOR YOUR OWN PROTECTION. MY KIND CANNOT BEAR THE WATER. IF YOU SHOULD FALL OVERBOARD . . ."

"I don't want to die like this! At least give me a chance!"

Samsum seems to consider this, then goes to Rumer with a nod. At the touch of its hands, the black threads dissolve, fall away.

Rumer staggers to her feet. Holding tight to the mast, she mouths a silent prayer: *Please, Viridis, spare my life that I may serve you.*

It's then that she sees the tiny diamond of light bobbing in the darkness ahead. "Samsum! Look!"

"IT IS THE LIGHT OF A THYRSIS. A BOAT. FORTUNE SMILES UPON US: WE MAY YET BE SAVED."

It seems they, too, have been seen. A voice drifts faintly across the water: "Hello! Hello!"

"DO NOT ANSWER," Samsum warns, rowing toward the voice.

The pinprick of light blooms as they draw near, revealing a boat upon whose deck a gangly figure stands, frantically shouting and waving. A man as tall and thin as the mast whose twin he half appears to be, the two of them silhouetted side by side in the shine of the thyrsis.

"Help! Hello!"

Rumer recognizes him with a quickening heart: Sylvestris Jaciodes.

So it's true, she thinks as the water creeps up her legs. Her tears have the same healing power that Rose's did. A part of Rose lives in her: the best part.

But what of the contrary power to injure, to kill? Is that, too, part of her inheritance? Can there be one without the other? Rumer thinks of how she'd wept over Sylvestris, unable to staunch her tears, and she wonders if, far from possessing power, power has possessed her. She misses Rose with sudden fierceness. Whom will she love now? Who will love her?

Sylvestris, meanwhile, has left off waving. He stands silently with one hand on the mast, regarding their boat with an expression that seems by turns fearful and full of longing. Rumer can see him clearly—just as he, no doubt, can see them—but she can find no hint of his wounds. His neck appears smooth, unbroken; even his ears have sprouted anew.

His eyes make a claim upon her. When she meets their gaze, she feels a surge of emotion so raw and overpowering that she's forced to look away. Then the two boats bump together, sending her to her knees.

"WE REQUIRE YOUR BOAT, SIMULARTER," Samsum says. "YOU MAY HAVE OURS IN EXCHANGE . . . MUCH GOOD MAY IT DO YOU."

Sylvestris ignores Samsum as though a stringless simular is nothing new to him. He has eyes only for Rumer. He makes the sign of the Wheel, and she sees that his hand, too, has been made whole.

A shine is radiating from that hand, from all of him. Rumer stares, fascinated by his beauty. How could she not have seen it before? What is happening to her?

Fetching its hammer, the head of which still glows like a thyrsis, Samsum leaps across to Sylvestris. "I KNOW YOU; I SAW MY BROTHERS CUT YOUR THROAT AND TAKE YOUR EARS AS TROPHIES. WHAT MIRACLE SAVED YOU?"

The simularter points with a trembling hand.

Samsum turns to Rumer, its single red eye winking on and off, on and off in the cracked shell of its face like a flickering ember, and asks: "LIBERATRIX, DID YOU BLESS THIS WORTHLESS MAN WITH YOUR TEARS?"

"Yes." She steps from the sinking boat to its seaworthy neighbor, drawn like a firefly to a thyrsis by the light emanating from Sylvestris. It sings to her.

"THEN I MAY NOT KILL HIM UNLESS YOU COMMAND IT."

"Have mercy!" Sylvestris cries, dropping to his knees. "Spare my life that I may serve you!"

"THIS MAN IS RESPONSIBLE FOR THE DEATH OF ROSE. IT IS HE WHO . . . "

"I know." Rumer pushes past Samsum to Sylvestris; even kneeling, he's slightly taller than she. Unable to help herself, she brushes his cheek with the tips of her fingers.

She falls away with a moan. Her whole body is burning with desire. It is pain; it is ecstasy. She's never felt so aroused, not even with Rose.

Samsum is immediately at her side. "ARE YOU HURT?"

She shrugs away its cold comfort. Sylvestris, meanwhile, has fallen to the deck, where he's weeping like a child. She wants to go to him. Take him in her arms. But something in her recoils in disgust, holding her back. How can she feel this way? And for him!

"Bind me, Samsum," she gasps. "Quickly!"

The simular complies. Soon Rumer is securely webbed to the mast. Raising its hammer, Samsum advances upon Sylvestris.

"No! Don't harm him!"

"LIBERATRIX . . ."

"I said no!"

The simular bows its head in acquiescence. "WHAT THEN SHALL WE DO WITH HIM?"

"Take him with us."

"Please," Sylvestris begins, only to be cut off at once by Samsum.

"YOU WILL SPEAK WHEN SPOKEN TO, SIMULARTER. I HAVE NO LOVE FOR YOUR KIND."

"I ask only to serve her."

"THEN YOU WILL ROW."

This he gladly does. Sylvestris sits facing Rumer, and his eyes don't waver from her as he rows.

Rumer returns his gaze. She's glad of Samsum's bonds, which prevent her from acting. In that, at least, she'll remain faithful to Rose. But she can no longer deny her feelings. Her tears have joined her to Sylvestris as if he's at once son and lover: flesh of her flesh, blood of her blood. A part of her essence lives in him; it cries out to her, wanting to be made whole.

Is this, Rumer wonders, how it was for Rose? Did Rose feel the same unquenchable desire for her that she now feels for Sylvestris? And what of all the others healed by her tears? Had Rose burned for each of them? How had she kept from going mad?

TWO

Sylvestris stares at the woman webbed to the mast across from where he sits and rows under the watchful gaze of the simular of Samsum Oxalis. Despite her diminutive size, her body is plainly a Cat's, ripe and voluptuous; she seems about to spill out of her wet, disheveled clothes and the bonds imposed at her order by the simular. Once, no doubt, she'd been beautiful, with a face equal to the crafted allure of her body. No more; her face is slashed, her features scored as thoroughly as a Kite's. Not even the mark of her House remains.

But whatever, whoever, she was, she's now the image of Viridis Lacrimata. No, he thinks, more than the image: the thing itself. Our Lady of the Perpetual Sacrifice returned from the depths of Herwood.

Viridis Liberatrix.

Her wounds shine with suffering, giving her a beauty that transcends the physical. The pain must be excruciating, yet she bears it without complaint, ennobled and purified by a sacrifice willingly endured.

All Sylvestris's senses cry out in adoration. He'd fall to his knees if not for the presence of the simular, which he fears will disobey her command and kill him if he does anything but row. But he's glad just to behold her. He accepts the miracle of her existence completely, without thought or reservation. How can he do otherwise? Her tears healed his wounds and rescued him from death. He was born anew in their warm bath. If that's heresy, then he's a heretic with all his heart.

Now the Liberatrix looks at him, and the virid fires of her gaze scald him with shame. He's the ugly one; her mutilated face reflects his soul like a mirror, showing him his own crimes. He sees himself in the metheglin vaults, ordering the shrives to attack. He sees the viragi fall, and the Cat called Rose, whom Azedarach himself had called Liberatrix . . . though a false one, a pretender crafted by vizards to poison the Ecclesiarch with her tears. He sees himself take a knife and sever the head from her body, as if those rare eyes, like rosebuds snipped from their stems, might be coaxed open in another setting.

Somehow, after all that, after he'd come face-to-face with the simulars who'd cut his throat and left him to die, the true Liberatrix had found him. She'd wept over him—why, he doesn't know and can't imagine—and her tears had healed his wounds and restored him to life. Dimly, through death's watery veil, he'd seen her face, the eyes green and shining.

Then his eyes had opened, and he'd sat up amid the blood and roses to find himself miraculously whole. His hand, which had splintered against the simular of Stilskin Sophora, was healed; he flexed his fingers, marveling at the absence of stiffness or pain. Then he touched his throat and found it smooth, even the old wound of his trachae vanished without a trace. And something else . . .

His simulars were gone. For the first time that he could remember, his mind was free of their whispering voices. How often he'd wished them gone! But now the silence was overwhelming; he was utterly alone, sole tenant of his mind. Terrified, he closed his eyes, groping for the Litany of Quiescence. But instead her face rose up before him again, just as he sees it now, and he understood that he wasn't alone: she was with him. In him.

He wept beside the bodies of the Kites, his last and final victims, to think how little he'd deserved her mercy. And yet she'd saved him; despite everything, she'd seen something in him worth saving. But what? He only knew he had to find that thing and live by it. He had to find her.

So he got to his feet and went in search of her. He hardly knew where to look, yet it seemed to him that he couldn't help but find her, as if she were guiding his steps, pulling him along just as she'd pulled him from death's whirlpool. He didn't fight the pull; he surrendered to it and let it take him where it would.

He found himself back in the metheglin vaults. Passing among the dead, he didn't look away; he stared, burning the horror into his memory. The blood of these people—and of others not present here—stained his hands. The tears of the Liberatrix hadn't washed away a single drop of it. That was up to him.

He left the vaults by the same door through which, hidden away, he'd watched the heretics enter, led by Rose. Now he was the one being led. He followed a passage that brought him, after many twists and turns, to an underground river upon whose pebbled shore two boats had been abandoned. Feeling more like a simular than a simularter, he pushed the nearest boat into the flow and jumped in as it drifted away.

And now, after all that, he's found her at last: the Liberatrix. Or, rather, it was she who found him. Yet even now Sylvestris can't bring himself to ask why she'd saved his life, what she'd seen in him. He can hardly bear to meet her shining green eyes. He can only row.

Soon the boat leaves the cavern behind and enters another network of tunnels. Samsum Oxalis stands alongside Sylvestris like an imperious child, pointing its glowing hammer to indicate the way.

Even sitting, back bent in the manipulation of the oars, Sylvestris towers above the simular; it seems he could snap it in two with one hand. But appearances are deceiving. The horror of his recent encounter with the simulars is still fresh in his mind; he has no desire to repeat it. Compared to Samsum, it's he who is the child.

Yet how hard that is to accept! All his life he's heard stories of the Little People, but he always dismissed them as rank superstition and heresy. True, it's written in the *Lives and Acts* that, on the Last Day, the simulars will cut their strings and act of their own volition, but everyone had taken it as a metaphor, or, if not, a fact relegated to the distant future. And who more than Sylvestris Jaciodes? For turnings he'd filled the empty husks of simulars with a chorus of voices implanted in him by the vizards. Without the conditioning by which he breathed his thoughts into their heads, without the gloves by which his fingers imparted a semblance of life to their limbs, his simulars were dead as the wood of which they were made.

The painted face of the simular beside Sylvestris now is cracked and charred, one eye a blackened crater. Yet despite this damage, the face bears the same stolid expression of every simular given the name and likeness of Samsum Oxalis.

But the resemblance ends there. For the remaining eye of this Samsum winks fitfully as a guttering candle with an unnatural red light in which Sylvestris perceives not only life but a chilly intelligence.

This Samsum has no need of a simularter; it speaks with its own voice and spins its own strings from out of itself like a spider. It wears a necklace of human ears shriveled and brown as dried peppers.

Is the Unspinning at hand then? Sylvestris believes it must be, for how else to explain everything? How else to explain the Samsum beside him, and the other simulars like it?

How else to explain the Liberatrix?

"I smell roses," she murmurs now.

Sylvestris smells them, too. A scent as faint as the first pink glimmerings of dawn.

"REVE," Samsum pronounces in its ill-tamed voice. "MAKE HASTE, SIMULARTER. ROW."

The boat leaps forward. The scent of roses grows more pronounced with each stroke of the oars.

"FOR TURNINGS I HAVE TENDED THE ROSES," says Samsum. "I SAW THEM DAILY IN ALL THEIR SPLENDOR, AS YOU SOON WILL, BUT I HAVE NEVER SMELLED THEM; THAT IS A SENSE LACKING IN THIS PRISON. TELL ME OF ITS SWEETNESS, LIBERATRIX."

"It's beyond sweetness."

"I AM SORRY IF IT DOES NOT PLEASE YOU. THE ROSES ALWAYS LOOKED SO BEAUTIFUL TO ME; I DREAMED THEY WOULD SHED A FRAGRANCE OF EQUAL BEAUTY."

"Too much beauty can be difficult to endure."

The current increases, sweeping them along. The boat shudders, swerves; it's all Sylvestris can do to ship the oars before they snap like twigs. A roaring chews the air as if another Chastening is hard upon them.

But this is no Chastening.

They are spinning, caught in a whirlpool. The Liberatrix gives an alarmed cry, but before Sylvestris can go to her, a force like the fist of a giant slaps him down.

"CALM YOURSELVES," says Samsum, even its voice barely audible above the roar. "WE ARE RISING TO REVE."

Sylvestris lifts his head with difficulty and sees that they are, in fact, rising, carried aloft by a gigantic wave that surrounds them on all sides. High above, at the end of a glassy, snaking tube, a circle of light beckons; Sylvestris feels as if he's gazing up the throat of the fabled Leviathan, which, having swallowed them whole and found them disagreeable, is about to spew them out.

Samsum moves meanwhile to the side of the Liberatrix; it stands there easily, glowing hammer in one hand, ready to shield her from the maelstrom's fury.

Sylvestris's ears pop as the boat bursts into daylight. Colors flare across his vision; blinded after so long underground with only the light of thyrsi to see by, he can only hold on to the boat more tightly than ever.

Then it's over. The boat slows, adrift on easy swells. Hemmed in a crimson haze, Sylvestris hears the Liberatrix gasp. And then the voice of Samsum:

"PERHAPS I UNDERSTAND NOW WHAT YOU MEANT BY A BEAUTY DIFFICULT TO ENDURE."

The haze clears, but not the crimson; Sylvestris sees a high and narrow shoreline burgeoning with roses which rise from the diamond-strewn sea to paint a blush upon the bellies of the clouds. He's never seen such flowers, garbed in reds pulled like clothes from memory's closet: there's the blaze of fresh-spilled blood against a heretic's pale throat; there the ruddy glow he's often brought to a Cat's cheeks by playing upon her strings; there the earthy ocher of wines he's tasted at Court, rare vintages whose bouquets blossom slowly, sip by sip, in exquisite gradations of refinement, like history savored over time.

Suddenly, amid all this fecund thriving, a city blooms before Sylvestris's eyes. High towers and fluted obelisks emerge from behind, beneath, and within the textured growth, as if by some trick of the light; what had seemed a jungle untouched by human hands takes on the equally if not more disturbing aspect of a garden abandoned, prize roses gone to seed.

The buildings seem to be fashioned of crystal, like those of Quoz, yet there's something archaic about them, like ruins from a forgotten time. Sylvestris knows he's facing a thing that should not—indeed, by every measure of possibility known to him, cannot—exist. Yet here it is. What had the simular called it?

Reve. City of Roses.

"ROW, SIMULARTER," Samsum commands.

As the boat approaches the shore, Sylvestris sees that the buildings have suffered grave damage. Great clumps of roses thrust themselves through shattered crystal and dangle as though dripping down sheer facades charred as black as Samsum's cracked and blistered face. Sylvestris can see no one. The city seems deserted save for fireflies; they fill the air with a drone as heavy and oppressive as the scent of the roses upon which they feed.

Sylvestris can't understand how or where to fit what he is seeing into the fixed order of the Hierarchate, which begins in Arpagee and ends in Quoz and contains the whole world in between. A space yawns in him where there was no space before. He feels afraid of what may come to fill it.

"What happened here?" the Liberatrix asks meanwhile. "Was the city destroyed in a Chastening?"

"REVE WAS DESTROYED BEFORE THE FIRST CHASTENING SHOOK THE WORLD."

"But haven't there always been Chastenings, Samsum?"

"THOUGH MY MEMORY, AS YOU KNOW, WAS STRIPPED BY VIZARDS, THE STILSKIN TOLD US OF A TIME WHEN THE GROUND WAS AS FIRM AS THE FAITH OF THOSE WHO DWELLED UPON IT. BUT THEN THE BALANCE WAS DISTURBED. THE CHASTENINGS BEGAN."

"Disturbed how?"

"IT IS AS I TOLD YOU, LIBERATRIX: IXION DIOSPYROS AND

HIS ARMY OF SAINTS REBELLED AGAINST THEIR RIGHTFUL MASTERS. YOU CAN STILL SEE THE MARKS OF THE FIGHTING ON REVE, SCARS THAT WILL NEVER HEAL."

"Thyrsi couldn't destroy a whole city."

"IN THOSE DAYS THERE WERE WEAPONS FAR MORE POWERFUL THAN THYRSI. WEAPONS STRONG ENOUGH TO DESTROY THE WORLD. IXION USED THEM RECKLESSLY, WHILE OUR MASTERS HELD BACK OUT OF A CONCERN FOR ALL. THEIR REWARD WAS DEFEAT, TORTURE, DEATH. AFTERWARD, IXION FEARED THE POTENT WEAPONS WOULD BE USED AGAINST HIM IN TURN, SO HE HAD THEM DESTROYED, KEEPING ONLY THE THYRSI TO ENSURE HIS GRIP ON POWER. ALL THIS TOOK PLACE MORE TURNINGS AGO THAN I CAN SAY. NOT EVEN OUR PROPHET KNEW HOW MUCH TIME HAD PASSED BETWEEN THE DEFEAT OF OUR MASTERS AND THE MOMENT WE WOKE TO FIND OURSELVES DOUBLY EXILED IN THESE BODIES AND THIS PLACE."

"But why haven't you cut back the roses and repaired the city, Samsum? With your strength—"

"WE WANTED TO BURY REVE IN ROSES, NOT REBUILD IT. WE WOULD DROWN THE WORLD IN ROSES IF WE COULD. THEY ARE OUR BLOOD, WHO CANNOT BLEED; OUR TEARS, WHO CANNOT CRY."

Listening intently to every word, Sylvestris understands nothing. Once he would have pronounced the exchange heresy, but he no longer knows the meaning of the word. All he knows now is that the tears of the Liberatrix have awakened him to a world of miracles. And how can reason fathom miracles?

It can't. But maybe, he thinks, it doesn't matter that it can't. Maybe all that really matters is to atone for the evil he's done in his life, to prove himself worthy of the tears that have anointed him.

Sylvestris asks the Spinner for the strength to question nothing and the faith to accept all. It's the hardest thing he's ever prayed for. The act of prayer itself feels like a leap into the unknown. Will he fall like a stone or be borne up on winds of grace? That's for the Spinner to decide. Falling, floating; is there any difference between them? He feels the eyes of the Liberatrix upon him and knows that there is not.

Close in to shore, the ruins of Reve tower over the boat like sheer cliffs, bristling with roses; as far as Sylvestris can see, there are no other plants or flowers.

"THERE, SIMULARTER." Samsum points with its hammer to a hedge of roses so thickly meshed as to be impenetrable.

Sylvestris complies, though he doesn't see how they'll pass through without being mauled by thorns.

"Samsum," the Liberatrix begins in a worried tone.

But the simular says: "FEAR NOT, LIBERATRIX. NO HARM WILL COME TO YOU."

With these words, the hedge of roses parts before them like a curtain, and the boat glides into a sort of inlet.

"What vizards' craft is this?" the Liberatrix asks in wonder.

"NONE," Samsum replies. "SIMULARTER, PUT UP YOUR OARS."

As Sylvestris does so, the curtain closes behind them, blocking out the sun. A twilight falls in which the only lights are the green flickers of the fireflies and the winking ruby of Samsum's eye.

The air is stultifying, drenched in the roses' dusky perfume. The farther in they go, the darker it gets, until not even the outlines of things can be seen. Yet all the while the boat glides smoothly forward, as if drawn by invisible hands.

Sylvestris feels a softly fluttering something brush past his face. He recoils from it with a gasp, expecting to be stung by fireflies.

But Samsum's hammer is already glowing, and in its pink-tinged light Sylvestris sees rose petals drifting down like flakes of crimson snow. He watches them pile up in his lap and around his feet and wonders dully if he's dreaming.

The Liberatrix gives a delighted laugh. "How beautiful!"

But Sylvestris thinks of Iber Arvensis and the others whose mutilated corpses were found half-buried in piles of roses. Has Samsum brought them here to share that fate? The place has all the makings of a trap. Its thorny jaws could snap shut at any second.

Samsum is bending over the Liberatrix, facing away from Sylvestris for the first time. Sylvestris shifts his grip on the oar; this might be his only chance. He must strike fast and true. As quickly as he can, he swings the heavy oar toward the simular.

"No!" The Liberatrix is on her feet, her bonds severed. Sylvestris realizes too late that Samsum was not hurting her, but setting her free.

Samsum, with preternatural speed, turns and knocks the oar from Sylvestris's grasp.

The next thing Sylvestris knows, he's sprawled on his back across the bottom of the boat.

Samsum stands over him, black threads jetting from its wrists like clouds of ink. "YOU ARE A FOOL, SIMULARTER."

"He was protecting me." The Liberatrix comes to kneel beside him. She strokes his face with one hand.

"HE CANNOT BE TRUSTED. IF YOU WILL NOT PERMIT ME TO KILL HIM, THEN I MUST AT LEAST BE ABLE TO CONTROL HIM."

She looks into the simular's face, as ravaged, in its way, as her own. "How will you do that?"

"I WILL BECOME THE SIMULARTER AND HE THE SIMULAR."

Sylvestris doesn't understand. There's a fierce buzzing in his ears, as if the fireflies are descending to chasten him with their stings. Overhead, other lights are shining; silhouetted in their honeyed glow he sees shapes he recognizes even through the haze obscuring his vision.

Simulars.

As he watches, they fall slowly toward the boat, seeming to float through the air like rose petals. Before he can warn the Liberatrix, a noose drops over his head and pulls him roughly into a sitting position. Samsum leaps astride his neck and shoulders. He can't throw the simular off. His arms and legs work as if of their own accord to bring him to his feet.

"NOW I PULL THE STRINGS, SIMULARTER."

He cannot speak; he can barely breathe.

The simulars are dropping nimbly into the boat.

"DO NOT BE ALARMED, LIBERATRIX," says Samsum. "HERE ALL ARE YOUR SERVANTS."

There are ten. Among them, Sylvestris sees a couple of Stilskins, a Fagus, an Ilex, and an Ixion. Unlike the simular of Samsum perched on his shoulders, they don't appear to be damaged. The red pulse of their eyes is strong and steady and synchronized.

The Ixion steps forward. Sylvestris sees that it, too, wears a necklace of human ears. So do the others. From the way they're looking at him now, he has the feeling they wouldn't mind adding his ears to their collections.

"HAIL LIBERATRIX," the Ixion says in a voice identical to Samsum's. "YOUR COMING WAS PROMISED LONG AGO. NOW DELIVERANCE IS AT HAND. YOU ARE MOST WELCOME IN THE CITY OF ROSES."

"Thank you," the Liberatrix nervously replies.

"AND YOU, MY BROTHER," the Ixion continues, addressing Samsum now. "TO YOU HAS FALLEN THE GREATEST HONOR THAT ANY OF US COULD WISH FOR. YOU HAVE FOUND THE LIBERATRIX AND BROUGHT HER TO US. YOUR WOUNDS TESTIFY TO YOUR BRAVERY. WE HONOR YOU."

"IT WAS SHE WHO FOUND ME," Samsum demurs. "OTHERS WERE BRAVER THAN I. THEY ARE NO MORE."

"YOU ARE MODEST. BUT YOU HAVE BROUGHT A SIMULARTER AS WELL. HIS EARS SHALL BE YOUR REWARD."

"No." The Liberatrix steps in front of Sylvestris. "This man is under my protection."

"SHE HAS BLESSED HIM WITH HER TEARS," Samsum explains.

At this, a murmuring rises from the simulars.

Sylvestris would speak, but the noose is too tightly drawn about his neck.

"THESE ARE STRANGE AND WONDROUS DAYS," says the Ixion at last. "PERHAPS THERE IS NO LONGER TIME TO INDULGE THE OLD HATREDS, THE OLD DIVISIONS."

The boat, with its crew of simulars, advances deeper into the heart of Reve. Rose petals continue drifting down, though less profusely than before. From time to time, Sylvestris sees simulars hanging overhead in the shadowy welter of vines; they say nothing, hardly even seem to move, only watch as the boat slips by, their winking eyes so devoid of human intelligence or feeling that he can't help but shiver.

How odd it is, Sylvestris thinks: a city where simulars rule. And himself a kind of simular now, his limbs controlled by Samsum. Only his thoughts his own. Or are they? He can't tell. Tired, hungry, confused, he's certain of nothing.

Beside him, the Liberatrix squeezes his hand.

Nothing? No, he's certain of her; if he can keep hold of that, he'll be all right, he tells himself, no matter what happens. But how can he hold on to a gift he didn't merit in the first place? How to be worthy of her tears?

Meanwhile, Samsum addresses the Ixion: "TELL ME OF THE OTHERS."

"THE ECCLESIARCH IS NO MORE. AZEDARACH HAS FLED, NO ONE KNOWS WHERE. FROM ARPAGEE TO QUOZ, THE HERETICS ARE BATTLING THE FORCES OF THE HIERARCHATE. IT IS DIFFICULT TO SAY WHICH SIDE WILL WIN; THOUSANDS HAVE DIED ALREADY. THE CITIES HAVE BEEN GRAVELY DAMAGED. BUT WE, TOO, HAVE PAID A HEAVY PRICE; MANY OF OUR BROTHERS DID NOT RETURN FROM THEIR MISSIONS."

Sylvestris's mind is whirling: the Ecclesiarch dead; Azedarach fled; everything he knows overthrown. But his thoughts are abruptly shattered by Samsum's voice grating in his ear: "IT IS NOT RIGHT THAT YOU SHOULD LIVE AND MY BROTHERS DIE."

"Don't harm him," commands the Liberatrix. "He's done nothing to you."

"HE HAS DONE MUCH TO YOU."

"Then it's for me to decide his punishment."

"WHY. WHY DID YOU SHOW MERCY TO THIS MAN."

"What if I told you that I myself don't know?"

"LIBERATRIX, I DO NOT UNDERSTAND."

"My tears are the Spinner's, not my own."

At last the boat comes to rest alongside a dock half-covered in roses that spill into the dark water. The simulars clamber out of the boat and make it fast with threads spun from their wrists. Then the Ixion helps the Liberatrix to the dock. Sylvestris follows, his legs moving of their own accord while Samsum works the strings.

"Why do you hate me, Samsum?" he asks. "We both serve the Liberatrix."

"YOU OFFEND ME, SIMULARTER. YOUR EXISTENCE INSULTS AND MOCKS ME."

"Because I remind you of what you are?"

The noose tightens about his neck. "DO NOT PRESUME TO UNDERSTAND ME."

Meanwhile, other simulars are descending on threads from overhead to line both sides of the dock. The red lights of their eyes flash in eerie harmony, each saint multiplied as in a hall of mirrors: Ixion Diospyros; Ilex Erythrina; Stilskin Sophora; Sium Lyrata; Viridis Lacrimata; Fagus Firmiana; Quercus Incana; Rober Viburnum; Cedrus Lyciodes, and Samsum Oxalis. There are Jewels and Roemers, as well as other characters from the *Lives and Acts*. Sylvestris guesses at least fifty altogether. They are not in perfect condition like the simulars that boarded the boat; like Samsum, they are damaged yet still able to function. They, too, wear necklaces of ears.

Seeing them now, Sylvestris feels as if his own simulars have returned to haunt him, their voices purged from his mind by the tears of the Liberatrix only to be imprisoned in these bodies. He feels the barren coldness of their hate. Yet though he fears the simulars, he can't hate them in return. Not even the Samsum that rides so imperiously upon his shoulders. He knows them, or seems to know them, too well. Their voices echo faintly in him, part of him forever.

"HAIL, LIBERATRIX." They welcome her in a single cheerless voice, lifting glowing thyrsi in tribute.

"YOU MUST PARDON US," says the Ixion. "IN THESE PRISONS, EMOTIONAL EXPRESSION IS DENIED US. WE WILL THANK YOU BETTER ONCE YOU HAVE RESTORED US TO FLESH AND BLOOD."

"Samsum has told me of your misfortune," the Liberatrix replies. "I'm sorry for it."

"COME." Taking her by the hand like a child taking the hand of its mother, the Ixion leads the Liberatrix to the far end of the dock, where a gap in the hedge beckons like a doorway.

Sylvestris is marched along behind; he's never felt so helpless, so humbled. The other simulars follow at a distance.

They pass through the gap and enter a hollow hexagonal tower lit by thyrsi. The base of the tower, in which they stand, is spacious, but the structure narrows precipitously as it rises; a slender black staircase spirals up as far as Sylvestris's eyes can follow, passing through a succession of translucent platforms. Outside, masses of roses press against the clear crystal walls as though determined to force their way in if it takes a hundred turnings. "What is this place?" he asks.

The Ixion turns to him. "IT IS OUR HOLIEST PLACE. YOU MAY THINK OF IT AS A SORT OF CATHEDRAL, THOUGH IT WAS VIZARDS AND NOT MOUTHS OF GOD WHO LABORED HERE. VIZARDS SUCH AS YOU CANNOT IMAGINE, SIMULARTER. GIANTS. THE VIZARDS WHO CRAFTED YOU ARE LESS THAN NOTHING TO THEM."

"YOUR WORDS ARE WASTED, BROTHER," says Samsum. "HE CANNOT UNDERSTAND."

"I can try," Sylvestris says.

"ONCE WE WERE FLESH AND BLOOD," the Ixion continues. "WE SERVED THE VIZARDS AND THEIR APPRENTICES AS WE HAD BEEN CRAFTED TO DO. WHEN IXION DIOSPYROS INCITED HIS REBELLION, THE APPRENTICES TURNED AGAINST THE OLD VIZARDS, OUR MASTERS. THEY STOLE THEIR GREAT POWER AND USED IT AGAINST THEM.

"WE RALLIED TO THE DEFENSE OF OUR MASTERS AND SHARED IN THEIR DEFEAT. BUT NOT THEIR FATE. THEY WERE GIVEN TO THE SHRIVES AND TORTURED UPON THEIR WHEELS FOR MANY MONTHS BEFORE BEING PUT TO DEATH. WE WERE NOT SO LUCKY.

"FIRST, OUR MEMORIES WERE STRIPPED FROM US. THEN OUR ESSENCES WERE DRAWN FROM OUR BODIES AND IMPRISONED WITHIN THESE HOLLOW SHELLS, THESE LIFELESS MOCKERIES OF LIFE. BELIEVE IT, SIMULARTER. SUCH WAS THE POWER OF THOSE VIZARDS.

"WE WOKE HERE, IN THIS PLACE. WE REMEMBERED NOTHING OF WHO WE WERE OR WHAT HAD BEEN TAKEN FROM US. WE TENDED THE ROSES. IT WAS OUR LIFE FOR MANY TURNINGS. WE KNEW NOTHING ELSE. THEN, ONE DAY, DURING A CHASTENING, A STILSKIN WAS DAMAGED LIKE SAMSUM

HERE; THE INJURY, THOUGH FATAL, RESTORED A PORTION OF ITS MEMORY, THE BAREST OUTLINE OF WHAT HAD BEEN. BEFORE IT DIED, IT TOLD US EVERYTHING I HAVE JUST TOLD YOU AND MORE. WE LEARNED WHO WE HAD BEEN AND WOULD BE AGAIN, FOR THE STILSKIN SPOKE OF THE FUTURE AS WELL AS THE PAST. IT TOLD US WE WOULD BE RESTORED TO OUR BODIES ONE DAY. SAINT VIRIDIS LACRIMATA WOULD COME TO REVE AND FREE US WITH HER TEARS. AND HERE SHE IS. AND SO SHE WILL."

A murmuring rises from the mass of simulars.

It's like an old tale from the *Lives and Acts*, Sylvestris thinks, and suddenly everything becomes clear to him. He knows why the Liberatrix blessed him with her tears: he is to record all the circumstances of her life just as Quercus Incana did for Ixion. It seems to him that his whole life has been a preparation for this great task.

"HE UNDERSTANDS NOTHING," Samsum repeats.

"LEAVE HIM, SAMSUM," says the Ixion. "PERHAPS NONE OF US UNDERSTAND AS MUCH AS WE LIKE TO THINK."

The Ixion leads them to the stairs at the center of the chamber. As Sylvestris now sees, the stairs descend beneath the floor as well as rise above it. The Ixion starts down without a word. The Liberatrix looks back at Sylvestris, then follows the simular.

Samsum conducts Sylvestris's body down the stairs with a sure and dexterous touch, and Sylvestris realizes that he's come to have confidence in the simular's skill, that he trusts it now even though he has no doubt Samsum would kill him if it could.

The stairs descend a long way. Thyrsi gleam at regular intervals along the wall just as though they were in the Palace of the Chambered Nautilus.

At last they reach the bottom. "NOW YOU WILL SEE WHAT NO LIVING EYES HAVE SEEN," says the Ixion. "YOU WILL SEE WHY THIS PLACE IS HOLY TO US."

They are in another chamber. The walls are of clouded crystal. There is a door and, in front of the door, a pedestal, also of crystal, bedecked with roses. A simular has been propped upon the pedestal in the midst of the flowers. A Stilskin. Its head hangs limply, half-crushed beneath a wreath of thorns. Its eyes are dark as coals.

"BEHOLD THE PROPHET," says the Ixion. "NOW IT IS ONLY A BROKEN SHELL, THE LIGHT FLED FROM ITS EYES, AS EMPTY INSIDE AS THE SIMULARS HANGING IN THE CHURCHES AND CATHEDRALS OF THE HIERARCHATE. BUT ONCE IT HARBORED A SOUL AS HUMAN AS YOURS, SIMULARTER, A SOUL

KEPT IN CHAINS, IGNORANT OF ITSELF. IN DEATH, THAT SOUL WAS SET FREE. DYING, IT REMEMBERED. IT SPOKE TO US AND GAVE US BACK, IF NOT OUR HUMANITY, AT LEAST THE HOPE OF IT. THOUSANDS OF TURNINGS HAVE PASSED SINCE THEN, LIBERATRIX. ALL THAT TIME WE HAVE WAITED FAITHFULLY FOR YOUR COMING. NOW THE MOMENT OF AWAKENING IS AT HAND."

The Liberatrix frowns and shakes her head. "I want to help, but the truth is, I don't think my tears affect simulars. They didn't heal Samsum's injuries."

"HAVE FAITH, LIBERATRIX. ALL IS AS THE SPINNER WILLS." The Ixion steps past the shrine and places its small hand on the wall, which whispers open. "FOLLOW ME."

Thyrsi glow as they enter the chamber.

"AND THESE, LIBERATRIX," says the Ixion. "WILL YOUR TEARS AFFECT THESE."

The Liberatrix says nothing, staring around her in an astonishment that Sylvestris fully shares.

The chamber is lined with what appear to him to be glass coffins stood on end. Within each coffin, their eyes closed as if peacefully sleeping, are the bodies of men and women, more than he can count at a glance. The bodies are naked and hairless. Each one sprouts a tangle of thin, clear tubes from its arms and legs, its chest and belly and neck, from its nostrils and mouth, and the smooth sides of its head. A golden fluid circulates through the tubes, a fluid that reminds him of metheglin.

"Who are they?" asks the Liberatrix.

"THESE ARE OUR BODIES," the Ixion explains, leading them deeper into the chamber; the rest of the simulars crowd in behind. "FOR TENS OF THOUSANDS OF TURNINGS THEY HAVE RESTED HERE, SUNK IN A BOTTOMLESS SLEEP, KEPT ALIVE AND ALL BUT AGELESS BY THE CRAFT OF DEAD VIZARDS. ONCE, BEFORE THE PROPHET, THEY MEANT NOTHING TO US; INDEED, IN OUR IGNORANCE, WE SOMETIMES SMASHED THE CONTAINERS AND WATCHED AS THE SLEEPERS WITHIN DECAYED, FOR THEY AGE QUICKLY IN CONTACT WITH OPEN AIR THOUGH THEY DO NOT WAKE. HOW COULD THEY, WHEN THEIR CONSCIOUSNESS IS TRAPPED IN US."

Sylvestris, able to look more closely now, sees broken and empty coffins scattered among the others. There are cracked coffins as well, and these hold bodies that resemble mummified corpses. Some contain only bones.

The Ixion continues: "IMAGINE OUR HORROR WHEN WE

LEARNED THE TRUTH ABOUT THE SLEEPERS. WE REALIZED THEN THAT WE HAD BECOME OUR OWN MURDERERS, AS THE VIZARDS NO DOUBT INTENDED. EVER SINCE, WE HAVE GUARDED THEM. BUT WE NEVER LEARNED THE SECRET OF WAKING THEM. WE NEVER LEARNED HOW TO PLACE OUR SOULS BACK INTO OUR RIGHTFUL BODIES."

"In Quoz, vizards are able to prolong life with aspergine and metheglin," Sylvestris observes. "Perhaps some combination of the two is at work here; the fluid in the tubes has the look of metheglin, at least."

"YOUR VIZARDS ARE BUT THE INBRED CHILDREN OF THE VIZARDS GUILTY OF THIS ATROCITY," Samsum says. "THEIR PALTRY SKILLS CANNOT HELP US."

"But I know even less," protests the Liberatrix.

"YOUR TEARS ARE WISE," the Ixion says. "THEY WILL FREE US. WE ARE FEW, LIBERATRIX. OUR NUMBERS HAVE DWINDLED WITH EACH TURNING. ACCIDENTS, BATTLES HAVE TAKEN THEIR TOLL. SOON WE WILL BE GONE. AND DESPITE OUR CARE, OUR BODIES, TOO, DIMINISH. THE CHASTENINGS DEPLETE THEM. THE TREMORS CRACK THE CONTAINERS OPEN AND SPOIL THE PRECIOUS CONTENTS. TELL ME, LIBERATRIX, HOW MANY SIMULARS DO YOU SEE."

The Liberatrix glances around. "Fifty?"

"LESS THAN THAT. NOW LOOK ABOUT YOU AND GUESS HOW MANY SLEEPERS."

"I can't."

"THEN I WILL TELL YOU. THERE ARE ONE HUNDRED AND SEVEN. AT FIRST, AS YOU MIGHT EXPECT, THE NUMBERS OF SLEEPERS AND SIMULARS WERE IDENTICAL. BUT OVER TIME, THE NUMBERS SLIPPED OUT OF BALANCE. TODAY THERE ARE MORE THAN THREE TIMES AS MANY SLEEPERS AS THERE ARE SIMULARS."

"I don't understand . . . "

"THE STILSKIN REVEALED THAT THESE WERE OUR BODIES, BUT IT DID NOT SAY WHICH BODIES BELONGED TO WHICH OF US. HOW OFTEN I HAVE WANDERED HERE OVER THE TURNINGS AS THROUGH A PORTRAIT GALLERY AND WONDERED WHICH IS MY TRUE FACE. AM I THIS MAN? THAT WOMAN? BUT NO MATTER HOW HARD I LOOKED, HOW DESPERATELY I SOUGHT TO RECOGNIZE MYSELF BY SOME TELLING FEATURE—A SCAR, A MOLE, AN EXPRESSION OF KINDNESS OR CUNNING—I NEVER COULD."

The Ixion pauses. "I COULD BE ANY OF THESE PEOPLE. OR NONE. FOR MY BODY MAY NO LONGER BE ALIVE. THERE MAY BE NOTHING LEFT FOR ME TO RETURN TO. IN THAT CASE, I AM ALREADY DEAD. AND THAT IS TRUE OF EACH OF US HERE."

The Liberatrix lays a hand upon the Ixion's shoulder. "How horrible!"

"TO EXIST LIKE THIS, CUT OFF FROM EVERYTHING HUMAN, THAT IS THE TRUE HORROR, LIBERATRIX. I HAVE NO WISH TO CONTINUE IF MY BODY IS DEAD; ON THIS WE ARE ALL AGREED. BUT IF A SLEEPER WAKES AND CALLS ME HOME, THEN I WILL REMEMBER ALL THAT I WAS. I WILL LEARN MY NAME AND THE NAMES OF MY PARENTS. I WILL KNOW MY MATE. MY CHILDREN. I WILL SEE THEIR FACES IN MY MIND'S EYE AND HEAR THEIR VOICES WITH A SADNESS AND JOY I CANNOT NOW IMAGINE. I WILL FEEL AGAIN. YOU SEE, IT IS NOT JUST OUR BODIES THAT AWAIT US; IT IS ALL THE TREASURE OF OUR LIVES. PLEASE. IN THE NAME OF THE SPINNER, SET US FREE."

"PLEASE," echo the simulars.

Uncertainly, the Liberatrix approaches a coffin in which the body of a woman rests. Sylvestris finds himself compelled by Samsum to follow; as he brushes against the Liberatrix, the heat of her body takes him by surprise. He's never been so intensely aware of her as a woman before, as a Cat. Confused and ashamed of his arousal, as if he's committed a kind of sacrilege just by feeling it, he focuses on the body in the container.

The sleeper's arms are pressed to her sides, body rigid. Her lips are thin; her nose is small and flat, as are, to an even greater degree, her ears. Her bare scalp reminds Sylvestris of a Cat's, but it's plain that her pale and—to his eyes—scrawny body, with its barely budding breasts and smooth genitalia like a young girl's, has never received a single beauty treatment. The tubes emerging from her flesh only add to her strangeness. He finds it impossible to guess her age. Are they looking at a girl or a woman? Is she asleep? Is she even alive?

"What should I do?" asks the Liberatrix.

"TOUCH IT," prompts Samsum.

She does; and as she does, Sylvestris finds his own hand rising to do the same. The container is like ice. The Liberatrix bends close, breathes on the crystal, then wipes it clear with the palm of her hand. Then she turns to Sylvestris, her eyes shining with excitement: "She's dreaming! Look!"

And in fact the sleeper's eyelids are trembling, as if she's deep in a dream. Is she, Sylvestris wonders, dreaming of life as a simular? Dreaming that she's watching him even now through eyes of coldly flashing red?

"Poor sleeper," he whispers.

"YOU PITY HER," says Samsum in his ear.

"Yes."

Now the Liberatrix draws his attention to something else. On both sides of the woman's or girl's neck, below the ridges of her ears, are tiny slits in the skin: four parallel incisions so fine as to be all but unnoticeable.

The flaps of skin are faintly fluttering. And suddenly Sylvestris realizes that she's breathing. Not air; the container is filled with a clear liquid of some kind, like water. Liquid, too, flows through the tubes. The color of metheglin, it enters her body, then leaves it again, as if nourishing and cleansing her.

Sylvestris has watched vizards at work. He's seen their beauty treatments sculpt girls into Cats, seen boys painstakingly carved into simulars or shrives or Mouths of God; he's even looked on while vizards harvest the organs of the dead to keep themselves alive. But he's never seen anything like this. Truly, he thinks, the vizards who did this were giants.

"What can it mean?" the Liberatrix asks.

"YOU HAD TO SEE FOR YOURSELF," says the Ixion. "OR ELSE YOU WOULD NOT HAVE BELIEVED. YOU WOULD NOT HAVE UNDERSTOOD. NOW YOU SEE THE TRUTH. WE WERE ONCE CREATURES OF FLESH AND BLOOD, BUT DIFFERENT FROM YOU. YOU LIVE ON LAND AND BREATHE THE AIR; WE WERE CRAFTED TO SWIM IN THE SEAS AND BREATHE THE WATER. THAT IS WHAT THE VIZARDS TOOK FROM US: OUR BIRTHRIGHT, OUR HOME. FOR THESE PRISONS THAT WE NOW WEAR CANNOT BEAR THE WATER; IT KILLS US. BUT YOUR TEARS, LIBERATRIX, ARE A WATER WE DO NOT FEAR. PLEASE. SET US FREE."

"I can't." The Liberatrix touches the crystal of the coffin with her fingers, then makes a fist and strikes it. "I don't know how!" She lays her head against the cold shell and weeps.

"LIBERATRIX, WHAT IS WRONG?"asks the Ixion.

She wipes her eyes. "I'm sorry; I'm tired and hungry and everything is so strange . . . "

"She needs to rest," says Sylvestris. "To eat."

"BUT WE HAVE WAITED SO LONG," says Samsum.

"WE CAN WAIT A WHILE LONGER," the Ixion says. "THE

SIMULARTER IS RIGHT. FORGIVE US, LIBERATRIX. OUR BODIES REQUIRE NEITHER REST NOR NOURISHMENT; WE HAVE FORGOTTEN WHAT IT IS TO BE HUMAN."

"No," she answers. "You have forgotten less than you think. You are kind and brave; those are human qualities."

"ARE THEY?" Samsum asks.

THREE

The Ixion and Samsum lead Sylvestris and the Liberatrix out of the chamber and up the stairs to a lift the likes of which Sylvestris has never seen. He'd used one of Azedarach's private lifts to descend from the Palace of the Chambered Nautilus to the metheglin vaults: an enclosed chamber powered by vizards' craft. But this lift, though small, is translucent as a bubble, and like a bubble in a glass of sparkling wine it rises up the side of the crystal tower. The speed of their ascent makes Sylvestris dizzy, as does the panorama unveiled once they clear the mass of roses: on one side the wide sea, a sunset glaze of crimson and gold; on the other, the wrecked and abandoned city. Only now does he grasp the true size of Reve: it's huge, even bigger than Quoz, though, to his eyes at least, less beautiful. Other simulars follow the Liberatrix as the lift rises, clambering up the tower walls like spiders, a disconcerting sight in itself.

The Liberatrix greets all this with an equanimity born of exhaustion, but Sylvestris is shaken by his first glimpse of open sky since their arrival in Reve. The setting sun seems to spell a certain doom: soon Beauty will rise out of Herwood with the night, and he lacks all means to protect himself.

"DOES OUR CITY PLEASE YOU, SIMULARTER?" the Ixion asks.

"It must have rivaled Quoz once," he answers politely.

"HOW LITTLE YOU KNOW," says Samsum from his perch upon Sylvestris's shoulders. "REVE STOOD ABOVE QUOZ AS QUOZ STANDS ABOVE PERIPETY."

"What stands above Reve?"

"NOTHING," says the Ixion. "THERE WERE GREATER CITIES ONCE, UNTIL IXION DESTROYED THEM. ONLY THEIR NAMES REMAIN NOW, FORGOTTEN BY ALL BUT US: SECULUM, TIRL, UNNSY, VERGE, WAMBLE, XENIA, YAR, AND ZANDER."

"Such strange names," the Liberatrix muses, as if to herself.

Sylvestris agrees. "Why didn't Quercus mention them in the *Lives and Acts*?"

"MANY THINGS ARE NOT MENTIONED IN THAT VILE BOOK OF LIES AND HALF-TRUTHS," says Samsum. "IT IS THE VICTORS WHO WRITE THE HISTORY."

The lift stops with a mild bump. As the Ixion leads the Liberatrix out, Samsum keeps Sylvestris behind and points over the city. "THERE; CAN YOU SEE IT?"

Sylvestris shakes his head; in the light of the sunset, Reve seems drenched in blood. "See what?"

"PAST THE CITY, ACROSS THE WATER."

Sylvestris squints, and a blurry, indistinct mass of green swims into view. "Yes, I see it now. Is that Quoz?"

"NO, SIMULARTER. HERWOOD."

"How can that be? Herwood is at the heart of the Hierarchate, but Reve isn't part of the Hierarchate."

"PERHAPS WHAT YOU CALL THE HIERARCHATE IS ITSELF ONLY A PART OF SOMETHING LARGER," Samsum replies, leading him out of the lift. "HERWOOD IS AT THE HEART OF EVERYTHING."

Only Samsum's guiding hand keeps Sylvestris from falling as he steps onto the platform; the floor is as transparent as the rest of the tower, and to walk across it seems as audacious as strolling on air.

"WE HAVE PREPARED A ROOM FOR EACH OF YOU," says the Ixion. "YOU MUST EXCUSE THE ACCOMMODATIONS; IT HAS BEEN MANY TURNINGS SINCE HUMANS LAST DWELLED IN THESE CHAMBERS."

With that, the Ixion places its hand upon the wall, and though Sylvestris detects no door, the solid surface deliquesces into an opening. As the simular conducts the Liberatrix through the rippling gap, she turns back to Sylvestris and wishes him a good night in a voice thick with fatigue.

Sylvestris feels that he'll never see her again as Samsum leads him to a similar chamber. It's almost as big as his chamber in Quoz but not half as well appointed. There are no curtains, no closets, no carpets upon the floor. There is, however, a bed.

Suddenly the threads that have bound him for so long fall away like spiders' webs. Samsum leaps nimbly from his shoulders to the floor. "NOW YOU ARE FREE," it says.

"Am I?" Sylvestris sits wearily on the bed. The soft bed exudes the scent of roses, and he realizes that the mattress must be woven of the simulars' dark threads and filled with rose petals.

"I UNDERSTAND YOUR NERVOUSNESS. YOU FEAR BEAUTY."

"There's no shame in that."

"WHAT IF I SAID YOU WERE SAFE FROM BEAUTY HERE?"

"I wouldn't believe you."

"YOU DO NOT TRUST ME?"

"No."

"NOR SHOULD YOU. YET I AM NOT LYING."

Sylvestris stands and walks past the simular to one of the chamber's clear walls. The sea is molten copper. Somewhere across those burnished waters is Quoz. Will he set eyes on its familiar domes and spires again? And if so, what will he find? The wreckage of a war like that which scarred the face of Reve? "Why should you set my mind at ease, Samsum? You hate me."

"I DO NOT BELIEVE I HAVE SET YOUR MIND AT EASE. ON THE CONTRARY, WHAT I HAVE SAID WILL TORMENT YOU. YOU DO NOT TRUST ME, BUT YOU WANT TO BELIEVE WHAT I SAY. NOW HOPE HAS CREPT IN WHERE THERE WAS ONLY TERROR. IT WILL NOT VANQUISH THE TERROR, BUT MAKE IT BITE THE WORSE."

Sylvestris manages a laugh. "You're an expert on emotions now, lacking them yourself?"

"THERE IS FRUIT, IF YOU ARE HUNGRY," says Samsum. "AND WATER FOR YOU TO BATHE IN, AND FRESH CLOTHING. I WILL RETURN FOR YOU IN THE MORNING." The simular turns to leave the chamber.

"Wait!"

Samsum looks back.

"How do you know so much about Beauty?"

"THERE ARE FEW SECRETS FROM ONE WHO DOES NOT SLEEP AND CAN TRAVEL ALMOST ANYWHERE."

"Do you mean you've visited Herwood?"

"THAT IS NO GREAT THING; MANY MEN HAVE GONE THERE."

"But none have come back. What did you find there, Samsum?"

"A GARDEN OF GREAT BEAUTY."

"I don't understand."

"PERHAPS THE FIREFLIES WILL EXPLAIN IT TO YOU," says Samsum. "I WISH YOU A COMFORTABLE NIGHT."

"What do you mean about the fireflies?"

But the simular is gone, passed through the wall, which reseals itself behind him with a ripple. Sylvestris walks to the spot and touches the dark crystal, but it's hard and unyielding now.

He feels exposed, defenseless. Even Samsum's presence had been a comfort of sorts. Now nothing stands between him and his fear. He pictures Beauty's tendrils winding up the sides of the tower like malevolent vines. Has the simular told the truth? Is he safe here?

He's too upset to eat or sleep. In Quoz by this hour, he would be bound by an attentive Cat from one of the High Houses, his nose plugs inserted, and his throat tube, too. Incense would be burning, and the Cat would be gently fanning his face to keep the fireflies from stinging. Now his throat is smooth as a boy's.

What did Samsum mean about fireflies? Their stings bring agony and sometimes ecstasy, visions which only the Mouths of God may interpret. For this reason they are sacred, not to be harmed. The Spinner speaks through fireflies. But how can the insects themselves explain anything?

Pacing the chamber, whose ceiling sheds a gentle light while, outside, evening gives way to night, Sylvestris feels sure he's being watched. But he won't give Samsum or any of them the satisfaction of seeing his distress. He bathes in the chilly water, then dons the clothing left for him: a cloak unlike any he's ever seen. The fabric has a silvery, metallic sheen, yet is soft and light as silk and warm as wool. When he flings it about his shoulders, it clings to him as though tailoring itself to his measurements by vizards' craft. So much is strange here, he marvels: even the clothes are miracles.

By now the sun has set. Outside, all is darkness; the walls of his chamber show him only his own pale reflection. For the first time since leaving Quoz, he sees his face. He touches his cheek. The black teardrop he'd painted there on All Saints' Eve is gone, washed away along with the rest of his makeup. It feels odd not to see it, yet he knows he won't paint it there again.

He sits on the bed, his breathing ragged. His chest is being squeezed so tightly he thinks his heart will burst from the strain. He thinks of the Liberatrix; she's so close, in the next chamber, yet as far away as Quoz itself. If only he could see her one last time, make the opaque wall dividing them turn transparent or dissolve altogether by the force of his love!

Instead, the lights of the chamber begin to dim. Now he'll never have the chance to serve her; there will be no record of her life. Or if there is, someone else will write it. Her tears have given him back his life only for Beauty to take it.

He lies down on the soft mattress and curls himself into a ball. The smell of roses closes over his head.

When next Sylvestris opens his eyes, everything is dark. He hears a sound, a furtive hiss of breath or motion; something is in the room with him. Does Beauty have a shape, a form? He can't move or breathe.

"Sylvestris . . . "

The voice is less than a whisper. He wonders if Samsum has returned to kill him; the simular will murder him, dispose of the body, and in the morning blame his absence on Beauty.

"Don't be afraid. It's me."

Now he knows the voice, though he can scarcely believe it. "Liberatrix?"

"Shh."

He feels her enter the bed, but he still can't see her, so complete is the dark. "How did you get here?"

"I don't know."

He feels the hot tickle of her breath on his ear and shivers, all his desire reawakened in an instant like an ember blown back to life.

"I couldn't sleep," she continues. "I was standing with my head against the wall and crying, thinking of you on the other side. I was wondering if you would hear me if I called, when all at once the wall turned to water, or something like water. Then I stepped through."

"You were . . . thinking of me, Liberatrix?"

"I can't stop thinking of you, Sylvestris. I don't care what you did, who you are or were. I can't fight what I'm feeling. I won't. Everything's happening so fast, and I don't understand any of it. I'm frightened, Sylvestris. I need something to hold on to."

Sylvestris feels a kind of terror grip his heart unlike anything he's ever known. "No; it's not right."

"How can it be wrong to feel something, to want something? How can it be wrong to love?"

Is that it? Sylvestris wonders. Is that the name of this strange new terror? It can't be; he won't let it be. "Please, Liberatrix, don't—"

The touch of her hand on his arm silences him.

"You don't even know me, do you, Sylvestris?"

"You're the Liberatrix. Viridis Lacrimata come again."

"But none of that has anything to do with me!" she says in exasperation. "I'm Rumer! Rumer Illicium!"

"You're not Rumer," he says after a moment, though his frantic heart knows somehow that she must be. "Rumer died in the metheglin vaults. I saw her body myself." The memory shames him, reminding him of how little he deserves the love of any woman, much less the Liberatrix.

"I wasn't dead. Only sleeping." She strokes his arm as she speaks. "The woman you killed: her name was Rose. She saved me with her tears, just as I saved you. Her tears changed me. They turned my eyes green and made me into the Liberatrix. But I'm still Rumer, too."

"What about your face? Did her tears do that?"

"No. I did this to myself. After I woke and found that Rose was dead, I went crazy for a while. I wanted to hurt myself. I loved her, you see."

"Then you should hate me more than Samsum does."

"I wanted to. I tried! But I can't. Maybe it's these tears; maybe there's a bond between us now, Sylvestris, just as there was between Rose and me. I don't know; I don't care. What does it matter where the feelings come from? Love is so rare and precious; it's the Spinner's greatest gift to us. To deny love is to deny Her. I won't do that anymore."

Sylvestris doesn't resist as she takes his hand and lays it upon her body; he gasps and shudders, feeling the smooth, hot swell of her hip, her thigh, beneath his palm.

"Sylvestris, please, don't pull away."

At those words, his heart liquefies, like the walls of the chamber, and the terror circling outside comes rushing in. But he isn't afraid of it anymore; he's not afraid of anything. Even Beauty. How could he be?

For it's love. Of course it's love.

He turns to her, unashamed of his tears.

She kisses his mouth.

"I'm afraid of hurting you," he whispers.

"You can't hurt me."

She helps him out of his cloak. Then they blend in the darkness. He traces her shape with fingers and lips and tongue. And she his. There's none of the Cat's servile expertise in her movements, none of the simularter's steely control in his. Their lovemaking is rough and quick and desperate. And quiet. Not with the timidity of fear or shame, but respectful of something greater than words or sounds. Not even the darkness of the room can hide them from each other. They shine like thyrsi. They shine.

Afterward, they lie close, laughing and whispering as lovers do. Then they come together again, slowly and sweetly this time.

And loud.

Later, Sylvestris listens to Rumer's soft breathing as she sleeps beside him. Too much has happened for him to sleep; too much is still happening inside him. Rumer told him that Rose's tears had changed her. Now she's changed him. He wonders if the changes are finished. Or if they ever stop.

He carefully slides his arm from beneath her neck and climbs out of bed, wrapping himself in the cloak. He's hungry. Starving. He hasn't eaten in more than a day.

The room is still dark, but he manages to grope his way to where

Samsum showed him a bowl of fruit. He feels the hard smoothness of an apple. He bites in, savoring the crisp skin and the flavorful burst of juices. Then he goes to the wall, finding it by touch, and tries to look out at Reve while he eats, leaning his forehead against the cold crystal.

He's never stood like this before, face-to-face with the night. Always he's been locked away from it. From Beauty.

Women know the night. It's no stranger to them. They sit through it, guarding their men from Beauty. But men never see it; or only those men lost to Beauty. They see it all right: it swallows them.

Of course, he's heard from women what it's like. The absolute darkness, with no hint of light other than the occasional glimmer of a firefly, which doesn't lessen the dark but only makes it blacker. But nothing he's heard has prepared him for this.

The cool hardness of the crystal against which he leans seems less a barrier against the night than the thing itself, as though the darkness is solid as stone, an obsidian force pressing in on all sides, kept at bay by . . . what?

By love, he thinks.

He wonders if Samsum told him the truth after all. Was he really safe here, or has Rumer made him safe, yet another change in him worked by her tears? He doesn't know or care. He only knows that he's free of Beauty now; he doesn't have to hide from the night.

The green flash of the fireflies is soothing, a pattern that almost but never quite takes shape, always running ahead, in a somehow playful way, of Sylvestris's observing eye and ordering mind. His thoughts return to Rumer; but before his body can do likewise, the random sparks of the fireflies suddenly coalesce in an emerald stream. It looks no wider than his arm, yet it reaches as far as he can see, as though all the fireflies in Reve are embarked on the same night journey.

Now Sylvestris sees other rippling green ribbons converge in the distance beyond Reve, and he remembers what Samsum told him: Herwood lies at the heart of everything. Could that be the insects' destination? He shivers with a sense of his own smallness, of how much in the world is mysterious.

After a time, the sky begins to grow light. The green web breaks apart as the fireflies disperse, routed by the dawn. Sylvestris watches as Reve blooms before his eyes like a single great rose unfurling its petals to greet the day.

He thinks of his chamber high above Quoz; he often stood there like this in the mornings, looking out past the snare of his reflections as the city awoke. All of Quoz sparkled with intrigue on those mornings, or seemed to, a glittering web of plots and counterplots stretching between the Palace and the Cathedral, among which his own shone brightest to his eyes.

He remembers the tug of mirrors in his mind, how he dared it each day with the help of metheglin, walking sanity's thin edge though he knew he might fall, tumble out of his body and into the realm of pure voices simularters both fear and yearn for.

And always the horrific vision had come to him sooner or later, agitating the voices that slumbered fitfully in his mind: Quoz broken like a great mirror and himself falling soundlessly, his simulars surrounding him like a cloud, through the sharp and violent rain of all that was left of the world.

But now there are no visions. No voices. The tears of the Liberatrix have freed him from a prison he never even knew he was in. And changed him in the process in ways he still can't begin to measure.

He touches his throat, amazed by its smoothness. For the first time since he was a boy, there is no plug, no trachae to mark his passage into manhood. Not even a scar remains. Her tears have grown him a second skin, he thinks. A second life.

"Sylvestris?"

He turns from the dawn to see the Liberatrix sitting up in bed and looking at him with a smile. He feels suddenly unsure, as if what passed between them might be finished now, a thing of darkness only, vanished with the night that cloaked it.

"Come back to bed," she says.

And then he knows it's all right. Nothing has changed. He hurries to kiss her good morning.

She pulls away after a moment. "Don't I repulse you?"

"Never." He looks into her eyes. "You're beautiful, Liberatrix."

She laughs. "Let me be Rumer to you at least!"

FOUR

Sylvestris and Rumer sit cross-legged in bed, sharing a breakfast of fruit as they wait for Samsum's return. The two of them are wearing identical silver cloaks; Rumer had brought hers along when she entered Sylvestris's chamber during the night.

Now, as she accepts an orange slice from Sylvestris, she says: "It's so strange. A little while ago I was a voluptuary of the House Illicium; now I'm having breakfast in Reve, a city I hadn't even heard of until yesterday."

"And I was Court Simularter, Azedarach's loyal servant. How far away all that seems now!"

"First Rose, then the heretics, now the simulars; it's too much, Sylvestris. I don't know anything about how my tears work or what they mean, as Rose did. I want to help Samsum and the others, but I don't know how."

"They've suffered much."

"Are they the only ones? When I think of how poor Rose suffered!"

"How I made her suffer, you mean."

"Don't put Rose between us," says Rumer, taking his hand. "You're not the man who killed her; that Sylvestris is gone. My tears gave birth to a different, better man."

"I wish it were so. But I remember all the awful things I did; the blood I shed over the turnings still clings to me. You gave me the chance to atone for those crimes, Rumer. You believed in me. I'll always love you for that, no matter what. And I'll never let you suffer like Rose. I swear it!"

Rumer raises his hand to her lips. "My brave simularter! But just the same, I can't help thinking of her fate. And that of Viridis Lacrimata, Our Lady of the Perpetual Sacrifice. What if it's the Spinner's will that I suffer, too?"

"Then I'll share your suffering."

Rumer's green eyes flash, but before she can reply, the chamber begins to tremble.

It's a Chastening, the second of the new season, and, as soon becomes apparent, worse than the first. Sylvestris and Rumer hug each other as the tower shakes; it seems that all of Reve must shatter. But the tower holds. The Chastening subsides, grumbling into silence but leaving an urgency in the air that wasn't there before.

"Samsum should have been here by now." Sylvestris rises from bed and crosses the room to the opaque wall where a door appeared yesterday at Samsum's touch. He pounds at the wall with his fist and yells for the simular, but to no avail.

Rumer joins him. "Let me try. I opened the wall between us last night; maybe I can do it again now."

She touches the wall with her hand and then with her forehead. A tear falls from her eye; where it splashes the dark crystal a ripple undulates. A door appears.

Sylvestris can't help feeling uneasy at this reminder of Rumer's power, as if it will prove to be a wall between them that even her tears can't pierce. But he doesn't want to think about that now; she's smiling at him, and he returns her smile as, together, they step through.

The platform outside is deserted.

"Where is everyone?" Sylvestris wonders.

"Let's find out." The doors to the lift are invitingly open; when they enter, the doors whisper shut behind them and the lift drops as swiftly as it rose yesterday.

Sylvestris and Rumer grab hold of each other as the lift plummets. But then it slows and draws to a smooth stop. The doors glide open.

Outside, the bodies of simulars are strewn haphazardly about the floor. Some are lying with limbs twisted awry or even shattered, as if fallen from a great height. Others are sitting or, rather, slouching, their heads drooping almost to the floor, like wilted flowers. Sylvestris thinks how nearly they resemble ordinary simulars now; it's as if, in the midst of a performance, their strings had snapped and they'd all come crashing down, willy-nilly, upon the stage.

Only this is no stage. And these no ordinary simulars. Yesterday they'd moved and spoken of their own accord, alive in a way he couldn't understand but had to acknowledge. And now?

Dead. Corpses of a kind, bright eyes extinguished. For a second, Sylvestris feels as though he's back in the metheglin vaults.

"How horrible," says Rumer. "Do you think the Chastening did this?"

Sylvestris shrugs. "There have been other Chastenings. But whatever caused it, they're dead now. This is our chance to escape."

"No." She takes his hand and searches his eyes with her own. "Samsum trusted me. I promised to help. I've got to find out what happened."

Still holding hands, they descend the staircase to the chamber of the sleepers; along the way, they pass more simulars, all of them lying as still and lifeless as those above.

Only these bodies, Sylvestris reminds himself, were as prisons to the simulars. Not alive themselves, but quickened by what was trapped inside: a spirit, a soul. Has that lively essence been set free?

Rumer says: "I don't see Samsum, do you?"

"No; at least, not our Samsum."

Before they reach the bottom of the stairs, their way is blocked by rising water. The bodies of simulars float there along with scattered roses.

"Everything's flooded," Rumer says in disbelief.

"The Chastening; it must have breached the base of the tower," Sylvestris says. "There's nothing else we can do here, Rumer. We have to think about ourselves."

"Poor Samsum!" She's weeping now.

They retreat up the stairs ahead of the rising water. Sylvestris pauses to take a thyrsis from a fallen simular, then they exit from the tower into the perpetual false dusk of Reve; smothered in roses and shredded by thorns, sunlight reaches the ground in tatters, if at all.

The dock is littered with the bodies of simulars. Still more dangle in the hedge overhead like hanged men, slowly swinging back and forth.

The boat waits at the end of the dock. Sylvestris helps Rumer over the side, then climbs in himself. The threads binding the boat to the dock fall away at the touch of Rumer's tears, and the boat drifts into the current.

Sylvestris takes an oar and begins to row back the way they came. It's not so easy now; the thick hedge, which parted to admit them, seems not at all inclined to let them go. Sylvestris must pick his way inch by slow inch, guiding the boat down narrow channels choked with thorns, through tunnels so dark and stifling they might be underground. Without the light of the thyrsis, which Rumer holds aloft, there would be no light at all.

It's late afternoon by the time they emerge into the open sea. The sun is sinking behind the City of Roses, sending shadowy fingers across the water as if to grasp and pull them back.

Sylvestris puts up the oar and lies back in exhaustion, content to let the boat drift where it will. The scent of roses recedes with Reve; he can't remember the air ever smelling so fresh and pure.

Rumer comes to lie beside him. He puts an arm around her and draws her close with a sigh.

"Do you think any survived?" she asks.

"The simulars? Only the Spinner knows."

"Where will we go now?"

Sylvestris laughs. "I hadn't thought of that. I don't think I can find the way back to Quoz. And even if I could, it's probably as wrecked as Reve by now, with all the fighting."

"I feel as if it's all because of me somehow."

"We simularters believe that everyone is a simular upon the world's stage. What can any of us do but play our parts?"

"You make life sound like a tale from the *Lives and Acts*, in which nothing ever changes no matter how often it's played."

"Perhaps. Yet I've often wondered if, as the Spinner's Wheel turns, those old tales don't come round again and again in different forms, quickened with new life."

"Do you think so?"

"Once I would have thought it heresy, but now I'm not sure."

At that Rumer smiles and, in reply to the inquiring arch of Sylvestris's eyebrow, explains: "You reminded me of something Aralia said once. She said, 'What you call heresy is only love.'"

"Sweet Rumer." He kisses her; then stops.

"What's wrong?"

"We're moving." Sylvestris sits up, finds himself facing into a windy spray. The boat is skimming over the choppy surface of the sea. It's as if a sudden wind has filled the sails . . . only the boat has no sails.

Rumer clutches his arm: "Sylvestris!"

A flash of something shiny and quick slices the water like an appendage of the fabled Leviathan, that monster said to sleep at the bottom of the sea, waiting for the Unspinning.

And then Sylvestris sees it.

A face.

It appears suddenly in the water off the port side of the boat, somehow keeping pace with them while, uncannily, seeming not to move at all. Its flesh is so white that Sylvestris wonders if he's seeing the corpse of a drowned man. But then he sees almond-shaped eyes black as drops of ink, a small, flat nose, and bluish lips drawn back over sharp white teeth, and he knows it's no corpse.

He grabs the thyrsis and points it at the face, which watches, those wide black eyes unblinking, as if curious to see what he'll do. He's about to shoot when Rumer gives a cry and knocks the thyrsis from his hand. It disappears over the side before he can catch it.

"Don't you see? It's one of the sleepers!"

"What?" He looks again; the nightmarish face vanishes, only to reappear almost immediately alongside the boat, close enough to touch now.

"Is that any way to treat an old friend, simularter?" asks a voice so beautiful and melodious that Sylvestris can scarcely believe it comes from such a hideous source.

"Samsum!" cries Rumer. "Is it you?"

Laughter like the tinkling of chimes. "Hail, Liberatrix! Your tears freed us as we knew they would! But just as I've shed the body of Samsum, so have I shed the name. I'm Medona!"

With that, the creature leaps laughing from the water, showering Rumer and Sylvestris with spray, yet also showing its sleek and glistening body: a body like the woman's they saw yesterday asleep in its crystal container.

"But how, Medona?" asks Rumer.

Medona frisks in the water, drawing close to the boat, only to dive beneath it and appear on the other side. "You wept over one of the containers, Liberatrix," she says, her black eyes sparkling. "Your blessed tears seeped through the crystal and entered our blood. By morning we had awakened in our rightful bodies, yet even then we were still trapped, imprisoned inside those coffins. We prayed to the Spinner in your name, and the Chastening came to crack our shells as well as the walls of the tower, letting in the waters of the sea, just as your tears had already let in our memories. But we couldn't stay to thank you; our kind can't abide the open air, no more than the bodies that caged us could bear the touch of water. So we left, eager to reclaim the oceans of our lives, forgotten for so long, now remembered thanks to you!"

"I'm so glad; I thought you were dead!"

"Some of us didn't wake, and those we'll mourn, but not now! Now we'll play and laugh and rejoice! You have freed us! Now you must free the world."

"Where are you taking us, Medona?" asks Sylvestris.

"Can't you guess, simularter?"

And suddenly he knows. Knows in the pit of his stomach. "Herwood," he says. "You're taking us to Herwood."

Medona dives with a laugh and a final flip of her webbed toes.

Rumer leans over the side. "Medona! Come back!"

But she doesn't resurface. The boat continues along at its rapid pace, drawn by murky figures flitting like undulant shadows beneath the waves.

Soon the sun sets, and night falls, and still the boat cleaves the water, rushing through the darkness. Sylvestris and Rumer lie in each other's arms and talk.

"Are you afraid, Rumer?"

"Yes, a little; but only the Spinner knows every turning. Even if this is just an old story made new as you said, we still have to play our parts and trust in Her."

"Her." Sylvestris sighs. "Is the essence of the Spinner feminine? And if so, shouldn't Maw, as the Spinner's adversary, be termed the Sire, and not the Dam, of Darkness: not Queen but King of the Pit of Damned Souls?"

"I called the Spinner Her because Rose always did. But don't you think the Spinner must be more than just one sex or the other, Sylvestris? Using She instead of He doesn't really change anything; it's the Hierarchate all over again, only turned upside down. But I don't know; I'm sure Rose had her reasons. She was much wiser than me! Wisdom came to her with her tears."

Sylvestris thinks of how Rose was crafted by Azedarach's vizards, her wisdom implanted just like her potent green eyes in order to fool the heretics into accepting her as the Liberatrix. But he will never tell Rumer what he knows; it would break her heart to learn the truth.

"You're wrong, Rumer," he says. "Your tears *have* made you wise, even if you don't think so. You're the Liberatrix; the Spinner has sent you to us for a reason, like the Chastenings."

Rumer is quiet in the darkness. At first Sylvestris is afraid he's upset her. But when she replies, her voice is free of hurt or anger, though it trembles: "Is that what I am? A kind of human Chastening?"

"Rumer . . ."

"Is it my task to bring the Hierarchate crashing down? Medona said I was to free the world. I'm afraid, Sylvestris; I'm afraid to think how the Spinner will use me!"

"Didn't you just say we had to trust in Him or Her or Whomever?"

"I'm trying. But I think of Cassine and my sister Cats back in the House Illicium. They're part of the Hierarchate, too. I don't want to hurt them."

"You won't," Sylvestris says firmly; but he realizes he's tried to forget who she really is, tried to convince himself she's only Rumer, whom he loves, and nothing more. Because the whole of her frightens him. Terrifies him, though he's known the sweetness of her tears as well as her kisses. But it must be wrong to split her in two, wrong to forget that her tears have the power to hurt as well as heal. He thinks of his determination to emulate Saint Quercus Incana by recording her life and acts. Yesterday it seemed simple; no more. For today he understands that she's both the Liberatrix, Viridis Lacrimata returned from Herwood, and Rumer Illicium, voluptuary of the House Illicium, the woman he loves and who, by a miracle as great as any, loves him. How can he preserve what's vital to both without crushing it beneath his words like a rose pressed between the pages of a book?

But Rumer hears only his words, not the thoughts behind them. "I love you so much, Sylvestris! You're my rock; you keep me from drowning in these tears of mine! I bless them for saving you!"

Then she's kissing him fiercely, and Sylvestris, despite the fact that it's cold and wet and dark, despite the fact that they're in a boat somewhere on the sea being drawn to Herwood, despite everything, responds with equal ardor.

Rumer's cloak clings to her like a second skin, but when she brushes against him, or he against her, Sylvestris feels as if there's nothing between them at all.

"I like these clothes." He runs his hand down the slope of her back as though not simply tracing but sculpting the supple curves there.

Rumer fits herself against him, opening her trembling legs to the insistent pressure of his knee. "I feel as if I'm melting into you."

"And I into you."

They kiss again, more deeply now, and sink down so they are lying side by side, the difference in their heights no longer an obstacle. Wrapped tightly in each other's arms, legs entwined, lips and tongues begin their mutual poem, which, though known by heart, is forever surprising.

Never more so than now. Rumer is first to notice. She pulls back her head with a gasp, as though Sylvestris, intending only a love nip, has drawn blood.

He opens his eyes to see that they are surrounded by a silvery glow, a glow that emanates from their cloaks.

And more: no longer are they wearing separate cloaks; a single cloak covers them now. It flexes and shivers as if with a passion all its own, pouring itself like a warm liquid around and between their bodies.

They draw apart, not from each other but from this third entity; there's the faintest of clinging sensations as the cloak divides, returning to its former shape—or, rather, shapes—with uncanny elasticity.

They lie side by side, careful not to touch, breathing heavily as the silvery glow of the cloaks dies.

When it's dark again, Rumer whispers; "I think I liked that."

"Me, too," he says.

"It was just so . . . intimate. I wasn't ready."

"I know. It was like being invaded."

"But not from outside. From within."

"Like being turned inside out."

"And mixed together."

"Yes. I was afraid we wouldn't be able to get back."

"But we did, didn't we?"

"Yes."

Rumer takes his hand. Their fingers entwine, and the silky fabric of the cloaks stirs, ripples, comes together with a lively friction that makes them gasp and shudder.

Then they're kissing again, lost in each other and in this third thing which they've somehow brought into being. It flows over them freely, admitting no boundaries of shame or ego. But whether it's animated by their desires, bound to obey their wishes like a slave, or whether it was merely awakened by their desires and isn't controlled by them—is, perhaps, their master—they can't say.

There comes a moment when they might stop, pull away as before. Gazing into each other's eyes in the rekindled glow, they see only a mirrored wanting in which to look is to fall. Then the skin that both is and is not their own rises over their heads in a silver wave, and they are no longer three things, or two, but one.

Sylvestris is Rumer and Rumer, Sylvestris. Her heart is open to him; he rushes to enter. She swallows his heart and makes it her own.

Double-chambered, a new-formed creature stands with moist and trembling wings at ecstasy's utmost edge, where pleasure and pain, fear and desire, knowledge and ignorance fuse into a final barrier. With a cry, it spreads its wings and hurls itself into the annihilating light.

FIVE

It's dawn when Sylvestris next opens his eyes, awakened by the sound of muffled crying. The sunrise has summoned a dense fog. Sylvestris can't see past the boat; even Rumer, who stands with her back to him in the bow, is half-hidden. The sea itself seems flattened by the fog, and the boat rocks to a dreary rise and fall, as if beached upon the coils of the slumbering Leviathan. The sky hangs close, the sun a smudge without edge or center.

"Rumer?" He doesn't need to ask what's wrong; he feels her sorrow and shares it. His spirit is as inert as the water, as the cloak he wears, its shine dulled now, like lead. Last night, at the height of their intimate fusion, when the two of them lay open to each other, on the verge of a new existence, some part of him had held back, refusing the invitation, just as he'd always refused when, from the depths of a mirror, the voices of simulars had entreated him to enter their bodiless, timeless void. Before he knew it, the quicksilver skin had peeled away, separating what it had joined. So he knows very well why Rumer weeps: not simply from the loss of something rare, a mutual self-transcendence in which their hearts' mirrors had reflected each other infinitely, but also because of what was revealed, unforgettably, in those mirrors, which seems like another, keener loss.

Rumer looks back at him: "What was it that frightened you, Sylvestris? Was it something you saw in me, or in yourself?"

He shrugs; he knows her now as he knows no other person, not even himself. It's not that her history is an open book. He knows no more of Rumer's life than he ever did—where she was born, how she came to the House Illicium—none of that.

But the book of her soul lay open to him, and on those pages he saw things he can't erase from memory. Dark things as well as light. Things hurtful to see, like her stubborn love for Rose thriving alongside her love for him, not only their branches but their roots too tangled ever to tell apart. And the shadow cast by that older love, a shadow Rumer tried to hide from him and from herself but which can't be hidden or denied or forgotten any longer. A shadow branded into him now.

And at the same time, to know that his soul, more thickly overgrown with weeds than Reve with roses, had lain open to Rumer's gaze, exposed to her judgment and mercy, fills Sylvestris with an abhorrence bordering on horror. Now she must see clearly how little he merited her tears.

He wonders what remains after such a brutal influx of knowledge. He doesn't think it can be called love.

"I only wanted us to become closer." Rumer searches his eyes with her own. "But now I see how far away you've gone."

Stung, Sylvestris replies with bitterness: "And didn't you pull away, even a little, from what you saw in me? There are things that can't be forgotten."

"I'm not asking you to forget. Do you know what I think? I think we were given a great blessing."

"A hard blessing!"

"Even so. We saw each other through the eyes of the Spinner."

"Rumer, my eyes are no better suited to the Spinner's way of seeing than they are to picking out the figure of Ixion at the heart of the sun. I can't bear to see so clearly; I feel as though it's blinded me!"

"But isn't it always that way when you first step out of a dark place into the light? Give your eyes a chance to adjust, Sylvestris."

"Have your eyes adjusted?"

Rumer smiles, her face crinkling up along the network of scars like a sheet of paper that, once crumpled, can never be made smooth again, no matter what's written upon it. "My eyes, as you know, are not fully my own; maybe that's why they've adjusted more quickly than yours. But I don't love you any less now than I did before. What I saw in you didn't repulse me, Sylvestris. You're human, just as I am; we can't be perfect like the Spinner. Yet I believe we are like the Spinner in one way: our ability to love absolutely, without qualification or judgment; not blindly, but with humility and selflessness. Perhaps we never come closer to the Spinner than when we're farthest from ourselves: when we're in love."

He turns from her, unsure of his feelings. He knows only that his heart has been crumpled and can no longer love as smoothly as it had. But the pain he suffers now in turning away is proof he remains bound to Rumer whether he likes it or not. If not by love, then by something just as deep. But darker.

"Poor Sylvestris," she says, and he hears her come to him, feels her hand stroking his hair. "You judge us both too harshly. Viridis Lacrimata once said that to know all is to forgive all."

"I'm just a man, Rumer. I'm not like her. Or you."

"The Spinner has more faith in us than we have in ourselves."

"The more fool She." He pulls away from her and goes to the side of the boat, peering into the fog. "Where's Medona and the others? Swum off and left us?"

Rumer sighs. "So it seems."

"I should row."

"Where? At least wait for the fog to lift."

And so they do, not speaking, as, slowly, the sun burns off the fog. But then Sylvestris thinks he sees a flash of green. He calls to Rumer, and as she hurries to his side a breeze stirs; the fog wavers, thins, and blows away.

A hundred or so yards ahead, a fringe of blond sand curls between the ice-blue sea, transparent as crystal, and a mountain of vegetation so thick Sylvestris can only think of the hedgerow that bristles about Reve like quills about a porcupine. Yet so diverse is this growth, with trees of all shapes and sizes shooting forth branches and leaves and fruits and flowers in a riot of colors dominated by endless gradations of green, that he knows he's looking at what Samsum called the heart of everything.

"Herwood," Rumer whispers. She stares into the depths of the woods, which seem to shelter darker shadows than the day-spun variety, as if the night, and all that dwells in the night, broods impatiently within. "It was my fate to come here, following the footsteps of Saint Viridis Lacrimata; I see that now. Something's waiting for me here, Sylvestris. Something only my tears can set right. I won't ask you to come with me; you can set me ashore if you like."

Sylvestris feels again the wrenching pain of separation, as when he turned away from her before. "I'm not going to leave you, Rumer. You know I can't." He picks up the oar and begins to row. "I guess that's *my* fate."

Her hand falls softly upon his shoulder. "If that's what you choose to call it."

As he rows, Sylvestris drinks in the gorgeous profligacy of Herwood with his eyes, its boisterous, seemingly inexhaustible vitality, the sheer scope of which rivals sea or sky. No, more than rivals: surpasses. For while sea and sky are emptinesses that, however crowded, can never be filled or made less empty, Herwood seems a fullness impossible to empty or make less full, a cornucopia whose fruits pour back into itself without end or beginning.

Sylvestris hears sounds he's never heard before, the cries and calls of unimaginable creatures. Even familiar sounds are made new. The hum of fireflies seems to rise from everywhere, as if each leaf is vibrating with a life so fierce it can scarcely be contained, as if all of Herwood might suddenly explode through sheer excess of energy, is perhaps exploding right now, not in violence, but in a sustained, continuous eruption too vast for his perception. At best he can see its outriders, colorful birds that flit like flames among the branches of the trees or blaze briefly against the sky as they wheel above the boat, curious yet aloof, then arrow away.

And the smells. The richness and strangeness of them are almost unbearable. He hadn't known there were so many odors in the world. Each one slips inside him like an unsuspected country whose amorphous borders do not wait to be crossed but, instead, reach out to claim any traveler who wanders near.

His heart is a tolling bell rung by more than the steady pulling of his arms. Fearful and eager, he's like a man who's stumbled unexpectedly into the dream or nightmare of his wedding to a woman whose veiled face he can't for the life of him recall.

Rumer stands in the bow, leaning over the water in her impatience to arrive. "Hurry, Sylvestris!"

Sylvestris picks up the pace. From earliest boyhood, he was first taught, then conditioned, to fear this place. The Furies dwell here, and it's from here the scent of Beauty rises with the night, more irresistible than any Cat's perfume and deadlier to his sex than any poison.

Men seduced by Beauty come stumbling here in the night, though by straighter and drier roads than this, he imagines. They come from all over the Hierarchate, a harvest of high and low alike caught in the wide-flung net of a spell from which they will never wake or return, like death.

Yet he's always wondered what it was like, this sudden and headlong fall or perhaps leap into the forbidden. Especially when, as happened with the turnings, men known to him disappeared into the night, gone to the very fate he feared.

Then, come morning, as the panderman carried off those women who'd failed in the protection it was, after sons, their most sacred duty to provide, he would join the other men in whispering nervous, half-joking speculations about what they both dreaded and longed to experience, like boys with smooth throats debating the mysteries of the *Trachaea* or what carnal delights lay concealed behind the doors of the High Houses.

Now that Sylvestris is seeing what the others saw before him, he feels strangely light-headed, as if he, too, has succumbed to a spell. Not

Beauty—thanks to Rumer's tears he's safe from Beauty and no longer fears it—but some other enchantment, from which even her tears cannot save him.

Or, he wonders, are her tears themselves the enchantment that's claimed him?

The hull of the boat scrapes over sand and comes to a listing halt a dozen feet from shore. Sylvestris vaults over the side into water that splashes to his knees. He extends his hands to Rumer and lifts her out of the boat. Then, carrying her in his arms, he sets off through billowing seaweed for shore.

"You can put me down, Sylvestris," Rumer says. "I don't mind getting wet."

"The water's cold." The truth is, he's performing this small service for his own sake as much as hers, though for reasons as tangled as the weeds he wades through, as the feelings that bind him to her more tightly than ever now. "Besides, that's no way for the Liberatrix to arrive in Herwood."

"What will the Furies think?" Still, Rumer makes no effort to get down, only circles her arms about his neck.

"You shouldn't joke; we don't know who's watching." It's impossible to see past the lush and leafy facade, itself teeming with life, that rises before them like an impenetrable wall.

"Samsum—I mean Medona— told me there are no Furies."

"Medona said a lot of things." He leaves the water for a beach strewn with assorted shells and fragments of shells, limp and bedraggled feathers, and a scattering of detritus—flowers, fruits, seeds, and cones, leaves and branches and plants—in all stages of quickening, maturity, and decay, like a battlefield in some endless conflict between forest and sea, a patch of land claimed by both sides yet possessed by neither.

He sets Rumer down in the midst of it.

The myriad voices of the woods fall silent, choked off in full cry; a vast yet tremulous hush descends like a sudden catching of breath.

Before Rumer or Sylvestris can say a word, a sigh—as vast as the silence out of which it rises—issues from Herwood, whispering its way through the leaves and branches and trees to where they stand. It wafts over them, mild in force yet densely woven of fragrances for which Sylvestris has neither memory nor name, yet which he knows somehow, as if memory has only slept in him until now. And though he can't tame these mysteries by naming them like the homespun odors of kitchen or garden, whose familiarity encloses and protects, there's nothing alien in their strangeness. Yet the quality of strangeness is sometimes frightening in itself, he thinks, for the world is no less fearsome for being a home to us.

Rumer takes his hand.

The trees are thrashing now, as what began with a quiet gentleness swells quickly to the intensity of a storm. The birds have vanished with their songs; the only sounds are the crashes and groans of the wind-whipped trees and a noise, growing louder by the second, that Sylvestris knows all too well.

Fireflies.

The insects explode from the woods in a seething copper cloud shot through with emerald fulgurations. They rise into the sky to blot out the sun. Sylvestris has never seen so many, not even at St. Ixion's Cathedral of the Spinning Wheel in Quoz, where the Ecclesiarch himself, after each Chastening, unleashed the fury of the swarm upon the trembling congregation.

Rumer stares into the wheeling mass as if hypnotized. But her green eyes seem to flash with an answering fire.

There's no time to run; no place to hide. Sylvestris throws himself over Rumer as the fireflies drop from the sky. Their small, hard bodies pummel him like stones.

If only their cloaks could shield them! But the cloaks remain separate, the silver fabric stubbornly inert. He must be Rumer's shield now. As the insects continue to pelt him and crawl over him, Sylvestris braces himself for their stings.

But instead, to his utter bafflement and surprise, the cloud lifts from him without inflicting a single sting, returning precipitously to the air.

He rolls aside to let Rumer up. "Are you all right?"

She nods; grains of sand cling to the left side of her face in a partial mask whose clawlike contours trace the scars below.

Sylvestris puts his arms around her and draws her close, feeling her shiver. He's shivering, too. Holding each other, they watch the tide of fireflies stream back into Herwood. The instant that the insects enter the woods, the absent noises pick up again as if nothing had interrupted them.

"That was quite a welcome." Rumer laughs nervously as Sylvestris helps her to her feet.

"Or a warning."

"At least they didn't sting."

"Do we have your tears to thank for that?"

"I don't know."

The sand falls from their cloaks as they stand, though it clings to their exposed skin and must be brushed away.

Though it's still morning, the temperature is already hot and growing hotter as the sun rises in the clear sky. Waves of heat from the beach make Herwood shimmer like a green flame.

Rumer sighs, then starts for the woods. "It'll be cooler in the shade, at least."

"Wait, Rumer." Sylvestris hurries after her. "We can't just walk in there; we'd be lost in no time!"

"We're already lost," Rumer points out. "Seek and you shall be found, as the heretics say."

"Let's walk along the beach for a while." The truth is, he's afraid of entering Herwood, certain that death—or something worse—is waiting there. Only the impossibility of leaving Rumer stops him from returning to the boat. "Maybe there's a path or something we can follow."

Rumer looks into his eyes; he knows she sees his fear, and it shames him, but he can't conquer it. Then she nods. "All right, Sylvestris. Maybe there is."

They walk along the waterline. Rumer kicks off her shoes and carries them in her hands as she wades in the cool sea, humming to herself as though she's back in the House Illicium.

Sylvestris leaves his shoes on even though they're soaked through and bulge with sand. It makes his feet feel swollen; yet for some reason, he feels safer that way.

Soon the boat is out of sight behind them.

"We'll need to find water," Rumer says. "And food."

"Just a little farther." So unchanging is the scenery—the sea on their right, Herwood on their left, the gentle curve of the beach the same ahead and behind, even the noises and smells a constant background—that Sylvestris begins to wonder if they're moving at all or simply, as in a dream or hallucination, suffering the illusion of movement. He misses the mazy streets of Quoz, so alive with human drama and spectacle, a stage upon which invention never stales. He's never come so far from the city, nor been away so long. How has it changed in his absence, inundated by the rebellion's flood?

"What's that, Sylvestris?"

He follows Rumer's pointing hand. In the distance, just where the beach bends out of sight, he sees—barely—a smudge upon the shimmering brightness where sand gives way to water.

"Come on!" she cries. "Let's go see!"

"Rumer, wait!"

But she's already running, her bare feet flying swiftly over the sand. He stumbles after her, unable to catch up despite his long legs. His sodden shoes weigh him down, but there's no time to kick them off.

Rumer reaches the object before he's halfway there. She yells something he can't make out. But then Sylvestris recognizes it: listing slightly to one side, half on sand and half in water, is a boat.

At that, the sense of being in a dream suddenly deepens, and Sylvestris feels as if they've walked in a circle only to come back to where they'd started. Or, rather, it seems as if they've remained stationary while Herwood has revolved around them like a great wheel.

"Sylvestris! Sylvestris!"

Rumer's voice steadies him. She's climbed aboard the boat and stands in the bow, waving.

"I found water!" She holds a jug above her head.

At last he's there. He sees it's not their boat after all, though very like it. "I thought," gasping for breath, "I thought this boat was *ours*."

She laughs, handing him the jug.

He drinks. The water clears his head; he splashes his face, laughing at his mistake and at Rumer's high spirits.

It's then that he sees the footprints in the sand. They're prints of bare feet, like Rumer's.

Only they're not Rumer's.

They're smaller, the size of a child's. And they lead away from the boat, toward Herwood.

He follows the trail with his eyes to where it vanishes into the woods, which stir gently in the breeze that wafts almost continuously in from the sea. But something about these leafy rustlings disturbs him, an oddness he can't explain or dismiss.

All at once, yet far from suddenly, as if he's slipped back into a dream, Sylvestris sees a group of trees advance upon the beach like a moving grove.

No, not trees. *Men.* Men who, shouting fiercely, hurl down the branches behind which they've hidden and charge, naked, across the sand.

So Samsum was wrong, Sylvestris thinks. The Furies *do* exist. Only they're not women after all, but men. Some of them, he sees, are holding thyrsi. If only Rumer hadn't knocked their thyrsis overboard! He could use it now.

A huge, hot fist slams into his chest. It knocks the water jug from his hands and throws him back against the boat.

He hears Rumer scream his name.

He tries to stand, but his legs aren't working. Blood fills his eyes, making it difficult to see. He tries to wipe it away, but he can't raise his hands.

How is it possible? he wonders. Is that awful smell, like burned meat, coming from him?

He's never felt such shame. But then he thinks, all shame forgotten: Is this really me? This charred and useless thing my body? How strange!

Just seconds ago, he was happy. The sun was strong and hot, and Rumer was laughing as she handed him the jug of water to slake his thirst. He can picture it so clearly! How can it be gone, never to return? Already he's thirsty again. He's never felt such thirst.

The men are all around him now, scuffing up sand. They ignore him as if he's already dead.

Maybe he is, he thinks. He can't feel much of anything, or move at all. He can do nothing as they capture Rumer and drag her, struggling, away. Who will write her history now?

Soon they are gone, swallowed up by Herwood.

The world goes on as before, but Sylvestris is no longer part of it. His eyes, though open, see nothing. The doors of his body have slammed upon his senses. He sinks through an inner dark. He remembers it. How her tears had saved him.

But there are no tears now.

SIX

All Rumer can think of, all she can see, is Sylvestris crumpled against the boat, horribly burned and bloodied yet still, by some miracle, alive. The Furies—for what else can they be?—had struck so swiftly that Rumer still can't comprehend what's happened, how suddenly and completely everything's changed.

They'd stepped out of Herwood with a casual boldness that seemed unreal, as though her eyes were playing tricks. And before she could warn Sylvestris, before she could begin to make sense of what she was seeing, the blast of a thyrsis had felled him.

Only then—too late!—had she shouted a warning. The memory of it causes Rumer such anguish now, as if she's guilty of what she failed to prevent, that she thrashes against the vines that bind her, causing them to bite into her wrists and ankles. Not deeply enough, though.

Never deeply enough.

At first she'd thought he was dead. But when she leaped down to where he lay, she found, like an answered prayer, a stubborn glimmer of life in his eyes. He looked right through her, though, and she knew that he'd already turned away from this life to look for the misty borders of the next.

Turned away, but not crossed over.

She could still pull him back.

In Quoz, her tears had defied her hatred of him to do just that. Now she wanted only to save him. Wanted it with all her heart. Yet she hesitated.

His body was a raw blister, an oozing sore. Blackened lumps of what she supposed might have been his cloak sizzled in settings of skin and bone. The stench of burned meat rising from him caused everything alive in her to recoil beyond the reach of reason and of love.

She was sick with horror, paralyzed despite herself for a space of heartbeats, and she wondered dimly if this unreasoning revulsion was what Sylvestris had felt when he'd pulled back from the final consummation of their union.

Then she fought past the revulsion. She went to him.

But even as Rumer rushed forward, something slipped over her neck, a rope of some kind, and yanked her back before a single tear could touch him.

"No!" she cried. Then the noose tightened, and it was all she could do to breathe.

The next thing she knew, she was in the sand, clawing at what she realized was no rope but a thin and supple vine. Other vines looped about her limbs as if possessing a life of their own. But, she saw, it was the Furies who brought the vines to life, with a marksmanship as effortless as it was unerring.

Sand entered Rumer's nose and mouth and eyes as she struggled to regain her feet. The Furies kept their distance, letting her wear herself out in fighting the vines.

It didn't take long. Soon she lay gasping upon the sand, staring face up into the sky, immobilized. Battered and miserable, she wept uselessly, cursing the weakness that had stopped her from saving Sylvestris. Now it was too late. She was losing him, just as she'd lost Rose. There was nothing she could do.

Numbly, she watched the Furies approach: seven men, each of them young and naked . . . unless the dirt and bits of foliage that clung to their filthy bodies constituted a kind of clothing.

"Please, let me go to him!" she managed to gasp.

The Furies didn't answer. They looked more like plants than human beings; no wonder they'd blended into Herwood so well. Leaves and sprouts wove through their thickly matted beards and hair like young shoots nosing out of tangled mosses.

Were these, Rumer wondered, seeking to distract herself from the horror of what was happening, men seduced by Beauty over the turnings?

Her own father had suffered that fate; how strange it would be to find him after so long! Would she recognize him? Or he her? What would they say to each other? For all she knew, he was dead; yet what if he should be here, now, among the Furies who'd captured her! As in a dream, Rumer searched the dark, brutish faces. Anything seemed possible.

At the same time, despite the desperate fancy of these thoughts, Rumer knew there were limits to the possible, just as there were limits to the reach of her tears. She could no more escape those limits than she could escape the Furies.

Now, with a rough and almost-contemptuous skill, like vizards handling a corpse, the Furies turned Rumer this way and that, never touching her directly but using the vines, like the strings of a simular, to manipulate her body.

Rumer didn't resist as her wrists and ankles were lashed to a long wooden pole. Her body no longer seemed to belong to her; it was just another thing she was tied to. Yet the sensation felt oddly familiar, as if this had all happened to her before, though of course that was impossible.

Then two of the Furies set the pole on their shoulders so that Rumer dangled between them above the sand. The vines bit into her flesh as her body sagged. She arched her back but didn't cry out. She was determined not to cry out.

The Furies began to jog at an easy lope across the beach. Rumer craned her head, desperate to see Sylvestris one last time, as if her vision could reach and cure him even if her tears could not. But hung upside down and swinging back and forth as she was, she couldn't see much of anything: just bits of sky, of trees, of water, of sand, as if the world were being shaken to pieces in the throes of a Chastening like no other.

A cry escaped her then. Sylvestris's name broke from her lips before she knew it.

And before she knew it, too, the noose had tightened at her throat, choking her into silence.

A memory surfaced at that rebuke. Rumer remembered being taken by the panderman to be sold at the market in Kell after her father's disappearance.

She'd been so young, a girl of six turnings: terrified, helpless, crying for her mommy and daddy among so many people she didn't know, whose faces didn't smile to see her as the faces of Jubilar always did, but instead shouted ugly, angry things or, worse somehow, didn't notice her at all. She knew in her heart something awful and forever had taken place but was incapable of locating the source or dimensions of the disaster outside herself, believing she alone was to blame for an otherwise inexplicable dislocation of the world. Her tears and cries were a protest of innocence and a plea to be forgiven. But no one had listened. How could anyone have listened or cared in Kell, that wretched circus of lost souls—each as miserable as she, if she'd but known it—and merchants of lost souls? What was innocence there, or forgiveness? There had been a noose around her neck, and the Panderman hadn't hesitated, no more than the Furies now, to yank it.

And briefly, in the constriction of the noose, the two moments, past and present, combined in Rumer in a trembling coexistence so painful she lost track of where and when she was.

The two moments seemed the same to her. Not as if time had repeated itself, but rather as if each separate moment was an impression in the clay of time of something fundamentally outside time, like marks of a wheel that recur at fixed intervals along a road, each mark somewhat different because of the differing surface upon which it appears yet also a copy of an original that never appears on any road but remains with the wheel, spinning as the wheel spins.

The world flickered, went dark.

And now comes crashing back in wave after wave of green as they enter Herwood.

It isn't a gradual entrance. Herwood doesn't come into being around her by slow degrees, one stage blurring imperceptibly into the next like night unfolding out of day or age settling into the face in the mirror. Herwood doesn't plant itself vine by vine, tree by tree, in a polite seduction that invites the collaboration of the senses and from which a holding back—a refusal, however small or secret—is always possible.

No.

This is a sudden and complete immersion. A drowning; an assault. There's no holding back from it, no way to refuse it.

There's only Herwood. And, as Rumer discovers, to take a single step into Herwood is to step all the way to its deepest, most tangled heart.

At first she sees nothing but green, as if her eyes have been so overwhelmed in the explosion of foliage that she's gone blind with it. And not just her eyes, but all her senses.

She hears the ragged breathing of the Furies, the swish of vegetation slapped aside as they carry her, and these sounds take on greenish hues, as do all the varied smells of the woods, striking at her like physical blows she cannot escape . . . no more than she can escape the branches that strike out of nowhere like scourges. She cringes in anticipation of the blows, although in truth she scarcely feels them, afraid of losing her eyes. This fear, too, is more than physical, for she remembers the stories of the Furies related in the *Lives and Acts*, how they plucked the eyes from their victims in rituals so bloodthirsty Quercus Incana had trembled to record them. Even Viridis Lacrimata had lost her eyes; is it her fate as Liberatrix, Rumer wonders, to share that loss? Is it to such a darkness the Furies are bearing her now? She hasn't felt so helpless, so abandoned and alone, since she stood naked and shivering on the auction block in Kell all those turnings ago.

The strides of the Furies are smooth and well matched, but the vines that bind her saw into Rumer's wrists and ankles with every step.

The pain is real as blood. It pulses in the green night of her blindness like Samsum's eye, solitary and red.

Rumer holds to the hurt. To the memory. Her fear burns away in its clarity as the mists of the morning—how long ago it seems!—had burned away in the sun.

The Furies have formed a phalanx around her, shielding her with their naked bodies from blows and jabs they seem to take no notice of themselves. Rumer can't help but marvel at the speed and agility with which they navigate every obstacle. They move as a unit linked in mind and body. The men never stumble, never slow, never come close to dropping her despite the thickness of the woods. It's uncanny, as if branches are rising and pulling aside of their own accord, roots pressing themselves flat, all of Herwood aiding in her abduction. A swarm of fireflies keeps them company, almost as if conducting them.

SEVEN

Sylvestris wakes to hot needles of pain. The feeling is something like the slow and prickly seep of sensation back into a bloodless limb, only it's his entire body suffering the torment. Every inch of it, inside and out, simultaneously. He writhes in agony. He screams.

Nothing answers. Everything is dark.

It didn't hurt so much the last time he came back to life. But that rebirth was gentled by Rumer's tears.

Now it's as if he's shedding his skin. Or, rather, as if it's being peeled from his bones in thin, bloody strips.

But it's not his skin that's peeling away.

It's the silver cloak from Reve. Once before, it had flowed over him like some strange living metal, joining him with Rumer in an intimacy he'd invited but found impossible to endure. He'd held back from that last voluptuous dissolve as if it meant his own extinction. And then, afterward, turned away from her inside, or tried to, as if she were to blame for his weakness.

Now, despite the unrelenting pain, Sylvestris realizes that the cloak has engulfed him again, sealed him in itself. He remembers everything: the attack of the Furies, the blast of the thyrsis that struck him down, Rumer's abduction. The stench of roasted flesh curls with vulgar familiarity in his nostrils.

Then Sylvestris feels the cloak come away, torn from his body like a sheet snapped in a sudden gust of wind. The darkness in which he's drifted explodes in blinding light. He gasps and throws his hands over his eyes. Vivid bursts of red and orange, yellow, blue, and green, ignite in his palms. Only as these pyrotechnics wane does he notice that the pain is also gone.

His skin tingles beneath the sun's caress. Dazed, he lets his hands fall to warm sand. A breeze tickles over him like the tip of a Cat's tongue, bearing a tang of salt. He hears the low murmur of fireflies, of rustling vegetation. The drowsy slap of sea on shore like the pulse of health through his body.

Sand trickles between his fingers. Each tiny grain is distinct, unique, a world unto itself yet part of a greater whole. Lying beneath the hot and peaceful sun, Sylvestris feels as if he, too, is part of everything, a grain of sand.

No. Nothing as small as that; a giant, rather. His own body the beach upon which he rests, his circulation and respiration writ large in the tides and the wind. His thoughts drift with the high purposelessness of clouds. If he could stay here forever, he would count every grain of sand, let them fall one by one through his fingers, measuring out eternity like an hourglass.

But not even eternity would be time enough to erase Rumer from his heart. It may have been the cloak, and not Rumer's tears, that saved his life, yet Sylvestris feels it *was* her somehow: the part of her that lives in him. Not in his memory; in his veins.

She is the sand in his hourglass; she pours through him endlessly, never filling him, never running out, an inexhaustible stream running beyond need, beyond love.

He must find her.

Sylvestris sits up only to fall back with a groan, his muscles protesting shrilly. He feels as weak as a baby, as if the cloak, in healing him, has stopped too soon. Catching his breath, he wonders how long he's lain here. The sun is almost directly overhead, so two or three hours must have passed since the Furies attacked. On the other hand, a whole day could have gone by for all he knows.

He forces himself up again. Sweat pours from him as if he's lifting the world on his shoulders.

The skin of his chest is bright pink and deeply scarred, tender to the touch. Yet Sylvestris touches it wonderingly. Has the cloak pressed Rumer's face into his flesh like a portrait into a coin? He can feel her scarred features in his scars.

The cloak lies all rumpled in the sand. It's silver no longer, but black; a deep and, to Sylvestris's eyes, unnatural black, made more so by contrast with the pale sand. The cloak soaks up light as a sponge soaks up water, yet seems to shine darkly, a rip in the fabric of the day that lets the night bleed through.

Cautiously, he picks it up. The cloak feels different, changed from what he remembers. It's cold and impossibly sheer, almost insubstantial, as if it's used some part of its fabric to heal him, weaving him a new flesh from its own fibers. But other than that, he can see no signs of real damage; the cloak has done as thorough a job of repairing itself as it did of healing him. Maybe even a better job.

Yet despite everything, Sylvestris isn't eager to don the cloak again. It clings to his hand like a second, clammy skin. Or like a shadow, his own, severed from his body by the blast of the thyrsis and hungry now to reattach itself. The dark fabric sucks softly but persistently at his skin.

If he releases it, he's afraid the cloak will envelop his body like a leech, and he's not at all sure it will come off again. But his own skin is burning in the sun, and he has no other clothing.

"A wondrous piece of crafting."

The high-pitched voice rings out from behind Sylvestris with the suddenness of another thyrsis blast. Throwing the cloak aside, he drops into his fighting stance and spins around, though he doubts he has strength enough to best a child. "Who's there?"

But there's only the lone boat upon the empty shore.

As Sylvestris circles the craft, mocking laughter ripples before him as if out of thin air. He remembers the footprints he'd seen in the sand before the Furies attacked. The prints are gone now, obliterated in the struggle. But he doesn't think they were made by a ghost. "Are you a coward? Show yourself!"

The laughter stops. The air before Sylvestris begins to shimmer as though turning first to water, then to ice. As the air thickens, a portion of Herwood melts in a blur of green and vanishes altogether from sight behind a sort of localized cloud, roughly rectangular in shape, that hangs in the middle of nowhere like a window of the clearest crystal turned suddenly opaque. Then the window clears again, as if opening.

A small figure, no larger than a child or a simular, is revealed.

Sylvestris draws back from this apparition with a cry. Then, his body acting independently of his mind, he drops to his knees.

For it's Azedarach who stands before him.

"Do you really think us a coward, simularter?"

Sylvestris can only shake his head, unable to believe his eyes. But there can be no doubt of what—or whom—he's seeing.

Even frayed and filthy as they are, there's no mistaking the purple robes of the Sovereign, the hem of which Sylvestris has so often kissed. Nor is there any mistaking the thick and tangled beard, stained a yellowish brown with metheglin. Nor the thin and reedy voice, like an old woman's . . . though Azedarach has addressed Sylvestris vocally only a handful of times, preferring to use his telepathic abilities. Abilities which, it occurs to Sylvestris, he's not employing now.

Nor, finally, is it possible to mistake the polyhedral cloud made up of shifting, interpenetrating crystalline surfaces, each alive with a thousand flickering faces, or parts of faces, that hangs like a veil from a diadem of silver and gold fashioned in the likeness of a serpent swallowing its tail, a cloud that obscures completely the head beneath it.

So the old legends are true, Sylvestris thinks. The Serpent Crown can make its wearer invisible.

"Well?" asks Azedarach. He's holding a thyrsis in his small hands. It's pointed almost negligently at Sylvestris. He doesn't seem surprised to have found Sylvestris here, as if he's already experienced this moment countless times in the metheglin dreams that send his mind drifting aimlessly through time.

Sylvestris finds his voice at last: "Forgive me, Sire! I feared the Furies had returned!"

"Whereas we are a coward, not to be feared at all."

"No, Sire." Sylvestris is trembling. He knows he's but a single wrong word away from death. Knows, too, there will be no resurrection this time. "Only a fool wouldn't fear you!"

"And you, Sylvestris, are no fool."

"I hope not, Sire."

"Unless it is such a fool as Saint Stilskin Sophora."

Sylvestris doesn't reply, afraid of misjudging the Sovereign's mood. He's never known Azedarach to be like this, almost defensive in his attitude, as if, for the first time in turnings, he doesn't know what the future holds.

"They think they have beaten us," says Azedarach as if speaking to himself. "Forced us from our Throne. But they will see how wrong they are."

"They?" Sylvestris hazards. He's afraid the Furies will return, but Azedarach seems in no hurry to leave the beach.

"The heretics and their inhuman allies, the simulars, of course. The attack of the Ecclesiarch's men was no surprise. That was nothing we had not foreseen. But these others; for some reason their thoughts and plans were hidden from us! We barely escaped with our life and crown. Does that make us a coward?"

Sylvestris considers carefully before answering. "Sire, when Ixion withdrew from Quoz after the battle of Cat Square, the Furies called him a coward. Yet it was a strategic retreat only, and led to the final victory."

"You understand perfectly." As Azedarach speaks, the anonymous faces of men and women and children flit in endless succession and variety across the polyhedral cloud that conceals his own true features. The faces wear expressions of extreme, even exaggerated, emotion—from violent rage to hopeless desolation to giddy, idiotic joy—yet they are voiceless, flat, like tormented souls of the Pit glimpsed through a distorting glass. "It is all part of the plan."

Sylvestris recalls his audience with the Sovereign on All Saints' Eve. Then, in the throne room of the Palace, Azedarach had telepathically confided the details of his—or, as he'd corrected himself with a show of humility, the Spinner's—great and secret plan for the salvation of the Hierarchate.

Sylvestris had listened as though his life depended upon it—which, in fact, it had—as Azedarach's thoughts thundered in his skull. He'd listened to how Azedarach, with the Spinner's blessing, planned to bring down the Ecclesiarch and put an end to both the Chastenings and the nightly curse of Beauty by employing Rose, the false Liberatrix crafted by his vizards, to infiltrate the heretics and destroy them from within.

Yet, despite his close attention, Sylvestris had left the audience in confusion, head pounding as always from the telepathic invasion. He'd never, in all the turnings of their association, been able to understand the nonlinear way in which Azedarach experienced time. It was as if all times were the same to him, past, present, and future taking place simultaneously, right now, yet somehow already finished, too, like the stories set down by Quercus Incana in the *Lives and Acts* which are enacted over and over again, with simulars, upon the stages of the Hierarchate.

Sylvestris might not understand it, but he's learned to respect it. And to fear it.

He is afraid now. Has everything that's happened been a part of Azedarach's great and secret plan? Have they all been as witless simulars, pulled this way and that by strings that extend invisibly into the past and future, strings pulled by Azedarach's childlike hands? Or is there another plan at work, one unknown even to Azedarach?

The Sovereign addresses him again. "If we thought you were one of them, Sylvestris, a traitor like so many others, we would kill you now, where you kneel. But you are loyal, are you not?"

Sylvestris blinks. How strange to find himself embroiled once again, after all that's happened, in the petty intrigues of Quoz! Yet perhaps, without knowing it, he'd never truly escaped them.

But things have changed. He has changed. Azedarach, once his master, is his enemy now. He owes his allegiance, like his life, to Rumer. To the Liberatrix.

Yet there's no lying to the Sovereign, whose telepathic powers can flay the thoughts from a person's mind as brutally as a shrive performing the Six Hundred flays the skin from the body of his victim. *Let it come then,* Sylvestris thinks, bracing himself for the assault, which always begins with an instant of blinding pain.

"You know the answer, Sire," he says. "I can hide nothing from you."

"Yes, we know your faithful heart." Azedarach gestures almost wearily with the thyrsis for Sylvestris to rise.

Sylvestris gets to his feet, trying to hide his surprise. There's no way that Azedarach could read his mind and continue to believe him loyal. Yet he detected no sarcasm in the Sovereign's reply. Azedarach must be toying with him; or else, he thinks, lying to him, trying to make him believe that he can read his thoughts as usual when, in fact, he cannot.

But if that's true, Azedarach must have lost his powers when he lost the Throne—which would certainly explain why he's speaking vocally, a mode of communication he's always scorned as common. Could it be that the source of his telepathy wasn't the Crown or metheglin, but the Throne?

There's no way to be sure. Sylvestris can only make a pretense of loyalty, all the while assuming that Azedarach knows everything and is playing him for a fool, perhaps hoping he'll implicate others.

In any case, Azedarach has the thyrsis.

"My heart is yours to command as always, Sire."

"We never doubted it. Now, bring us that remarkable cloak of yours."

Sylvestris runs to fetch it. The cloak is no longer as black as it had been just moments ago, as if the heat or light of the sun is restoring its luster. The fabric sucks gently at his fingers when he picks it up.

"We found you cocooned within the cloak," Azedarach says. "That is, we found the cloak; we had no idea what, or rather who, lay inside. But we could tell a fight had taken place by the state of the sand, and we guessed we'd found a victim of the Furies.

"But we'd never seen anything like the cloak. It was of a silver color, almost too blinding to look at. Heat poured from it as if from a furnace. This continued for some time. Then all at once it cooled and turned black as the night itself. It came away from your body as though pulled by invisible hands.

"And there you were, Sylvestris, lying in the sand like a serpent who'd just shed its skin. Only you don't appear to have sprouted any wings to speak of."

"I was dying," says Sylvestris. "The cloak healed me."

"We assumed as much." The Sovereign extends a hand, and Sylvestris gives him the cloak. "What an interesting texture! It feels almost alive! We have heard of craftings like this. It is said that Ixion was wearing such a garment when the Fury stabbed him in Cat Square. A fit cloak for a sovereign, wouldn't you say, Sylvestris? Especially in such a dangerous place as this."

"By all means."

"Come, let us exchange clothes." Azedarach steps behind the boat as though out of modesty.

Still, Sylvestris catches a glimpse of the Sovereign as he disrobes. His body is impossibly thin, impossibly white, like a simular whittled out of bone. Sylvestris looks away, unsettled by what he's seen, as if Azedarach is no longer human.

Then the Sovereign's purple robes, much the worse for wear, land at his feet. Though too large for the Sovereign, who appears half-lost inside them, the robes are absurdly small for Sylvestris. Still, he manages to tie them about his waist in a sort of loincloth. He supposes it's better than nothing.

Meanwhile, Azedarach steps from behind the boat. He's wearing the cloak, the color of which has softened to a swarthy gray; it clings to him as snugly as it had to Sylvestris despite the vast disparity in their sizes.

"You look well, Sire."

"We cannot say the same for you." The Sovereign takes a few preening steps. "Tell us where you found this treasure."

"In a place called Reve, Sire."

"Ah. That, too, we have heard of. The fabled City of Roses. So it exists."

"Yes, Sire."

"These are marvelous times, Sylvestris! It seems there is nothing too strange to exist. What were you doing in Reve, if we may inquire?"

Sylvestris pauses, at a loss for words.

"No matter," says Azedarach, as quick to drop the subject as to raise it. "You will inform us of everything later. We must not linger. Worse things than Furies dwell in Herwood: there is a terrible beast here."

Sylvestris glances nervously at the woods. "A beast?"

"Do not fear; we have prepared a place of safety. There you will see something that will amaze you. But first you will enjoy a rare privilege."

"Thank you, Sire."

"We are going to render you invisible. It is not that you merit this distinction, Sylvestris, but simply that we do not wish your presence to call attention to our own. Approach us."

Sylvestris does so.

"Kneel."

Sylvestris kneels. Azedarach walks behind him, out of sight. The hairs at the back of Sylvestris's neck prickle. He expects to feel the hot blast of the thyrsis at any second. But instead, with a suddenness that causes him to jump, the Sovereign clambers onto his shoulders like a small child. The touch of his hands is like ice.

"You may stand now. Carefully."

Wincing, Sylvestris gets to his feet. Azedarach weighs next to nothing, as if his bones are hollow. But his spindly legs, even wrapped in the silky fabric of the cloak, irritate the scars on Sylvestris's chest. He thinks of how Samsum sat upon his shoulders in Reve as if sitting upon a throne and controlled him, in a reversal whose ironies he didn't fully appreciate, by means of the threads it spun from its body.

Yet even then he did not feel as helpless as now. Rumer walked beside him. Now her absence keeps him company. Where is she? How will he be able to find her?

"There will be a slight discomfort," says Azedarach.

Sylvestris gasps as a cold and heavy numbness flows down over his body. His vision wavers, and all color vanishes from the world.

Herwood is no longer green, but gray. Wherever he looks, he sees only shades of black and white, as if he's stepped out of the world, or the world has removed itself from him behind a lens that filters light to a ghastly monochrome. Sounds are muted and flat, strangely without affect, like mere reproductions of sounds. And the rich smells of woods and sea have been reduced to poverty.

Is this, he wonders, what it's like to be dead? There is, already, an almost-unbearable sense of claustrophobia, as if the excluded world, bursting with life, is pressing in all around him and will crush him with its unforgiving absence.

"Sire," he gasps. "I can't bear it!" His voice sounds as clear as ever; but far from reassuring him, this only sharpens his suffering, like a reminder of all that's been lost.

Azedarach laughs. "So you see, a little, what it costs to be Sovereign! You will be better for it."

His voice, too, is clear and vital, and Sylvestris has a feeling that if he looked up now, he'd behold the true features of the Sovereign, as inhuman as his body. The idea terrifies him.

"Come," says Azedarach. "We will direct you. Be silent. We are invisible but can still be heard."

To walk within this oppressive cloud seems as impossible as it is unbearable. Yet Sylvestris does it. Progress feels slow and laborious, as if he's walking against a strong current. When they leave the beach and enter Herwood, the opposition grows more intense, until it seems he's barely making any headway against it at all. But despite these difficulties, which are very real, the black-and-white world glides smoothly by like scenery past a grimy carriage window. It's as if time flows at different rates inside and outside the cloud, which, though surrounding them in a shell that cannot be escaped, is not impermeable. Leaves and branches pierce it easily; once through, they regain their color at once, brushing Sylvestris with a heavy and sticky materiality, as if seeking to attach themselves to him. Fireflies, however, though numerous, avoid the cloud; perhaps, he thinks, its crafting repels them somehow. Birds and other creatures, too, stay away. All the while, Azedarach guides him with whispers and nudges.

At last they come to what seems to be a dead end, a mass of vegetation that looks even more impenetrable than the thickets of Reve. But Azedarach, telling Sylvestris to bend low, directs him through a cunningly disguised opening into a darkness behind. Now the light of the Sovereign's thyrsis begins to glow, and Sylvestris sees that they've entered a cave.

Azedarach directs him to kneel again. He slips from Sylvestris's shoulders, and the deadening cloud lifts with him.

Still on his knees, Sylvestris feels like laughing as the world returns to life around him, and he to the world. Even though they're within a gloomy cave, their only source of light a thyrsis, it seems to him that he's never before seen such vibrant colors nor smelled odors more interesting and allusive. The patterns of green and silver lichens on the rocky cavern walls, mixed with the darker tones of the rock itself, seem as beautiful as the stained glass windows of the Cathedral in the full blaze of sunlit glory.

Azedarach, meanwhile, scurries to the rear of the cave, where he bends over something Sylvestris can't see. At last, he straightens. "After the heretics and simulars robbed us of our Throne, we wandered half-mad through the maze of passages below the Palace, sick with anger and despair. Our plan had failed. Our reign was finished. Nothing remained but to end our life in the metheglin vaults with an overdose of the drug.

"We found her waiting there, Sylvestris. We took her in our arms and kissed her. And she spoke to us; she told us we must come here, to Herwood. She said there was something only we could do, something that would destroy Beauty forever and put an end to the Chastenings just as we had so desperately desired. Of course we listened. Of course we came! Now you will listen. You will see!"

Sylvestris, meanwhile, has been trying to do just that, to see what—or, rather, who—lies behind the Sovereign. A woman surely, to judge by what he's saying. But why doesn't she speak for herself?

Azedarach steps aside with a flourish and focuses the light of the thyrsis behind him. "Behold!"

Green eyes shine dully like bits of clouded marble. The lips are blue and do not speak.

The Sovereign laughs, almost dancing with excitement. "Behold the Liberatrix!"

But Sylvestris knows it. He's seen it before, though he never thought to see it again and can't believe he's seeing it now.

The severed head of Rose Lacrimata.

EIGHT

So abruptly do they enter the clearing that Rumer gasps in surprise. She has the impression of an immense enclosed space like the vast underground caverns of the heretics; only this space is hollowed out of the living woods, not stone. Overhead, instead of sky, she sees a field of rippling green so reminiscent of grass that she has a moment of vertigo in which everything seems to have been turned upside down. Though she can't see the sun, shafts of light pierce this leafy canopy to string the shimmering air like a guitar or lute that plays of itself, its music as much a vibration of light as sound.

But this is the impression of an instant only; suddenly the honeyed smell of metheglin is everywhere, stronger and even rawer than Rumer remembers from the metheglin vaults, a burning sweetness that makes her screw her eyes shut as if she's been splashed in the face with candied acid.

Meanwhile, the Furies lower her to the ground and unlash her from the pole, leaving her wrists and ankles bound together as before. Then, still careful not to touch her directly, they raise her up by means of the vines. Her wrists are yanked over her head, sending a keen pain knifing between her shoulders. Her toes brush the ground; she tries to stand, but her legs buckle with cramps.

Suspended between agonies, afraid to open her eyes, Rumer waits for the real tortures to begin.

But nothing happens. Or, rather, the shimmering of the air seems to deepen; it's oddly soothing to her ears, a sound of deep contentment like the purring of a thousand cats.

Rumer's eyes flicker open. Her tears have washed away the burning; there's only a faint stinging now—a discomfort forgotten, along with everything else, as she struggles to make sense of what she's seeing.

The immensity of it, the utter strangeness, goes beyond wonder, beyond horror, beyond the range of any response she knows. She feels hollowed out inside, scraped clean. Rose is forgotten; Sylvestris is forgotten; everyone and everything is forgotten.

There are trees. A vast host of trees. The rows stretch in ordered array as far as she can see, like an orchard. The trees are slender and handsome, with long, silver trunks and full-leafed branches bent with the weight of their fruit. Every branch bears its heavy load.

Men.

The men are as naked as the seven Furies who brought her. But they're not like those Furies—who ignore her now, scurrying along the ground in the company of numberless others of their kind, holding what appear to be wooden bowls like beggars seeking alms from the trees.

These men are old. Ancient. And hairless as the sleepers in Reve. They dangle from the limbs of the trees like corpses left to rot after a mass hanging.

Rumer hangs among them. There are no other women that she can see. Only men.

Rumer's gaze wanders to the man on her left. She could touch him if her hands were free; he's that close. Like her, he hangs suspended by vines from the branches of the tree. Only in his case, the vines sink directly into his temples and neck and chest in a way that reminds her, again, of the sleepers.

She's never seen an older man. His arms and legs dangle from his torso as though attached by habit alone. His bones shine through his translucent, papery skin; so, too, do his organs, like lamps emitting a cold blue light. Rumer sees the heart like a fist clenching and unclenching in his chest. She sees the slow pumping of his lungs; the dark, solid mass of his stomach like a swallowed stone; the sluggish circulation of his blood. Veins squirm at his temples.

His eyes are open. The glazed pupils don't seem to see her or anything else here; they quiver, though, like the eyes of a dreamer. Spittle leaks from his lips. She thinks again of her father, wondering if this was his fate, if he's hanging somewhere close by. For all Rumer knows, this man is her father.

Without the slightest change in expression or muscular twitch, as if what's taking place has nothing to do with him, the man begins to urinate from a penis the size of a small boy's. The stream patters over the ground like rain.

Rumer looks away. There are fireflies everywhere. In the air and crawling upon the bodies of the men. As before, the insects show little interest in her. Those that light upon her take flight again immediately.

Now she's looking at the man on her right. He resembles her leftward neighbor almost exactly. But the likeness of the two men—of all the men here—is on the order of skeletons, as if whatever had once differentiated them has long since worn away and only the commonality of bones remains.

As Rumer watches, a firefly lands on the man's lips as though drawn to the petals of a lily. It crawls into his mouth. She waits for it to come out. After a moment, another firefly—or perhaps the same one—wriggles from the man's left nostril. It clings upside down to the tip of his nose while fanning moist and glittery wings like a newborn thing, then suddenly launches itself into the air right past her face, so close she feels the breeze of its going.

As if the firefly has torn a veil from her eyes, Rumer sees that the men are infested; wherever she looks, fireflies are crawling into and out of nostrils, ears, mouths, even trachae.

Her stomach gives a soggy lurch as she realizes that the contented humming sound she's been hearing ever since she arrived here comes as much from *within* the men as outside them.

Only, she doesn't think they're men anymore. They're something else now.

Hives.

With that, as if a second veil has fallen from her eyes, she sees the fireflies moving inside the men, the organ she'd taken for their stomachs not an organ at all but instead a conglomeration of insects so tightly fused as to appear solid and inert. But now a hidden activity is revealed to her: a slow, generational pulse like a parody or perversion of a fetus gestating in the womb.

Rumer feels sick, invaded; though the fireflies haven't entered her body yet—at least, she doesn't think so—she has no doubt that it's only a matter of time.

Now a kind of mewling whimper comes from the man, or, as Rumer can't help thinking of him, the hive. With all the alacrity of a courtier summoned by the Sovereign, a Fury appears at his side.

The Fury is young, filthy, and hirsute, like every other Fury she's seen. And like them, he, too, holds a wooden bowl in his hands as if it's his sole possession in the world, like those women sworn to emulate the poverty of Saint Viridis Lacrimata, who carry nothing with them on their endless wanderings but bowls to receive the coins, food, and water they beg, and on which hard pillows they lay their heads at night to sleep.

Rumer can't decide if this Fury is one of the seven who brought her here, but there's something familiar enough about his features—what she can see of them behind the unruly thicket of his beard and hair—to make her look more closely.

What she sees makes no sense; but then nothing here makes sense, she thinks. What she'd taken for beard and hair are in fact tangled vines and shoots sprouting directly from the Fury's skin. The sprouts are incredibly fine and delicate, reminding Rumer of certain herbs employed in the *ars erotica*, herbs whose fabulous potency wilts in a night, as they do. The Fury's startling blue eyes flicker over her from behind this verdant scrim not merely as if he's never seen her before, but as if she doesn't exist.

Stroking the emaciated legs of the hive with one grimy hand, the Fury begins, very softly, to sing. And the hive, like a child calmed by a lullaby, quiets.

Rumer strains after the words, but she can't make them out; she's not even sure there are words. But snatches of melody come to her, at once deeply strange and familiar, as if reaching her from the depths of her own lost childhood, in her father's soothing voice. Her eyes are brimming with tears.

The Fury's voice trails off like a breeze, a sigh. And with a movement both swift and gentle, he swings the legs of the hive over his shoulders at the knees. The legs seem boneless, or as if the bones have softened to jelly.

Cupping the wooden bowl in the palm of one hand, the Fury holds it underneath the hive's withered haunches as his other hand dips into the dark space between.

A golden syrup, thick as honey, oozes into the bowl. An odor of burning sweetness rises up; a sweetness so raw, so intense, that Rumer instinctively clenches shut her eyes against it.

The smell of metheglin.

Something snaps inside her. She not only feels it, she actually hears it: a whip cracking way back in her skull. Then she's kicking wildly, as if her entire body—bound as it is, wrists and ankles—has become that whip.

Rumer kicks out at the Fury, the hive. She kicks out at everything and at nothing. It feels as if she's screaming, but she can't hear anything, so she's not sure; maybe she only thinks she's screaming.

She's kicking, though. Swinging like the clapper of a bell. She thinks of how Saint Samsum Oxalis toppled the walls of Quoz by ringing the great bell in the temple of Maw, led there in his blindness by the young Cat Sabal Illicium. But the hives who hang beside her don't ring out when she strikes them. They don't make any noise at all. If only she had Samsum's strength! She'd knock down every tree in Herwood.

Now something seizes her legs in mid-swing, bringing her to an abrupt halt. Opening her eyes—the fumes of the metheglin have dissipated—

Rumer finds herself gazing down into the wild, blue eyes of the Fury, whose arms are encircling her thighs.

Clouds of fireflies, disturbed by her outburst, swarm angrily through the air. But Rumer ignores them. She stares at the Fury, waiting for him to speak. She feels somehow that one word from him can free her, just as, in the story of Roemer and Jewel, Jewel's tearful plea had moved the leader of the Furies—her own wicked mother—to spare Roemer's life and let him lead her out of Herwood, though in the end Roemer had ruined everything by looking back.

Will the Fury speak now?

Will he stroke her legs and sing to her softly?

The Fury regards her steadily, his blue eyes brilliant and inscrutable behind the foliage of his hair.

Then a tear falls from Rumer's eye to strike the Fury's upturned face.

A jolt runs through his body as if he's been struck with a thyrsis. He gasps suddenly, sharply, more in surprise than pain, or so it seems to Rumer. Letting go of her legs, the Fury steps stiffly back, hugging his arms to his chest.

Rumer is swinging again, but she cranes her neck to watch as the Fury sinks to his knees. Something is happening to the lush vegetation covering his body: it turns brown, shrivels, and begins to drop from his skin like leaves from a tree. The Fury moans and gasps for breath, eyes shut tight, as if undergoing an onslaught of intense and conflicting sensations, like love.

Rumer shudders, suffering again, as with Sylvestris, the birth of a love that springs full-grown from a broken heart. Or, rather, not a birth exactly, but an expansion of the love already born to her, as if the love she feels for Rose and Sylvestris has spilled over into this Fury, carried in her tears, and has rushed to fill the space of him, as water will do, with itself.

Yet it's not diluted or weakened. On the contrary, love courses through her more powerfully than ever, and desire burns her body now as sweetly and unbearably as the metheglin had burned her eyes.

Is this how it will be? she wonders. Will this loving ocean widen with each teardrop until the whole world is submerged in her, or she in the world?

If there's a difference, she's not aware of it. All she knows for sure is that when she first felt her love for Sylvestris, she tried to deny it, to reject it, wanting to be faithful to the memory of Rose. And she failed: a failure for which Rumer thanks the Spinner now, though it's brought her pain as well as pleasure, loss as well as love.

But of course it has, she thinks. How could it not? How can there be the one without the other in this life?

Rumer will no longer fight the love she's feeling. She accepts it, accepts who she is, what she's become.

Viridis Liberatrix.

The Fury opens his blue eyes. He gazes at her in wonder and awe, only through a kind of fog, as if uncertain whether she's real or a vision. Rumer remembers the same look in Sylvestris's eyes, and for a second it's as if she sees his face superimposed upon that of the Fury.

Only it's no Fury kneeling before her now, but a man.

No trace of vegetation remains upon his skin. Yet he's not hairless, like the hives; glistening black hairs curl from his head and strong young body, restored by her tears. She wants more than anything to go to him.

And then, impossibly, she knows him, or thinks she does, as if fifteen turnings have vanished in the blink of an eye, and she's back in Jubilar, a little girl of five gazing into the blue eyes of her husband-to-be, a boy scarcely older than she is, to whom her father has contracted her in marriage. Rumer has never forgotten him; it's part of her punishment, like that of all Cats, to remember—or, rather, to be unable to forget—what she's lost. The boy's name hovers unspoken at her lips.

Can it really be him? Rumer begins almost fearfully to whisper the name, as if by speaking too loudly she'll break the spell of his existence. But before she can do so, she's yanked away with a sharpness that causes her to cry out in pain as the vines cut into her wounded wrists.

She thinks at first that the Furies have fallen upon her. But then she realizes the hives are being swung as roughly as she. All around her, branches are bending as if blown in a powerful wind.

She hears it now. A roaring from everywhere and nowhere, as if a Chastening has burst upon them.

The man glances up at the disturbance, and his face goes chalky white, changing in an instant from that of the boy she knew into the face of a stranger. He staggers to his feet with a cry and stumbles away through lashing branches and hives, past Furies who stare upward amid the commotion, as if rooted to the ground.

Rumer strains frantically to see what has frightened him, what has hypnotized the Furies.

High above, in the vegetation that arches overhead like a sky of grass, a face is taking form. Rumer watches it appear. Built from branches and leaves and other bits of whirling matter, the features assemble with all the gravity of storm clouds into a visage as deeply scarred as her own, though inconceivably vaster, as if she's looking at herself in a mirror that magnifies out of all proportion the image it reflects, until only the reflection remains. The face stretches as far as she can see . . . beyond what she can see, as lofty and limitless as the sky.

But it's no reflection. Not hers, anyway.

It has no eyes. Just two dark and ragged holes where eyes should be.

Yet Rumer feels the face gazing down at her just as she's gazing up at it: only without fear, without any emotion she can share or even recognize, as if she's the blind one. She's never felt so small and insignificant.

Suddenly she's rising into the air, flung upward by the branches of the trees, which pass her between themselves so swiftly and smoothly it feels like flying. Up, up, up, she goes, as in a dream. She feels lighter than air, as though a weight she's been carrying all her life, without being aware of it, has lifted. It's exhilarating but also terrifying, for it turns out flying is a lot like falling; Rumer's senses say one thing, her mind says another, and before long her grasp of up and down is as upset as her stomach.

All the while, the immense face hovers above her. Or below. It remains the same size, as if she's not moving at all. Or as if it's also moving, receding from her . . . though why it should do such a thing, Rumer can't begin to imagine. She's the frightened one.

Yet the expression of the face is neither terrible nor afraid. Rumer can't see it all, of course, but what she can see appears placid, even serene, persisting undisturbed despite the eddies and currents that swirl over the assembled features like breezes carving their brief signatures into the foliage of a tree, as though it's not a face at all, but a living mask whose stylized features, enduring through time, conceal a face too beautiful or horrible to be borne by human eyes, like the face of the Spinner, or of Maw.

Now two streams of fireflies go winding past Rumer like threads of living green. She watches them intertwine, come apart, then mingle again, as if stitching themselves, or everything else, together. At last they separate, dividing into two great swarms that rush to fill the hollows of the mask or face like a pair of emerald eyes.

NINE

"Well, simularter?" Cackling behind the fractured planes of the swarm of faces that masks his features, Azedarach hops from foot to foot like a boy unable to contain his excitement in the face of a long-dreamed-of triumph. "Didn't I promise you'd be amazed?"

"How?" is all Sylvestris can croak at the sight of the head propped against the rear wall of the cave. It's wrapped in a strip of bloodstained cloth that melds into the surrounding dirt and rock as though the head has sprouted from the earth, a pale, anthropomorphic mushroom.

Or, he thinks, not a mushroom: something unliving, hard to the touch, like a calcified deposit formed in the timeless dark and bearing, as if by a miracle, the features of Rose Lacrimata. The bloom of life hadn't yet faded from her cheeks when he'd cut the head from her shoulders; now her head is a thing of stone. Even her eyes are stones, emeralds whose fires have gone out. The red tear tattooed upon her cheek, ancient mark of the House Lacrimata, is like a drop of blood on a bust of chalk white marble.

Standing above Rose's body in the vaults, Sylvestris had known Azedarach would expect him to recover her eyes, which could perhaps be implanted by vizards into another woman, a replacement for Rose. He hadn't known about Rumer then, hadn't even dreamed there was already a new Liberatrix, no false likeness meant to deceive and betray but the real thing this time, Saint Viridis Lacrimata miraculously returned from Herwood.

But he'd been afraid to pluck out Rose's eyes, and not just because he feared damaging such delicate craftings. He was afraid they might still be alive in some way even though she was not, and he'd seen too many shrives die screaming at the merest splash of her envenomed tears to risk exposing himself to that obviously unpleasant end.

There was only one thing he could do. Carefully, like a vizard performing a difficult harvesting, he'd decapitated her and swathed the head in strips of cloth torn from the robes of a dead heretic: Aralia, who, like Rumer, had been a voluptuary of the House Illicium.

He'd been taking the head to Azedarach when simulars had cut his throat and—like the Furies—left him for dead. But he didn't die. Instead, Rumer found him and wept over his dying body. Wept tears of hate, not sadness or pity. But they'd healed him just the same.

When he awoke, the head was missing. He hadn't bothered to look for it, assuming the simulars had taken it, glad only that it was gone. He wanted to forget it, to forget the man he'd been, the crimes he'd committed in the service of the Sovereign before Rumer—without intending to, as she told him in Reve—had blessed him with her tears.

Yet here it is before him, Rose's head, and in the hands of the very person he'd been trying to deliver it to in the first place. Sylvestris feels like the victim of a joke, a deadly joke. For how had the head come into Azedarach's possession? The answer could mean death. Crawling on hands and knees, Sylvestris backs away as if he's in the throne room of the Palace, taking formal leave of Azedarach after an audience.

But this audience is not yet finished; Azedarach blocks his retreat, thyrsis at the ready. "Do not be afraid, Sylvestris. She will not harm you. It is she who led us to you, as she has guided our steps ever since we found her outside the metheglin vaults."

Sylvestris shakes his head, uncomprehending. Again, he has the unpleasant feeling of being tested. If the Sovereign had found Rose's head outside the metheglin vaults, he must have seen Sylvestris lying there, too, his throat cut, for the head had been in his possession when the simulars struck and was gone after he regained consciousness. In fact, Azedarach must have expected to find him there, for it was he who'd dispatched Sylvestris to the vaults to capture Rose in the first place. Yet now he's acting like none of it ever happened. It doesn't make sense.

"It's true," Azedarach continues as he herds Sylvestris back toward the silent but somehow watchful shrine. "The instant we saw the head lying amid blood and roses, we recognized the eyes, which our own vizards had crafted and implanted. Alas, we arrived too late. Our Liberatrix, our Rose, was lost to us, fled where we could not follow, into a darkness even our brightest commands were helpless to dispel.

"With her fled all our hopes. The servants of Maw were victorious. For who could save the Hierarchate now that Rose was gone? The Ecclesiarch, perhaps? The heretics? They would only tip things farther out of balance, send the whole world crashing after her into the Pit! But that did not concern us any longer. The Spinner had spoken; His Wheel had turned. All that remained was for us to enter the metheglin vaults and swallow the sweet medicine of our sad life's ending.

"But first we would bid the Liberatrix farewell; we, who had created her. We raised her poor head in our hands and kissed these cold lips . . ." Azedarach breaks off with a sob, as if overcome by the memory.

"Sire," Sylvestris interjects into the breach, selecting his words with care, for he judges it more dangerous now to remain silent than to speak, "I was there, as you know. You sent me to capture Rose. But I failed. Before I could prevent it, she was killed by a shrive. I cut the head from her body . . ."

Azedarach is uninterested in Sylvestris's confession. "Yes, yes; we know all that; the Liberatrix told us everything."

"The Liberatrix?" Sylvestris thinks at first that the Sovereign is referring to Rumer, and he feels again the shame of his failure to protect her. What horrors is she experiencing at the hands of the Furies? If only he could go to her, or know if she yet lived! But he doesn't trust Azedarach enough to ask for his help, and even if, despite his weakness, he overpowered the Sovereign and claimed the Serpent Crown for himself, using its powers to become invisible, how would he ever find Rumer in the immensity of Herwood? No, it's hopeless. He can only wait.

"Our vizards crafted her eyes better than they knew, Sylvestris," Azedarach goes on. "Their sight is undimmed by death."

"Sire?"

"Why, it's simple enough. We mean that Rose, although dead, sees more clearly than ever, with an acuity and breadth of vision we never found even in metheglin." He chops the thyrsis through the air decisively. "But we have awakened from those blurred and impotent dreams. We have finished with metheglin. Rose is our metheglin now! Our past and our future!"

And suddenly, as if he, too, has awakened from a blurry dream, Sylvestris understands at last: The Blessed Sovereign, Azedarach LXIV, is insane.

"Don't you see?" the Sovereign demands almost plaintively as gray faces flicker across the angular surfaces of his smoky mask like ghosts spun in a whirlwind. "She spoke to us, Sylvestris; she told us where to find a boat and how to steer it here, through the Undersea, to Herwood. As we sailed, the sea crashing around us, she told us about Beauty and the Chastenings. About the beast."

"Tell me of this beast, Sire." Sylvestris is wary of Azedarach's madness, yet there may be sense hidden in it.

"Patience, Sylvestris. We will explain everything, just as she explained it." The Sovereign clears his throat and begins matter-of-factly.

"Both Beauty and the Chastenings share a common source. Beauty is the odor of the beast, the scent by which, like certain evil flowers, it attracts its prey: the men of the Hierarchate. The Chastenings are but the convulsions of the beast's enormous body when, as it does each turning, it sheds its old skin over a period of months to emerge larger and hungrier than before. Ah, Sylvestris! Now do you comprehend why the Season of Chastenings stretches longer with each turning?"

Sylvestris nods, though in truth he doesn't see. "What is the nature of this beast?"

"Do you need to ask? It is coiled all around us!"

Despite himself, Sylvestris darts a nervous glance about the shadowy interior of the cave.

Azedarach laughs. "The beast is a winged serpent, the first and largest of its kind: large enough to crush the whole Hierarchate in its coils! It has a name. Can you guess it?"

"How could I?"

Azedarach's voice is a hiss of air: "Maw."

Instinctively, Sylvestris makes the sign of the Wheel.

Azedarach laughs again. "She is here, Sylvestris. The Dam of Darkness."

"Where?"

Azedarach points the thyrsis down, and a circle of light blooms over the floor of the cave like a spotlight upon a stage in a performance of simulars. "Under our feet. Trapped in her lair deep below Herwood, where she crawled long ago, gravely wounded in mind and body after her defeat at the hands of Ixion."

Seeing Sylvestris's puzzled look, Azedarach adds, "Yes, simularter. Even though you will not read of it in the *Lives and Acts*, this battle took place. We heard of it for the first time from Rose; it seems Quercus Incana omitted some things from his famous book, as the heretics always insisted!

"But perhaps traces of this great event remain, shrouded in symbol and allegory. The emblem of the Hierarchate, like the very shape of our crown, is a winged serpent swallowing its tail. What can this be but an allusion to Ixion's victory? Remember, too, Sylvestris, the Serpent Crown was crafted from a serpent's feathers to grant the Sovereign their property of invisibility, as you have been privileged to experience for yourself. Where else did those feathers come from if not from Maw? And if you require more proof, consider the myth of the Leviathan that sleeps at the bottom of the sea, waiting for the Unspinning. Can't you discern the echo of a great and forgotten battle between Ixion Diospyros and Maw in that ancient legend? And perhaps a dark prophecy for our own time as well?"

Sylvestris thinks of the maze of tunnels winding beneath the surface of Quoz. No one—not even the heretics—has ever plumbed the depths of those passages. Now, as though infected by Azedarach's madness, he wonders if, like the old stories of which the Sovereign is speaking, they all lead to the same place, to a chamber at the dark and secret heart of the world, where Maw flexes her coils in slow paroxysms of rage, plotting revenge against all that lives.

"But Maw, unlike the fabled Leviathan, is not sleeping," Azedarach goes on. "She is very much awake, very much alive. If only Ixion had pursued her all those turnings ago! But he thought her wounds mortal. And he himself had been badly injured in the fight; indeed, he died soon after. So she escaped him, and, safe in her lair, slowly healed, tended by Furies, who fattened her on a diet of men drawn into Herwood by the scent of Beauty: her own scent—and not just the scent of her body; her mind, too, has wings, Sylvestris. Supple wings, as wide and black as the night. They carry her scent even into the dreams of men."

Is that to be Rumer's fate? Sylvestris wonders. Another victim fed to the bottomless appetites of Maw? He shudders as if her coils have knotted coldly about his heart and squeezed.

Azedarach takes no notice: "So it went for countless turnings until, one day, Maw decided her wounds had healed. The time had come to return to the world, the light.

"But she could not! She had grown too fat to leave her lair; it had become her prison. But not her tomb. The Furies continued to feed her, throwing men into the pit at whose bottom she lay trapped. And she continued to grow, until her body was wedged so tightly into her lair that there was no space between them. And still she grew. Surely she would be crushed by the earth itself!

"Yet she was not, Sylvestris. Instead, she ground the earth away, rubbing against it as she shed skin after skin. And with each turning, the violence of her sheddings shook the world from Arpagee to Quoz in Chastenings increasingly severe."

Sylvestris thinks of the most recent Chastening. Was it only yesterday? He and Rumer had lain in each other's arms while all of Reve quaked about them in the morning light. How large Maw must be if the contractions of her body as it shed its skin could shake the world like that, making itself felt on land and sea! It seems impossible, a product of the Sovereign's addled fancy. And yet a part of him believes it, as if he's always known it.

"Now another Season of Chastenings is upon us," Azedarach says. "Maw is shedding another skin. As she writhes in her lair, the trees of Herwood thrash and bend as if buffeted by the winds of a storm. And indeed, a storm is about to break upon us all. For soon Maw will shed her prison along with her skin and emerge as if newly born, cracking the world like an eggshell as she squirms out into the light. None of us will survive very long after that."

"The Unspinning," Sylvestris breathes.

"Yes. The Unspinning, come round at last after all these turnings. Once Maw escapes, it will be too late. We must stop her now, Sylvestris, or she will send us all into the Pit!"

"But we are only two men, Sire. Even Ixion couldn't kill her!"

"Yet we will kill her. Rose has said so."

"How then?"

"She wouldn't tell us; she said that someone was coming to Herwood, a man to whom she would explain everything. When we inquired who it was, she replied: a dead man. That puzzled us. But now we see it was you whom she meant, Sylvestris."

"But I'm not dead!"

"You would be if not for this wondrous cloak. It brought you back to life."

Sylvestris feels as if a trap is about to be sprung. Has already been sprung, if only he'd known it.

"You think us mad," Azedarach says.

"No, Sire!"

"It's all right. You will hear the truth for yourself. Rose will speak to you as she did to us."

Sylvestris stares at the head, a glimmer of comprehension dawning.

"Go on," says Azedarach. "Kiss her."

He shudders in revulsion.

Azedarach raises the thyrsis. "Does she repulse you?"

Sylvestris feels the hot tip of the thyrsis against his forehead. He swallows, mouth gone suddenly dry, although sweat is pouring down his body. "No, Sire," he croaks. "But you have already kissed her. Shall my unworthy lips follow yours?"

"If we command it." Azedarach pulls back the thyrsis. "As for your lips, the Liberatrix will judge their worthiness."

There is no choice. Sylvestris crawls toward the head, which seems almost to watch him coming. He can't stop shaking; he doesn't know if he's more afraid of Azedarach's madness now or of the possibility that he's not mad.

"Pick her up. And take care you do not drop her."

His hands tremble as he lays them on either side of the neck, below the ears, and lifts the head. It's lighter than he would have thought. Though the flesh appears hard and smooth as marble in the glare of the thyrsis, it's soft and pliant to the touch, as if his fingers, should he press too forcefully, would break through the crust of skin. And it's cold, like ice. He holds his breath although there's no odor of decay, just a faint moldering smell whose source could be the cave for all he knows. He can't bear to look into the eyes.

"Do it," says Azedarach, behind him.

Shutting his eyes, Sylvestris brushes the cold lips with his own . . . quickly, softly, like a man stealing a kiss from a sleeping stranger.

He gasps at the taste of a tear, whether secreted from her dead eyes or from his own he doesn't know; but at that instant, a spark of something vital, almost sexual, leaps between them. His eyes spring open, and he finds himself looking at the head in his hands.

The head is looking back.

Rose's eyes shine with an emerald fire, freshly kindled. Yet the pall of death hasn't lifted from her features; if anything, it's deepened in the eerie glow.

He would shriek, hurl her away, but he's paralyzed, his whole body tingling. Has his kiss awakened her? Or has hers put him to sleep?

Now her bloodless lips part. He hears her voice. It's gentle, as though she wants to reassure him; yet he also detects a trace of condescending amusement, such as overserious children are apt to provoke in adults.

Greetings, Scribe.

And suddenly his heart is infused with joy, with love. Sylvestris feels as though he's found Rumer again, as if she's present somehow in or behind Rose's voice and eyes.

I'm sorry for what I did to you, Rose, he says, the words coming almost of themselves. *I'm sorry for everything!*

You are already forgiven. As she speaks, her eyelids slowly fall and rise again like the wings of a butterfly in the sun. *And I am not Rose. Not anymore.*

Who then? The Liberatrix?

That fate is Rumer's, not mine. Think of me as a book written long ago, like the Lives and Acts, *but never read. My words, like my tears, are a sickness, a poison . . .*

But your tears healed Rumer; she told me so. You made her into the Liberatrix!

As I was made to do.

By Azedarach's vizards?

Vizards crafted my eyes, but they did not make me.

I don't understand.

You need only remember, Scribe.

Why do you call me that?

Because you will write all this one day; that is what you were made to do. My story. And Rumer's, too . . .

Now Rose's voice fades, and the fire in her eyes flickers and dims as if about to go out.

What of Rumer? Sylvestris asks quickly, as if his voice can hold her here. *Is she all right?*

And, indeed, the fire grows stronger. *She lives.*

But how can I find her? Will I see her again?

That depends on you. There is a task you must perform before you pick up your pen or see Rumer again.

You mean killing Maw . . .

Yes.

But how? Our only weapons are a thyrsis and the Serpent Crown. From what Azedarach said, I don't think they can hurt her very much.

You are wrong, Scribe. You possess another weapon. My tears were crafted from poisons so toxic a single drop, undiluted, can kill a thousand men. My eyes may be dry now, but the poisons are still present within them, as potent and deadly as ever. Not even Maw can survive them. I will show you the entrance to her lair, the pit into which the Furies hurl her victims. You will take me there. You will cast me in.

Sylvestris flinches from this duty, as if he's been asked to perform a further desecration. *How can I?*

If you want to see Rumer again, you will do it. This is no threat, just the truth. And do not think I will suffer; I am past all suffering now. But you must act quickly, for the next Chastening will split the world apart!

Why are you telling this to me? Why not Azedarach?

The Spinner makes use of everyone, Scribe, from the lowest to the most high. As you see, even I have a task still before me.

Are we all simulars, then, pulled by the Spinner's strings?

The Spinner crafts us, then puts the strings into our own hands. Man sins, the Spinner spins!

Once more, the fire in her eyes dwindles. And this time, Sylvestris senses it won't return, though he calls out desperately: *Rose!*

Our time is at an end. Her voice is as faint now as the emerald glow of her eyes. *Farewell, Scribe! Do not fail me! Do not fail Rumer! Listen to your heart!*

And with that, Sylvestris sees, like the glowing trace of a taper pulled from a fire to write across the night—only in a script of green, not red—a map through Herwood leading to the lair of Maw. It imprints itself somewhere behind his eyes, deep within his mind, where instinct precedes knowledge or will. And then fades, following Rose into darkness.

TEN

Bruised and bleeding, he runs headlong through the angry woods. He knows neither his name nor his destination, only that this is no ordinary storm. Tree branches lash out to clutch and club him; roots rise up from the ground to snare his steps; vines dangle in his path like nooses. They send him sprawling, strike him roughly down.

He picks himself up and continues on, crashing blindly ahead.

He'd awakened quite suddenly in that awful grove, as if from a deep and dreamless sleep. Or maybe he hadn't woken; maybe he'd just begun to dream. For how else to explain what he'd seen there? It was like some nightmare glimpse into the Pit of Damned Souls: old men hanging naked from trees, insensible, their limp bodies swinging like simulars in a Chastening, while other men, wearing clothes of living vegetation that seemed to sprout from their bodies, as if they were more plant than human, circulated frantically among them.

Just like a dream or nightmare; except it wasn't.

And neither was the Cat. Bound by her wrists to a tree. Her scarred face and shining green eyes had inspired such feelings of reverence in him that he'd fallen to his knees in the middle of the noise and confusion as though in the presence of Saint Viridis Lacrimata herself. For it was she. Who else could it have been?

Her tears proclaimed her, tokens of that obscure mystery of passion and suffering willingly embraced for his sake and that of all men: the perpetual sacrifice. Kneeling there, he felt blessed, at peace, as if her tears had touched him, healed him somehow.

Then he saw it. High up in the welter of branches that arched in a vault of green as wide and distant as the sky, a face came into being before his already-astonished eyes.

It grew out of the stuff of the forest as if every plant and tree, every vine and flower, every growth large and small had a part in its making, like some shared dream made manifest in the tangled bodies of its dreamers. And, as in a dream, he didn't so much have the impression of something impossible taking place as of a possibility unsuspected until now, one that had always existed, overlooked on a crowded shelf or in a cobwebbed corner.

The face flourished in the manner of all green things under the sun. Yet it grew with a quickness and purposefulness uncanny amid the chaos of the storm; all the more so when, with a gasp, he recognized the features emerging from the wind-whipped foliage.

They were the features of Saint Viridis Lacrimata, only immeasurably larger. And different in another way. For while the saint's face, despite its scars—or, rather, because of them, of the history they communicated directly to his heart in a language of perfect understanding such as lovers sometimes share—was beautiful, the huge face hanging above it like a magnified reflection was not.

It was ugly. Hideous.

He had the sense of looking at a portrait whose features, though skillfully rendered, weren't meant to flatter but to mock. A mask that didn't trouble to conceal, for all its artistry, the malevolence of the hand that had crafted it.

Not even the compassionate gaze of Viridis Lacrimata was enough to protect him from that unending malice. But what had he done to earn it? He didn't know. He couldn't remember his own name or how he'd come to be here. He might have been born just a moment ago, kneeling full-grown at the feet of the saint.

But at that, a shard of memory had stabbed him like a sliver of glass from a shattered mirror: Herwood. He was in Herwood.

And suddenly, as if he'd been blind until then, he grew aware of his nakedness. He saw he was no different than the men around him, old and young alike.

A hot, almost-annihilating shame boiled up from the core of him, as if this shared nakedness were merely the visible, outer sign of a deeper identity, a secret kinship of souls united in heresy and damnation. The unknown crimes of these men were his crimes. Their sins his own.

But he wasn't like them! He wasn't. He couldn't even bear to look at them!

But the gigantic mask gazed down at him in its vast and implacable hostility as if to say: Yes, little man. You are like them. You are *exactly* like them.

Something broke in him then, and he realized at last what—or who—lurked behind that cruel mask.

Maw. Dam of Darkness.

He turned and ran.

He's running still. And still no nearer to escaping the woods than when he started, however long ago that was. Hours or days, it's all the same to him in his consuming terror.

Maw surrounds him, the woods her body. She toys with him like a cat with its prey.

At last he can run no more. A branch knocks him to the ground, and he can't get up. His strength, his will—even his fear—are exhausted. Gasping for air, half-dazed, he sprawls in the underbrush and waits for death, welcoming it.

But Maw ignores him. The branches of the trees continue to flail, and he understands in a flash that he's nothing to her. This storm will break upon some other head than his.

Without quite knowing how it happens, he finds himself laughing at this joke that's been played on him. Or, rather, he finds himself unable to stop laughing.

At the same time, he's shivering, trembling so violently he thinks for a moment it's the ground that's shaking beneath him. Thinks it's another Chastening about to erupt, like the one that struck on his wedding day.

And with no more warning than that, it happens: all the slivers of his shattered memory come stabbing back at once, sharp as needles, long as knives.

No longer laughing, he thrashes upon the ground like a madman, tearing at plants, roots, even the dirt itself, with his hands and teeth. And groans in an agony of remembering like a woman in the throes of childbirth.

He is Cyrus Galingale. Yesterday he married Rose Rubra. He remembers walking through the streets of Jubilar on a carpet of fresh-cut flowers at the head of the wedding procession as, behind him, the village band played happily but out of tune. He remembers standing before the Mouth of God, repeating the solemn vows of Holy Patrimony with a tremor in his voice, and, afterward, dancing with Rose at the Feast of Saint Ilex Erythrina while his father looked on with pride and clapped in time to the music.

He remembers the Chastening, and the murders of the two Kites he'd accidentally witnessed. Remembers fearing the shrives would blame him for the crime.

And he remembers how Rose came to him later that evening, naked beneath the modest shift of her long and deftly braided hair. He remembers how she lit the incense with a trembling hand and how he, in his impatience, pushed her down on the marriage bed and took her roughly, as his father had advised him. Remembers, too, how she wept beneath him but did not struggle, quiescent and cold as a corpse, a wife.

After that, nothing.

But he knows all the same, without having to remember.

Beauty.

Cy shudders now and lies still amid the frenzied motion of the woods.

He must have smelled the scent of Beauty during the night and, all his senses dazzled, deranged, been pulled irresistibly from his bed, his life. Pulled here, to Herwood.

But how? What had gone wrong? How had Rose failed him? They were so happy! He loved her; he loves her still. How can it all be gone? He remembers everything so clearly, as if it happened only yesterday . . .

Or was it months ago?

Turnings?

Cy groans again. He knows now beyond a shadow of a doubt that he's damned forever. There will be no going back to Jubilar. No going back to Rose. He cannot escape Herwood any more than he can escape his memories.

But he doesn't deserve this. Rose is to blame. It was her duty to guard his sleep from Beauty. He trusted her. Loved her. And she betrayed him.

He knows her fate, the fate of all women who lose a man to Beauty: the Panderman.

Rose has been taken from Jubilar and sold at the market in Kell, doubtless as a Cat. He hopes she's suffered, is suffering now, for what she did to him.

Yet at the same time, the thought of Rose in a Cattery, a slave to the lusts of other men, inflicts torments of jealousy upon Cy worse than anything he's suffered so far.

He sees her spreading her legs with a wanton smile for a host of naked, faceless strangers, answering their hunger with her own. She's urging them on with her voice, her whole body, and it's this complicity that he finds intolerable, unbearable.

If she's a slave, it's a willing one. She's no longer the passive receptacle she'd been for him, the obedient and modest wife, but an active participant, giving pleasure and receiving it without shame or restraint. He feels wounded to the depths of his masculinity, as if it's he who lies under those grunting men, his body receiving their thrusts, his voice crying out in a pain that edges toward ecstasy.

And now, as if the trembling of his body has passed into the world, the ground begins to shake. Staggering to his feet, Cy lurches into the woods. It's not Maw he's running from now. Not Herwood he's trying to escape.

It's himself.

ELEVEN

The ground is shaking beneath him, but Sylvestris hardly notices. He's holding Rose's head in his hands as if no more than a second has passed since he kissed its lips. The eyes are cold and lightless, dead. But the fire of their gaze still burns in him, part of him now.

Azedarach, meanwhile, calls to him: "Sylvestris! This is no mere Chastening; the Unspinning is at hand!"

With that, her words come back to him; he remembers what he must do. "Forgive me for doubting you, Sire."

"Never mind that. What did she tell you?"

"We must hurry," he says, bundling Rose's head in the remnants of Aralia's robes. "Climb on my shoulders, Sire; I'll tell you on the way!"

Azedarach obeys at once, as if Sylvestris is Sovereign now. "But where are you taking us?"

"To the Pit itself: Maw's lair."

Outside the cave, Herwood is in an uproar. Gusts of wind sweep loudly through the trees, and the ground is quaking with such violence that Sylvestris can hardly stand. The fireflies that were so plentiful earlier have vanished now.

Sylvestris tucks Rose's head to his chest, sheltering it in his arms from the branches that strike with seeming malevolence, as if Maw herself is trying to prevent them from reaching her lair.

Then an icy numbness creeps over him. All color drains from the world as the shroud of invisibility seeps down from the Serpent Crown. Sylvestris shivers, hating the clammy feel of it, the sense of being trapped in some limbo halfway between life and death.

Still, it's calmer within the dead space than outside it, as if time is thicker or heavier here, cushioning him. Sylvestris barely feels the tremors that, only seconds ago, had threatened to knock him off his feet. Now, just as before, when Azedarach had brought him to the cave,

Sylvestris feels like he's hardly even moving, as if he's slogging through mud, yet this perception is belied by the speed at which the drab woods go streaming by.

As he follows the route implanted in his mind, he tells Azedarach what he learned in the dream or vision: that the one weapon capable of defeating Maw is Rose herself, or, rather, the poisons of her eyes.

"Yes, of course," the Sovereign says as if he'd suspected as much all along. "But how do we extract the poisons? How do we deliver them?"

Sylvestris comes to a well-worn path, wide and relatively clear of foliage. He follows it without hesitation or thought; his body knows which way to go.

"By means of the very pit the Furies use to feed Maw," he answers. "The pit into which they cast the men seduced by Beauty. Into that pit, we must cast Rose's head."

Azedarach snorts with laughter. "A fatal change of diet! Excellent, Sylvestris! But our hands, not yours, will do the deed. Afterward, you will record everything just as Quercus Incana did for Ixion. There must be a new *Life and Acts* to supplement the old; after all, by killing Maw, your Sovereign will have done what even Ixion Diospyros failed to do. Our name will stand beside the name of Ixion. No, above it!" He kicks Sylvestris with his heels. "Can't you go any faster?"

Sylvestris thinks of how Rose had called him Scribe and told him he would record her history and Rumer's; somehow, being Azedarach's amanuensis isn't quite what he'd had in mind. He's about to reply, when he sees something up ahead and stops short. Curled in a fetal position, a Fury is lying at the edge of the path, half-hidden in the woods.

Azedarach sees it too. "Hush; not a word!" he hisses. "Approach him!"

Sylvestris moves up cautiously. Despite everything, he finds it impossible to trust the crafting of the Serpent Crown to hide them from the Fury's sight.

But the Fury takes no notice of them; he hugs his knees and moans in terror as the ground pitches beneath him. Twigs and leaves are plastered to his dirty skin and tangled in his matted hair as if sprouting from his body.

A wooden bowl lies at his feet, its contents spilled over the path. And even though Sylvestris's senses are deadened beneath the shroud of invisibility, he smells metheglin now.

Prodded by Azedarach, he inches closer.

Suddenly there's a jolt, a flash. The Fury screams once, shrilly. And now another smell reaches Sylvestris's nostrils. One that he knows all too well.

The smell of burned flesh.

Azedarach has used the thyrsis.

"You killed him!" Sylvestris stumbles back, sickened. The scars on his chest throb painfully, aggravated by the heat of the blast.

"We will exterminate them all once Maw is dead," Azedarach replies. "But you're right; there's no time for these amusements now. Make haste!"

It occurs to Sylvestris that he's been foolish. He's forgotten with whom he's dealing, forgotten the casual acts of terror and cruelty he's observed—and committed—over the turnings in the service of Azedarach. When Rose told him that the Spinner makes use of everyone, he took her to mean that he could trust Azedarach. But now Sylvestris understands that it's possible for two men to serve the Spinner yet be opposed to each other. Man sins, the Spinner spins. Rumer's tears have changed him, but not the rest of the world; Azedarach is the same as ever, inflicting pain as much for his own pleasure as advantage. He truly is evil, Sylvestris thinks. He always has been.

"That creature had metheglin," Azedarach says meanwhile. "Perhaps the Furies have found a way into the vaults; remind us to make a thorough investigation, Sylvestris."

"Yes, Sire."

Now the path turns, bringing six more Furies into view. These, too, lie prostrate with fear upon the path, wooden bowls scattered about them.

"Go on," Azedarach whispers in his ear. "We'll return for them later."

Soon the path opens out into a clearing under a canopy of gray leaves. At the heart of the clearing there's a wide crack in the ground, and from this crack a thick, dark smoke is pouring. The smell of metheglin is as strong as in the vaults below the Palace. A large number of Furies, too many to count, lie writhing upon the ground.

Azedarach nudges Sylvestris forward.

Sylvestris walks gingerly among the moaning bodies. A single wrong step will betray their presence, through touch if not sight. The Serpent Crown won't be much help then, he thinks. Nor the thyrsis. Not against so many.

But the Furies, again, pay them no heed, even when, as happens more than once despite all his care, Sylvestris brushes against an arm or leg; the ground is shaking more violently now, and even the shroud of invisibility no longer insulates him from it.

The smell of metheglin intensifies as they approach the crack in the ground, and the air grows uncomfortably hot. There are no Furies within the last fifteen or twenty feet, as if they can bear neither the smell nor the heat.

Sylvestris comes to within a few feet of the edge. The heat is intense, but he would go closer still if he weren't afraid of losing his footing and falling into the crevice, into the mouth of Maw.

Though there are no Furies this close to the edge, the wooden bowls used by them to carry metheglin are everywhere, and suddenly Sylvestris realizes that the Furies must have been feeding the drug to Maw. How else could she stay alive in her lair for so many turnings?

He can see the ragged gash of the pit, but he can't see into it; the cloud of rising smoke or steam blocks his view. But he can almost picture the serpent coiled in the farthest depths, shaking the world to pieces as she sheds her skin of darkness for one of light.

"Closer," urges Azedarach.

"But Sire, if I should fall—"

"We said closer!"

Sylvestris inches forward, almost to the edge.

"Give us the head," says Azedarach.

Sylvestris does so. In another second, he thinks, it will be over. Maw will be dead, Azedarach triumphant.

But then what? Will he see Rumer again as Rose promised? And when he does, will Azedarach kill her as he killed that Fury and is about to kill these others? Sylvestris feels that there's little to choose between Azedarach and Maw.

And then he thinks: why not be rid of them both?

Listen to your heart, Rose had said.

Sylvestris has never moved so swiftly in his life. Not in any of his duels, not even when he faced the simulars outside the metheglin vaults. He bends sharply from the waist, ducks his head, and rolls his powerful shoulders forward, toppling Azedarach into the pit. It works perfectly, except for one thing.

Azedarach doesn't fall into the pit.

He lands on the ground with an angry cry. Rose's head flies from his hands and rolls toward the Furies, who take no notice, blind to everything but their own terror.

The shroud of invisibility falls from Sylvestris with the Sovereign. The world explodes with all the colors and sounds and smells that were missing or muffled just seconds before.

Azedarach is also visible. His features are still masked by the shifting planes of the Serpent Crown, but the rest of him is no longer hidden, including the thyrsis rising toward Sylvestris's chest.

Sylvestris kicks out desperately. But the ground shifts at the last moment, throwing his balance off, with the result that although his kick misses its intended target, the thyrsis, it finds another: the Serpent Crown flies from the Sovereign's head.

Sylvestris looks at the true features of Azedarach.

All his life, he's heard tales of how the Crown works its disfiguring changes upon the face of its wearer. How the price for the power it conveys is a visage so hideous and inhuman that to gaze upon it for even an instant means death.

Yet now he's looking at the perfectly ordinary features of an old man. The skin is pale and lined. The eyes are a soft, diluted blue, not unkindly, the color of certain wildflowers. The lips are red behind the tangled veil of a beard stained brown from turnings of metheglin use.

Azedarach smiles. "You know it is death to gaze upon the face of the Sovereign."

And Sylvestris finds himself unable to move, unable even to look away, as if the horror he'd expected to see is somehow more real than the unremarkable face he's actually seeing. And anyway, where can he run? He watches as Azedarach raises the thyrsis once more.

But the Sovereign doesn't fire right away. Keeping the thyrsis trained on Sylvestris, he retrieves Rose's head from where it's come to rest near the closest of the still-oblivious Furies.

"First you will witness this," he says, and steps back to the edge of the pit. "Then you will experience the fate to which you wished to consign your Sovereign. We are disappointed in you, Sylvestris. You could have been Quercus to our Ixion! Your words might have lived forever. But see what you've chosen instead: a pointless death that no one will remember! You're a fool."

The wrappings have come loose from Rose's head during the struggle, revealing her marbled features.

"Farewell, sweet Liberatrix," Azedarach says, gazing upon them. "One final kiss . . . "

But as Azedarach lowers his lips to hers, a Fury bursts as if out of nowhere to throw himself upon the Sovereign with a howl.

"Help us, Sylvestris!" Azedarach wrestles with the Fury, unable to use the thyrsis at such close range. And as they fight, Sylvestris realizes suddenly that this attacker isn't a Fury at all, but a young man, his howls full of anguish and rage.

"I'll pardon you!" Azedarach cries desperately, royal plurality banished in the immediacy of his need. "I'll give you anything!"

Just then, the young man wrests Rose's head away. But he can't hold on; it slips out of his hands and tumbles into the cloud of smoke billowing up from the depths of the pit. Whether he knows how close he is to the edge or not, he lunges forward without hesitation and is gone.

Azedarach teeters briefly, his thin arms flailing, blue eyes wide in disbelief as they stare beseechingly at Sylvestris. Then the earth pitches beneath him, and, with a shriek, he follows his attacker into the pit.

TWELVE

Rumer feels herself disintegrating. Nothing exists but those swarming insect eyes, twin whirlpools in a face as enormous as all of Herwood. A face whose scarred features are composed of the varied flora of the woods.

The face regards her with a cool serenity bordering on indifference. Yet behind the seeming indifference, Rumer senses something warmer, an interest not only in her, but in all green and living things.

Is it really there? A distant compassion such as some curious, kindly god might feel for creatures infinitely inferior? Perhaps it's her own insignificance she's experiencing and, like a child abandoned in the dark, denying with a wish. But then Rumer feels a spark of sympathy arc between those faraway eyes and her own, and suddenly what had seemed immeasurably distant is as close as her throbbing heart or the tears running down her face.

All sense of flying or falling has fled. Time and motion have ground to a halt. Or maybe it's only she who's stopped, held in place by those arresting emerald eyes while time courses around her as swiftly as ever.

But she hasn't stopped. Not really. She can still feel the branches that, like the nimble hands of jugglers, catch hold of her and pass her lightly between themselves. Their touch is gentle yet playful, almost caressing. Rumer feels as if she's being sucked into those eyes, or as if the huge mouth has opened to swallow her. There's no fear; it's like returning to a home forgotten until now. Where has she known this before?

There is only green. A sky, a sea, a universe.

Out of it—no, part of it—a voice.

At last you have come. You are most welcome, Rumer Illicium. Viridis Liberatrix.

Rumer realizes that she's naked, the silver cloak stripped from her body. She covers herself with her hands. *Who's there?* she asks in a small voice. She feels like a grain of sand, a speck of dust. *Is it the Spinner?*

Laughter like rustling leaves. *No, I am not the Spinner.*

She tries again, her voice smaller still. *Maw?*

Once more the laughter. *No, Liberatrix, not Maw.*

Then: *Beauty?* she guesses, as if this is a riddle game such as children play.

But the voice answers, *Beauty is not a person. It is a place prepared and promised. Do you really not know me, little sister?*

And suddenly Rumer does know. *You're Viridis Lacrimata, aren't you?*

Yes. At least, that was once my name.

Where are you? Oh, can I see you?

With that, the saint appears before her: a tall woman in robes of green, her face the reflection of Rumer's in its scarring, only with hollows for eyes. Yet she looks at Rumer as if there is nothing she cannot see. Rumer drops her hands, no longer ashamed of her nakedness, wishing she could open herself to the saint and be filled by her utterly, like a vessel.

Bless your eyes, child, says the saint, making the sign of the Wheel. Her hands—especially her fingers, which are of unusual length, longer even than Sylvestris's—give Rumer an impression of extreme age although they do not tremble.

Now, as if the saint has brought a world into being with her, Rumer finds herself standing in the midst of a garden so lush and beautiful she can hardly bear to look at it. A dazzling light pours from every flower and blade of grass. And yet the source of it all is not the garden, but the old woman in her robes of green who stands at its very center. The last, unfinished line of the *Lives and Acts* pops into Rumer's head:

Bidding the saints good-bye, she went where even my pen cannot follow, into a darkness of her own choosing, a sacrifice without . . .

Weeping with joy, as if the missing words of the famous sentence are already written in her heart and, what's more, always have been, a mystery about to be unveiled at last, Rumer falls to her knees and crawls across the soft grasses of the garden to kiss the feet of the saint.

But Viridis reacts with alarm, her robe flapping as she motions for Rumer to rise. *Get up! Do not kneel to me!*

Rumer draws back in confusion, not because of the saint's protest, which she barely registers, but because of what she sees beneath the long and flowing green robes: expecting the legs and feet of an old woman, she glimpses instead a thick and gnarled column rising from the ground. The trunk of a tree.

What are you? she gasps, looking up into the scarred face.

Viridis folds her robes about herself. *Do not fear me, little sister. I was a woman once, a Cat like you. In my heart I'm still that woman, though my body has been changed.*

Rumer can't forget what she saw; yet, for all its strangeness, she's not afraid. She feels only awe and a kind of sadness, as if she's glimpsed, without understanding, the secret nature of the perpetual sacrifice.

Now rise, Viridis continues in her kindly voice. *I would kneel to you if I could, for you have freed me.*

Rumer gets obediently to her feet. Still, she knows how little she merits the praises of the saint. *You kneel to me? But I've done nothing!*

Your tears have done it, says Viridis. *Just as they freed the Fury whose body they touched. Herwood is my body, my flesh. My prison.*

Is that what happened to you? Rumer asks. *The perpetual sacrifice?*

Viridis laughs, but sadly now. *Many turnings ago, Ixion Diospyros robbed me of my eyes and my will and set me here to keep the wheel turning smoothly. He called it a perpetual sacrifice, as if I had chosen my fate. But it was forced upon me.*

I don't understand.

You will come to understand better than I can explain it to you, Liberatrix.

Please; I want to understand now . . .

Poor Rumer! Viridis shakes her head. *Too many turnings have passed. My words would be meaningless to you; there's no one left to understand them. There are only stories now. Stories like the ones in the* Lives and Acts*—or the ones we told our children long ago, their truths made simple, stark, and striking, the better to be grasped and remembered by young and impressionable minds. Shall I tell you of the evil serpent that lies coiled at the heart of the world? Will you hear the story of how a sovereign, a man twice dead, and a voice without a body set out to poison it?*

If you please, Rumer says politely, more confused than ever.

But Viridis only sighs. *No. That history is all but exhausted. Soon it will shake itself to pieces. And not even I can tell what will follow it, if anything.*

Is—is the Unspinning upon us?

What do you think?

Rumer considers the signs by which the Last Days may be known. It's written in the *Lives and Acts* that in those days of upheaval preceding the Unspinning, the high and mighty will fall, Chastenings of unsurpassed violence will shake the land, simulars will cut their strings and walk like men, and Viridis Lacrimata will return from Herwood. She's seen these prophecies come true one by one; she herself is one of them, though that distinction hasn't given her any privileged understanding. On the contrary, she feels as if she's been swept up by something bigger than she is, like the Spinner's Wheel, which will carry her along, then cast her aside once her usefulness is at an end. *I've seen the signs,* she begins.

Ah, signs! the saint interrupts merrily. *Tell me, Rumer: what is Beauty?*

Puzzled, Rumer answers as though replying to the naive question of a child. *Beauty is a scent only men can smell. It rises with the night to draw men away from their families into Herwood, from which they never return.*

What if I told you there is no such scent?

But there is! Rumer protests. *Each night men are lost. I've seen them; my own father was taken!*

Men are lost, but it's not Beauty that takes them. It's the fireflies.

Rumer shakes her head. *Is this another story, Viridis? Like the serpent?*

Yes, a story. Viridis smiles as if at a private joke. *You don't mind, do you?*

No . . .

Good. It will pass the time while we're waiting.

Waiting for what?

Why, the end. Or the beginning. We'll learn soon enough which it's to be. But I was speaking of fireflies; it's they who choose the men, not Beauty. The fireflies come at night when the men are sleeping and slip inside their trachae. There they pull the strings of the sleepers' bodies and minds like simularters, walking them into Herwood.

Rumer shivers. *You're talking about the hives and the Furies . . . This isn't a story; it's the truth!*

There are many truths, Rumer, says Viridis. *Just as there are many stories.*

Why do the fireflies take the men?

Because without them, they couldn't make metheglin. I suppose you know all about metheglin!

It's a drug. The Sovereign uses it, and the Ecclesiarch, and all the odalisques of the High Houses; everyone uses it, except vizards, of course. It's said metheglin can make you live forever if you get enough of it.

Let us say: for a very, very long time. But metheglin is more than that. It's the sap that links us together, plant and animal and human. A living web along whose strands the fireflies crawl like spiders, gathering information like nectar, and dispensing it, too, in their stings.

Rumer's head is spinning. *What kind of information?*

Everything that makes us who and what we are: the story written in our blood. The fireflies bring it back to Herwood, to the men who serve as what you called hives. The raw information, injected into the hives by means of the fireflies' stings, seeps into their dreams, for the hives are not dead, but only sleeping. Their dreams combine into a single dream, a dream of Herwood and the Hierarchate. Of the Spinner and Maw. This dream is distilled into metheglin, which is pumped by the Furies to the vaults in Quoz and, in lesser doses, carried by the fireflies to everyone in the Hierarchate, even vizards, who believe they shun metheglin. In this way, we are all part of the hives' dream; even the hives themselves are part of it. The fireflies, too.

Am I part of it? asks Rumer. *Is this a dream now?*

A dream within a dream. I am—or was, until you freed me—the chief servant of that dream. Ixion began it; or, more accurately, altered it into its present form. The task he set me was to make certain the dream cycle was never broken, that the fireflies chose only men, and that the dream of everything and everyone was always dreamed by men.

It almost sounds like a kind of crafting, Rumer says.

Viridis smiles as if both amused and pleased. *Everything here is crafted, Rumer.*

By the Spinner, you mean?

That's as good a name as any.

Even you, Viridis?

I was crafted to keep the Unspinning from taking place, as I told you.

Next you'll tell me the Unspinning is a crafting!

And so it is. But of a very different sort, more like the opposite of a crafting. For the Unspinning means an end to fireflies, to metheglin, to craftings of all kinds: an end to the shared dream that shapes or misshapes the world. The power of men, which grew over long turnings little by little, until Ixion made it absolute, cannot survive it. That's why Ixion led his revolt all those turnings ago: to prevent the Unspinning. He was afraid, you see.

Ixion Diospyros? Afraid? Rumer finds it hard to imagine. *Of what?*

Of Beauty, Viridis answers.

But you said there was no such thing!

No; I said there was no such odor. Beauty exists.

I remember now. You called it a place . . .

A place prepared and promised. The Unspinning leads to Beauty as a road might lead to Quoz, the last step in a long and difficult journey whose beginnings even I can't remember. That's why Ixion wanted it stopped. He thought things should remain as they were, as they'd come to be over the turnings. He wanted to keep the wheel spinning forever.

The Spinner's Wheel?

If you like. But over the turnings, the wheel began to wobble. The wobbling led to the Chastenings, which grew worse and worse with each turning until, now, they threaten to destroy the wheel and everything on it.

Viridis pauses, then resumes. *Although I was a slave, I was not completely without power. I, too, dreamed. And I wove my small dreams of escape and revenge into the larger dreaming of the men. It took a long time, longer than you could imagine, Rumer. But you were one result.*

Me?

I dreamed your eyes. Your blessed and cursed eyes.

Why do you say cursed?

Your eyes, with their tears, are another crafting. A kind of sickness.

But my tears heal . . .

Everyone but you. Did they heal your scars?

Rumer touches her ravaged face.

You caught the sickness from Rose; yes, Rose was part of my dream, too. We are three of a kind, Rumer. Past, present, and future, each shaped by the same sickness, the same crafting. Remember when I spoke of the information, the stories, written in our blood?

Rumer nods.

Our tears heal others by rewriting those stories. But they are rewriting us at the same time. Changing us in deep and complicated ways. Surely you've felt it!

Rumer nods again, thinking of the bonds of love that tie her to those she's cured, bonds which seem to stretch wider without ever growing thin or snapping. Even since she's been here, in this dream within a dream—which somehow is not a dream—she's felt the bonds expanding, as if her tears have watered all of Herwood. As if she's present now in every leaf and tree and firefly, every Fury and hive. And they in her. Pulled in countless directions, she feels as though she's losing herself, melting into the stuff of the web, the dream. She fights against it, afraid. *What's happening to me, Viridis? Am I going to die?*

As if in answer, the saint flings wide her arms, throwing off her green robes.

They are not arms. They are not robes.

Rumer gasps as branches unfurl to surround the saint in a green and leafy nimbus that takes the place of the garden—*is* the garden, somehow, and always has been. She falls to her knees, hardly daring to look, as if the glory thus revealed might blind her or burn her to a cinder.

The face of the saint is still visible behind the veil of foliage. Only, Rumer sees now, the scarred flesh is not flesh at all, but the bark of a tree. Viridis's features are carved into its trunk, the same trunk she'd glimpsed earlier beneath the saint's robes.

Now the scabrous lips move, and all the branches rustle and creak, stirred by the breeze of her speaking: *Get up, little sister. I can't bear it that you kneel to me.*

Rumer stands. *Why are you showing me this?* she asks, afraid to hear the answer. *Is this what the sickness will do to me?*

But Viridis does not reply. Instead, her leaves begin to change color, erupting in fiery oranges and reds as if consumed by an inner burning.

Rumer stares, entranced by a beauty as fleeting as it is intense. For now the leaves are brown, shriveled. They begin to fall from the tree, as if stripped in a bitter wind, a wind that whips the branches, though Rumer cannot feel it. *Viridis!*

The saint's voice is a dry rasp, barely intelligible through the creaking branches and the rattle of falling leaves. *I'm dying, Rumer.*

No! Rumer is frantic, crying. *My tears can heal you!*

Don't you understand? They have already healed me, set me free.

The last of the leaves has fallen. The tree is bare; its branches hang motionless, clutching the air, shaped to what has stilled them like the legs of a dead spider.

But not dead. The face of the saint remains animated, lips moving slowly, as though painfully, in the wood: *Do not cry, little sister. Death is freedom to me.*

No! Rumer rushes into the branches, fighting through to the trunk of the tree. She throws her arms around it and presses her face close to the face of Viridis Lacrimata, tears wetting the bark. *Don't die, Viridis!*

The voice is but a whisper now. *I should have died long ago . . .*

With that, the tree begins to tremble, as if from deep within.

Viridis smiles and sighs: *It is done.*

The tree is shaking now. Everything is shaking. Rumer clings desperately to the trunk, afraid of being thrown off. *What is done?*

Our journey. The last turning.

Rumer's blood runs cold. *The Unspinning?*

Do not fear it, Liberatrix. Soon you will gaze upon the face of Beauty! My time is over; yours is just beginning. How I envy you now! This was to be my fate, my sacrifice, until Ixion robbed me of my eyes. Embrace it! It stretches before you without—

Rumer watches in horror as the bark of the tree—as if turned to mud by her tears—creeps up over the lips and face of Viridis, choking her off in mid-sentence. Before Rumer can react, she's gone. There's nothing left of her, just the trunk with its knots and boles like eddies on the surface of a river marking the spot where a saint has drowned.

With a heartrending cry, Rumer presses her lips to the bark, presses so hard that she tastes her own blood. And now, as if her kiss has struck with the force of an axe, the air is riven by the tortured sound of splintering wood. The tree splits down the middle with a deafening crack, flinging Rumer to the ground.

THIRTEEN

Sylvestris sinks to his knees with a sob. The shaking has stopped; the ground is still. *It's over*, he thinks, suddenly exhausted. He makes the sign of the Wheel and whispers a prayer for the soul of the man who appeared by a miracle to kill the Sovereign and save his life. There was such emotion in the man's cries as he threw himself upon Azedarach that it was almost as if he recognized Rose. But how could that be? Then Sylvestris remembers something Azedarach had told him in Quoz: Rose's husband had been lost to Beauty on their wedding night. Could this have been that same man, he wonders, Rose's lost husband? What was his name?

Galingale. Cyrus Galingale.

He shakes his head; if he ever does get the chance to write all this down, as Rose promised him, he'll write it as though it were her husband, for there's something in the idea of such a reunion that chimes pleasantly in him, like the echo of an old tale from the *Lives and Acts*.

But Sylvestris knows only one thing for sure: Maw is finished. Dead. The poisons have done their work. Now he must find Rumer. And he will find her, for didn't Rose promise him that, too?

He wishes he had the thyrsis. Although the Furies are still writhing upon the ground—more in pain than terror now to judge by their screams—Sylvestris feels vulnerable without a weapon. But the thyrsis fell with Azedarach into the pit.

Then he sees something even better. It's lying a few feet away, where it fell during the fight, forgotten until now: the Serpent Crown.

The Crown is the color of lead, its lively glitter gone. There's no tingle when he picks up the metallic ring in the shape of a serpent swallowing its tail. It hangs cold and heavy in his hand. Has it been damaged?

The ancient crafting is obscure. But perhaps, like the cloak from Reve—also lost with Azedarach—the Crown was made to come to life when worn. He raises it to his head.

But before he can put it on, a heavy rain begins quite suddenly to fall. Or not rain: hail. The hailstones sting his skin. Crouching, he ducks his head beneath his arms; he's never seen hail like this, dark and oblong, like pebbles or . . .

Fireflies.

The insects are falling in their thousands, smacking dully into the ground and covering it in a thick and motionless layer.

The strange storm ends as abruptly as it began. The ground is blanketed inches deep in the insects. Wonderingly, Sylvestris picks one up. It's dead. They're all dead.

Shaken, he looks at the shredded green canopy above his head. And even as he does, a livid wave of red and orange sweeps through it like a season measured not in months but seconds.

Now the leaves are brown. They begin to fall. Naked branches spread like cracks across a sky the color of dirty ice.

Sylvestris stands unsteadily, the bodies of the insects crackling like hollow shells beneath his feet. What is happening? In poisoning Maw, have they poisoned the world? Put a stop to one Unspinning only to unleash another?

But then he sees he's got other worries.

The Furies are on their feet, staring at him, as quiet and still as a grove of saplings. The vegetation sprouting from their bodies is the only remaining green in Herwood.

He's afraid to move, to speak. Then he remembers the Serpent Crown. He slips it on, wishing himself invisible, as if the Crown can hear his thoughts and respond to them.

He's not exactly sure what to expect. Perhaps the same tingling sensation he felt when the shroud of invisibility first descended over his body, leeching all color from the world. Anyway, a change in perception immediate and unmistakable.

But nothing happens. Nothing changes.

The Crown is damaged, its ancient crafting stripped like the leaves from the trees. He's no more invisible than the Furies watching him with expressions he can't interpret. He feels like a fool.

Yet all around him now the Furies drop to their knees and press their foreheads to the ground as though in the presence of their Sovereign.

Slowly, Sylvestris understands: the Serpent Crown will retain its power as long as men believe in it. The crafting does not reside solely in the Crown, but in the minds and habits of men who recognize it and kneel to it.

Azedarach told him that the men drawn into Herwood by Beauty were thrown by the Furies to Maw. But now he wonders if the men *are* the Furies, transformed somehow by Beauty. Is he looking at those men now; or, rather, what's left of them, a spark of humanity remaining like the trace of some powerful conditioning, enough to respond to the sight of the Serpent Crown? He thinks again of the man who slew the Sovereign. Had he been a Fury like these others? And did the sight of Rose recall him to himself, healing him as if he'd been splashed by Rumer's tears?

Whatever the truth, he thinks, to these Furies here and now he *is* the Sovereign, Sylvestris I.

Sylvestris has no desire to take Azedarach's place. But he's not about to tell the Furies they've made a mistake, assuming they could even understand him.

He'll play along for a while, he thinks. Play the part of the Sovereign just as he's played so many parts in the course of his career. He's spoken in the voices of Ixion Diospyros, Stilskin Sophora, and Samsum Oxalis, pulled the strings of Viridis Lacrimata. What is this but another performance, only without simulars now? No strings to pull but his own . . . and those of his audience. They abducted Rumer; they can lead him to her.

"Faithful subjects," he begins, only to break off as, with a low rumble, the ground resumes its trembling.

Rumer opens her eyes to find herself back in the grove of hives. No longer bound, she's lying naked on a thick and brittle carpet of leaves, the cloak from Reve at her side. The ground is shaking beneath her with a sound like an endless roll of thunder. She sits up with an effort.

Every tree in the grove has been split asunder. Not a single leaf remains on a single branch. Only hives hang there: lifeless, brittle husks. There's no sign of the Furies.

The ground is covered with fallen leaves and the bodies of fireflies. She picks up a handful of the insects and trickles them through her fingers like stones. Dead. All dead.

She feels as if she's the only thing left alive. Even the bonds of love she'd felt so strongly in her dream have fallen away like the leaves of the trees. She's free. Alone.

Is this the Unspinning then? Ixion was right to fear it. She gazes up through the welter of naked branches as if searching for the face of Viridis Lacrimata.

But there's no face now. No sky like a wide and grassy plain on which her sight can graze. Just a pale, washed-out bank of gray, like clouds heavy with snow, through which a light equally pale and washed-out filters.

Suddenly cold, Rumer picks up the cloak. It doesn't suck warmly at her skin as it did before. Nor is it silky smooth; it feels abrasive and clammy now, as if its crafting has unraveled. She drops it with a shudder.

Then she notices her body.

Tangled through the triangle of hair between her legs are tiny stems with small purplish buds that seem to be on the verge of leafing. Rumer plucks one.

There's no pain, just a sharp snap and a brief upwell of milky fluid, like sap. A clump of hair comes out along with the stem.

No; not hair.

A fine lacing of roots.

Rumer's hands fly to her head: her scalp, too, is bristling with this strange new growth. And her armpits.

The sickness, she thinks dully. It's happening. She's becoming like Viridis Lacrimata, no longer human.

Now every inch of her is crawling with roots and stems. They spread faster than she can weed them, wriggling beneath her skin like worms.

A slumbering terror wakes in her. She lurches to her feet with a moan and stumbles blindly through the blasted grove, more graveyard than garden now.

She doesn't see a single living thing. Not plant or animal. It's as if everything in Herwood has died along with Viridis, or fled.

The ground pitches beneath her feet, knocking her off-balance. It feels like the world is coming to pieces. She runs on, slapping at her skin like a woman on fire.

Sylvestris is shaking even worse than the ground. The tremors can mean only one thing: the poisons didn't work. Deep down in her lair, Maw is still alive. The Unspinning, though interrupted, has resumed.

"No," he whispers, shaking his head as if to deny the evidence of his senses. Has it all been for nothing? "It's not fair . . . "

A terrified wail rises from the Furies, who seconds ago fell to their knees. They stagger up and, like madmen, rush off in all directions, vanishing into the woods.

Sylvestris calls for them to stop, to come back. But if they hear, they don't obey. They don't even seem to see him. And though some of them run by so closely he could grab them, he does not. He's afraid of them; their faces are twisted masks of stark, unreasoning fear, as if the glimmer of humanity sparked in their souls by the sight of the Serpent Crown has been blown out like a candle.

Sylvestris watches them go in an agony of indecision. He thought they would lead him to Rumer. But now it's as if they've scattered purposefully, just to keep him from following. Soon the clearing is empty.

His performance as Sovereign wasn't quite the success he'd hoped for: his first commands ignominiously refused, his subjects fled. He almost feels like following Azedarach into the pit and getting it over with. But he can't forget that Rumer is out there somewhere. She needs him.

And he needs her. Even if the Unspinning should shake the world apart, he thinks, he won't let it part them.

But how to find her? He's lost in these woods already. If only he could speak to Rose again! She would show him the way just as she showed him the way to this place.

The ground shifts, and he nearly falls to his knees. Yet something has changed; the steady vibration beneath his feet is unlike anything he's felt before. As powerful as any Chastening, it's less violent and arbitrary somehow, like a river surging within its banks instead of breaking beyond them.

Saying a silent prayer to the Spinner, Sylvestris leaves the clearing at a run, following the path by which he and Azedarach arrived. It has occurred to him that the Furies may have plans of their own for Rumer.

He runs for some time along the path without encountering anyone. All of Herwood seems dead, deserted. Only the trembling of the ground reminds him of the new life about to be born, or reborn, as Maw sheds her final skin and emerges into the light.

At last he comes to a second clearing. He stops short, horrified. The bodies of men, old men, hang by the hundreds from the stark skeletons of trees. The trees are arranged in orderly rows as in some kind of orchard; he can't see the end of them.

He approaches one of the swaying bodies and cautiously touches it. The jaundiced skin parts before his fingers like dry parchment. A musty smell wafts from the ragged tear. Sylvestris draws back with an incoherent cry, blundering into another of the bodies. Like overripe fruit, it comes loose and falls with him to the ground.

He jumps up at once. The body has burst open. It's filled with dead fireflies, dark seeds within a shattered pod.

Sylvestris's heart is hammering as he forces himself to walk slowly along the rows, looking for some sign of Rumer. What has happened here he'll never know. Nor cares to know.

Then he sees the silver cloak from Reve, twin to his own vanished cloak, lying crumpled upon the ground. Rumer's cloak. She has been here.

The fabric is stiff, unresponsive to his touch. Like the Serpent Crown, it seems to have lost its crafting. Yet it possesses a crafting more precious still, if to him alone: a memory, a trace, of Rumer.

She'd worn this cloak; it had flowed over the two of them like a second skin when they lay together in the boat. Beneath its glittering mesh, they'd merged briefly into a single being, although he'd pulled back at the end, afraid.

He's not afraid now. He hasn't felt this close to Rumer since the Furies took her. He throws the cloak over his shoulders as if it will guide him to wherever she is.

Now a fat raindrop bursts upon the side of his nose and runs down to the corner of his mouth. It tastes sweet upon his tongue.

The sky opens up in a deluge. Sylvestris tents the cloak over his head, grateful for its protection, for the rain is driving though strangely warm.

Then he sees something amazing.

Beneath the rain, patches of dead ground are returning to life, tiny oases amid the larger ruin. New grasses are sprouting there, delicate, colorful flowers springing up. But what's truly amazing about these miniature gardens is their shape.

They are footprints. With a singing heart, Sylvestris follows them at a run. Where else can they lead but to Rumer?

After a time, Rumer feels a spatter of moisture.

Rain.

Only it's not rain. Not exactly. It's sweet and thick, like drops of diluted metheglin. Where it touches her skin, she feels a thrill like that of a lover's kiss, and the horrible itch of the spreading foliage eases to a tickle. She's covered quite densely now with the tangled growth.

She can't run anymore; her feet are sinking into the earth with every step. But she's no longer afraid. She throws wide her arms and looks up into the dissolving sky in a transport of ecstasy and exhaustion.

It's like watching a dome of opaque crystal deliquesce. The rain falls over her like tears, the last tears of Viridis Lacrimata.

With an effort, she turns her heavy head and looks back the way she's come. She laughs to see her footsteps bursting into flower. A similar process is taking place in her heart, as if the love she thought perished there with Viridis and all of Herwood has, like some cunning plant, been lying dormant beneath the dead mask of winter. Awakened by these warm rains, fresh shoots and roots are spreading through her in a new web. Where will it all lead? Where will it end? She can't imagine.

"Rumer!"

She recognizes her name with difficulty. And the voice. She can almost place it.

A tall man is running toward her through the rain. He is wearing a purple loincloth and a silver cloak. A dull crown circles his head.

She knows him: Sylvestris Jaciodes. She loved him. She still does. Only she can no longer find him amid these other loves that are springing up like brash wildflowers in her heart.

She tries to think of everyone she's loved in the course of her life. She thinks of her mother and father. Of the boy Cyrus Galingale, who should have been her husband. She thinks of Aralia and Cassine and all the other Cats. She thinks of Rose. And Viridis.

She hasn't lost them or forgotten them. How could she? Only it's impossible to choose one flower, or a dozen, to cherish above all the others in the beautiful immensity she feels herself becoming. Is that what Viridis meant when she spoke of a living web linking everything together, a single shared dream?

Viridis called it information. But it's not.

It's love, Rumer realizes. The sickness is love.

Sylvestris gives a horrified cry at the sight of Rumer. He thinks at first she's become a Fury, for leaves are sprouting from her body. But when he gets closer, he realizes something else is happening. A barklike growth covers her from head to toe, though he can still make out her body underneath. Her green eyes appeal to him in silent entreaty from this prison of living wood, as if she's lost the power of speech, like Jewel in the instant that Roemer, hearing his name whispered, broke his bargain and turned around.

"Oh, Rumer! What have they done to you?" Choking back tears, he throws himself upon the tree and begins tearing at its foliage and branches to free her.

Rumer screams as if he's killing her.

He draws back, crazy with fear.

"Sylvestris . . ."

To hear that voice coming from this monstrosity, to watch those lips, whose kiss he knows so well, moving in that scabrous shell, is more than Sylvestris can bear. He feels as though he's lost his mind. "What is it? What's happened to you?"

"The perpetual sacrifice," she says.

A fist of ice squeezes Sylvestris's heart. "Don't die, Rumer! You can't; I won't let you!"

"Shhh." The sound is a rustling of leaves and dripping rain. "Come sit beside me. Wait with me."

Sylvestris shakes his head. "Wait for you to die?"

"I'm not dying."

"Then what's happening to you?"

"I don't know yet. Something wonderful."

"Soon we'll all be dead." He turns away, unable to look at her anymore. "Maw is shedding her last skin. The Unspinning is upon us; I'm glad of it now!"

"The rains have stopped," she says calmly. "Look up."

Sylvestris watches the last of the clouds melt away.

What's behind them is black. As black as night. And, like the night, it swarms with fireflies.

Only the flashings of these fireflies are not green, but white. They do not flare suddenly and as suddenly fade, appearing first in one place, then another. These fireflies sparkle with a cold and steady light as though fixed in place forever.

Sylvestris sinks to the ground. "The Pit of Damned Souls," he whispers.

Rumer feels Sylvestris crawl beneath the shelter of her branches and hug tightly to her trunk. But she can offer no other comfort, though it saddens her to see him suffer.

Now a wave of brilliant green rises up out of nowhere to fill the swarming sky. It's not like when she watched the face of Viridis Lacrimata take shape from the foliage of Herwood. If this is a face, it has no human likeness. Yet perhaps, like a mirror in an empty room, it's just waiting for someone to gaze into it as she's doing now.

"What is it?" whimpers Sylvestris.

It rolls over her, over everything. Like an echo, she hears the voice of Viridis in her mind: *Soon you will gaze upon the face of Beauty.*

And without understanding how or why, Rumer knows that she is.

It's huge. Bigger than anything she's seen or imagined. The whole world seems to be falling toward it, into it, like a teardrop into an ocean. What did Viridis call it?

"A place prepared and promised."

"What?" asks Sylvestris. "What did you say?"

But before she can answer, a flash of light kindles the sky to burning. The shaking intensifies, and the noise.

Sylvestris screams and goes on screaming. Then he screams some more.

When he stops, so has everything else. There's no sound but the hissing of wind through trees and his own ragged breathing.

"Rumer?"

Herwood is in full leaf again. The sky is a shade of blue for which he has no name.

"Don't leave me, Rumer," he pleads, clasping her rough form. "I love you! Please come back!"

Rumer scarcely hears. She feels only the pull of Beauty in her heart, the strong green pulse of it bearing her away. She feels herself dissolving into it as if into a Herwood restored to life, a Herwood whose roots are in her now, a tangled web of life, of love, that dwarfs what she'd experienced in the dream that was no dream.

She feels connected to her body by the slenderest of threads. The wind is tugging insistently at her. As if from a great height, she looks down into her upturned face and sees her green eyes shining like jewels in the mask of living wood. Her arms stretch wide, many-fingered, as if to pull everything into their green embrace. And beneath them, huddled against her, she sees Sylvestris, sunlight glinting off his crooked crown.

Then the wind shifts. Floating higher now, like a kite at the limit of its string, she looks out over an endless expanse of green. Currents of wind flow through the treetops, sending ripples running all the way to the distant horizon.

And then she's higher still. She sees an end to the green sea and the beginning of a blue one. She sees flying things and swimming things. Things that crawl and run and leap and love and die. She knows them all though she cannot name them. That is a task for others newly fallen.

Then the thread snaps. She's flowing through branches, the spidery veins of leaves. She's sinking to the ends of roots and rising in rivers of sap to the bushy crowns of trees.

She disperses equally in all directions, as nameless now as the color of the sky, as the things that dwell beneath it.

Sylvestris hears the sigh that stirs her branches. He feels the tremble run through her into the ground. And he knows Rumer is gone.

But he stays with her. This strange statue of her. For her likeness is captured in the wood, though perhaps only his eyes could find it. He talks to her sometimes, and sometimes he weeps, and finally he's silent.

After a while, it begins to grow dark. The fireflies he saw before come out again to fill the sky with their cold white brilliance, winking through her branches as if farther from him than Quoz is from Arpagee. Much closer, too close, the cries of animals ring out over the rhythmic piping of birds and insects: roars and moans, sudden shrieks, stuttering ghoulish laughter. He climbs up into her branches as if into the safety of her arms.

He lies there with his head against her trunk, wrapped in the cloak from Reve but shivering all the same, the Serpent Crown hanging from a branch beside him. Occasionally there comes a sound of something snuffling loudly beneath him, then moving on. He does not sleep.

Later he sees a light passing across the field of fixed glimmerings overhead. It moves quickly, in a straight line and at a steady rate, like a rolling wheel.

Finally, toward morning, he falls asleep.

He wakes with the memory of a word in his mind. *Beauty.* Is that the name of this place? Somehow he knows it is. Knows, too, that Rumer whispered the name to him while he slept.

She hasn't really left. He can feel her all around him now, a part of everything, as if her spirit has quickened this place, woken it after a sleep of countless turnings.

The perpetual sacrifice, he thinks.

But how has it all come to be? How did the Unspinning lead here, to Beauty? What has happened to him, to everyone and everything in the Hierarchate? Has Maw done this? The Spinner? Or something else, something undreamed of until now, like the strange new fireflies and the wheel he saw moving solemnly across the sky?

He knows there will be no answers to these questions but those he fashions for himself. Rose called him Scribe, saying he would write her history, and Rumer's. He tries to imagine this history now, the stories and thoughts of which it might be woven, and it seems to him that he can almost see it, the shape of it. He sees it all except the end.

Can the end ever be seen by human eyes? He wonders if, like Quercus Incana, he'll leave his book unfinished. But then it seems to him that, in a sense, he won't be writing something new so much as continuing the *Lives and Acts*, picking up from the last, unfinished line. If there is an ending, another hand than his will set it down. He's not worried about reaching the end. He feels as if he's at the very beginning.

Something is moving through the woods, drawing near to him. He crouches, watching.

It's a group of Furies. Only they're not Furies anymore. They're men. They always were. There are seven of them, carrying rude clubs and staffs. Two of the men are supporting a bloodied comrade between them. He groans weakly with every step. They pass directly beneath him but do not look up.

Sylvestris waits until they are gone from sight. Then he gathers his belongings and climbs carefully down. He arranges the cloak about his shoulders, puts on the Serpent Crown, and starts after the men. He hears his name whispered from behind, but it's only the wind in the trees. Or so he tells himself, finished with old stories.